Praise for

The Family Game W9-BXT-313

"Harriet has just announced her engagement to the preternaturally rich and charming Edward Holbeck—but his family, it turns out, is what you might come up with if you took the Roys from *Succession* and blended them with the Murdochs, the Macbeths, and the Borgias. Even worse, they're obsessed with bizarre psychological games."
　　　—*The New York Times Book Review* (Editors' Choice)

"*The Family Game* is both sharply modern and timeless, with strains of *King Lear,* Dickens, and P. D. James's postwar holiday chillers."
　　　　　　　　　　　　　　　　　—*The Washington Post*

"[A] terrifically twisty thriller . . . Think *Succession* on steroids!"
　　　　　　　　　　　　　　　　　—*Good Housekeeping* (UK)

"If you thought your in-laws were less than ideal, you can take solace in novelist Harriet Reed's predicament when she goes to meet her fiancé's powerful family."
　　　　　　　　　　　　　　　　　　　　　　—*E! Online*

"A powerful family and a deadly game: Be prepared for a nail-biting roller coaster of a ride in Catherine Steadman's classy and ingenious new thriller."
　　　　　—B. A. PARIS, *New York Times* bestselling author of
　　　　　　　　　　　　　　　　　　Behind Closed Doors

"Millionaires, marriage, and murder make for a potent cocktail in this compelling tale set among the super-rich of New York's elite."
　　　—T. M. LOGAN, internationally bestselling author of *Lies*

"Instantly compelling and filled with ingenious twists and brilliant characters . . . This is sublime thriller writing."
　　　　　　　—B. P. WALTER, author of *The Couple's Secret*

The Family Game

a novel

Catherine Steadman

BALLANTINE BOOKS

NEW YORK

2023 Ballantine Books Trade Paperback Edition

Copyright © 2022 by Catherine Steadman Ltd.
Book club guide copyright © 2023 by Penguin Random House LLC

Published in the United States by Ballantine Books,
an imprint of Random House, a division of
Penguin Random House LLC, New York.

BALLANTINE is a registered trademark and the colophon
is a trademark of Penguin Random House LLC.
RANDOM HOUSE BOOK CLUB and colophon
are trademarks of Penguin Random House LLC.

Originally published in hardcover in the United States
by Ballantine Books, an imprint of Random House,
a division of Penguin Random House LLC, in 2022.

LIBRARY OF CONGRESS CATALOGING-IN-PUBLICATION DATA
Names: Steadman, Catherine, author.
Title: The family game: a novel / Catherine Steadman.
Description: First edition. | New York: Ballantine Books, [2022]
Identifiers: LCCN 2022012427 (print) | LCCN 2022012428 (ebook) |
ISBN 9780593158081 (trade paperback) | ISBN 9780593158074 (ebook)
Subjects: LCGFT: Thrillers (Fiction)
Classification: LCC PR6119.T436 F36 2022 (print) |
LCC PR6119.T436 (ebook) | DDC 823/.92—dc23/eng/20220422
LC record available at https://lccn.loc.gov/2022012427
LC ebook record available at https://lccn.loc.gov/2022012428

Printed in the United States of America on acid-free paper

randomhousebooks.com
randomhousebookclub.com

2 4 6 8 9 7 5 3 1

Title page photograph by Ysbrandcosjin/Adobe Stock

Book design by Elizabeth A. D. Eno

I dedicate this book to my readers,
with thanks and huge gratitude.

The Family Game

Damaged people are dangerous. They know they can survive.

—Josephine Hart, *Damage*

Our most basic instinct is not for survival, but for family.

—Paul Pearsall, neuropsychologist

Prologue

I come to on the parquet floor of the entrance hall, my face pressed hard against its antique wood, with the clear knowledge that this is not how Christmases should go.

Around me the Gothic grandeur of The Hydes slides back into focus. The Holbecks' family seat, everything multiple generations of wealth and power can buy you; this imposing Hungarian castle ripped brick by brick from the Mecsek Mountains, packed, shipped, and grafted into upstate New York soil. Their ancestral home a literal castle in the sky dragged to ground and anchored into the American landscape and its psyche. A testament to sheer bloody-mindedness and cold hard cash.

In the 1800s a Holbeck bride wanted her beau to "lasso the moon," and here's the solid proof he did. He made a dream real. Some might say: more money than sense, maybe, but from down here, bleeding on their floor, even I have to admit this place is beautiful. And who, in love, doesn't hope for a lassoed moon? After all, that's what love is, isn't it?

Across from me the front door stands ajar, so close and yet so, so far. A crisp winter breeze tickling my face as I watch snow-flakes float peaceably through the air outside, freedom just beyond my reach. Past that doorway the grounds roll out in all their splendor, snow-blanketed ornamental gardens, an ice-crusted boating lake, crystalline lawns that finally give way to miles of thickly packed Holbeck woodland. And at the limits of that moonlit forest a fifteen-foot-high perimeter wall, encircling us, separating the Holbeck family from the rest of the world. A sovereign state, an enclave, a compound with its own rules and self-regulating systems.

I have been found lacking, by one, or all. And steps are in motion. I might not survive the night.

If I could stand right now, if I could run, and scale the perimeter wall, the nearest town would still be over an hour on foot. If I had my phone, I could call the police. But given who I am, who they are, I can't be sure the way things would go when they got here. There is a way to read any story and I might have found myself with a slight credibility problem.

A girl with a past tries to marry into money and all hell breaks loose. We all know how that story ends.

It's funny: in-laws are supposed to be problematic, aren't they? That old cultural stereotype. I guess it's funny because it's often true. In-laws can be difficult. Families can be difficult. And I can't argue with the facts, here, bleeding on their floor.

I carefully ease up onto my forearms, the dark stone of my engagement ring shifting moodily in the light. A sleeping creature woken.

If I could go back now, to the day he proposed, would I do things differently? That is the billion-dollar question.

My temple throbs as I carefully wipe blood from my eyelashes.

They say head wounds seem more serious than they are, because they bleed so much. They say the human body can do incredible things in a crisis. People walked for miles to hospitals on broken legs after 9/11, women give birth in war zones, new mothers lift cars to save their children. I hope that's true.

Twenty years ago, I almost died. I hung in silence, death all around me, but somehow, I survived. And if I could survive that, I can survive this, because since you showed up, I have so much more to lose, and so, so much more to gain.

We're going to survive this, you and I. They say you can't choose your family but they're wrong. You can. It just takes way more effort than most people are willing to put in.

And with that thought in mind, I slowly push up and stumble to my feet.

1

Fairytale of New York

MONDAY, NOVEMBER 21

Christmas lights twinkle in the rain as I duck down Fifth Avenue—reds, greens, and golds glimmering in reflection on puddles and glass as I dodge along the busy sidewalk, my phone pressed tight to my ear.

"And the good news is, it's looking like we're going to hit the million-copy sales mark by the end of this week! We did it, Harry!" my literary agent, Louisa, cheers on the phone. Her voice is as warm and close as if she were bundled up against the cold beside me in the sharp New York City chill. I try not to think of the three and a half thousand miles of distance between New York and London—between me and my old home and its soft, damp grayness—but every now and then the pangs of homesickness wake and stretch just beneath the surface of my new life. It's been four months since I left England, and the pull of home is somehow stronger now that winter is setting in. New York can be cold in so many ways.

"For all intents and purposes," she continues with glee, "here's me saying you are now *officially* 'a million-copy bestselling author.'" I can't help but yelp with joy—a surreptitious half skip in the street. The news is incredible. My first novel, a runaway bestseller, has been on the charts since publication, but this new milestone isn't something I could ever have dreamed of until now. New York swallows my ebullient energy greedily. I could probably lie down on the sidewalk and start screaming and the festive shoppers would just weave unfazed around me. It's an oddly terrifying and yet reassuring thought.

"We'll be getting another royalty payout from the publisher at the end of the quarter," Louisa continues. "So Merry Christmas, everyone!"

It's funny, it's only November and yet it feels like Christmas is here already. I look up to the halos of light hanging above me, holiday decorations, sparkling from shop windows, strung in great swaths high over the main drag of Fifth. Everything seems to be moving so fast this year, a whirlwind, a whirlpool.

"How's it going over there?" Louisa asks, snapping me back to reality. "Settled? Happy? Are you living love's young dream?"

I let out a laugh of surprise because *yes,* as smug and as self-satisfied as it may sound, I really am. After so many years alone, after pushing relationships away, perhaps I've paid in full for my mistakes and I can put them to bed. Maybe I'm finally allowed a little happiness.

I shake off the dark thought and grasp back onto my new life with both hands. "Well, we've got furniture now at least. Not sure I've quite worked out the subway yet but I guess I'll get there in the end. Or I guess I won't," I add jokingly.

The truth is, while I know I am beginning to get a feeling for New York City, I realize I am trying to settle into a city that does not settle itself. The crowds, noises, faces, people, that frenetic fight-or-flight energy. I suppose it's only been four months—

I know it can take a lifetime to become part of a city, to find your place. And the world I've landed into here, with Edward, the new circles I find myself moving in, his rarefied life, that is something else again.

"And how is your dreamboat, how is Ed?" she asks, as if reading my thoughts. I slip past a gaggle of tourists in front of St. Patrick's Cathedral, its bells tolling anachronistically alongside towering glass and steel.

Louisa was with me the night I met Edward; I shiver at the memory of the look she gave me when I first brought him over to meet her. That silent swell of pride I felt to have my arm hooked through his, the pride anglers must feel cradling their outsized shimmering catches. Though I can only credit chance and timing with my iridescent prize. In fact, it would probably be more accurate to say Edward plucked *me* from the stream than the other way around.

I would be lying if I said Edward's background, his habits, his rituals—so alien to me—hadn't lent him a strange additional attraction. His world is different from mine, everything he does invested with the subtle shimmer of something gilded. Not that I knew who he was when he first spoke to me.

We met at my publisher's annual Summer Gala in London, a lavish, star-studded party packed with bestselling authors, high-flying editors, and superagents. That year it was being held at the Natural History Museum, the vaulting Victorian architecture festooned with bright bursts of tropical flowers: orchids and heady-scented lilies. Waiters in white tie, ferrying champagne high above the heads of the mingling household names, debut authors, and reviewers. It was my first big author event, my book having only just come out the week before and exploding directly onto the Top Ten. I'd bought a ridiculously expensive emerald dress in celebration and then spent half the night trying not to spill booze and canapés down it. Nervous, and completely out of my depth, I let Louisa usher me from important contact to important contact until I finally managed to escape the madness for the relative calm of the loos. I am no shrinking violet but too much noise, too many faces, trigger old wounds and set my senses to a different frequency.

It was on the way back from the toilets, empty champagne glass in hand, that it happened. At first I thought it was nothing, just my heel snagging on something, causing a little stutter in my step. But the snag turned into a halt, a tug, and a hot blush rising as a glance back confirmed that my high heel was firmly wedged in one of the museum's tiny, ornate floor vents. Victorian central heating.

I gave another tug and the heel seemed to loosen, but a few passing eyes found their way to me and I panicked. I tugged again, harder. And with a retrospectively impressive show of strength and an extremely loud metallic clatter I somehow managed to completely dislodge the 150-year-old wrought-iron grate from the stone floor, still attached to my Dior heel. The noise and spectacle now attracting the gaze of everyone in the vicinity.

With a deep desire not to prolong the experience but totally unsure what else to do, I hitched my dress and—drained white with shame—half lifted, half dragged the entire wrought-iron grate back toward its gaping floor hole. The grate clanked and banged as I tried to get it back in, all the time with my heel firmly attached. And that's when he saved me, a firm hand on my back, that warm American accent, his voice low, reassuring, like home.

"Okay, okay. I see the problem." His first words to me. And though, of course, he meant the problem with my shoe, and the grate—and that he could fix it—to this day I like to think he meant he saw the larger problem, with everything, with my past, with the holes in my life, and that he could fix those too. Listen, I'm no damsel in distress, trust me, I've survived a lot more than most, but you can't underestimate the overwhelming power of someone swooping in to save you after a lifetime of having to save yourself.

Those eyes looking up at me, filled with such a disarming calm, with an inborn certainty that everything would all work out just great. The warmth of his skin against my bare shoulder blades. I did not have time to put up my usual barriers, to insulate myself or pull away from intimacy, because there I was, stuck.

He dropped down on one knee, like a proposal, like the prince in Cinderella, this impossibly handsome man, and as he gently wriggled my mangled shoe loose from the grate with my hands on his strong shoulders, I felt something inside me shift. A hope, long tamped down, flickered back to life in the darkness. And the rest is history.

Here I am a year-and-change later, having moved a continent and my entire life to be with him.

"Ed is doing great," I answer, though we both know it's an understatement. Ed's start-up company turns over more money in a month than the literary agency Louisa works for does in a year. Edward is doing immeasurably well, but we're British and we don't talk about stuff like that. Besides, Louisa is well aware of who Edward is, the family he comes from. He's a Holbeck and with a surname like that, even without family investment, success was almost inevitable. "I'm actually on my way to meet him now. He's taking me skating."

"Skating?" I hear the interest pique in her tone. She's desperate to hear about him. About the Holbecks. Somehow I managed to bag one of America's wealthiest bachelors without even trying and everyone wants to know how I did it, why I did it. But more important, they want to know: what are they like?

For that, of course, there is Google. And God knows I did a deep dive or ten in the weeks after meeting Edward. Generations of wealth, woven into the fabric of America since the Gilded Age, shipping, communications, and of course that ever-present shadow of questionable ethics. There is no end to the op-ed pieces on them, the gossip column space, the business section dealings with the Holbeck name, and yet the air of mystery they maintain around themselves means one can never quite be satisfied. They remain elusive, mercurial. That, with their presumably ruthless brand of magic, is a heady and alluring mix.

"He's taking you skating? Like roller-skating?" Louisa asks, incredulous, though I doubt anything I told her about Edward would really surprise her.

"No," I say. "No, he's taking me ice-skating. It's a family tradition, The Rink at Rockefeller Center, start of the season. He wants us to go together this year."

"Oh my God, will his whole family be there?" Louisa erupts. She's dying to hear more about them but I haven't been able to furnish her with any more information than I've gleaned from the internet so far.

"No. Still haven't met them. No family yet. Edward's terrified they'll scare me off." I cringe as I say it; I know how it sounds. Millionaire playboy won't introduce girlfriend to family. I'm aware I've moved my life for Edward and I haven't even met his parents yet. But it isn't like that. I see the look in his eyes when we talk about them. He has his reasons and the time will come. Besides, I didn't just move over here for him. I've needed a fresh start for a long time now, and the success of the book and meeting Edward made that a very real possibility.

Funny, I always thought I'd end up over here. My mother was an American. Sometimes, if I close my eyes, in coffee shops and restaurants I can almost imagine her voice among the crowd, her round open vowel sounds all around me, the warmth of it, like the past.

It's funny I don't recall my dad's voice at all, but I was only eleven when it happened. Twenty years of new experiences having scribbled over what was once so clear. Though I miss him just as much. It's only natural to forget when remembering hurts so much.

Louisa chuckles. "I'm not surprised he's wary. They sound terrifying. Well, you know what I mean, fascinating but . . . hive inducing." Her tone becomes playful, confidential. "Although between you and me, bloody hell, I would definitely be willing to put in some awkward in-law hours if Simon had looked half as good in a suit as Edward does." Louisa and Simon split up last year. He was pretty useless by all accounts, but her compliment stands.

And she's right. I would be willing to put up with an awful lot to be with Edward.

"Oh, and how's the new book coming?" she asks with a studied nonchalance that almost has me fooled. I'm three weeks past the deadline for my second book.

I shiver in the winter breeze, waiting for the crosswalk light to change. The truth is I haven't been able to focus for about a month now. Even the thought of sitting down to finish drains me. The crosswalk *pip-pip*s and I join the swarm of commuters flowing across Fifth.

"Harry?" Louisa's voice drags me back to reality. "The book?"

"Sorry, yes. The book is coming," I say, which is true. "I'm almost there," I say, which is not true at all. "I just need—"

"—another month?" she interjects. She knows me too well.

"Um. Yes. That would . . . that would be great."

"Okay. I'll hold the publishers off one more month. Listen, the first book is still flying off the shelves so we're in a good place. People will wait for the next. But you need to be honest with me about where we are, Harry. You're definitely nearly there?"

The seriousness of her tone hits me hard. "Yes. Four weeks, probably less. I swear. First draft done." As I say it, I realize it will be hard, but I can do it. I just need to break my funk.

My eyes catch the time blinking high on the side of an office building. I need to finish this call. Rockefeller Center is right ahead and Edward will be there waiting.

"Oh, and I forgot to say: the publishers want to have a meeting about the paperback edition this Wednesday afternoon. At their main office, does that work?"

Ahead the glittering frontage of Saks comes into view opposite the entrance to The Rink and I realize the rain has stopped.

After I agree to the time and hang up, I pop my phone on silent, pull off my winter hat, and shake out my hair, checking my reflection in a shop window. Edward and I have already been together just over a year, but I can't imagine a time when I won't still get those date-night nerves.

Tonight will be special, I feel it. I'm being introduced to a family tradition and God knows I could do with some of those. Orphans don't tend to have many.

As I round the corner of Rockefeller Plaza, my breath catches, the scale of the Christmas decorations bringing me to a stuttering halt.

In front of me is a tunnel of pure light created by the forms of angels heralding, golden trumpets raised. Color, light, and warmth. And beyond them, the famous tree, rising up into the New York skyline. I'd read in the paper this morning that it's over eighty feet tall, but standing beneath it now that number finally sinks in. It's the largest Christmas tree I've ever seen. I stand slack-jawed as I stare up. Around me a few other kindred spirits look up transfixed as the rest of New York jostles past us. Eighteen thousand lights twinkle golden into the night air, thick with the scent of Nordic pine and the delicious aroma of Christmas treats wafting from the vendors dotted about the plaza.

A hand grasps my shoulder and I whip around to a familiar touch. Edward. Wrapped up warm against the chill in a cashmere scarf and coat, his hair tousled, his eyes smiling.

"You scared the shit out of me," I lie, too embarrassed to say I would know the feel of him anywhere.

"Sorry," he says with a smile. "I called your name but I guess you didn't hear." He nods up to the tree, slipping his arms around my waist as I lean back into him, his warmth against mine. "It's really something, isn't it?"

Beneath the lights of the tree, on the sunken ice-skating rink, we watch as people glide effortlessly across its pristine surface, bobble hats on, bundled in scarves. Amid the young, old New York is still present, an elderly man in a full suit and hat, two women of equally advanced years wrapped in thick furs, their hair set hard as rocks.

"I'm a terrible skater," I warn Edward later as we fasten our skates and hobble out of the enclosure toward the ice.

"Lucky I'm here then." He grins, pulling me tight. He backs out onto the ice first and offers me both his hands for stability. I take them, my breath held in concentration as he glides us out into the middle of the rink. It's not that busy. A handful of new skaters slip and weave around us, and after a moment my muscles loosen into his rhythm, his movements reassuring and fluid. He was an athlete—I suppose he still is.

Christmas music blares merrily over the ice rink's loudspeaker, and as a new song begins Edward loosens one of his hands from mine. "May I have this dance?" he intones, grinning as he slowly spins me. I realize the song they're playing is "Fairytale of New York" by the Pogues—its craggy lilt kicking in as we slip and slide across the ice, grinning like idiots. One verse in and everyone on the ice is gliding in time with the jaunty tune as above us one of the more vocal market vendors starts to sing along with the lyrics, his accent an appropriate lilting Irish brogue. Other skaters instinctively join in, merrily blasting out the odd phrase, tongue firmly in cheek, but we're all singing. And just for a microsecond New York is made of magic. I find myself thinking: *God, I love Americans*. British people just aren't like this, our toes curl at the slightest inkling of real sentiment, and yet here *I* am, singing, dancing, on ice. Everyone's caught in the moment as the song crescendos and we belt out the chorus. Edward releases my hand again and I wobble slightly as he swoops down in front of me, one wet knee on the rink. He's got something in his hand and suddenly my stomach tightens with soul-capsizing embarrassment as I realize what it is.

Oh, please, no.

This is too much. He can't be doing what I think he's doing. I swallow hard. People are looking at us now, smiling at us, clapping for us, and I keep smiling because what the hell else can I do.

God knows I want him to ask, but this, here, is too much, too public. I feel my panic rise as he opens the box and starts to speak and suddenly the world around us fades away. I feel tears come and my voice catch and he's taking off my glove and sliding a ring onto my finger. A small crowd has formed on the walkway above the rink and they're cheering and whooping as the song ends and "Chapel of Love" blasts out into the chilly air around us. The lights twinkle in time as I struggle to take everything in.

Edward pulls me close. "I love you, Harry," he whispers. And for a second nothing else matters, because when I look into his eyes, I know it's true. This is him trying to give me new memories, strong, bold, undeniable memories. This is him sharing his life, his past, and his future with me. I touch his face, so handsome I often marvel at being allowed to. His lips are warm on mine and the city around us disappears. The sound of cheering muffled by his hands over my ears.

Later in the rink's Christmas café, I inspect the ring on my cold-numbed finger while he fetches us hot toddies. The stone glimmers in the light, the color caught between a rich claret and a warm brown. I've never seen anything like it. A ruby, I imagine. Large, deep, expensive. The setting, and cut, old. It must be an heirloom, yet the fit is perfect.

Edward heads back over, balancing our drinks and two mince pies in his hands.

"Did you plan that?" I ask, taking a tentative swig of the sweet heady drink. "The music, the singing?" It fleetingly occurs to me that, with the means at his disposal, Edward could have rented out the entire rink and peopled it with ensemble actors twice over if he had so desired. It's a terrifying thought but thankfully a million miles from anything Edward might actually do.

He splutters a laugh and shakes his head, wiping mince pie dust from his upper lip. "No," he says. "I mean, I knew I was going to ask you tonight. I had the ring on me, but I wasn't planning for it to turn into a Broadway number out there. Guess that's New York for you; everyone's got something to say." He looks suddenly concerned. "Ah God. It was too much, wasn't it? Damn it, sometimes I forget you're British."

He's genuinely mortified.

"No, stop. It was perfect. I mean, I'm not likely to forget it," I quip. "And for the record, I'm not British anymore, am I? My US passport is as real as yours."

"Good, well then, consider what just happened out there on the ice your swearing-in ceremony. It's all going to get pretty un-British from here on in. But seriously, if anything gets too much, you have to tell me. No harm no foul. I don't want to scare you off. At least . . . not yet anyway."

He means his family. They must know he was planning on asking me; I'm guessing he had to ask them for the ring. And now that we're engaged meeting them must be in the cards. I raise my hand and consider the deep-red jewel in the light. "What stone is this?"

"Garnet. It was my great-grandmother's. Mitzi's." He studies my reaction. "You like it, right? No? We can change it. Get something new?"

"No, no," I blurt. He's so worried about the effect his family will have on me he can't read me at all. "Edward, *I love it,*" I tell him, taking in its gleaming facets. "I mean, God, I think I might love it more than I love you," I joke. "Seriously, though, I love that it means something. To you, to your family. That it's important. What was she like? Mitzi?"

I would be lying if I said I didn't already know as much as the internet can tell me about Edward's family.

John Livingston Holbeck, Edward's great-great-great-grandfather, was one of the original Gilded Age tycoons who made their fortune in the 1800s during a period of massive expansion across America. J. L. Holbeck created monopolies and reaped the rewards of a captive market by controlling a large percentage of all shipping, railways, and communications at the time. One of the handful of men who built America in an era predating taxation, J. L. Holbeck amassed a mind-boggling fortune and innumerable holdings; he was a contemporary of Cornelius Vanderbilt, Andrew Carnegie, and the father of the man who built the building we're now sitting beneath. Which makes me wonder if this skating-on-the-first-day-of-the-season tradition dates a lot further back than I had previously considered.

"What was Mitzi like?"

Edward ponders my question. "She was beautiful. And talented. She was an artist, she trained as a ballerina. German, but she left between the wars, then she met my great-grandfather. They had this great love affair, so the story goes, this intense love

affair. Famously, theirs was the first marriage for love in the Holbeck family."

I choose not to open that can of worms. Though I have no
experience of wealth I can understand the instinct to protect it, to
fortify what you have. Love is an unknown quantity after all. It's
a gamble at the end of the day. I'm more than happy to gamble
with the few chips I have, but give me the GDP of a medium-sized
country and I might at least consider a prenup. I'm sure the Holbecks have learned the hard way to question that first flush of
passion.

"And your family's okay with this. With me? They let you
have Mitzi's ring?"

I wonder what they'll make of me now that I know for certain
they're aware of my existence. What Edward has or hasn't told
them about me. Perhaps they've looked into me themselves? I
shudder at the thought, then quickly reassure myself that while
they might be able to research me, they can never know my
thoughts, my memories. I am just a British novelist with no real
credentials—except one bestseller to her name—no real history,
no Ivy League anything, no Oxbridge. I can't imagine I'm what
they had in mind for their firstborn son. I don't even have a family, let alone a notable one.

Maybe they just want Edward to be happy. Edward has promised me time and time again that not meeting them has nothing
to do with me. He's had problems with them in the past, they like
to exert control, he tries to keep his life at a distance from the
madness of theirs. Things tend to get dragged into their orbit.
Which makes the sudden appearance of this family ring now on
my finger all the more interesting.

"Yes, they know about you," he says with a grin. "A worrying
amount actually. Mother was over the moon when I asked for
the ring. Insisted I use it actually."

"Really?" I ask, trying to mediate the surprise in my voice. It's
not that I have a self-esteem issue, but it's slightly puzzling that a
woman like Eleanor Holbeck would be insisting her firstborn
child jump at the chance to marry an orphan from England.

"Really," he echoes and takes my cold hand in his across the table. "Listen, I know it's weird you've never met them. But I wanted to be sure we were in a good place before"—he pauses, trying to find the words—"before I let them loose on you. They are a lot to handle. But if you want to meet them, they *really* want to meet you. Especially now." He thumbs the ring on my finger gently. "We haven't had anyone like you in our family be-fore," he says lightly, and the words imprint themselves in my mind. What does that mean? *Someone like me.* "And God knows we could do with fresh blood."

I feel my throat tighten at the thought of the type of person I actually am. But they can't know that. They cannot know what happened to me on the edge of that road twenty years ago; I was alone.

I shudder, and Edward lifts my hands to his lips to blow warmth back into them. "If you're worried about what they think about us, don't be. My great-grandfather had all the money in the world, and he married a woman without a penny. Granted, he was the only one ever to do it—point is, there's precedent." He laughs at my reaction. "I know, I know, you're hardly on the breadline! Plenty of pennies in bestselling author Harry Reed's coffers. But you know what I mean," he adds seriously. And I do, because whatever I have is only ever going to be a drop in the Holbeck ocean.

"Why did your great-grandfather choose a garnet? For Mitzi's ring?" I ask.

"She loved pomegranates."

I look down at the ring and smile. It looks just like the top of a ripe pomegranate seed.

"He knew he could make her happy and that she would do anything for him. They just fit. Two peas in a pod. And together no one could stop them," Edward says, studying my expression.

I take him in, this fiancé of mine, in all his glory. Tall, athletic, in cashmere and tailored Italian wool, and I can't hold back the grin. God knows how I found him. God knows how it got this far, this serious.

"When am I going to meet them?" I ask.

A smirk forms. "Apparently, my sister has been chosen to *ease* the transition. The powers that be have deemed her the most accessible family member to make an introduction," he says jokingly. "After me, obviously."

I can imagine Edward is the most normal—if that's the right word—of the Holbecks. He's clearly spent his life trying to be. After graduating from MIT, he actively moved away from the family business, handing his control of that side of things over to his brothers. He's a *self-made* man—as much as a Holbeck descendant can ever be, that is. He established his own tech start-up and grew the company into what it is today. Although I'm sure the glamour of his surname can't have hurt his success, alongside his intelligence and easy, affable charm.

"So I'm going to meet your sister first. Matilda?" He nods before I continue. "And she has my phone number?"

"Oh yes. That she does." Edward grins. "She's got your number, email address, *actual* address, dress *size*, blood type, donor consent status . . . kidding."

I narrow my eyes. "I thought you said I shouldn't be scared of her?"

"Oh no. You should *definitely* be scared of her. She's absolutely terrifying, they all are; you'd be mad not to be. But I think you want this, don't you? To be included, part of the family? A family?" He finds the answer in my eyes. "Just don't change your mind about me after all this, that's all I ask," he says, then kisses the ring on my finger lightly and grins.

2

An Invitation

TUESDAY, NOVEMBER 22

"His family could literally be insane. You've never even met them and you've already agreed to marry into it. You have no idea what you've signed up for. As your agent and friend, I've got to say it's dicey territory."

I can't help but bark out a laugh in spite of my throbbing head. Edward and I stayed out celebrating last night, and my champagne hangover is showing no sign of diminishing even after a pint of water and two paracetamols. I only rang Louisa for more details about my publisher meeting on Wednesday, but here we are. I wedge my mobile into a more comfortable position between my ear and shoulder and continue to tap away at my computer as I talk.

"Every family is crazy, though, right? In their own way. Money just highlights what's already there." I chuckle. "Plus,

I've only agreed to be his fiancée. It's hardly a legally binding contract."

"Oh, okay? So, you'll cut and run if they're all mad as hatters then, will you?" she challenges.

I take a moment to genuinely consider how bad the Holbecks would have to be in order to put me off Edward. "No. You're right," I concede. "They could basically be the Fritzls and I'd still try to make it work with Ed."

Louisa bursts out laughing. "I'm glad you're in a place where you can admit that, at least. My God, that proposal though. Singing, dancing, Christmas. Wowzer. I'm surprised your head didn't explode. No half measures there. You remember when Simon proposed to me? In our old back garden after breakfast? You and Ed make me sick."

"Hey, it *was* snowing in your back garden. Give Si some credit. Though probably best you turned him down in the end, all things considered."

"Yeah, I have quite the instinct for these things," she jokes. "Which brings me back round to Ed's family. Random Holbecks are just going to descend on you at some point, are they?" She must hear the sound of my keyboard, as she doesn't wait for an answer. "Hey. Are you writing now? While I'm talking to you?" she asks, mock-incredulous, then cheers loudly.

I pull back from the noise, my hungover brain reeling. "Please, Lou, I am very tender today. No loud noises."

"I'm just glad you're getting sucked into the draft. I knew you'd rally," she adds proudly.

I look at my screen. I have not rallied.

"I'm not writing, Lou. I'm googling Mitzi Holbeck."

An image of Edward's great-grandmother stares back at me on Google Images. A grainy black-and-white wedding shot from *The New York Times* in 1923.

"Oh. Hang on . . . there was a Mitzi? My God. *Fabulous* name."

I stare at Mitzi, and Alfred Holbeck beside her, a paparazzi shot from their wedding day for some old society column. They were celebrities back then. Alfred holds open a town car door for Mitzi as she beams out at the camera in her wedding dress, a knowing twinkle in her eyes. God, she was beautiful. Alfred too, gallant, handsome, a rough-hewn old-world prototype of Edward.

"I know, right, and she was really something too. An artist. She fled Germany between the wars—her family was originally from Bohemia."

"Bohemia? Is that even a place? Who are these people?"

"Bohemia is just a fancy name for Czechoslovakia, pre-1918, basically before—" A loud knock on the front door interrupts me.

I push my study chair back and stare down our long apartment hallway to the front door. Odd, I'm not expecting anyone this morning, and Edward left for a tech conference in San Diego earlier. "Sorry, Lou, one second."

"Everything okay?" Louisa asks.

"Yeah, just the front door." A second knock comes, more insistent this time.

"Probably a package or something."

As I make my excuses and hang up, another knock comes hard. I head out into the hall, scraping back my hair quickly as I pass the hall mirror. A brief glance at my reflection reminds me I haven't yet showered this morning. But then I'm supposed to be in full deadline mode. Perhaps with Edward away for the next few days I'll actually get time to write, to finally finish my book.

As I reach for the front-door latch, I freeze. Edward said I'd meet Matilda soon. My heart skips a beat as I realize she could be on the other side of this door.

My fingers hover over the latch; I am in no fit state to meet someone like Matilda Holbeck. I look down at my comfy writing clothes, my bobbly wool socks and cardigan, and groan internally. This is not the first impression I should be making. I've seen photographs of Matilda Holbeck and I'm pretty sure a wool sock has never even made it into her *Architectural Digest* apartment, let alone onto her feet. I squint through the peephole but our new Christmas wreath blocks my view.

Another loud knock comes, this time incredibly close to my face.

I could pretend to be out but I've hardly been stealthy this side of the door. If she knows I'm here and hiding that would be an even worse first impression than my appearance.

I take a deep breath, remind myself I am good enough as I am, and open the door.

Instead of Matilda's pale angular features, I'm met with the brisk outdoor energy of a bearded city courier. Disinterested, he hands me a crisp white envelope, gesturing for me to sign. I quickly scribble my name, half relieved, half spooked by my own paranoia, then watch as he wordlessly disappears around the corridor toward the elevators.

Back in the apartment I turn the thick card of the envelope over in my hands. On the front, my name and address are carefully inked onto the paper. I don't need to open it to know who it is from: no one I know owns stationery this nice; no one I know couriers mail. Matilda has sent me a letter. She could have called, sent a text message, emailed, but she didn't; she sent a hand-couriered letter. Hardly as accessible as advertised, but I can't deny there is a certain thrill to the feel of the watermarked correspondence in my hands.

In the kitchen I flick on the kettle and perch on a kitchen island stool, slipping a finger under the envelope's gum seal and carefully tugging out the note card from within. The thick white card is embossed at the top with the silver swirling initials MBH.

Matilda Beatrice Holbeck. Edward's sister. The next in line to the throne. Unmarried, five years my senior, the Holbecks' only daughter. Beneath her initials an elegant handwritten request to join her, tomorrow, at a fashionable Upper East Side members club for afternoon tea. Four P.M.

My stomach flips as I read; my publisher meeting is at four P.M. tomorrow. I am already in tricky territory with my deadline, so meeting the publisher is definitely not the kind of appointment I can push. It would send all the wrong signals. Which means I need to rearrange with Matilda.

At the bottom of the card in silver leaf is an RVSP email, her assistant. My shoulders relax slightly at the idea I won't have to turn her down directly. Her assistant can just reschedule—I'm free pretty much any other day.

I shoot off my RSVP and head back to my desk with purpose, to address my word count.

Four minutes later a reply pings into my inbox. Matilda's assistant, Max, writes: *That is unfortunate timing-wise. I will pass on your deepest regrets to Ms. Holbeck.*

My stomach tightens. He'll pass on *my deepest regrets*? Well, that sounds incredibly dramatic. Almost like I'm refusing to meet her at all rather than asking for a raincheck. Mild panic begins to brew but I tell myself I do not have time for this right now. I can only hope Max passes on my actual reasons. I force myself to stop rereading my email, and his, and I dive back into the novel.

An hour later I almost jump out of my skin when an extremely loud phone starts ringing in our hallway. I didn't even know we had a landline, and it's certainly the first time anyone has ever called it in the four months since we moved in. Edward must have had it installed at some point.

The shrill ring continues, impossible to ignore. I head out to answer it.

"Hello?"

"Hi, Harry, it's Amy at Grenville Sinclair."

My publisher. That's odd.

"Oh, hi, Amy?"

"Hi. So, I'm calling about the meeting scheduled here at the office tomorrow. Just to let you know we're rescheduling our end."

"Rescheduling?"

"Yes. We're happy to. So, that's fine," she says curtly. There's something odd in her tone. "Can you do next week, perhaps? Or if not, there's really no rush for this meeting at all. We could just postpone until the New Year if that's easier . . . for you? Timing-wise."

And suddenly I realize exactly what's going on here and I am genuinely speechless. It takes me a second to give voice to my thoughts, so bizarre is the conclusion they seem to come to.

"Amy? Did someone else just call you? Is this something to do with—wait, Grenville Sinclair is part of the Laurence Group, isn't it?"

She gives a nervous laugh. "It is, yeah."

"Right. And . . . the Laurence Group is a subsidiary of . . . ?"

"ThruComm Holbeck."

"Yep. Okay. Yep," I manage. "I think I see what's happened here."

While I of course knew that my publisher was in some way connected to the business interests of my future in-laws, the idea that they might ever use this fact as some kind of leverage had not even crossed my mind until now.

Matilda has canceled my meeting so that I can eat cake with her.

"Um, Amy, I am so, so sorry about this, I . . . if any—"

"No, no, no. Harriet, *please*. Really, it is absolutely fine. I mean, whatever we can do to accommodate our authors. That's always our primary concern here. So let us know, about next week or next month. Whenever you're ready. We're here."

"Okay. Okay, thank you, Amy."

The line is silent for a moment. "Yes, thank you, Harriet." And she's gone.

I stand in silence in the hallway for a moment to let what just happened sink in. And the realization hits me that however weird this situation is, this is only the start of my dealings with the Holbecks. Matilda is supposed to be the most restrained member of Edward's family, and if this is restrained then God help me.

Dazed, I head back to the study and grab my mobile, bringing up Edward's number, my thumb poised over the DIAL button. This is exactly what he was worried about. His family being too much for me. I take a breath and close the app.

I can do this. I knew his family would be tricky but this is what I want. I want to be with Edward, to start a family with him, to be part of something bigger than myself. I'm going to have to buckle in if I'm going on this ride. I can't balk this early. After moving continents for this, after leaving my old life and friends behind, I won't let this knock us off course. And I don't want Edward to be forever pulling me out of sticky situations. I can deal with this on my own.

I place my mobile back down on the desk beside me and type out a short email to Matilda's assistant, Max.

Am now available for 4 P.M. tomorrow.

My email swooshes out into the ether.

I sit motionless for a moment wondering if I have made the right decision or if I have allowed things to start off on slightly the wrong foot. I feel the mild panic of earlier rise again inside me and my hangover pound back to life. I try to breathe through it but suddenly I realize it's too late. I shoot up from my chair, an unstoppable urge to vomit surging through me. I burst from the room and hurtle toward the bathroom, hand clamped firmly over mouth as behind me I hear the ping of a new email landing in my inbox.

3

Two for Tea

The nausea hasn't abated when I arrive at Matilda's private members club the following day. The website listed the dress code as *smart casual* so I'm wearing heels even though I feel like death warmed up and have an irrationally strong desire to take them off and hurl them as hard as I can at the ten-foot ecru marble sculpture in the club lobby.

Pre-meeting nerves and illness have twisted my previously hopeful attitude into one of full-blown irritation at being forced into this situation. I should be working; I should be meeting my publisher, not here at the beck and call of a woman I've never even met.

And I have no idea why my hangover decided to stick around but it seems to have somehow morphed into some kind of stomach flu. Either way it's safe to say that—after a day and a half of nausea, vomiting, and lack of sleep, in spite of being absolutely exhausted—there is nowhere on earth I would rather be less than waiting to be seated for a formal afternoon tea.

But here I am, because I have to be. The truth is I want Edward's sister to like me way more than I care to admit, and postponing again, this time due to illness, might look a little too deliberate.

As I'm led into the club's lounge my eyes find her almost immediately, that vibrant pop of auburn hair, a shot of red in a sea of New York neutrals. She's even more beautiful in real life than in the photographs I've seen. Perhaps they all are, the Holbecks.

I glide past tables of elegantly dressed, artsy, Museum Mile hipsters. At her table she is turned away from me as she points to something in a menu, an attentive waiter leaning in to catch her order. I imagine she knows exactly what she wants. She must feel eyes on her because she looks up and meets my gaze with alarming precision, almost as if I'd called her name. A fresh wave of nausea hits me and I pray that Matilda's first memory of me won't involve me being sick.

I hazard a smile, but immediately realize that given her statuesque demeanor, she might not be a big smiler. A suspicion quickly confirmed when she raises a pale hand in acknowledgment of my arrival, her face remaining perfectly still.

My already queasy stomach tightens. This could be a long tea. Or a very short one. I'm suddenly reminded of Matilda's *helpful* phone call to my publisher yesterday and how easy it is for a Holbeck to make things happen or stop them dead.

Matilda's waiter unobtrusively pulls out a chair for me as I arrive, before smoothly exiting.

Matilda's eyes play over me as I settle and take her in: her crisp white shirt, that immaculate tailoring, those pillowy red lips and the two perfect emerald earrings twinkling through her flame hair. From her unwavering expression, I cannot help but wonder, for the first time, if Edward might have outright lied to me when he said his family couldn't wait to meet me.

She stretches out an alabaster hand across the table and then, to my unending relief, cracks a giddy smile. "Harriet. It's *so* wonderful to meet you," she says, her voice a bubbling brook of warmth and friendliness. I take her cool hand in mine and shake. "*Argh,*" she continues, animatedly. "I'm *supposed* to be on my best behavior but—wait, do I call you Harriet? Harry? What do you like? Harry, right?" I nod and she barrels on. "Great. So, *Harry,* I'm *supposed* to be on my best behavior, representing the family, yada yada, but can I just get out of the way how excited I am about all of this? You and Edward. Edward settling down. With you. This is so good. Your move, the engagement, all of it. He's a tough little nut to crack but looks like you cracked him. He's had us in the dark completely. But then he barrels in asking for Gran-Gran Mitzi's ring. And here we all are." She takes a heady breath in through her nose before letting out a sigh. "It is so great that we are finally doing this. Meeting. Edward is such a grouch for keeping you to himself this whole time." She pauses, her beautiful features resetting into their statuesque stillness.

She's not the person I expected at all. She's easy and affable, with a girlish ebullience that instantly dissolves my preconceptions. It's hard to believe she'd make a power move like cancel my publisher meeting through anything other than presumed helpfulness. Unless this is all part of some elaborate act. But right now, with Matilda sitting in front of me, I honestly can't imagine us not becoming fast friends.

"Matilda, it is so wonderful to finally meet you too. I've heard so much about you from Edward—"

"All good I hope?" She smirks.

"Mm-hmm," I answer, my pitch a little higher than rings true. "Yeah, yes, all good. Well, you know . . ."

"Don't worry. I know Edward *very well*. He can be sensitive about his relationships. And about the family." She sobers slightly, her tone serious. "But rightly so, I understand why completely. He's had problems in the past with relationships and with Dad." Yes, Robert Davison Holbeck. Edward's father. Now, there is a terrifying man if ever there was one. Terrifying in the way rich, attractive men always tend to be. There are rumors of the type of man he might have been in his youth, the type of man he still might be. Allegations, payoffs, blackmail, business dealings in countries where there shouldn't be, and insider trading. But never anything more than allegations. His ability to ride anything out seemingly unstoppable.

"But you know it's hard, for any of us, to find a partner who's okay with all this," she adds conspiratorially, gesturing to the air around her. "At least that's my excuse for being perpetually single." She smiles, lightening the mood. "Hey, shall we order? I could eat a horse, hooves and all."

Tea poured, and Jenga-stacked truffle-infused finger sandwiches and French confections towering beside us, I force down my nausea and steer the conversation back to me and Edward. I need to get a feel for the lay of the land in the Holbeck camp.

"You said the ring was the first you'd heard about us, is that really true?" I ask tentatively. "Edward didn't mention me at all?"

"Oh gosh no. Of course, we all *knew* about you. It's impossible to keep things quiet in this family. We just weren't allowed to ask him about it. We were told in no uncertain terms to back off. That you might be the one."

"By Edward?"

She nods and I can't help the flush of happiness that comes from the thought of Edward saying those words.

"We knew he had a new girlfriend. You," she continues. "And that you met in London. That you're an author, which by the way is beyond fascinating to me—but we'll put a pin in that and circle back; I have a million questions. But regarding Edward, we gave him space, because we've made mistakes in the past. Forced issues that perhaps we shouldn't have. Anyway, this time things seem very different. You seem *very* different from his previous girlfriends."

I feel my hackles rise. I dread to think what it could be that makes me so different. But she's moved on before a sentient question can even form in my mind.

"He's never talked about anyone the way he talks about you. He has this certainty—that you're the one."

"The one?" I ask.

"Uh-huh." She nods, then leans forward, her elbows on the linen of the tablecloth. "And he's so much happier now. He came by the house a couple of weeks back to talk to us about everything, to get the ring. We hadn't seen him, God, not since last Christmas. It was a tough one between him and Dad. They're cut from the same cloth, you see. Before you, Edward was *work, work, work*. For years now. But since you he's mellowed. We thought he'd stopped trying to find someone, that he'd end up an old bachelor. Then you." Her voice lowers conspiratorially once more. "I'm going to be honest with you, Harry, because I like you. I'm not sure how much you know but things have not been great between Dad and Edward for a long while now. Dad pushes him, sometimes too far. It's a lot of pressure and in the past, with Ed's romantic choices, things haven't worked out at all."

I'm leaning in now too. "What do you mean? What went wrong?"

"Well, not to put too fine a point on it, Harry, but we-gotta-lotta-money." She lets out a little girlie snort at her own words.

"And that's caused problems? His exes had the wrong intentions?"

"Well, we'll never know now, will we? They never lasted. I'm not gonna lie, we can all be a little much, but we've got a nose for bad intentions, it kind of comes with the territory. Sometimes Ed lets his emotions get in the way of self-preservation. I know how the world views us: cutthroat, dog-eat-dog, sociopaths, or whatever. But we're only reacting to what we face every day. It is brutal out here. And you should know, coming into all this, everything we have, everything we are, other people want it. We developed tough skins because by God, we've needed them just to survive. But we love Ed, we want him to be happy. Here's the thing. Since the last girlfriend—he's kept his distance from the family. He got it in his head Daddy scared her off. That he'll scare you off." She shrugs lightly. "And maybe he did scare the last one, but maybe it was for the best. Some people aren't built for this, some people aren't strong enough to run with the pack." Her eyes flick across my features before she adds, "I see you, though. You're a strong one. I see it in your eyes. To get this far, to leave a life behind, to get that ring on your finger, you're a strong one, a survivor. Like us." She gives my hand a rallying squeeze across the table and I realize that even though she doesn't know me, she kind of knows me. "Listen," she continues, "don't worry about meeting Daddy, he's mellowed. The upshot is Dad wants Edward back in the fold, and you make him happy. Edward wants you and if any of us stand in the way I'm under no illusions that we'll lose him completely. I think I understand your intentions toward him. He's always been a good brother to me. So my question to you is: will you help us out?"

"Help you out?"

"Yeah, honey. Will you help the family out? We want him back; we want to keep him where we can see him. We think this engagement is just wonderful."

A strange warmth permeates me as I begin to understand what is going on here. They *have* to have me; they *have* to like me; they have *no* choice. As I said, I don't have a self-esteem problem but the idea of their immediate acceptance of a nobody from England as their new daughter-in-law was completely baffling, until now. Why would one of the wealthiest families in America endorse the engagement of their oldest son to a woman they'd never met? Here is the answer. It's reassuring in its simplicity. They pushed him away and vetoed his choices too many times and they've run out of *no*s. They either accept me or they lose him.

Edward's already chosen me over them, so they need me on their side if they want him back. I'm the missing piece that can bring them together again.

I'm no business tycoon but I do know that you can't sell anything without first creating a need. However uneven our power differential might be I have something that the Holbecks want: their son.

My blue eyes find Matilda's green ones. "I understand. And I'll see what I can do," I say with a smile.

"Fabulous." She grins. Then a thought seems to occur to her, almost in passing, almost as if she's only just thought of it. Almost.

"Oh, and listen, what are you both doing tomorrow?"

"Tomorrow? I'm not sure. Not much, I don't think. Why?"

She pauses, confused in some way by my response. Then she smiles. "Oh, of course, right. Well, we're having a little family dinner. It might be a nice occasion for you to meet everyone. There'll be a big crowd, but everyone's girlfriends/partners will be there too so there'll be lots to take the pressure off you. Just a quiet family dinner. I just think everyone's going to love you. I wouldn't suggest it otherwise, trust me."

"Tomorrow? Yeah, okay, I don't see why not. I'll tell Edward we're coming over."

Matilda squeezes my arm in solidarity. "That would be perfect. This is perfect. I can't wait."

Out on the street Matilda hails me a cab and slips the driver a wad of bills as I slide in.

"Oh, and honey," she barks through my open window. "Forgot to say. I am so sorry for that situation with your publisher. I thought I was helping but Mother tells me, 'All totally inappropriate.' So, lesson learned. Don't worry. It won't happen again, Sis." And with that she blows me a kiss and slaps the roof of the taxi, sending us off into the busy traffic.

Edward's still in San Diego so I tap out a text to let him know I've agreed to the family dinner. He'll be back tomorrow morning and there will be more than enough time for us to make it across town for the evening. Although the idea of meeting everyone tomorrow is incredibly daunting, I can't think of a better way to acclimate myself to them than in a large group where the focus will be spread out.

Edward's reply comes back almost instantly.

Tomorrow night?!

Yeah. Why?

And you told them we were free?!

Um, yes . . . we are free, aren't we? Is everything ok? Xx

You know what tomorrow is, right?

What do you mean?

Tomorrow is Thanksgiving!

I stare at my phone screen unblinking. *No. Oh my God, no.* I did not know that. I feel my face throb with heat, my nausea re-surfacing, until colors speckle my vision of the city through the cab window.

She tricked me. Matilda straight up tricked me into a Thanks-giving dinner.

I may be British but I know Thanksgiving is a big deal and definitely not something to be wandered into lightly, the day be-fore it happens, having never met another soul at the table. My stomach flips as I picture the scene in my mind's eye.

I open my cab window, letting the cold air cool my flaming cheeks. New York rushes past, and life goes on, the world keeps turning even though I am heading directly into the heart of the Holbeck clan, tomorrow evening, like a lamb to the slaughter.

Matilda tricked me and I didn't even notice it happening. If she's the presentable face of that family, then I will need to be on my toes tomorrow night. A shudder runs through me as I close the window and it hits me that I will finally be meeting Robert Holbeck.

I stare down at Edward's replies. He's worried. He's annoyed with them already. He thinks they're up to their old tricks. But if there's one thing Matilda said this afternoon that I can be sure is true it's that, her Thanksgiving trick aside, this time things will be different.

Edward's family needs me. They can't afford to push me away, because if they do, they'll lose him forever.

I carefully tap out a reply to Edward.

> Of course, I knew it was Thanksgiving.
> Matilda and I thought it might be a good
> way to kick things off x

4

The More the Merrier

THURSDAY, NOVEMBER 24

Edward gets back from San Diego earlier than expected the next morning.

When I hear the front-door latch lift I rush to quickly shut down the open tab on my screen, fumbling to delete the recent search history. I've been googling Edward's ex-girlfriends, the ones that didn't make the Holbeck cut. As if, somehow, I might uncover the secret reasons they failed.

Of course Edward has told me about them, and God knows I've looked them all up before now, but back in the early days I was only concerned with torturing myself through comparison; now I have my business brain on. I want to know the details.

I want to know what exactly made them sub-Holbeck in Edward's family's eyes. I have less than twelve hours till I meet them and I want to be armed, at least, with knowledge of how my predecessors failed.

Evidence of my deep dive erased, I head out to meet Edward as he lugs his suitcase into the hallway.

He looks up at me as he unlatches his case and smiles, impossibly fresh for this time of the morning—especially considering the flight he's just taken. I on the other hand look exhausted. I've been ill now for three days straight, the nausea and lethargy unabated. "You look awful," he says with a grin. "Did you miss me that much?"

It's just a joke and I know he loves me, regardless of my pallor, but to my utter horror tears burst from me unbidden. It must be the emotional buildup and low-key stress of the last few days breaking to the surface, though I hadn't really been aware of its presence until now.

I throw my arms around him, burying my face in his sweater to inhale the warm, fresh scent of his cologne. Cedar and citrus. This is very unlike me; I never cry. And I dare not look up at him now, crippled with the sheer weight of my own awkward need. I feel his hand in my hair, his mouth close to my ear as he speaks.

"I missed you a ridiculous amount too," he whispers, then kisses the top of my head. "How did it go with Sis? I'm guessing good given our Thanksgiving plans tonight."

I look up to check his expression, to see if Thanksgiving is a problem that we need to address, but his face shows nothing more than mild surprise at my sudden clinginess.

"So you're okay with tonight?" I check.

"I am if you are. But—and don't take this the wrong way—you don't seem like you're in quite the right frame of mind for tonight?"

He takes in my pasty, tearstained face. "It's food poisoning or something," I tell him, quickly wiping the tears away and pulling myself together. I am not going to be the reason tonight fails. "I'm fine. I'll be fine. I've had it a few days now. But it's manageable."

I untangle myself from him and head to the kitchen, hoping to locate something that might perk me up. "Tea? Coffee?" I ask him.

"Err, yeah, coffee, thanks," he calls after me.

From my research into Edward's exes this morning, being from a wealthy, notable family doesn't seem to be enough for the Holbecks. Edward's first girlfriend out of university was the daughter of a Fortune 500 founder and that didn't work out. I found a few society-page magazine photos of them on Reddit. Girlfriends of the super-rich. I know, I'm a terrible person. In the shots they both look so young, squinting in the harsh pop of a paparazzi flash. Rosy-cheeked, clammy hands held tight, like two wholesome Ralph Lauren models. Lily was beautiful, a good match for him in looks and height and breeding. She's married to a senator now, with three freckle-faced angel kids and a choco-late Labrador. So the Holbecks must require something else from their potential daughters-in-law, something more than money and looks and prestige. God knows what the Holbecks had against Lily, or—if Matilda is to be believed—what Robert Hol-beck in particular had against her; I couldn't imagine a more perfect match for Edward.

Edward's second internet-documented ex was more recent, a relatively well-known French actress with an impossibly cool air. I stare at my own distorted reflection in the metal of the toaster and feel a kick of inadequacy. A lifetime without a family, con-stantly adapting to fit into new groups and situations, stripped me of any kind of default insouciance long ago—I might be able to look relaxed but I rarely actually feel it. Especially today. Now, apparently, I cry for no reason. I try to remind myself that I have been sick for three days, I'm just tired.

The kettle rattles to a boil and clicks off triumphantly. But as I fill the cafetière the rich scent of the coffee grounds hits me with overwhelming force. Do they usually smell this strong? My hand flies to my mouth and I run, full tilt, sprinting past a puz-zled Edward as I race for the apartment's bathroom. I reach it just in time, retching into the porcelain of the toilet bowl until there is nothing left in my stomach. After a moment of hiatus, I catch my breath, my shaking body sinking down onto the cool tile floor.

A concerned tap comes from the door: Edward.

"You okay?" he asks, poking his head around.

"Yeah, fine," I lie, quickly wiping my mouth and pulling myself up to sit, with a modicum of dignity, on the rim of the tub. "It's just this virus thing."

"Virus? Okay. 'Cause it kind of seems a lot like you're—" he says, leaving the words hanging as if we're both in on a secret. Except I have no idea what he's talking about.

And now he's grinning at me. "You're not, are you?" he asks.

"Not what?" I croak.

"Pregnant?"

I stare at him, dumbstruck. Of course I'm not pregnant.

I'd know if I was pregnant. Wouldn't I? My mind races back over the last few weeks, my inability to focus on my writing, my bizarre fatigue, my complete loss of appetite, my intense sense of smell, nausea, vomiting, crying?

Oh shit.

Ten minutes later we're in the bodega beneath our building purchasing three boxes of pregnancy tests, Edward a ball of contained excitement by my side.

The cashier eyes us both with suspicion as I pay, a bleary-eyed, bedraggled woman and an immaculate, beaming man in a suit.

Back in my bathroom I rip open the tests and go to town. Three minutes later it's official: we're having a baby.

Edward scoops me up into his arms and spins me around the sun-filled sitting room, the trees of Central Park visible through our terrace windows, and I can't help but cry, happy tears this time, because I realize with sudden unearthly clarity what this means. After a lifetime alone, I am going to make my own family. *We* are going to be a family.

And with that surge of happiness comes, too, the relief of knowing that the writer's block, the unproductivity, of the last month or so isn't me losing my creative spark. I have been making a person. Growing the beginnings of a human brain and body deep inside my own.

I check my calendar and a quick calculation tells me that I must be close to eight weeks; what with settling into my new life here and everything associated with that, I must have missed my last period completely.

Edward looks up how long morning sickness lasts and I'm horrified to learn I have at least another month of this never-ending hangover feeling. Though right now, in this moment, I have never felt happier.

Edward makes a call to his family doctor and by lunchtime we are holding hands in Dr. Leyman's wood-paneled office as he looks at my hormone levels and blood test results.

My dates and maths seem to add up so Dr. Leyman books us in for a scan the following week, where we'll be able to see the fetus for the first time.

I'm prescribed pregnancy-safe anti-nausea tablets for the constant vomiting and Dr. Leyman talks me through all the things I should and shouldn't be doing from now on, but all I can think of is the future. The life beginning to take form inside me and what it means for us.

It's late afternoon when Edward and I get back to the apartment and we remember our almost forgotten Thanksgiving dinner plans.

"We can cancel," he says, a sliver of hope in his voice. And he's right in a sense, because just the idea of meeting *everyone* in a few hours sends adrenaline coursing through my already depleted body. But I know that now that we are becoming a family in our own right, there is even more reason to meet his.

"I have to meet them at some point, Ed. If we do introductions now it won't be such a bombshell when we tell them about the pregnancy. I'll be in the second trimester soon and we can tell them then. That gives them three weeks from now to get their heads around the idea of me before we land a baby on them too. It's probably best to get the ball rolling as soon as possible, right?"

Edward weighs my words. "Put like that, yeah. But I don't want you feeling pressured by any of this. Dr. Leyman said you should avoid anything too stressful until we get through the first trimester. We'll go tonight but if it gets too much you need to tell me straightaway. If anything concerns you, you tell me. Right?"

His tone has a seriousness that makes my stomach flip. He's not messing around; all joking aside, his family is going to be hard work. I think of Matilda, her smile, her ebullient warmth, and then the fact that she completely screwed me into a nonconsensual Thanksgiving. I'll be walking into a whole nest of Matildas tonight. A building full of people I might not even realize are manipulating me until well after the fact.

"Who's going to be there, again?" I ask.

His eyebrows lift. "The usual crowd, I'm guessing. Mom. Dad. Matilda. My brothers and their partners." His younger brothers, Oliver and Stuart, and their partners. "Then there's Nancy, my dad's general counsel—"

"Wait, wait, wait. Your dad's general what?"

Edward smirks. "General counsel. Nancy, she's head of legal at ThruComm Holbeck." He takes in my incredulous face. "She's been around awhile. He trusts her."

"I see. And his legal counsel comes to family functions. Okay, good to know. I hadn't realized we were living in Wolf Hall. Please continue. Anyone else?"

"Nunu will be there too, I'm guessing, with the kids."

"Don't understand any part of that sentence."

He laughs. "The family nanny, Nunu. She'll be there but at the kids' table."

"Family nanny, *Nunu*, right," I say, making a mental note to remember these names. "Wait, the kids have a separate table?"

"Trust me, you'll want to be at the children's table too once you've experienced the adult one."

"Okay," I say with a smirk. "There's a lot to unpack there. I'm going to want to hear a lot more about this whole family nanny/Nunu situation later—you never said you had one growing up. But put a pin in that . . . who else might be there tonight?"

"Marty Fullman's usually there. COO of ThruComm. And his dog, Grog."

"Oh for God's sake."

"So twelve adults, four kids, and a dog. Plus the staff, but I'm not counting them." I feel my eyebrows shoot up before he adds, "You know what I mean, it's house staff, maids, kitchen staff, a chef . . ."

"Right, so basically, I'm meeting everyone. But your brothers' partners will be there, right? How did their first dinners go?"

Edward takes a moment before answering. "Varies, but it was sort of different for them."

"Different how?"

"Well, because I'm the eldest. The firstborn."

I can't repress a laugh. "Oh, I'm sorry, Mr. Bingley."

"Ha, ha. Yes, very good. But technically, and legally, lineage is still very much relevant. Certainly, in my family. Primogeniture is part of the family trust. It's like entailment but it doesn't matter what gender the firstborn is—whoever they are they get the lion's share. You can refuse to be part of the family business but you can't get away from genetics—or the law. Unfortunately."

"So it matters more who *you* marry than who they marry?"

"Yeah. It does. To my family . . . and to the outside world."

"To the outside world?"

"Who I marry has repercussions. I'll control it all one day and they'll be part of that. It affects shareholder confidence, market valuation, future projections—our reliability, sustainability," he says with unvarnished simplicity.

"Oh," I answer, and though I try to stop myself from asking I can't. "What will marrying me indicate?"

"To the world: that times are changing. To my family: that I love them but they will not hold me back from doing what I want with my life. I waited a long time to find you. And now I have. You can read any story in a million different ways but I think my family and the world in general will understand the story of us. Don't you think?"

"Um, yeah. If I'm honest, I'm really glad I bought a new outfit for this now," I say, half joking, then I catch his expression. "You are worried about what they'll think of me too, aren't you? Honestly?"

"Honestly? Of course I am. They're my folks. I want them to like you. I want you to like them. Mom likes what she hears about you. There's no way she'd have handed over Great-Grandma's ring otherwise. And what Mom thinks trickles down to the rest of them eventually. Dad's trickier. But it's going to be fine. Matilda didn't say anything weird about it all, did she? When you met?"

Aside from flexing her undeniable power in a single phone call to my publisher and then tricking me into meeting every single person in her family, no, she didn't say anything weird.

But clearly *weird* is a relative term, excuse the pun.

I wonder if he suspects that Matilda asked me to help bring him back into the family.

That thought sparks another: After all, Matilda is second in line to everything directly after Edward. There could be more going on here for her, in particular, than I had ever previously considered.

I realize Edward is waiting for my answer. "She didn't say anything that strange, no. It was nice . . . meeting her, she wasn't anything like I expected her to be. She seemed to be happy, about us, the idea of us. And I'm guessing she isn't someone who'd shy away from brutal honesty if she had real issues." I give him a reassuring smile, even though now I'm not so sure at all. "I think it's all going to be fine, Ed," I tell him.

And it will be, I just need to stay on my toes. Which is never a bad thing, especially now that I have a growing family to protect.

And with that warm thought in mind I lean in and whisper softly into his ear, "Hey. We're going to have a baby."

5

Introductions

THURSDAY, NOVEMBER 24

The immense façade of 7 East 88th Street towers above us. At its red-brick summit, a golden weather vane flashes and fades as it wavers in the evening light, guarded at every corner by stone gargoyles. I watch as its arrow swivels high above the city roof-tops like an omen of what is to come—an instrument to divine which way the wind is blowing.

I slam the car door and the Holbecks' town car pulls away, leaving Edward and me on the curb. Of course they sent a driver. I stare up at the grandeur of their Manhattan townhouse, one of the many Holbeck homes dotted across the globe. A six-bedroom, three-floor city pied-à-terre just behind the Guggenheim. They possess such incredible wealth that I find it hard to comprehend what it all really means.

Edward takes my hand in his, and I drag my eyes from the

glowing windows high above us in time to catch his expression. He's grinning at me. He's clearly enjoying the effect that fifty-seven million dollars' worth of real estate is having on me. I give his hand a firm squeeze; I'm going to need a little help tonight. Help is something that I'm slowly learning to ask for, and thankfully he responds on cue.

"It's just a house," he tells me, pulling me close. "Everyone gets nervous meeting their in-laws."

"But this isn't quite the same, is it?" I reply.

"No," he says with a smirk, following my gaze back to the warmly lit penthouse windows. Then he looks back down to me, pushing a strand of loose hair behind my ear and kissing me lightly on the lips. It's a promise. A reminder of why we're here.

I close my eyes and let the feel of him, so close, so real, clear my head. We are here tonight because he gave me a ring; because I will become a part of this family.

Beginnings are always hard, almost as hard as endings, I remind myself.

From behind the gold and glass of the building's entrance a doorman appears, in off-black livery. He holds open the door with a silent professionalism that does nothing to put me at ease.

Inside: a marble lobby and a buttonless elevator activated by the doorman's magnetic card.

As we travel up to the Holbecks' penthouse triplex I try to imagine what it must have been like to grow up with all this, the Guggenheim next door. "Did you spend much time here, as a kid?" I ask Edward over the gentle hum of the elevator. I can't really imagine a tiny flush-faced Edward dashing around this place in the 1990s Tommy Hilfiger sweatshirt I've seen in his childhood photos.

"No, not really. Dad stayed here, during the week, for work. Mother went between here and home. We were always either at school or at The Hydes."

The Hydes. The Holbeck family home in upstate New York. I can only speculate, along with the rest of the world, on what Edward's family house looks like inside. There are no pictures online, only paparazzi shots of the gates bordered by dense wood-land and a high perimeter security fence. Its interiors have never been photographed for a magazine or an architectural supple-ment and it hasn't been on the market since J. L. Holbeck built it in the late 1800s. Edward has mentioned it and clammed up when pressed on it. The place has remained a mystery, and while I try not to press him on it, each new crumb of knowledge slowly builds a picture of something more than I dare to think about right now.

He squeezes my hand as the lift slows. "You doing okay?"

I nod and attempt a smile, then watch as he straightens his collar in infinite reflections in the elevator mirrors. He's nervous too, I can tell, though he's hiding it well. That tightness around his strong jaw I've noticed during work calls, the same tightness the evening of our first official date. An almost imperceptible tell that I've picked up on over time; an oddly comforting glimpse of his human vulnerability beneath. This matters to him, a lot.

I tuck my errant strand of hair back into my loose chignon. Under my coat a dark-red jumpsuit, to match Great-Grandma Mitzi's ring. I wonder if Edward's mother will notice the gesture.

The lift pings and glides open to reveal a Carrera marble atrium, a sculptural glass chandelier glistening high above us. There isn't a Thanksgiving pumpkin or turkey decoration in sight.

Edward leads me from the elevator, our shoes tapping on mar-ble, the quiet murmur of voices and music drifting to us from somewhere deep within the apartment. I try to quell the sudden surge of fear and nausea rising up inside me; I need to stay calm. But when a man in gray suddenly appears from a doorway to our left, I literally jump.

"Mr. Holbeck, Ms. Reed," he murmurs, sotto voce, giving a muted apologetic smile. He's British. A British butler, of course they have a British butler. I'm going to sound like the help, aren't I? I squeeze Edward's hand as our guide gestures for us to con-tinue on down the corridor. "The family's just taking drinks in the drawing room."

"Who was that?" I whisper as we round the corner away from him.

"No idea, never seen him before in my life." Edward shrugs. "There's a pretty heavy turnover around here."

"Oh."

The voices coming from the door ahead of us become clearer as we approach, then I catch the jovial tinkle of Matilda's laugh. They sound friendly at least.

At the closed door Edward holds my gaze for a second; he's waiting until I'm ready. I take one last fortifying breath before giving him the nod, and he opens the door.

Three oversized white sofas face one another around a low glass coffee table, over which the entire Holbeck family and friends have arranged themselves.

All eyes in the room find us as we enter, and for a heart-stopping second Edward and I come to a halt, hands held, smiling like idiots. A silence, punctuated only by the gentle spit and crackle of the log fire in its marble fireplace and the dull clink of ice cubes in glasses, fills the room. I feel Edward bristle beside me.

My eyes flick across the group hungrily as I take in as much as I can. Visible, beyond the drawing room's far door, a lofty dining room opens out, its table set and glimmering in soft candlelight. This is where our evening will play out.

After an eternity that almost certainly stretches only a few seconds in real-world time, Edward's mother speaks, breaking the tension. "Harriet," she says with genuine warmth as she rises to welcome us. "Edward, darling."

The rest of the family seems to relax, life coming back to the room around us. In a microsecond they have, no doubt, made their judgments on me and on our relationship—if they hadn't already.

Glasses are raised in acknowledgment; smiles beam and positions shift as Eleanor glides over to us. I take her in, tanned and immaculately made-up, her gray hair cut into a razor-sharp bob. She modeled in the 1980s; I know this from Ed, but mostly from the internet. Her wide eyes and thick brows are hallmarks of a bygone age. I recall an image of her in profile, balanced on tiptoe in a ballerina costume, aged eighteen, for American *Vogue*. No wonder Edward looks the way he does. No wonder all his siblings do, with parents like Eleanor and Robert.

I scan my periphery for him, for Edward's father, but I know he's not here. I do not sense him and judging by the family's now easy demeanor, I know I must be right.

Eleanor takes my hand in hers in greeting, her skin warm and soft to the touch, the scent of her perfume fresh and powdered as she leans in to air-kiss my cheeks.

"I cannot tell you how pleased I am, Harriet," she tells me with a twinkle in her eye, "that you could both make it tonight. And at such short notice." There's something in her tone that tells me that she knows the favor Matilda asked of me and she appreciates my help.

She holds me back at arm's length and playfully makes a show of inspecting me, genuine joy lurking just beneath her surface. "Radiant. Absolutely radiant." I let out an evasive chuckle. I certainly don't feel radiant.

"I know. I don't know why she said yes either, but she did," Edward quips, making his way over to plant a kiss on Matilda's cheek. Beside her sits a kind-faced woman that I do not know, who pats Edward on the arm supportively as he shifts past her. In fact, there are five people in this room whom I don't recognize. Actually, that's not strictly true. I recognize some of them.

Eleanor gently slips my arm over hers. "Now, yes. I need to introduce you to everyone. Don't I?" she says, with a conspiratorial glint in her eye. "You know Matilda, of course." Matilda raises her gaze to us and flashes a ruby-red smile.

"Of course." I smile back.

"And you've met Edward," Eleanor jokes, to a couple of chuckles. "And that poor woman he's trying to squeeze to death over there," she says, indicating the woman with the kind face, "is Fiona, my son Oliver's wife."

Fiona is about my age, with soft features and a maternal glow. I try to remember what Edward told me about her and Oliver.

Fiona is a stay-at-home mom; she and Oliver have three sons and a Portuguese water dog. Oliver took over Edward's responsibilities in the family business alongside Matilda when Edward decided not to take them up.

Fiona rises and offers me an outstretched hand across the huge coffee table, and I shake it thankfully. She gives me an encouraging look; she's clearly run the gauntlet of meeting this family for the first time herself. She feels my pain.

"Marty and Nancy are old family friends," Eleanor continues, pointing over to a cheerful-looking older couple seated near the window, a black dog asleep at their feet.

Nancy gives me a wry smile and raises her glass, with Marty quickly following suit.

"We're not married," Nancy quips with a wink. "Just old. And the dog's his."

"Then there's Stuart there," Eleanor says, directing my gaze to the other side of the room, "my youngest son, and his partner, Lila." My gaze follows Eleanor's and I flat-out stare. Beside Stuart—who appears to be a shorter, thinner, and more irascible version of Edward—sits an incredibly familiar face. I recognize Stuart's girlfriend from glossy magazine adverts, gossip columns, paparazzi pictures, and a notable role in a new action franchise. Stuart's girlfriend is Scandinavian model-turned-actress Lila Erikson.

She looks up from her phone at the mention of her name, her perfect mouth pulling into a friendly albeit slightly tight smile. "Hey-hey, Harry. So nice to meet you," she says with a Nordic accent heavier and deeper than expected. In her lap her phone screen begins flashing up a call. She groans. "I'm so sorry, everyone, it's them again, I really have to take this. So embarrassing." She sighs in apology, shaking her loose blond hair. "Sorry, Harry, it's very rude. It's so great to meet you. I just need to sort out this total *fucking shitshow* of a double booking. My *asshole* agent."

"Li, it's fine," Stuart interjects, jumping on her expletives, "just take the call." I watch as his nervous eyes flit quickly back between his girlfriend and his mother and then he catches me staring, surprised to have pulled my focus. He studies me quickly as beside him Lila slips from the room, then turns back to chug from his glass bottle of Coke as Lila's voice wafts back to us in Swedish from the hallway.

Mrs. Holbeck gives me a contained smile. "Poor Lila, such long hours. What with work and little Milo and her charities it's a wonder she's still standing." It's unclear if this is a compliment or a sugarcoated criticism. "Well, it's just nice to have the whole family together for once," she continues. "We all have such busy lives these days."

As if on cue another member of the Holbeck family ambles in through the dining room doorway, the family resemblance unmistakable. I'd put him in his mid-forties, so I'm momentarily thrown as to who he could be. Too old for a younger brother, too young for a father. Edward is meant to be the eldest at only thirty-eight. The new arrival is a bear of a man, bigger and stockier than Edward, with an imposing footballer's physique.

"There he is. Oliver," Mrs. Holbeck coos. "Oliver, this is Edward's Harriet."

Edward's Harriet. The words are loaded, but again it's hard to tell with what exactly.

Oliver raises an eyebrow in mild surprise as his eyes find mine. I'm not what he expected, clearly, but then neither is he. Oliver Holbeck, the third child, is supposed to be four years younger than Edward but looks half a decade older. Gray peppers his stubble and temples. And then as if in answer to my unspoken question I hear the crescendoing shrieks of children as Oliver and Fiona's three young boys hurtle into the room, drawing up short at the sight of me. Three little sets of eyes join those already on me.

Having three young sons certainly might explain the apparent age differential between Oliver and the rest of the Holbeck siblings, although looking back at Fiona, the same can't really be said of her. Perhaps it's that the Holbeck family business has taken its toll.

"Wonderful to finally meet you, Harriet," Oliver says, his voice deeper than Edward's, with an almost transatlantic, New

Hampshire lilt to it, like Eleanor's. Edward doesn't have that. Perhaps New York beat it out of him. Oliver's greeting sounds genuine, heartfelt. I see something in Edward shift. Oliver must be important to him, his support valued but not taken for granted.

Edward moves to pull his younger brother into a tight bear hug, and Oliver reciprocates, his arms fully enveloping Edward's taller frame. "There he is," Oliver chuckles, the two slapping each other's backs. "Big bro's back."

Watching them it's clear that tonight is as much a reunion for the family as it is an introduction to me. I find myself wondering if Oliver ever begrudged having to take on Edward's mantle, if he wanted a different life or if he cannot believe his luck from one day to the next.

When the brothers pull apart Edward greets the young boys, ruffling his eldest nephew's hair, the boy dodging away and causing the whole group to dart off in different directions.

"Stay close, boys," Oliver booms after them. "No running, no shouting. Stay away from Granddad's study. Dinner in twenty."

"And where is Dad?" Edward asks, turning back to the room in general. Odd to think that anyone could refer to a man like Robert Davison Holbeck as Dad, or Granddad for that matter, but I suppose they have to call him something.

"Call," Matilda responds, absentmindedly twisting her braceleted wrist into a telephone gesture.

"And he shall appear," a resonant voice intones from the doorway. I catch Edward tensing at the sound of it before turning to take in the tall, brooding frame of his father standing, scotch in hand, in the doorway.

I feel my expression freeze in place as I take him in for the first time, a strange sensation fizzling through me. It's undeniable—his questionable past and ethics aside—and as much as I would never admit this to another living soul, there is something overpoweringly attractive about him. I hate myself for thinking it, but there it is. If it looks like a duck and quacks like a duck . . .

Of course I've seen him before in magazines and on newspaper stands, but in the flesh, the resemblance between him and Edward knocks the breath from me. Though clearly older, Robert Holbeck looks almost exactly like the man I've agreed to marry. Edward's looks, his rakish smile, the knowing behind his eyes, are as present in the father as in the son but somehow, unsettlingly, more so. More present, more dangerous, more elusive.

Robert Holbeck's eyes find mine, the deep brown of them eerily similar to eyes I have stared into for over a year, but these eyes are filled with a different history, an unknown past I will almost certainly not be given access to.

I feel the heat rise in my face.

Of all of the reactions I thought I might have on meeting my father-in-law, sexual attraction is not one I would have ever considered being a problem. I suppose I could blame my hormones: I am pregnant after all. If ever there was an excuse. Perhaps R. D. Holbeck is my own personal version of craving a jar of pickles in the middle of the night. If pickles were incredibly powerful billionaires.

Robert releases me from the hold of his gaze, his eyes gliding back to Edward.

"Edward," he says. There's a careful humility to it, an offering not of peace so much as acceptance that some things must be taken as they are in life.

"Dad." Edward nods and I feel an infinitesimal tightening of his hand around mine, the fully grown man beside me thrust unwittingly back into the role of son.

Eleanor deftly breaks the weight of the moment. "R.D., this is Edward's Harriet," she coos.

Edward's Harriet. There it is again.

I watch this new information pass across Robert Holbeck's features as his eyes find mine once more.

He takes me in fully now and I realize I've stopped breathing. I couldn't break his gaze if I wanted to, and for some reason it suddenly seems deeply important that I'm not the one to look away first. Half challenge, half invitation—though to what I do not know.

After a moment the skin around his eyes creases, something amusing. For not backing down I am rewarded with a smile.

One thing is for sure now: I have Robert Holbeck's attention. For better or for worse: he sees me. And I see him.

6

Dinner

The table is laid, twelve crystal glasses gleaming in the candle-light.

On the walls above us hang oil paintings that seem to date back as far as the first Dutch American colonies. The Holbecks' ancestry. No doubt the paintings are priceless, but I wonder how the living Holbecks can stand to have the dead ones staring down at them. Family members long gone, their milky eyes watching while the living make merry, oblivious, or long inured, to their persistent gazes.

At the head of the table Robert is flanked to his right by Nancy and a glistening-eyed Matilda. He clearly appreciates the company of women.

As my eyes play over the other guests, I understand that the family's ranking system is in evidence in tonight's seating plan:

the heart of the Holbeck machine, and its inner workings, made visible. I'm placed as far from the seat of power as it is possible to be, slotted neatly between two other minor plus-ones: Oliver's wife, Fiona, and Stuart's girlfriend of two years, Lila Erikson.

Lila leans in conspiratorially as she unfurls her napkin. "They're creepy, right?" For a second, I'm certain she means our hosts, but then her eyes travel up to the faces hanging silently above us, the gaunt white visages looming from the walls. "I hate them," she chuckles and grabs for her drink. "Bunch of creepy-assed colonists. Oh yeah, and lest we forget, Happy Thanksgiving." I let out a snort of laughter and she clinks her glass of wine with my glass of water. "Cheers."

Across the table Edward throws me a rallying smile. I smile back, grateful to have been placed beside someone I can actually talk to.

"No wine, Ms. Reed?" a voice behind me inquires loudly. The gray-clad butler proffers a decanter that I had seamlessly managed to swerve on its first round of the table. But this guy isn't going to back down quite as easily as the previous server. I weigh my next move.

What would draw less attention: outright turning alcohol down or pouring it and not drinking it?

Lila's interest is piqued by my hesitancy, so I bite the bullet.

"No, no wine, thanks." I give a grateful smile, but the butler doesn't flinch.

"Perhaps you'd care for a white instead? Or a *cocktail*, maybe," he asks, managing to imbue the word *cocktail* with a whole spectrum of negative connotations. I notice a few eyes around the table flit to us with interest.

"No, no thank you. I'll just stick with the water for now. No need to—"

Eleanor chips in now too. "It really is no trouble, Harriet, if you'd like a different drink. Whatever you'd prefer we can get for you. I should have checked beforehand, your drink, of course," she admonishes herself. Now that our hostess is involved conversation drops off around the table, and as Edward goes to speak, I start to babble.

"No, no. I love red wine. Love alcohol in general but I'm just not . . . tonight. Honestly, water is fine. I'm . . . basically . . . I'm not drinking at the moment."

God, now I just sound like an alcoholic.

Stuart must agree because it's his turn to dive in. "Yeah, I'm *not drinking* at the moment either. We unhappy few, we band of brothers." He toasts me with his glass Coke bottle. Great, they all think I'm in AA now.

Matilda leans forward in my defense. "Not quite, Stu. Harry's recovering from a bout of food poisoning. Right, Harry? She was an angel to come to tea with me this week and she's a positive saint to take on a Holbeck Thanksgiving, all things considered. So let's give her a break, shall we?" I watch her words work on the group, their interest in me waning, except for R.D.'s. His eyes fix on me and I catch the ghost of his curious smile again before he breaks the connection.

Heads dip in concentration as the food is served, and intermittent conversation bubbles along. My eyes catch Matilda's and she winks.

After the first course I take the opportunity to swivel in my seat to gently insert myself into Lila and Oliver's conversation about their respective children.

"I don't know how Fiona does it though, Ollie," Lila croons. "Your boys are so independent. Milo is—" She breaks off, throwing a look across to the children's table where her son, Milo, sits with his halo of soft curls. Her child from a previous relationship. "He's sensitive, you know," she continues. "He needs to know I'm around or he goes crazy." She grimaces. "I mean, like, crazy crazy, *all* the time."

"You should talk to Nunu," Oliver says. "She spent some time with Billy before he started preschool. He wouldn't leave Fi's side but now he's fine. Some boys are just that way."

I look over at Billy, the youngest of Oliver and Fiona's boys.

He sits happily playing beside Milo, the Holbeck profile already taking hold of his tiny features.

My gaze flits to the much-feted Nunu, a jolly-looking woman in her fifties. She must have been so young when she nannied Edward and his siblings back in the 1990s. She looks across, feeling all of our eyes on her, and gives a warm smile before signaling for Oliver to come over.

Oliver leaves me with Lila, and I take the opportunity to try to fill in some gaps in my family knowledge.

"Nunu's quite young, right?" I ask, and when Lila raises an amused eyebrow, I can't suppress a giggle. "No, I mean she's much younger than I expected her to be. She was their nanny too, right? Edward, Matilda, Oliver, and Stuart's?"

"No, they had someone else back then," she says with a smile. "But that one left after the whole thing with Bobby," she adds casually.

"The whole thing with Bobby," I echo, trying to remember if Edward ever mentioned a "Bobby" to me.

"Yeah," she says, her tone suddenly sobering. "Can't say I blame her for leaving. You couldn't have paid me enough to stay after that. The whole thing was just—"

Oliver's hand firmly lands on Lila's shoulder, interrupting her. He smiles down at us both. "You're up next, Lila, Nunu will see you now. I put in a good word for Milo. And *apparently,*" he says with raised brows, "Milo is already asking if he can stay over tonight with the rest of the boys. Without Mumma."

"No. Oh my God." Lila rises and turns to me with a yelp of excitement. "Hey-hey. Nunu certainly doesn't mess around, does she?"

As Lila glides away, two questions drift in her wake. Who the hell is Bobby? And why have I never heard of him?

7

Billy, Bobby, Strudel, and Port

THURSDAY, NOVEMBER 24

As the second course is taken away, a wave of nausea resurfaces and I calmly make my excuses to head off in search of the nearest bathroom.

Safely installed in a large cream marble bathroom I let my shoulders relax, releasing a tension I had forgotten I was even holding. Nausea temporarily abated, I lean on the basin and inspect myself in the mirror. My makeup is still in place despite my strong expectation of it having completely melted from my face through a combination of hot flashes and social anxiety. My hormones are all over the shop.

I place a hand on my abdomen. *What are you up to in there?* I ask my tiny raspberry-sized passenger. *Whatever it is I need you to stop, just for the next few hours, just till we're in the car home.*

A knock on the door sends my pack of mint gum flying out of my hand and skittering across the immaculate bathroom floor.

"Shit." I sigh, hunkering down to fish it out from behind an oversized potted fig tree. "Just one second."

After dusting myself down I crack the door but there's no one there. Until I look down. Little Billy stares up at me, his expression blank save for two tellingly tearstained eyes.

"Oh, hey Billy," I say, and hearing the uncertainty in my own voice I suddenly remember for the first time in a long time how terrible I am with kids. I never had the benefit of siblings, or babysitting jobs, or friends with kids—absolutely no day-to-day experience to draw from. Which obviously doesn't bode well at all for the future.

Billy must have been looking for his mum and found me instead but decides I'll do for now. He grasps both my legs in a surprisingly robust hug.

"Oh, okay," I say, a hand patting him gently on the head as I check the corridor for literally anyone else. Not a soul in sight. I guess this is up to me. I bend to meet him on his level, his grasp loosening to let me. "Hey, honey. Billy? Look at me, sweetheart."

He looks up, his little angel face tear-blotched and puckered. His tawny hair so like Edward's. God, what a beautiful family. Billy stares at me, his eyes expectant.

"What is it, honey?" I ask him. "Did you hurt yourself?"

Billy shakes his head, suddenly shy, suddenly doubting whether he should have come to me with this. He turns to look back down the hall.

"Did one of the boys do something? Did they upset you?"

Billy pauses and then nods firmly.

"I see," I say, and some unknown reflex makes me gently push the hair from his eyes. "Do you want to tell me what happened?"

He looks back down the hallway again, the sound of adult laughter reaching us from the dining room. Then after a moment, satisfied no one else is coming to help, he nods.

"Uh-huh," he mumbles, feet shuffling.

"What is it, sweetie?"

"The boys. They said I had to sleep in Bobby's room on my own tonight, or I can't play w'them," he manages before the tears slowly return and he buries his face from me once more.

Bobby's room. Again with Bobby.

Billy continues, muffled now into the dampened cotton of his sweater. "I don't like it. I don't want Bobby's room."

This is my chance to find out who Bobby is, I suppose. Decisively I take his tiny hand in mine and squat down beside him. Then face-to-face I calmly say, "Okay. Why don't you show me Bobby's room?"

I flick on the lights and the room bounces into view: An anonymous-looking guest room. The same well-appointed furnishings as the rest of the apartment, nothing that would look out of place in an interior magazine's spread, but there is nothing personal here. Whoever's room this is, or was, it certainly isn't occupied anymore.

So the question is: why does this innocuous room scare Billy?

"It looks nice, don't you think?" I ask the little man in my arms.

Billy surveys the empty room discerningly then turns to me with mild concern. "Yeah, nice. But closet?"

"Oh right, yeah." I forgot kids get scared of wardrobes. "Okay. Let's see," I say and head over to the cupboard to crack the door open. The internal lights click on. It's empty save for six cedarwood hangers, a stack of freshly laundered towels, and a bathrobe.

"Looks like the coast is clear in there, right."

Billy leans into the closet to inspect it further before confirming solemnly, "Yeah, coast all clear, Auntie Harry-ept."

I feel a warmth spread through my chest. *Auntie Harry-ept.*

"Right, then," I say in all seriousness, matching his business-like tone, "I think a sleepover in this room might just be okay after all, mightn't it?"

"But . . . *Bobby*?"

I pause, unsure where to go next before landing on, "Well—I don't see Bobby? Do you?"

Billy looks around worried for a second, then lets out an embarrassed giggle. "Nope."

"Nope is right. So . . ." I say carefully, letting him get down onto his feet, "why don't you go tell the other boys that you don't care where you sleep tonight and if they *do,* then they are just big babies, right?"

Billy finds my joke hilarious. "Big *babies,*" he echoes, gratified. "Okay. Okay thanks Auntie Harry-ept," he adds, quickly bolting from the room and disappearing down the hall.

I flick off the lights of Bobby's room, pulling the door closed, and bump directly into a man standing right behind me.

"Jesus Christ!" I gasp, jumping back.

Edward stands bemused and amused in front of me. "Er, sorry? I guess." He grins. "Just wondering where you'd gotten to. Thought you might have made a break for it between courses."

"Who the hell is Bobby?" I demand. Edward's eyebrows rise at the question, then, distracted, his eyes catch someone coming toward us along the corridor. Eleanor.

"There you both are," she calls, her voice merry and alcohol-infused. "Come on, you two lovebirds. Dessert's ready. Marcia made your favorite, Eddie, she'll be heartbroken if you don't have some." She turns on her heels expecting us to follow. "Shall we?"

It's funny she makes no reference to where we are standing, or why. Perhaps this Bobby thing isn't quite the secret I think it is.

I look back up at Edward inquiringly, then whisper, "Bobby. Later, okay?"

He gives me a firm nod. "Okay."

Back in the dining room the warm, flaky pastry of a fourteen-person apple strudel is ceremoniously sliced, the scent of cinnamon and sugar hanging in the air.

"This was Great-Grandma Mitzi's strudel recipe, Harry," Matilda calls down the table. "Marcia, in the kitchen, makes it for us every year. It's Ed's favorite." She grins at him, delicately forking a morsel into her mouth, her eyes oddly locked with his. I watch Edward stare back at her, and though his expression is patient it's obvious there is some family stuff going on here that I do not understand.

"Has Edward told you much about her?" Matilda continues. "Mitzi?" My eyes flash to Edward. I suppose I know an above-average amount about his great-grandmother. Edward smiles back at me encouragingly. "I know Alfred and Mitzi married for love," I hazard. I notice, in my peripheral vision, R. D. Holbeck pulling back from his conversation with Nancy, his focus now on me. "And Edward told me she loved pomegranates!" I add lightly, hoping to God someone will step in.

The corners of R.D.'s mouth curl, and he looks down. "Well, it sounds like you've covered all the key points there, Edward. Well done."

Edward's eyes fly to his father but R.D. has already moved on, reaching now for his wine.

Matilda's voice drags my gaze back to her. "Show us," she demands, waggling her own ring finger. I raise my left hand oblig-ingly into the candlelight and watch Mitzi's garnet glimmer.

"Beautiful," Nancy sighs as Fiona, beside me, takes my hand gently in hers, turning it and sucking in a breath.

"They don't make them like they used to, do they?" She chuck-les softly. I realize I've hardly said two words to her since we sat down, so engrossed in conversation has she been with Eleanor. I make a mental note to try harder with Fiona going forward. She seems nice.

"No. They do not," R. D. Holbeck intones. It's clear his mean-ing extends beyond jewelry. "I think it's time for a port, what do we all think?"

And I can't help but feel that this is code for dinner being over.

"I'm game," Marty concedes.

"Port for anyone who's having it. We're celebrating after all." The butler in gray steps forward as his employer rises from the head of the table. "I'll take mine in the study."

Before turning from the table, Robert lifts his wineglass and waits for the rest of the table to follow suit. "To the happy couple," he booms. "Welcome to our family, Harriet Reed." Eyes flit from family member to family member, giving the distinct impression that Robert doesn't do things like this very often. Stutteringly the assembled diners echo his sentiment before sipping liberally from their glasses.

Edward is first to lower his glass. "Thank you, Dad. We appreciate it, and dinner, so, thank you." He gives a diplomatic smile.

Robert studies him for a moment before replying, "Very good." He smiles. "Very good."

Then Robert turns to me. "Harriet," he says lightly, "would you mind joining me for a port in the study. Ah, no, on second thought, for you a tea perhaps? James?" He gestures to the butler in gray.

All eyes in the room flash to me, and my heart flutters with panic in my chest. If a sinkhole opened up beneath me and took me from this world forever right now, I'd be glad of the quick death.

"The night is young and we have much to discuss, Harriet. Indulge an old man."

I look to Edward for help; I was not warned about this, I had not planned for this. But Edward looks as pale as I feel. No help there.

"Um, sure," I answer, rising from my seat and somehow managing to sound halfway human. "Yes. That would be lovely. Thank you." I throw Edward a bewildered smile.

"Wonderful." Robert grins. "Shall we?"

I gulp back the last of my water, avoiding Edward's no doubt very concerned and concerning expression, and follow one of the most powerful men in America out of the room.

8

The Game Begins

THURSDAY, NOVEMBER 24

"I hope I didn't put you on the spot back there," Robert says as we enter the vast green cavern of his study.

I give a shake of the head though fully aware it's a rhetorical question. He barely acknowledges my presence as I follow him and hungrily absorb as much as I can from this new environment, and this unexpected access to his inner sanctum.

I know I should be nervous; this man, so much more powerful and self-possessed than me, has me on his own ground. And yet I'm not. Well, I am, but not to the extent I should be. Because here's the thing: I have a secret; a warm cozy secret that I hold close to me, like a comforter in situations just like this. No matter what happens here, I know I can handle myself—better than most. I have been through too much to doubt that fact. I know I can do what I need to do when my back is to the wall.

My eyes fly up as the room opens out above us: a mezzanine library. Books line the room, breaking up the obsidian walls, a cursory glance at the shelves revealing everything from thick reference tomes to cutting-edge releases and thin poetry periodicals. Ahead a jewel-toned Persian rug proffers two low club chairs facing each other in front of a crackling fire. The lighting in the room gives a warm glow, and a wooden staircase, spiraling up to the mezzanine, slips into shadows, the covers of the books beyond it indiscernible.

But the thing that stands out the most is the subdued but persistent flashing and flickering coming from above the bookcases where wall-hung plasma screens display a constant rolling stream of live news channel feeds. Each screen a different network, on mute. Newscasters stare down at us, not dissimilar to the oil paintings in the dining room, except these move.

Text scrolls. An oil spill off the coast of Brazil, a Hong Kong billionaire under house arrest, another police shooting, the GDP growth of the Indian economy.

"Take a seat," Robert says, gesturing to one of the club chairs, and I head over to the fire to sit as instructed.

I watch him, this older, more storied Edward, move across the room and push the heavy door of the study closed, eclipsing the sounds of the apartment beyond.

He notices my eyes flit to the screens above. "I like to keep my finger on the pulse," he says, wafting a hand up at them dismissively. "Let's call them the pulse."

I smile at the remark and he turns from me, seemingly at ease with me in his space. Wordlessly he heads across the room to a cabinet beside the spiral staircase and, lifting the lid of a brightly colored box, he pulls something out from within. "Does it bother you?" he asks, without looking over, and I can't tell if he means the silence or the situation. But when he turns, I see that he actually means neither.

He lifts his hand, showing me an unlit cigar.

"It doesn't bother me, no," I answer after a moment. "I've always quite liked the smell if I'm honest."

That smile again. "Well, it is always important to be honest, isn't it? Especially with one's self." There's something in his eyes a little too knowing for comfort. He cuts the cigar end and sets about lighting it. It's only then that I stop to consider the impact his cigar smoke might have on the raspberry-sized fetus growing inside me. But it's too late to turn back now. Embers flare red as the dark tobacco leaves transmute to wavering white ash when he takes a puff and sinks into the armchair opposite mine.

Beyond the flickering screens, in the deep darkness, I make out his desk, a wide monstrous thing lurking in the half-light, its wires, cables, hard drives like tentacles reaching into the shadows.

R.D. leans back in his chair, his eyes cast up to the rich smoke pooling above us. There is a painting above the fireplace. J. L. Holbeck, Edward's great-great-great-grandfather, the man who started it all.

It must be hard to look at him every day, to know that everything in your life is due to the hard work of another man. And no matter how hard you strive, no matter how much you achieve, in your heart you'll always question how much of it was due to you. Hard to be faced with that kind of legacy every day.

But here I am feeling sorry for a billionaire.

I study Robert's features again as he looks up at the screens and feel the strangely familiar ache of excitement I felt the first night I met Edward.

That dangerous fizzle of possibility. A desire to possess, to be possessed. To smell him, feel him, close. I feel a blush rising up my neck and try to shake off the thought. I know it's deeply inappropriate; a sharp twang of guilt pelts me from within for my thoughts. I love Edward, I am here because of Edward, and I know the only reason I am feeling this right now is because the man sitting in front of me reminds me so much of the man I love. But with a thrill of something else.

After a moment he looks back at me. I wonder if he can read my thoughts, if he can feel this strange pull between us too.

Shut up, Harriet.

God, I want him to like me. I've seen pictures of Robert as a young man; I've seen the magazine interview photos of him in the 1980s, lithe and dangerous in Wall Street double-breasted suits. But at sixty-five, his hair silvered, it's clear that right now is his real peak.

There's a gentle knock on the study door.

"Come in, James," Robert calls, breaking the silence. I look away as the butler glides in with our drinks, certain he can read every one of my inappropriate thoughts.

"The Fonseca '84, sir," James says placing the bottle down on the table. "The family has withdrawn to the drawing room, sir."

"Wonderful. Thank you, James," Robert answers absentmind-edly, thumbing his cigar.

"Not a problem, sir. Is there anything else I can get you?" James asks, eyeing me as I pour my tea.

"No. That will be all, thank you, James," Robert says, looking up now and noticing James's gaze. "And close the door on your way out," he adds curtly.

As the study door closes, Robert's focus returns to me. "I'll be honest with you, Harriet—having determined, as we have, that we both value honesty, I'll share the truth about my son." He pauses for a moment, taking a swig of his port. "I am sure he's told you; we've had our problems. But I want to be clear about things with you. To be clear *for* you."

"Of course. I appreciate that," I say. "He's told me a little. About previous relationships—I know things have been difficult between you and him."

"Do you?" he asks. "I wonder." That wolfish smile again.

I feel that dark tug of desire again. *Oh, for fuck's sake.* Is it normal to fancy your father-in-law?

No.

But then look at him. That little tell behind his eyes, that world-weary calm, the feeling that at any moment he could switch on me, the tone could change, and a man like him would have the power, the ability, to do almost anything and get away with it. I don't see how that couldn't be both terrifying and intoxicating. Edward has it too, that deep undertow of power, that sense that I may not be good enough, smart enough, quick enough to live in his world.

He studies me, in my silence. "You love him? My son?" I feel a knife twist of guilt at my thoughts, their direction.

"Yes," I answer honestly. "More than anything."

Robert's expression softens. "Be careful of that: 'more than anything,'" he warns. "Never quantify."

"Why?" I ask.

"As the saying goes: If you can measure it, you can manage it. People can rarely be managed." He lets the words settle before continuing with a boyish grin. "Oh, I read your book by the way."

I feel suddenly exposed. The fact that he has read my book puts me firmly on the back foot. Which I imagine was the idea. I'm learning very quickly that Robert likes to play linguistic games. He's testing my boundaries, mapping my character.

"I enjoy a thriller every now and then," he continues with a wry smile. "Fictional horror as a balm for the everyday sort." He takes a long puff on his cigar. "You're good at it. Telling stories. Untangling them." He dips his head at me in congratulations. "It's hard to surprise me . . . but you did," he adds lightly.

I sink into the warmth of the compliment.

"Thank you." I hear my tone veering toward the edge of flirtation. I need to work on my poker face—then again, judging by the reemergence of his grin, perhaps I don't. He's enjoying whatever strange game we're playing as much as I am.

"You liked it, then?" I ask, every nerve in my body alive to his response. "The twist?"

The curl of his lip, the tap of ash into an ashtray, the slow release of rich tobacco smoke.

His eyes level with mine. "I did. Very much. You're clever, very clever, young Harriet, but I suspect you already know that, don't you?" He pauses before adding, "We could certainly use another clever girl in the family."

Girl. I know my feminist hackles should rise but they don't.

There's something in his tone as he says it, something incredibly self-aware, the noun carrying a respect I haven't often heard it imbued with. I think of the women who work for him, with him—perhaps he's come to recognize the no-frills, relentless efficiency of female energy.

He liked my book. I absorb his very particular brand of acceptance, aware that there is a kind of understanding growing between us.

"Thank you," I tell him with genuine gratitude, "that means a lot."

"Coming from *me*?" he asks, amused. Another test. Am I playing the game of elder statesman and grateful young woman? And if I am, am I doing it deliberately?

That smile again. If this isn't flirting it's definitely in the ballpark. So I guess the question is, will I play ball?

"Yes," I say, my eyes on him. "It means a lot—*coming from you.*"

And just like that we both know where we stand. I am game and so is he. Anything could happen.

He nods to himself and raises his port to me in acknowledgment.

It makes sense that he would be this charming in person; people don't tend to get, or stay, in his position without knowing how others tick. But I know how people tick too. After a lifetime of trying to fit in, working people out has proven essential.

I watch him refill his port glass. "We have something in common, you and I," he tells me.

"Aside from Edward. And our love of thrillers?" I quip.

He takes a slow puff of his cigar, watching me. "Indeed, our cups runneth over already. No. We are orphans. You and I both suffered loss at a young age. Your parents died. My parents died."

He's gone straight for my weakest spot, my soft underbelly. He knows. Edward must have mentioned it to his mother, and I know how these things spread. Like wildfire.

And just like that my brain lights up like a Christmas tree with memories I do not want. An upturned car, bodies hanging in the air. Fire and pain. Images press in on me fast and hard. Before and after. Driving down that early-morning road, the chill in the air, the startling, the bracing, my mother's face turning to me, the look in her eyes, the words I never quite heard. Then sound, pain, and darkness. Even here in the Holbecks' penthouse I smell that mix of country air and petrol. After all these years, no matter how far I go, it follows.

"I'm sorry," Robert says, after a moment. "That was unnecessary. I should know better than that. Especially at my age. The past can catch us if we don't see it coming, can't it? I apologize, Harriet."

He really can read me. But then perhaps he speaks from his own experience.

I recall his words. "How did you lose your parents?"

"My mother went first. When I was seven." He breaks off, looking back into the darkness of the room. "She was a good woman. Full of love. Maybe too good. She left a hole when she died; my father lost his way. As I said, one must be careful not to love any one person 'more than anything.' Life is fragile. We both know that. My father was a case in point."

"He killed himself?"

"In a sense, but no. Illness. He put up little fight. It was quick."

"And what happened to you? Afterward?" I ask.

"Alfred and Mitzi Holbeck happened to me. My grandparents took me in. The woman who wore the ring on your finger raised me."

I look down at it, the garnet's arterial red glimmering in the firelight, and I wonder for the first time exactly whose idea it was to give me this ring. Either way Edward must know its significance to his father.

"Was it hard after they died?" I ask, more to hear him speak than to hear the answer I already know.

"It was. And for you? You miss them."

"Yes. I try not to think about them," I say simply. "But they come back. Every day. A tune, a laugh, a memory. Every day."

"Every day," he says almost to himself. "But do you still look for them in crowds?"

My eyes snap to his in surprise. A laugh of recognition. "I do. Do you?"

He nods warmly, leaning in to top up my tea. "Always. Even now, when time has meant that they would be long gone regardless."

I watch him as he pours. To have all this and no one to see it.

"I'm glad Edward found you, Harriet. You're not his usual. But then the woman you ask to marry you never is, is she?" I don't know why, but something about the way he says this unsettles me.

I'm reminded of Edward's exes, and the power Robert has had in the past to decide who is or is not right for him. I remind myself that it is only a quirk of fate that Robert has decided to approve of me. And that approval is conditional.

"I don't know how much he's told you?" he continues. "About our history? About the family."

"Not much, to be honest," I say carefully.

He studies my face for the truth of that and seems to find an answer there. "That's interesting," he says, "very interesting."

He seems to come to a conclusion, leaning forward on an elbow. "He left ThruComm. He wanted to make a go of things on his own. His own way in the world." He leans back now with a nod. "A noble idea, of course, to build a life from scratch. But a family business is a group endeavor. We take from the past and give to the future. We add more and pass it on. Edward is my eldest, the company should be his. But he chose another way." He gives me a wry look. "Now, Harriet, don't misunderstand me. I've made peace with that part of the story. My concern now is for my family. I want him back here. Eleanor wants him back with the family. Matilda spoke with you, I understand. We all want him back, and we think this engagement is a good thing. You're good for him. I see that."

Robert stops speaking and the crackle of the fire fills the space.

I look down at my tea, and I can't help but feel a little disappointed. All of this just to get to Edward.

"You're willing to put up with me because you need *him*," I say, addressing the elephant in the room directly. "That's what this is about?" I ask, gesturing between us.

A chuckle of surprise. "No, no, Harriet," he says, his tone precise, "I did this to see if I was right about you. You are going to be a part of this family so it's very important we understand each other, it's important we both know the facts about who we are. Because you'll have to believe me when I say, I know the facts about you. I'm sure you won't be surprised to hear that you were vetted. Due diligence. All possible concerns noted, flagged."

A slow blossoming of dread at the possibility of what a man like Robert Davison Holbeck could dig up on me. Ghosted boyfriends, broken promises, weakness. But I know he can't know the worst—no one can—because I was alone the day my parents died. Only I know the things that happened that day.

He knows the shifts and ebbs of my life, the everyday missteps and the mistakes of youth. Things that do not touch the sides of what it is possible to truly regret.

"You're everything I hoped you would be, Harriet," he says, then gestures between us. "*This* is not about Edward. This is about us. If I lose a son in all this, I hope at least that I might gain a daughter."

9

A Novel Idea

As we rise to rejoin the family, he gestures for me to wait, heading back past the flickering television screens into the darkness where his desk lies. He flicks on a green desk lamp and slides open a drawer.

The rattle of brittle plastic on plastic, the very particular sound of a cassette tape in its case. The lamplight clicks off and Robert wanders back to me.

"Now, as we know, we have several things in common, Harriet." He smirks, leaning against the arm of the nearest club chair. "I wasn't sure about sharing this. But I have a good feeling about you, and from what I've seen I'm almost certain you can handle a challenge." He looks suddenly younger, enlivened by whatever is about to happen.

He reveals what rests in his hands. It's a relic from before my time: a tiny little cassette in a miniature case. He lets out an involuntary laugh as he catches my puzzled expression, his face more handsome than ever.

"It's a Dictaphone tape, Harriet, not a carrier pigeon. Don't look so baffled or I'll start to feel my age."

His ease with me is almost as intoxicating as whatever the hell he's up to right now.

"What's on it?" I ask.

He holds my gaze, danger crackling in the space between us.

"I'd like your advice, Harriet. Your expertise—shall we say—on it," he says, tapping the tiny tape, his expression hard to read for a moment before he cracks an uncharacteristically sheepish smile. "Let's call it an idea for a novel, maybe. It's not a book, yet, but perhaps it's the bones of one." He rattles the case, the bones of Robert Holbeck's story. "It's a start, to something," he continues. "Perhaps we'll find out the story I have to tell together." He looks at me, and I catch the heady glimpse of an offer.

Robert Holbeck has written a story. Or at least recorded one. His voice, his words, on tape. I shiver with excitement at the thought of all that potential.

I watch him turn the tiny tape in his hands absentmindedly and wonder if it's fiction or not. Because whatever is on that tape could be of interest to a lot of people. I can only imagine what a publisher would pay for it, given the author. Given its possible content.

"You wrote a book?" I ask carefully, then quickly correct myself. "You recorded one?"

He nods, amused by my clear interest.

"What's it about?" I ask.

"Well, now, that would give the game away wouldn't it," he replies breezily. "Let's call it a thriller, shall we?" Then after a pause, "It's definitely in your wheelhouse."

This isn't the first time I've been asked to look at someone's idea for a thriller. Friends, acquaintances, taxi drivers, baristas, plumbers, you name it—as soon as people know you write, they want to tell you their story. Everyone's got a book in them, as the saying goes. Though sometimes that's probably where it should stay.

Though something tells me Robert Holbeck's story might be worth a read.

"Why a thriller?"

He casts his eyes up at the flickering screens, stories upon stories feeding through to us in silence. "I like their mechanics, their intricacy. But in the end, all is explained." He shakes his head, lost in thought, and finally looks back at me. "That kind of clarity, it's so rare we find it in life."

"I see," I say, then echo his words from earlier. "'Fictional horror as a balm for the everyday sort'?"

He raises an eyebrow, amused. "Quite. One must be careful of what one says around writers, mustn't one? Or risk being remembered a little too accurately."

"You have nothing to worry about, Robert," I reassure him, my tone soft. "I could never fully do you justice if I tried."

He rises then, closing the space between us, a panic instantly flexing within me. And before I know it, he's close enough to touch. The warmth of him is tangible, and then I feel his warm hand take mine, pick up the scent of expensive soap and cigars. He folds his tape into my palm, nothing more, then steps away. "I would appreciate it if you kept this between us. At least until I know what you think?"

I nod almost reflexively.

Adam offering Eve an apple, a small, brittle plastic apple. And there's nothing I can do but accept it.

10

Nobody Puts Bobby in the Corner

11:43 P.M.

THURSDAY, NOVEMBER 24

In the back of the car, Edward's silent presence beside me, I watch New York glide past the window as I replay the events of the evening in my mind.

"What did you talk about?" he asks, finally, with a commendable lightness. The question must have been burning a hole in his thoughts since I followed Robert out of that dining room. I pause before replying because, the truth is, I've been trying to figure that out myself since I left Robert Holbeck's study.

"Well, we spoke about writing, how he lost his parents—and he spoke about you." I say this in a very particular order.

"Wait, he told you about his parents?" Edward repeats, surprised.

I nod and he raises an eyebrow, incredulous. "Right. Okay.

Why? He never talks about them. In what context did he talk about *them*?"

There's an edge in his tone that I don't quite like, a glimmer of derision, and it's my turn to look incredulous. "In the context of what he and I have in common, Ed. His parents died young; my parents died young. Remember? He was trying to find common ground with me."

Edward considers this for a moment before responding, "I see. Common ground. And he managed to find some." It's the first time I've seen Edward be genuinely skeptical of someone's motives. "He didn't mention anything else—about his parents, or our family?"

It's an odd thing to say.

Suddenly I remember Bobby, the intensity of the rest of the evening having overshadowed him until now.

"Talking of family, who the hell is Bobby, Ed? Because I get the distinct feeling I could have used that information tonight or, I'm guessing, at some point over the last year! Am I supposed to know who he is? Everyone else there tonight seemed to."

"My father mentioned Bobby?" Edward asks, suddenly direct.

"No? Lila did. And then your nephew Billy seemed to know all about him too, and he's a child."

"Billy talked about Bobby?" he echoes, and there's an odd timbre to his voice.

"Yeah, the older boys were scaring him with stories."

"Jesus," Edward breathes, rubbing his eyes. A weariness seems to overtake him, but looking at me he senses he really needs to start talking.

"This is not how I would have done this . . ." he continues, his voice trailing off to such an extent that I can suddenly see where this story is going. Bobby is dead.

In the silence that follows I give Edward's hand a squeeze to let him know I am here for him, no matter what. After a moment he squeezes back, straightening in his seat.

"I should have told you this before. Someone was bound to mention him eventually but I've always found remembering so much more unhelpful than forgetting." He looks away from me, eyes glistening in the passing streetlights.

"I think I really need you to remember for me at this point, honey," I nudge gently, my tone sensitive but clear.

"Yeah. So." His features scrunch with discomfort. "I find it hard to talk about growing up. The tough bits, whatever," he says, finding the words as he speaks them. "I mean, people like us, we've hardly had it hard. What goes wrong is easy to box up and store. There's an expectation we won't dwell."

"Who was Bobby, Ed?" I repeat.

"My brother. Our brother."

I study Edward's face for the truth of these words. "You had another brother?"

"Older. Oldest," he clarifies, and the significance of this doesn't pass me by.

"He was next in line, before you," I say piecing things together. "How the hell do I not know this, Ed?" I ask as gently as I can, because this is definitely the kind of information fiancés should be sharing with each other.

Edward grimaces, but my thoughts are gathering speed. "Wait, Ed, *seriously,* how do I not know about this? I mean, there's not even anything about this online. Nothing anywhere about another Holbeck son. I would have seen it. There's no mention of a *Bobby* at all."

"I know," he says, almost to himself, trying to wrap his head around the fact that he will have to explain a lot more than he would like to. "That's deliberate. Not my choice. It was kept out of the papers, the press. For the family, insurance, or investors, I don't know. I was eighteen when it happened, I did what I was told. We all did. The investigation went through all the proper channels, then disappeared. Press embargo. Favors called in; deals made. Things were easier to control back then, pre-internet craze, before everyone filmed everything, before everyone had a platform; it was easier to make things fade away."

I shiver and pull my cashmere coat tighter around me. I know how easy it was for things to disappear back when we were kids.

I doubt I would be sitting beside Edward now if that weren't the case. The details of what happened the day my parents died were only a byline in the local papers, columns long pulped, facts forgotten by all except those involved.

"Bobby was twenty, a junior, at Columbia," he continues, trying to keep his voice in check. "He got into Yale too," he says with an unexpected chuckle, "but Columbia was closer to the New York apartment, and he wanted to stay close for Marcia's dinners. That's the kind of guy he was. He used to drive back to see us too, at The Hydes on weekends. Always family first." He breaks off.

"You were eighteen when it happened?" I ask.

"Yeah. Matilda was sixteen, Ollie fourteen, and Stuart must have been, what, twelve? It messed with him the most, I think. Bobby loved Stu. He was a cute kid." He looks at me, his eyes full of regret. "We don't talk about it to each other, so it surprises me that Billy knew, that Lila was talking about it. After Bobby died, our parents sent us to see separate therapists. A therapist for each of us. I think they were scared we'd cross-contaminate, or something, if we all went together. Or maybe that's how therapy works for kids, I don't know. We just stopped speaking about him with one another after that. We had designated people to talk to and talking about it at home only made Mom cry so—it was easier to box it up and time just passed. The years passed and it became the way we did things."

"How did he die?" I ask as delicately as I can, still reeling from the knowledge that Edward could keep such a formative part of his life from me for so long. I push from my mind the thought that I am guilty of doing just the same, because that is, of course, different. "Did he get sick?"

"He was healthy, thriving, playing varsity, grades impeccable; they always were," he answers, eyes cast out at the city rolling by. "But little things started to change. He switched from economics to law. In retrospect there were signs. He became a little snappy, short-tempered—that wasn't like him. Things between him and Dad became difficult; the pressure Bobby had on him to be the best, to toe the line. An *A* student, popular, the guy who does it all and makes it look easy. Always cheerful, always thinking of others. We didn't know until it was too late. The autopsy found traces of meds—we knew about the pain medication, an old football injury; that wasn't the problem, but it had mixed with something else. He'd been cramming his work between football practices, on weekends, whenever he could fit in the time. It was just Adderall or something similar but the drugs interacted. That's what they call it when two drugs mix and poison you without you even realizing. *Interaction.* All those tiny shifts in personality, his sudden fear that it would all slip through his fingers, the anxiety, insomnia, and finally . . . a seizure. No one saw it coming. He wouldn't have realized himself, why he suddenly felt the way he did. Why everything was becoming so hard for him. He must have thought he'd just reached his limit. I can't imagine how scared he must have been in the days before it happened."

Edward's words sink in, Bobby's death infuriatingly preventable. Mixed meds. A simple mistake that could have so easily been avoided, and for the Holbecks to know *that,* how arbitrary and preventable the loss of their son and brother was. It's realizations like that that can change a person.

I should know; what happened to me at eleven changed who I am.

"Edward, I love you, but at any point over the last year could you not have told me this? We've discussed my family, their deaths, multiple times. Did you not even think to share this with me then?" I can't help but be unsettled by this fact.

"I'm sorry," he says, fully aware of the inadequacy of the apology. "I know. I should have. I'm an idiot and I took the coward's way out. I don't know what I thought would happen, that it would just disappear? I mean, it's not as if no one was ever going to mention Bobby."

Guilt seeps in through the tiny breach opened in our relationship and fills me. I have not told him everything about my childhood. In the same way he kept this from me, I still keep my biggest secret from him. But that is for the best.

"Your father didn't mention Bobby," I say, a question implicit in the statement. I can't help wondering if the family doesn't talk about Bobby because they feel culpable—for applying too much pressure, for not noticing until it was too late.

"We really don't talk about it, I promise you. It isn't just you. I should have told you. Please don't think that I price my own loss higher than yours. I just, I guess when he left, the burden passed on to me. I try not to think about the bad places things can go."

Edward studies me for a moment. "Did you like him? My father?" Edward asks.

"I did," I answer honestly. After a moment I add, "I think I passed whatever test that was."

Edward laughs, and his eyes catch mine in the pooling light of streetlamps as we weave on through the streets. "Of course you did," he says, his tone changing as he observes me.

They say sex and grief are inextricably linked; I feel the shift between us.

He takes my cheek in his hand, almost appraisingly, then softly brushes a thumb over my lip. "How could you not. You're a very unique individual," he whispers with an oddly familiar tone and suddenly I'm back in Robert's study, the air thick with cigar smoke and dangerous ambiguity. I try to block Edward's father from my thoughts but in my mind father and son have become mixed; they morph seamlessly.

I feel Edward's lips on mine, but Robert is there too. I let them happen, the thoughts, even though I know I shouldn't. I know the warm ache rising inside me is for both of them, and it is tinged with danger and a bitter twist of guilt. It feels wrong, but by God do I want it.

They say your sex drive can go wild during pregnancy. That must be it. A chemical reaction, nothing to do with me, or with my character.

As Edward pulls me close, I become aware of the scent of Robert's tobacco on me, in my hair, on my clothes. I open my eyes and there is Edward, Robert thirty years younger. I bury my hand in his still-dark hair, my body pressing into his, as I desperately try to separate the man I am thinking about from the man I am kissing. The hard ridges of Robert's tape cassette dig into the skin of my upper thigh through the velvet of my jumpsuit, less than an inch from my silk underwear. I wonder if I should pull away and stop this before it goes any further. But I do not.

As Edward's lips travel to my neck, my gaze flutters to the Holbecks' driver, a thick sheet of glass dividing us. His eyes are glued to the road, oblivious.

Back in the apartment, hours later, I sit on the edge of the bathtub, my feet cold against the tiles. I can't sleep but it's not morning sickness this time; it's everything else.

Bobby, Edward, and Robert Holbeck himself.

I tap Bobby's name into the search bar of my phone. The apartment is silent around me, Edward fast asleep back in our bed.

The search results load but to my surprise have autocorrected to *Robert Holbeck*. For a second I'm baffled, but then it clicks and I kick myself for being so stupid.

Bobby and Robert have the same name. Father and firstborn son. The weight of that tradition hits me afresh as I stare at the screen. Bobby never really even had his own name.

I scroll past the autocorrected business articles and op-ed pieces on Robert Davison Holbeck's empire, its reach, its impact. Google images of Robert's roguishly handsome face slip past and I try to squash the bizarre mixture of feelings they give me, shame, desire, and anger at myself.

I don't locate what I'm looking for until the third page of the search results. There is a straightforward, no-frills obituary in *The New York Times*.

Robert Alfred "Bobby" Holbeck, aged 20, died on October 18, 2002, at Mount Sinai Hospital, New York, after therapeutic complications. Born on January 3, 1982, to business magnate, investor and philanthropist R. D. Holbeck and his wife, Eleanor Belinda Holbeck, a former model and Goodwill ambassador. Robert was in his third year as an undergraduate at Columbia University in the city of New York, studying law. He was a bright student, a valued member of the undergraduate community, and a highly skilled young athlete. He will be greatly missed by all who knew him and his family kindly ask for privacy, and the space to grieve, during this difficult time.

A memorial service will take place on November 18 at St. Paul's Chapel on Columbia's Morningside Heights campus for those who wish to pay their respects.

I notice the date of Bobby's memorial service. The anniversary of it would have been last week, just three days before Edward proposed to me. I can't help but wonder if thoughts of Bobby somehow influenced Edward's decision to ask me. A sense of carpe diem perhaps.

I look down at the glimmering jewel on my finger. Did he give me this ring out of love or out of fear that he might end up like Bobby? That his family might slowly push him to the edge?

I skim the obituary again, shuddering at the strangely bureaucratic language used to describe his death. *Therapeutic complications.*

There is precious little else about Bobby online. Edward was right, the Holbecks really did manage to keep Bobby off the internet. A year after 9/11, I guess the city, the world, had bigger fish to fry. Easy to lose one accidental death in the abundance of human tragedy around that time.

I know from writing research how search results can be made to disappear; the EU has its own online right-to-be-forgotten law. Anyone can request that their personal information be removed from search results. You just have to prove it is more damaging to the people involved for it to remain in the public sphere than it is beneficial to the public for the information to be available.

The US doesn't have a similar law yet, but there is legal precedent. I'm sure the Holbecks could avail themselves of that fact.

Matilda rearranged my work life in under thirty minutes. Given a long enough time frame, I'm sure that for people like them, anything is possible.

Robert must have gone to extraordinary lengths to protect his family after what happened to Bobby. I feel that odd ache again and push the feeling away angrily. But it's not just for Robert, it's for all of them, the family, their strange history, and the aura surrounding them. They are utterly terrifying and bewitching.

The tape Robert gave me is safely nestled in my bedside drawer—a glow blossoms in my chest at the thought of it. I have been entrusted with something special. If I had something to play it on, I would play the whole thing now, but I don't.

In spite of the extremely early hour, I suddenly have a desperate urge to write, a desire I haven't felt in months. I pad swiftly through the apartment to my study, ease myself into my writing chair, and flip open my laptop. Through the window New York twinkles and I get the thrill that every early riser gets, of being the first to live the new day.

I open a fresh document and the words just come. A new story. The story of an intoxicating family with a secret.

11

The Man in the Carriage

Dawn breaks across the city skyline, pinks and apricots giving way to crisp azure as I close my laptop. I have three new chapters. I am back. Robert and the Holbecks have reignited the fire inside me.

I let the sun warm my face as I remember with an illicit thrill that Robert's tape is waiting for me, like an early Christmas present demanding to be unwrapped. The sooner I can find something to play it on, the better.

In the kitchen I make a plump stack of silver-dollar pancakes with streaky bacon and wait for Edward to emerge from the bedroom. I know I should tell him about the tape, about the conversation with his father last night, but selfishly I want to hear what's on it first. That, and I promised Robert I would keep it between us, for now.

When Edward finally enters the kitchen, bleary-eyed and hungover, my desire for total honesty has thankfully passed.

Once I'm showered and dressed, I slip Robert's tape into my pocket. I need to do a little research. If I want something to play the miniature cassette, I'm going to need to find a specialty store.

As I head out the door, Edward kisses me goodbye, a portrait of hungover shame. "Thank you for breakfast. You're too good to me," he says with a shake of his head. "And listen, I'm sorry again about last night. I should have prepared you better. I should have told you about . . . I'm sorry if you felt thrown in at the deep end."

"It's okay. It's always weird meeting someone else's family. Probably good I didn't know about Bobby. It would have been another thing on my mind."

He takes my hand across the table. "How did I get so lucky with you?"

I feign remembrance of our first meeting. "I think you picked me off from the herd while I was trapped. That sound about right?" I ask with a grin, the hard plastic angles of R.D.'s cassette tape digging into my thigh with almost anthropomorphic insistence.

Out on the blustery streets of Manhattan I check my route again before heading down a set of subway steps. The temperature has dropped in the city in spite of the cobalt-blue sky, my fingers already red and numbed as I swipe my MetroCard. I was warned about New York winters; they sneak up on you.

After a little googling, I managed to find a secondhand electrical store down in the Financial District. The store specializes in used audio and recording equipment, so if I can get my hands on a Dictaphone, I could be listening to Robert Holbeck's story before the day is out. I would be lying if I said the idea of that alone wasn't enough to propel me across town.

The tiny tape Robert handed me last night is an Olympus XH15 microcassette, placing its time of manufacture firmly in the late 1990s. According to the internet, I need a similar micro-cassette recorder to listen to it.

Although the tape is old, it's impossible to know when he recorded it. I get a jolt of excitement at the thought of hearing a younger Robert's voice, his words coming to me directly from the past. I wonder what the tape will tell me about his life, his family, his children.

As every writer knows, even if a story is pure fiction, there are truths hidden in there—about the writer, about the time it was written—that are incontrovertible. I get a now familiar shiver of guilt as I hop through the doors of the subway carriage and slide into one of its glossy plastic seats. I shouldn't be this excited about hearing Edward's father's voice.

But thoughts are just that: thoughts. It's impossible to police them, and as long as they stay just thoughts, I have no reason to feel guilty—do I?

I put this odd little infatuation down to two very simple things: early-pregnancy hormones and novelty. I haven't had access to Edward's family until now and I'm getting carried away. This mild obsession with Robert is just an obsession with everything to do with that family, with Edward's life before me, as shrouded in mystery and exoticism as it is.

I'm no psychoanalyst, but I'd say there's definitely some orphan/daddy stuff thrown in there too for good measure. But fantasies are fantasies, and I haven't actually done anything wrong.

I relax back into my seat, my eyes flitting over the packed subway carriage. A sleeping girl with headphones on catches my attention, her face so peaceful as the subway rattles on around her. I used to be able to do that back in London, sleep on the Underground, but I don't think I ever could here. Then, breaking the tranquility of the moment, I notice a man beyond the sleeping girl staring at me.

He isn't looking at the girl; he's looking directly at me. As soon as I catch his eyes, he stands and calmly slips deeper into the busy train car, as if caught. As if I knew him or he knew me.

I repress a sudden urge to jump up and follow him, to confront him. Oddly, I can't help but feel this has something to do with the Holbecks. The knowledge of Robert's tape and what might be on it is burning in my mind.

The train doors slam open and a fresh batch of travelers bustle on, replacing those that disembark. I watch the crowded platform beyond, hoping to catch a glimpse of him disappearing, but he is nowhere to be seen.

I run his appearance back through my mind. White, mid-forties, short brown hair, dark trousers, dark sweater, nondescript jacket, and a dark baseball cap. All deliberately unassuming.

Before I can stop myself, I am up on my feet and making my way farther into the car, in the direction he went. I dodge through the packed carriage as it shudders on, my nerves tightening into a ball in my throat. I know how irrational I am being right now. I have no logical reason to be doing what I am doing. I'm just following an instinct.

Then, just as that instinct begins to wane, a woman ahead of me shifts position and I see through to him in the next car. The baseball cap, that same oddly calm energy. His eyes meet mine, and I see a flash of concern.

The carriage doors behind me clatter open at the next stop. Another passenger pushes roughly past me, my focus momentarily breaking as my bag is knocked from my shoulder onto the carriage floor, its contents scattering chaotically. Keys, wallet, phone, and everything else, suddenly tumbled between the legs of strangers.

I dip, frantic to gather what I can as more passengers surge on and off the train past me, jostling my loose possessions. But as I squat to gather them, Robert's tape slips from my pocket and ricochets away from me in the melee. I watch it skitter across the carriage floor, wedging itself precariously in the rubber gap between the closing doors and the carriage floor. I lunge toward it to stop it from slipping out onto the tracks below, but when I reach it it's thankfully stuck solid in the closed door, until I give it a good yank and free it still in one piece. I deposit it safely into the pocket of my coat, much to the interest of everyone watching.

When I rise and look back toward the next carriage, the man in the black baseball cap is gone.

12

MH Electricals

"We got it, but you gotta wait—few hours, maybe," the short, animated electrical store worker tells me with a little more vehemence than my question really warranted.

"No, no, that's fine. I don't mind waiting," I lie politely. Because, of course, there is a rush. I need to listen to Robert's tape *now*, this very minute. I need to know what's on it.

I watch the short man tap through his computer system searching for what I need as my mind wanders back to the incident on the subway. The more I replay it, the less sure I am that the man in the other carriage was the same man after all. Had he been wearing the same black cap, or had his been a blue one? I get a twinge of concern at the direction of my thoughts; I've been on the lookout for this very feeling since I packed up my things and moved here from London four months ago.

Throughout my twenties I had recurrent bouts of PTSD, from the trauma I experienced the day my parents died. Major life overhauls always seem to trigger them: a job loss, a breakup, change. These periods are marked by hypervigilance, paranoia, familiar faces seen in crowds, with all the physical symptoms of panic though without the actual feeling of being panicked. But I haven't felt anything like that in years. The pregnancy could be to blame for what happened earlier, or this sudden and intense introduction to my new family.

I knew change would have consequences, and besides, a brief google on the walk here from the subway station told me that twenty percent of pregnant women experience anxiety and paranoia at some point during their pregnancy anyway.

"So you definitely have something I can use?" I ask, refocusing. I notice the store worker's name tag: SYLVESTER.

His brow creases, followed quickly by a pained expression at the computer screen. After a moment he calls out to the back room: "Marv? *Marv,* you got an Olympus? Ready now? Microcassette." Marv and Sylvester.

Marv's voice comes back throaty and loud. "What model?"

Sylvester looks back to me and—finding no help there—answers for me. "Er, Pearlcorder? Or whatever you got."

A pause before Marv's gruff voice rejoins, "Yep. Got a compact. Spruce it up in an hour."

Sylvester lifts an eyebrow in my direction. "Compact sound good? You happy with that?"

I pause, with absolutely no idea. "Will it play the tape?"

"Sure," he says, shrugging.

It suddenly occurs to me that Robert could have just loaned me one of these players, but chose not to. This is part of the test, no doubt—the thrill of the chase. And I can't say it isn't working. I need to listen to what's on that tape more than ever.

Sylvester pulls a calculator from his overall pocket and tots up some unknown figures. "Okay, for the wait I'll do you a deal. Fifteen percent sweetener. So . . . let's just call it . . ." He sucks his teeth. "How does a hundred and sixty dollars sound?"

"A hundred and sixty dollars?" I repeat with slight disbelief, though I had no idea how much an old Dictaphone would cost in the first place.

Sylvester, misreading my signals, comes back hard and fast with an amendment. "Okay, okay: one forty, final offer."

None the wiser, I agree. I hand over my credit card and settle into the idea that I will be hearing Robert's voice in just over an hour.

13

A Word to the Wise

Safely cocooned in an end-of-aisle subway seat, coat tight and scarf pulled high, I slip my new gadget from its MH Electricals bag. It's a relic from another time. I notice a few interested glances flit my way as I prize open its anachronistic wire band headphones and slide the red foam earpieces over the surface of my ears. It's crazy to think this is how people used to listen to music, the foam pieces barely balancing over my earholes let alone covering them, and yet I feel an ache of nostalgia for a simpler time. A time before me, before upgrades and updates and digitization. I tuck the plastic bag away and inspect the device.

Sylvester gave me a brief tutorial in the store but there's precious little that can go wrong with the player. *Unless*—and I have been resoundingly warned by both Marv and Sylvester—unless I accidentally hit RECORD/PLAY instead of PLAY; the buttons are tiny and right next to each other. If I do that, then I'll record over the tape, erasing its contents.

But that will not be happening, because unlike Marv and Sylvester, I do not have giant bear hands. And now that I've been forewarned, I am forearmed. Robert's tape is safe with me.

I fish the cassette from my pocket, open the player, and slide the tape in. It shuts with a satisfying click.

I press PLAY and the machine responds with another gratifying clunk, then a low fizz and an ambient crackle as sound bursts to life in my ears. I brace myself for Robert's voice.

Through the headphones, I pick up the distant muffle of speaking, then I distinguish the low rumble of fabric rubbing on the mic, as if this were recording in someone's pocket.

It could be the murmurs of a private conversation or something already badly recorded over. I spin the volume dial up in the hope of hearing more, but the words remain indistinct. And then I get the odd feeling that I am listening to something I shouldn't be.

There's a chance Robert might have given me the wrong tape. He retrieved it in the half-light, after all.

I consider turning it off but suddenly the quality of sound changes in my headphones; the muffling lifts. I strain to hear more, sliding the volume up to its highest, and then I hear it. The sound of breathing first, and then, in earsplitting volume, the unmistakable voice of Robert Holbeck.

Reflexively I yank the headphones from my ears with a yelp. In front of me an elderly woman is staring directly at me angrily, her face slack with age, her expression unambiguous. "What are you, deaf?" she shouts, her tone implying she knows I'm not. "You gonna answer it? Or we all gotta put up with it?" she spits, jutting a bony finger toward my bag, and I realize what the hell she is talking about. My phone is ringing, loud and persistent in the car.

"Oh, er, thank you," I manage, and she shrugs dismissively as I fumble the offending article from my bag and answer it.

"Sorry, yes, hello?"

"Oh hi, Harriet. Is this a bad time? It's Amy at Grenville Sinclair. Is everything okay?"

I straighten in my subway seat. It's my publisher. Again. I dread to think of what could be sparking this second call in a week.

"Amy, no, no, I'm free. What can I do for you?"

I look down at the Olympus microcassette player on my lap. Through its small window I watch the reels of the tape continuing to turn. It's still playing. *Shit.* I clunk down the STOP button and then the REWIND and watch the reels reverse their movement.

"Oh, fantastic. Wonderful," she says with relief. "I'm so glad I caught you. I tried you on your home phone but there was no answer. My mistake. I thought I recalled you once mentioning in an interview that you write from home. Where are you writing these days? It sounds busy there. Do you write out and about?" Her tone is friendly and conversational but the unspoken upshot of the call is that we both know I am not writing right now. And I should be. My deadline has passed and I am under contract.

"No, actually, I'm just out doing a little research," I lie. And yet considering the new direction my novel has taken, perhaps calling Robert's tape "research" isn't such a stretch.

"Oh, fascinating. Can you tell me more, or is it all still bubbling away?" she asks.

"Bubbling, yeah," I say, floundering. "Listen, Amy, I am so sorry about what happened the other day. I think wires got crossed and—"

"Not a problem at all, Harriet. I totally understand the situation. And your agent, Louisa, has emailed about your extension request, which is actually why I'm calling."

"Oh, great," I respond optimistically, though something in the change of her tone makes me realize this is not a good call.

"Yes, so Louisa mentioned you're almost there with this draft. More than two-thirds. Now, you know how much Grenville Sinclair loves you; we even looked at pushing publication dates. But the thing is, not much more can be done at this end. We're in a bind. I know this is a lot to throw at you, but we're really going to need that manuscript by the second week of December."

I swallow hard, my mouth suddenly arid. "The second week? As in . . . ?"

"Two weeks? Is that doable?" Her voice is a little crisper now, a little more businesslike. "It sounds like you're nearly there anyway, right?"

"Right," I lie. I have fifty thousand words of a ninety-thousand-word novel and last night I entirely reworked the plot.

Two weeks to write forty thousand words and pull the whole thing together. I feel my pulse skyrocket but force myself to remain calm. This isn't the moon landing. It's a curveball, for sure, but it's doable. It's a high daily word count, but I've managed it before. After all, I got seventy-five hundred done last night alone. I seem to be back in the game, which is the most important thing.

"Okay. Okay. I can do the eleventh. That is not a problem. Thank you for letting me know, Amy."

After I hang up, my eyes drop to the cassette player on my lap. I definitely do not have time for this now. I need to be working all day, every day, until December 11. No interruptions, no distractions. I click off the cassette player's power, carefully wrap the headphone cord around it, and open my iPhone Notes app.

Robert will have to wait. All the Holbecks will have to wait. Though judging by their previous track record, that doesn't seem like something they're used to doing.

14

Red Rag to a Bull

FRIDAY, NOVEMBER 25–TUESDAY, DECEMBER 6

It turns out, as predicted, the Holbecks don't take kindly to other people's commitments.

The first call comes that evening. As I hole up in my study with ten pages already under my belt and a half-eaten sandwich at my elbow, Edward pokes a tentative head around the door. He knows where things stand with the book and what I need to do in order to get over the line. He lifts the phone muffled in his hands apologetically.

"I know you're right in the middle of it. I told her. She knows. But *my mother* wants a word," he says, his face sheepish. Something about Edward plunged into the role of put-upon son makes me laugh—though I doubt I'd find any of this quite so amusing if my word count weren't as high as it already is this evening.

"Yeah, it's fine. I can speak to her. I might stop for the night now anyway," I say, taking the phone from him. "What's it about?" I ask before raising it to my ear.

He shrugs. "Won't tell me."

I twitch an eyebrow in interest, and he smirks, slipping out of the room, leaving me to find out.

"Hi, Eleanor, it's Harriet. Everything okay?"

"Oh, hello, darling. Now, listen, Edward has explained the situation. You're a Trojan; good for you. And I'll be out of your hair imminently. I just want to get your advice on something. Gauge your thoughts really. Robert and I, of course, want you *both* over for Christmas this year, but as you're aware it's a delicate topic with Edward. I don't want to cause a fuss, scare him off, so I thought I'd hold off asking him at all if you thought it was perhaps too soon . . . for him?"

This is not the conversation I was expecting. "Um, I—"

"You see, last Christmas was the first we all spent apart," she blusters on. "We tend to cluster together at The Hydes most holidays. But of course Edward was in London with you last Christmas and everything was a bit fraught between us, as you know. The whole family comes to us usually. It's very festive. We'd love to get back to the way things were, you understand."

I think she is inviting me over for Christmas. But it's hard to be sure.

The idea of it is terrifying and thrilling in equal measure. A chance to look inside The Hydes, a chance to study Edward's family in its natural habitat and absorb their strange magic free from constraint. But in order to do that, I would actually need to *spend* Christmas with them.

"Um, well, it sounds lovely, Eleanor. I really appreciate the offer, and I'd personally love to, but I really don't know how Edward would take to that idea at the moment. Or, to be honest, how he'd take to you asking me the question in the first place," I say gently, my voice lowered in spite of the fact I can hear Edward pottering around in the kitchen.

"I see," she says, circumspectly. "Noted. Well, in that case, perhaps we just need a little more time to ease him into the idea. Softly, softly, catchee monkey, as they say." She sighs, though a smile is evident in her voice. I can't help but relish her old-world familiarity with me given the fact we've only met once. "Well, thank you for your honesty, my dear. We'll give it a little more time perhaps." She pivots. "Now, listen, Edward told me about your situation with Grenville Sinclair. Is there anything the family can do to help—?"

"No!" I blurt, but quickly recover myself. "No, it's all good. Thank you, Eleanor. It's actually very motivating, a hard deadline. I've never been so prolific," I add lightly.

"Oh, that's so good to hear. But you must take care of yourself, Harry dear. You must be exhausted with the house, and your work."

The question blindsides me to the extent that I find I don't really understand it. "The house?"

"Running the house and working full-time," she clarifies.

"Oh, well, it's just an apartment really. And we don't make much mess, so—"

"Yes, Edward mentioned you hadn't managed to find a suitable housekeeper in town yet? You know, I'm not surprised. I know it can be a real nightmare when you first move to the city. People hoard the good ones."

I find myself once again lost for words. Edward thinks we need a housekeeper? "Er, well, we actually don't really need a housekeeper, I don't think." Yet even as I say it, I'm wondering if I'm wrong. Apparently, Edward needs to make excuses for the fact that we don't have one. Suddenly I wonder if he finds it weird that we don't have a cleaner, that I hoover and tidy myself, that he sometimes has to cook?

"Harriet, darling, you're not cooking and cleaning yourself, are you? Not on top of everything?" she asks, as diplomatically as it is possible to, given the inference. I look at the limp half-eaten sandwich beside me as she continues. "You will run yourself ragged trying to do it all. But who am I to tell you how to do things? I'm sure you know your own mind. Here's the thing: We're dyed-in-the-wool Democrats, my dear, to a man. We're all liberal, woke, pro-union, patrons of the arts, what-have-you, but let's be honest here: chapped hands help no one."

I stifle a giggle. This is the strangest conversation I've had with a partner's mother. And I'm pretty sure there's some blurred definitions in there.

"You certainly make a robust argument for it, that's for sure, Eleanor. I'll give it some serious thought," I tell her, and bizarrely I mean it. I don't want to fight any battles I don't have to, especially as I get further into pregnancy. I chose to enter Edward's world and it looks like this is what it is.

"Do, my dear. And thank you for the advice. I'll let you get on with your important work. All my love."

There's a knock at the front door early the next morning. Luckily I'm up and dressed this time and already two hours into my day. The view through the peephole is still blocked by the Christmas wreath, so I'm none the wiser when Edward quizzically pops his head out of the bathroom and asks who it is.

"No idea," I tell him.

"Right, if it's any of them, I'll deal with it. I promise, just give me a minute to put some clothes on," he calls, disappearing back into the steam of the bathroom.

I wonder if it's odd that I don't mind his family's attention half as much as he does. But then this is all new to me. I've never really had *relatives* before, and now there seem to be a lot of them.

I lift the latch and swing open the front door to reveal a beaming and incredibly tall Maori woman in her forties. She's dressed in a pristine gray uniform, and in her arms she is carrying cleaning supplies and a large brown bag of groceries.

"Ms. Reed? My name is Ataahua. Mrs. Holbeck asked me to come over, if it's okay? I'm so excited to be helping you with the house for the next few weeks. Is it okay if I come in?"

I stare completely dumbfounded at my newest employee. Eleanor sent us a housekeeper.

"Hi, Ataahua. This is, wow, *yes,* this is so exciting. Thank you so much," I say with a smile as I wonder how in God's name I am going to explain this to Ed when he gets out of the shower.

By the end of the month my phone is filled with missed calls from various Holbecks and I already can't imagine life without Ataahua—though I'm perfectly aware that once my deadline has passed, we'll both just be standing around in the empty apartment together. I can't deny, however, that the last few days with her have been a writer's dream: everything clean, ironed, and spotless when I emerge at the end of a working day after locking myself away.

I'll miss her gentle knock on the door and her maternal face peering around it offering me delicious home-cooked food. Eleanor almost certainly overstepped the mark, but I can't deny that part of me is so glad she did.

On this occasion the Holbecks' interference was much welcomed, though Edward has been quick to warn me that thinking that way could be a slippery slope. But then he doesn't know what I know, the reason they are on their best behavior: they need me or they lose him.

And boy, have they gone all-out to pull me in. During the past few days, I have been inundated with calls, texts, and offers to get to know me better. The strangest coming from Stuart, who suggested I join his tennis doubles group on Thursdays. I've never been so relieved to admit I don't play tennis.

And then there was a request from Fiona to join her for coffee and a *chat* that I grudgingly had to raincheck, desperate as I am to glean some insider gossip from another Holbeck partner. I think perhaps Fiona's world might intersect most comfortably with my own, and I'm curious to know how her start with them went when she got serious with Oliver.

Speaking of which, even Oliver managed to send a short but friendly email a couple of days after Thanksgiving, welcoming me to the family and saying how wonderful it was to finally meet me.

The only offer I have accepted is one from Lila, not because of who she is but due to the fact that she seemed to be the only one in the family who was willing to postpone until after my book is in—something that hasn't seemed to occur to a single Holbeck.

With one week to go until my deadline, I am slightly ahead of myself in terms of word count, my story coming together with pleasing clarity. The tale of an incredibly wealthy family and their secret history. Of course, I have concerns about the content, the idea that Robert might read my story, that any of them might—but this is what I do. I can only go where my mind will let me go, especially now that my focus is so split. And now that I finally seem to have my flow back, I can't let embarrassment or fear of what other people might think stop me from moving forward. Besides, I would assume that the Holbecks would appreciate the difference between fact and fiction, and I can only hope be a little flattered at the fleeting similarities. But perhaps that's too much of a stretch.

I think of Robert reading my first book and imagine him reading this one too, my mind naturally going to his tape, safely shut away, hidden in the suitcase under my bed, the only thing I own with a lock. I had to move the tape player there two days ago after Ataahua wandered into the kitchen holding it and, oblivious to its content, started asking where she should put it. I had thought it was safely buried under my side of the mattress until then. Clearly not.

Every fiber of my body wants to listen to what is on that tape. And every Holbeck text, call, and email I have received this week has reawakened that urge. But I know if I start listening, I will keep listening until the end. I'll lose a day, or two, and if what is on there is good, I might lose my focus altogether. I cannot risk missing my deadline. I am not a Holbeck, and to think I can get away with the things they get away with would be to delude myself.

I cannot risk being drawn into the Holbecks' orbit. At least not for five more days.

15

Lila

It's just past midnight on the twelfth when I push send on the email to my publishers, ten minutes over my deadline. As the manuscript wings its way through the ether and out of my sphere of control, I slump back into my chair and let out a sigh of internal surrender.

My Herculean challenge finally complete, I contemplate a cold glass of wine before quickly remembering I can't do that for another seven months. Unless I take the Continental approach to pregnancy and start on a glass a night for good measure. At this stage the idea has a certain ring to it, but perhaps a hot bath and a bar of chocolate might do just as well.

I close down the sent document triumphantly. Two days ago, I set a password on my manuscript. Call it paranoia, call it cowardice, but Edward asked about the plot that morning and I got the jitters. I was so close to the finish line, and I didn't want to run the risk of him balking at the hook of my story before I sent it. Not that there's anything in it to balk at, and I can amend things in the edit, if anyone raises concerns. The point is: the family in my story isn't the Holbeck family, and the lost son isn't Bobby. In my story, the son doesn't really die. He comes back.

The fact remains I password-locked the document, to stop Edward from reading it, whatever that means in terms of trust. It's not that I don't trust him, and there's nothing wrong with curiosity and it's flattering to imagine he might want to sneak a peek, but I didn't want to feel encumbered at the first-draft stage by outside judgment. The truth is I am pleased with it, come what may. It might be the best thing I have written. We'll see.

The next morning, after a well-deserved lie-in, I take a short walk from the apartment to meet Lila at an open-air Christmas market at Columbus Circle. I've seen it in passing since it went up last week, on the few rare occasions I've left the apartment for writing breaks.

I considered making a start on Robert's tape this morning, but wanted to enjoy it without having to break it up. If Edward's not home before me tonight, I will begin.

The Christmas market is a small, festive shantytown of painted alpine huts, glowing warm and each stocked to the brim with crafts and imported delicacies from across Europe. There's something so nostalgic about it that as I approach, it almost feels like coming home. The market's walkways are swathed with thick pine garlands that twinkle with fairy lights, and the air is filled with the spiced scent of glühwein and roasted nuts.

I catch sight of Lila ahead of me in front of a large Christmas tree, totally at home in the anonymous crowd, though she stands a few inches taller than passersby. She looks amazing, every inch the Swedish Christmas dream: snow boots, leggings, and a shearling coat wrapped tight against the cold. She smiles as she catches sight of me.

"Harry," she cheers. "You did it! You finished." She pulls me into a hug and claps my back harder than I expect her to, making me cough slightly. "You're finished. Yes? Deadline over?"

I crack my own smile now. "Yep, all done."

"In that case, let's celebrate," she says, looping an arm through mine and guiding me purposefully into the tightly packed market.

As we go, she tells me about herself, how she moved to New York as a young model, her childhood in Sweden, her disastrous first marriage to a well-known Boston Irish basketball player that led to the birth of her gorgeous son, Milo, and finally how she met Stuart.

"Zermatt. Skiing with friends. We were thrown together. I'm sure you know, Stuart doesn't drink. No alcohol, no substances. Our friend groups, well, they can all get a bit cokey, you know. A bit much. I grew up modeling. I've seen some things, too young, you know. I don't touch any of that stuff, never have. It scares the bejesus out of me. My ex always got messy drunk. I don't like it." She studies my expression for a second, then continues. "I know what you're thinking. She's going from one guy with a drink problem to another, right?" I go to protest but she smiles. "It's fine. Stuart isn't like that. He's ten years sober, still goes to meetings; he's a lifer. Trust me, I've met a lot of addicts in my life, a lot of liars, and you get a sense for people, of who's kidding themselves . . . Stuart is a good man; he might seem like a black sheep, but that's just another way of saying how rare he is. He's a good stepdad to Milo."

We stop at a hut selling glühwein, glögg, and hot chocolate. The vendor clearly recognizes Lila and becomes mildly awkward. In the short time we've been together I have already noticed a few roving eyes and open mouths.

"You ever had glögg?" she asks me.

"I don't think so. What is it?"

"It's like glühwein but much better. It's Swedish." She grins. "It'll warm you up from the insides."

That's exactly what I'm afraid of, and I politely decline and settle instead for a fully loaded hot chocolate with marshmallows and a crumbly chocolate stick valiantly wedged into its creamy summit.

We wander on, sipping our hot drinks, and I steel myself to ask a question I've been longing to ask since Thanksgiving. "Did you know about Bobby?"

Lila's focus turns to me, an eyebrow raised. "Of course. I know they are very sensitive about it. The whole family. You didn't know?" she asks, interested by this new information.

I shake my head, and after a moment's thought she pats my arm in sympathy.

"Well, Stuart talks a lot. I blame AA. He's an open book. But Edward, he's different. More like Robert, I think. A tougher nut to crack. I think you're a good match, though. Me, on the other hand," she adds with an impish smile, "my nutcracking days are over. I like to keep it simple."

The market complete, Lila flags us a taxi downtown. In the sheltered warmth of the cab, she turns to me excitedly with a question. "Are you scared of heights?"

I only fully understand the question when we're deposited outside One Vanderbilt and I look up at the jutting steel and glass towering skyward above us. I've read about it. It's been closed most of this year while they changed the internal exhibits.

Lila pulls two lanyards from her bag and they jostle in the wind. "It officially reopens on Friday night; social posts are embargoed till then, but we can get content anytime. VIP passes." She slips one over my head and for the second time today I remember she's a celebrity. It's odd to think how one can forget that so quickly in the context of the Holbecks. Even fame like Lila's seems to fade in significance beside the reach of that family.

We're fast-tracked up to the ninety-first floor, our ears popping at the speed of the elevator's ascent as a guide straps an electrical bracelet to our wrists.

When the doors open, I see the relevance of Lila's question. The entire cavernous ninety-first floor of Summit Vanderbilt is made of glass and mirrors suspended a thousand feet over Madison Avenue, reflecting everything in it back ad infinitum. Lila steps out of the elevator first, her wristband light blinking as the sounds of birds and the ocean fill the space.

"The bracelets map each wearer's vital signs," the guide tells me, gesturing for me to step out of the elevator too. "The space responds to the people that fill it. Think of the building as a massive mood ring. Different types of stimuli, reflecting you back to you."

A sensory hall of mirrors. The idea is a terrifying one for a person like me, who fears truly being seen, but I have little choice but to follow Lila as our guide disappears.

I feel my wrist vibrate gently, and the sound of fire crackles to life around us. Lila spins to face me, a Cheshire-cat grin blossoming. The sounds I am unwittingly producing are so unexpectedly telling that it sends a hot flush of fear up my throat and into my cheeks.

"Harry, that's you. The sound of you. It's beautiful," she says, beaming. I feel my pulse beat faster at the intensity of her focus but force myself to stay calm, to center. I cannot let the sound, or the memories associated with it, overwhelm me.

As the fire's roar settles into the low crackle of a campfire, I follow Lila across the building's glass floor to the full-height windows and the panoramic view of the city beyond.

I watch, strangely disconnected, as Lila takes the shots she needs for her social content before finally returning to my side.

"Look down," she says. And when I do I see that where we are standing a thick sheet of glass is all that holds us both suspended a thousand feet above Madison Avenue. I feel my heart rise an inch higher in my chest at the realization. Lila holds my gaze playfully and starts to crack her high heel against the glass beneath us, grinning the whole time.

I am not scared of heights, but my limbic system, millions of years old and incapable of understanding the modern world, causes my blood pressure to drop ever so slightly. I feel the woozy vertiginous rush I am supposed to.

Lila must feel it too, because the reactive sounds around us seamlessly mellow, soften, to the slow, pulsing beat of rain drumming on a roof. Through the glass, New York City is laid out in lines and blocks. So tidy and easy to understand from up here.

The Empire State Building, Top of the Rock, and the Chrysler Building. Model skyscrapers made by men like Robert Holbeck— the building we're standing in now just the same.

"This is a good test," Lila says with a chuckle.

"Of what?"

"All sorts of things. But it's good to know," she answers simply. "You don't scare easily."

16

Krampus Is Coming

MONDAY, DECEMBER 12

On my way back to the apartment, my phone rings in my bag. It's an unknown number. It's too early to be hearing back from my publisher about the book; I only sent it last night. Curiosity piqued, I answer.

It's a female voice I don't immediately recognize. "Oh, hi, Harriet. Is this a bad time? Are you still working? I wasn't sure if you would be. Sorry, it's Fiona here. Fiona Holbeck."

"Fiona? Oh, hi." Weird that Fiona is calling me, I think, given I have just left Lila. For a second I wonder if they're all in constant contact on some kind of family WhatsApp group, but then realize the thought of Robert Holbeck on WhatsApp is ridiculous. Plus Fiona has been trying to get hold of me for a few days now. "No, I'm free, now is fine," I tell her, slipping into a shop doorway to better hear her. "What's up?"

"Wonderful. I'll cut to the chase," she says conspiratorially. "It's a madhouse here," she adds. "The boys are taking part in the end-of-term show at their school and it's like wrangling cats trying to get them to practice."

I can't help but smile at the idea of little Billy in a tiny costume, singing, and the logistics involved in that. "It sounds very cute, though," I say in what I hope is a supportive way.

"Ha. *Never* have kids, Harry," she chuckles wryly, in the way that only mothers can. "Now, listen, I'm calling because every year we have a thing at the house, a party, and I was wondering if you'd like to come along to this one? Billy has been especially insistent about me asking you," she adds.

"Really?" I ask, a sliver of pride in my voice.

"Oh yes. He's been asking if you can come since the Thanksgiving dinner. To be honest I don't think he's going to stop asking until I give him a definitive answer. And of course we all want you there too." She breaks off for a second, her attention elsewhere, her tone of voice changing as she talks to someone beside her. "I'm asking her now, honey. Yes: Auntie Harry. I'm asking her now. Okay, then. No, let Mama talk to her first, okay?"

It's Billy. I get a fuzzy aunty feeling followed by an odd ache, which I guess must be broodiness. Thank God that just kicks in at some stage; I had thought it might not for me.

"Okay, Harriet," Fiona singsongs. "Are you free on the sixteenth of December? You and Edward, of course?"

"Um?" I answer hesitantly, suddenly wary of being tricked into another unwitting Thanksgiving situation. It occurs to me that this invitation might be a slow preamble toward Eleanor's Christmas. But perhaps that's not so bad. "Sorry to ask, Fiona, but the sixteenth isn't some big American holiday I don't know about, is it? Nothing like that?"

Fiona chuckles. "Definitely not. It's just a regular American Friday evening. Though it is something we do every year. It's this Friday," she adds helpfully.

"Then I guess we're free," I tell her. It works out perfectly, as

Fiona is next on my list to get to know better. I'm dying to hear more about the family from her perspective.

"Oh, that's just great. Billy is going to be over the moon. All right then, so just to tell you a little bit about it. It's family tradition, every year, for Krampusnacht." She says it breezily, as if I will know what that means. Her German pronunciation is perfect and immediately intimidating. "I mean," she continues, "technically Krampusnacht is supposed to be on the fifth, but we always push it to the last weekend before the Christmas break. It's just easier for everyone." Sensing my lack of comprehension, she chuckles. "I've lost you, haven't I? It's a silly German thing— a Holbeck Christmas tradition. I took over organizing from Eleanor when we had kids. It's ostensibly for the children but there's fun to be had for the grown-ups too." There's a smile in her voice that tells me food and booze will be involved and, while I can't drink, I can almost certainly eat.

"That sounds fun. I'd love that. Krampusnacht," I say, testing the word in my mouth. "Do I need to bring anything? Wine?"

"Oh no. No need to bring anything at all. Well, unless . . ." She pauses a second. "Do you own a flashlight?"

"A flashlight?"

"Yes, a battery-operated flashlight? A big one."

I frown at the glass beside me in the shop doorway and catch my own bewildered expression in it.

"No. But I can get one, I guess, if I need one?"

"Great. Well, that's settled," she says brightly. "Yes, I know Edward has one. He used it last year, but, anyway, we'll get a car over to you on the evening too, so don't worry about all that. Does seven P.M. work?"

Edward was at their house last year while we were still doing long distance from England. It must have been one of the last family events he took part in before he came over to spend Christmas with me.

"Seven P.M. Yeah, great," I say, remembering the question. "Wait, will Billy be up if it starts then?" Though as soon as I've said it, I recall how late the boys were up for the Thanksgiving dinner.

She chuckles. "Oh yes. The kids don't tend to sleep on Krampusnacht. They'll be exhausted the next day, of course, but they always stay up for Krampus."

After we hang up, I google Krampusnacht on my phone and stop dead in my tracks, an immovable object on a bustling sidewalk, pedestrians forced to flow past me, an island in a cursing, jostling stream. I stare at my phone's screen absolutely dumbfounded as the results for *Krampusnacht,* or *Krampus Night,* load.

I gawk at the main Google image. A towering monstrosity of fur and teeth with barely recognizable human features, its body twisted in pain and rage. Jesus Christ, what the absolute hell is a Krampus? And why in God's name are Fiona and Oliver having a night for it? I must have typed the word in wrong, or perhaps this is Fiona's idea of making a joke—a very strange, very worrying joke? Again, I remember what Lila said earlier about me not scaring easily. Perhaps that's a good thing if this is the Holbecks' idea of humor. But then, thinking of Fiona, with her friendly, open face, I doubt she would make a joke like this. I must have just misheard the German word she used. There has to be a rational explanation for this, I tell myself, yet at the same time I read on.

Krampusnacht is celebrated as an accompaniment to the feast of St. Nicholas. The feast of St. Nicholas? Father Christmas has a feast? It occurs to me possibly for the first time in my life that while I've celebrated Christmas every year since I was born, I have absolutely no understanding of most of the traditions surrounding it.

The Krampus, I read on, *in Central European folklore, is a horned anthropomorphic creature; a mythical half-goat, half-demon monster who must punish misbehaving children at Christmastime. Krampus is the evil brother or "shadow self" of St. Nicholas. Traditionally the pair appear as a team, working together, with St. Nicholas (the patron saint of children) rewarding the good once a year while Krampus punishes the bad. The leg-end of the Krampus is believed to have originated in Germany and Eastern Europe, the name deriving from the Germanic word* Krampen, *meaning "claw." The Krampus is often depicted as a Christmas devil carrying chains and birch sticks, which he uses to whip bad children, and a sack on his back in which he can drag them to hell.*

Drag them to hell. Jesus, actual, Christ.

Krampusnacht celebrations often include an appearance of the two characters and usually end in children receiving presents, in shoes they have left out—something nice if they have been good and birch sticks or coal if they have been bad.

Okay, so they don't get dragged to hell, at least. That's a relief. I suppose, in a way, it kind of sounds like trick-or-treating. Perhaps Krampusnacht is a sort of Christmassy Halloween for Eastern Europeans. It could be a fun night, I reason tentatively, though it does potentially sound like low-level child abuse. But then I guess even the tooth fairy could take on a sinister edge viewed through other cultures. Why would a fairy need to collect so many human teeth? What does she do with them?

Krampusnacht games: races are popular in some European countries such as Austria, Germany, and the Czech Republic, where a costumed Krampus will terrorize excited children into behaving themselves throughout the year.

Outdoor games. I suppose that explains why I might need a torch. Fiona said Edward had brought one last year. How did I not know he attended this event last year? You'd think he might have mentioned it at least in passing on one of our long-distance Zooms. I guess he'd have worried it would sound weird, but as weird as it does sound, I am interested. Still, it would seem I'm interested in everything to do with Edward and his bizarre family.

I round the corner of our building, stride into the lobby, and head straight for the lift up to the apartment. I have a lot of questions for Edward, and I presume he has answers.

17

Forewarned Is Forearmed

MONDAY, DECEMBER 12

Edward face-palms when I tell him that I've signed us up for Krampusnacht. "You've done it again, haven't you?" he asks, half amused, half incredulous. "Accepted an offer with absolutely no idea of what you're getting yourself into. Why the hell didn't you just say we were busy?"

"Because we're not busy, and your family is making a lot of offers and I can't turn them all down. Besides, I thought it might be fun. Festive."

He snorts a laugh. "Yeah, it'll be festive. You've basically signed us up for a night of babysitting, you know that, right?" he says with a light shake of the head.

"We're hardly babysitting, Ed. It's a party? Or a dinner, isn't it? I don't know," I admit. "But I think it's sweet that Billy wants me to come. He likes me; it's cute."

"Of course he likes you. You are the most caring person I know. It's crazy that you don't see that. Even Billy sees it." He pulls me close to him, his arms round my shoulders. "It's the first thing I noticed about you. Beautiful *and* kind. It's rarer than you'd think."

I give him side-eye. "Thanks for the flattery, but it's not going to get you out of explaining to me what the hell a Krampus is."

He laughs, releasing me. Perching on a kitchen stool, he splays his hands out on the countertop. "Okay, where to start? A potted history of Holbeck Krampusnacht. I guess it started with Mitzi; her family did it and she brought it over from Germany with her. Alfred and Mitzi did it for their kids when they had them—that was my father's father and his uncles. Then when my dad was a kid, his parents did it until they, you know—"

"Died?" I offer.

"Yeah, and after that Dad moved in with Alfred and Mitzi at The Hydes and they did Krampus Night there for him and his friends. Then we came along, and Mom and Dad did it for us at The Hydes. Then Oliver had kids and now it happens at their place. It's just kept going. It's fun, I promise you. Weird, but—"

"How weird?" I chip in again.

He laughs. "Pretty. But . . . mostly just harmless fun. Hide-and-seek, parlor games, scary masks and costumes. Kids love it. Well, it terrifies them, but you know what I mean. It's character building. That's why Dad kept it going for us and why Ollie does it for his kids. Maybe one day we'll do it for our—"

"Whoa there!" I interject quickly. "Let's just get through *one* Krampusnacht before we start making sweeping statements, okay?"

"Okay," he says with a shrug of acceptance.

"Great. Now, why exactly do I need a torch?"

As I lie in bed that night, not for the first time, I try to imagine the bizarre childhood Edward and his siblings must have had. I picture Robert as their father, how he must have been with them, how he must have wanted to share a piece of his own childhood with them. And then my thoughts move to Eleanor, the woman holding the whole family together, her old-world connections and diplomacy capable of anything but discussing death with her own children. The Holbeck siblings sent off to their respective psychiatrists and the gap Bobby left filled with other things. The day Bobby died, all of the expectations and responsibilities heaped on him fell to Edward. No wonder things have been hard between Edward and his family; this was never his birthright. All of this duty should never have been his to bear; I can't blame him for running scared from a family that ostensibly killed the last guy who had the job before him.

I wonder if Robert mentions any of this on his tape. If his story is a memoir or a thriller, or if that was just a joke. I didn't have a chance to listen to it as I had hoped when I got home earlier, but I could listen now with Edward sleeping beside me. I feel a jolt of that illicit thrill at the idea of hearing Robert's voice, but I'm not sure I could stand the shame if Edward found out what I was doing next to him. No, best to wait until he's out tomorrow. Edward stirs in the sheets as if my thoughts had seeped into his dreams and I can't help wondering if I am a bad person.

But I know the answer to that: I *am* a bad person. Good people don't do the things I have done. There are no mitigating circumstances. What I did was not in self-defense, or in the heat of the moment, or by accident. I did what I did in cold blood. My pulse was steady and I was thinking straight, and *that* is how I know I am a bad person.

Edward loves me, but he wouldn't if he knew what I was capable of, what I did on the side of a road on a cold morning twenty years ago. We all have something inside us that we fear would repel the world if it ever came out. But for most people that thing is something that the light of day would only render harmless. My secret would put me in jail for the rest of my natural life.

I shake off the thought and tell myself I am not that person anymore. We change, we grow; I will never be her again. Though

I know that's not true. I feel her inside me down dark alleys; late at night when things get scary I know she is there in the shadows with me. I know she has my back; our back.

I try to imagine what Robert Holbeck would think if he really knew who his son was marrying. If he knew he'd chased away so many perfect partners and ended up letting me slip through the net.

Unless of course he does know.

That thought hits me hard. I look at the digital clock on the bedside table beside me. It's three A.M. This is insomnia, this is anxiety, this is PTSD. Robert Holbeck does *not* know. He might have a sense for people, he might have a feeling about me, but he cannot read minds. No one was there that day. You could call it a perfect crime except it wasn't perfect; it was horrific.

I turn in my fresh Egyptian cotton sheets and try to clear my mind. The past is gone, my family is gone, and right now, I need to think of the future.

The next morning after Edward leaves for work I slide my suit-case out from underneath the bed and spin its combination lock until the numbers align and retrieve the microcassette player.

It's finally time to listen to Robert's story. I want to hear it—him, his voice, his words.

I make sure the front door is locked as I pass by it and set my-self up in the sitting room, the chunky Olympus player nestled in my lap. I slip the red foam headphones over my ears, carefully adjust the volume, and press PLAY.

18

The Tape

PART 1

Things I remember from that morning. The warmth of sun on skin, dust hanging in light, her hair in the street breeze.

There would be a tent, eventually, to cover him. His college sweatshirt, with all but the A of COLUMBIA obscured. I often recall her face looking up at me as she explained what happened, her expression serious, her words lost in the traffic and the wind. It did not need explaining, what happened. Although it would be explained. Thoroughly.

His head hit the sidewalk at thirty miles an hour. He did not brace himself; he did not break his fall from six floors up, which initially mystified at autopsy. My boy, my good, kind boy, lying broken on the sidewalk like leaking left-out garbage.

Her face again as she spoke words I could not hear, her eyes filling with tears as the wind played with that soft blond hair. The weather vane glinting high above us.

I would hear the story again. Many times. And then later the police would, in turn, ask me. Lawyers. I would search for you in each detail she told me. Knowing the truth was hiding somewhere in there. Knowing she knew *why* you did it but was unable to articulate it, and I could not hook it out of her.

Things had gone wrong between me and you, my son, that much everyone knew. He was good, a good boy, better than me, and there is a particular pain to knowing that the one you want the world *for* does not want your world. That your way is the wrong way. You wanted change, and though I feared it, deep down, I wanted you to prove me wrong. To show me this great change. To prove me wrong about the way the world works, and show me that good triumphs and kindness wins the day. But you did not show me that, unfortunately. You showed me this. And the world kept turning.

The blood was so dark it looked black on the sidewalk.

He jumped, so the story goes, but why?

After lunch, he went back to his room to study, she would tell me. He was tired. He had bitten off more than his still-adolescent mind could chew, more responsibility than he could shoulder unaided. And the poison inside him. But she did not know this then. It would be weeks until we knew what he had taken. The medication, a slow daily drip of meds on top of meds, the results unnoticed at first. And what could be more like him than choosing a drug that pushed him to *be* more, to *do* more. So clever, so undetectable to everyone who knew him, it's no wonder it passed for so long.

If I think on it long enough the blame always lands on me.

I pushed you too far.

What you did. What I did after.

A hasty word to you, a lack of malleability in myself, my poor show of example. But it was done, and it cannot be undone: my work, your work. The solution to it all writ large.

After the funeral she would not come back to the house. I started to suspect she knew. I am not a bad man. But my family is sacred to me.

What you did that day, the mess you made, what you forced me to do to protect those you left behind did not end then. That was the beginning of something. A loosening of something. The boundaries loosened.

I found her.

Her elegant neck, its pale skin delicate, leading down to an alabaster carved clavicle. Beautiful, and all that soft-spun hair, the velvety scent of peony. She made noises as she struggled. She fought. But it did not help. As close as lovers in those last moments. Her breath warm against skin. Her eyes inexplicably calm, as if she knew something the rest of the world did not. Perhaps how little fighting might help in the long run.

She slipped away, and was dealt with. She knew too much about those final hours.

Then a two-hour drive. A two-hour hike, with only the sky and the wind and the rain as companions. There I left her. In the shadow of a green mountain past the calm of a lake. To the wolves. To the wolves because that is where she would have thrown us. And I will never let that happen to us. To my family. Let it not ever be said I let others do my dirty work. I dealt with the mess. That is what we must do.

That was the first.

This is not a threat, *Harriet Reed*. Take this as you find it: a work of fiction, a parable? But take from it that my meaning holds. My family will protect itself. Know that.

19

The Name of the Game

TUESDAY, DECEMBER 13

I gasp and whip off the headphones at the mention of my name, flinging the machine and Robert as far away from me as I can. Across the room the machine spools on undeterred beneath the coffee table, the slow murmur of Robert's gravelly voice still audible.

He recorded that tape for me. To give to me. It's about Bobby's death—and a girl. And it sounds a lot like a confession.

No, I think again. It sounds like a warning.

He must know what I am. What I am capable of. And he's warning me to be very careful.

He wants me to know he won't let me hurt his family. That he will do what is necessary to protect them. It occurs to me with razor-sharp clarity that I have to see this man again in three days.

I leap to my feet and grab the whirring tape player, shutting it off, then perch on the sofa and catch my racing breath.

The recording is so personal. His thoughts about Bobby, his guilt, his culpability. And to tell me about the girl, that he killed a girl. What is he hoping I do with this information? I think of the man on the subway yesterday and suddenly my behavior doesn't seem quite so paranoid.

I wonder if I should call someone. I should call the police, or Edward. But what would I say? I listened to a tape that may or may not be fictional? This could just be another Holbeck test—a game, a cruel joke even. It must be. I look down at my trembling hands, the sight of them shaking a clear indication that I need to calm down.

I remember Lila's words. I'm not supposed to scare easily. Is this what she meant? Does every Holbeck girlfriend get a bizarre tape? Surely someone would have said something, wouldn't they?

I blow out a few slow deep breaths. This is too much for me, so I'm guessing it's not great for the baby. I don't want to push my luck. The first trimester is the most fragile, according to Dr. Leyman; I don't want to miscarry. I need to calm down.

I stride into the hall, grab my coat and bag, and slam the front door behind me.

Out on the street, the cold air hits my flushed cheeks, cooling them as the sounds of the city drown out thoughts and my pulse begins to regulate.

I have found over the years that mindfulness works best for me when panic sets in: the wind on my skin, the sound of the city, the feeling of the cold sidewalk through my shoes.

As I walk, my thoughts reshuffle.

Robert Holbeck gave me that tape for a reason. It's either a warning, or a test. Another game. He clearly enjoys those. It's hard to know if the story is even real; it sounds like Bobby's story, and the building Robert mentions sounds like 7 East 88th Street—its weather vane glinting in the afternoon light—but Bobby didn't jump to his death, did he? His medications interacted.

I pull out my phone and rack my brain for the year Bobby died as I hit Central Park. Edward was eighteen, so it would have been 2002.

I type in: *suicide, East 88th Street, 2002.*

The first search result is a photo. I draw in a sharp breath as I catch the unmistakable shape of a white incident tent erected beneath the Holbecks' apartment building. It discreetly covers something. I blink away the thought of Bobby's black-stained Columbia sweatshirt.

Edward lied to me. Bobby jumped; he didn't die from a drug interaction. The story on Robert's tape is true. That dignified, quiet death Edward described is fiction.

I feel my knees weaken. I need to sit down. Edward kept the extent of this horrendous event from me—he must have known how much more seriously I'd take his reticence to spend time around his family.

And that's when I feel it; eyes on me. Surprised, I stop mid-stride and scan the park, not entirely certain what I'm looking for. I dodge a woman and stroller caught short by my sudden stop, looking back up just in time, and then catch sight of something. The man with the baseball cap, from the subway, across the park. His eyes lock with mine and I realize now with absolute certainty: Robert has had someone following me since he gave me the tape.

In a reflexive act of self-preservation, I let my eyes slide from his as if nothing had happened, and I continue on my way. If Robert is monitoring me, waiting for me to listen to his tape, then I need to make sure my next move is well thought out. I need to buy time.

Thinking fast, I calmly take the next left and exit the park, heading toward my favorite local diner. I must have spent almost as much time writing in there as in our apartment since I moved here. I'm pretty sure the man in the baseball cap won't follow me inside.

I slip into the warmth of the place, a waitress nodding me over to an empty booth. I slide in, my eyes locked on the door as I wait.

After twenty minutes, I let myself relax. My shadow didn't follow me, and I didn't catch him passing the large condensation-misted windows. I can't be sure he's not waiting out there, but that won't be a concern until I leave at least.

I order a coffee and a Danish, sipping the hot liquid gratefully as I pore over the internet for more on Bobby's suicide. The few articles that mention the East 88th Street suicide do not name the deceased, but the description on the tape appears to be true. I can't find anything about a blond girl, though, so she could be fictionalized. I suppose the question is whether or not a girl disappeared after Bobby died. I know from Lila that the Holbecks' old nanny left after Bobby, so this could be the person Robert is referring to.

I shiver at the thought of everyone at that Thanksgiving table knowing that Bobby jumped from that apartment. No wonder Billy was so terrified of sleeping in Bobby's room. For all I know, that's where he did it. I push the morbid thought from my mind and try to focus on the issue at hand: whether the Holbecks' nanny resigned after Bobby's death, or if she simply disappeared.

I cast my eyes across to the fogged diner windows and watch the huddled shapes of pedestrians glide by. Somewhere out there Robert is watching and waiting to see what I do next. If he *has* killed before, and if he has done so more than once, I am in serious trouble. And yet I was alone with him in his study, we sat opposite each other; it would be impossible to deny the strange connection we had with such seeming ease. The confusing thing is, Robert Holbeck likes me. And suddenly it dawns on me: *that* is why he is telling me this. He has chosen me because he likes games, because he likes thrillers, and because he has decided I am a worthy opponent.

I search on my phone for *Holbeck family nanny* and a couple of grainy paparazzi shots of Nunu standing beside the family celebrity, Lila, come up alongside gossip columns. No sign of the old nanny, though. All I have to go on is that she was blond.

I realize the best way to find a photo of her is to search for ones of Edward and his siblings as children. I head to Getty Images and search Edward's name.

Photos of the Holbeck brood at various ages fill the screen. Then I catch one. A young Eleanor carrying a swaddled Edward in her arms, beside her a youthful Robert holding her hand, then, in the deep blurry background, out of focus, a figure pushing the two-year-old Bobby in a stroller, a baseball cap covering her hair. The nanny.

Halfway down the page, I find an in-focus shot. Her face is turned away, half in profile, but I can see she is a woman in her early twenties, beautiful and fresh-faced with her soft blond hair pulled back in a loose ponytail.

My breath catches. It's her. The woman described on the tape. He was talking about the Holbecks' nanny.

I squint at the photo credit caption beneath.

(L to R) Robert Holbeck, wife Eleanor Holbeck, with their two sons, Edward and Robert, and a family friend, as they attend the Children's Aid charity luncheon, July 31, 1985.

A family friend. No name. I scroll on, skipping ahead to the late 1990s, getting closer to Bobby's death date. And I see her again, at some kind of garden party. She gets her own photograph this time, beside Eleanor, Pimm's glass in hand, as they are caught mid-laugh. The nanny's soft blond hair is swept back up in a French twist, her pale neck and delicate collarbone bare. She is older here: but now that I consider it, there is an eerie similarity between us. I can't help but wonder if it's ever crossed Edward's mind how much his fiancée looks like this willowy figure from his childhood; I imagine it has crossed Robert's.

The photo credit reads: *(L to R) Eleanor Holbeck and Sa-*

mantha Belson at the Melfort annual Summer Gala, August 7, 2002.

Samantha Belson.

I have a name. Now I just need to find out if she's still alive.

My next move depends very much on the type of game we're playing here, and I've got exactly three days in which to find that out.

20

The Plot Thickens

THURSDAY, DECEMBER 15

"So, this is for the new book?"

Retired NYPD lieutenant Deonte Hughley sits across the table from me in a cozy booth at Tom's Diner in Prospect Heights. He gives me a wry smile as he takes off his pristine cowboy hat and places it gently down on the bench seat beside him.

My American publisher put me in touch with Deonte two years ago after I requested they connect me with someone in the NYC police force who could fact-check my first novel.

Lieutenant Hughley was keen to help, having recently retired, and was an invaluable resource on my first book, always sparking creative ideas and handling my layman's knowledge with diplomatic kid gloves. During the final edit, I spoke with him regularly, running legal and sometimes infuriatingly granular procedural questions by him. At what temperature is DNA evidence completely destroyed? Can a cause of death always be determined? Do cops really like donuts?

It always helped that he answered with a certain lightheartedness, given the sometimes unsettling nature of the content. We've kept in touch via email since, and spoke most recently last week, in the final frantic throes of my new novel's first-draft deadline.

We know each other fairly well by now, a shared language emerging from his honest disclosure and my unending interest in his answers. We've certainty duked out a lot of plot strands together, though this might only be the fourth time we've actually met in person.

"Uh-huh. Second book. Exactly. Just piecing it all together," I say with a smile. And in a way it's true. My questions are about a family, a family with the power to cover up anything. But it isn't my book I need Deonte's help with this time. It is my life.

He shakes his head, slow, and stirs his coffee. "I don't know where y'all come up with these ideas. So in this one, a girl finds a cassette tape with a confession right there on it. Ha. Now, that is a case I would have killed to be on."

"Why, because it's a sure thing? Convictable? Given the evidence?" I ask, perhaps a little too hopefully.

Deonte raises an eyebrow. "Nah, because it sounds like a fun one. I think you know by now, at least from our conversations, most crime, well, it ain't fun. It's a god-awful, draining, soul-destroying slog. But this tape, that sounds tasty—juicy, exciting, you know. Like a movie. I'm in. Hell, I wanna read it now."

"Well, that's a good sign." I give a reassured smile. "So my main character, the girl, is given this tape by the perpetrator of the crimes. But here's the thing: the crimes mentioned on it, it's not clear if they really happened or if this man is stringing her along, toying with her. She doesn't know if the events described are real," I add, then break off, unsure how to get to the nub of what I'm asking. "I guess I want to know what evidence she'd need in order to take this to the police? To be sure it wasn't a fake, or to ensure a conviction without leaving herself open to reprisal."

"Reprisal? Who's the tape maker? What type of guy? What type of killer? You know, background, motive?" he asks, his tone serious now, his old NYPD instincts kicking back in and lifting Deonte from friendly graying retiree back to a force to be reckoned with.

"He's rich, well connected . . . incredibly powerful," I say carefully.

He winces. "Trump-y?"

"Definitely not. Old, old money. Ingrained in everything. Establishment."

Deonte studies my face for a moment, and I suddenly wonder how much he knows about my private life. If he knows about Edward and the Holbeck family. If he does, he doesn't mention the glaring equivalence. But then why would he? Authors write close to home, and I am just an author with a few outlandish questions.

"Damn. So he's playing cat 'n' mouse, taunting her. Okay, now we're talking. She can't let on she knows, until she's sure it's real. Can't tell the police, can't be sure if this whole thing's a scare tactic. And she's got to be careful who she trusts, because if that tape's real, and this guy is that powerful—anyone could be feeding what she does back to him. Leaks in departments, hired hands—yeah, got it: one false step and she's toast."

A flicker of doubt blossoms inside me. Leaks in departments, hired hands, trust. I suddenly wonder if I should even be speaking to Deonte. My connection to him comes through my publisher, after all, and the Holbecks have proved their reach on that front already.

I push the paranoid thought away. If push comes to shove, I'm confident Deonte's got my back. "Exactly. She can't trust anyone until she has real evidence that the tape is an actual confession. Then she can decide whether to hand it over to someone."

"Sensible. She's got a job, reputation, I'm guessing? Doesn't want to make a fool of herself if the tape maker refutes the validity of the recording." I nod. "So, seems reasonable she'd need to be sure the people mentioned in the confession are real people, and they're dead people. Best not to go to the police until then, if she doesn't want a libel case or worse hanging over her. Even then, if she does find a death, she'd need to find something suspicious about it; she'd need to look at cause of death. If it's murky, though, or in keeping with that confession—well, then, she's cooking with gas." He looks momentarily pained. "Thing is, if these victims are just missing, you got problems. That's trickier. It'll be easier for your plot if she finds an actual body; then they can exhume, run a fresh autopsy if there wasn't one first time round. Things are much more accurate these days, if they got missed the first time—less cracks to slip down."

"And if the girl finds something? If the tape is real?"

Deonte lets out a puckish whistle. "If the confession is real. If she finds a body, and the circumstances of death are hazy, then it's go-time; she needs to lawyer up and hunker down. Then it'll be a legal battle there on out. Full O.J." He ends with a flourish before adding, "Oh, and before I forget—this girl, she damn well better copy that cassette tape. I don't wanna be screaming at this book: *Why didn't you copy the damn thing?*"

"Noted," I say gratefully. It hadn't occurred to me until now, but the import of this hits home.

"Why does he choose her? This cold-blooded killer?" Deonte asks, catching me off guard. It's a good question, but then that's Deonte's profession, asking the right questions. And the answer to it is just a little too close to home for me.

Whether or not Robert knows what I am capable of isn't clear, but what is clear is that he knows I am the kind of person with more to lose than appearances might suggest. He sees me.

"I can't tell you that. It'd spoil the ending," I say with a grin, thinking on my feet.

His eyes sparkle in recognition at my swerve.

"Okay. So, Deonte," I continue, "if this girl wanted to find someone and she only had a name to go on, how would she go about doing that, do you think?"

"This girl's just an ordinary person? Not a cop?"

"Just an ordinary person."

"And . . . this is for the book?" Deonte asks with a wry smile.

Back at the apartment I put the tape recorder back in the suitcase and lock it safely under the bed, its cassette not even a quarter played yet. If I'm honest, what's on it scares me, and until I know what exactly I'm dealing with here I need to be careful what I expose myself to. Besides, somehow, I will need to act normal tomorrow night when I see him again. The more I know about his crimes, the less successful I am going to be at pretending I haven't heard any of it yet. Given how busy I have been with my deadline, I can still safely hide behind the idea of my own ignorance.

I have thought about bowing out of the party tomorrow night, but I'm sure that kind of reaction would be a red flag for Robert, and I would have to explain my reasoning to Edward.

I open up Facebook and search for Samantha Belson. Within an hour I've emailed twenty in the right age bracket; she would be around sixty this year. If she's still alive. Unless Robert made up his story just to scare me.

That night, by the time I hear Edward's keys in the door, I've already received five replies. But none are from the Samantha I'm looking for; they never worked either in New York or as a nanny.

I head out to the hallway just as Edward walks in.

When he looks at me, his face is a pale mask of concern; for a second I am absolutely certain that he knows everything. That he knows about Robert's tape, about the confessions and my unintended complicity. About my own secret.

"Your cell is dead," he says, his tone panicked.

I pull it from my pocket. He's right; the screen is blank, the battery long dead. "I couldn't get hold of you most of the day," he continues. "I thought maybe something might have happened. How are you feeling?"

"How am I feeling?" I ask, confused by the question.

"The baby, Harry? You're pregnant, remember? I couldn't get

you; I've been trying all morning. I've been worried. But you're okay, right?"

I had completely forgotten about the pregnancy.

"Harry," he prompts me again, coming over and placing a cool hand on my forehead. "Are you hot?" he asks solicitously.

"No, no, I'm fine," I say apologetically, pulling away. "I'm sorry, honey. I didn't realize I'd run out of battery. Was everything okay today? Did you need me?"

"No, I just wanted to check in. Oh, and to tell you I'm out for dinner tonight. A Chinese company wants to press the flesh. That okay for you?"

It's not. I don't want to be in this apartment on my own tonight. I don't want to sit here thinking about that tape. Worrying if I'll get an unexpected call or visit from a Holbeck. I want Edward to stay home, but I realize from the look on his face the significance of this Chinese company. Edward has been wanting to expand his tech company into the Chinese market for a while now and this sounds like inroads.

"Yeah, of course. Go," I tell him, though for a microsecond I consider spilling everything. The tape, the confession being drip-fed to me, my rising concern.

"Thank you," he says, kissing me lightly on the lips and heading into the bedroom to change for dinner.

Down the hall in my office, I hear the unmistakable electronic ping of fresh email landing in my inbox. I swing a look back to the office. Another reply from a Samantha Belson. I left my laptop open.

Once Edward is dispatched, showered and suited, I dash back to my computer and read the new email.

This one is only three words long, but it's enough.

Who is this?

The concern implied in those three words is telling. I emailed her through an anonymous account, a brand-new Gmail address; I could be anyone. I gave a plausible reason for reaching out and signed off with my initials, but whoever wrote this reply needs more than that, which is interesting.

I type out a response, and attach the Getty Images photo of Samantha Belson laughing beside Eleanor Holbeck.

> Is this you? Did you work for this family between 1982 and 2002? <u>I am not a journalist.</u> It's an entirely personal, and confidential, matter. You are guaranteed complete discretion. Would you be happy to talk? Your help would be greatly appreciated as I believe you are the only person qualified to set the record straight around a certain matter.

Her reply comes back almost immediately.

> Are you a member of the family? Or do you work, in any capacity, for them?

I wonder how best to answer, fingers poised over the keys. I'm guessing it will not help my case in any way to explain I'm about to marry one of them.

> I am not involved yet. That really depends on you, and what you might be able to tell me.

I stare at my inbox and wait. After half an hour I consider giving up for the night and checking in again tomorrow. And then it comes.

> It is me, in the photo. I'll meet with you. I will pick the venue and time. Come alone.

> If I feel unsafe, I will leave.

I bark out a triumphant *whoop* at the empty apartment. The woman in Robert's confession is alive; he did not kill her. Whatever this tape *is,* it's a game, nothing more, and I've won the first round.

A new thought surfaces and my smile withers: I have no way of knowing if that was Samantha Belson messaging me, or if I've just made a plan to meet someone else entirely.

I open her Facebook profile and scroll through her photographs. The account looks real, and while she might not have quite the same soft blond hair she had as a young woman, I see the same curve in her smile, the same crinkle around her eyes. This is Samantha Belson, aged sixty. Whatever happened, she didn't die in 2002.

I type back a quick reply.

Thank you, Samantha. I have lots of questions.

21

Krampusnacht

FRIDAY, DECEMBER 16

And just like that, it's Krampusnacht.

We're standing on a Brooklyn curb in front of the glowing windows of Fiona and Oliver's five-floor brownstone as it looms over us, its door festooned with foreboding Christmas decorations.

I look at Edward beside me. "This is weird," I say. "Your family is weird." Somehow the weight of everything I can't tell him is in those words, as well as the weight of my fear at having to see Robert again. I will feign ignorance tonight, but I know he will be watching me carefully. The truth is I'm scared of what could happen next, of what Robert might do.

Edward nods in solemn acknowledgment. "Oh, I know they

are. Believe me." His expression softens as he looks down at me with a smile. "Remember, tonight is just an Austro-Hungarian version of Halloween. Nothing to worry about, right?"

"Got it," I agree, allowing only a sliver of the vulnerability I actually feel to surface.

He offers me his hand and I take it, letting him lead me briskly up the brownstone steps to the elaborately carved dark-wood-and-glass front door.

Edward pushes the doorbell and through the glass I just about make out its ghostly tinkling. In the hallway beyond I can make out rows of shoes already lined up against the thick eighteenth-century baseboard, shoes lined up for Krampus. It looks like there's quite a crowd in there already. I note that there are adult shoes mixed among the children's and my stomach tightens. We all have to take part in the Krampusnacht games it seems.

Edward looks at his watch, then back into the dim hallway, light and movement visible at the end of the corridor. "We're late," he mumbles. "They probably just can't hear us."

It's my fault we're late. I had no idea what to wear, and I don't mean in the usual sense. I mean I genuinely had no idea what to wear to a Krampusnacht.

After another minute, the front door flies open in front of us, revealing a beaming Fiona.

"Hello, hello, hello," she cheers merrily, and through another doorway along the hall Oliver appears, a bottle of red in hand and a smile on his face.

"Hello, strangers," Oliver bellows, clearly making an extra effort. It seems to settle Edward. In all of my own very particular terror about tonight, I had forgotten that Edward is the prodigal son. Oliver pulls him into a hug before bending to plant a quick peck on my cheek. "Shoes off, both of you," he orders us merrily. "You definitely know the rules by now, Ed. No excuses."

I look between the brothers, an easy familiarity beginning to settle in alongside both parties' hypervigilance. Fiona places a reassuring hand on my arm.

"You told Harry about the shoes, right, Ed?" Fiona asks, half teasing, half concerned.

"He did," I say, answering for him as I slip mine off, as instructed, and into the immaculate row. "Yeah, we have to leave them out for Krampus," I add with a smile, as if Krampus were the milkman and not a seven-foot-tall deformed goat-demon. "Right?"

"She's got it," Oliver replies, winking in such a mock-theatrical way I can't help but laugh.

"That's the spirit," Fiona tells me, and there's a hint of apology in her voice as she takes me conspiratorially by the arm and pulls me toward the kitchen.

"I know you're not drinking," Fiona whispers, with a level of knowing that slightly concerns me, "but I have something you might be interested in seeing in the kitchen." She raises an impish eyebrow that suggests to me there is food involved and I follow gladly, looking back just in time to see a relaxed Edward follow Oliver into the party.

My appetite has skyrocketed over the past week, but whether I'm eating for two or just making up for the nausea and loss of appetite of the preceding weeks, I do not know.

"How much has Edward told you about tonight?" Fiona asks.

"Not much—just hide-and-seek, costumes, masks, that kind of thing," I say lightly, my mind on the room Edward just walked into and the prospect of whether or not Robert Holbeck is in it.

"Okay. Well, listen," Fiona tells me, slowing us down to a halt. "I don't want you going in blind tonight. My first time, Oliver thought it would be hilarious not to tell me anything at all, so I almost had an aneurysm when it all kicked off. Not that it's that bad. It's fine," she adds quickly, catching my expression. "I'm probably just a scaredy-cat. And I wasn't expecting it. Anyway," she says brightly, pulling me along again.

The kitchen is a massive stone-floored affair with a large provincial farmhouse table and Le Creuset–lined shelves. Hired caterers and chefs bustle about the space transferring beautifully crafted savory creations onto small dishes and shucking fresh oysters over at the sink.

The air is filled with the fresh scent of salt and sea, and the aroma of something sweet baking. My hunger dips into a groaning ache just as I catch a face I recognize bent over by the range cooker.

Lila looks up from the tray of blood-red cookies with a broad smile, her cheeks rosy with the kitchen heat, her hands stained red by the dough. "Hey, Harry!" she calls, sliding her cookies into the oven. "You made it." She gives me a gooey-handed wave. "I'm making Krampus cookies," she continues with a grin. "Pretty weird, right?"

"Krampusnacht? Sure is," I agree. *As is the thought of having to see Robert Holbeck and pretend I'm normal and he's normal,* I think. "Is this your first Krampus too?" I ask Lila as Fiona busies herself with the kitchen staff.

Lila pulls an expression that I don't really understand, then says, "No way. We sometimes do it in Sweden. It's my third here, I think." She counts on blood-dough fingers. "Yeah, third one. Milo loves it." She shrugs as if to say she comes for Milo but stays for the weirdness.

I know if Lila is here everyone is here, and that anyone could walk into this kitchen at any moment.

I reorient myself against a kitchen counter in order to keep the kitchen door in my periphery. I want a little warning before I have to put my guard all the way up.

I am not meeting Samantha Belson until next week. I know Robert didn't kill her as he suggested, but I'm sure there's more to uncover there. I don't know yet how far this all goes—though there is a world in which Robert's tape is just a joke and I'm just a bad sport. I suppose I'll see.

Fiona joins us with an exasperated sigh. "I need to learn to delegate if it's the last thing I do. I'm a real pain in the ass," she groans, then hands me a tall glass of sparkling water with a wink. "So the plan is: drinks, canapés, and snacks until around nine P.M.

The kids play among themselves until then. But at nine o'clock you'll hear a bell—"

"Like a cowbell," Lila chips in helpfully, though it clarifies absolutely nothing for me.

"A cowbell, okay," I echo.

"The kids will flip out at that point," Fiona continues. "Then there'll be three loud knocks on the front door; that's Krampus arriving. And that's the beginning of the Krampus Race, which ends when the Evergreen is found, at which point Krampus *disappears*," she says with a finality I'm not sure she's earned. "Oh, and after Krampus disappears, we unwrap the presents in our shoes."

I'm not sure Fiona knows how mad she sounds.

"Right. Krampus, Evergreen, presents in shoes. I think I've got it," I say regardless. Edward's explanation didn't mention anything called an Evergreen.

I take a sip of my icy water and wonder when Fiona will drag us out of the relative safety of the kitchen into the main party and closer to Robert. My stomach flips with dread.

"Now, Harriet, you're doing the Krampus Race with Billy this year. As a team. Is that okay?" Fiona asks.

I splutter a little of my water back into the glass.

"Don't worry. I'm doing the Krampus Race too, with Milo," Lila says.

"Oh, um, sure. If that's . . . Is everyone doing it?"

"No, just you and Lila and the kids. If you're happy to? Billy asked for you especially."

I gulp back the rest of my water and try to ignore the emotional blackmail, resigning myself to the fact that I have to play a weird game with a bunch of kids while the rest of the adults, including Robert Holbeck, stay in another room. Which actually works out perfectly.

I put down my empty glass with a triumphant smile. "Great," I say. "In the meantime, could I get some of those canapés we saw go past, Fiona? I'd better get my energy reserves up or the kids might not be able to tell the difference between me and the Krampus."

Lila gives a high giggle. "I don't think there's much danger of them getting confused about *that*." Something in the pitch of her laugh unsettles me, and a concerning question slowly begins to form in my mind.

"Hang on. Who plays the Krampus?" I ask with a grin.

The two exchange a look, then burst out laughing.

"No one *plays* Krampus, silly," Fiona giggles. "Krampus is Krampus." She gives me a stage wink that does nothing to settle me—if that was its intention. "Let's get you some food, though," she continues, making her way toward the kitchen door with a beckoning gesture. "We'll go through to the others."

I feel a pressure drop within me, my anxiety shifting into a higher gear, as I reluctantly follow in Fiona's wake, leaving Lila and the safety of the kitchen behind.

"Are Eleanor and Robert here yet?" I ask as we go.

Fiona nods with a smile, her eyes playing over me with interest. "They are," she says, then, seeming to sense something off, she stops, pulling me into a hallway recess beside the sitting room door.

"How many weeks along are you?" she whispers conspiratorially.

"You know?" I ask, my voice breathier than I expect it to be. "Did someone tell you?"

Her eyes hold mine. It's clear she's off the family script; she's the only one who knows. "No. I have three children, Harry. The signs kind of burn into your brain," she says quietly, her eyes checking the door beyond my shoulder. "How far?" she asks again.

"Early. Eight weeks," I answer simply. There seems like little reason to deny it.

"Still too early to tell anyone then," she says, before clarifying, "No one else in the family knows?"

"Just me and Edward."

She looks surprised. "Edward knows! And he was okay with you coming tonight?"

I frown. "Of course he knows. And why wouldn't he be okay with me coming to a party?"

Fiona pauses, then gently shakes her head. "Oh, no reason, I guess. If he's okay with it then it's fine. Just be careful tonight, please. I know it's just a children's game, but people can get carried away, you know, in the heat of the moment."

It's unclear if she is deliberately trying to scare me or annoy me. The idea that I might somehow get so caught up in a child's game that I would actually hurt myself is frankly insulting.

I bite back the desire to follow that line of response. She's just trying to be nice, I assure myself, to offer pregnancy advice, even though with three kids of her own she should know how badly that tends to come across.

"Noted," I say with a smile. "I'll take it easy. What gave me away?" I add. I should probably stop doing whatever that is if I want to keep this pregnancy quiet for now.

"Not drinking, of course. But mainly, when you took your shoes off earlier. Edward put his hand on your lower back, to steady you." She absentmindedly looks down at the ring on her finger. "Oliver does that—did that—during my pregnancies. He'd steady me. It's an unconscious thing, a protective instinct. Maybe it's a Holbeck thing or a man thing. But it's impossible to miss if you know what to look for." She shrugs off the thought. "Anyway, my lips are sealed. Your secret's safe with me." She gestures toward the sitting room. "Shall we?"

Fiona's sitting room is filled with people, warmth emanating from a large fireplace that laps and crackles beside two large sofas. Through the milling guests I make out an enormous Christmas tree positioned between the two large sash windows. At its tip a glittering golden star almost skims the paintwork of the brownstone's high ceiling; its thick branches are festooned with red and gold ribbons, twinkling baubles, and softly glowing lights.

The gentle babble of polite conversation and unseen music steadies my nerves as my eyes rove the faces for one in particular. It's mid-December but in this room, with its soft flickering candles and heady aroma of fresh spruce, one might imagine that it could be Christmas forever.

My eyes find Edward first, by the fire in conversation with Oliver. They seem intent on something—not a disagreement so much as a debriefing of sorts. I make a mental note to ask Edward about what later. He catches me watching, his serious expression lightening as he raises his glass in my direction.

"I can introduce you to everybody, if you like?" Fiona says. I had almost forgotten her beside me. "There's family here you haven't met yet. Robert's cousins, their children; the extended family." I still can't see him in the crowd but I can feel he is here. Fiona points out an elderly couple milling by the piano in conversation with the only biracial couple present. "That's my side of the family. My parents. And my brother and his wife. Their daughter, Olivia, my niece, is here too somewhere with the boys—" She breaks off suddenly as a waiter beckons her from across the room. "I'll be right back. Will you be okay alone for a moment?" I start to speak but she is already gone.

The room is filled with faces I do not recognize; waiters weave among them with food and drink. I pluck a few things when they glide by and as the crowd shifts, I spot him sitting beside Matilda on one of the low chintz sofas, my chest constricting slightly as I prepare for his gaze. I take him in before he notices me, his tall, powerful physicality at odds with the soft domestic setting. I watch Matilda talk to him, their expressions serious, and I can't help but wonder if there is a problem. If something I do not know about is happening in the Holbecks' world, if there is an issue with the company, or worse.

Robert must feel eyes on him. He looks up, his gaze magnetically finding mine.

A shiver runs through me as his words from the tape come

back to me. Visceral apprehension, and a desperate curiosity to know why he is doing what he is doing to me, fizzling through every fiber of my being.

He looks younger than I recall from Thanksgiving—stronger, smarter, even more of a credible threat. He tips his head in acknowledgment of my presence and taps Matilda deftly on the knee. She stops talking, her eyes following his to me, her energy changing seamlessly, like Edward's and Oliver's—a lightness seeming to click on inside her, her features blossoming into a smile. "Harry!" she calls across the room. "There you are."

Robert watches me carefully as I tentatively sink into the sofa beside Matilda. He's trying to figure out if I've listened to the tape yet. He can't ask with Matilda here but the quiet calm in his eyes tells he's not averse to waiting.

"How have you been?" Matilda inquires enthusiastically. "We've all been desperate to see you. How's the book?"

I realize with a wave of relief this might be the closest I get to talking to Robert tonight, so I can indirectly sell my excuse for not listening to his tape yet. "Great. I handed it in just the other day. I've barely come up for air since we last met; no time for anything."

Matilda's hand flies to my back in congratulations. "Oh my God, Harry. That is so exciting. You must be exhausted. When can we read it? Did you hear that, Dad? Harry's been at the grindstone with her book."

It suddenly occurs to me, in earnest, that the Holbecks might genuinely be concerned about what I write in my next book. I suppose if I become part of the family, I will ultimately fall under the same scrutiny that they are prey to—or I could be kidding myself about my own importance. That said, my last book was read by over a million people, and that's a sizable reach.

And then another thought emerges from the shadows of my mind. The idea that Robert gave me his tape for that very reason, to have me write his story. But that would bring the entire house of cards crashing down around him. That can't be his intention.

I snap back to the present at the sound of his voice. "The new book is complete. That's wonderful news, Harriet," he says lightly. "I look forward to reading it." He gives me a polite smile, his expression otherwise unreadable.

There's a scuffle by the door and I see that the children are beginning to flood into the room. It must be time for the race and for my time with Robert to end.

The party crashes into silence and after a moment I realize why. A cowbell is clunking somewhere beyond the room. I watch the children's features fizz with terror and excitement as adults exchange knowing glances.

I see eight children in total. Fiona's boys: Sam, Tristan, and Billy. Lila's Milo and three other boys around Sam's age. Olivia is the only girl present and clearly the eldest. She sticks close to Fiona's middle son, Tristan; I imagine she's been told to pair with him. He can't be more than two years older than Billy.

"You're taking part in the race, aren't you, Harry?" Matilda whispers, her voice low as the bell clunks again ominously.

"I am. Though I'm not entirely sure how it all works. I didn't realize Edward wouldn't be playing with me," I answer, suddenly realizing I might have left everything a bit late. "Any tips?" I ask, an entirely new clutch of nerves stirring inside me.

Matilda grins, her red lips parting to show a perfect set of white teeth. "Yeah," she says with a throaty chuckle. "Run for your life."

22

Run for Your Life

FRIDAY, DECEMBER 16

I join the rest of the players congregated in the hallway, the children, me, and Lila all sectioned off from the adults now, the sitting room doors closed behind us as we wait for whatever is about to happen.

Lila is busy hushing an anxious Milo as they wait by the staircase, my way to her blocked by jostling children who skitter about the entrance hall with pre-game excitement. There simply isn't enough time now to ask what the hell I'm supposed to do other than run. Besides, I too have more pressing matters to deal with. Billy tugs my trouser leg again and I crouch to meet him at eye level.

"What's our plan then, team captain?" I ask brightly, but his concerned little face makes it clear it's going to take a lot more than my casual optimism to quash his mounting fear.

"We gock to run away and hide, Auntie Harry-ept," he tells me with solemn decisiveness.

"No problem. We can do that, easy-peasy. I know loads about hiding spots. Is that all we need to do in the game, honey?"

I'm aware I should have dug deeper into the actual rules of the game before now, instead of trying to decipher them from a terrified toddler at the absolute last minute. But I had other things on my mind. And a game's a game; you only really pick it up as you play anyway.

"You good a' games, Auntie Harry-ept?" Billy asks, giving me a quizzical look I find oddly exposing.

"Um, yeah. I think so." He looks unimpressed, so I follow up with a perhaps overly confident, "No, yeah! Best hider ever! I've got you covered, little man."

Billy thinks for a minute, then puffs out his chest, buoyed by my certainty. "I guess then we could look for *stick*? If you fink you know hiding places."

"Look for a stick? Is that part of it?"

"Yep. Ebbergreen stick." He gives a firm nod as he tests the word in his mouth again.

I remember Fiona's sketchy explanation from earlier. "Yes, the *Evergreen*? If we find that the game stops, right?"

"Yeah, *Ebber*. You got to show the Krampus the Ebbergreen, then you win; he goes away."

Right, so we need to find a hidden stick and not get caught while we do it. It sounds like the game Capture the Flag. "We just show the stick to the monster—I mean the Krampus—and that's the end?"

"Yep. Das it." He stares up at me, wide eyes filled with a mix of fear and hope that I realize I am supposed to make good on.

I'd like to ask Billy: Why a stick? Why an evergreen? Why a Krampus? Why any of this? But he's three and it all seems a little above his pay grade.

Thankfully, Sam, Billy's older brother, must have overheard our conversation, as he leans in to elaborate.

"Basically, you need to find the Evergreen because Evergreen wood is the Krampus's weakness, so the only way to kill him is to run Evergreen through his heart."

I frown. "Oh, right. But we're just *showing* the stick to the Krampus, right? We're not running it through anything?"

Sam smirks as if I'm playing a trick on him. "No, of course not, that would be stupid. You just find the stick then you shout 'Evergreen' as loud as you can and stay exactly where you are and the Krampus stops chasing everyone. Then he'll come and find you and the stick." I feel myself frown and Sam continues, "He has to check you have it. If you do, you'll be safe from him, don't worry. As soon as he sees you have it, you win."

I turn back to Billy with a big smile. "Well, that sounds great, right?"

"Yep, great," Billy agrees, trying his best to be brave. "Up, up," he adds, his arms outstretched, and I scoop him up onto my hip, the flashlight looped around my wrist thumping heavy against my thigh.

"Oh, and one more question, Sam," I say turning back to him. "What do I do if I get caught by the—"

But I do not get to finish as the house plunges into darkness and the children begin to scream.

From outside the front door, the cowbell clunks mournfully and the shrieks stutter to a halt. The darkness is suddenly filled with nothing but the sound of muffled breathing and fear. Then three reverberating knocks hit the front door and echo through the house. All eyes turn to the grotesque and towering silhouette beyond the glass of the door. Then the sound of something barely human screams out into the night air, cutting through everything. *Jesus fucking Christ.* I was expecting an uncle in a costume, and maybe a little growling, not whatever the hell that is.

The door handle turns and, at that point, the kids go absolutely berserk. Bloodcurdling screams filling the house as panicked feet pound up the staircase and away, down hallways, into the darkness of unseen rooms. Only Billy and I remain in the silence, Billy completely frozen on my hip as I gently try the handle back into the adults' room. I don't think I want to play anymore.

But the sitting room door is locked; beyond, only silence. They've locked me out. The front door slowly creaks open, the last barrier between us and the silhouetted creature. Billy wriggles with blind panic in my arms.

"Run! Harry-ept, run!" he screams, and I spin in time to see what he sees, the blood draining from me. I don't know what I was expecting, but it was not this. This is not a Holbeck brother in a furry suit; this is not something digestible, or child-friendly.

My breath comes in short, tight gasps. It stands seven feet tall even as it crouches under the frame of the front door, panting wet animal breaths, haloed in streetlight against the night sky. Its face, partly stripped of skin, is bleeding, its teeth jagged, yellowed, and slick with strung saliva. Its distorted face is part human, though its jaw is distending in pain. And around its neck a rusty dented cowbell *tunk*s with its every movement.

I reel back instinctively, the wall knocking the air clean from me as I hit it, and Billy's grip tightens. The creature's eyes watch us carefully, the slowest of the herd, left behind. It cocks its head, taking in the stairs to our right as it anticipates my next move, but I do not think twice; I bolt as fast as I can, because whatever this is does not feel like a game.

Behind me the creature lunges as I scramble up the stairs, Billy clinging tight to me. When we reach the top, I dart behind the landing wall where, pressed against the paintwork, breath coming high and fast, I try to listen. There is no sound from the stairs.

I cannot hear him. *It. Krampus.* Only the rasp of my own tight breaths.

The house is silent save for the muffled sounds of children's feet in the darkness. The cowbell must have been silenced, because I can no longer hear the creature coming.

Whatever that thing is downstairs, it won't be announcing its presence anymore; it'll come stealthily and slowly and God knows what will happen if it finds you.

Of course, I'm a rational person; I know the thing down there is someone in a suit. It has to be. I just wasn't expecting the suit to look quite so terrifying, to be quite so real. But I suppose with all the money in the world you can afford realism. And this Krampus is just that—a movie-grade prosthetic marvel. I know monsters are not real, my rational mind knows that, but like it or not my heart will not stop pounding. First Robert's tape and now this; games definitely don't feel like games in this family.

After a few more seconds of recovery, I carefully heave us both up to standing. In the half-light I make out Billy's terrified face. He watches me silently, the unfathomable trust in his eyes demanding clear action.

"Which way goes up?" I whisper to him calmly. I know from the outside of the building that it has five floors including a basement level. There should be another two more floors above us. The higher we are, the safer we'll be for now.

Billy holds my gaze for a second then raises a tiny hand in answer, pointing across the landing to a corridor that disappears into the darkness.

We'll need to pass the open stairwell again to get there. I look back at the blackened void between us and then, in the corridor beyond, a flashlight beam swings through the darkness and I see Olivia peek around the doorframe. Catching us in her beam, she quickly clicks the light off, but I am already blinded by its afterglow. Vision spangled, I need a moment to readjust, and when I do I see she has crawled to the edge of the landing wall on her side. Behind her, little Tristan shuffles into view, timid and silent.

I catch Olivia's attention and indicate we should both cross the landing at the same time. She thinks a moment and then nods. We double our chances of not getting caught that way. If there's something waiting in the stairwell, he can't catch us all.

I hitch Billy higher on my hip and signal Olivia to go on three. But we don't reach three when a shrill and bloodcurdlingly real scream rips through the house from downstairs. It sounds like Milo. I tell myself it's fine, Lila is with him, but for the first time since the game started I think of Robert's tape. Of the girl on Robert's tape.

Olivia breaks cover, yanking Tristan along behind her as she pelts past the stairs toward us. Reflexively we burst from our hiding spot, barreling forward across the landing too.

We pass Olivia and Tristan mid-landing and plow on in our respective directions, plunging back into the darkness of opposite sides. In the safety of the dark corridor, I look back in time to wonder what Olivia's plan is, but a gentle tug on my hair refocuses me.

"Up," Billy whispers, his mouth close to my ear, his breath warm on my skin.

"Up," I agree as I move us onward into the darkness.

We round a bend in the corridor and I clink on our flashlight for the first time. The beautifully restored interior wood paneling of Fiona and Oliver's house bursts into view as we creep around another bend and a thin staircase appears ahead. In spite of everything, as we stride toward it, I can't help but wonder how many staircases this place has and what something like this might be worth in the current climate.

But the hot warmth of urine spreading across my hip from Billy's trousers snaps me to reality.

"You okay?" I ask him, concerned. "You scared?"

My anger at the Holbecks, and in particular at Fiona, resurfaces. Why would she put her child through this? Why would any of them make me do this? And why on earth didn't Edward tell me what this was really like?

"Yeah, scared, but mainly soda," Billy replies with a judicious shake of the head. "Should have gone before." He looks circumspect, then adds, "Sorry, Harry-ept."

He's scared but dealing with it incredibly well. "That's okay, sweetie. We'll sort it out later. You're doing a great job." I smile for his benefit, in spite of the fact that his family has put me in a totally inappropriate position and my whole left side is soaked in hot piss.

I hoick Billy a little higher on my hip, try not to think of all the damage I could be doing to the growing fetus inside me, and shine my torch up into the dark stairwell above us.

It's just a game, Harry. An incredibly weird one, granted, but just a game. The baby will be fine. Billy will be fine. Whoever that was screaming downstairs will be fine. And Robert did not kill Samantha Belson because I am meeting her in three days.

When we reach the next landing, Billy nods up again, the staircase narrowing, closing in around us as we reach the top of the house.

A pink door comes into view above, cracked paint and a lift latch, something ominous about it making me slow as we approach.

The door swings open with a creak and I can feel the sheer size of the space beyond it; it's cavernous. The whole top floor of this house must be open-plan. I sweep my torch beam into the murk. Odd things catch in the light's path: the edges of a circus tent at one end of the room; a full-sized horse frozen mid-gallop, its body accurately rendered except for the bright red plastic of its saddle and reins. At one end of the room a small network of road markings covers the floor, littered with child-sized cars and bikes, a street in miniature, and beyond it in the far distance I make out the backs of eight teddy bears in a picnic circle of more. It's a playroom. The whole top floor of Fiona's brownstone is a massive, creepy playroom.

"Is there anyone up here?" I call carefully into the darkness. Billy presses a finger to my lips.

"Sshh," he whispers with a shake of his head.

Wind chimes jangle from somewhere in the darkness and, nerves frazzled, I jump, my shoulder bumping on a light switch in the stairwell that clicks on and bathes the penthouse playroom in bright light.

The lights work here. Without a second thought I dash into the playroom and shut the pink door firmly behind us, blocking the light's path down the stairwell.

I scan the brightly colored room, its proportions ludicrous, larger than our whole apartment put together. The sound of a scream from many floors below springs me into action. I plop Billy down onto the floor, head over to a large bookcase filled with crates of toys, and speedily remove them all. I then slowly drag the bookcase across the carpet to block the doorway, reinserting the toy crates one by one to reinforce our barrier.

Pink door blocked, I flop down onto the carpet completely exhausted. "Come 'ere," I huff to Billy, my arms outstretched, and he totters over, wet pants sagging. "We should be safe in here."

He collapses into my arms too. "Yep," he says simply, then looks up. "Where's Mumma?"

I consider.

"I really don't know. But I'm sure she's fine. You definitely don't need to worry about her." I look at Billy's little face, his soft blond curls, and I wonder what the hell Fiona was thinking letting him play this game. Then I conjure the image of a three-year-old Edward pissing himself, thirty-odd years ago, on some unknown nanny's hip. What was it Edward said? *Character building.*

I look around the playroom and can't deny it's cute. Fiona and Oliver clearly care about their kids, in spite of what tonight might make one think.

"Is this your place, then?" I ask my little friend.

He splays his hands, indicating both indifference and pride. "Yeah. My toys." He looks thoughtfully around before adding, "And Tristan and Sam's."

"It's nice up here."

"Yep."

I look down at my watch. Thirty minutes have passed already. "How long till the game is over, Billy?" I ask.

"Not till Ebbergreen."

I look up abruptly. That can't be right; it just keeps going indefinitely until then? "Are you sure, Billy? It doesn't stop until someone finds the stick?"

He nods.

"And how long does that usually take?"

He shrugs. "Sam said they stayed up past midnight last time. And only Uncle Edward could find it 'cause he was a grown-up."

Lila is, given Milo's scream earlier, probably already out of the game and I am the only adult left playing.

It's nine-thirty now; I cannot do this until midnight. I'm already exhausted and freaked-out, but all that aside, I need a wee now too and I don't want to have to piss my pants like Billy.

A thought occurs and I scan the room, hoping that Billy's accident might be less of an anomaly and more of a regular occurrence demanding contingency plans. I find what I'm looking for in a corner of the room near a large industrial-looking metal unit. A small wardrobe.

I rise and head over to the wardrobe, Billy following me wordlessly. If we're staying here until midnight, we're sure as hell not doing so covered in piss.

The wardrobe is full of costumes. Magician, unicorn, Marvel characters, frog, fireman, cowboy, and lederhosen.

"Okaaaay," I say, as Billy peeks into the wardrobe beside me and lets out a tiny, world-weary sigh.

He kneels down and pulls open a drawer revealing a fresh stack of clean underwear and socks.

"Great work, little man. That'll do for underneath. But what about on top?"

Five minutes later a urine-free lederhosen-clad three-year-old stands before me. I try to stifle a giggle but it's his anger at the outfit more than the outfit itself that gets me.

"Stop, Auntie Harry-ept. Not funny. Stupid."

"I'm not laughing at you, sweetheart, I prom—"

A knock sounds abruptly from the pink door and we both freeze.

The knock comes again. Billy's eyes are wide like saucers. But a Krampus wouldn't knock, would it? And just like that I'm up and across the room, my ear pressed to the pink door. "Who is it?" I whisper.

"Olivia," a soft voice answers.

After a couple of minutes huffing and shuffling, I open a gap big enough for Olivia and Tristan to slip through the doorway, and together we all reassemble the barricade.

Once it's back in place, Olivia turns to me. "Have you found it yet?" she demands.

"Found what?"

"The Evergreen."

"Um, no," I say with slightly more vehemence than antici-pated. "Wouldn't this be over if I found it?"

Her face falls. "Yeah, but I thought maybe you'd found it and you didn't know what to do." She looks to Tristan, disappointed, then rallies. "Where have you looked, then?"

I pause, genuinely considering whether or not to lie to a child, but deciding it's probably not a great precedent to set. "Nowhere. We've just been hiding up here."

"Oh. Okay." She's disappointed, and I try not to let the shame drown me.

"To be honest," I say, leveling with her, "I have absolutely no idea what is going on here, Olivia, or what I'm supposed to be looking for. I'm just trying to keep him safe." I eye Billy in his lederhosen.

"Why is he wearing that?" Olivia begins, before thinking bet-ter of it. "Never mind. We've checked the second and third floor already but we haven't been up here yet or in the basement."

"What about the ground floor, where everyone started?"

"That's out-of-bounds; the only open doors there lead upstairs or downstairs."

"Okay, so if it's not here, it will be in the basement."

"Yeah."

"And how do you know where to look? Are there clues?"

She looks aghast. "Are we the first people you've talked to since the game started?"

"Yeah," I say, noting her derision.

"Oh, okay, I guess that makes sense. It's you. The clue is your name. It's always the name of the oldest player. If you'd asked anyone, after the game started, they would have told you the clue is hidden in the letters of your name."

"I was supposed to ask someone after—" I begin, but quickly lose the will to continue. "Okay, so . . . The clue to where the

Evergreen is hidden is in the letters of my name: Harriet Reed. An anagram?" I ask.

Olivia nods, pulling out her iPhone and tapping away furiously, her brow furrowed. "Maybe I'm spelling it wrong. Here, you try."

She hands me the phone, the screen open on a letter-reshuffling app. She has typed my name in correctly: H-A-R-R-I-E-T—R-E-E-D. The best suggestion comes up beneath it: *reheated*.

"Reheated," I mutter. "Could there be a microwave, or an oven, in the basement?"

Olivia shakes her head. "Kitchen's on the ground floor. And out-of-bounds."

I look at the letters again. "Oh my God," I say, my own slowness surprising me. I tap in the initial of my middle name, Yasmin, and I press RESHUFFLE once more.

The letters of my name rearrange into a new word and I shake my head at the nerve of the clue. *Hereditary*. Someone in the Holbeck family's got a real sense of humor all right. I spin the phone back to Olivia.

"I don't know what that word means; I'm thirteen," she says.

"It means inherited characteristics, or inherited property," I tell her. "Is there anything up here or in the basement that the word could refer to?" That said, I think, is there anything in this house that it wouldn't?

Olivia grins broadly, her eyes suddenly alive. "Oh my gosh. I know what it is. This was J. L. Holbeck's first home in New York. It's been in the family ever since. There's a placard in the basement. Like a foundation stone. Everyone who's ever lived in this house has inherited it."

"Great," I cheer, the prospect of the end almost in sight. "Now, how in hell do we get down to the basement from here?"

Billy raises his tiny hand once more, his finger pointing toward the large industrial-looking unit in the corner of the room. "Hatch," he says with authority.

23

Down the Hatch

FRIDAY, DECEMBER 16

Olivia slides the hatch doors shut on me and I flick on my torch in the darkness of the service lift.

I try not to think about the empty lift shaft beneath me and content myself with the fact that I am not above the maximum weight warning on the hatch door.

Olivia would have been lighter, but there was no way I was going to let a child travel down five flights in a service hatch lift on my watch.

Besides, if you want a job done right, do it yourself. I want this game over.

The lift clanks down and I think of the Holbecks and the bizarre drinks party they must still be having in a different part of the house, pure anger burning through me. I could laugh at the situation, sure, but cramped up in a service lift covered in toddler piss at eight weeks pregnant, it doesn't seem like that much of a joke.

I flick off my torch as the lift rattles to a stop and sit in silence for a moment. No sound from the basement beyond. No seven-foot monsters. Or men in seven-foot monster suits, I should say.

Gently I slide my fingers into the gap between the hatch doors and prize them open. The room beyond is dark.

I slip from the hatch then follow the right-hand wall along as per Olivia's meticulous instructions. I need to follow this corridor and pass two doorways before I reach up. Above the final door-frame is the placard, and the Evergreen should be there. I count the doors to my right as I pass them.

One.

I shuffle on in the blackness, noises of the party above just audible from down here: faint music, laughter. Then I hear an-other noise. I freeze. Ahead of me, the sound of breathing. My hand flies to my mouth to mask my own.

I stay still for a second listening, but the noise is gone as quickly as it came. I hold a moment longer then remind myself that if I don't end this, no one will. I force myself to continue, to creep on past the second door.

Two.

After three more steps I feel the lip of another doorway. This is it. With incredible care I raise my arms above the doorframe and sweep my hand along the lip. My baby finger makes contact first but I react too slowly and the stick rolls away from me, my stomach clenching with primal terror as I wait for it to clatter to the ground. There's a moment's hiatus in the thick blackness and then it does just that.

I drop immediately into a low crouch, scrambling to grab it before it rolls away. There's the sound of breathing again; deep, hoarse, animalistic breathing. I freeze. It's here; *he's* here. Who-ever it is in that suit is down here with me. The Krampus.

I wonder who could be inside that costume. And how odd it is that whoever's in there is still keeping up their monster act when it's only me and them down here.

I push the thought away. The Holbecks obviously take their traditions very seriously. As I reach in the dark, images of who it might be flash through my thoughts: Oliver, Stuart, Edward. Then my mind inevitably lands on Robert, and it will not budge. I think of the girl on his tape, of what he said he did to her, and the silliness of being down here in the dark melts away, leaving only dread. I push the thoughts away and try to locate where the sound of the creature is coming from.

It is to my right, about six feet from me. Two large strides away.

But the Evergreen stick is near, and the end of the game is tantalizingly close. I want to go home.

I tentatively let my fingers search for it. But I need to stretch farther, and I realize that if I want this game to end, I'll need to turn on my torch, come what may.

Every nerve in my body rebels at the idea, but the truth is that all I need to do is grab that stick on the floor right in front of me, and shout the magic word. It doesn't matter if he sees me. It'll all be over. I can grab it before he reaches me.

I clutch the torch tight and flick it on.

The space around me bursts into vision, the terra-cotta of floor tiles and, three feet ahead of me, the thick Evergreen stick, a rod about a foot long. I dive for it and as I do I hear the rush of movement behind me. I fumble the stick into my hand as I spin around and point my flashlight back at the massive form rushing toward me. I dodge and scramble desperately up to my feet, the Evergreen branch firmly in my grasp, but he does not stop. He plows into me, his dank fur pushing me back against the basement wall. The wind is knocked out of me and my torch clatters to the floor. I look up at the dim figure pinning me to the wall, its wet mouth inches from mine. It studies me, now that it has me pinned, its head tilting as if it were trying to work something out. I try to call out the word *Evergreen,* its wood held tight in my hand, but, like in a nightmare, the word does not come.

The creature, still so real, even at this proximity, forces a wet hand over my mouth. I think again of who is in that suit and the nature of what is happening suddenly changes.

Is it Robert pressing me hard against the wall? Is it Edward? Is he trying to scare me? Humiliate me? Paralyzed by anxiety and confusion and the sheer strength of him, I cannot do anything but let him continue. His breath is hot on my neck as his free hand traces lasciviously down the side of my body to where my hand hangs, gripping the Evergreen branch firmly. The nature of the situation changes again to something threateningly sexual, bordering on assault. It is only when his clawlike fingers reach my thigh, wet with toddler piss, that my paralysis is broken. My anger bursts its banks as I think of the night I have had. The night Billy has had. I am incandescently angry—at this family, at this game, at all of this bullshit.

I summon all my strength, then pull back and slam my elbow as hard as physically possible directly into the creature's face, not caring who is in the suit, and not caring about the consequences. The creature howls and reels back, releasing me. I choke in a lungful of air and I yell with every ounce of anger I possess, "EVERGREEN."

Instantly all the lights blast on. Throughout the house, around me and above, I hear the sound of doors electronically unlocking.

It's over. The game's over. I won. But my anger is not replaced by triumph. If anything, it hardens into something denser.

Around the corridor, I hear a door open and the gentle hubbub of the party, and laughter, carries along to me.

I hear Fiona before I see her. "We have a winner. Good job, Harriet!" She appears around the corner smiling with an excited round of applause. "That was fantastic."

A medic appears, moving past her to attend to the prone creature on the floor behind me. He hoists it up to sitting and gently helps to remove its mask.

The man inside it is finally revealed, but he is no one I have ever seen before. He takes a glug from the water bottle the medic offers him and wipes the moisture from his sweat-stung eyes. I try to make sense of who he is but can't. He's in his late twenties, hair slicked to his tanned skin with sweat from the heavy suit. His red eyes squint up into the light, his breathing still snagging from exertion and my blow to his head. I feel sick with guilt. And yet whoever he is ruined my night, felt me up, and scared me half to death.

"How are you, Mikhail?" Fiona asks him cheerfully. He looks up and flashes a handsome if exhausted smile punctuated by an athletic double thumbs-up. "Remarkable performance again, Mikhail," she continues. "Best yet." I get the impression from Fiona's tone and volume that Mikhail doesn't speak much English.

"We hire a motion capture performer every year," she tells me, taking my arm in hers and leading me away from him. "To be Krampus. Mikhail is a special effects CGI performer. He's done Krampus for us for two years running now. He's a phenomenal find; we're very lucky to have him."

I let her lead me, dazed, up the basement stairs into the bright light of the hall, my anger morphing into bald incredulity now. The house around us is alive once more with the sound of children, as if nothing out of the ordinary has happened. I stare at Fiona as she leads me to a ground-floor toilet and starts to dab a wet flannel onto my damp, piss-covered trousers. I stare at her, dumbfounded.

"I always tell Billy to go before things start but he never listens," she says ruefully.

I stop her hand mid-dab and she looks up at me.

"What the absolute hell was that game, Fiona? You think that was okay?"

Fiona looks at me, confused for a second, then touches my forehead. "Why? Do you not feel well? Was it too much?" she asks. "For the baby?"

"Are you fucking kidding me? It was too much for me. Why the hell didn't you explain it to me? Why didn't anyone?"

Her gaze flits to the bathroom door and then back to me, conflicted. "Because that's part of the game," she tells me, her tone low. "You're not supposed to tell new family members how to play; they have to find it out, like everyone else. It's a test. Of character. Of working together, as a team, one generation with the next. Teamwork." She smiles. "And you won. You should be happy." Her tone is tight now, slightly irritated, as if she'd laid on the whole evening for me and this was all the thanks she'd gotten.

"And what about Billy? Weren't you worried about him?" I ask, and a question falls into place. "Wait, how did you know he wet himself? Were you watching us?"

She nods. "Of course. I'm not going to let a stranger run around in the dark with my child, am I?" she says softly, and I can tell I've hit a nerve. "This house got broken into fifteen years ago. The whole building is rigged with cameras now. You'll see next year. We all watch the game." Her attention returns to my wet trouser leg. "I'm not sure how much I'm actually helping here," she says. "Let's leave it, shall we? I'll get you a fresh pair of mine instead. But right now, we need to get moving. It's time for presents," she says brightly, then, assessing my expression, she adds, "If you're ready, that is?"

I give her a look that I hope conveys exactly how ready I am.

"Right. I see," she says carefully. "Well, the children are waiting for their auntie Harriet. And I think they'd be very excited to see the winner, don't you think?"

I decide I hate Fiona and that feeling that way is okay. I grab the flannel from her hands, briskly rub my own wet hip, and toss it away.

"Yeah, let's get it done."

24

Diamonds Don't Come from Coal and Other Facts

SATURDAY, DECEMBER 17

The lights in Mount Sinai Hospital make the diamond bracelet around my wrist sparkle. My present, my prize, for beating the Krampus. I was a good girl; I protected the children and saved the day. I'm a regular hero.

It's a beautiful bracelet, I can't deny it, twinkling on my wrist in the strip lighting of the pregnancy ward.

The Krampus, or St. Nicholas, or whoever the hell, left it in my shoe. All the shoes along Fiona and Oliver's hallway were stuffed with gifts, good or bad.

My shoes alone were coated with black coal dust; a joke, apparently. Coal for the naughty. If only they knew how naughty I have actually been in my life. Though, given Robert's tape, perhaps they do.

In my left shoe there was a leather box. Inside was a note, and beneath that note, a gift.

As I watch other couples head in for their scans, I try not to think about last night. I try to let the anger dissolve. I would be lying if I said I am not concerned that being chased by the Krampus might have done more damage than any of us realize, that this morning's scan—instead of showing me a heartbeat—will show me only stillness. Life can be fragile sometimes.

I look down at the diamonds throwing light into colors, the only shimmer in this sterile ward.

Edward fastened it onto my still-trembling wrist in Oliver and Fiona's hallway last night, silent in the knowledge of the almighty shitstorm coming his way as soon as we got home. He saw on camera the hand sliding down my body, the look in my eyes.

Matilda sidled up beside us to inspect the winner's spoils. "You get coal and diamonds, ha. That's funny; Dad's sense of humor all over. It's a common misconception, that diamonds come from coal. Not true obviously. Coal is compacted rotten matter. Diamonds existed long before anything organic could even rot." She grins knowingly. "Coal comes from coal and diamonds come from diamonds."

I straighten at the sound of a nurse's sneakers squeaking down the corridor. Edward's hand slips into mine. I look him in the eyes, heavy from lack of sleep, and I do not pull away.

Last night was our biggest argument. Don't get me wrong: we're a normal couple; we argue. But last night was a big one. It didn't so much end as run out of words. In a nutshell, Edward didn't warn me about the game.

"You're supposed to go in blind; that's part of it. I thought you'd get a kick out of it. How could I know you'd take it that seriously? I warned you it was weird—*they* were weird—and you told me it was fine. That you wanted this," he'd argued, his pillow and bedding stacked in his arms, as baffled and upset by the extremity of my reaction to the evening as I seemed to be by his. "I didn't know you'd freak out, did I? How could I know that? You should have just stopped."

"I don't know, Ed, I was scared. Maybe if you'd told me about the seven-foot deformed goat-man I'd have been able to make an informed decision? Maybe me being pregnant should have twigged something for you? That, and having to run around all night carrying a toddler up and down a five-fucking-story house?"

"I didn't know you'd carry him. And not to undermine your, whatever, but Fiona's played it pregnant. I'm pretty sure Mom did too. I didn't know it would be an issue. I just thought you'd be good at it; that you'd find it good weird. Was I wrong? I mean you won it, didn't you? And in record time. You did that; I didn't make you do that." He stops, looking at the now stony aspect of my face before continuing: "It was a game, Harry. Part of it is you didn't know the rules. You could have stopped—you didn't need to run, or win. You know, the kids who get caught by the Krampus get taken to the kitchen and have ice cream!"

And that fact had put the nail in the coffin for me.

"Oh my God, Edward. How could I have possibly known that? Jesus fucking Christ! You didn't tell me anything. Anything at—"

"That's the point, Harry! To see how you do under pressure. Teamwork. And it turns out you do incredibly well. Okay. And you're fine."

"Do I look fine, Edward? Do I? Having been chased around and felt up by a motion capture guy? Do I look like I'm avoiding stress like Dr. Leyman said?"

And so on, and on, in circles, until sleep caught up with us.

Lying on the scanning table, warm goo spread liberally across my only slightly swollen belly, I try to calm my mind, to think positive thoughts.

"Today is just an initial look to see if everything is going according to plan with the pregnancy," the sonographer tells me.

"And hopefully we should be able to ascertain a due date." Her hand finds my shoulder. "Now, I need you to know, in case you have any concerns, that if we *don't* pick up a heartbeat today, that doesn't necessarily mean there is a problem. Okay? So bear with us. There's always a chance we have our dates slightly wrong; it happens every so often. We wouldn't expect to hear a heartbeat until at least six weeks, okay?"

It's like she can read my mind. Or, on second thought, maybe it's just my face she's reading.

Edward shifts beside me too. I can feel his concern, his expectation, as keenly as my own as I look up at the Styrofoam ceiling, like innumerable women before me, and wait for the sonographer to find life.

After a moment she turns her screen, wordlessly, around to show us. My eyes dance across the black and white trying to make sense of the undulating picture. And like an optical illusion, you appear.

A tiny butter bean, a sea creature, a little life wriggling and squirming inside me—of me, but independent from me.

I hear a gasp and I cannot tell if it's Edward's or my own. The sound kicks in now. The aortic *whoosh, whoosh, whoosh* like a deep-sea vent, pumping life in and out, hard and fast. And somehow, even though I've only just met you, I already love you.

An imagined future for you spools out ahead of us in my mind. Baby, toddler, child, teen, and adult. I see you, though you flick between genders, heights, looks, and ages, but I love every iteration of you. Birthdays, Christmases, fun and heartbreak. All of it. I want it all for you. Everything, all at once.

The sonographer smiles and turns the screen back deftly. "Congratulations, Mom and Pops," she says, carefully wiping the goo from my stomach. "We're at eight weeks today. You're welcome to get dressed and we can book you in for your next scan and a gender blood test as early as next week if you want to?"

On the subway journey home, we sit close, our argument now forgotten, our hands entwined. The game last night, so important before, has already slipped into memory, a funny story to tell our child one day. The bracelet on my wrist a Holbeck rite of passage. A talisman of how brave I can be when it is required.

Back at the apartment I help Edward pack for another work trip; his dinner with the Chinese investor last week went well, necessitating a trip to Hong Kong. We let name ideas flow between us. Our quiet contentedness morphing into full-blown excitement at the idea of knowing our child's sex a few days after Edward returns, the speed at which this is all happening thrilling and daunting.

I push the tape and Robert from my mind. I do not mention it to Edward. I won't until I have spoken to Samantha, until I know what this new game is.

"I'm serious when I say this," Edward tells me later as he lugs his bags into the building's elevator. "If you don't want to be so closely involved with them, if it's too much—which I think anyone might agree it could be—then we can step back from them. *You're* my family now. Both of you," he says, placing a warm hand on my slowly doming belly.

I think of the family—of Lila, Billy, Eleanor, and Matilda, their friendship, their glamour, and their approval—and I can't help but feel a pang at the thought of losing what we could become. "Can we play it by ear?" I ask him. "I don't want to throw the baby out with the bathwater, as they say. Once we pass the twelve-week mark and tell them about the pregnancy, they might settle down, right? Besides, I want our child to have a big family—grandparents, uncles, aunties. If they don't get yours, then they don't get any."

I watch from the building's lobby as Edward's cab pulls away and disappears into the flow of traffic.

I have three days on my own; three days to decide if I want to be part of this family, three days to work out exactly what Robert's game is and how I can beat him at it.

25

What the Nanny Saw

Samantha Belson looks surprised as I catch her eye across the busy service station cafeteria. Perhaps she was expecting someone different, someone older or less whatever it is I am.

I recognized her as soon as I entered the food court, her once blond hair now dyed a natural brunette, her petite shoulders bundled up thick against the Pennsylvania weather. I don't know where she lives but I agreed to meet her here, at a busy freeway service station, just outside of Philadelphia, a two-hour drive from Manhattan.

Up close she looks younger than her sixty years. Good bone structure, I guess; a simple, stress-free life. After the Holbecks, I'm sure that's what she would have wanted.

She rises to shake my proffered hand.

"Harriet?"

I nod; her guard is still up.

"It's Harriet Reed," I say, introducing myself formally, and I note she bristles slightly at my British accent—another thing she wasn't expecting, another potential barrier rising between us. "Thank you so much for meeting me," I continue, trying to exude a trustworthiness that I have no idea whether I possess. "I really appreciate you coming here today. I know it's a pretty unusual request."

I pull out my chair and sit, hoping she will do the same, and after a cautionary scan of the cafeteria she does. We face each other, two strangers, across a bright-yellow table.

Something about me, or the situation, seems to have settled her enough to make her stay. She must sense I'm no direct threat, and it's glaringly obvious I'm here alone.

"How did you find me?" Samantha asks, leaning back into her seat appraisingly.

"Using a very blunt instrument," I answer honestly. "I messaged every single Samantha Belson in her sixties that I could find online."

Samantha chuckles in spite of herself. "Fair enough. I suppose it worked. Was I the only one who responded?"

"No. But you were the only one who responded in the right way. You seemed concerned about being contacted in relation to the family at all, concerned about the questions being asked. The questions wouldn't really have bothered anyone but you."

She tenses as she realizes the truth of my words. Her own caution gave her away.

She toys with her empty takeaway cup. "Yes, well, no one had mentioned their name to me for years. They were ghosts to me. Ghosts I didn't want to stir," she says, her voice gentle as a primary school teacher's. "So who exactly are *you* in all this, Harriet Reed?" She looks at me with fresh eyes, as interested in what I might have to tell her as I am in what she can tell me.

"Nobody. Just an observer. With concerns," I answer, deciding it's probably best not to tell her I'm marrying directly into the

Holbeck family just yet. "I'm not a reporter, or anything like that, if that's what you're worried about. I was just concerned about what happened to you after the accident. I thought perhaps something might have happened—after you left their employment."

"I see," she says, shifting forward in her seat.

"The Holbecks are an unusual family, we both know that, but it's hard to know exactly how unusual they are, if you catch my meaning. I needed to see to what extent they stray from the norm."

Samantha gives a terse laugh that confirms she knows exactly what I'm talking about.

"You want to know why I left the family?" she asks, her expression settling into something more serious.

"I do."

"I left because of what happened."

"With Bobby," I push.

"You know I can't talk about Bobby," she says curtly, her gaze flitting back on me, suddenly on edge. "You're a wife, aren't you?"

I flounder, caught out by the directness of the question.

"No, I'm not. Not yet," I say carefully, and as I say it the reality of that fact hits me for the first time in weeks. I have made no promises; there are things I might learn that might make marrying into Ed's family impossible. "Why can't you talk about Bobby?"

"The NDA."

I feel my eyebrows rise. "They made you sign a non-disclosure agreement—about Bobby?"

She looks irritated by the question. "No. Everyone who works for the Holbecks signs an NDA the day they start. It's not unusual in wealthy families. It gives them a sense of security. Families discuss their private lives, their businesses, their family relationships, we hear it all—" She breaks off, with a look to me. "I wish I could help; you seem like a nice girl, but I'm afraid I can't speak to specifics. Especially around something as delicate as Bobby. If they were to sue—I have nothing except my house, Harriet. I'm sure you understand. I bought it with the payout they gave me."

"Why would they give you a payout if you chose to leave yourself?"

She looks at me mutely. I've caught her out.

"Samantha, please. I just need to know what I'm getting into here," I beg, then quickly change tack. "Why agree to meet me, if you can't or won't say anything? Why come?"

"Because you dusted off the past and presented it back to me. I needed to know who you were; if this might become a problem for me."

And then, as much as I hate myself for doing it, I use my trump card. "It might become a problem for you. I'm pregnant and I'm concerned about my safety around these people. I need you to tell me about them. It will go no further, I promise you. I don't want to put you in a compromising position."

Her eyes drop to my stomach and I feel her take me in in an entirely different light.

"Oh, I see," she says. "Well, at least now I understand why you're here. That makes sense. One of the boys. Yes, yes, I suppose you had better ask me what you want to know and we'll see where we get."

"Bobby. Was there something strange about the way he died?" I ask immediately.

"Strange how?" she asks.

"Did he jump or—"

"Or was he pushed? He jumped," she says with a firmness that tells me this is not the area I should be looking into.

I throw my mind back to Robert's tape. He describes Samantha's death because she knew something incriminating about that day. If Bobby jumped, then what could she have had over Robert? "Did something make Bobby jump? Was the suicide triggered by a person or an event?"

Samantha holds my gaze, then her mouth pulls into a pinched

line and she gives me a tight nod. "Mm-hmm. Bobby was having trouble with his father at the time. Too much pressure on him for sure. But *he* jumped all by himself."

Something in me loosens slightly at the reiteration of that point. Bobby killed himself and Robert killed no one. He made up the murder and Samantha is alive. The tape is a trick.

"The Holbecks like playing games, don't they?" I ask.

She straightens in her seat. If I didn't have her full attention before, I have it now.

"Oh yes. Yes, they do. Some of them can be very cruel."

"Some of the Holbecks?" I clarify.

"No. Some of the games."

I let her words sink in. There are other games; I have only experienced the tip of the iceberg.

Another question springs to mind about her role as a nanny.

"You were there in New York that day, the day Bobby died; you ran down to him on the street, after he fell; you were the first responder. Robert Holbeck joined and you tried to explain what happened, but who was looking after the other children while you were—"

"Wait, what?" Samantha interrupts me, her face blanching. "What did you just say?"

I freeze, her tone raising the hairs on the back of my neck. I flash back through what I've just said but she beats me to it.

"I wasn't there the day Bobby died. I wasn't at the New York apartment; I was at The Hydes with the children. I was always with the children. Why would I be in the city? Bobby was a twenty-year-old man; he certainly didn't need a nanny."

Something crystallizes inside me. Samantha isn't the blonde on Robert's tape. It wasn't her hair blowing in the breeze that day; it was someone else's. Samantha Belson might be alive, but that has little to do with anything. I've found the wrong woman.

I think carefully before I speak next.

"Samantha, there was a woman with blond hair at the apartment that day. Do you know who that might have been?"

Samantha considers. "Um, I so rarely went there, I'm not sure who came and—" Suddenly her eyes flare. "Oh my God, wait, no. It can't have been her," she falters. "Are you sure there was someone there with *blond* hair? You're certain?"

"I'm not certain, but I am extremely concerned that something might have happened to a woman of that description, yes. I thought I'd found her in you and that she was safe. Who came to your mind just then?"

Without warning, Samantha rises to her feet and hastily buttons her coat. She's realizing now how serious this could be, how close she is to being dragged into the past and the consequences of it. Our interview is over.

"You know who it is, don't you? Please, Samantha, could something have happened to her?"

Samantha grabs her bag and slips it onto her shoulder. "I think that's enough," she says with finality. "I can't be involved in *this*. I can't get sucked into their world. Please don't contact me again. Don't mention my name. If I find out you have, I will pass on your information to the police." She goes to leave, then pauses, a tug of guilt pulling her back to me.

"Do yourself a favor: Don't mess with these people, do you understand me? Not in your condition," she says, her tone serious. "They aren't like you and me; they don't operate in the same way; they don't even operate in the same world. Just walk away. I don't know your situation but my advice is: Drop whatever it is you think you're gaining from this. Think about yourself. Think about your child." She stops abruptly, a thought occurring. Her face sharpens with focus. "Which one are you marrying?"

"Edward," I say after a second's hesitation.

"Oh," she says simply before continuing. "The blonde—the one who sprang to my mind just now—was Bobby's college girlfriend. They broke up a month or so before Bobby died. I don't know why she might have been at the apartment that day. But she was young and she was blond."

"Do you remember her name?" I ask.

"It didn't seem important at the time," she answers, looking outside at the parked cars, her eyes flitting from one shadowed windshield to the next. "Don't contact me again," she reaffirms, her voice low and vulnerable. "And if you want my advice, Harriet Reed? Be very careful what you do around the Holbecks."

26

Who Is She?

MONDAY, DECEMBER 19

Be very careful what you do around the Holbecks.

Samantha's warning echoes in my mind as I drive home and it occurs to me, not for the first time, that given her advice, I probably should not have just written a thriller loosely based on a wealthy family who loses a son. What seemed like an interesting idea at the time now has the potential flavor of outright baiting. But I can fix that in the edit. Or not.

Though right now, I have more pressing matters. I need to find the name of Bobby's college girlfriend and check whether she's alive, for starters.

And if she's not, I need to go to the police. I try not to think of what will happen to me and Edward if I am the one to bring down his father, his family. Which raises the question of why on earth Robert gave me his tape in the first place. Does he have a death wish?

I can't help but wonder if Edward ever had his own suspicions about his father. He lived in the same house as the man for years. Perhaps I might have stumbled on the real reason they fell out.

Samantha's question about who I was planning on marrying sticks in my mind. She didn't seem that concerned about Edward, which makes me wonder who she *might* have been concerned about me marrying.

Oliver, Stuart, or even Robert himself.

Edward's car safely returned to the parking lot under our building, I head back up to the apartment, shedding my winter layers as I pull up a chair at my desk.

I type *girlfriend Bobby Holbeck* into my internet browser.

But once again, the results autocorrect to Robert Holbeck, filling the screen instead with a plethora of images of Robert Holbeck and various models and heiresses from the 1970s and '80s. In among them, I spot a young Eleanor, doe-eyed and mysterious—the woman he would eventually marry.

Without a name, I know I won't find Bobby's girlfriend.

In the kitchen I grab a consolatory snack to pep my energy and consider my options.

I could just ask someone. I could just call Edward, or Matilda, or Eleanor. Granted, it would be an odd question—what was your dead brother/son's ex-girlfriend called?—but it would save me a lot of time and anxiety. But then I recall Samantha's words and for some reason I am reminded of the conversation Matilda and Robert were having in Fiona's living room the other night and I'm suddenly not sure I can trust any of them with a question like this.

But Edward was his brother, and this is his house, so there're bound to be photos of Bobby somewhere in the apartment. All I need to find is one from Bobby's time at college, a party, a mixer, a ball game, anything. If they were a couple, she'll be in one of them. Bobby's stuff must have gone somewhere after he died, because it sure as hell wasn't in his old room.

Standing in front of Edward's closet, I suddenly balk at the idea of rooting through his personal belongings. Since the night of the proposal, I realize, I've unwittingly been chipping away at the bedrock of trust between us. Do I really want to rifle through Edward's things, his dead brother's life? Because I wouldn't want him to do the same thing to me, and I know exactly what he'd find if he did.

But if I can just find out who this ex-girlfriend is and whether she's okay, then I'll know Robert's tape is a trick and I can go to him and end this.

Buoyed by my resolution, I grab a chair so I can reach the high shelves above, where shoeboxes peek out over the edge. Up there I find exactly what I thought I might: an old school trunk, and a sun-bleached file box.

I pause, a dark thought blossoming. If I find a photo, and the girl is dead and Robert's tape is real, I will have to do something about all of this, and if I do there's a chance my own past might be dragged into things. I push the thought away. I'll have to cross that bridge when I come to it.

An hour into my search, legs numb from sitting on the floor, I come up for air, taking in the chaos fanned out around me. Photos from Edward's school days, university, weekends, and holidays. Friends, partners, family members I do not recognize and a precious few I do. Hugs, kisses, alcohol-rouged cheeks, and practical jokes. Wet hair, Bermuda shorts, and suntan-lotion-smeared books I didn't even know he'd read. Snapshots of Edward's life lie all around me. I try not to focus on the other girls. The fresh-faced women he has known and loved. I try not to judge myself against a poem written to him on the back of a postcard.

I try to have eyes only for Bobby. But I cannot find him among the old letters, gap-year trinkets, and report cards.

I stand to better take it all in, the relics of Edward's life so far. Bobby is not here.

It's only natural that he wouldn't be, I suppose. That he'd keep

Bobby in a separate place. I do not keep the soft-focus 1990s disposable-camera shots of my own long-dead parents with the other memories of my life. I lock them away; I can only see them if I make a conscious effort to see them. No surprises. It's easier that way.

If my own experience is anything to go by, then Edward's photos of Bobby will be somewhere else, somewhere safe, possibly somewhere locked.

I jiggle life back into my legs and head out to Edward's home office. His is larger than mine and rigged to the gills with cutting-edge computer tech, hard drives, and multiple screens. The similarities between the studies of father and son suddenly hit me.

I slip past the double-banked screens and head to the wooden filing cabinet next to Edward's desk, but fifteen tiny drawers later I am none the wiser. Invoices, statements, correspondence, but no personal items. I turn back to his desk and try the drawers. Nothing.

I let my eyes scan the room: bookshelves, hard drives, paperwork. On the bookshelves across the room, I find a row of dog-eared old coding books bookended by a small lockable steel storage box. My eye snags on the box. I remember noticing it before. Something so analog in a room so full of new tech.

I head over and gently lift the dark-gray metal box from its resting place. It's heavier than I expect. Full. There is no helpful key slotted in the lock, but looking at the rudimentary design I know I can open it. My aunt used to keep my maintenance allowance in a similar steel petty-cash box in the short time I lived with her after the accident. It took me a while to pluck up the courage, to get the knack, but back then days rolled into one another with nothing but reminders of what was gone. I had time.

These boxes can be opened with a paper clip, nothing more technical than that. It's a wonder the companies that make them are still in business given the—I'd imagine—widespread knowledge of this fact.

I slip a small metal paper clip off one of the documents on Edward's desk and take the box into the sitting room, placing it on the couch while I straighten out one side of the clip, leaving the other end still hooked. Then I crick my neck, lift the box onto my knees, and set about revisiting the magic touch I had at age eleven.

There is the satisfying slide of the simple wafer lock and, just like that, the small catch releases. The people who buy these things must know they offer no protection. I think of Edward and I can only assume he's aware of the box's flimsy nature. I suppose they offer more of an honesty system than anything else; the person who uses one is telling other people that they'd prefer you not to look inside.

I flip the lid. Inside is a thick stack of photographs. *Jackpot.*

The first is a shot of the Holbeck children, arm in arm, grinning broadly. Bobby and Edward in their teens; Matilda, Oliver, and Stuart younger. They look so happy, and it occurs to me that in spite of having an incredibly strange upbringing, at least they had one another. For a while, anyway.

The photo beneath is of a girl I do not know, her dark, wild curly hair as showstopping as her unselfconscious smile. I've never seen her before, but she's beautiful. One of Edward's undocumented ex-girlfriends no doubt, or a crush. I feel a sharp twang of jealousy at the idea of him keeping this photo under lock and key. But I know I have similar pictures hidden in my still-unpacked boxes.

I shuffle quickly through these special, chosen photos, trying not to dwell too long on each. I know what I'm looking for and halfway through the pack I find it, my hands stuttering to a halt as I catch sight of his Columbia sweatshirt.

Bobby beams out at me standing in front of a lush green football field. It must be after a game; smiling spectators and players mill and beside him, his arm encircling her, pulling her close, an equally happy blond girl. Her sweatshirt is a carbon copy of his, a cheerleader's skirt beneath it, her soft pale hair pulled back from her face in a shining ponytail.

My breath catches. I found her. She went to Columbia too. I turn the image and find, written on the back:

'01.
Bobby 'n' Lucy.

Lucy. Her name was Lucy. She looks the same age as Bobby, which means she would be forty this year. She could be alive somewhere out there right now—or she could be out there in the woods, two hours outside New York City, as Robert described on the tape.

I shiver looking at the blurry noughties photo, the happiness of it, the promise.

I have a first name; now all I need is a last.

27

Lucy

That night I dream I am on East 88th Street again.

It's 2002 and the sun is low in the sky, giving the evening a warm glow. On the other side of the road a small cluster of people mill. Something terrible has happened down there, and I realize it is the Holbeck building. And an understanding of what I am witnessing hits me like a punch to the gut.

With sickening dread, I head toward the crowd, drawn inexorably to what they are staring at. The noises of the street are muffled as if heard through a wall, or through water, everything caught in a kind of slow motion.

I cross the street in a daze, picking my way through stopped traffic as drivers, like sleepwalkers, slowly rise from their cars, having witnessed something fall. The weather vane high above us glints and swings in the evening breeze. There is an open window in the eaves, a net drape caught in the wind. And below, on the sidewalk, amid the legs of strangers, I make out a huddled shape on the ground, blackness all around it.

I feel Robert's presence before I see him, his strong, angular frame, from behind. Over his shoulder, a woman is just blocked from view, a wisp of her pale hair visible, fluttering in the wind.

Suddenly I am kneeling in front of Bobby, his sweatshirt thick with blood, his hair matted wet. I look down and I am wearing a Columbia sweatshirt too. I am Lucy. I am Bobby's girl.

I feel a gentle hand touching my shoulder and I turn as if drugged, as if trapped in resin, my movements heavy and slow. It is Robert Holbeck, but younger than I have ever known him.

He recognizes me for who I am and looks surprised to see me here. He knows I am not Bobby's girl; he knows I come from a different time and should not be here, in this scene, in this memory. He seems to understand the problem and slowly lifts a finger to his lips. Behind us a car horn blares and I gasp awake.

I bolt up in the darkness of the bedroom, my heart pounding, sweat-soaked. I wriggle free of the heavy duvet and lurch to the edge of the bed, my feet gratefully finding solid ground. I try to reorient myself. I am safe, I am here; it was a dream. I am not Lucy. My eyes adjust to the darkness of the bedroom and I look down at my chest. The Columbia sweatshirt is gone; instead my pajamas stick to my skin with perspiration.

As my mind focuses, a thought clarifies itself. I grab my bedside water, drain it, and head straight for my office.

I click on the desk light, drag my chair up to the computer, and open Google. I don't know why I didn't think of it before.

I type *Lucy, Columbia University, 2002, missing person* into the search box.

Lucy must have been a junior at Columbia too; if she went missing, people would have noticed.

I let out a yelp of triumph as thumbnail after thumbnail of Lucy fills my screen, the sound curdling in the silence of the room as I read the results.

Search for Missing Columbia Student Lucy Probus in Its Fourth Day

The parents of Columbia undergraduate Lucy Probus, 20, are "deeply concerned" for her welfare following her disappearance last Saturday night. The student was last seen returning to campus at around midnight on the night of October 27.

Lucy was reported missing after failing to attend scheduled activities the following day.

The third-year anthropology major, a dedicated member of the Columbia University cheerleading squad, formerly a resident of Pittsburgh, is described as petite and slim with blond hair and green eyes.

She was last seen wearing a burgundy jacket, jeans, and a gray hoodie bearing the distinctive blue C of the Columbia cheer squad. (photo insert above)

In a statement, NYPD chief Jim Westerly said: "We remain open-minded as to the circumstances behind Lucy's disappearance, but naturally, as the search enters its fourth day, our concern for her is growing. We are aware that Lucy had recently undergone significant trauma due to the loss of a close friend, and family and friends have described her recent actions as 'out of character.'

"I would like to appeal to Lucy directly. If she sees this, please make contact with the police or with your family."

Jesus. I close the tab and scroll down, opening up an article published earlier this year. Perhaps they found her?

Family of Columbia student Lucy Probus, who went missing 20 years ago, mark her milestone 40th birthday by appealing to those "haunted" by knowledge of what happened to come forward.

I stop reading abruptly. The girl with the soft blond hair was never found. The girl Robert described in his tape was never seen again.

The tape is real. It's a confession. He left Lucy's body in the woods two hours outside New York City.

Without missing a beat, I lunge back toward the bedroom and pull my suitcase out from under the rumpled bed to retrieve the tape player. I pull its red foam pads over my ears, fumble REWIND until it clicks off, and press PLAY.

Back in the office, in sweat-soaked pajamas, I listen to Lucy's story again, as New York glitters beyond my dark windows.

The thing is, there are a *lot* of woods two hours outside of New York. I bring up an online map of New York State, a search perimeter website I've used before for researching my novels.

Pen in hand, I scribble out the maths on a pad. The time it takes to get out of Manhattan, the average miles per hour a car is likely to maintain on the interstates and highways surrounding the city—the distance achievable in the space of two hours. I drop a boundary line down on the map and within its wide circle assess all the possible wooded areas where Robert could have left her in a 360-degree perimeter around Manhattan.

I then add another circle beyond that one. After his drive, Robert mentions hiking with her for another two hours. I do the maths once more: the average person can hike between two and three miles an hour, but he was carrying her, so let's say only two miles an hour. My second circle extends another four miles out past the original circle. It's a huge area. She could be anywhere out there.

But then Robert mentions other factors: a mountain and a lake. Still, the huge catchment area is peppered with mountains, lakes, and reservoirs. Two whole mountain ranges lie within my circles: the Catskills and the Adirondack Mountains.

I will never find her out there. But then, that is why he told me.

I need to tell Edward everything. We need to go to the police.

I shudder at the thought of Lucy out there in the cold. But

she's been there so long already. I can't do anything right now, and after two decades, one more night will change nothing.

The clock on the desk reads three forty-five A.M. I'm not going to get any sleep tonight, and Edward will be back from Hong Kong in just five hours.

I look down at the tape player in my hands. As much as I do not want to hear more, I know I have to; I need to see how deep this goes. I need to find out why he is telling me any of this and what he wants.

With grim determination, I sink back into my chair, slide the headphones back on, and pick up where I left off.

28

The Tape

PART 2

I have no doubt you will feel resistance to this recording. To this story. But I also know you will use your inquiring mind to sort through what lies before you. All I can ask is that you bear with me, dear Harriet, as I continue, because there is more for you to know.

I suspect you have already thought of telling my son about this recording. But the fact that you are still listening tells me you have not. I suspect you have weighed the pros and cons of such a decision. The knock-on effects of that choice. You are an intelligent, resourceful woman; that is why I have chosen to confide in you. But I advise you to tread with incredible care.

God knows, I love my son. I love all of my children, but I am not above taking action to protect the future of our family. Too many have given too much for us to let it all slip away, for it to be squandered by one unknown quantity. In his way Edward knows what I have done for this family, not in the details, but we know the men we are.

So I ask you for his sake, do not act rashly. This cassette recording is meant for you, and you alone. Listen carefully to what I tell you, weigh the content, use your faculties, and when you are ready to talk, talk to *me*.

I have faith in you, Harriet. We are alike, you and I. In what we have done for our families. As you will see.

The second girl was harder than the first. And Gianna fought. She screamed and clawed and left marks. She wanted to live but she saw too much.

A fashion party, 2004, a warehouse loft on New Year's Eve. There were red balloons, and a drive for the future as present and tangible as the glitter on young faces. Her eyes did not waver as she danced. That look of hers, intent, determined, a challenge. And she was beautiful, her lips stained dark, her thick curls tumbling around her. She had pushed and pushed for more but she could not have more. She was not suitable. Good fun, but not worth the investment she seemed to require, or demand. And so, to her place.

The boom and the pulse of the warehouse left behind. An argument, a scuffle, but, once words were spoken, she calmed enough to come willingly. Her rooms were dark and full of foreign objects. Low light, blue-black linen sheets, and the smell of jasmine. Mirrors everywhere so that she could watch what happened. Her lipstick imprinted on a crystal tumbler, the kiss of her wet lips as she drained the fluid, as her slender throat swallowed. She looked like she knew what she was drinking, but she did not know.

Do not worry, Harriet Reed. I did not touch her as I lay her in the fresh sheets, only softly arranged her for whoever would find her. Her breathing already too slow, already ebbing away.

In the drained glass: too much of what she had already had. A mixture of excess. That is what she was given, simply more of what she had already had, because that is what she wanted in a sense. It was what she wanted to give us. More of the same. More of her. So you see, she had to go.

Sitting in the corner of the room, I watched her slow to a stop. You could say watching is cause enough to give up on a person, and perhaps you would be right, my dear. After all, who would do such a thing? Who would watch another person die?

But we both know the answer to that, don't we? We know the kind of person who would watch another die and do nothing. We both know the kind of person that takes, don't we, Harriet Reed?

The question is: Is there a difference between you and me? Between what I have done and what you have done? And you must believe me when I say I *do* know what you have done. I imagine you reason that I cannot possibly know about that lonely morning on a country road, and my answer to you is simple: I do. I know enough.

Enough to fill in the gaps, enough to color the picture and present you with my findings. I am not the writer here, Harriet, but indulge me if you will.

I see you. Little girl in the back seat of a car, in a world of your own, safe. The babble of parents up front. Perhaps you felt the air change as the moment came, an unexpected intake of breath from the driver, a tensing, a sudden movement of the wheel, a jerk. Your gaze flashing forward too late. Did she turn to you, your mother? Did she catch your eye before it hit, her last instinct to protect you?

I cannot presume to know what happened in those last moments. The life you came from, the ones who loved you, taken from you.

The car impacted, flipped, skidded, and came to a stop in a gully beyond the road. In the silence that followed that deafening noise you slowly came to, your own cries inaudible beneath the buzz in your ears. Around you glass and twisted metal, the taste of blood and the thick fug of gasoline. Your left arm broken, torn muscles in your neck and both shoulders. Broken ribs. You hung suspended by nothing but your seatbelt.

You all hung; a silent family suspended as if stopped in time. Your mother's auburn hair swaying just out of reach, the car's windshield decimated, plant life inching deep into the car. Whether you said her name or not, I do not know. Whether you leaned forward to try to wake her I do not know; but she would not have stirred. She was an object jostled, nothing more. Your father beside her, equally silent.

I don't know how long you waited and hoped and tried to rouse those silent bodies. But after a time, an animal instinct moved you. Even at eleven years old you knew to cut your losses, to chew through a trap. Or perhaps you thought you could save them, get help, that someone else would come.

You disengaged your seatbelt and tumbled into the roof well, scrambling out on bleeding hands and knees. In my mind, Harriet, you did not look back as you passed them. You did not want to remember them that way.

The dead feel different, don't they? Once the light has gone, the people we love become strangers, don't they? We cannot reach them and something different is left in their place.

You clambered out of that broken windshield, snagged by branches and barbs of twisted metal. You did not pull a phone from their pockets; you did not think to do so in your rush.

I have no doubt that over the years you have stewed over why you did not think to do that in the moment. But rest assured, there was nothing you could have done for them; I have seen the medical reports. They left you before you even knew.

Back on the road, shaking and bruised, you saw what hit you. He was there. His car tipped, immobile, its windshield shattered milky by the impact. You saw him, pinned by his own steering wheel, shivering, crying, his body trapped in the twisted metal.

Did you speak to him? Did he scream for help, shriek his regret? I imagine, even at your age, you could tell he was drunk, that this was why you had lost everything. Judging by what you did next, I think there can be no doubt about that.

Crashed cars rarely explode in real life, but small fires are common. A spark at the front of his vehicle. A fuel leak at the back. The two so rarely connect.

There was a witness. A local woman, a farmer. She heard the sound of the crash and rushed across her fields toward a pillar of smoke. As she ran, she saw a girl standing by the wreckage. She saw flames lick along the ground, from one end of the car to the other. A rush of burning heat along the tarmac like a magnesium strip, there and then gone. She watched as the car's cabin exploded into flames, as you stood motionless beside it. The screams from inside it jolted her into a run. She ran to you but by the time she reached you the screaming had stopped.

A short sharp shock and your work was done.

Later, when questioned, she could not be sure what she had seen: if you had tried to put the flames out as they went past you or if you had been doing something else. When the police arrived, you did not speak.

We both know what happened that morning. And Harriet, my dear, let me tell you as an outside observer, what you did that day could never have been different.

I would have done the same. A man took your family, through his own stupidity, through his poor choices. You acted in everyone's best interests. A child forced to do an adult's work. Actions must have repercussions. They must.

I have seen the reports, the files. It is always important to know the type of person one is welcoming into one's home. After all, one's home is one's sanctuary. I wanted to know the type of person you were, Harriet, my future daughter-in-law. I had the logistics run, and that is why you are listening to my voice now. Because that road was level, and fluid—water, gasoline—can never travel unaided, Harriet. I do not know if they suspected then, if it crossed their minds, but the facts stand.

If it were to happen today, Harriet, with the technology we have, with the procedures now in place, you would not be marrying my son. You would not be who you are in the world.

I am in absolutely no doubt that you are fully acquainted with the law in your country. I am sure you have checked in on it many times since you were a child. The minimum age of criminal responsibility in the United Kingdom is ten years old. *Ten*, Harriet.

You were eleven when your parents died.

And again, I am certain you know this, but there is no statute of limitation for criminal offenses in the English courts.

It must plague you. Or perhaps you reasoned that after all this time you might be safe. Well, you are safe with me. Whatever succor that might bring.

So you see, we *do* have a lot in common, Harriet Reed. We both lost the ones we loved and found new ones. We would both do anything for our families.

For what it is worth, Harriet, I like you. I forgive you. We must remember, you were just a child; your parents killed and the man responsible there in front of you. It's at moments like these that our true nature is revealed. You did a terrible thing, but you did it for your family. And I have done the same for mine.

Now, I believe, we are singing from the same hymn sheet.

As I said earlier, I would prefer it if you did not share this tape with my son, or with anyone for that matter. And I will return the favor. We both have skin in the game.

You may be asking yourself now, why is he telling me any of this? On that front, I will ask you to bear with me, Harriet. I am telling you this because I know who you are; I know what you are capable of given the right circumstances. And I have chosen you for just that reason. I will ask something of you. I will ask something of you very soon.

29

Gagged and Bound

WEDNESDAY, DECEMBER 21

The tape crackles and clicks off. Side A complete.

I sit, stricken, in the silence of the apartment.

It's funny having your worst fear realized and the world still spinning. A sigh shudders from me, and with it something dislodges deep within me.

A wave of jumbled emotion erupts, overleaping itself, bursting up and out. Warm tears roll down my face, the taste of salt hitting my lips, because this is the first time anyone has articulated what happened that morning. What happened to me. What I did. And why. A tightness held for twenty years begins to loosen.

I know I should feel shame, dread, fear—and in part I do, though those feelings are old friends. The new feeling weaving and twisting among them is a surprise, something I never even considered: acknowledgment. Hearing his words—even given who he is and the terrible things he has done—I feel known. For the first time in my adult life, I have been seen by another person. And they did not shrink away in disgust. I know Robert Holbeck is no arbiter of moral character, no great judge of human worth, but someone knows and they have done worse, and they understand. Of course I fear what this means, that a man like Robert knows and can wield my darkest moment over me, and yet I cannot lie: it feels good to be known.

And however confusing it might be, I feel oddly grateful. Grateful to him.

We are not alike, he and I; I refuse to acknowledge that, but in a terrifying way I feel a tiny bit less alone in the world than before.

I slowly pull myself together, wiping my eyes and nose with my sleeve and carefully removing the Olympus headphones from my ears.

The tape is clear. Robert Holbeck kills women. He kills them when they know too much, or when they get too close and threaten his family. Both women knew enough about the family's dealings to pose a grave threat to their future. I recognize the description of the second woman, Gianna, from a photograph in Edward's locked box earlier. The girl with wild curly hair and fearless eyes. Gianna must have been seeing Edward in his first year at MIT. A distraction, who was asking for more attention than the family was willing to give. Robert must have feared that Edward, now next in line, might go the way of Bobby. Robert took her out of the equation.

Did Edward suspect foul play or did he think the overdose was fueled by her unhappiness at not being able to be with him? People around the Holbecks seem to find life harder to deal with than most.

Robert had already lost one son; he couldn't risk losing another. He drugged Gianna and made it look like an overdose while he sat back and watched.

I understand the predicament I am in now; I understand the

terms. I cannot expose Robert because he will expose me. But I know why he has chosen me and what he wants—a favor.

I roll-call the dead in my mind: Bobby, Lucy, Gianna. Bobby started it all; he could not handle the weight of the Holbeck name and jumped, but something else happened there that day. And Lucy Probus knew too much. She knew Robert was in the house, and rumors can build and take on a life of their own.

But both Gianna's and Lucy's perceived crimes against the Holbecks are not worse than mine. I am a murderer who is trying to marry their firstborn son. I set a man on fire and watched him burn. It's a wonder I'm still alive.

I suppose, as long as Robert needs something from me, I am safe.

Robert knew about me the night we met. He knew who I was, what I did. I recall the electricity between us, in his study that night, the intoxicating danger. The way he looked at me, the connection we had, instinctive; he knew who I was and he was comfortable with me. But perhaps only a man like Robert Holbeck could ever feel comfortable with me. Edward can never know; the thought alone makes me sick to my stomach.

Laurence Fletcher was his name—the man I killed. He begged, but I was not listening. I took my chance and I made him pay, because men like him don't change.

It would be a misreading to say I did what I did with the best of intentions. I did not. I wanted him to suffer; I wanted to *see* him suffer. I didn't do it to protect the world, or others, or because I could sense he was a *bad* person. I didn't know anything about him the day he died, except what he had just done to me, to us.

I got to know him over the years that followed, though. I'd find out all there was to know about the man who changed my life. His divorce, his addictions, lost visitation rights, harassment, and abuse. Somehow, through it all, he'd kept his job; I guess he saved his worst for those he loved. He wasn't a great person, it turned out, but that wasn't why I killed him.

I killed him because I wanted to and because I could. And because, for a second, it took the pain away.

In that sense, Robert and I are alike. We are not on the side of the angels. The only difference between us is that I only killed once.

Once was enough for me—enough to put me in prison, enough to ruin my life. Enough to end a career. Enough to make Edward hate me if he were ever to find out. Once was already one time too many.

I cannot go to the police about the tape and I cannot tell Edward. Not if I want him to love me. If I want him to love me, he can never know who I really am.

I scour the apartment for traces of my search for Lucy Probus. I erase my computer search history and put Edward's steel lockbox back on its shelf in his office, replacing the paper clip I took from his documents with a fresh one. When Edward returns it will be as if none of this had ever happened. And I will bide my time until I can work out what Robert wants.

Edward's "hello" from the hallway wakes me with a jolt. He's back.

I sit bolt-upright in the bedsheets, panic coursing through me as I try to remember my plan, or if I even had a plan, my thoughts ricocheting through my mind.

From the safety of the bed, I listen to him moving about the apartment, dropping his bags, removing his coat, and wonder how I am going to get through what is coming next without Edward, without anyone, to share this with.

I force myself out of the bedroom and into the kitchen, where I find him making breakfast. He looks up with a smile that I do not deserve and I head straight to him, squeezing him as tight as I can.

He leans down to kiss me, mistaking my silent embrace for a warm welcome home.

"Hey, sleepyhead. How have you been?" he asks. "Get up to anything exciting while I was away?" I do not answer and when I unbury my head from his chest he laughs.

"Let it be noted," he says, breaking away from me to flip whatever he is cooking in the pan, "that I am actually *cooking*."

He's happy; his trip must have gone well. "Listen, I love Chinese food," he says, by way of explanation, "but I have not been able to stop thinking about bacon and eggs for two days straight." He stops while pulling milk from the fridge, suddenly noticing I haven't said a word yet. "Are you okay?" he asks with concern. "You look a little pale, or something. Is the baby okay?"

I give him a halfhearted smile, the desire to tell him and not tell him almost unbearable. "No. I'm fine. Still half asleep."

He slips a hand around my waist, resting it on my abdomen. "How's it all going in there? When's the next scan again?"

"Day after tomorrow," I answer, as cheerfully as I can, the idea of bringing a baby into the current situation beyond terrifying. I tell myself it's going to be okay because somehow, I am going to fix all of this. I will make sure that we are safe and that Edward's father can't ever hurt us, that my past can't hurt us.

Edward looks at me with so much love in his eyes I want to burst.

"Okay, no laughing. I'll say a boy's name, you say a girl's. Ready?"

"Ready." I smile.

"Okay. Three, two, one. George."

"Iris."

"Iris and George," he repeats back, testing the sounds. "Love 'em. Hell, let's have two kids and use both."

He mistakes my sudden tears for joy, or hormones.

I pull back and quickly wipe them away.

"You okay, really?" he asks, unable to decipher my emotions but aware something is very wrong. "If there is something happening, if you need to tell me, I'm here," he says, his expression gentle but serious.

I hold his gaze a moment, taking in his handsome face, the look of concern in his eyes, and I realize I can do this. I can do this alone, for us, for him, because this man is worth fighting for.

"I'm fine," I tell him finally. "I'm just really glad you're back."

We gorge ourselves on Edward's breakfast while he updates me on his business trip to Hong Kong.

"They've made a preemptive offer on the company." His eyes glisten in the morning sun that streams through the apartment windows as he lets that fact land on me.

"Wait, what? The whole company? They want to *buy* the whole company? I thought the plan was expanding over there?" I ask, my surprise obvious enough to draw a snort of laughter from Edward.

"Yeah, I know. That was the plan, then Li-Chen wrote a number on the back of a business card, pushed it across the table, and suddenly the plan changed. It's a healthy number," he tells me, his smile broadening into a grin. "A really goddamn healthy number."

I feel my chest tighten; Edward doesn't use superlatives. I feel my head swim at the idea of a figure he'd be genuinely impressed by, a price he'd be willing to sell his entire company for.

"And what did you say to Li-Chen?" I say carefully, the unpredictability of our conversation destabilizing my already scrambled senses. "Is that something you'd want to do, sell the company? You've built it from the ground up—"

"There will be other companies. I can do all this again and the next time I'll have capital behind me." He loses the smile, becoming serious. "I have a few days to consider, to approach other investors, or buyers, if I want, but with an opening offer like this, not many players would be in the running."

"What about ThruComm? Couldn't your family buy it, subsume it?" Even as I say it, I realize what an unattractive prospect that is, even to me. Nobody wants to be subsumed, especially by their domineering family.

Edward's eyes crinkle into a smile. "ThruComm's already priced out. They're not capable of matching this."

"Holy shit!" I gasp, my hand flying to my mouth. "You're serious?"

"Yeah." He nods, pleased that I am finally getting the scope of what he is trying to tell me. "We've just got to play it right."

"Okay. How long do you have to decide?"

"Close of business tomorrow."

"And when will it—"

"As soon as I sign the documents."

The extent of what Edward is telling me slowly dawns on me. If I thought he was wealthy before, this deal could make what he has now a drop in the ocean. The sheer level of protection, and power, that money would give us hove into view. Whatever methods Robert Holbeck has used to avoid his own past will suddenly be available to me, to us. It won't solve the problem of Robert, but it could certainly even the playing field.

Edward rises from the table, his energy infectious. "Right, I'm going to get going. I've got meetings all day. I love you," he says, then, from the doorway, he adds, "You are okay, aren't you?"

"Yes, I am. Go, go," I order him.

He heads out of the kitchen with a grin then circles back.

"Oh yeah. Did Matilda get hold of you yesterday?" he asks.

"Yesterday?"

"Yeah, about Christmas?"

My blood freezes in my veins. I have no idea what he is talking about but I can tell I am not going to like it one bit. "What about Christmas?" I ask.

"Damn it. I thought they'd have called by now. I said if you were happy to do it, we'd do it."

"Do what, Ed?" I say, finding it hard to keep the snap out of my voice.

"Um, Christmas," he says, surprised by the bite in my tone. "They want us over for Christmas; three nights, at The Hydes.

It's family only. They've never invited anyone not married into the family. They want you and Lila there this year. Call it a stab at modernization. It's a step in the right direction. You said we'd play it by ear so I said maybe. I think it's sort of an apology for Krampusnacht. Though I know I'm as much to blame for what happened then as anyone else. Up to you, though?"

I struggle for how to respond to this appropriately because I absolutely cannot sleep under the same roof as Robert Holbeck.

"When would we go?" I ask, buying myself a few seconds to think.

"The twenty-third. Day after tomorrow. The deal should be all wrapped up by then so it works for me."

A palatable excuse drops into my mind and relief floods my body. "Ah, damn, we can't. That's the day of the scan. The twelve-week scan. We need to be in the city for it, remember?"

He tilts his head as if I'm joking. "Yeah, but the scan's only in the morning. We'll drive out of town after. It's not like we had big Christmas plans anyway. Or are you thinking we should maybe put a bit of distance between them and us? Because that's fine too. I can just call Mom and tell her we're doing our own thing?"

I have to physically stop myself from leaping up and kissing him in gratitude. But the relief is short-lived because I know there is no getting away from Robert. He knows what he knows and if Edward says we're not coming, his family will think I have stopped playing ball, and Robert will know I am scared of him. He will know I have listened to his tape.

My mind flies through my options and comes up blank. There is no excuse that won't sound like I'm running scared.

"Is there something you want to tell me?" Edward asks, after I fail to reply. "Did one of them do something, say something, while I was away? Was it Matty? Fiona? Dad?"

I search his eyes, careful not to react to any one name. "Why do you ask?" I answer, trying to gauge how much he knows of anything.

"I don't know. Has someone upset you?"

"No. I just, I'm sorry, I'm just not over our last visit yet, Ed-

ward. I don't want you to upset them, or tell them I don't want
to go, but I just can't do anything like that game again," I say. It's
risky but worth a shot; perhaps he can think up an excuse to give
them for me.

"You don't need to worry about that. Christmas won't be anything like Krampusnacht. No one is going to make you join in
any of our weird family stuff if you don't want to, okay? Besides,
everyone will know you're pregnant by then. We'll tell them as
soon as we get there. You won't have to lift a finger. This way,
Christmas, everything, is done for us—zero effort; festivities covered. We don't have to decorate, cook, clean up. Sounds pretty
good, right? We don't have to live in their pockets either. We usually only get together for meals and drinks. It's a big place. The
rest of the time we'll do our own thing," he says, then lets out a
surprised laugh. "And if you want to go at any point, we go."

I mean, what the hell am I supposed to say to that?

I find myself wondering if the fact I'm pregnant will change
Robert's plans for me, because one thing is for sure: I will not be
able to avoid him at The Hydes.

30

Bigger Fish to Fry

10:34 A.M.
WEDNESDAY, DECEMBER 21

While Edward showers and changes for work, I set about preparing for Christmas at The Hydes.

Carefully listening for sounds from the shower room along the hall, I roll the combination lock on my suitcase and relocate the tape player to its old hiding place under my side of the mattress.

I fill my now empty case with travel essentials, then turn toward my wardrobe to examine what clothes I own that might in some way be appropriate for a Holbeck family Christmas.

I pull out the ridiculously expensive emerald-green slip dress I wore the night I met Edward, its silk like liquid in my hands as I hold it up to myself. Perhaps too much, but who's to say. If the Holbecks don't dress up for Christmas, then who does? And who's to say I'll last that long anyway?

I carefully fold and pack it. Three nights of festivities; who knows what will happen?

I inspect the best of what I have as I play Robert's words back in my mind. His description of the day I lost my family is achingly redolent. He is so far ahead of me in this game, I wonder if it might ever be possible to catch up.

I take a black velvet Versace dress from the rail, one I bought for my last birthday, egged on by Edward, and pack it neatly.

I try to guess what the tone of their celebrations might be, and pack some more casual items too. It's impossible to know what the other Holbeck women might wear over this short but no doubt telling visit. This Christmas invitation feels like a kind of Balmoral test. A test to weed out those who do not fit in with the family from those who do. If I manage to match some unspoken codes, hell, if I manage to survive, then perhaps they will accept me as one of them.

Christmas seems to have become the final stage of a Holbeck test triptych that I didn't know I was signing up for: Thanksgiving, Krampusnacht, Christmas. Each one, I'm guessing, progressively harder than the last.

Finally, I pack the claret jumpsuit I wore for Thanksgiving and three dressy outfits, then I add shoes and call it a day. I have bigger fish to fry. I need to listen to the rest of Robert's tape, but I can't do that with Edward in the house.

I listen for Edward still busying himself along the hall. If I want to listen, I'll need to do it away from the apartment, even though leaving the safety of the building means potentially being followed again. The man with the baseball cap springs to mind. While I made sure I wasn't followed the day I went to meet Samantha, I was in the car and that made it somehow easier. I deliberately wound through the streets of Manhattan before I headed for the Lincoln Tunnel. I could take the car again but I would have to think of a reason to tell Edward now that he's back. No, I'd better go on foot—I just need to go somewhere the man with the baseball cap can't follow.

Somewhere men aren't allowed.

The first place that comes to mind is my gym, and the women-only changing rooms. Going to the gym isn't going to raise any alarms, and there are lockable stalls there. I could listen in safety.

I grab my gym bag and swim things from the closet and slip on my sneakers before retrieving the tape player from under the mattress.

Edward's head pokes out of the bathroom as I make my way to the front door and raise my gym bag in explanation. Toothbrush in mouth, he gives me a cheerful thumbs-up as I head out the door.

The desire to slip on my headphones and start listening as soon as I leave the building is almost too much, but I hold off. I need my wits about me until I can get someplace where I can't be disturbed. Robert's confession isn't an interesting podcast to be listened to on the go—the future of my family entirely depends on the words on that cassette.

I swipe through the turnstiles at the gym, heading straight for the women's changing rooms, which I find, thankfully, empty. I slip into a cubicle, lock the door, and plop down onto the cubicle bench. After a moment of welcome silence, I pull my gym bag onto my lap, unzip it, and retrieve its precious cargo. I take a breath and shuffle into a more comfortable position, then flip the tiny cassette over onto the B side, slide the headphones on, and press PLAY.

31

The Tape

PART 3

Before we discuss the future—and what it holds for us—I want you to be in full possession of the facts. The body count, if you will.

Bobby started this story. He jumped.

Then Lucy had to go.

Then Alison. And Gianna.

Gianna was the easiest. Her family accepted the version of events presented to them. Their daughter was like that, you see: hard to manage. It was only a matter of time, they concluded, before something like that happened. And accidents do happen. Losing friends can be hard. But I digress.

The point is, if one does one's homework, people can disappear with surprising ease. It is possible to briefly come into contact with someone and make them slip out of the everyday flow of life. Subtly, ambiguously, conveniently. Gone.

Not *your* chosen technique for ending a life, I know, Harriet. And while I have never tried your fire-and-brimstone approach, I can see its warm allure. Forgive me if I am being facetious.

My point is, if ending a life is unavoidable, it is usually best to be ambiguous about it. Better *not* to burn out than to fade away.

I am getting old, Harriet, and the truth is I cannot continue to do things as I have in the past. I cannot contain all of this indefinitely; I alone cannot hold this family together. And that is where you come in. I must share what I know, pass on the baton. These are the names, the places, the dates.

It seems only fair, given I know the details of yours, that you should know these. Quid pro quo, as they say. Do as you wish with the information, but know the consequences.

I expect you'll want to get a pen.

Lucy Probus, 2002.

Alison Montgomery, 2003.

Gianna Scaccia, 2004.

Aliza Masri, 2020.

Melissa Brown, 2021.

I thought for a period of time that the urge had passed. That it was over and I would not need to intercede in matters again. But it came back—the need, the necessity to correct the errors of others.

These are the facts and this is your area, Harriet Reed. Do your best. Use that sharp mind of yours, but move with care, because I think you know how this all goes if you make the wrong move.

You are not the first person I have divulged these secrets to, but you could be the first person to survive the knowledge. I have faith in you, at least.

32

Cat 'n' Mouse

I jab the PAUSE button and scramble in my gym bag for a pen, settling instead for my iPhone Notes. I rewind the tape, then, phone resting on knee, I hit PLAY.

Once the final name is spoken, I click off the recording and look at my list.

Lucy Probus—2002
Alison Montgomery—2003
Gianna Scaccia—2004
Aliza Masri—2020
Melissa Brown—2021

Five names. Five women.
A gap of sixteen years between the two sprees. Two of the

deaths are recent. I shiver as I look at the final date. I met Edward around the time of Melissa Brown's death. I can't help but wonder if Robert gave her a tape too.

I notice a new name wedged between Lucy and Gianna, one I have not heard before. Alison Montgomery. Robert hasn't mentioned her until now.

There's a soft rap on the changing room door and I jerk up, sending my iPhone clattering across the floor.

"Sorry," an apologetic voice comes from beyond the cubicle. "Just wondering if you're nearly done in there?"

Shit.

I notice the bustle now coming from the changing room. I hadn't registered it till now, but the lunchtime rush has begun. "Um, yeah, yeah, sorry, one minute." I quickly shove everything back into my bag, iPhone slightly wet and stinking of chlorine. I'm just about to pull open the door when it dawns on me that I've come into a changing room and done nothing. I can't just leave the gym. If anyone was following me, it would almost certainly raise suspicions if I never even made it out of the changing area.

I dump my bag back on the seat, strip off, and slip on my bathing suit.

Outside the cubicle I find a woman in her late forties, patience waning, with a towel wrapped tight around her. Behind her a full changing room, bodies in various stages of undress. I find a free combination locker, store my bag securely, and head to the pool.

On the subway ride home, hair now suitably damp and redolent of swimming pool, I google Gianna Scaccia and find what I expected to, what Robert has already described. Death by accidental overdose. I stare at her beautiful face, her eyes alive with possibility, her caramel skin and tumbling curls.

But as I tap through the article, something unexpected jumps out at me, stopping me dead in my tracks. I reread the paragraph to be sure I haven't misunderstood.

"It's important to understand," Marion Scaccia, 58, Gianna's mother, tells us, "that while someone with an addiction might appear to have things under control, relapses can be triggered by anything. Gianna was going through a lot. The loss of a close friend is always hard, but in the case of suicide doubly so. I think she was having trouble processing it. The fact that Gianna hadn't seen Alison's suicide coming, at all, hadn't noticed her friend's troubles, plagued her. After all, there was no outward explanation for why Alison did what she did. My daughter blamed herself for not seeing the storm cloud coming. And she turned to substances to lighten her pain."

I sit bolt-upright in my subway seat. Alison Montgomery, the second girl on Robert's list, was Gianna's close friend.

Alison can't have committed suicide, though. She wouldn't be on Robert's list if she had. Gianna must have worked out what happened to Alison, that the Holbecks were involved, and she must have let them know.

I type Alison Montgomery's name into my search engine.

Death of MIT Undergraduate Alison Montgomery Highlights the Abnormally High Suicide Rates at the University

Legal questions are being asked about the extent to which educational institutions can be held responsible for the deaths of their students after Alison Montgomery, 21, was unexpectedly found dead in her dormitory last week. Alison becomes another student in a long list who have committed suicide at the institution since the 1990s. Alison, in her final year of study majoring in data, systems, and society at Massachusetts Institute of Technology, was described as "a warmhearted and brilliant young woman." Her death has come as a shock to many and has raised questions about why the warning signs were not picked up sooner by the university.

I look up from the article abruptly.

Edward was at MIT the years both girls died. My heart thunders in my chest as his proximity to Alison hits home. My mouth is suddenly dry. *Oh God.* Edward must have known both Alison and Gianna. Did he date them? Did Robert consider Alison a distraction and Gianna a complication?

I lean forward, head on hands to keep from fainting, as I try to push the thought away, but it will not go. Edward must have known. He must have suspected something strange was going on. Is that why the rift opened between him and his family? And if so, why in God's name are we cozying up to them now?

Edward told me he had a girlfriend at MIT, but that they broke up after the first year. I feel like I'm going to be sick as the subway car rattles into the next station and I bolt for the door, managing to reach the nearest platform bench before a wave of dizziness drains the blood from me and my vision blurs.

I try not to think of the fact that I'm almost twelve weeks' pregnant, and how totally trapped I am in my situation. I take a deep slug of water from my gym bottle and force myself to stay calm, to think. How could I get so far into all this without noticing what must have been right in front of me? Edward did not want me to meet his family, and since I have, he has been on guard to make sure no one oversteps a mark. I pushed to meet them. He could have, *should* have, told me if he knew any of this, but then could he really know? I push my cold hands into my burning cheeks and try to calm down.

First of all, Edward didn't really know Lucy Probus; Lucy was Bobby's girlfriend. Edward was living back at The Hydes when Bobby was attending Columbia; he was just a teenager. He wouldn't have had anything to do with Lucy. He might not even have been aware that she went missing.

The simple truth is, Edward must have been seeing Alison, and Robert didn't like it. He broke up with her at the family's behest and as her exams approached Alison took her own life. And as far as Edward knew, Gianna, her wild and guilt-ridden best friend, overdosed shortly after. It's not as if Edward would have had a tape to explain all of this. Alison's and Gianna's deaths were made to look innocent. And life can be hard for some people—tragedy, while awful, is rarely more than that.

As my faintness subsides, I rise, carefully, and board the next train as it pulls in.

Finding a seat, I turn my attention to the two most recent women on Robert's list: Aliza Masri and Melissa Brown. If I can work out their connection to the Holbecks, things might come fully into focus.

Wikipedia tells me Aliza Masri is a visual artist.

Born in Lebanon to an American mother and a Lebanese-Syrian father, Aliza attended international school in Beirut before moving back to the US with her mother. Aliza's work has appeared in notable galleries across Europe and the US.

Masri slipped into notoriety in late 2019 when it was alleged, after controversial comments made on social media, that she may have supported the contentious movement the FFI, who are known to have strong international links to Hezbollah.

As of January 2020, Masri's exact whereabouts are unknown, though it is thought the artist may now be residing in her native Lebanon.

I search for her name in conjunction with the Holbecks and my phone screen fills with pictures.

My breath catches at what I see.

Matilda looks back at me, from Instagram, beaming beside Aliza, her thick red curls and pale skin unmistakable. A photograph of the pair attending a gallery opening of Aliza's work. Matilda looks beautiful, and so happy, her free hand tenderly placed on the small of Masri's back in a gesture I recognize as entirely Holbeckian.

Aliza and Matilda were together. I look at the two of them, in love, caught in the amber of the moment. It's undeniable—the happiness, the hope, in their eyes. So much ahead of them, and yet somehow it—their relationship—went wrong.

I pull my phone closer and zoom in on Matilda's features, her intelligent green eyes, the soft curl of her lips. Could she have killed Aliza? Could she be capable of that? Did she kill them all? But there would be no reason for her to kill Lucy, Alison, or Gianna. Besides, she wasn't older than sixteen when Lucy disappeared; younger than Edward.

The tape is trying to tell me something, but it's not yet clear exactly what. I kick myself for not being able to piece it together. Unless, perhaps, the next name on the list might be connected to either Oliver or Stuart. Could each sibling have lost someone they cared about?

I google *Melissa Brown, 2021,* but the only online result is for a LinkedIn account. No social media, nothing. The account tells me she has been a personal assistant to the CEO of Lefroy Henshaw since 2014. A sliver of hope glimmers as I quickly bring up the Lefroy Henshaw website. There's always a chance she could still be alive.

Lefroy Henshaw is a hedge fund firm. I read the "About Us" section until my hope curdles in my veins. Lefroy Henshaw is part of the Laurence Group. It's owned by the Holbeck family; Stuart is listed as its CEO.

Melissa Brown was Stuart Holbeck's personal assistant, and I'm guessing, being on Robert's list, she isn't still alive.

I look at Melissa's photograph on their website—her soft, friendly features a far cry from Lila's ethereal beauty—and I wonder if she and Stuart might have been having an affair. All the other women on Robert's list got too close to his children. And while Melissa is clearly not a catwalk model like Lila, there is a soft, gentle beauty to her. She might have made Stuart happy, made him laugh, understood him. But then I think of the way Lila spoke about Stuart and I'm not so sure he didn't have someone to do that already. Perhaps Melissa simply saw too much, knew too much?

Robert said on the tape that she died in 2021, but she hasn't been removed from the Lefroy Henshaw website.

The train rattles into my station. I grab everything and disembark.

Up on street level, I decide to cut to the chase and call up Lefroy Henshaw and just ask if she still works there.

After eight minutes I am plucked off the automated system by a friendly voice.

"Hi there, sorry, you're calling about Mel, right?"

"Um, yes. Melissa Brown. I'm trying to track her down. Is she still working there?"

"Technically, yes. But she doesn't work from the office anymore. She's satellite. Can I ask who's calling?"

My mind scrambles for a story and bizarrely lands on, "Yeah, sure, I'm calling from her dentist's office. We can't seem to track her down. We have an unpaid invoice for . . . two hundred and seventy dollars that I need to get paid. She has Lefroy Henshaw down as her primary address for some reason."

The other end of the line is silent for a second. "That's weird. Really? I can email her?"

"Yeah, I've tried emailing, but nothing," I add quickly.

"How odd. She's usually super on it. Maybe you're going to junk. I'll email now from here. She should get that."

That's interesting, I think. She must still be answering emails. In which case I definitely don't need this call flagged to whoever is answering them.

"Okay," I reply, "that'd be fantastic. Actually, why don't I forward you her bill and you can pass that on to her directly too?"

The voice on the end of the line hesitates, clearly not keen on being dragged into a credit control situation. "Me? Um, actually, you know what, why don't I just give you her postal address. What's your office name again?"

"Morningside Dental," I answer, using the name of a dentist I used shortly after moving to New York.

I hear the tap-tap of a Google search and a grunt of acknowledgment.

"Oh yeah, I see you, perfect. I'll give you the address I have listed for her. That's the best I can do, I'm afraid."

"That'd be great, thanks," I affirm, with the appropriate level of enthusiasm that I assume a dental receptionist might have for this offer.

As I pass a bodega, I grab a chained-up pen and carefully scrawl Melissa's address and phone number onto the back of my cold hand.

33

Melissa

Edward has left for work before I'm up the next morning.

I lie in the warmth of the sheets a little longer, pushing my life and the facts of it away for another few more precious minutes before slipping a hand beneath my T-shirt and noticing the gathering swell of my tummy there. Twelve weeks tomorrow.

I force myself from the bed. I have one day left to find the connection among the women on Robert's list and to work out how I survive what's coming next.

The address and phone number written on my hand are long gone, safely stored on my phone. The phone number I tried before Edward returned last night was out of service, as I predicted it might be, but I still have the address.

I shove everything I need into my handbag, grab a baseball

cap, and call down to the doorman for a taxi. I figure I'll be harder to follow in a car.

As the taxi slips out of the underground pickup zone, I lower the peak of my cap and scan the sidewalk outside the building; the street is clear. I lower my gaze as we roll away and I don't look up or behind until we clear a full block.

Standing in front of Melissa Brown's apartment building in the winter sun, a knot of nerves forms as I realize the reality of following through with my plan to see if she's there, alive and well, or if she's not.

I stare up at the building, its windows glinting in the morning light, before I head along the landscaped garden path to the glazed front door and gingerly press her buzzer. I wait with the warmth of the sun on the back of my neck, the sound of birdsong reaching me from a small park across the street. I press again, almost resigned to the fact I won't get an answer, when the speaker crackles to life.

"Yep, hello. What's up?"

My heart leaps into my throat and my mind goes completely blank. "Um," I stumble. "Hi, is that Melissa?"

The voice hesitates. "What? Who?"

"Melissa?" I know I'm playing a dangerous game here, because (a) if this *is* Melissa, then who the hell am I supposed to be? And (b) if this *isn't* Melissa, then who the hell is it?

"No, I'm not Melissa. I'm Nina. Who's Melissa?" she asks with annoyance.

It's a curveball question. I definitely have the correct buzzer number so I leave the question hanging a second longer. I hear the sound of a muffled conversation, then:

"Oh shit. Sorry, sorry. Yeah, Mel's not here. Actually, you know what, I'm coming down. Wait there." The intercom cuts out and I wonder if I should run.

I rack my brains for an answer as to who I am when Nina inevitably asks again, but my musings are cut short by the arrival of a bouncy, pastel-crop-top-wearing twenty-year-old.

"Hey, man. Sorry, who are you again?" she asks with an easy affability.

"I'm, just, I'm a friend of Mel's." She raises an eyebrow at my accent. "From England," I add.

"Oh, okay. So you're not on the board, right?"

"The board?"

"The residents' board?"

"Er, no. Why—"

"Oh, okay. That's cool. Yeah, so," the girl continues, relaxing her weight against the doorframe, "Mel's been subletting to us, which we thought was fine but, well, she's been leasing to Karen actually, but we're all paying. Anyway, point is, Mel's not here. She doesn't *live* live here right now. Sorry, man. I think Karen might have her cell, though, if you want it? Did you come all the way from England to see her?" she asks.

"No. No, I didn't. Listen, odd question, but," I push on, "did Mel's place come fully furnished? Are all her things still in there?"

"Like her books and stuff? Yeah. Why? We moved them into the small room, though. Like, they're safe and everything, so—"

"No, it's fine. I just wasn't sure. Sorry to bother you. I didn't know she was away. I'll call her. I have her cell already. Thanks."

"Oh, okay. Cool. So, we're fine?" she asks, more concerned about how she will come out of this interaction than with who or what I might be.

"Yeah, you're fine," I tell her. She smiles and shrugs, then disappears back into the building.

I wander back toward the park, a sinking feeling dragging me down to the truth of what I just witnessed. This is what Robert meant by people "fading away." Melissa is gone, but the cogs of her life are still turning. Someone is keeping it all going, for now—subletting her apartment, paying her taxes, and responding to emails when necessary. Melissa has become a ghost.

I am now as sure as I can be that every woman on Robert's list is dead: Bobby's girlfriend, Edward's girlfriend, Matilda's girlfriend, Stuart's assistant, and a girl who got caught in the crossfire.

I feel anger fizz inside me at the fact I cannot untangle the knot Robert has presented me with. There is really nothing more I can do but go to The Hydes and face whatever he has laid in store for me.

I plonk myself down on a bench in the park opposite Melissa's old apartment and let my eyes play over the treetops as the breeze sways them. And then it hits me. Oliver is the only Holbeck not to have lost someone. Fiona is alive and well. They are happily married with kids and, now that I think about it, Oliver is the one who took over the company after both Bobby and Edward stepped aside. He seems to have come out of it all a lot better than the rest—could he be the key to this in some way?

Time is nearly up, and I'm almost out of avenues to explore. There is a reason Robert is telling me all this. He thinks I can piece it together, but I wonder if I can—if there is enough; if *I* am enough.

I place a hand on my abdomen as I wonder if the life growing inside me might be any kind of protection against Robert and his family. I can't assume being pregnant grants me immunity, although he has given me his word that I am safe for now because he needs me to do something.

If I'm really going to The Hydes tomorrow, and going in blind, then I'm going to need more protection than his word.

I pull my phone from my bag, scroll through my contacts, and press DIAL before I can talk myself out of it. I might be stretching my luck by bringing things this worryingly close to home. The phone rings four times before he answers.

"Hi, Deonte, it's Harriet. You free to talk?"

"Ah, it's Ms. Reed. Yes, you caught me at a good time. Out walking the dog. What can I do for you, ma'am?"

"Okay, plot holes. You remember the girl with the recording, the taped confession?"

"Sure do," he singsongs, happy to dive back in.

"So, it turns out she's got a secret of her own and the guy who gave her the tape knows it."

"Ooo, juicy. She killed someone too?"

"She did," I say.

"But hers was accidental, right?"

I hesitate. "No, no, she straight-up killed someone. She's occupying a . . . gray area."

He takes a moment to consider this twist, and I can't help but wonder if he senses something off with me. If he can read me like my own open book. "Ha. Okay, interesting. So, he's confessed his crimes but she can't report it 'cause he's got something over her. Blackmail kinda thing."

"Correct. And he wants her to meet him, to come to his home, to be with his family. He says he's chosen to confide in her because of what she did, and he needs her to do him a favor," I explain.

"Oh, okay. He's gonna ask her to kill someone for him?"

I pull up short, my eyes immediately focusing on the park around me again.

Robert wants me to kill for him.

My mind hadn't gone there, but now that Deonte has articulated it, that seems entirely probable. I suppose my only USP, in his eyes, could be the fact that I've killed a person. I recall Robert saying he wanted to pass on the family baton. Is that what he meant?

I realize I've left Deonte hanging. "Um, yeah, it could be that. I haven't entirely decoded what the favor is yet, but possibly," I manage with what I hope sounds like creative reticence.

"Um," he muses, "but we're still rooting for her? She's still the hero, right?"

"I think so," I answer, tentatively, unsure anymore if we're speaking about a plot or my actual life.

"Well, if she goes to meet him, to hear out this request, she needs to leave a trail. And she needs this guy to know she's left one, too. He's got to know it won't be easy to get rid of her without drawing a lot of focus. She's copied that confession tape, right?"

I grimace into the receiver. "No. But I'm not sure she would. The tape has her crime on it too."

Deonte laughs. "That a joke? This some kind of historical drama? She can just edit her crime out. She's only gotta cut out that one bit, and then carry on, right? Easy. Done. Confession gone."

"Sure, but she can't erase the fact that the guy who gave her the tape knows. If his crimes come to light, he'll drag her down with him."

"Well, then, I guess she's got two choices. She does what he asks her to do and hopes it ends at that, or—"

"Or?" I nudge.

"Or she kills the tape maker and hands in the edited tape to the cops. If she's killed someone before, she should be okay, right? In a way it's a kind of self-defense."

"Is it?" I ask, incredulous. "What, legally?"

"Legally? Hell no! That's first-degree murder right there. I meant in the book; in the story it seems like self-defense. We'd buy it as necessary, right—poetic justice? But, ha, no, *legally* it's premeditated murder. We'd be talking life without parole."

I swallow hard, my mouth so dry again. "Yeah, no, I thought so, just the way you said it was . . . weird."

"But here's the thing with your stories, Harriet. Morally, it's different. I don't know, your characters are likable, we side with them; that's gold dust. People can get away with almost anything if they're likable."

"Thanks, Deonte. God, I hope you're right."

After I hang up, I sit in silence and wonder to what degree Deonte was aware of the levels of that phone conversation. And to what degree I may have legally screwed myself if anything was to happen over Christmas. That said, I am certainly starting to leave a trail.

34

Leaving a Trail

THURSDAY, DECEMBER 22

Back at the apartment I pull some stationery from a drawer, grab a pen, and begin to hand-write, for the first time in God knows how many years, an actual letter.

The clock on my desk reads four fifty-six when I lay them out before me: three thick card envelopes inlaid with my initials, my cursive clearly spelling out the names and addresses. Former NYPD officer Deonte Hughley; Dermot Jones, my solicitor back in London; and my agent, Louisa.

I keep my letter to Louisa fun and incidental, and it would only be on a second reading, in a certain set of circumstances, that anything might pop out to her. I tell her about my pregnancy, my excitement about the future and our child. And then, buried deep within the text, I fleetingly mention the tragedy of Bobby, and of Alison Montgomery, Edward's first girlfriend. And I am confident that if anything was to happen to me, she would be perfectly capable of putting two and two together.

If Robert wants to kill me, he had better make sure it doesn't look like a suicide.

Inside the envelope to my solicitor, I place another carefully sealed envelope. On the front is an instruction to only open it in the event of my death. In the cover note I apologize for the dramatics but respectfully ask that they carry out my request.

Inside is a written account of the events of the day my parents died—my own confession. And in a separate letter inside the sealed envelope, I put a written account of Robert's confession, his list of names, adding my own to the end.

My letter to Deonte is simpler and fits on a small note card.

Thank you for your wise words and help, Deonte. You are a lifesaver. I don't know where I'd be without you.

Also, I forgot to mention when we last spoke that I am getting married next year. Into a rich and powerful family. Guess I'd better watch out! I don't think you ever got a chance to meet Edward Holbeck, my fiancé, but I would love it if you and your wife Regan would be able to make it to our wedding when that happens. It would be great to have some friendly faces on my side of the congregation— I've never been over-subscribed in the family department.

I'm sure the similarities between my life and the new book won't have passed you by—life imitating art. But let's hope not too much so, given everything we discussed.

As a wise man once told me: always leave a trail.

Speak soon,
Harriet x

I drop them in the mailbox across the street. They won't make the Christmas post, but the letters will arrive eventually, and the threat of that is all I need.

Back in the apartment, step one complete, I open a new email and address it to my publisher, Grenville Sinclair. In a flurry of keyboard taps, I outline the changes I intend to make to my manuscript in my next round of edits.

It will be the same story I have told Deonte and the story I am living through now. A story where an author finds herself trapped when her father-in-law gives her a tape, the contents of which force her into a terrifying and complicated position. I fire off my email and delete my SENT folder. The trail Deonte told me to lay is laid. Robert will not find it easy to make me disappear.

I retrieve the tape player from my gym bag, set up my iPhone beside it, and when it's rewound, press PLAY and start to record it on my iPhone. I leave the recording to do its thing while I head to the bedroom to arrange one last thing.

I don't have a gun, and a knife is too premeditated a weapon to take. I need something that isn't a weapon but can be used as one. On a shelf in the bedroom, I find what I'm looking for: the palm-sized glass paperweight I won as a secondary school prize for writing. A good-luck charm, a talisman. Inside its translucent heft is a smoky swirl of lilac, a ghost of a color caught in tiny bubbles. This will do.

I know from hours of research that the weakest point of the skull is the pterion, the area just behind the temple. The bone is the thinnest here, where three sections of skull meet, and a solid blow can easily rupture the meningeal artery hidden just beneath. I remember, after I unearthed that horrifying little fact, I went straight out and bought myself a cycle helmet.

Back in the bedroom, I tuck the glass ball neatly inside a rolled-up pair of socks and bury it deep in my suitcase. It might not be a loaded gun, but it's all I've got. I can explain away my paperweight as an old Christmas gift with sentimental value if ever questioned on it.

The rattle of keys in the apartment door snaps my eyes to the bedside clock. It's six o'clock and Edward's home.

"Harry?"

I close the lid on my case, flick the clasps, and spin the combination lock, heaving it up to standing. Packed. Ready. "Just coming," I holler back. "One second."

He's in the kitchen with a smile on his face when I find him. He raises both hands, a bottle of Bollinger champagne in one, a gift bag in the other. His grin broadens and I know what it means.

"It's done. Signed," he cheers, pulling me into a tight bear hug.

"Oh my God, Ed."

"Two point eight," Edward says meaningfully.

I stare at him for a moment, the number too abstract to grasp. "Two point eight?" I ask.

His eyes have an almost electric charge. Billion; he means billion. My stomach clenches at a number that doesn't sound quite right, quite healthy.

"Two point eight billion." I mumble the words, their meaning gone. I set down the two glasses in my hands carefully. If there was ever a time to make an exception to my no drinking rule, this might be the time.

Edward laughs but I do not. He carefully removes the foil on the bottle, twists the wires, and pops the cork. Foam rises.

The numbers terrify me. Like a sudden timer set on my life. Like a price on my head. The numbers are too high. Fate, karma— whatever—will not allow it.

I swallow hard and try to think of the right thing to say as he pours for us.

I try to focus on Edward, how happy he is. I try to remember who we are, who I am, why we are doing any of this. I close my eyes and bury my face in his chest. There he is—his smell, his touch, the sound of his heart. I breathe in the scent of the man I met at the Natural History Museum a year-and-change ago, the man I have laughed and cried with, who has been beside me ever since. I let my body relax into him.

He's still here; I just need to focus on him.

He pulls back with a smile, a thought occurring. He lifts the thin rope handles of the gift bag and hands it to me.

"It's a lot to take in, I know. Give it a minute. But, in the meantime, I wanted to get you a thing," he says with a grin. I feel my cheeks flush hot as I take the gift and carefully unwrap its delicate tissue paper. The bag is discreet but the tissue sticker reads BALMAIN, and when I unfurl the folded article within and hold it up against myself, I see it is a dress. But nicer than any dress I have ever worn. The weight of its fabric is heavy in my hands. It's beautiful, something from another world, another life—black bouclé, thick gold embossed buttons, shoulder pads, the tailoring immaculate. A Balmain blazer dress. I have never owned anything like it. It's a work of art. I catch my reflection in the kitchen window, the dress pressed to me.

"It should fit perfectly. I wanted to get you something to wear for Christmas. Holbeck Christmases can be dressy," he adds with a smirk, downing his glass.

"I'll go try—" I nod toward the bedroom, grateful for the excuse to take a moment to process.

In the bedroom I sit in silence and try to calm myself. Everything is moving too fast, the world around me changing at breakneck speed. I try to order my thoughts, to keep my mind on why I am doing any of this. To be with Edward. To have a family. I let my hand linger on my swelling bump and pull myself together.

In the large bedroom mirror, I step carefully into the dress, its lining cool against my skin. I need to get back to Edward; I've taken way too long. I untie my hair and shake it out, and when I take in the full picture I have to stifle a giggle. I look like someone else; I look amazing. Like a 1990s CEO, or a coffee-commercial singleton, an Italian *Vogue* editorial. A late-twentieth-century idea of what "having it all" might look like. Who'd have thought? Shoulder pads really do make you look thinner and feel more powerful . . .

I pull on a pair of heels and stand back.

"I'm ready," I call out to Edward, but the apartment is silent. I wait a moment before calling again. "Ed?"

Nothing.

Something is not right; I feel it instantly. "Ed, is everything okay?" I call again, moving to the doorway.

I strain my ears but there's nothing but the rumble of New York beyond our walls. The bathroom door remains ajar, as do all the others along the hallway. I swallow, softly, a lump having formed in my throat. Something has changed in the air.

I duck back into the bedroom instinctively, certain there is someone else in the apartment. I dash to my discarded pile of clothes to find my phone. And it's then that the crashing realization hits me. My phone isn't here; it's recording Robert's tape out loud in my office. But why would Edward be in my office?

"Ed?" I yell through the apartment. I hear the sound of movement from my office and I bolt from the bedroom, barreling down the hallway, my heels snagging on the carpet as I fly into the room using the doorframe for leverage. Edward looks up at me, the bright-red headphones now on his ears, the tape cassette out of the player and in his hand. He gives me a confused smile before sliding off the headphones.

"What is this?" he asks simply.

"Um," I flounder, my breath snagging in my throat. Before I can speak, he gives a low whistle and looks me up and down.

"Wow. You look insanely hot," he says plainly, his eyes surveying my body.

"Er, thanks, yeah, it's a good fit." I fumble for an understanding of the situation. "You okay? You good?" I ask with a little too much vigor.

I don't know how else to find out how much he's listened to. If he's heard his father's voice, why is he acting like this? Why is he acting so normal?

I point to the tape player in his lap. "Did you . . . ?"

"Listen? Yeah," he says happily. "Well, I tried to, but this side is blank, right? Was there supposed to be something on it?"

"What?" I say, the blood draining from me. "Blank?"

Then it hits me. Oh my God, I must have accidentally nudged

the RECORD button when I pressed PLAY. A flood of relief bursts through me; Edward heard nothing. I sink down onto the carpet with a groan, half grateful, half gut-punched that I have lost all recorded proof of Robert Holbeck's confession. The most important piece of advice Deonte gave to me, to copy the recording, and somehow I managed to fuck it up with my stupid bloated pregnant fingers.

"You okay, honey?" Edward asks, crouching down in front of me. "I don't want to be that guy, but you probably shouldn't be running around at this point, you know? At least probably not in heels," he adds carefully. "Was there something important on the tape?" he asks when I don't respond.

I straighten up and let out a sigh that could pass for many things. "No. No, it's fine. It was just research," I say, rubbing my face as if somehow I could rub the truth of my words into existence.

He leans in and kisses my forehead. "Ah, annoying. Sorry, honey. That sucks. Still, at least it was just research, right? Love this retro tech, though. Very analog, very nineties. Dad would love it. Heck, *I* love it," he chuckles, reaching back to the chair to grab it. "Is this for the book research too?"

A shiver runs up my spine at the meta nature of the conversation we are now having.

"Er, yeah," I answer. "It's a split timeline. The next book. Present day and the nineties. Lots of fun period stuff in there." I smile, gently taking the Olympus recorder back from him. "I just need to get the edits back and have a reshuffle before I start talking about it."

As I look down at the cassette window of the recorder in my hands, I suddenly realize that all might not be lost. Only one side will be wiped. While Side A is lost, Side B should be untouched.

"Sounds great. Can't wait to read it," he tells me, getting to his feet and offering me a hand up. I rise like a hobbled Bambi.

I watch Edward's back as he leads me through to the kitchen, and our champagne, then I steal another fleeting look down at the Olympus in my hands. A question reemerges. Why was Edward in my office in the first place? And a doubt slowly forms. Did I accidentally wipe the tape, or did he?

When I look back up, he's looking directly at me.

35

Road Trip

FRIDAY, DECEMBER 23

Bags packed and ready to go in the trunk of the car beneath Mount Sinai Hospital, we wait on the bleach-scented ward for our names to be called.

I try to think only one step ahead, of seeing the face of my baby, of finding out if I have a daughter or a son. My due date is July 7 next year. Hard to process that I have been pregnant for three months already without anyone but us knowing. I try not to speculate on what will come after that. I do not want the baby to feel my fear.

Edward looks up from his phone as a couple exits the scanning room. I watch his profile and wonder how long he was alone with that tape player in my office. Ten minutes? Fifteen? Twenty? I sat paralyzed by rumination in our bedroom for long enough.

I checked the recording I tried to make on my iPhone later that night, and it turns out it was my fault; I did accidentally wipe one side of the tape. There was an hour-long recording of an empty office on my iPhone with only five minutes of Edward and I talking at the end.

But I can't prize my thoughts from the image of the microcassette out of the player and in Edward's hand. He had enough time to turn it and listen to what was on the other side. There's no way I can be sure he didn't hear his father's voice.

A nurse rounds the corner and gives us a smile that asks if we're ready.

Moments later in the darkness of the sonography room, we are asked if we want to know the sex of our child from my blood results, and as the nurse tells us, something beautiful bursts open inside me.

The drive to The Hydes is long. After two hours of freeway and an hour of forest-flanked highway, we stop at a local gas station. It's the only sign of civilization we've seen for miles and it looks unstaffed. Edward jumps out to fill us up and I catch sight of an attendant in the cramped kiosk across the forecourt.

The GPS says we have another forty-five minutes before we arrive at The Hydes, and I still haven't had a chance to listen to the rest of the tape. I plunge a hand into my bag in the footwell and make sure it's still there, the dry foam of the headphones brushing reassuringly against my wrist. The tape is stored in a separate zip pocket. I feel safer with the two apart. The rest of Side B is waiting for me, and the sooner I can listen the better. I haven't had a second away from Edward since last night, though.

I look out at the gas station hoping for signs of a restroom. I could listen to it now, lock myself away in a grotty toilet for as long as I need and refuse to come out. But even as I imagine it, I know it's a terrible idea. What would Edward think? I watch as he ambles back to the car and slips in beside me, blissfully unaware of the thoughts and fears racing through me. He's certainly not acting as if he heard anything on the tape. He would have said something, surely, and we certainly wouldn't be on our way to his childhood home to meet his family if he'd heard what was on it.

He restarts the engine, handing me a chilled bottle of water and a gas station snack with a smile. "This'll keep you going," he says, and I think how great a husband he's going to be; a great father, if we ever get that far.

We roll out of the station and I let my gaze skim the landscape rushing past, mile after mile of thickly packed forest still standing between us and them.

As we drive, Edward tells me more about The Hydes and I try to picture it.

"John Livingston Holbeck bought the land back in 1886, but the house wasn't there then. He demolished the original building, razed it to the ground and rebuilt something bigger, grander. Something with more history."

"He built something with more *history*? What the hell does that mean? How would a new building have more history?" I interject, my European sensibilities ruffled.

"Because it wasn't a new building. He bought a stone mansion from somewhere in the hills outside Budapest. A castle. He had it taken apart and shipped over here to the US. They rebuilt it, stone by stone, and it became The Hydes. Alma, John's wife, had remarked on it from a carriage on their honeymoon. The building had fallen into disrepair, so the story goes, and it had made her sad."

"It made her sad so he rescued it, brought it home to America? Like a dog at the pound?"

Edward chuckles. "Yeah, I guess. But you have to remember, J.L. basically owned logistics back then, so it was nothing to him to move things. To build. If you wanted to get anything in the US from A to B, you had to pay John Livingston Holbeck's companies to do it for you. So he could cover a lot of ground on a whim."

I nod, conceding the point. He had a monopoly, or close to one. Back then you had no choice but to make J. L. Holbeck richer.

"So," Edward continues, "he shipped the house over, bricks and all, and had it reconstructed here. It was an enormous project, took them two years to finish. He brought over Hungarian stonemasons, landscapers, set up a kind of village of workers. He wanted it to be perfect for Alma."

"Romantic," I mutter under my breath, because if I'm honest I have to wonder whether Alma really did want a giant stone house erected in the middle of nowhere, miles from anyone she knew. Then again, perhaps she did, and maybe I'm being unfair.

"I can't wait for you to see the place," he says, his eyes on the road. "You know, you can get used to things, having things, and it's only when you show other people that you see them again. With fresh eyes."

The blue arrow on the satnav glides on, unstoppable; we're nearly there. Nerves flutter inside me like something trapped.

The trees on one side of us begin to recede from the road and are suddenly overtaken by a high and ominous wall. The perimeter of the vast Holbeck property, its stone topped with razor wire, like a federal complex, a fortress. So much wealth within its walls, I imagine it probably warrants such fortifications.

Edward clicks on the car's hazard lights, even though we are the only car on the road, and we begin to slow.

We idle in front of an enormous set of wrought-iron gates, their Hieronymus Bosch tangle of vines and creatures shuddering open to reveal a long evergreen-lined driveway beyond. Edward's hand slips into mine and squeezes.

"It's okay to be nervous," he tells me. "I'm nervous too." We begin our steady crawl up the winding drive and I watch in the rearview as the twelve-foot-high gates swing firmly shut behind us.

As we proceed along the winding driveway, the sheer size of the estate becomes apparent. The house is still nowhere to be seen but the road spools on with no sign of ending. After a while the trees flanking us loosen to reveal the rolling parkland beyond.

I pick out the slow-moving forms of deer, their tawny hides coming into view as they raise their heads from the grass.

Then I catch sight of it, in the distance, rising from the landscape. The size of it is breathtaking.

Immaculate ornamental gardens rise up to meet its wide stone steps and there, the hulk of the building crouches, like a creature lying in wait. Four floors, glinting window upon window all the way up to the spire-like crenellations that top each of its four wings. It is monstrous and overwhelming in its scope.

Another tunnel of trees swallows us and my view is blocked once more as I feel our speed creep up. When we break through into the open again, I catch sight of a massive maze, growing in the center of the lawns that lead up to the house. Beyond it a long ornamental fountain flows right up to the stairs leading up to the house.

I marvel at the money it must have cost J. L. Holbeck to create this place—the extent of it, the vision required to even conceive of the idea, as if somehow with enough money reality can become malleable.

"Jesus," I say with a sharp intake of breath, and I feel Edward's eyes on me, concern tangibly pulsing from him. He's worried I don't like it, that it's too much, but I cannot pull my eyes from the building as we glide toward it. Pale, weatherworn marble statues stand sentinel on the edges of the lawn running all the way up to The Hydes, their plinths staggered at intervals, their bodies arranged in classical poses like so many frozen people. And above them the quiet darkness of the building rises up to a castellated summit, its darkly balustraded peaks popping starkly against the cloudy winter sky.

"It's so big," is all I manage as the car bends around to the front of the building, the flutter inside me morphing into dread. Robert is in there; they all are.

The Hydes is a foxhole and I am a rabbit. A stupid, pregnant rabbit.

Edward cuts the engine and turns in his seat to look at me.

"You okay? You look a little . . ."

I decide to be as honest as I can. "I'm fucking terrified, Ed," I huff out.

He gives my hand a quick kiss.

"You are amazing and I love you. They love you. Look at me. This will be fun; Christmas will be fun." I must look unconvinced because he chases it up with more. "We can go home. Right now. If that's what you want?"

I take in his concern. The idea alone is more than I dare to allow myself to indulge in. I can leave this place, but I can't stop what's going to happen from happening.

"No, it's fine. I'm just—"

"You don't need to impress anyone. Everyone likes you. Matilda, Mom, Ollie, everyone. Even Dad, and he's a tough nut. And you don't need to worry about what they'll think of the pregnancy. They'll love it, trust me. They will *love* it."

"That's kind of what I'm worried about, Ed. I'm not sure I want them to be too into it. I'm not sure I want them to be too into *anything*."

He nods, taking in my words. "I see. Yeah. Stealing the first-born. Hexes, et cetera. Could be an issue, for sure." He grins; he's joking. Nothing seems quite so bad when Edward shines his warm light of rationality on it.

He tucks a stray strand of hair behind my ear and I feel my heart rate beginning to settle. He gives me a supportive nod, then briskly unfastens his seatbelt and pops the car door.

"Okay, let's do this," he says, getting out, his energy propelling me out into the crisp December air too.

36

The Hydes

"Why is it called The Hydes?" I ask as Edward carries our bags to the front door. I've meant to ask the question so many times before, but it's only standing here on the doorstep that I realize I still don't have an answer.

"This was all forest once," Edward says, gesturing out at the parkland. "When J.L. bought it, he leveled the building the previous landowner had erected and rebuilt. It was just wild North American forest before us, before them. Hunting ground," he says, leaning past me to rap the door's heavy knocker, the slow reverb of metal-on-metal echoing within. After a few moments in the cold, he shakes his head, leans around the doorway to a nearby window, and bellows into the glass of the house, "Someone, let us in!"

I raise an eyebrow and he shrugs innocently. "They know we're here. They opened the damn gates."

I feel a smile creep across my face at the normalcy of what he just did. After everything, it's a relief to see evidence that the Holbecks are just another family, with all that that entails.

Edward sighs as he tries to recapture his train of thought. "Hunting ground, yeah. It was all forest, all hunting land. White-tailed deer, wild turkeys, waterfowl, black bears. Mitzi had a thing for bears," he says with a shake of the head. "When the house fell to her and Alfred, she filled it with Black Forest crafts. Carvings, art. Black bears, the forest. There's hardly any of it left now—Mother is a minimalist at heart—but there's the odd relic. Anyway, New York State still has some of the best hunting in the country, thousands of acres of game. So the name, The Hydes, kind of came from that, but there was a mistake. No, wait, what's it called—a . . . an orthographical error? You're a writer, you must have heard of those. Someone, somewhere, at some point, mishearing, misunderstanding a name, writing it down wrong. An auditory error. Or a conceptual error." He catches my perplexed expression and explains further. "The name was written down wrong in the deeds. It was meant to say The Hides. Like hiding. With an *i*. Because of the old hunting hides that used to pepper the property. But someone wrote it down as The Hydes, with a *y*. Like the family name. I guess they thought the family that bought the land were called Hyde."

"Like Jekyll and Hyde?"

"Ha," he scoffed. "Yeah."

"Wait, there are hunting hides here?" I interject. "Like hidden lookouts?"

"Yeah, hidden shelters in the forest, in the undergrowth, up high. Hunters would set up in them and wait to pick off game below. Like snipers."

"Are they still there?" I ask cautiously, the idea of them nestling in the forest strangely unsettling.

"What, the snipers?" he teases.

"No. The hides."

"Yeah, I guess," Edward says with a chuckle, unsure why the idea has hooked me so much. "We used to play in them as kids. They wouldn't be in great condition now, but they'd still be there."

I look to the edges of the dense woodland across the lawns. I let my thoughts slip between the gaps in the tall trees and fly up to those unseen structures deep within.

The sun breaks through the winter clouds, forcing me to look away. "So the house's name is spelled wrong," I say, returning to his story. "Couldn't J.L. have fixed that? With all the money in the world, couldn't he just have corrected the deeds?"

"No way. He loved it," Edward tells me with a grin. "The Holbecks have a weird sense of humor. J.L. had one for sure. He liked it as an origin story. He liked the reminder that no matter what you do, how much work you put in, it will always be misunderstood. There's something in there about the inadequacy of the human condition—I don't know. The human element in any enterprise will always be its sticking point. My family loves myth creation. They managed to turn a simple spelling mistake into some kind of life lesson. Hence The Hydes."

As if on cue, the front door's bolts are drawn back, its oak façade creaking open to reveal Matilda, her pale face beaming in the dim hallway.

"Well, hello, strangers. It's about time. What kept you?"

Unimpressed by the wait, Edward bends to pick up our baggage as I follow Matilda into the warm darkness of the house.

Our bags left in the hall, Matilda leads us briskly through the vast carved stone hallway. "Everyone's waiting in the sunroom," she says as I absorb the house flowing past me. The hallway opens out to an enormous stairwell, and on its opposite wall gapes a monstrous fireplace carved directly into the Hungarian stone of the building. From the staircase walls, portraits rise and disappear around the bending flights.

"The whole mob's been scratching around for tea for the past half hour," Matilda explains, turning back to us with a smile. "It fell to me to beat them off with a stick. You see, we only have two staff over the holidays, Harry."

I can't keep the ghost of a smirk from flickering across my features. "Only two? Wow," I say innocently as we turn another corridor.

"Uh-huh, so I always end up doing more than my fair share of the grunt work over the holidays. Point is, I was holding everyone off for you lovebirds. I sent tea back to keep it warm. I've told them to bring up some more now, fresh." She suddenly stops dead in her tracks in front of a door and I narrowly avoid bumping straight into her.

"They're in here," she sighs, clearly already too full of Christmas spirit. The dread I'd been managing to push down until now crests inside me at the thought of them all in there. "Tea in the sunroom," she trills as she swings the door open.

Walking into the light of the sunroom after the dimness of the halls is blinding as warm winter sun floods through the vast orangery windows. The room is high-ceilinged and airy, giving an immense sense of space. My eyes struggle to adjust as I try to make out their faces in the blazing light, one face in particular more important than the rest. In front of the massive glare of the windows a table is laid with a brilliant white tablecloth, silverware flaring in the light, glasses refracting, the shape and blur of stacked tiers of cakes, savory fare, petits fours.

"Welcome to The Hydes," Matilda adds with self-aware grandiosity.

The figures at the table rise, in silhouette, as we enter, their shapes beginning to make sense. "Harriet, Edward," comes a voice I recognize as Eleanor's. I shield my eyes and she comes into focus. "We thought you'd slipped off the face of the earth," she quips with a light shake of her chic gray bob. "We were expecting you this morning."

"We had a little appointment this morning," Edward answers, just holding back, and I realize we have to tell them imminently.

Over Eleanor's shoulder I notice the view beyond the colossal sunroom windows, and it snatches my breath clean away. Beyond the twinkling glass, the full panorama of the Holbecks' palatial gardens stretches out in all directions; the epic sprawl of it, a god's-eye view. The ornamental gardens spill with bright bursts of color set against tight evergreen borders, winter blooms in full flower pouring over crisp paths. Out toward the splashing fountain, a long shallow pool of rippling water carries on deep into the lawns. The fountain itself is an elaborate sculpture, water pouring from mouths, claws, eyes, and hands, creatures twisting as the sunlight catches and refracts in the water.

Past it, the green carpet of lawn rolls out to the edge of the dark forest.

Eleanor follows my gaze. "Ah, the grounds. Yes, they're quite lovely this time of year, aren't they?" she says with a modest smile. "Tea?"

Edward pulls out my chair and I sit, letting out an audible sigh when I realize Robert is not here.

"Yes, I'd love some," I say, the dread inside me loosened. I watch the rest of the family as they slip back into conversation. Two uniformed maids enter, unacknowledged, with steaming tea in silver pots.

I take in everything, this family in its natural environment, the warm scent of lemon cake, buttery scones, the bubble of conversation, dust particles sparkling in the air, and the delicate roll of heat off the tops of teacups.

I let my eyes flicker over the Holbecks: Matilda and Eleanor, Stuart and Lila, Oliver and Fiona, Edward and me.

The children aren't present, and neither is Nunu. Which brings me back full circle to Robert.

"Is, ah—" I begin, but my voice catches as eyes find me. I clear my throat. "Is Robert joining us?"

I feel Edward's gaze on me now too, surprised by the question.

Eleanor dabs her mouth with a napkin. "Mm, sorry, yes, I should have said. Robert is just tying up a few loose ends," she answers, then chuckles, giving her children a solicitous look.

"Though Robert missing our pre-holiday tea is as much an annual tradition as the tea itself."

A surge of relief buffets through me. He's not coming. I might not see him until tonight. Which means I will have time to listen to the rest of the tape.

Edward's hand slips onto my thigh, making me jolt slightly. His look is inquiring: *Why are you asking about my father? Is everything okay?*

I shake my head lightly, chasing his question away with a quick smile. But he holds my gaze and I suddenly realize I have misunderstood him. He thinks I want Robert here so that we can tell everyone about the pregnancy together.

He's asking if I want to tell them now.

"Oh, okay," I say, hearing the surprise in my own voice.

He gives a decisive nod then takes my hand in his and places both down on the white linen tablecloth pointedly.

Eleanor raises an eyebrow at our clasped hands. "I have a feeling something's coming, Ed," she says softly. "What's coming?"

Silence descends around the table, teacups caught halfway to mouths, chewing paused.

I flush as Edward speaks beside me, his words somehow muffled as I feel a flutter in my chest. Palpitations. The obstetrician told me the hormones might do this. No stress, he warned me—no stress and plenty of fluids. I down the cool glass of water in front of me.

Smiling eyes flit between Edward and me.

". . . And this morning we found out that we are having a baby girl," Edward finishes, beaming.

Eleanor's hand flies to her mouth. "Oh, Edward, a little girl," she gasps with genuine joy.

Words of congratulations cascade around us. Oliver nods his, but beside him I note Fiona's blank expression. She looks concerned—for me perhaps? for our child?—and for the first time I wonder how much she really knows about this family. My focus is pulled by Lila squeezing me into a tight hug, her eyes twinkling with excitement.

"A girl," Stuart intones wryly. "Dad's going to love that. He's always said we could do with more female energy in the place. Right?"

Matilda smirks. "I think he just says that to you, Stu."

"Do you have a name yet?" Eleanor asks.

"Her name is Iris," I say.

Iris: a beautiful flower. Or the sharp aperture of a human eye—a jewel-toned, star-speckled universe in miniature.

"Iris," Eleanor repeats, savoring the word. "Beautiful."

37

A Moment's Peace

After tea, the family peels off, promising to reconvene for supper at seven. For a moment I think I might get the opportunity I've been waiting for to slip away and listen to Robert's tape, but Eleanor intercedes.

"I'll show you around, Harriet, if you're not too tired from the journey?"

I think of making an excuse but realize I don't even know what room I'm staying in yet, so I have nowhere to escape to anyway.

Eleanor ferries me and Edward through the property, creaking open door after door to opulent rooms filled with beautiful objects, the house a curated marvel of fine textiles and artwork.

However, when we reach the farthest wing, the aesthetic changes.

"This is the new wing," Eleanor informs me as underfoot the floor switches abruptly from antique parquet to polished concrete. Ahead of us through a glass corridor the walls are lime-washed and minimalist. We stop, our way on blocked by a state-of-the-art glass security door with a keypad entry system.

Beside me Edward's phone bursts to life. He attempts to ignore it for a few rings before Eleanor gives him a look that says she will go no farther until it is silenced.

"I'll leave you two to it, then?" he says, pulling the phone out. "I should probably take this." He plants a kiss on my cheek. "I'll catch you back in the room before dinner."

"Sure," I say, nodding.

"Blue room, Mom?"

Eleanor nods. "Yes, your bags should be up there already. Don't work too hard, Eddie. It's Christmas, remember? And you have a very special guest to look after."

"Forty-five minutes max," he calls back as we watch him disappear around the corridor.

I do not see the numbers Eleanor keys into the system, but once we are inside I realize the new wing is actually the most impressive part of the house.

Glass doors puff open into beautiful rooms constructed with glass, concrete, pale wood, and rough quartz. The lighting is ambient, the temperature climate-controlled, and everything in this wing has a beautifully designed function. It must have cost millions.

"The old wing burned down back when the children still lived here. Absolutely terrifying, as you can imagine, but everyone survived. Robert's old study was lost, though. The whole wing was rubble and ash. I blame the cigars. But the new wing can withstand anything. The insurance otherwise"—she rolls her eyes—"you wouldn't believe."

"Do you like it?" I ask Eleanor, her sharp gray bob swishing as she turns to me.

"The new wing? I do," she answers after a moment's consideration. "Truth be told I like it a lot more than the rest of the house. I like knowing what everything is for and that everything works. I've never been a fan of the needlessly complex. Of collections. You?"

I don't get the chance to answer as the sound of a voice raised in anger and the smashing of glass reaches us from the room at the end of the corridor. It is Robert's, and he's arguing with someone. I can't make out his words but the tone is clear.

Eleanor gives me an apologetic, indulgent look. She shakes her head.

"I swear to you, Harriet. Every Christmas, without fail. He won't let things go. Work, work, work. And that Holbeck temper. Every year he winds himself up into a filthy mood." She looks at her watch. "Don't worry, he'll boil over by six and be as soft as a kitten for suppertime."

That Holbeck temper. As she says it, I realize I'm not sure I've ever witnessed it. Edward is the calmest man I know; compared with previous boyfriends he's a positive saint. And Oliver and Stuart seem more tired than angry, from my experience. But then I know what is on Robert's tape. Perhaps temper can be measured in different ways.

I listen once more but the new wing is silent.

Ten minutes later, pregnancy excuses made, I am lying on a duck-egg-blue bed in a duck-egg-blue room, surrounded by duck-egg-blue curtains and cobalt objets d'art. On the bedside table beside me a cool glass of water sits next to a small vase of freshly picked hothouse cornflowers.

Once I have heard Eleanor's footsteps tap back down the wide stone steps of the main staircase, I scramble over to my bag, lock the bedroom door, and slip on the headphones.

38

The Tape

PART 4

I am under no illusions that you have not done your homework. You will have looked into the names I have given you.

The thing about us orphans is that we find it incredibly hard to relinquish control, don't we? If we want a thing done, then we do it ourselves. I would not expect you to take my word on anything, least of all the veracity of what I am telling you. Just as I would never take you at your word, my dear Harriet, at least not yet. We both have much to prove to each other. Perhaps we will get there. Perhaps we will not. Time will tell.

But again, I digress.

As I'm sure you have gleaned, it is wise to be wary of my whole family at this stage. I know your past; I will continue to keep an eye on who and what comes in and out of your life. But I am not the only one who may have taken this precaution. Other members of my family will always have their own concerns and access to similar resources, and perhaps they will not hold you in quite the same esteem as I.

You will be invited, if you haven't been already, to an event at my son Oliver's house. A family tradition, Germanic as so many of ours are. It's a child's game but not so childish if the rules are not known. That is how we play it. You will not know what is real and what is not; it only works on the imagination this way. But whatever you fear, do not fear exposure from me; do not fear the things you have heard on this tape. If you have listened to this tape in its entirety before Krampusnacht, then do not discuss it with me at that house. There are no private places there; everything is seen. Play the game as well as I know you can, because everyone will be watching.

Wait and I will bring you to me. I will bring you to The Hydes. It is there that we will speak and I will ask my favor of you.

People have died, Harriet—not because of bloodlust; I think you know that. Necessity is often the only real motive anyone can hold in their head and act on.

You have done things out of necessity—as have I.

You will receive an invitation to The Hydes. Do not be scared; accept it and have faith in the knowledge that I keep those of value close to me.

Here is what I need you to do.

We play a game on Christmas Eve, another tradition from the old country. I'm sure you're surprised that a family like ours plays so many childish games, but, Harriet, that is the common misconception about the nature of games. Games take us as close as is acceptable to the strategies we use in life. Games reveal our most base instinct: the instinct to survive. Under the mask of enjoyment, we reveal ourselves, we reveal how we play at life, our methods, how we navigate others' strengths and weaknesses.

A game is only a game if you do not fully understand it. We play as we live. And I want you to play a game with me, Harriet. The stakes will be high but there is everything to play for.

The game begins at eight P.M. on Christmas Eve, and it is a

treasure hunt. Edward will want you to sit it out, or to play with him. He will try to shelter you from us, but you must play and play alone. We all play alone.

Each player will have a present waiting for them at the end of their hunt, and clues that will lead them there. Follow your clues, watch your back, and when you find what I hope you will find, all will be revealed. I have no doubt that everything will come together in your mind before you reach the end.

If you have listened to this recording by the time we meet at The Hydes, I would ask you to show me a sign. There will be flowers in your room. Wear one to supper and we will understand each other. Until then: good luck, Harriet.

Oh, and a point of interest: my children no longer sleep in their childhood bedrooms. Those old rooms are kept just as they were. Eleanor wanted to have them cleared, but I like the memories. It might be worth taking a look if you're interested. You can tell a lot about a person from the mess they leave behind.

39

The First Night

FRIDAY, DECEMBER 23

The tape clicks off. I fast-forward, hoping for more—more explanation, more anything—but there's only the crackle of virgin tape. Robert is gone. That is all I get.

It's clear I should have listened to the entire tape long ago. Before Krampusnacht, and well before I arrived here. Robert must have assumed I'd listen to it the day after he gave it to me. I would have had so much more time to try to decode it if I had, but life got in the way.

I rewind the tape and press PLAY again, carefully recording Robert's list of names onto my phone. I may have lost the whole first half of the cassette, but I still have the list of dead girls. It might just be enough to save me. Once the recording is finished, I email it to myself. It should be waiting on my laptop back at home. If anything was to happen to me out here, the trail is laid and it will lead straight back to Robert Holbeck.

Edward doesn't get back to the room until after the tape player is finished and packed away, my work done.

He's finalizing things with Hong Kong, signing off on the little details still remaining. And he had a beer with Oliver. I smell the sweet hops on his breath.

"What have you been up to?" he asks.

I give him the same pregnancy excuse I gave his mother and his hand flies to my head solicitously to check my temperature.

"I'm fine, Ed. It's just been a long day."

He holds my gaze as if to test the truth of my statement and, seemingly satisfied, removes his hand. "Luckily, we're skipping the family dinner tonight. Dad's in the middle of something."

I stop breathing, my eyes trained on Edward. "No family dinner?"

"Well, we'll eat, just not together. God knows what he's in the middle of. But we'll see everyone at dinner tomorrow anyway. He can't avoid Christmas entirely."

"You think he's avoiding us?" I ask before I can stop myself.

Edward seems surprised at the question. "No, of course not. Turn of phrase. But who knows? Who knows what goes on in his mind? He'd certainly never deign to tell us. But we'll see him tomorrow for sure. We play a game on Christmas Eve. Family tradition. There are clues; you find presents. He wouldn't miss that. But don't worry, after what happened at Fiona and Oliver's, no one's going to expect you to take part in any of that."

"How come you didn't tell me about it before?"

"Because there's no way I'm letting you do it, not after Krampus."

"Letting me?" I inquire archly, though the sentiment is oddly comforting given everything going on right now. "Is it similar to the Krampus Race?" I ask, fully aware that I need to take part in the game willingly or this will never work. "I did okay in that, right?"

Edward looks amused. "Um, yeah, you did amazing, but, I mean, you hated it, right? No offense, honey, but I really don't think this one is a good idea. I'll be honest with you, it's a really weird game. And sure, there's no monster chasing you in this one, but there is my family. Besides, no one is expecting you to do this. You're pregnant. You can definitely sit it out."

"No way am I sitting it out," I say with as much enthusiasm as I can muster. A look of confusion passes over his features and I quickly continue. "I might have overreacted about the whole Krampus thing. It was fun, in retrospect. I just should have known a bit more about it before it started. But the rules of this game aren't a secret too, are they?"

His expression lifts. "No, it's just clues. A treasure hunt. You're racing the other players but no one's going to be chasing you."

That's what you think, I reply in my mind.

While eating a dinner in our room later that evening, I decide to broach a question that's been niggling me since I first listened to Robert's tape. I can't get the idea out of my head that in some way Edward, and the rest of the family, must have an inkling of what their father is really capable of.

I know it's a risk bringing this up, but I need to know the answer and there will never be a good time to ask.

"Edward, why didn't you tell me the truth about Bobby? That he jumped?"

He looks up at me, startled.

"He didn't die from the drug interaction," I continue gently. "Well, I suppose in a way he did, but why didn't you tell me he committed suicide?"

I watch him flinch at my choice of words and immediately I regret them. "Because I was ashamed. For him. Of him. He wasn't like that, you see. I don't want him remembered like that. He was strong, and suicide seems so—"

"I feel like you should have told me, Ed," I say, not harshly, but I can't deny I am starting to feel a little alone on a limb. "I had to hear it from Lila," I lie.

He gives a slow nod, a question answered.

"I'm not good at talking about my emotions," he tells me, and I feel his vulnerability for the first time in a long time. "Stuart is better at it. Heck, they all are. Being the eldest has been hard. If I don't mention it then it didn't happen and if it didn't happen then it can't happen to me. I don't know . . ." He trails off, embarrassed, like he has said too much.

There I was thinking the man I found was too perfect, but it turns out he's just under more pressure to hide his fears than the regular guy. "It's okay. I understand. And you don't have to worry about that happening to you, Ed, because I am here with you. Every step of the way. Nothing ever has to be that hard again. I promise you." As I say it, I know I mean it even though it's not true. Because I don't even know if I'm going to make it through the next two days let alone be with him for a lifetime. But my words seem to salve his worries.

"I'm trying, Harry, I can't tell you how hard, to be open with you. I'm glad you can be with me. This is the closest I have ever gotten to—" He stops himself with a gentle shake of his head. "I just love you. I'm glad we're here, together. I'm glad you came."

Beyond the bedroom window, thick flakes of snow are beginning to drift. We watch it swirl and settle, dusting the moonlit gardens as far as the eye can see. A winter wonderland in the making. I try to imagine the view through Edward's eyes, try to imagine the feeling of owning all of this, owning the grass, the snow, the walls, the windows, the moon bone white in the sky. But the idea, like quicksilver, is too mercurial to hold in my mind.

We sit in our moonlit rectangle of light, one hand grasping the other's, and finish our meal as virgin snow blankets The Hydes.

40

The Players and the Game

When we wake, the snow has settled and continues to fall. The Hydes has been blanketed in white and the branches of the forest hang laden.

From the bedroom window I take it in and that age-old Christmas feeling flexes itself awake inside me, in spite of everything.

My thoughts are interrupted by a knock on the door and Sylvia, the maid who brought up our dinner the night before, enters with a heavy breakfast tray.

"It's a beautiful morning," she says, singsong, as she lays out freshly brewed coffee and a selection of pastries.

"What's everyone up to this morning?" Edward asks from the bathroom doorway. He's shirtless, with a towel about his waist.

She blushes noticeably as she lays the cutlery and plates, pouring us two steaming cups of coffee. "Mr. Robert is in his office.

Mrs. Eleanor is in the orangery. Your brothers are planning on fishing this morning. Jimmy is preparing the kit in the boot room." She looks up at Edward. "Shall I ask him to prepare your things too?"

"No, thank you, Sylvia. I think I'll show Harriet around today. Maybe we'll take lunch in the snug? Is it free?"

"It is, sir."

"Say one-thirty?"

"Perfect." She smiles. "And, er, I don't know if you've been told, but the children are staying in the keeper's cottage with Nunu tonight. Something about staying up for Santa," she adds with a knowing smile.

"God, Nunu is a saint," Edward remarks, causing a sharp flirtatious giggle to erupt from Sylvia. Sometimes I forget how attractive Edward is until I see him in action and it's like a kick in the head.

"Oh, and Ms. Erikson is swimming," Sylvia adds, seemingly without judgment. Edward's gaze snaps up.

"What, in the lake?" Edward asks, clearly taken aback.

Sylvia nods slowly. "She's Scandinavian," she offers, by way of explanation, then shrugs, leaving it at that. We grunt our understanding. Swimming in freezing water in the snow makes a little more sense in that context.

The breakfast served and the whereabouts of the entire Holbeck clan accounted for, Sylvia takes her leave.

After breakfast, Edward and I trek out into the garden bundled up in layers, our breath fogging in the cold air. Edward leads us out across the crunchy snow toward the bulk of the maze.

"There's a trick to the maze," Edward says with a smile as we approach its entrance. "Want to hear it, or prefer to try your luck first?"

From the driveway it looked fun, but standing right in front of it, its size really hits home and I find myself wondering what would actually happen if you got stuck inside it. The densely packed hedges making up its walls must be over fifteen feet high. It's unlikely you could climb it or crawl through it if you had to break the rules.

"I don't know. Be honest: how hard is it?" I ask.

He raises an eyebrow. *"Hard."*

"Well, then, I think I'm going to need the trick. It's going to be a long day otherwise."

Edward lets out a laugh. "Yeah, maybe a maze, my family, *and* a treasure hunt is a bit much for your first Christmas."

In front of the maze's opening, I notice a small wooden sign at knee height with the words ENTER HERE hand-etched onto it.

"Creepy," I say.

"Yep," he says with a sigh. "Now imagine being seven and having to celebrate Krampusnacht here."

"Bloody hell."

"Exactly," he says. "So the trick with mazes is . . ." He lifts his right hand in demonstration. "You know this one, right?" he says, checking.

I shake my head and then he places his right hand on the maze wall. "In that case, this works on most mazes. It certainly does on this one. Keep your right hand on the maze wall from start to finish. No matter what happens, you keep that hand on. Dead end? You keep your hand on the wall and walk around. All the walls are connected, you see, so if you follow one wall all the way through, you'll get there in the end. It's a much longer route, but it's a route."

He starts walking, his gloved hand brushing loose snow from the hedging as we disappear into the towering green maze. "FYI, this method is particularly useful if you're running away from something terrifying and it's pitch-black. At least, it was when we were kids," he adds with a self-deprecating laugh.

He's talking about Krampuses long passed, but I can't help but feel the very real possibility of this advice becoming necessary at some point during my stay.

"And you're certain this method works?" I ask, casting my eyes up to the high edges of the maze walls.

"Yeah, it'll get you in and out. But it only works on a simple maze," he says.

"Wait, this is a *simple* maze?" I say, pulling him up.

"*Simple maze* is a term. It doesn't mean it's easy; it's a technical description of the structure. A simple maze is a maze with one connected wall. A complex maze has bridges, unconnected walls. To get out of one of those you'd need to use Trémaux's algorithm."

I look up at Edward, suddenly getting a glimpse of what his childhood must have really been like.

"Trémaux's algorithm? Bloody hell, Ed. How many you been stuck in?"

"Enough," he says with good humor. "I won't bore you with Trémaux. Unless we go to the place in Rouen, it won't become relevant."

As we turn the next corner, I bump directly into a sweaty, red-faced Lila.

"Jesus Christ," she yelps, grabbing her throat. Wet hair pokes out beneath her thick bobble hat, her cheeks flushed with cold and exertion. "Oh my God. Thank God—people," she gasps, letting out a convulsive giggle. "How the hell do you get out of this fucking hedge? I was on a call with Milo's dad and I wandered in here. Thought the distraction might calm me down. It did not," she declares, shivering deeply. She must be absolutely freezing after her swim.

"It's fine. We'll walk you out," I tell her.

"Yes. Yes, please," she says, a sigh juddering from her. "I need to get back and sort Milo out."

"I thought Milo was staying at his dad's until Boxing Day?" I ask as we lead her efficiently back the way we came.

"Yeah, it's not going well. Milo won't leave his room. Just screaming for me to come pick him up. They can't do anything with him. I feel guilty but then, you know, I also don't. The new girlfriend is a real number—"

Lila clocks my apparently not-so-masked surprise at the judgment.

"I would never say it around Milo, of course," she adds, horrified at the thought. "Anyway, they want me to come pick Milo up. Now. And they want me to arrange therapy for Milo for next year." She shakes her head.

"Jesus," Edward intones. "I wish there was something we could do. Do you want to talk to Mother about it? She knows some people in the city."

Lila looks up, suddenly a little lost. "Um, yeah. God, maybe they're right, maybe the whole thing hit him harder than I thought." She sighs.

"I'll get Mother to pass some names on to Stu for you," Edward says gently. Lila cracks a weak smile before nodding.

"Great. Only thing is now I've got a five-hour drive. Stuart should definitely stay here; I do not need him meeting my ex on top of everything else. I'll pick Milo up, stay overnight at a hotel, and we'll make it back here for Christmas morning."

"I'm so sorry this is happening on Christmas Eve. That you can't stay and relax," I say with sympathy for her, but the truth is I feel like I'm losing an ally here at The Hydes.

"No, God. I'd cross the country ten times over for my child. Besides, it'll be fun. Road trip. I just wish I didn't have to drag him through this kind of thing every holiday. Every birthday. This back-and-forth bullshit." She grimaces as she turns from us to head back inside. "Sorry, I'm cold and cranky. Thank you for listening."

Edward and I spend the rest of the morning exploring the grounds before feeding and grooming the horses at the stables. I make peace with not being able to ride, given the pregnancy, and offer up a few handfuls of oats to a gorgeous dun mare instead while Edward fills me in on Matilda's teenage equestrian glories.

The estate is a positive menagerie; we cuddle goats, feed chickens, peek into deer shelters, pass hay over paddocks to llamas, and all the while I try to piece together the childhood Edward must have had.

Our tour moves on to outbuildings, the majestic glass orangery filled with thick palms and a cozy reading corner. We pass groundskeeper workshops where men who I presume work for the Hol-becks potter away with wood and metal. Matilda gave the impression that only two people were working at the house over the holidays, but now I see she must have meant *inside* the house.

As we head into an overgrown patch of land, Edward directs my gaze into the undergrowth, where I can just about make out a well. "The house isn't connected to a main water source; all our water comes from wells. That one's ornamental, but you get the idea."

The low stone well is a perfect circle, moss visible beneath the thin layer of snow. It's pretty.

I peer over the edge into the dripping darkness beyond and a thought occurs to me. "Why wouldn't you be connected to the water mains?"

"The wells mean we don't need to be. Besides, we're too far from the nearest pipelines anyway. The water companies would need to run new lines out here to reach us," he explains.

"How far are we from the nearest town?" I ask as I watch flecks of snow sail down and disappear into the murky depths.

"From town? Twenty minutes in the car. Ten, fifteen miles. Why?"

"Just curious," I say, pulling back from the well's edge. Ten miles is a long run—over an hour and a half without a break.

He pulls me close, oblivious to my fears, and plants a kiss on my forehead. "Shall we head back and get some lunch?" he asks.

"Sure," I say. "Can you just show me one last thing? Is that okay?" I pitch my voice sugar-sweet. "Can you show me the hides?"

The nearest town is ten miles away. If worse comes to worst, I won't be able to run; I'll have to *hide*.

The structure hangs in the air above us, moss-greened and hid-den. Its sheer height throws my stomach through loops.

"Is it safe?" I ask as Edward wraps his arms tight around me and cranes his neck up, taking in its off-kilter angle.

"Who knows now," he says with a grin. "We used to go up all the time as kids, and it was fine. But that was a long time ago and we were a lot smaller." He gives me a squeeze, then an idea seems to excite him. "Why don't I test it out?" He takes in my concerned expression then adds, "Probably best you stay here—"

I watch him apply pressure to the first few rungs, then, with a hopeful glance back at me, he slowly begins to climb.

I watch, heart in throat, as he rises one moss-slimed rung after another, checking each foothold firmly before trusting it with his weight. At the top he uses a free hand to give the platform above a solid shake. Surprisingly, it doesn't budge.

"Seems okay," he calls down. He must be at least thirty feet above the forest floor. He lets out a half laugh, half grunt as he hauls his weight onto the platform.

"Careful," I call up as the whole structure shifts visibly. Everything in me is clenched. Edward, unfazed, calmly shifts his weight into a better position, settling on the platform, hands tightly gripping a low branch as he takes in the view across the forest and finally dropping his eyes to me.

"You look so small down there," he says with a chuckle, and for the first time today I feel the cold.

41

We Play Alone

SATURDAY, DECEMBER 24

At around seven o'clock, Christmas music begins to fill every room of the house, a soft jingle with an almost recognizable melody I can't quite put my finger on. It's unclear where it's coming from, but it fills the building like the scent of oranges, wine, and roasted meats coming through from the kitchen.

It's nearly time for dinner.

Up in the blue room, I slip into the dress Edward bought me and examine myself in the full-length mirror. Behind me, Edward shrugs on a crisp suit. I watch his reflection as he fixes his cuff links, take in his dark, tousled hair, his strong features, so similar to his father's but so different. He grins as he catches me looking and I feel desire stretch awake inside me.

"You look good," I tell him.

He slips an arm around my waist as he holds my gaze in the

mirror, his lips traveling to kiss my bare neck as far down as my dress allows. I try to push my fears about tonight from my mind. I try to be present, with Edward, but I cannot stop my thoughts. Robert is waiting for me downstairs. The only man in the world who knows what I truly am and the only one who can destroy everything. I let my eyes bat closed as Edward's hand slips into the opening of my dress and over my breast. I lean back into him, giving myself over to my animal need for him. I let my mouth find his, warm and wet, as the distinctions between father and son blur once more.

Matilda and Stuart are seated by the fire when we make it down to the drawing room. Eleanor, elegant in a white rollneck complimenting her sharp gray bob, turns from the candles she is lighting as we enter.

"There we are," she coos, gesturing for us to settle wherever. I take a seat on the sofa opposite Stuart and Matilda. Matilda's wearing green cigarette pants, an emerald necklace popping against her red hair. Edward perches on the sofa edge beside me, protective.

"We were just talking about how Stuart always scares women off." Matilda grins, nudging Stuart. "Lila's cut and run already."

Edward splutters out a laugh as Fiona and Oliver walk in.

"What's so funny?" Oliver asks, slipping into an armchair.

"Stuart," Matilda says simply.

"Dinner in ten, everyone," Eleanor declares as she hands around drinks. "We're just waiting for your father to come down."

Fiona sinks into the sofa beside me with a sigh. She pushes her brunette waves to one side, revealing the thin red spaghetti straps of her figure-skimming dress. She leans back heavily into the sofa cushions.

"The kids are with Nunu for the night. In the lodge." She exhales with a shake of the head. "God, I love coming here for Christmas." I take in her outfit, her incredible figure. Up until now I had no idea she even *had* a figure hidden under her casual everyday clothing.

She looks at me conspiratorially, an oddly different person now that her children are elsewhere.

"You look amazing," I tell her beneath the hubbub of conversation.

"You too," she says, smiling, then leans in to whisper, "I guess you got the dress code memo."

"Edward bought it for me," I say, looking down at my dress.

"Oh, and cute flower."

I follow her gaze to my lapel and the bright pop of blue there. The flower Robert told me to wear if I understood his instructions. My secret admission of knowledge visible for all to see.

I sip my sparkling water, wishing it were something stronger as the conversation ebbs and flows around me, one eye constantly locked on the doorway.

He must have used another entrance, however, because I hear his voice behind me before I see him.

"Well, here we all are," he says, cold and warm all at the same time.

"Drink, Robert?" Eleanor asks, handing him a glass of scotch with a peck on the cheek as he enters my field of vision.

I look away.

And when I look back, Robert is looking straight at me. "Harriet Reed, I hear congratulations are in order. You're with child." He raises his glass to us both and Edward responds in kind, the air between them crackling.

Robert's gaze dips to the blue flower on my breast, his expression unfaltering. "Not that we didn't take you seriously before, Harriet," he says carefully. "But this certainly changes things. Wouldn't you say, Edward?"

As we file out of the drawing room for dinner, Edward is plucked from beside me by Eleanor.

"You don't mind if I steal him away, Harriet, dear?" she asks. "There's one more clue to arrange before this evening. And I need someone tall." She pats her son on the shoulder.

"Of course," I demure, aware that if I'm unchaperoned I am open to Robert.

Edward plants a quick kiss on my cheek and mother and son slip back into the drawing room while I follow the rest of the Holbecks to dinner.

Robert's hand finds my elbow on the threshold of the candlelit dining room, strong but gentle, tender almost. "A word?" His voice goes straight through me, hitting all my sweet spots.

I look up at him as the rest of the family find their seats, too busy juggling drinks and conversations to notice. We're as alone as we could be.

"Yes," I say carefully.

"Good." His gaze falls on the flower on my lapel. "Thank you for following my instructions. The color suits you," he says with a smile that undercuts everything, and I feel a giddiness for which I hate myself.

I cannot take my eyes off him, and I do not want to, partly because I fear what he would do if I did, and partly because I do not want to break this spell. It's like he's devouring me and I, in turn, him.

"You listened to it," he says simply. "And you're here. That's a good start. I had a feeling you would be capable of engaging with this."

"I'm here because I have to be," I answer, and hope my meaning is clear. I am here to end whatever this is so I can live my life. My life with Edward.

"Aren't we all, Harriet? Aren't we all? We can speak more after the game tonight. I think you should have a better understanding of things by then." He rips his gaze from me, eyeing his seated family. "Remember, whatever happens, you must play alone tonight. Do you understand?"

I nod.

"Of course you do," he says with finality.

42

The Rules

SATURDAY, DECEMBER 24

At the gleaming, opulently laid Christmas table, I find my seat
next to Matilda's.

Conversation bubbles on, crystal glasses sparkle, eyes crease
with laughter. Down the middle of the table candles flicker in a
braided evergreen centerpiece, the whole scene reminiscent of a
Dickens illustration; a cornucopia.

Stuart is holding court on the Lila situation. Updating those
who do not know on why she is absent.

I keep silent. I watch Robert in the flickering light; I watch
them all. This odd family who are now my family, my future. I
remember Robert's warning about them, how any one of them
could know about me. That they, like him, are not to be trusted.
I wish I were Lila; I wish I were not here; I wish I were free. But
then I would not get Edward, and that is all I want.

When he and Eleanor finally rejoin us, he slips into the seat beside his father's with barely a look to the place card. I wonder if he knew he would be sitting there, beside his father, or if he's just covering well.

"So you're, what, twelve weeks now?" Matilda asks, snapping me back to reality. "When does that make you due?"

I rip my eyes away from father and son to answer her.

"Oh, so a summer baby," she trills. Robert looks over and holds my gaze.

Sylvia and the other maid, Anya, flit silently in and out of the room with the first course. I watch the others delicately fork food into their mouths and force myself to do the same. It's going to be a long night and I will need my strength.

The courses flow into one another. Voices rise and fall, peaking and troughing with the flow of conversation, and I watch the evening swirl around us. There are two murderers at this table, and I have no idea how many of them know that.

Coffee is served back by the fire in the drawing room. The family's eyes are glazed with festive cheer and alcohol as the clock in the hall sounds ten.

The first chime silences the room; the second summons knowing smiles and a sharp giggle from Fiona. Robert places his coffee down and stands.

"I should probably say a few words before we start this year. Unfortunately, Lila could not attend tonight, but Harriet is here. So for those who do not know, or possibly for those that need reminding, here are the rules," Robert says gently as I watch Matilda shove Stuart hard in the ribs.

"There will be only one present on Christmas Eve. If you find your present, then you get to keep it; if you do not find it, then you do not. Most of you here know the rhyme well, but for Harriet's benefit I'll say it again:

"Nothing in this life is free
we work for what we have and see

if you cannot in the time you're given
then harder harder you should have striven."

The last phrase is said with such singsong cadence, it is clear that the words are ingrained in Holbeck family history. In my mind's eye I picture Mitzi Holbeck, decked in 1930s evening wear, German accent thick, as she recites the rhyme Robert just intoned.

The sentiment of the poem is extremely questionable given the extraordinary wealth these people inherited before any of them lifted a finger, but perhaps that is the point of the rhyme.

"Players, your first clues are on the cards marked with your names," Robert continues, and all eyes fly to the green baize table beside the fire. On it I see one of Mitzi's carved Black Forest bears standing, paws aloft, behind eight cream envelopes. He holds a silver dice cup in his claws. "No conferring, no hints, no help," Robert continues.

Edward shifts uncomfortably beside me. "Wait, I'm not sure it's appropriate that Harriet play. Given everything," he says lightly. He takes my hand in his, giving it a supportive squeeze, though I know what's coming before Robert even opens his mouth.

"Well, hold on for a moment now, Edward," Robert says with almost theatrical caution. "Perhaps we should ask Harriet herself if she wants to play. After all, if memory serves me correctly, she's a very capable young woman. She won the last game she played in record time, didn't she?"

All eyes turn to me, expectant.

"Are you happy to play, Harriet? Or would you like to sit this one out? Lila has been removed from the game. It's perfectly possible for you to be as well." There's something in the way he mentions Lila that makes me suddenly worry for her safety.

"Yes, I'll play," I say conclusively, as if I ever really had a choice. The rest of the gathered faces fizz with a new kind of excitement.

"Now we're talking." Oliver grins.

"Then it's decided," Robert says, clearing his throat, a glimmer of triumph in his tone. "Harriet plays, like everyone else. In which case, you should hear a bit more about the game you'll be playing, Harriet. Your first card will be a riddle, and it will lead you to the next. There are three clue cards in total, with the third location holding your Christmas gift. It is a traditional treasure hunt in that respect. You may have played similar games before, but this version is slightly different. In our game, the prizes are tailored specifically to the needs of each player. Would anyone care to explain, by example?" The room around me goes silent, smiles fading with discomfort.

"No, I didn't think so," Robert continues. "You see, Harriet, the gifts involved are extremely personal, and always very timely. They are things that the receiver may need badly but may be unable to achieve unaided. Sometimes they might not even know they need them, or that anybody else is aware of their need." I tense at his words; the thought occurs that somehow my secret will be involved in this game.

Robert elaborates, his focus now entirely directed at me. "To save the blushes of those in this room, I will use Great-Uncle Nelson as an example of how the game works."

Stuart snorts out a laugh, which Eleanor quickly shushes.

"Great-Uncle Nelson," Robert continues, my discomfort rising, "had something of a gambling addiction. Perhaps Stuart finds my choice of example amusing given its simplicity, but I think it sums up the game's core drive. In 1969 Nelson Holbeck's Christmas Eve gift was the complete erasure of his debt, professional and personal. Nelson had accrued over three-quarters of a million in backroom poker debt as well as significant losses through bad investment. If he had won the game that year, he would have had all his debts paid off in full by the family, his balance sheet balanced."

Robert falls silent.

"But what? He didn't play?" I ask, eyes surveying the silent Holbecks. "Or he couldn't solve the clues and find the present?"

"Oh no. Nelson played," Robert answers. "He played his heart out. But he lost. You see, someone else won that year, and there is only one winner. We play against one another. It's a family game. Whoever gets to their present first wins and the game stops." He pauses, waiting for his words to sink in. "One winner; one gift. No one else receives theirs, and the winner is told what the other players' gifts were—what each other player needed more than anything in the world."

"But how could you possibly know what people need?" I ask with a lightness I realize we are long past.

"There are ways to find these things out. I think you might have an inkling how. We do our research—all in the service of picking the perfect gift, you understand?"

I look at the benevolent faces around me and realize this game, its cruelty and its indulgence, is normal to these people. Even to Edward.

"Okay, I buy it," I reply grudgingly, after a pause. "But what then?"

"The winner can use their newfound information in any way they see fit. Whoever won in 1969 could have helped old Uncle Nelson, or at the very least they could have kept his embarrassment to a minimum, but they chose otherwise. If you win, Harriet, you win what you need most *and* the knowledge of what everyone else needed. But if you lose, you lose what you need most as well as the secret of that. I think you'll agree, the stakes are high. So we all play to win here, because we know everyone else will do the same."

I look at the other players then back to Robert before choosing my words carefully. "You think you know what I need?"

"You'll have to play to find out, won't you?" he replies, with a degree of kindness.

Edward puts a hand on my leg in reassurance.

"You don't have to play," he reiterates. And I suddenly wonder what on earth Edward could have to gain from playing this game.

I turn to the rest of the family. "But, I mean, why would any of you want to play this? How is it even a game? I mean, it's meant to be Christmas, for God's sake! Isn't it all a bit . . ." I struggle for a word to describe what *this* is.

Edward leans in now, taking charge. "Okay, why doesn't Harry just sit it out this year? Considering everything," he says lightly, gesturing in the direction of my stomach, "it might be worth taking the stress out of her first Christmas with the family. She can play next year—if she wants."

Robert looks across at me expectantly. "Would you like to skip this year, Harriet?"

It's not a question.

"No, I would not," I answer by rote. "I'll *do* it. I just, I don't get how it's a *Christmas* game, that's all. I mean, where's the Christmas spirit?"

Robert sips his scotch and perches on the arm of a sofa with an amused smile. "What could be more in the spirit of Christmas than offering everyone in the family a chance to *do the right thing*? Whoever wins has the opportunity to act with kindness as much as greed, you see? You choose. The game gives us a chance to rebalance the scales, once a year, to rectify the power balance in the family. It reminds us that we must be good to one another all year long or risk the consequences if the tables are turned." He breaks off, Eleanor topping up his glass. "But as Edward rightly says, it is just a game. No one gets hurt here; by the end there are just bruised egos, some damaged pride, and it has always meant a lot to those who play it. The only reason you might have to fear the game is if you have something to hide. Do you have something to hide?"

"Nothing you wouldn't already know," I answer.

"Then you'll play," Robert concludes.

"Of course," I say with a smile that I hope presents as authentic. "After all, it's not the winning that counts, right?" I ask hopefully. "It's just the taking part. That's what they say, right?"

"Ha, I bet they do," Stuart mutters, a sharp look from Oliver quickly shutting him down.

"Well, then. I think we're decided. If we're ready," Eleanor suggests as she lifts the silver dice cup from the black bear's wooden claws and jostles it. Inside, dice rattle. "Highest number starts the game," she instructs, offering up the cup to the group. "Who wants to roll first?"

43

One Clue. Two Clue.

SATURDAY, DECEMBER 24

Standing in front of the card table, the fire roaring, I pull my card from its envelope. Two players have already gone before me.

I can feel the family's eyes on me, but having watched both Fiona and Stuart take their turns, I know not to give anything away as I read my card.

Up the wooden hill to Bed-ford-shire,
Heading for the land of dreams.
When I look back to those happy childhood days,
<u>Nothing is quite what it seems.</u>

I look up at the faces staring back at me.
"Who writes these?" I ask.

All eyes swivel to Robert, answering the question for me. "And who writes yours?" I ask.

"I do," Eleanor answers, then gestures to my card. "Does everything there make sense?" she asks with generosity.

I look down at it again.

"I think so, yes," I reply.

Like the players before me, I drop my card into the roaring fire, carefully watching as it burns to nothing.

"Wonderful." Eleanor beams. "Then good luck, Harriet, and happy hunting."

I feel Edward's eyes on me but I do not engage with him, or anyone else, for fear that somehow the truth will pour out of me, out of my face, my eyes. Instead, head high, I make my way straight past the remaining players and directly out of the room.

I need to go up the wooden hill—the stairs—to find a bedroom, that much is clear. A *childhood* bedroom. I'm reminded of the ones Robert mentioned in his tape, his children's childhood rooms. There I will find my next clue, and hopefully the trail Robert is leaving me will start to make sense.

My heels tap a sharp rhythm across the parquet hallway and muffle as I take the carpeted stairs up two at a time. Time is against me. The previous players have a decent head start already. I listen ahead for the sound of Fiona or Stuart, but the low hum of Christmas music is all that greets me.

At the top of the stairs, I catch my breath and take in the landing, its four wings branching off in different directions. To my right are the guest bedrooms we have been staying in, to my left the wing where Robert and Eleanor sleep; which leaves the two wings behind me as possibilities.

I turn and face them, the right-hand corridor dimly lit and matching the style of the rest of the house, the left-hand corridor bright and new, part of the new wing protected by a glass security door. The childhood bedrooms certainly won't be in the new wing.

I grab the banister and propel myself around the landing toward the old wing, unsteady in my heels.

I pull up short. I can't spend the rest of the evening like this. I listen for movement from downstairs, checking if I can hear the next player beginning, but the hall is silent. Taking my opportunity, I squat down, unstrap my heels, and abandon them in the hallway as I race back to the blue room and grab my trainers. After shoving them on, I bolt back in the direction of the old wing.

I dash around the staircase, following the bend of the corridor away from the main building, and as the hallway doors appear, I throw one open after another looking for anything that resembles a childhood bedroom.

I don't know why, but Bobby's name springs to mind as I go. My clue mentions nothing being "quite what it seems," and nobody knew how ill Bobby was before he died, so perhaps I need to find Bobby's old room.

The first childhood room I stumble across is all in pink. Matilda's, I surmise, and quickly move on. The next room is green and filled with sports trophies, wrestling, football, boxing. A photo of a young man padded up for a football game—broad, muscular, his helmet raised in triumph. Oliver's room.

The next is red, on its walls jet fighters twisting in the air, miniature supercars lining the shelves, a faded 1997 Pirelli calendar hanging dog-eared by the window. Stuart's room. I fly on down the corridor.

The next room is blue. I pause, instinct telling me to. This room is harder to read. It's eerily impersonal. A computer, a 1990s beige plastic box, dominates the sparseness of the space. Pictures line the walls; a young man sailing, rowing, swimming. Again, trophies. Bobby rowed, but so did Edward. It's impossible to tell from the doorway whose room this was, but the computer edges me toward it being Edward's.

A door slamming somewhere deep in the house forces my gaze back down the corridor in the direction I have just come, but of course there is no one there.

I check the time on my mobile phone in the pocket of my blazer dress. I have been going for sixteen minutes already. Time is ticking, and I'm pretty sure I know what will happen if I lose this game.

I walk into the blue room and head for the nearest photo. It's of Edward—younger, his face fuller, with an expression I do not recognize. There is something different in his eyes. I scan the room for another photo and find a framed one on the dresser; Edward sits beside Eleanor and someone else at a garden table, flowers in bloom around them. I gasp. The boy in the photo isn't Edward, because Edward, much younger, is sitting right beside him.

The boy is Bobby. This is Bobby's room. They looked so alike as children, and I realize that up until now I haven't seen a photograph of them together when they were young. The uncanny thing is that young Bobby looks incredibly similar to Edward as he is now, as an adult. And now that I think about it, this whole room, its aesthetic, had felt like Edward's room when I entered it. The computer, the color, the tidiness, the simplicity. Which makes me wonder: were they always so similar, or did Edward become more like his brother after the accident?

I leave Bobby's door ajar and head to the next room.

Edward's bedroom door swings open and I feel my brow pucker with confusion. This last room is incredibly busy, the walls lined with lithographs of historical architecture, intricate blueprints of elaborate and complex buildings. Columns and cornicing depicted in forensic detail, cross sections, elevations. I step into the room, uncertain; I must have mixed the rooms up somehow, because nothing about this room is Edward. I let my eyes sweep the surfaces for anything that reminds me of him but there isn't even a computer in here. Just books; books on books: Roman history, the Greeks, the American Civil War, the world wars. History.

I take a photo from the bedside table. It is the whole family, except him; Edward must have taken it himself. I replace it carefully, my eye drawn to another photo hanging back by the door, Edward flanked by his mother and father. Eleanor is beaming, while father and son are serious; the usual spark behind Edward's eyes is not present.

I try to shake off the odd feeling swelling inside me that I do not recognize the man I love from this photo, from this room. Bobby's death must have changed him more than I ever considered, I think. But then my parents' death made me who I am. The hairs on the back of my neck prickle; this must be what Robert wanted me to see. That Edward changed, after Bobby's death. That Edward was not always as he is today. My Edward seems to fit the childhood bedroom of Bobby more than his own, but then he had to fill Bobby's shoes, didn't he?

The sound of a clock chiming somewhere in the house shakes me from my reverie. I need to keep moving. I need to find the next clue.

A childhood bed, not what it seems, I puzzle, paraphrasing the first clue.

On an impulse, I head toward Edward's bed and slip a hand under his pillow. My fingers come into contact with the stiff card of another envelope.

Another clue.

> You know me well, but not well enough.
> Come look harder, though you scramble and scuff.
> Peer into my darkness, it's cold and deep,
> <u>But to win you must find the secrets I keep.</u>

My hand goes to my mouth as I realize this clue leads me outside. I need to scramble and scuff in the cold and dark.

I try to shake off the dread of what I don't quite understand yet. I carefully reread my clue.

"You know me well, but not well enough," I repeat out loud, and just like that the words jump into focus. "You know me *well,* but not *well* enough." I will find the next clue out by the well.

The well that Edward showed me earlier today—the well that used to supply the property with water.

You must find the secrets I keep.

There's something in the well. I have to get in it. *Scramble and scuff.* I think of the inky blackness I stared down into this morning. The damp hole spiraling down into darkness. Whether I want to do this or not, whether it is safe or not, I have to go.

I gave up my right to an easy life when I did what I did twenty years ago. My secret must be kept, because there is no excusing it.

You can say I didn't know what I was doing back then, but I did. I wanted him to hurt like I did; I wanted him to pay. And this is the price *I* now have to pay.

This game might be my shot at wiping the slate clean. Robert hinted that my prize might just be that: my secret safe.

I shove the new clue in my pocket and leave Edward's childhood behind me. After all, we all used to be different people, didn't we?

And with that thought, my walk breaks into a run.

44

Stiff Competition

SATURDAY, DECEMBER 24

I emerge back onto the central landing and dart across to the blue room to grab what I need. Safely inside, I scramble through the pile of clothes gathered on the chair beside my suitcase and shrug on my warm puffy coat over my dress. Then, dropping back down to my suitcase, I forage for something else, and in among the shoes, hair tongs, and straighteners, I come into contact with its hard solid form. The paperweight. I slip it from the sock and hold it in one hand. I might not need it, but better to have it; who knows what I'll find out there in the darkness. I slide its smooth glass into my coat pocket and fumble for the cold metal of my torch. I had a feeling it might come in handy at some point during this trip, and I was right.

I flick it on in the dim lamplight of the blue room and its bright beam fires out, flaring against the dark glass of the sash windows.

Shit. I quickly turn it off as its light tunnels out into the dark night air beyond the glass. The last thing I want is someone seeing the light and following my next move. I now know this game is competitive, but I don't know to what extent. I'm guessing slowing other players down might be strategically worthwhile for some players, however, so best to avoid all contact with Holbecks until the game is over. If Robert is leading me to something that he wants only me to see, the last thing I need is an audience.

I zip up my coat, slip my phone into the other pocket, and head out of the blue room as stealthily as I can.

The house is quiet as I steal through it, silent save for the ghostly piano music and the soft crackle of the hall fire. No people stir; there is no movement at all. At the back door I ease quietly out into the sharp chill outside.

The white-sprinkled gardens sparkle in the moonlight. Around me the air is full of snowflakes tumbling down in slow fluffy clusters. Deep snow is setting in, and as I look down I realize what this means for me: footprints.

But there's little I can do about that. If the snow continues to fall they should disappear before too long anyway. I can only hope no one stumbles across them before then.

Outside the main house, I head quickly toward the maze, casting a look back at the house, its insides lit up, warm and cozy, a toy house hinged open for all to see.

On the second floor I catch sight of Eleanor searching through a bookcase, illuminated in her endeavor. Below her, at the corner of the building, I see Oliver in the flicker of candlelight through the giant windows of the sunroom, intent on unearthing something from the fireplace. But I don't have time for spying. I turn and break into a run but only make it a few yards before someone rounds the corner of the maze and propels straight into me, knocking me to the ground.

I look up and the figure towering over me is Fiona, her floor-length red silk dress hitched up over rubber wellies and partially covered with a waxed jacket. Her expression is as confrontational as the shovel grasped tightly in her hand.

"Of course. It's you," she says, rubbing her shoulder. She offers an unapologetic hand to pull me up. Her usually soft, open demeanor is gone to such an extent that I have to wonder if I imagined it in the first place. It's funny how wrong I could have been about the type of person Oliver's wife was. I guess I made the mistake of assuming all stay-at-home mums are cut from the same cloth. Fiona's cloth is not quite as forgiving as I had supposed.

I give her my hand and she yanks me up to standing.

"Have you seen any of the others?" she asks with a directness that tells me we are not playing as a team.

"I saw Oliver and Eleanor through the windows. The others I don't know."

She nods, looking back toward the house, then seems to decide something. "Yeah, I think I saw Edward or Stuart a minute ago," she says, absentmindedly casting her gaze toward the driveway. Then she looks me up and down. "And where are you going?"

"I'm not going to tell you that, Fiona."

She laughs humorlessly. "Whatever. I'll find out anyway." I try not to focus too much on the shovel in her hands, or on the fact that she will be able to track my footprints in the snow and doesn't seem like a very forgiving winner who might keep my secret. Something in my demeanor amuses her.

"Oh my God. You're terrified, aren't you?" she registers with a chuckle. "That's hilarious. What have they got on you? What's Robert got on you? God, it must be good."

"I don't know what you're talking about, Fiona," I say, walking away.

"Wait," she shouts after me, pulling me up short, her tone aggressive. "Whatever it is, I don't care. I'll make you a deal. Your secret, if Oliver or I win, we'll make it go away."

Her eyes gleam in the moonlight, snowflakes catching in her tumbling brown hair.

"And what would I have to do in return?" I ask tentatively. "You want me to keep your secrets if *I* win?"

Fiona lets out a bright burst of laughter. "Oh my God, you're

not going to win, Harry! That's so sweet. Did you really think—"
She gives me a cartoonish expression of mock-sympathy. "That
is so cute. You really don't know who you're playing against
here, do you?" she says with a shake of her head, before adding
seriously, "No, the deal is: if Oliver or I win, then you and Ed
don't have kids."

"What?" I snort out a laugh. "I'm already pregnant. How the
hell does that work?"

She frowns at my stupidity. "Have a think about it, Harry,
you'll get there in the end."

What she's suggesting suddenly hits me square in the chest.
"Jesus Christ. You want me to get an abortion? For a game?
Jesus Christ, Fiona."

"This is not a game—we both know that. I want you to have
an abortion and not to have any children with him, at all. That is
the deal. They have something on you, and believe me I'll find out
what it is. You've done something bad, I can tell. It must be fucking awful, because there's no way you'd have agreed to play tonight if it weren't. You had to play, didn't you? You might be able
to fool Edward, but I see you."

I pull myself up to full height. This is taking too long; I need
this to end.

"Fiona, get a fucking grip. I am not aborting my child for you,
so fuck off. Is this about inheritance or some bullshit? Because I
don't want their money, or need it. We've got more than enough.
How much does anyone need anyway?"

Fiona hardens. "Right now, my children are the only grandchildren, do you understand that? If you have that child, if you
have *Edward's* child, you are taking from my sons. And I am
their mother. Does that make sense to you? If you want to keep
whatever dirty little secret you've managed to keep hidden from
Ed, then you'll do exactly what I tell you to do. Do you understand me?"

"Ed and I aren't even married. My child won't even be a Holbeck. They wouldn't be able to inherit anything, so they'll take
nothing from your kids. What is the problem here?"

"God, you're a stupid little bitch, aren't you?" she snarls, casting her eyes back to the house in disbelief. "I guess this is why he fell for you. Because you're easy. You don't know anything about this family, do you? You haven't looked into the entailment, have you? Holbeck inheritance runs by *blood*."

"What? What does that—"

"Edward is the firstborn. If he has a child with anyone—married, not married, whatever—then that child inherits everything. It doesn't matter about you, if you're married to him; you mean nothing. Only blood counts. Only our children count. Even their gender is irrelevant. Blood counts. Children count. We are nothing."

"We're nothing?" I repeat, turning the idea of that over in my mind. "Okay," I say finally, her eyes boring into me. "Well, in that case, I guess you're completely fucked, then, aren't you, Fiona? Because I'm having this baby and *I* don't give a shit what happens to you either. If you win tonight, which I highly doubt, I'm still having this baby, and this family will have no choice but to accept my child no matter what I did or didn't do—according to you. So the question is, really, do *you* understand? Because it sounds to me like you probably should have done a bit more research yourself, shouldn't you? Before you got knocked up by the wrong fucking brother, you stupid cunt."

Fiona's mouth drops open in a satisfying gawp. There it is. I guess she must have read me wrong too.

I turn with a hot ember of triumph glowing inside me and crunch on at a jog through the swirling snow.

Once I've passed the maze, I slip behind some bushes and let out the tension I've been holding in my body. A quick look back toward the house confirms that she isn't following me, and I'm relieved to see she's gone.

I shove my burning-cold hands into my pockets and continue on, replaying Fiona's words. My baby, the creature growing inside me, will inherit everything. Everything here, everything in New York and London and France and Italy and LA and Switzerland. All of it. Everywhere. Everything. The whole Holbeck empire.

The idea is beyond real understanding. The weight of all that shouldn't rest on one person. You only have to look at history, at the lives of all those who have inherited, at *Bobby,* to know what a mixed blessing inherited wealth can be.

I don't want that much weight for my unborn child. I want a new world for her. A fresh world for her to find her own happiness in.

But Fiona's words throw new light on my situation and on Robert's interest in me. The fact that I am still here is perhaps more due to the life growing inside me than I ever realized. He must have known. Somehow, before we met that Thanksgiving evening. And suddenly I remember Dr. Leyman. We visited him the morning before Thanksgiving dinner. A simple phone call between old friends could have told him everything. Given what I know of the Holbecks I doubt doctor/patient confidentiality has ever stood in their way.

Finally I reach the lip of the well, and with one hand resting on the icy stone I lean over to shine my torch into the darkness. The hole's dripping walls disappear down into a void, and I fumble in the snow-covered dirt beside the well for something to drop down into it to gauge its depth, but as I do my hand comes into contact with something and I quickly pull away. It felt like human hair. I yelp, jumping back, my heart thumping erratically in my chest. There I was expecting to find horrors down the well, but here they are right on the surface.

Every fiber of my body tells me to run, to forget the game, to forget Robert and Edward and even the life growing inside me. The sudden possibility that I might die here tonight finally hits me with its cold, hard reality. A pure animal instinct for survival overtakes everything but I do not move, because if I run now, how long will I last out in the world with enemies like the Holbecks? If I make an enemy of Robert, I'm as good as dead.

I suck in a lungful of frozen air and force myself to pull it together. I've seen dead bodies before; I have seen those I love still and quiet; I am certainly strong enough to bear the death of a stranger.

I dip my hand back into the snow, keeping the beam of my torch on my hand as I tunnel into the gap. My fingertips find it again: a thick tendril of matted hair, coarse and frozen by the cold. I carefully brush the snow away and see I am wrong. It is not hair. It is not a body. Held in my hand instead is a frayed length of hemp rope. I pull at it and the snow all around the well shifts as the rungs of a rope ladder emerge from beneath. I rise to standing, dragging it up and out of the snowy scrub. At one end of it is a large double-claw hook.

I guess I will have to go down the well after all.

45

The Point of No Return

SATURDAY, DECEMBER 24

There are times in your life when you really do question where it all went wrong; and if scrambling into a pitch-black well at night, in a snow flurry, wearing a Balmain blazer dress, just shy of three months' pregnant, with a torch rammed in your mouth isn't one of those times then I don't know what is.

The rope creaks but it does not give. It held my weight when I tested it on the outside of the well wall but now, looking down into the darkness, doubts surface regarding its reliability.

I know there's water down there—a dropped stone proved that—so if I do fall, at least I'll hit water, even if it is freezing. The question is, how would I get out if I fell?

I pat my pocket for my iPhone and feel its reassuring bulk. It can survive being fully submerged in water, or so popular advertising would have me believe. If worse comes to worst, I can call someone. Edward. He can get me out. I might lose this game; I might have to tell him everything, but at least I wouldn't die of hypothermia. Granted, I may lose him in the process, but I'd have to call him if it came to it.

The opening of the well recedes above me, the midnight sky visible in blue through the breaks in the clouds as white flakes land delicate and cool on my upturned face.

I'd estimate the ladder to be approximately fifty feet long, and watching the shimmer of water far below, fifty feet seems about right.

The smell hits me a few more feet down. It is so overwhelming that I have to stop, take the torch from my mouth, and bury my face in my elbow crease to keep from retching. It's the unmistakable smell of rot, of something dead. I force my mind to picture a rat, a fox, a coyote—anything but the dead thing I fear is actually waiting down there for me.

> Peer into my darkness, it's cold and deep,
> <u>But to win you must find the secrets I keep.</u>

For the first time this evening, I wonder if I'm really playing the same game as the rest of the family. There's a chance my clues lead me only down here and nowhere else. For all I know, I might have crawled into my own grave.

My gaze shoots up to the opening of the well, fully expecting to see a figure above me—a figure who will send me splashing down into the darkness, unable to find a way out. But there is no one there.

Another terrifying thought occurs and I fish the iPhone from my pocket, careful to hold it with the firmest grip as my eyes fly to the signal bar. I let out an audible sigh of relief because I do not live in a horror movie; even down here in this well, there is a signal. If I fall, I can still call for help.

Robert is no fool; if he'd planned to kill me down here, he'd have damn well made sure I didn't have a phone on me.

I secure my phone back in its zipped pocket and pull out an

old tissue. I rip it in two with one hand and my teeth, dampen each section with saliva, and force them up my nostrils to block out the vomit-inducing stench.

Below me, the ladder meets the water and the well opens out into a small cavern, its walls no longer man-made but craggy rock.

I shine the flashlight into the water beneath me. It's clouded, so impossible to gauge its depth. I swing the torch beam around the cave walls, their wet slime glimmering and flaring in the roaming light. Then something catches my attention and I swing back. The pop of a bright envelope. My next clue. The third clue. I could still win this. I just need to get that envelope.

I hover above the water, the envelope still a good six feet away from me, positioned high on a jutting section of rock. I'll need to get in the freezing water if I want to reach it. I shine the torch into the murk beneath once more.

I plunge a trainer in and let the cold seep through and fill it. My breath catches; it's freezing. I tell myself I can do this; people swim in cold water every day. Lila did this morning. As long as I'm in and out quickly, as long as I can get dry, I'll be fine.

I push the smell from my mind as I gently ease my body into the water. I take in a sharp breath as it seeps through my clothes and reaches my skin, the cold somehow burning hot, but I sink no deeper. The cave floor is solid underfoot, and the water only reaches to my waist.

I wade to the ledge and haul myself up from the waterline, grabbing the card from the rock shelf. I rip it open and read.

You've come so far, you're almost there.
The next clue is something she would wear.
You can sense her, she's right here,
Reach out and check,
Your present is under what's around her neck.

There is someone here. Oh my God. I swing my torch back over the milky water. One of the women from Robert's list is here. It could be Melissa, Aliza, any of them. Though the smell suggests one of the more recent women on the list.

The cold is inside me now, my whole body quaking. I need to get out. I need to find this body and get out of here.

I stuff my clue card into a pocket above the waterline and shine my torch across the dark pool. I know what I need to do. I don't want to do it, but that's irrelevant. Someone's in here and I need to see whatever is around her neck.

I wade through the foul water, my arms searching for something solid in the soup.

It touches my bare right leg first, and in spite of knowing it's coming, I leap back, causing stinking water to splash up as far as my hair. I quickly wipe putrid water from my eyes using my dry shoulder, then I shine my torch into the water above the submerged object. It's funny, there's knowing something, and then there's experiencing it. I have experienced dead bodies, I have felt them, the strange weight they suddenly have, the cooling and hardening of once soft skin, the difference life makes to flesh, to bone, to hair.

I know and yet, inches from this person, I am scared. An animal instinct, a reflexive fear of death overriding my system. It's strange, because the dead are really the only things in the world who can't hurt us anymore.

I push away thoughts of who this girl might be, of how she ended up down here. All I need to focus on is what is around her neck.

Do not look at her face, I remind myself. *If you do see it, you will never forget it. Do not look at her face.*

I thrust my hands deep into the brown water. They make contact as expected with cold slippery flesh and tangled-up clothing. She is hard and soft at the same time, like rotten fruit. I slip one arm under her and cradle her body up toward the surface.

Do not think, I remind myself, *just do.*

She breaches the surface white and bloated, the stench overwhelming. I gasp in spite of myself. A bare shoulder comes into view but I keep my gaze elliptic, skimming over the edges of what

I see as I handle it. Mousy brown hair tangled into wet swirls curled against the gray-white flesh. It's Melissa. Aliza had jet-black hair. Melissa is wearing a red blouse, rotten and water-logged. Khaki slacks, a belt. Each image I let in is an image I know will haunt me. I've played this game before. I know how it goes. Then I locate it: a silver necklace around her bruised throat.

I focus only on that, my torch gritted between my teeth. I catch the edges of her chin, a bottom lip thick and purpled. Her hair is so close to my face; the smell, too much.

The silver of her chain twinkles, and as her head tilts back into the water I use my free hand to turn her necklace. The charm on it glistens into view, winking in the torchlight. It's a star. A sparkling diamond star.

That is all I need.

I let her sink back into the water and she disappears, the pool eddying around her until it is still once more. I do not have time to mourn. I think of Melissa's family, her friends perhaps unaware she is even gone yet, and my heart is full of sadness.

I am shuddering enough to ripple the water around me now. I need to get warm or risk hypothermia. I need to get out.

I scramble across to the ladder and haul my soaking body out, cold hands raw against the rope.

My Christmas Eve present, and whatever fresh hell that might entail, is hidden under a star. And I know exactly where I might find one of those.

46

Something Clicks

I barrel back across the lawn toward the house. There's a chance I could still win this, if everyone else has been going through the same awful things I have.

I push from my mind what might happen after this game ends. My desire to call the police and confess everything just so I can drag the whole Holbeck family kicking and screaming to justice is pretty heady, though I know I'd only go down with them.

Right now, I tell myself, I just need to finish this game. I need to win—and when I know every single thing each of these people has done, I will decide what I should do with that knowledge. I'm going to beat them at their own fucked-up game and then I'm going to beat them for real.

I scramble past the maze and on to the ornamental garden, my trainers slipping in the snow, my muscles erratic and juddering from the cold. Ahead, the lights of the house are warm and inviting and so close.

Something catches my trainer and sends me sprawling forward into the snow, knocking the air from me.

I roll over, arms up to protect myself, but there is nobody there. I rise on my elbows and look at what tripped me. There's a half-buried wellie jutting from the snow.

Immediately I know whose boot it is; she was standing here with me in them spewing bile less than an hour ago. Dread rises inside me as I clamber to my feet.

"Fiona," I call softly, but there is no one there.

I scan the ground for footprints, and in the beam of my torch her tracks appear heading back toward the maze. Judging by her gait, and the fact that she didn't stop to retrieve her boot, she must have been running. Something must have scared her so much that losing a boot seemed irrelevant. Something tells me to ignore this diversion and carry on with my own game, but if something happened to her, even though I don't like the woman, I'm not sure I could live with that.

At the maze's entrance, I notice a torn piece of red silk flapping, snagged on a low branch.

Oh God. Not in the maze, seriously?

If I'm going in there, I need something with a bit more heft than the paperweight in my pocket. I look around the maze's entrance for something, anything, I can use as a weapon. I really only have one option. I squat over the wooden maze arrow sign and heave it from the frozen ground. It pops out of the earth after a few wiggles and I fall back, a sharp wooden stake in hand.

At the maze's entrance, I raise my right hand to the wall and start to run, branches whipping across my open right palm as I go.

"Fiona," I call ahead, doubting a response but eager to interrupt whatever might be going on ahead of me. Then I recall that when I was talking to Fiona earlier, she was carrying a shovel.

It's only now that I wonder why.

It crosses my mind that she might be waiting for me in here. She has a weapon; this could all be a trick of some kind. And just as I'm thinking how unlikely it is that Fiona might want to hurt me, I remember what the baby inside me stands to inherit. Everything she would get would be taken from Fiona's children. People have killed for much, much less.

I round the next corner and pull up short. There is a spray of blood in the snow, the ground disturbed, like in the aftermath of a struggle. Beyond the patch of scrambled mud and meltwater, I see another set of footprints in the snow. Someone was waiting in here for her. She must have run straight into them. The new set of footprints is the only one that continues on into the maze, but the red drip continues with it, a red dotted line in the whiteness.

Something about the trail of blood up ahead makes me steel myself. I finally release my right hand from the maze wall and raise my weapon in both hands. I pause again before the next corner as I take a steadying breath before propelling myself around it.

A monstrous stone fountain looms over me and I stumble back, surprised to find myself at the heart of the maze. My gaze darts around the center of it, searching for a person, but there is no one here. I shuffle hesitantly around the fountain to make sure. Snow fills the fountain's tiers; no water is flowing from the gaping mouths of fish and sea creatures, which instead seem to scream silently up into the moonlight. I shiver. Lila was right; it is a creepy fountain.

Carefully I continue to make my way around the center of the fountain, following the line of blood, and as I do the shovel Fiona was carrying comes into sight. The soil beneath it has recently been turned. It is a mound; there is something buried beneath. A shallow grave.

In the silence the soil gently moves and I fly back from it, letting out an animal noise as I do. Whatever is under there is still alive. I edge closer to it once more.

"Fiona," I whisper gently, and from my tone it's clear I don't really want an answer.

The mound remains still and I step closer. It suddenly shifts and I leap back again, hand to heart, as its soil crumbs tumble and settle.

I dive to the ground and use my numb hands to scrape the soil away from her. A hand, an arm, a nose, lips, and, for a second, I really think she might be okay. But when I clear the soil from her face I see the wide set of her mouth and the dirt filling it. I continue to uncover her, scooping her onto her side, into the recovery position, but as I turn her, I feel a warmth spread across my own stomach, across my arms. I look down and see the thick blood pouring from her, congealed and soupy brown. I release her back onto the dirt and see the wound in her abdomen: deep and wet and dark. I gently place a hand on her chest; she's warm, but not warm enough. I hold for a heartbeat but there is none.

One of her legs kicks out again, reflexively, and I realize what is going on. Cadaveric muscle spasms. You can learn a lot of things researching novels. Bodies can move even after death: muscles contract, mouths open, faces twitch. I pull back from her, my arms and coat thick with her blood, the skin of my arms and thighs drenched in it. Fiona is dead.

I jerk up to standing, my breath coming in sharp snatches.

The game, already terrifying, just kicked up a gear into something else entirely.

Robert is picking off members of the family. It suddenly occurs to me why I might be here: my USP. I have a history of violence, and now Fiona's blood is all over me. I was also one of the last people to see her.

I realize how easily her death could be pinned on me. Anyone's death could be pinned on me. Robert has literally invited me here to get away with murder. He's sent me on a wild goose chase around the property in order to give himself time. I will take the blame for this if I don't end up dead myself. I need to stop him.

I rise, remove my phone from my blood-soaked puffer coat, and pull it off, wiping as much of Fiona's blood from me as I can before discarding the coat entirely.

I abandon the paperweight, grabbing the shovel instead, and

head out of the maze. Fiona said she'd seen either Stuart or Edward outside too, and with a jolt of terror I wonder if I am too late to warn him.

I dial Edward's number on my phone. The game has changed; none of us are safe.

Edward answers after one ring. "Where are you?" he huffs, his breath short, his concern knocking the emotion clean out of me. Wherever he is, he knows what's happening too. Floodgates open inside me.

"Ed, something awful is happening," I say to him, my voice quivering with cold and fear. I look down at my trembling body in a blazer dress and trainers, my arms filthy with mud and blood and God knows what else.

His voice is a whisper when it comes; he must be hiding inside the house. "I know. Same here. Listen, listen to me, Harry. Are you safe where you are?"

I look around at the moonlit garden. "Um, I think so," I tell him.

"Great, where are you, exactly?" he asks, and there's an urgency in his voice. "Tell me and I'll come get you."

"Is everyone okay there, Ed? Is everyone in the house okay?"

Silence and then, "No. No. I don't think so. No."

"Oh my God," I hear myself say. But the truth is, this is my fault; I thought I could fix this by myself. I selfishly tried to protect my secret by not going to the police and now Edward is in danger.

"Where are you, Harry?" Edward repeats, trying to focus me.

"I'm outside. It's so cold. I need to come in. I can't stay out here. Where are you? I'll come find you."

He is silent for a moment. "Okay, yeah, come find me," he says, but I can tell it's not what he wants. And now there's something strange in his tone. "I'll meet you in our room," he continues. "But listen, be careful, coming in the house. Don't talk to anyone. Don't stop for anyone until you find me. Don't let anyone see you. Do you understand? You need to make sure you get up to me without talking to anyone, okay?"

"Yeah. Yes, I can do that," I say, though every bone in my body is telling me there's something not right about this. Edward sounds different.

Robert could have Edward already; he could be forcing him to say this to draw me in. But my Edward wouldn't do that; he wouldn't lure me anywhere, even at gunpoint. Besides, Edward wanted to come to me; it was my idea to go back inside.

And just like that, Samantha Belson, the Holbecks' nanny, comes back to me. I thought *she* was the blonde at 7 East 88th the day Bobby jumped, but she was here, at The Hydes, with the children. But who were the children? *Bobby was a twenty-year-old man*, she'd said. *He certainly didn't need a nanny.*

It occurs to me now that Edward was eighteen years old when Bobby died. He certainly didn't need a nanny either. And with terrifying ease, a series of thoughts slot themselves into place and a question forms in my mind.

"Edward?" I ask.

"Yes."

"Where were you the day Bobby died?"

The line is silent for long enough for my creeping dread to blossom into something worse. "I was upstairs," he says after a moment.

Inside me, something yawns wide open with panic.

"Okay," I say as neutrally as I can, buying myself a precious moment to order my mind.

"But I love you, Harry," he says simply, and I feel my tears come. Edward was there the day his brother died. Something triggered Bobby to jump, and Lucy knew exactly what. Edward was with Bobby when he committed suicide.

The silence between us is thick, and I feel his sadness down the line.

"I know what you are too," he tells me cautiously. "But I still love you."

His words hit me viscerally, knocking the last remaining doubt from my unwilling mind. Edward had a hand in Bobby's death. He killed Lucy, and then Alison and Gianna, Aliza and Melissa.

And now Fiona and who knows who else. As the facts come together, I feel the Edward I know disintegrate.

I've had the wrong end of the stick this whole time. Robert's tape is real, but it's not Robert's confession. He fed me the truth, but in the only way I would be able to hear it. If he'd told me outright, I would have thought he was lying, trying to scare me off his son. I would have told Edward. All this time, I've been condemning the wrong Holbeck, terrified Edward might find out my own awful secret. But he knows. He knew all along; in me, he found someone as broken as he was.

And suddenly I get an inkling of what the favor Robert Holbeck requires from me might be. He wants me to know who his son really is, to know whose child I am having and what that might mean. Robert wants me to stop Edward.

I squeeze my eyes tight shut to block out what is happening, but I am instantly barraged by flickering images of the bloated body in the well. Images of Lucy's hair caught in the wind outside 7 East 88th, of Gianna dancing on that New Year's Eve, of Alison's family alone and still waiting after twenty years. These women did nothing to warrant their fates.

And suddenly, with a seismic shift, I feel myself break away from Edward.

I feel him being ripped from me, not by Robert, or by his controlling family, but by the real Edward.

My Edward—my good, kind, funny Edward—never really existed. I created him. Well, Edward Holbeck created him, a copy of the brother he killed.

I feel the loss of the man I knew with aching clarity as warm tears stream down my face. I will never see that man again; he will never hold me again. He was only ever the idea of a man, the ghost of one that I saw reflected in Edward Holbeck.

My eyes glide back to the house ahead, its lights warm and welcoming, but the man in there isn't who I thought he was. He's a killer, and not the kind of killer I am. That's why Edward chose me: my past. He thought perhaps he'd found a kindred spirit. That's why I've survived this long; that's why he asked me to marry him, why I'm carrying his child. He thinks we are the same.

Everything clicks into place, just as Robert told me it would, and I realize what Robert wants me to do. What his tape has been leading me toward.

I don't have a family of my own; I lost them long ago. But I do have something.

I gently place a hand on my abdomen and slow my breathing. Robert is offering me a chance at a new family. I have a little girl growing inside me, whose family needs me to keep them safe.

"I'm coming back now, Edward," I say into the receiver. "I'll see you soon."

47

The Whole Family

SUNDAY, DECEMBER 25

Light spills from the crack beneath the boot room door as I listen for voices. I don't know what has been happening in the house since I left, but it can't be good. After a moment I try the door handle, hands numb with cold.

The stark white corridor beyond must be one for staff, as it's unlike any other part of the building I've seen. I follow it along until I see a room ahead, shadows dancing within, and only once I'm sure it is silent do I peer inside.

A small television plays on mute, a Christmas movie. Beside it, a small table covered with well-leafed magazines, and at the end of the room a low gray sofa on which Sylvia and Anya slump, seemingly asleep.

"Hello," I try softly, but the two women do not stir. "Shit."

I approach carefully, kneeling before the unmoving pair. I

touch Sylvia's shoulder gently. She slips onto Anya. I raise my fingers to her nose; she's still breathing, just unconscious.

I let out a huff of relief. Both have drained coffee cups abandoned in their laps. Drugged but alive.

I leave them where they sit, carefully closing the door to their break room behind me.

Farther along the corridor, I find myself in a cavernous working kitchen. Leftovers from tonight's dinner are covered in wrap, ready to be stacked and refrigerated. Breakfast trays are laid out, ready to be filled for the morning. On the kitchen island, mince pies cool on wire. The smell of them mixes with the scent of rot coming off me, making me want to vomit.

There's another smell in the kitchen, though. I look across to my warped reflection in the copper pots hanging over the gas cooker. Then my eye catches something on the ground jutting out from the other side of the kitchen island. An ankle, a shoe, a foot. Tom Ford heels and green nail polish. It's Matilda.

I dash around the island unit where I find Eleanor and Matilda propped against the cupboards in front of the cooker, the doors of which are open. The soft hiss of gas fills the room. I grab a tea towel and thrust it over my face, leaning past their bodies to twist off the gas dials.

Then I drop to a crouch beside Matilda, checking her pulse. She stirs, sluggish, eyes fluttering open, drugged and dazed. I move to Eleanor; her pulse is slow and stable too, though she does not stir.

"Harry. Harriet," Matilda groans, her eyes glazed. "Careful. He's in a mood," she slurs.

"Who's in a mood, Matty?" I ask, though I know the answer.

"Little Eddy Teddy Bear." She giggles. "I feel mushy."

They've been drugged with whatever Sylvia and Anya got, I'm guessing.

"I know," I tell her. "Do you think you can stand up, Matty?"

She looks at her towering shoes with a frown and shakes her head. I dutifully remove them.

"How about now?"

She shifts forward slowly, making her way up onto all fours. "I think someone put something in my drink," she mumbles, more to herself than to me. "Not the first time," she giggles. Then, after a moment, she pulls herself up to a very wobbly stand using the kitchen island as leverage. "I'm up. I'm up."

"Okay, we need to keep it quiet, Matty, okay?"

Matilda lifts a finger to her lips and nods earnestly.

I take her hands in mine and hold her gaze, focusing her. "Matilda, it's very important you do what I say now, okay?" She nods, squinting at me with concentration. "I need you to take your mother somewhere and hide. Okay? Can you do that?"

Matilda suddenly seems to notice her mother for the first time down on the floor beside her, and she covers her mouth to stifle a giggle. "Oops. Her too. Oh, okay. I can, we can, do that. Safe. Yep." She nods for an extended period.

"Great. But you need to hide away from here. Do you understand? It's not safe in the house. Something is going on."

She nods and juts out her lower lip. "Yeah, Daddy and Eddy are fighting again. We can hide. I'm a good hider," she whispers, tapping the side of her nose.

"Do you know where the hunting hides are, Matty? The hide at the edge of the forest?"

She grins.

"Good, go there. If I don't come get you by the morning, you need to call the police, okay?"

She juts her lip out. "No phone."

Fuck.

There's no way around it. I fish my own phone from my pocket, remove my passcode settings, and hand it to her. "Do not lose this. And do not use it until the morning. I'm going to sort this out, but if I can't, you need to call the cops when it gets light."

Matilda looks baffled at the concept but gives an undaunted shrug. "Good for you, Harry," she says cheerfully, then claps me on the back and raises the phone. "No cops till daytime." She uses the phone to salute me then promptly turns to inspect her prone mother.

I watch her pocket the phone and when I'm certain she knows what she's doing, I pick up my discarded shovel and head out of the kitchen.

As I shift through the house, heart thumping light and fast in my chest, a plan begins to form. I know what I need to do. I need to find Robert. He set this game in motion; he must have a solution, a plan. I'm aware my plan is basically to find out what Robert's plan is, but I think it's fair to admit that he's had longer to think this through than I have. And it's definitely time we had our chat.

At the entrance to the new wing, I see Edward slumped against the glass on the other side of the security door. I only catch him from the back, his suit jacket crumpled and rucked on the transparent wall, his white shirt collar stained with the blood still dripping from his hairline. He's locked himself in there, his bloody fingerprints smeared across the control panel. Someone must have gotten to him before me.

I watch his shoulders gently rising and falling as I approach and, safe in the knowledge that glass door is locked, I sink to the ground behind him, my breath fogging as I crane to get a better look at his face.

Over his shoulder I can see his lap, his bloodstained hands, and the small pinkie ring on his little finger. It's not Edward; it's Stuart. Something inside me unclenches.

I tap delicately on the glass next to Stuart's head. He jolts up, shocked at my proximity, and as he turns, I can see that his movements are as slow and fuzzy as Matilda's. There must have been something in the drinks this evening, or the coffee. Stuart wouldn't have been drinking, so it must have been the latter.

His face is a mess, his right eye swollen, bruised shut, the wound to his right temple congealed, but there are bloodstains on his cheek and neck all the way to his collar. He must have just gotten away from Edward, crawled in here where he knew he'd be safe. Edward doesn't know the passcode to the new wing. I remember him trying to ignore his call the other day before Eleanor tapped in the keypad code. He wanted to see it, to get in here.

Stuart is saying something, but the glass is soundproof. I shake my head and he squeezes his eyes tight shut with annoyance. After a moment he regroups, and with great effort turns his body to face me fully, pointing past me, his eyes flaring. Suddenly certain Edward is directly behind me, I spin, grabbing my shovel, but the main hallway beyond is empty.

I wheel back to Stuart and he shakes his head slowly, trying to make me understand, a characteristic smirk blossoming beneath his injuries. *No,* he mouths carefully. He gestures past me again and I follow his gaze out into the hallway. When I look back at him, he jabs a finger left, indicating through the hall and left. *Edward,* he mouths, then, with finality, he slumps back against the glass wall, exhausted. Edward went that way. He closes his eyes and unseeingly raises a hand to wave me off.

I grab my shovel and leave Stuart behind, safe in the knowledge that he's protected by two inches of security glass.

So far only Fiona is dead. Stuart is safe; Matilda is safe; Eleanor is safe. The kids are safe down in the lodge with Nunu—now it seems to make more sense why Robert chose this year to allow that. Some of my new family is safe. Which leaves only Edward, Robert, and Oliver unaccounted for.

I creep into the main hallway, careful to watch where I place my trainers on the creaking parquet, my shovel raised and ready, and it suddenly occurs to me that I have no idea what happened to Oliver. Or where he went. He's the biggest and strongest Holbeck, the family's very own all-American linebacker. Why isn't *he* doing something about all this?

And at that exact moment, my vision flashes white as pain crests at the back of my skull, and everything goes black.

48

Merry Christmas, Harriet

SUNDAY, DECEMBER 25

And this is where we started.

I come to on the hall floor. I cannot tell how long I have been out, and I cannot lift my head. Around me the house twinkles on, Christmas music still jingling softly through the hallways.

I just need a second, I tell myself. I know this because it took time to move after our car rolled to a stop twenty years ago. I hung in the creaking cold for what seemed like an eternity that morning. But my body came back to life.

The smell of gasoline is thick on the floor around me, making my eyes water as the breeze from the open door wafts it into my face. I swivel my gaze across to the hall fireplace, its logs burning brightly. It could catch so easily, but I imagine that is someone's plan, when the time is right. Whether it is Robert's plan or Edward's or even Oliver's, I no longer know.

If I could stand, I could run. I could just leave them all, save myself, bolt and call the cops—but then I see the story being constructed around me and I understand what it is designed to look like.

The gasoline, the flames, the bodies. What is happening here is being carefully staged, and if this building goes up in flames, I have no doubt who will be held accountable. Whoever is doing this has enough on me to ensure that.

If I run, I don't get a say in how this ends.

I try to lift my face again. Straining every sinew, I manage to lift myself a few inches from the floor, just enough to turn my head in the other direction.

I gasp. Oliver's lifeless face rests inches from mine, his mouth open, his eyes glassy. I stifle a yelp. His hand is still pressed tight to the wet wound across his throat, though blood no longer pumps from it.

By the look of things, it's safe to say that Oliver is not the mastermind behind all of this. At least, if he ever was, he's not anymore.

On the floor beside him I see a wrought-iron fireplace poker; that must be what he hit me with. He must have thought I was responsible for all of this. Then the sound of a scuffle must have brought the real perpetrator straight to us, to him. I am still alive, though, which can only mean one thing: either Edward or Robert needs me to play my part in what happens next.

I become aware of the weight of Oliver's legs on mine, pinning me to the floor, and I slowly edge myself out from under him. From there I struggle up to all fours and then carefully onto unsteady feet. I wait for my dizziness to settle, then quietly stalk to the stairs, where I see my shovel kicked to the side.

As I creep, I hear the muffled noises of someone moving about in the sitting room. The sound of furniture being rearranged. I freeze, crouched beside the shovel. Something is happening in there. I could run, but I know what that will bring down on me. I will spend the rest of my life in jail, framed as the woman who burned down the Holbecks' mansion with the whole family inside. But they can't say that if I try to stop it—if I save everyone.

I carefully rise, lifting the shovel and hefting it in both hands.

The sitting room looks different when I enter: the log fire roars on, the Christmas tree lights twinkle in hazy halos, and beneath, brightly wrapped presents silently wait, but now all of the furniture has been moved to the edges of the room. All that remains in the center is a rug, wet with gasoline, and two armchairs facing each other.

In the armchair facing me sits an unconscious Robert Davison Holbeck, his head peacefully resting against the high back of the chair. Beside him stands his son Edward. If Edward did not have a shotgun pointed directly at Robert's head, the scene might easily resemble one of the family's historic oil paintings.

"Harry," Edward says, with an oddly welcoming tone, as he takes in my blood- and mud-smeared appearance. "It's been a long night, hasn't it? But you made it." His voice has a sardonic lilt to it that I do not recognize, which gives me the distinct impression that I'm meeting this man for the first time.

There are a million things I could say to him, that I want to ask him, but only one question really matters.

"How long did you know?" I ask, careful not to play the idiot. "What I was?" I'm pretty sure we both know what's going on here; I just need some of the gaps filled.

"Very early," he says gently. "I had you vetted the day after we met. A week later I had everything. But in a sense I knew from the beginning. I felt it. Your strength, your loyalty, your love. I loved you the night I saved you but by God did I love you more when I found out what you were capable of. How you responded under pressure. That man took from you, but you took straight back, without hesitation. What you could do for love, what you had done—" He breaks off with a shake of the head. "I spent a lifetime looking for you. Looking for someone I could be honest with, finally be myself with."

Robert stirs slightly in the seat beside him, but Edward's focus is on me. I don't know what his plan is, but I know I need to keep his attention.

"But you weren't honest," I nudge gently, careful to stay the right side of empathetic. "All this time you knew about me, but you said nothing. Why?" I ask, and in spite of everything I hear the rattle of emotion in my voice, because however twisted his thought process was or is, I loved him.

"I wanted *you* to tell *me* first. It might seem childish, but I wanted you to trust me enough to show me who you were," he answers. "Then I would know what I felt was real. But you never said a word, did you?"

A sickening wave of guilt hits me in spite of what he has done, and who I have found him to be, because he is right: I have never, in my life, trusted anyone with my truth. Least of all the people I have loved. I feel myself bristle at the accusation.

"I was scared you wouldn't love me. That I'd lose you if you knew," I tell him honestly. "Isn't that what you felt too? You didn't trust that *I* could love *you*. The real you. If I knew what you had done, that you had killed Bobby and Lucy, and Alison, and Gianna. And all the others."

He looks away fleetingly. "I didn't kill Bobby."

"You had something to do with it."

"Yes," he says, taking the hit with a strange, disarming honesty. "He wasn't taking Adderall. I was slipping it to him, in his meals back at the apartment. I found a way to make the drugs interact. He would never have taken a stupid drug like that. I think they all knew, afterward. Dad knew. He was pulling away from what Dad wanted. He would have taken the company, everything, in the wrong direction. I wanted to take him out of the game, that's all. I wanted to force him to step aside, for his health; I wanted to break him. But it went much further than I anticipated; he had a mind of his own and I lost control of things. I tried to stop him that day; I told him it was all in his head, what he was feeling wasn't real, but it was too late. He wasn't listening. It was my first time and I made mistakes. I didn't mean to kill my brother. He did that to himself."

"You wanted to be Bobby? To have the company? Why did you hand it all over to Oliver, then?"

He looks down at the man beside him. "We made a deal, Dad and I. He would keep it all quiet if I waited until he thought the time was right for me to take over. Oliver was only ever supposed to be there until Dad stepped down," he says. "And that hasn't happened yet. I thought it best to do my own thing until full control passed to me. But by God did they want me back in the fold, where they could keep an eye on me. I'm not the only one in this family with secrets, but I'm sure you know that."

Robert stirs once more in the seat beside him, his eyes flickering hazily open, disoriented.

"Why did you kill them, Ed?" I ask, desperate to buy more time for Robert to come around.

He studies me for a second before speaking. "Why did you kill him?"

I'm momentarily back-footed by a question no one has ever asked. I think about obfuscating, but there is little point, and part of me desperately longs for the release of unfettered honesty. "Because I wanted him to pay, to suffer, to understand what he did."

"And do you think he did?"

I consider the question for the first time in my life. "Yes, actually. Yes, I think he understood."

"So you got what you wanted?" he asks simply.

"In a way, but I have to live with that. That a momentary whim of mine cost an entire human life."

"His whim cost you two lives, though, didn't it?" he argues, and I see what he is doing.

"We aren't the same, Edward."

He tilts his head to one side. "No, we are not. You meant to kill your first; mine was a mistake."

The distinction smarts. "But the second wasn't, was it?"

"The second was necessary. Lucy was there the day he died; she heard everything. I had little choice."

"And Alison. She was your first real girlfriend, wasn't she? Did you have no choice then?"

He flinches at my words. "Yes, I had no choice. I thought I loved her, that she loved me. I tried to tell her everything, about Bobby, about Lucy; I tried to be honest. She ran from me. I don't know what I expected; she was young and good and it was naïve to think she'd forgive anything, but I had to try. You know that impulse, I'm sure, even if you've never followed through. I thought it would be safe to share my secrets, but it was not. I had no idea what she might do, who she might tell. And then Gianna. I pulled her close in the hope I might be able to uncover how much she knew or suspected. But she had a strange way about her. I could never be sure what Alison had told her; how much she knew. Is this what you want to hear?" he asks suddenly. "The why of everything?"

There's a pragmatism to the question that I suddenly realize means he is still hoping for the other shoe to drop with me. There's still a part of him certain that if he is honest enough, open enough, I will somehow understand and I will be able to continue loving him. But what if I don't?

"Are you going to kill me, Edward?" I ask.

He studies me silently. "I know what's been going on between you two," he says gently, looking to the slumped Robert in the chair beside him.

He knows about the tape. He must have heard Robert's voice that night I found him with it in his hands. He must have known what it was as soon as he heard that list of names. He knows I've lied to him for weeks.

"You heard him on the tape?"

Edward nods. "I expected it from him. But not from you. He tried to avoid me, to manipulate the situation. To gain your trust."

In my mind, I desperately rewind the events of the past few

days. I recall Edward getting a phone call and leaving me with Eleanor to see the new wing, then, moments later, Robert arguing and smashing something in his office. He was on the phone with Edward. It is possible Edward confronted him in that call, which resulted in dinner being canceled.

"I brought you here to force the point," he continues. "I hoped you might listen to the tape and tell me who you were of your own free will. I hoped maybe it could be good for us. Has it been good for us?"

In the chair beside Edward, Robert straightens slightly as he takes me in, a muted smile blooming on his face. "Harriet," he croaks, his voice hoarse. "You made it, just in time." He shifts in the seat with difficulty, nursing a wound on his side. "Did you find your final clue?" he asks hazily.

Edward watches intently for my reaction, clearly as invested in the answer as Robert. I try to recall what my final clue was—the game now a distant memory. Then I remember the well, the stench, the weight of Melissa's body in my arms.

"Harriet, I need you to tell me if this relationship is still what you want," Edward says with disarming simplicity.

Robert gives me a pointed look and I force my mind back to the final clue.

Your present is under what's around her neck.

My gift is under a star, I'm guessing a Christmas tree star. Though the house is full of them and unless my gift is another shotgun, I don't see what use it could possibly be to me now.

I nod to Robert. I understand the clue. His eyes flick behind me and suddenly I recall what lies there, in the corner of this very room.

A Christmas tree!

"What happens tonight if I say yes? If I say I still want this?" I ask Edward, with care.

He pauses before responding. "If you say yes, what happens here tonight is an accident. We walk away, we survive, everything becomes ours. Together, like Mitzi and Alfred."

I do not want what he is offering. I do not want that life. I do not want to be that person. It must only be a micro-reaction I give, but it is enough. He sees it, and I cannot pull it back. I watch the disappointment crest inside him as his last hope fades and a cold calm settles over him.

"Okay," he says after a moment. "I need you to sit in that chair, Harry." He tips the barrel of his gun toward the armchair opposite Robert's. "Can you do that for me?"

Robert is silent beside him but everything about this situation tells me not to do as Edward says. I think of the star, and it takes every ounce of willpower I have left not to spin around and look straight up at the star sparkling on top of the Holbeck tree behind me.

"I don't want to sit in the chair, Ed," I say, shifting the weight of my shovel. I know a shovel is useless against a shotgun, of course, but there is only one of Edward and two of us, and Edward can't point the gun at both of us. If Robert and I both move, one of us might survive.

"Just sit in the chair, Harry," Edward barks.

My present is right behind me under the tree. That's what Robert is telling me, and from the look on his face, it seems like it might really help our current situation.

I desperately play for time.

"Why kill Aliza? She wasn't even close to you. Or Melissa?" I ask, scrambling for a break in his concentration, or a sign from Robert.

"Aliza asked too many questions, about the past, about our family. Matilda is too trusting and Aliza got a little too close to the truth. But she had secrets as bad as yours. Worse, perhaps. I warned her, but she was dangerous, so—"

"I found Melissa, by the way," I say, for Robert's benefit. I want him to know I have worked out where my gift is and I am ready to get it.

Edward shrugs. "An assistant working above her pay grade," he says without further explanation. He lifts the gun directly at me. "Sit. Down."

Robert gives an almost imperceptible nod and I make a show of slowly lowering my weapon to the floor for Edward.

I place my shovel down gently on the edge of the rug. "I'll sit in the chair if you put the gun down."

Edward gives a surprised smile. "I'm not going to do that," he says.

Hands still gripping the shovel, I catch a glimpse of something in my periphery beneath the tree. It pops out, bright yellow against the reds of other wrapped presents, completely out of place. A palm-sized canister of Ronsonol lighter fluid decorated with a massive red bow.

That's my gift: a very dark joke. I look back at Robert in disbelief and he gives a barely perceptible lift of the brows.

I guess I know what the gift was meant to symbolize: a release from the past; evidence removed, lost, my slate wiped clean. But that is no help now. And then what Robert is trying to tell me clicks into place. I catch sight of the fire still raging in the hearth behind Edward and I understand Robert's thinking. I need that can.

I gently let go of my shovel and raise my hands to Edward in surrender, my eyes trained on him as I rise to stand. As far as Edward is concerned, I am unarmed; I am doing as he asked.

"Thank you, Harriet," Edward says, his tone gentle as he gestures for me to make my way to the chair.

In my peripheral vision Robert raises a finger a few inches above the armrest of his chair and my eyes flick to him, then back to Edward. Robert raises two more fingers above the armrest. A countdown.

"You're going to burn it all down?" I ask Edward. "You've already killed Fiona and Oliver. You're going to kill everyone else and frame me?" I add, keeping Edward distracted as I prepare to make my move.

"The facts will tell a story of their own," Edward answers wearily.

The first of Robert's three raised fingers taps down.

Three.

"And you? You'll be alone. No family, no wife, no daughter. Can you live with that? All the money in the world but no one to talk to."

"The human element in any enterprise will always be its sticking point. It's always best to keep things simple," Edward says, his tone resigned.

The second of Robert's fingers taps down.

Two.

"I think we've all done enough talking, Harry," Edward continues.

The last of Robert's raised fingers hits the fabric of the armrest and everything happens at once.

One.

Robert suddenly makes a grab for Edward's shotgun barrel, yanking it down and away toward the ground, giving me an opening. I spin and dive for the bright yellow of the can beneath the tree. My hands grasp it just as a shot reverberates behind me and my gaze snaps back to the pair just in time to see Edward wrest back control of the weapon and whip the rifle butt into his father's face. Robert crumples down to the floor, blood oozing from his thigh. Edward spins, pointing the gun back at me.

He holds me in his sights for a second and then we both seem to realize the same thing at once. Edward's gun is a single-barrel shotgun; he needs to reload.

We both move at exactly the same time. He cracks open the gun, plunging a hand into his pocket for a cartridge, as I snap and twist the cap from the lighter fuel and run straight for him.

With terrifying efficiency, he slips a fresh cartridge into the weapon and snaps it shut before raising the weapon. But I am on him; I plow straight into him at full tilt, knocking him back as hard as I can. He bowls backward, losing his footing, having to grab the mantelpiece to stop himself from falling into the fire, the gun flailing now in his one free hand. And that is when I do it.

I squeeze the lighter fuel canister as hard as I can and a tight pressurized stream dances across Edward's clothes and face as he struggles to regain his balance. The acrid smell of butane fills the air and without stopping to think, I let the canister's stream hit the roaring fire behind Edward's back.

The flames flare white and engulf him, the gun clattering to the floor as his hands desperately fly to his face.

I do not stop to think. I advance on him even though I see his pain, his newfound terror. I see his openmouthed screams but I can barely hear them over the throb of blood in my own ears, the pounding of my heart, because I know I cannot stop until this is over. *He* will not stop until this is over.

I empty more and more of the fuel canister onto him as he lunges and swings madly toward me. The pain must become too much because suddenly he throws himself down to the rug to tamp out his flames. But he does not think it through; the gasoline-soaked rug beneath him leaps to life, flashing even brighter as fresh flames engulf him and creep out toward the rest of the room.

I look to Robert's prone form. We don't have much time before this fire is completely out of control. Robert and I need to leave.

I know what I need to do. I circle around Edward and pick up the discarded shotgun, its handle hot from the flame-engulfed floor, and raise it toward Edward's shuddering figure.

I get him in my sights, flames from the rug now lapping at my own bare legs, sending white-hot pain through me as I try to steady the weapon. I exhale calmly and pull the trigger. There is a rip of sound and Edward stops moving before the flames swallow him whole.

I drop the weapon and run to Robert's side, tearing an antique wall hanging from the wall above him to muffle out the flames approaching him. I thrash them out and pull him, coughing, up to sitting.

"We need to get out," I tell him. "Keep pressure on the leg wound." He nods, and with my help stumbles up to his feet.

"The other children? Eleanor?" he croaks.

"They're safe," I tell him. It's a half-truth. Eleanor is safe. Matilda is safe. Stuart I'm not so sure about, and Oliver and Fiona are dead.

We stumble from the sitting room into the hall where I steer Robert clear of the sight of Oliver's body and out the open front door.

We burst out into the snow and take in lungfuls of clean winter air. Robert is safe, but Stuart is still inside the building, and I am not like Edward. I cannot be responsible for any more death.

"Can you make it out to the woods?" I ask Robert as we stumble clear of the house. "Eleanor and Matilda are in the hide at the edge of the forest."

"Yes," he tells me, then grasps my wrist protectively. "Wait. Where are you going?"

"Stuart is still inside."

Robert shakes his head, grasping my wrist harder. "No. Don't go back in, Harriet. Think about your child."

I remember the life inside me, half Edward, half me, and I hesitate. Then I carefully remove his grip from my arm. "I am thinking of her," I say delicately. "She needs me to be a person who goes back in. *I* need me to be a person who goes back in."

The heat is hard to bear when I reenter the building, and the snow-drenched strip of fabric I thought might protect my lungs does not stop the hot burn in my throat. I dash back through the heat of the flaming hallway, my eyes stinging.

When I reach the new wing, Stuart is no longer behind the glass. He must have made it out another way.

I turn to leave again, but with a sudden jolt remember Sylvia and Anya propped up beside each other in their break room. I turn and sprint toward the staff quarters, through smoke-clogged corridors that lead back to the gas-filled kitchen.

I know nothing I can do will change the past; nothing can change what I did, or who I am in consequence. But the past can stop here. I can change. I can be better. A fresh start, a new me— a more honest me.

After all, isn't that what I want for my child? For my daughter?

We all make mistakes and live with them, but we can make a

virtue of that fact. We can turn one bad day into a hundred good ones. One bad choice into a lifetime of good choices.

Ahead of me I hear the sound of flames hitting gas and exploding as the force blows the kitchen door clean off its hinges, the backdraft knocking me off my feet. My hands fly to my buzzing ears as I choke on the cloud of smoke.

I stumble up to my feet and dart forward into the kitchen, dodging the flames lapping cabinets and bursting along the fabric of the half-rolled blinds.

I bolt into the white corridor beyond and then I see her. Anya freezes mid-step, the weight of a barely conscious Sylvia leaning against her, her expression terrified as she tries to work out if I am here to help or hurt.

But there is no time to explain. Wordlessly I slip an arm under Sylvia's other shoulder and take half her weight.

The three of us burst out into the frozen white of the garden and spill onto the snow gasping in clean air.

After a moment, Anya catches her breath and speaks. "The phone lines don't work. We need to call the fire department, the police. Do you have a phone? We aren't allowed our own phones in the house."

Of course they aren't.

"Matilda has my phone," I answer honestly.

Anya suddenly seems to remember the rest of the Holbeck family. "Oh God, where are they? I completely—" Her hand flies to her mouth. "Are they okay? I didn't think— There was only time to save Sylvia," she gabbles, emotion taking hold of her.

"Everyone else is okay," I lie. "Everyone is gathered down by the forest, away from the fire. We can walk down to meet them—call for help there."

Anya looks between me and her barely conscious friend and seems to come to the conclusion that I am, at least, the devil she knows.

"Okay," she says, "let's go."

49

Iris

MONDAY, JULY 10

Iris. Apple of my eye.

You stir in the clear bassinet beside my hospital bed as I shift into a more comfortable position.

Beyond the windows of Mount Sinai, the sky is blue. You are a summer baby; you arrived a little later than everyone expected, but you survived that night in the snow seven months ago. We both did.

We stood in the cold, the remaining Holbecks and I, and we watched The Hydes burn to the ground. The new wing would be all that would remain. A wing rising from the ashes. They say the rebuild will be completed by next spring, to Eleanor's minimalist specifications.

In the hospital corridors beyond my private room the ward buzzes with life, but you sleep on peacefully after the storm of hours before. I watch your tiny chest rise and fall—the life inside me now outside.

The last Christmas I spent with your father will always be burned into my memories and into my skin: the flesh of my hands, my calves, warped forever; my lungs scarred. I'll never run a marathon, but I was strong enough to keep us both alive.

They cut you from my abdomen in the early hours of this morning. Not because there was a problem, but because there wasn't. You just didn't want to leave; you were happy, *too* content nestled safe inside me.

But the world was waiting to see you. So they shucked me open, like an oyster, and popped you out, my pearl. My little Iris.

Granddad Robert paid for this room. He paid for everything, and he always will. He chose Mummy, you see, for a very important task: he saw something in me, a strength or a usefulness—whichever you prefer. Granddad knew one day we would do something amazing, you and I, that we would save him, that we would save the whole family. You won't hear it from me, but you will from them. You see, Mummy won a game—an old Christmas game. But we don't play that game anymore.

That last year we played, everyone got their presents—Mummy insisted. Auntie Fiona got a trust for her boys; Uncle Oliver got a company stake for them; Uncle Stuart got to take over Oliver's position in the company; and Mummy got a new family. And lest we forget, Granny and Granddad got you.

They found a gas leak at The Hydes; it could have killed us all. And while the insurance company would not pay out, the lawyers and investigators found enough evidence to close the case. An unforeseeable accident. Of course, we wish there was someone to blame for the deaths of three dearly loved people, but life takes as often as it gives. The temperatures reached in the main building meant only DNA could be recovered. Uncle Oliver, Auntie Fiona, and your father, all lost.

Sam, Tristan, and Billy became orphans that night, like Mummy. But you still have me.

I will not tell you how they moved their parents, how the scene was set, how the men that came in the early hours made everything go away. Your grandfather set wheels in motion. Money, power, leverage make the world go around. Sometimes knowing the *right people* for the job means knowing the *wrong people*.

But my hope is you never have to find that out.

Though, know this, if you ever need me to, my love, I will move the world for you. But no more than once. I have seen how chasing one mistake with another can become a habit.

They stayed up late, you see, after the rest of us went to bed. They must have fallen asleep in front of the fire, the rug caught and wooden doors warped with the heat. The smoke would have gotten them while they slept, and the fire did the rest. If it hadn't been for you, keeping me awake at night, I might not have noticed the heat, the smoke. I might not have been able to save those that I did.

I want you to know, Iris, my love, that Mummy tried to save Daddy. I mean that in the truest and the realest sense, but it was too late. And though he is no longer here, the man I met that one magical night, the man I fell in love with—he will live on in you. You are the best of him and he would have loved you so much. And while Daddy might be gone, you will have so many people who love you.

And when you are older, I will tell you the story of the family I lost, and the family I gained. The favor Granddad asked of me and the price he paid for it. The son he lost and the daughter he gained. My story might not be a perfect rendition of the facts, but sometimes it's easier to understand the truth of our lives through stories. Sometimes stories cut to the heart of things straighter, truer.

I know a mystery surrounds us, but the global interest in us, in my latest book, will be long gone by the time you are old enough to understand. They say the book is too close to life for comfort. That to write a thriller based on a real-life tragedy is distasteful in the extreme, but we all cope with what life throws at us in different ways. And people love a mystery.

Better fictional horror than the real sort, as your granddad would say.

Years from now you will inherit it all. The Holbeck fortune, the empire, the history, because you are the firstborn's first child. You take your father's mantle. Granddad and Uncle Stuart will hold down the fort until you are ready—if you want to be ready.

The family name is a heavy crown to bear if you overthink it. But I promise you, things will be different for you, my love. I will be here for you every step of the way—if you need me to be. You can choose the life you want to live, because you are not a Holbeck, not really. You're a Reed, and us Reeds—we have no history to live up to at all.

We only have our future.

Acknowledgments

Thank you to my wonderful editors: Kara Cesare at Penguin Random House in the United States and Bethan Jones at Simon & Schuster in the United Kingdom, who both added so many layers to this story with their invaluable thoughts, questions, and nudges. Huge thanks for making the editing process on this, and on every book, so creatively engaging and fun! I'm incredibly lucky to have you.

Massive thanks to the rest of the team at Penguin Random House and everyone who helped to get this book safely into your hands: Jesse Shuman, Allyson Lord, Allison Schuster, Yewon Son, Jennifer Hershey, Kim Hovey, Kara Welsh, Kelly Chian, Carlos Beltrán, Elizabeth A. D. Eno, and many more. Thank you for your hard work, enthusiasm, and creativity.

Special thanks go, as always, to my brilliant agent, Camilla Bolton at Darley Anderson, the best advocate an author could hope for—thank you for your continued support, dynamism, and knowledge of the industry.

Thank you, also, to the booksellers, reviewers, podcasters, and libraries for getting my books out there onto shelves and into people's hands.

And, of course, unending thanks to my husband, Ross, and my two daughters for everything else under the sun.

The Family Game

Catherine Steadman

Random House
Book Club

Because
Stories Are
Better Shared

TM

A BOOK CLUB GUIDE

Dear Reader,

I don't know about you but I love a festive movie—those atmospheric classics that we all know and love so well and that have the ability to fast track us directly into that holiday feeling: a cozy, magical comfort blanket as the weather turns cold. Well, I wanted to write a twisty, turn-y popcorn thriller with all those festive vibes but with an added pinch of page-turning terror, and I hope I've delivered that with . . . *The Family Game*.

The story of British novelist Harriet Reed's introduction to her incredibly wealthy future in-laws takes place in Manhattan and upstate New York over the period from Thanksgiving to Christmas morning. Cue lights down Fifth Avenue, ice skating at The Rockefeller Center, parties, festive cheer, family gatherings, and very unusual seasonal games. . . .

Harriet, an orphan, is desperate to make it work with her fiancé Edward's estranged old-money family, but in order to win their approval and secure their affections she finds out that she must run a gauntlet of holiday season games, a kind of Balmoral test, to gain their respect. The only thing is these in-laws are not your average in-laws, and their traditions, their family games, prove to be just as strange as they are. And when Harriet's father in-law, the incredibly powerful patriarch of the Holbeck clan, gives her a tape that appears to be some kind of confession, she will have to be very careful about what move she makes next.

This Christmas Harriet Reed will find out that while it might just be a game . . . losing could cost her everything.

I hope you enjoy *The Family Game,* become immersed in its snow-clad, log-fired, festive world, and follow right along with Harriet through every twist and turn on her holiday season from hell.

Good luck and remember . . . the Krampus is coming!

Happy Holidays,
Catherine Steadman

Questions and Topics for Discussion

1. "They say you can't choose your family but they're wrong. You can. It just takes way more effort than most people are willing to put in" (7). Do you agree?

2. Why do you think Robert decides to tell Harriet about Edward through a tape recording? Why do you think he chooses to tell her the truth as though *he* were the culprit? Do you think Harriet would have believed the truth if it were told to her outright?

3. Do you think Harriet's career as a thriller writer aids in her investigation? How so?

4. Why do you think Robert feels powerless to stop his own son? Why do you think he entrusts that responsibility to Harriet? Does

it have anything to do with her own past? What did you make of the "HEREDITARY" clue?

5. What do you make of the Holbeck's bizarre family traditions? Do you find them particularly eccentric? Do you think they were a kind of test, or all in fun? Do you have any traditions that might strike others as out of the ordinary?

6. What do you think of the ending? What does Harriet addressing Iris in a letter say about the nature of storytelling and how we choose to tell the story of our lives?

7. How does Holbeck Estate play into the plot? Did the estate feel like a character of its own?

8. Do you think Edward was born bad? Or do you think that wealth corrupted him?

9. How does *The Family Game* subvert our notions about "the Christmas novel"?

10. "Games take us as close as is acceptable to the strategies we use in life. Games reveal our most base instinct: the instinct to survive. Under the mask of enjoyment, we reveal ourselves, we reveal how we play at life, our methods, how we navigate others' strengths and weaknesses. A game is only a game if you do not fully understand it. We play as we live" (248). Discuss this quote. How does it tie into the themes of the book? The title? How does understanding this quote help to reveal and deepen Catherine Steadman's shocking twist?

PHOTO: © RACHELL SMITH

CATHERINE STEADMAN is an actress and author based in London. She has appeared in leading roles on British and American television as well as onstage in the West End, where she has been nominated for a Laurence Olivier Award. She grew up in the New Forest, Hampshire, and now lives in North London with her husband and daughters. Catherine's first novel, *Something in the Water,* was a *New York Times* bestseller with rights sold in over thirty territories. She is the author of *Mr. Nobody* and *The Disappearing Act.*

Twitter: @CatSteadman
Instagram: @catsteadman

MEMORY OF FIRE

By the same author:

Memory of Fire: I. Genesis
Memory of Fire: II. Faces and Masks
The Book of Embraces
Walking Words
We Say No: Chronicles 1963-1991

Eduardo Galeano

MEMORY OF FIRE

III. CENTURY OF THE WIND

Part Three of a Trilogy

Translated
by Cedric Belfrage

W. W. Norton & Company
New York • London

Translator's Acknowledgments

To Monica Weiss, and all the wonderful young people who formed a human word-processor to get this on paper; and above all to Fernando Molina, who back-stopped the work of all three volumes.

Translation copyright © 1988 by Cedric Belfrage
First published as a Norton paperback 1998
Reprinted by arrangement with Pantheon Books

Originally published in 1986 in Spain as *Memoria del fuego III: El siglo del viento* by Siglo Veintiuno de España Editores, S.A. Copyright © 1986 by Siglo XXI de España Editores, S.A.; copyright © 1986 by Siglo XXI Editores, S.A.; copyright © 1986 by Catálogos, S.R.L.; copyright © 1986 by Eduardo Galeano.

Library of Congress Cataloging-in-Publication Data

Galeano, Eduardo H., 1940–
  Memory of fire.
  Translation of: Memoria del fuego.
  Includes bibliographies.
  Contents: 1. Genesis—2. Faces and masks—
  3. Century of the wind.
  1. Latin America—History—Anecdotes, facetiae, satire, etc. 2. America—History—Anecdotes, facetiae, satire, etc. I. Title.
ISBN 0-393-31807-9 (v. 3)   85-42866

W. W. Norton & Company, Inc.
500 Fifth Avenue, New York, N.Y. 10110
www.wwnorton.com

W. W. Norton & Company Ltd.
Castle House, 75/76 Wells Street, London W1T 3QT

Contents

Preface

This Book

is the last volume of the trilogy *Memory of Fire*. It is not an anthology but a literary creation, based on solid documentation but moving with complete freedom. The author does not know to what literary form the book belongs: narrative, essay, epic poem, chronicle, testimony . . . Perhaps it belongs to all or to none. The author relates what has happened, the history of America, and above all, the history of Latin America; and he has sought to do it in such a way that the reader should feel that what has happened happens again when the author tells it.

At the head of each text is given the year and place of each episode, except in certain texts which cannot be situated in any specific moment or place. At the foot, the numbers show the chief works the author has consulted in search of information and reference points. The absence of numbers shows that in that particular case the author has consulted no written source, or that he obtained his raw material from general information in periodicals or from the mouths of protagonists or witnesses. The sources consulted are listed at the end of the book.

Literal transcriptions are italicized.

Acknowledgments

To Helena Villagra, who helped so much at each stage of the work. Without her, *Memory of Fire* would not have been possible;

To the friends whose contributions were gratefully acknowledged in the previous volumes, and who also helped here with sources, trails, and suggestions;

To Alfredo Ahuerma, Susan Bergholz, Leonardo Cáceres, Rafael Cartay, Alfredo Cedeño, Rosa del Olmo, Enrique Fierro, César Galeano, Horacio García, Sergius Gonzaga, Berta and Fernanda Navarro, Eric Nepomuceno, David Sánchez-Juliao, Andrés Soliz Rada, and Julio Valle-Castillo, who provided access to the necessary bibliography;

To Jorge Enrique Adoum, Pepe Barrientos, Álvaro Barros-Lémez, Jean-

Paul Borel, Rogelio García Lupo, Mauricio Gatti, Juan Gelman, Santiago Kovadloff, Ole Østergaard, Rami Rodríguez, Miguel Rojas-Mix, Nicole Rouan, Pilar Royo, José María Valverde, and Daniel Vidart, who read the drafts with Chinese patience.

This book

is dedicated to Mariana, the Little Flea.

and clawing ourselves out of the wind with our fingernails

—Juan Rulfo

1900: San José de Gracia
The World Goes On

There were some who spent the savings of several generations on one last spree. Many insulted those they couldn't afford to insult and kissed those they shouldn't have kissed. No one wanted to end up without confession. The parish priest gave preference to the pregnant and to new mothers. This self-denying cleric lasted three days and three nights in the confessional before fainting from an indigestion of sins.

When midnight came on the last day of the century, all the inhabitants of San José de Gracia prepared to die clean. God had accumulated much wrath since the creation of the world, and no one doubted that the time had come for the final blowout. Breath held, eyes closed, teeth clenched, the people listened to the twelve chimes of the church clock, one after the other, deeply convinced that there would be no afterwards.

But there was. For quite a while the twentieth century has been on its way; it forges ahead as if nothing had happened. The inhabitants of San José de Gracia continue in the same houses, living and surviving among the same mountains of central Mexico—to the disenchantment of the devout who were expecting Paradise, and to the relief of sinners, who find that this little village isn't so bad after all, if one makes comparisons.

(200)*

1900: West Orange, New Jersey
Edison

Through his inventions the new century receives light and music.

Everyday life bears the seal of Thomas Alva Edison. His electric lamp illumines the nights and his phonograph preserves and diffuses the voices of the world, no longer to be lost. People talk by telephone thanks to the microphone he has added to Bell's invention, and pictures move by virtue of the projecting apparatus with which he completed the work of the Lumière brothers.

* The numbers at the foot of each item refer to the documentary sources consulted by the author, listed on pages 281–301.

In the patent office they clutch their heads when they see him coming. Not for a single moment has this multiplier of human powers stopped inventing, a tireless creator ever since that distant time when he sold newspapers on trains, and one fine day decided he could make them as well as sell them—then set his hand to the task.

(99 and 148)

1900: Montevideo
Rodó

The Master, the talking statue, sends forth his sermon to the youth of America.

José Enrique Rodó vindicates ethereal Ariel, the pure spirit against savage Caliban, the brute who wants to eat. The century being born is the time of anybodies. The people want democracy and trade unions; and Rodó warns that the barbarous multitude can scale the heights of the kingdom of the spirit where superior beings dwell. The intellectual chosen by the gods, the great immortal man, fights in defense of private property in culture.

Rodó also attacks North American civilization, rooted in vulgarity and utilitarianism. To it he opposes the Spanish aristocratic tradition which scorns practical sense, manual labor, technology, and other mediocrities.

(273, 360, and 386)

1901: New York
This is America,
to the South There's Nothing

For 250 million dollars Andrew Carnegie sells the steel monopoly to banker John Pierpont Morgan, master of General Electric, who thereupon founds the United States Steel Corporation. A fever of consumption, a vertigo of money cascading from the tops of skyscrapers: the United States belongs to the monopolies, and the monopolies to a handful of men; but multitudes of workers flock here from Europe, year after year, lured by the factory sirens, and sleeping on deck they dream of becoming millionaires as soon as they jump onto the New

York piers. In the industrial era, El Dorado is the United States; and the United States is America.

To the south, the other America hasn't yet managed to mumble its own name. A recently published report states that *all* the countries of this sub-America have commercial treaties with the United States, England, France, and Germany—but *none* has any with its neighbors. Latin America is an archipelago of idiot countries, organized for separation, and trained to dislike each other.

(113 and 289)

1901: In All Latin America
Processions Greet the Birth of the Century

In the villages and cities south of the Rio Grande, Jesus Christ marches to the cemeteries, a dying beast lustrous with blood, and behind him with torches and hymns comes the crowd, tattered, battered people afflicted with a thousand ills that no doctor or faith-healer would know how to cure, but deserving a fate that no prophet or fortuneteller could possibly divine.

1901: Amiens
Verne

Twenty years ago Alberto Santos Dumont read Jules Verne. Reading him, he had fled from his house, from Brazil, and from the world, until, sailing through the sky from cloud to cloud, he decided to live entirely on air.

Now Santos Dumont defies wind and the law of gravity. The Brazilian aeronaut invents a dirigible balloon, master of its own course, that does not drift, that will not get lost in the high seas or over the Russian Steppe or at the North Pole. Equipped with motor, propeller, and rudder, Santos Dumont rises into the air, makes a complete circuit of the Eiffel Tower, and lands at the announced spot, against the wind, before an applauding crowd.

Then he journeys to Amiens, to shake the hand of the man who taught him to fly.

Settled in his rocking chair, Jules Verne smooths his big white beard. He takes a shine to this child badly disguised as a gentleman, who calls him *my Captain* and looks at him without blinking.

(144 and 424)

1902: Quetzaltenango
The Government Decides That Reality Doesn't Exist

Drums and trumpets blast in the main plaza of Quetzaltenango, calling the citizenry; but all anyone can hear is the terrifying thunder of the Santa María volcano in full eruption.

At the top of his voice the town crier reads the proclamation of the sovereign government. More than a hundred towns in this section of Guatemala are being destroyed by avalanches of lava and mud and an endless rain of ashes while the town crier, protecting himself as best he can, performs his duty. The Santa María volcano shakes the ground beneath his feet and bombards his head with stones. At noon there is total night. In the blackout nothing can be seen but the volcano's vomit of fire. The town crier yells desperately, reading the proclamation by the shaky light of a lantern.

The proclamation, signed by President Manuel Estrada Cabrera, informs the populace that the Santa María volcano is quiet, that all of Guatemala's volcanos are quiet, that the earthquake is occurring far from here in some part of Mexico, and that, the situation being normal, there is no reason not to celebrate the feast of the goddess Minerva, which will take place today in the capital despite the nasty rumors being spread by the enemies of order.

(28)

1902: Guatemala City
Estrada Cabrera

In the city of Quetzaltenango, Manuel Estrada Cabrera had for many years exercised *the august priesthood of the Law in the majestic temple of Justice upon the immovable rock of Truth.* When he got through stripping the province, the doctor came to the capital, where he brought his political career to a happy culmination, pistol in hand, assaulting the presidency of Guatemala.

Since then he has reestablished throughout the country the use of stocks, whips, and gallows. Now Indians pick plantations' coffee for nothing, and for nothing bricklayers build jails and barracks.

Almost daily, in a solemn ceremony, President Estrada Cabrera lays the foundation stone of a new school that will never be built. He has conferred on himself the title Educator of Peoples and Protector of Studious Youth, and in homage to himself celebrates each year the colossal feast of the goddess Minerva. In his Parthenon here, a full-scale replica of the Greek original, poets pluck their lyres as they announce that Guatemala City, the Athens of the New World, has a Pericles.

(28)

1902: Saint Pierre

Only the Condemned Is Saved

On the island of Martinique, too, a volcano explodes. As if splitting the world in two, the mountain Pelée coughs up a huge red cloud that covers the sky and falls, glowing, over the earth. In a wink the city of Saint Pierre is annihilated. Its thirty-four thousand inhabitants disappear—except one.

The survivor is Ludger Sylbaris, the only prisoner in the city. The walls of the jail had been made escape-proof.

(188)

1903: Panama City

The Panama Canal

The passage between the oceans had obsessed the conquistadors. Furiously they sought and finally found it, too far south, down by remote, glacial Tierra del Fuego. But when someone suggested opening the narrow waist of Central America, King Philip II quickly squelched it: he forbade excavation of a canal on pain of death, because *what God hath joined let no man put asunder*.

Three centuries later a French concern, the Universal Inter-Oceanic Canal Company, began the work in Panama, but after thirty-three kilometers crashed noisily into bankruptcy.

Now the United States has decided to complete the canal, and hang on to it, too. There is one hitch: Colombia doesn't agree, and Panama is a province of Colombia. In Washington, Senator Hanna advises waiting it out, *due to the nature of the beast we are dealing with*, but President Teddy Roosevelt doesn't believe in patience. He sends in the Marines. And so, by grace of the United States and its warships, the province becomes an independent state.

(240 and 423)

1903: Panama City
Casualties of This War:
One Chinese, One Burro,

victims of the broadsides of a Colombian gunboat. There are no further misfortunes to lament. Manuel Amador, Panama's brand-new president, parades between U.S. flags, seated in an armchair that the crowd carries on a platform. As he passes, Amador shouts vivas for his colleague Roosevelt.

Two weeks later, in Washington, in the Blue Room of the White House, a treaty is signed granting the United States in perpetuity the half-finished canal and more than fourteen hundred square kilometers of Panamanian territory. Representing the newborn republic is Philippe Bunau-Varilla, commercial magician, political acrobat, French citizen.

(240 and 423)

1903: La Paz
Huilka

The Bolivian liberals have won the war against the conservatives. More accurately, it has been won for them by the Indian army of Pablo Zárate Huilka. The feats claimed by the mustachioed generals were performed by Indians.

Colonel José Manuel Pando, leader of the liberals, had promised Huilka's soldiers freedom from serfdom and recovery of their lands. From battle to battle, as he passed through the villages, Huilka returned stolen lands to the communities and cut the throat of anyone wearing trousers.

With the conservatives defeated, Colonel Pando appoints himself general and president, and, dotting all the *i*'s, proclaims: *"The Indians are inferior beings. Their elimination is not a crime."*

Then he gets on with it. Many are shot. Huilka, yesterday's indispensable ally, he kills several times, by bullet, blade, and rope. Still, on rainy nights, Huilka awaits the president at the gate of the government palace and stares at him, saying nothing, until Pando turns away.

(110 and 475)

1904: Rio de Janeiro
Vaccine

With the slaughter of rats and mosquitos, bubonic plague and yellow fever have been vanquished. Now Oswaldo Cruz declares war on smallpox.

By the thousands Brazilians die of the disease, while doctors bleed the moribund and healers scare off the plague with the smoke of smoldering cowshit. Oswaldo Cruz, in charge of public health, makes vaccination obligatory.

Senator Rui Barbosa, pigeon-chested and smooth-tongued orator, attacks vaccination using juridical weapons flowery with adjectives. In the name of liberty Rui Barbosa defends the right of every individual to be contaminated if he so desires. Torrential applause, thunderous ovations interrupt him from phrase to phrase.

The politicians oppose vaccination. And the doctors. And the journalists. Every newspaper carries choleric editorials and cruel caricatures victimizing Oswaldo Cruz. He cannot show his face on any street without drawing insults and stones.

The whole country closes ranks against vaccination. On all sides, "Down with vaccination!" is heard. Against vaccination the cadets of the military school rise in arms, and just miss overthrowing the president.

(158, 272, 378, and 425)

1905: Montevideo
The Automobile,

that roaring beast, makes its first kill in Montevideo. An innocent pedestrian crossing a downtown street falls and is crushed.

Few automobiles have reached these streets, but as they pass, old ladies cross themselves and people scamper into doorways for protection.

Until not very long ago, the man who thought he was a streetcar still trotted through this motorless city. Going uphill, he would crack his invisible whip, and downhill pull reins that no one could see. At intersections he tooted a horn as imaginary as his horses, as imaginary as his passengers climbing aboard at each stop, as imaginary as the tickets he sold them and the change he received. When the man-streetcar stopped coming, never to pass again, the city found that it missed this endearing lunatic.

(413)

1905: Montevideo
The Decadent Poets

Roberto de las Carreras climbs to the balcony. Pressed to his breast, a bouquet of roses and an incandescent sonnet; awaiting him, not a lovely odalisque, but a gentleman of evil character who fires five shots. Two hit the target. Roberto closes his eyes and muses: *"Tonight I'll sup with the gods."*

He sups not with the gods but with the nurses in the hospital. And a few days later this handsome Satan reappears perfidiously strolling down Sarandí Street, he who has vowed to corrupt all the married and engaged women in Montevideo. His red vest looks very chic decorated with two bulletholes. And on the title page of his latest book, *Funereal Diadem*, appears a drop of blood.

Another son of Byron and Aphrodite is Julio Herrera y Reissig, who calls the foul attic in which he writes and recites the Tower of Panoramas. The two have long been at odds over the theft of a metaphor, but both fight the same war against hypocritical, pre-Colum-bian Monte-idioto, which in the department of aphrodisiacs has progressed no further than egg yolks mixed with grape wine, and in the department of literature—the less said the better.

(284 and 389)

1905: Ilopango
Miguel at One Week

Señorita Santos Mármol, unrespectably pregnant, refuses to name the author of her dishonor. Her mother, Doña Tomasa, beats her out of the house. Doña Tomasa, widow of a man who was poor but white, suspects the worst.

When the baby is born, the spurned señorita brings it in her arms: *"This is your grandson, Mama."*

Doña Tomasa lets out a fearful scream at the sight of the baby, a blue spider, a thick-lipped Indian, such an ugly little thing as to arouse anger more than pity, and slams the door, boom, in her daughter's face.

On the doorstep Señorita Santos falls in a heap. Beneath his unconscious mother the baby seems dead. But when the neighbors haul him out, the squashed newcomer raises a tremendous howl.

And so occurs the second birth of Miguel Mármol, age one week.

(126)

1906: Paris
Santos Dumont

Five years after creating his dirigible balloon, the Brazilian Santos Dumont invents the airplane.

He has spent these five years shut up in hangars, assembling and dismantling enormous iron and bamboo Things which are born and unborn at top speed around the clock: at night they go to bed equipped with seagull wings and fish fins, and wake up transformed into dragonflies or wild ducks. On these Things Santos Dumont wants to get off the earth, which tenaciously holds him back; he collides and crashes; he has fires, tailspins, and shipwrecks; he survives by sheer stubbornness. But he fights and fights until at last he makes one of the Things into an airplane or magic carpet that soars high into the sky.

The whole world wants to meet the hero of this immense feat, king of the air, master of the winds, who is four feet tall, talks in a whisper, and weighs no more than a fly.

(144 and 424)

1907: Sagua la Grande
Lam

In the first heat of this warm morning, the little boy wakes and sees. The world is on its back and whirling; and in that vertigo a desperate bat circles, chasing its own shadow. The black shadow retreats to the wall as the bat approaches, beating at it with a wing.

The little boy jumps up, covering his head with his hands, and collides with a big mirror. In the mirror he sees nobody, or someone else. Turning, he recognizes in the open closet the decapitated clothes of his Chinese father and his black grandfather.

Somewhere in the morning a blank sheet of paper awaits him. But this Cuban boy, this frenzy called Wilfredo Lam, still cannot draw his own lost shadow, which revolves crazily in the hallucinating world above him, having not yet discovered his dazzling way of exorcising fear.

(319)

1907: Iquique
The Flags of Many Countries

head the march of the striking nitrate workers across the gravelly desert of northern Chile—thousands of them and their thousands of women and children—marching on the port of Iquique, chanting slogans and songs. When the workers occupy Iquique the Interior Minister sends an order to kill. The workers decide to stick it out. Not a stone is to be thrown.

José Briggs, leader of the strike, is the son of a North American, but refuses to seek protection from the U.S. consul. The consul of Peru tries to save the Peruvian workers, but they won't abandon their Chilean comrades. The consul of Bolivia tries to lure away the Bolivian workers. The Bolivian workers say: *"With the Chileans we live, and with the Chileans we die."*

General Roberto Silva Renard's machineguns and rifles cut down the unarmed strikers and leave a blanket of bodies. Interior Minister Rafael Sotomayor justifies the carnage in the name of *the most sacred things*, which are, in order of importance, *property, public order, and life*.

(64 and 326)

1907: Rio Batalha
Nimuendajú

Curt Unkel was not born Indian, he became one, or discovered that he was one. Years ago he left Germany for Brazil, and in Brazil, in the deepest depths of Brazil, he recognized his people. Now he accompanies the Guaraní Indians as they wander the jungle as pilgrims seeking paradise. He shares their food and shares the joy of sharing food.

High aloft rise their chants. In the dead of night a sacred ceremony is performed. They perforate the lower lip of Curt Unkel, who comes to be known as Nimuendajú: *He who creates his house*.

(316, 374, and 411)

1908: Asunción
Barrett

Perhaps he once lived in Paraguay, centuries or millennia ago—who knows when—and has forgotten it. Certainly four years ago, when by chance or curiosity Rafael Barrett landed here, he felt he had finally reached the place that was waiting for him: this godforsaken place was his place in the world.

Ever since then, on street corners, mounted on a soapbox, he has harangued the people, while publishing articles of revelation and denunciation. In response, the government throws him out. Bayonets shove the young anarchist to the border—deported as a *foreign agitator*.

Most Paraguayan of all Paraguayans, true weed of this soil, true saliva of this mouth, he was born in Asturias, of a Spanish mother and English father, and was educated in Paris.

Barrett's gravest sin, unforgivable violation of a taboo, is to denounce slavery on the maté plantations.

Forty years ago, when the war of extermination against Paraguay ended, the victorious countries in the name of Civilization and Liberty legalized the enslavement of the survivors and the children of the survivors. Since then Argentine and Brazilian landowners count their Paraguayan peons by the head as if they were cows.

(37)

1908: San Andrés de Sotavento
The Government Decides That
Indians Don't Exist

The governor, General Miguel Marino Torralvo, issues the order for the oil companies operating on the Colombian coast. *The Indians do not exist,* the governor certifies before a notary and witnesses. Three years ago, Law No. 1905/55, approved in Bogotá by the National Congress, established that Indians did not exist in San Andrés de Sotavento and other Indian communities where oil had suddenly spurted from the ground. Now the governor merely confirms the law. If the Indians existed, they would be illegal. Thus they are consigned to the cemetery or exile.

(160)

1908: San Andrés de Sotavento
Portrait of a Master of Lives and Estates

General Miguel Marino Torralvo, glutton of lands, who tramples on Indians and women, governs these Colombian coastal regions from the back of a horse. With the butt of his whip he strikes faces and doors, and shapes destinies. Those who cross his path kiss his hand. In an impeccable white habit he canters along the roads, always followed by a page on a burro. The page carries his brandy, his boiled water, his shaving kit, and the book in which the general notes the names of the girls he devours.

His properties increase as he rides by. He started out with one cattle farm and now has six. A believer in progress, but not to the exclusion of tradition, he uses barbed wire to set limits to his lands, the stocks to set limits for his people.

(160)

1908: Guanape
Portrait of Another Master of Lives and Estates

He orders: *"Tell him he'd better carry his shroud on the back of his horse."*

He punishes with five shots, for nonperformance of duty, the serf who is late with the bushels of corn he owes, or who makes trouble about delivering a daughter or a plot of land.

"Don't hurry it," he orders. *"Only the last shot should kill."*

Not even his family is spared the wrath of Deogracias Itriago, supreme boss of the Venezuelan valley of Guanape. One night a relative borrows his best horse to go to a dance in style. The next morning Don Deogracias has him tied face down to four stakes, and skins the soles of his feet and his buttocks with a cassava grater to cure him of the urge to dance and show off on someone else's horse.

When in an unguarded moment he is finally killed by some peons he himself had condemned to death, for nine nights the family chants the novena for the dead, and for nine nights the people of Guanape go wild celebrating. No one tires of making merry and no musician wants payment for the marathon.

(410)

1908: Mérida, Yucatán
Curtain Time and After

The train is already disappearing, and the president of Mexico with it. Porfirio Díaz has examined the henequén plantations in Yucatán and is taking away a most favorable impression.

"A beautiful spectacle," he said, as he supped with the bishop and the owners of millions of hectares and thousands of Indians who produce cheap fibers for the International Harvester Company. *"Here one breathes an atmosphere of general happiness."*

The locomotive smoke is scarcely dissipated when the houses of painted cardboard, with their elegant windows, collapse with the slap of a hand. Garlands and pennants become litter, swept up and burned, and the wind undoes with a puff the arches of flowers that spanned the roads. The lightning visit over, the merchants of Mérida repossess the sewing machines, the North American furniture, and the brand-new clothes the slaves have worn while the show lasted.

The slaves are Mayan Indians who until recently lived free in the kingdom of the little talking cross, and Yaqui Indians from the plains of the north, purchased for four hundred pesos a head. They sleep piled up in fortresses of stone and work to the rhythm of a moistened whip. When one of them gets surly, they bury him up to his ears and turn the horses loose on him.

(40, 44, 245, and 451)

1908: Ciudad Juárez
Wanted

A few years ago, at the request of Porfirio Díaz, North American Rangers crossed the border here to crush the striking copper miners of Sonora. Later, the strike in the Veracruz textile plants ended in arrests and executions. Still, strikes have broken out again this year in Coahuila, Chihuahua, and Yucatán.

Striking, which disturbs order, is a crime. Whoever does it commits a crime. The Flores Magón brothers, agitators of the working class, are criminals of the highest order. Their faces are plastered on the wall of the railroad station in Ciudad Juárez as in all stations on both sides of the border. The Furlong detective agency offers a forty-thousand-dollar reward for each of them.

For years, the Flores Magón brothers have flouted the authority of eternal president Porfirio Díaz. In journals and pamphlets they have taught the people to lose respect for him. With respect once lost, the people begin to lose their fear.

(40, 44, and 245)

1908: Caracas

Castro

He shakes hands with just the index finger, because no one is worthy of the other four. Cipriano Castro reigns in Venezuela, his crown a cap with hanging tassel. A fanfare of trumpets, a thunder of applause, and a rustle of bowing shoulders announce his appearance, followed by his retinue of bullies and court jesters. Like Bolívar, Castro is short, quick-tempered, and addicted to dancing and women; and he plays Bolívar when posing for immortality; but Bolívar lost some battles and Castro, Semper Victorious, never.

His dungeons are crammed. He trusts no one, with the exception of Juan Vicente Gómez, his right hand in war and government, who calls him the Greatest Man of Modern Times. Least of all does Castro trust the local medics, who cure leprosy and insanity with a broth of boiled buzzard. Instead he decides to put his ailments in the hands of learned German physicians.

At the port of La Guaira he embarks for Europe. Hardly has the ship cast off when Gómez seizes power.

(193 and 344)

1908: Caracas

Dolls

Every Venezuelan male is a Cipriano Castro to the women who come his way.

A proper señorita serves her father and her brothers as she will serve her husband, and neither does nor says anything without asking permission. If she has money or comes from a good family, she attends early morning Mass, then spends the day learning to give orders to the black staff—cooks, maids, wet nurses, nannies, laundrywomen— and working with needle or bobbin. At times she receives friends, and even goes so far as to recommend some outrageous novel, whispering: "You should have seen how I cried . . ."

Twice a week, in the early evening, seated on a sofa under an aunt's attentive gaze, she spends a few hours listening to her fiancé without looking at him or letting him near. Every night, before bed, she repeats her Ave Marias and, by moonlight, applies to her skin an infusion of jasmine petals steeped in rainwater.

If her fiancé deserts her, she becomes an aunt, condemned forever to clothe saints, corpses, and new babies, watch engaged couples, tend the sick, teach catechism, and spend the night in her solitary bed, sighing over the portrait of her disdainful lover.

(117)

1909: Paris

A Theory of National Impotence

The Bolivian Alcides Arguedas, sent to Paris on a scholarship by Simón Patiño, publishes a new book entitled *Sick People*. The tin king feeds Arguedas so that Arguedas may reveal that the Bolivian people are not just ailing, but incurable.

A while ago another Bolivian thinker, Gabriel René Moreno, discovered that the native and mestizo brains are *cellularly incapable*, and that they weigh from five to seven or even ten ounces less than the brain of the white man. Now Arguedas proclaims that mestizos inherit the worst characteristics of their forebears and this is why the Bolivian people do not want to wash or learn, can't read, only drink, are two-faced, egoistic, lazy, and altogether deplorable. Their thousand and one miseries thus spring from their own nature, not the voracity of their masters. Here is a people condemned by biology and reduced to zoology. Theirs is the bestial fate of the ox: incapable of making his own history, he can only fulfill his destiny. And that destiny, that hopeless disaster, is written not in the stars, but in the blood.

(29 and 473)

1909: New York

Charlotte

What would happen if a woman woke up one morning changed into a man? What if the family were not a training camp where boys learn to command and girls to obey? What if there were daycare for babies, and husbands shared the cleaning and cooking? What if innocence turned into dignity and reason and emotion went arm in arm? What if preachers and newspapers told the truth? And if no one were anyone's property?

So Charlotte Perkins Gilman raves, while the press attacks her, calling her an *unnatural mother*. Yet the fantasies that inhabit her soul and bite at her guts attack her far more fiercely. It is they, those terrible enemies inside, that sometimes bring her down. She falls but recovers, falls and recovers again, some impulse to go forward never abandoning her entirely. This stubborn wayfarer travels tirelessly around the United States, announcing a world upside down.

(195 and 196)

1909: Managua
Inter-American Relations at Work

Philander Knox is a lawyer and a shareholder in the Rosario and Light Mines Company. He is also secretary of state of the United States. The president of Nicaragua, José Santos Zelaya, does not treat the company with due respect. He wants Rosario and Light to pay taxes. Nor does he respect the Church enough. The Holy Mother has judged him to be in sin ever since he expropriated her lands and suppressed tithes and first-fruits and profaned the sacrament of matrimony with a divorce law. So the Church applauds when the United States breaks relations with Nicaragua and Secretary of State Knox sends down some Marines who overthrow President Zelaya and put in his place the accountant of the Rosario and Light Mines Company.

(10 and 56)

1910: Amazon Jungle
The People Eaters

Overnight the price of rubber collapses, and the Amazonian dream of prosperity comes to nothing. With a rude slap the world market abruptly awakens Belém do Pará, Manaos, Iquitos, all the sleeping beauties who lie in the jungle in the shade of the rubber tree. From one day to the next the so-called Land of Tomorrow turns into Never-Never Land, or the Land of Yesterday, abandoned by the merchants who have extracted its sap. The big rubber money flees the Amazon jungle for new Asian plantations which produce better rubber at cheaper prices.

This has been a cannibalistic business. *People eaters* the Indians called the slave hunters who cruised the rivers in search of labor. All that is left of substantial villages is the scraps. The people eaters sent the Indians, bound, to the rubber companies. They sent them in the holds of ships along with other merchandise, appropriately invoiced for sales commissions and freight charges.

(92, 119, and 462)

1910: Rio de Janeiro
The Black Admiral

On board, the order for silence. An officer reads out the sentence. Drums beat furiously as a sailor is flogged for a breach of discipline. On his knees, bound to the deck balustrade, the condemned man receives his punishment before the whole crew. The last of the lashes—two hundred and forty-eight, two hundred and forty-nine, two hundred and fifty—fall upon a flayed body, bathed in blood, unconscious or dead.

Then the mutiny breaks out. In the waters of Guanabara Bay, the sailors rise up. Three officers fall, knifed to death. The warships fly the red ensign. An ordinary seaman is the squadron's new commander. João Cándido, the Black Admiral, leans into the wind on the command tower of his flagship, and the rebel pariahs present arms to him.

At dawn two booming guns wake Rio de Janeiro. The Black Admiral issues a warning: the city is at his mercy. Unless flogging— the custom of the Brazilian fleet—is prohibited and an amnesty granted, he will bombard Rio, leaving no stone upon stone. The mouths of the warships' cannons are pointed at Rio's most important buildings.

"We want an answer now, right now."

The city, in panic, obeys. The government declares the abolition of corporal punishment in the fleet and an amnesty for the rebels. João Cándido removes the red kerchief from his neck and surrenders his sword. The admiral transforms himself back into a sailor.

(303)

1910: Rio de Janeiro
Portrait of Brazil's Most Expensive Lawyer

Six years ago he opposed smallpox vaccination in the name of Liberty. An individual's skin is as inviolable as his conscience, said Rui Barbosa. The State has no right to violate thought or body, not even in the name of public hygiene. Now, he condemns *with all severity the violence and barbarity* of the sailors' rebellion. This illustrious jurist and preeminent legislator opposes flogging but denounces the methods of the flogged. The sailors, he says, did not make their just demand in a civilized way, *by constitutional means, using the proper channels within the framework of prevailing juridical norms.*

Rui Barbosa believes in the law, and bases his belief on erudite quotations from imperial Romans and English liberals. But he doesn't believe in reality. The doctor shows a certain realism only when, at the end of the month, he collects his salary as lawyer for Light and Power, that foreign enterprise which in Brazil exercises more power than God.

(272 and 303)

1910: Rio de Janeiro
Reality and the Law Seldom Meet

in this country of legally free slaves, and when they do they don't shake hands. The ink is still fresh on the laws that put an end to the sailors' revolt when the officers resume flogging and kill the recently amnestied rebels. Many sailors are shot on the high seas; others are buried alive in the catacombs of Cobra Island, called the Isle of Despair, where they are thrown quicklimed water when they complain of thirst.

The Black Admiral ends up in a lunatic asylum.

(303)

1910: Mauricio Colony

Tolstoy

Exiled for being poor and a Jew, Isaac Zimmerman ends up in Argentina. The first time he sees a maté cup he takes it for an inkpot, the straw for a pen, and that pen burns his hand. On this pampa he built his hut, not far from the huts of other pilgrims, exiles like him from the valleys of the Dniester River; and here he produces children and crops.

Isaac and his wife have very little, almost nothing, and the little they have they possess graciously. Some vegetable crates serve as a table, but the tablecloth is always starched and very white, and on it flowers lend color, and apples perfume.

One night the children come upon Isaac collapsed at this table, his head buried in his hands. By the candle's light they see his face glistening with tears. And he tells them. By sheer accident, he says, he has just learned that over there, on the far side of the world, Leo Tolstoy has died. And he explains who this old friend of the peasants was, this man who knew how to portray his time so grandly and to foretell another.

(155)

1910: Havana

The Cinema

Ladder on shoulder, the lamplighter goes on his way. With his long pole he lights the wicks, so that people can walk without tripping through the streets of Havana.

The messenger goes by bicycle. Under his arm he carries rolls of film from one cinema to another, so that people may walk without tripping through other worlds and other times and float high in the sky with a girl seated on a star.

This city has two halls consecrated to the greatest marvel of modern life. Both offer the same films. When the messenger dawdles with the rolls, the pianist will entertain the audience with waltzes and dance tunes, or the usher will recite selected fragments from *Don Juan Tenorio*. But the audience bites its nails waiting for the femme fatale with the bedroom circles under her eyes to dazzle in the darkness, or for the knights in coats of mail to gallop at epileptic speed toward the castle wreathed in mist.

The cinema robs the public of the circus. No longer does the crowd queue up to see the mustachioed lion-tamer or Lovely Geraldine, sheathed in sequins, glittering erect on the horse with enormous haunches. The puppeteers, too, abandon Havana to wander the beaches and villages, and the gypsies who read fortunes depart along with the sad bear that dances to the rhythm of the tambourine, with the goat that gyrates on a stool, with the gaunt acrobats in their checkered costumes. All quit Havana because people no longer throw them pennies of admiration, but only of pity.

No one can compete with the cinema. The cinema is more miraculous than the water of Lourdes. Stomach chills are cured by Ceylon cinnamon; colds by parsley; everything else by the cinema.

(292)

1910: Mexico City ·

The Centennial and Love

Celebrating a hundred years of Mexico's independence, all of the capital's whorehouses display the portrait of President Porfirio Díaz.

In Mexico City, out of every ten young women, two engage in prostitution. Peace and Order, Order and Progress: the law regulates the practice of this crowded profession. The brothel law, promulgated by Don Porfirio himself, prohibits carnal commerce without the proper façade, or in the proximity of schools and churches. It also prohibits the mixing of social classes—*In the brothels there shall only be women of the class to which the customers belong*—while it imposes all sorts of sanitary controls and penalties, and even obliges the madams *to prevent their pupils from going into the streets in groups that might attract attention.* They are allowed to go out singly: condemned to exist between bed, hospital, and jail, the whores at least have the right to an occasional stroll through the city. In this sense, they are better off than the Indians. By order of the almost pure Mixtec Indian president, Indians may not walk on the principal avenues or sit in public plazas.

(300)

1910: Mexico City

The Centennial and Food

The Centennial is inaugurated with a banquet of French *haute cuisine* in the salons of the National Palace. Three hundred and fifty waiters serve dishes prepared by forty chefs and sixty assistants under the direction of the renowned Sylvain Daumont.

Elegant Mexicans eat in French. They prefer the *crêpe* to its poor relation of native birth, the corn tortilla; *oeufs en cocotte* to the humble rancheros. They find *béchamel* sauce more worthy than guacamole, that delicious but excessively indigenous mixture of avocados, tomatoes, and chili. Faced with foreign peppers or Mexican chilies, the gentry reject the chili, although later they sneak back to the family kitchen and devour it secretly, ground or whole, side dish or main dish, stuffed or plain, unpeeled or naked.

(318)

1910: Mexico City

The Centennial and Art

Mexico celebrates its national fiesta with a great exhibition of Spanish art, brought from Madrid. To give these Spanish artists the presentation they deserve, Don Porfirio has built a special pavilion for them in the city center.

In Mexico, even the stones for building the post office come from Europe, like all that is considered worthwhile. From Italy, France, Spain, or England come construction materials and architects, or when money is lacking for imported architects, native architects undertake to put up houses just like those of Rome, Paris, Madrid, or London. Meanwhile, Mexican artists paint ecstatic Virgins, plump Cupids, and high-society ladies in the European mode of half a century ago, and sculptors entitle their monumental marbles and bronzes *Malgré Tout, Désespoir, Après l'Orgie.*

Beyond the boundaries of official art, far removed from its star performers, the genius engraver José Guadalupe Posada strips naked his country and his time. No critic takes him seriously. He has no pupils, although two young artists have been following him since they were children. José Clemente Orozco and Diego Rivera haunt Posada's little workshop and watch him labor, with devotion as if at a Mass, as the metal shavings fall to the floor at the passage of the burin over the plates.

(44 and 47)

1910: Mexico City
The Centennial and the Dictator

At the height of the Centennial celebrations, Don Porfirio opens a mental asylum. Soon afterward he lays the foundation stone for a new jail.

Don Porfirio is decorated from his paunch up to his plumed head, which reigns above a cloud of top-hats and imperial helmets. His courtiers, rheumatic antiques in frock coats and gaiters, with flowers in their buttonholes, dance to the strains of "Long Live My Misery," the latest hit waltz. An orchestra of a hundred and fifty musicians plays beneath thirty thousand electric stars in the National Palace's grand ballroom.

The festivities last a whole month. Don Porfirio, eight times reelected by himself, makes one of these balls the occasion for announcing the imminence of his ninth term, while conferring ninety-nine-year concessions of copper, oil, and land on Morgan, Guggenheim, Rockefeller, and Hearst. For more than thirty years the deaf, rigid dictator has administered the largest tropical territory of the United States.

On one of these nights, at the peak of this patriotic binge, Halley's Comet bursts into the sky. Panic spreads. The press announces that the comet will stick its tail into Mexico and set everything on fire.

(40, 44, and 391)

1911: Anenecuilco
Zapata

He was born in the saddle, a rider and breaker-in of horses. He navigates the countryside on horseback, careful not to disturb the deep sleep of the earth. Emiliano Zapata is a man of silences, someone who talks by keeping quiet.

The campesinos of his village Anenecuilco, little palm-thatched adobe houses peppered over a hill, have made Zapata their leader, entrusting him with papers from the time of the viceroys. The bundle of documents proves that this community, rooted here from the beginning, is no intruder on its own land.

Anenecuilco is being strangled, like all the other communities in the Mexican region of Morelos. There are ever fewer islands of corn in an ocean of sugar. Of the village of Tequesquitengo, condemned to die because its free Indians refused to become a gang of peons, nothing remains but the church-tower cross. The immense plantations advance, swallowing up land, water, and woods. They leave no room even to bury the dead.

"If they want to plant, let them plant in pots."

Gunmen and conmen see to the actual plundering while the consumers of communities hold concerts in their gardens and breed polo ponies and pedigreed dogs.

Zapata, leader of the enslaved villagers, buries the viceregal land titles under the Anenecuilco church floor and throws himself into the struggle. His troops of Indians, well turned out and well mounted, if badly armed, grows as it goes.

(468)

1911: Mexico City
Madero

Meanwhile, the whole of the north is rising behind Francisco Madero; and after thirty continuous years on the throne, Porfirio Díaz collapses in a few months.

Madero, the new president, is a virtuous son of the liberal Constitution. He wants to save Mexico by judicial reform, while Zapata demands agrarian reform. Confronting the clamor of the campesinos, the new deputies promise to study their misery.

(44 and 194)

1911: The Fields of Chihuahua
Pancho Villa

Of all the northern leaders who have raised Madero to the presidency, Pancho Villa is the most loved and loving.

He likes to get married and keeps on doing it. Pistol to head, there is no priest who balks nor girl who resists. He also likes to dance the *tapatío* to the strains of the marimba, and to get into shoot-outs. Bullets bounce off his sombrero like raindrops.

He took to the desert early on: *"For me the war began when I was born."* He was little more than a child when he avenged his sister. Of the many deaths notched up since, the first was that of his boss, leaving him little choice but to become a horse thief.

He was born as Doroteo Arango. Pancho Villa was someone else entirely—a gang compañero, a friend, the best of friends. When the Rural Guards killed the real Pancho Villa, Doroteo Arango took his name and kept it. Against death and forgetting, he began calling himself Pancho Villa, so that his friend should continue to be.

(206)

1911: Machu Picchu

The Last Sanctuary of the Incas

isn't dead; it only sleeps. For centuries the Urubamba River, foaming and roaring, has exhaled its potent breath against these sacred stones, covering them with a blanket of dense jungle to guard their sleep. Thus has the last bastion of the Incas, the last foothold of the Indian kings of Peru, been kept secret.

Among snow mountains which appear on no maps, a North American archeologist, Hiram Bingham, stumbles upon Machu Picchu. A child of the region leads him by the hand over precipices to the lofty throne veiled by clouds and greenery. There, Bingham finds the white stones still alive beneath the verdure, and reveals them, awakened, to the world.

(53 and 453)

1912: Quito

Alfaro

A tall woman, dressed all in black, curses President Alfaro as she plunges a dagger into his corpse. Then she raises, on the point of a stick, a flaming banner, the bloody rag of his shirt.

Behind the woman in black march the avengers of Holy Mother Church. With ropes tied to his feet they drag away the nude body. Flowers rain from windows. Saint-eating, host-swallowing, gossipy old women cry *"Long live religion!"* The cobbled streets run with blood which the dogs can never lick away nor the rain wash off. The butchery ends in flames. A great bonfire is lit, and on it they throw what remains of old Alfaro. Then gunmen and thugs, hired by the landed gentry, stamp on his ashes.

Eloy Alfaro had dared to expropriate the lands of the Church, owner of much of Ecuador, and used the rents to create schools and hospitals. A friend of God but not of the Pope, he had legalized divorce and freed Indians jailed for debt. No one was so hated by the surpliced, nor so feared by the frock-coated.

Night falls. The air of Quito reeks of burned flesh. As on every Sunday, the military band plays waltzes and *pasillos* in the Grand Plaza bandstand.

(12, 24, 265, and 332)

Sad Verses from the Ecuadoran Songbook

Don't come near, anyone,
Stand aside or go.
My disease is contagious,
I'm full of woe.

I'm alone, born alone,
Of a mother forlorn,
All alone I stay,
A feather in a storm.

Why should a painted house
Make a blind man sing?
What are balconies to the street,
If he can't see a thing?

(294)

1912: Cantón Santa Ana
Chronicle of the Customs of Manabí

Eloy Alfaro was born on the coast of Ecuador, in the province of Manabí. In that hot land, region of insolence and violence, no one paid the least attention to his recent divorce law, pushed through against wind and tide. Here, it's simpler to become a widower than to get caught up in red tape. On the bed where two go to sleep, sometimes only one wakes up. Manabís are famous for short tempers, no money, and big hearts.

Martín Vera was a rare Manabí. His knife had rusted from remaining so long in its sheath. When the neighbors' hog invaded his little garden and ate his manioc plants, Martín went to talk to them, the Rosados, and asked them nicely to shut the creature in. On the second occasion, Martín offered to repair the rickety walls of the Rosados' pigsty for nothing. But the third time, as the hog romped about in his garden, Martín took a shot at it with his gun. Round as it was, the baneful animal fell flat. The Rosados hauled it back to their property to give it a porcine burial.

The Veras and the Rosados stopped greeting each other. Some days later, the executioner of the hog was crossing the Calvo cliffs, holding on to the mane of his mule, when a bullet left him hanging from one stirrup. The mule dragged Martín Vera home, too late for any kneeling woman to help him to a decent death.

The Rosados fled. When Martín's children hunted them down in an empty convent near Colimas, they lit a fire around the place. The Rosados, thirty in all, had to choose death. Some expired by fire, burnt to a crisp; others by bullet, riddled like colanders.

This happened a year ago. Now, the jungle has devoured the gardens of both families, leaving only a no-man's-land.

(226)

1912: Pajeú de Flores
Family Wars

In the deserts of northeast Brazil the elite inherit land and hatred: sad land, land dying of thirst; and hatred, which relatives perpetuate from generation to generation, vengeance to vengeance, forever and a day. In Ceará there is eternal war between the Cunha family and the Pataca family, and the Monteses and the Faitosas practice mutual extermination. In Paraíba it is the Dantases and the Nóbregases who kill each other. In Pernambuco, in the Pajeú River region, every newly born Pereira receives from his parents and godparents the order to hunt down his Carvalho; and every Carvalho comes into the world prepared to liquidate his Pereira.

Today, Virgulino da Silva Pereira, known as Lampião, fires his first shots at a Carvalho. Though still a child, he automatically becomes an outlaw, a *cangaceiro*. Life is not worth much around here, where the only hospital is the cemetery. If Lampião were the child of the rich, he would not have to kill on others' account; he would have it done for him.

(343)

1912: Daiquirí
Daily Life in the Caribbean: An Invasion

The Platt Amendment, handiwork of Senator Platt of Connecticut, is the passkey that the United States uses to enter Cuba at any hour. The amendment, part of the Cuban Constitution, authorizes the United States to invade and stand fast, and gives it the power to decide who is or is not a proper president for Cuba.

The current proper president, Mario García Menocal, who also presides over the Cuban American Sugar Company, applies the Platt Amendment, calling in the Marines to put unrest to rest. Too many blacks are in revolt, and none of them has a high enough opinion of private property. Two warships steam in and the Marines land on the beach at Daiquirí to protect the iron and copper mines of the Spanish American and Cuban Copper companies, threatened by black wrath, and the sugar mills all along the Guantánamo and Western Railroad tracks.

(208 and 241)

1912: Niquinohomo
Daily Life in Central America: Another Invasion

Nicaragua pays the United States a colossal indemnity for *moral damages*, inflicted by fallen president Zelaya when he committed the grave offense of trying to impose taxes on North American companies.

As Nicaragua lacks funds, U.S. bankers lend the necessary monies to pay the indemnity, and since Nicaragua lacks guarantees, U.S. Secretary of State Philander Knox sends back the Marines to take charge of customs houses, national banks, and railroads.

Benjamin Zeledón heads the resistance. The chief of the patriots has a fresh-looking face and startled eyes. The invaders cannot bribe him because Zeledón spits on money, so they defeat him by treachery.

Augusto César Sandino, a no-account peon from a no-account village, sees Zeledón's corpse pass by, dragged through the dust, hands and feet bound to the saddle of a drunken invader.

(10 and 56)

1912: Mexico City

Huerta

looks like a malignant corpse. His shiny dark glasses are all that seem alive in his face.

Veteran bodyguard of Porfirio Díaz, Victoriano Huerta converted to democracy on the day the dictatorship fell. Now he is President Madero's right-hand man, and has dedicated himself to hunting down revolutionaries. In the north he catches Pancho Villa, in the south Zapata's lieutenant, Gildardo Magaña, and orders them shot. The firing squad are stroking their triggers when the presidential pardon interrupts the ceremony. *"Death came for me,"* sighs Villa, *"but missed the appointment."*

The resuscitated pair end up in the same cell in Tlatelolco prison. They pass days, months, chatting. Magaña talks of Zapata, of his plan for agrarian reform, and of Madero, who turns a deaf ear, so eager is he to offend neither campesinos nor landlords, *riding two horses at once.*

A small blackboard and a few books arrive. Pancho Villa knows how to read people, but not letters. Magaña teaches him, and together they enter, word by word, sword-thrust by sword-thrust, the castles of *The Three Musketeers.* Then they start the journey through *Don Quixote de la Mancha,* crazy roads of old Spain; and Pancho Villa, fierce warrior of the desert, strokes the pages with the hand of a lover.

Magaña tells him: *"This book . . . You know? A jailbird wrote it. One of us."*

(194 and 206)

1913: Mexico City
An Eighteen-Cent Rope

President Madero imposes a tax, a tiny tax, on the heretofore untouched oil companies, and North American ambassador Henry Lane
Wilson threatens invasion. Several warships are heading for the ports
of Mexico, announces the ambassador, while General Huerta rebels
and his troops bombard the National Palace.

The fate of Mexico is discussed in the smoking lounge of the
U.S. embassy. It is decided to invoke the shot-while-trying-to-escape
law, so they put Madero in a car, order him to get out of town, and
riddle him with bullets when he tries to.

General Huerta, the new president, attends a banquet at the
Jockey Club. There he announces that he has a good remedy, an
eighteen-cent rope, for Emiliano Zapata and Pancho Villa and the
other enemies of order.

(194 and 246)

1913: Jonacatepec
The Hordes Are Not Destroyed

Huerta's officers, old hands at massacring rebellious Indians, propose
to clean up the southern areas—burning villages and hunting down
campesinos. Anyone they meet falls dead or prisoner, for in the south,
who is not with Zapata?

Zapata's forces are hungry and sick, frayed, but the leader of the
landless knows what he wants, and his people believe in what he
does; neither fire nor deceit can prevail against that. While the capital's newspapers report that *the Zapata hordes have been totally
destroyed*, Zapata blows up trains, surprises garrisons and annihilates
them, occupies villages, attacks cities, and moves wherever he wants
across impenetrable mountains, through impassable ravines, fighting
and loving as though it's all in a day's work.

Zapata sleeps where he likes with anyone he likes, but of them
all he prefers two who are one.

(468)

Zapata and Those Two

We were twins. We were both named Luz for the day of our baptism and Gregoria for the day we were born. They called her Luz and me Gregoria and there we were, two young girls in the house, when Zapata's boys came along, and then their chief, trying to persuade my sister to go with him.

"Look, come with me."

And precisely one September 15 he came by and took her.

Afterward, in this continuous moving around, my sister died in Huautla of a disease that they call—what do they call it?—Saint Vitus, the Saint Vitus disease.

Three days and three nights chief Zapata was there with us, not eating or drinking a thing. We had only just lit the candles for my sister when ay, ay, ay, he took me by force. He said I belonged to him, because my sister and I were one . . .

(244)

1913: The Plains of Chihuahua
The North of Mexico Celebrates
War and Fiesta

The cocks crow whenever they feel like it. This land has caught fire, gone crazy. Everyone is in rebellion.

"We're off to the war, woman."

"But why me?"

"Do you want me to die of starvation in the war? Who'll make my tortillas?"

Flocks of vultures follow the armed peons over plains and mountains. If life is worth nothing, what can death be worth? Men roll themselves like dice into the tumult, and find vengeance or oblivion, land to feed them or to cover them.

"Here comes Pancho Villa!" the peons exult.

"Here comes Pancho Villa!" cry the overseers, crossing themselves.

"Where, where is he?" asks General Huerta.

"In the north, south, east, and west, and also nowhere," replies the Chihuahua garrison commander.

Confronting the enemy, Pancho Villa is always the first to charge, right into the smoking jaws of the guns. When the battle gets hot, he just horse-laughs. His heart thumps like a fish out of water.

"There's nothing wrong with the general. He's just a bit emotional," his officers explain.

And so he is. With a single shot, for pure fun, he has been known to disembowel the messenger who gallops up with good news from the front.

(206 and 260)

1913: Culiacán
Bullets

There are bullets with imagination, Martín Luis Guzmán discovers. Bullets which amuse themselves in afflicting the flesh. He has known serious bullets, which serve human fury, but not these bullets that play with human pain.

For being a bad marksman with a good heart, the young novelist is assigned to direct one of Pancho Villa's hospitals. The wounded pile up in the dirt with no recourse but to clench their teeth, if they have any.

Checking the jammed wards, Guzmán confirms the improbable trajectories of these fanciful bullets, capable of emptying an eye-socket while leaving a body alive, or of sticking a piece of ear into the neck and a piece of neck into the foot. And he witnesses the sinister joy of bullets, which, having been ordered to kill a soldier, condemn him never again to sit down or never again to eat with his mouth.

(216)

1913: The Fields of Chihuahua
One of These Mornings I Murdered Myself,

on some dusty Mexican road, and the event left a deep impression on me.

This wasn't the first crime I committed. From the time I was born in Ohio seventy-one years ago and received the name Ambrose Bierce, until my recent death, I have played havoc with the lives of my parents and various relatives, friends, and colleagues. These touching episodes have splashed blood over my days—or my stories, which is all the same to me: the difference between the life I lived and the life I wrote is a matter for the jokers who execute human law, literary criticism, and the will of God in this world.

To put an end to my days, I joined the troops of Pancho Villa and chose one of those many stray bullets zooming through the Mexican sky these days. This method proved more practical than hanging, cheaper than poison, more convenient than firing with my own finger, and more dignified than waiting for disease or old age.

1914: Montevideo
Batlle

He writes articles slandering the saints and makes speeches attacking the company that sells real estate in the Great Beyond. When he assumed the presidency of Uruguay, he had no alternative but to swear before God and the Holy Evangels, but explained immediately that he didn't believe in any of that.

José Batlle y Ordoñez governs in defiance of the powers of heaven and earth. The Church has promised him a nice place in hell; companies he nationalized, or forced to respect their workers' unions and the eight-hour work day, will feed the fire; and the Devil will avenge his offenses against male-supremacists.

"He is legalizing licentiousness," say his enemies when he approves a law permitting women to sue for divorce.

"He is dissolving the family," they say, when he extends inheritance rights to illegitimate children.

"The female brain is inferior," they say, when he creates a women's university and announces that women will soon have the vote so that Uruguayan democracy need not walk on just one leg, and so that women will not forever be children passing from the hands of the father to those of the husband.

(35 and 271)

1914: San Ignacio
Quiroga

From the Paraná River jungle where he lives in voluntary exile, Horacio Quiroga applauds Batlle's reforms and *that ardent faith in noble things.*

But Quiroga is indeed far from Uruguay. He left the country some years ago, fleeing the shadow of death. A curse has darkened his life since he killed his best friend while trying to defend him; or perhaps he was cursed from the beginning.

In the jungle, a step away from the ruins of the Jesuit missions, Quiroga lives surrounded by bugs and palm trees. He writes stories without detours, just as he opens paths through the thicket with his machete. He works the word with the same rugged love as he does the soil, and wood, and iron.

What Quiroga seeks he could never find away from here. Here, yes, though only very occasionally. In this house which his hands built by the river, Quiroga has at times the joy of hearing voices more powerful than the call of death: rare and fleeting certainties of life, which while they last are as absolute as the sun.

(20, 357, 358, and 390)

1914: Montevideo
Delmira

In this rented room she had an appointment with the man who had been her husband. Wanting to possess her, wanting to stay with her, he made love to her, killed her, then killed himself.

The Uruguayan papers publish a photo of the body lying beside the bed: Delmira struck down by two bullets, naked like her poems, all unclothed in red.

Let's go further in the night, let's . . .

Delmira Agustini wrote in a trance. She sang to the fevers of love without shame, and was condemned by those who punish women for what they applaud in men, because chastity is a feminine duty, and desire, like reason, a male privilege. In Uruguay the laws march ahead of the people, who still separate soul from body as if they were Beauty and the Beast. Before the corpse of Delmira flow tears and phrases about this irreplaceable loss to national letters, but deep down the mourners feel some relief: the woman is dead, and better so.

But is she dead? Will not all the lovers burning in the nights of the world be the shadows of her voice and the echoes of her body? In the nights of the world won't they make a small place where her unfettered voice can sing and her radiant feet can dance?

(49 and 426)

1914: Ciudad Jiménez

Chronicler of Angry Peoples

From shock to shock, from marvel to marvel, John Reed travels the roads of northern Mexico. He is looking for Pancho Villa and finds him at every step.

Reed, chronicler of revolution, sleeps wherever night catches up with him. No one ever steals from him, or ever lets him pay for anything except dance music; and there's always someone to offer him a piece of tortilla or a place on his horse.

"Where do you come from?"

"From New York."

"Well, I don't know anything about New York, but I'll bet you don't see such fine cattle going through the streets as you see in the streets of Jiménez."

A woman carries a pitcher on her head. Another, squatting, suckles her baby. Another, on her knees, grinds corn. Enveloped in faded serapes, the men sit in a circle, drinking and smoking.

"Listen, Juanito, why is it your people don't like Mexicans? Why do they call us 'greasers'?"

Everyone has something to ask this thin, bespectacled, blond man who looks as if he were here by mistake.

"Listen, Juanito, how do you say 'mula' in English?"

"Goddamn stubborn—fathead mule . . ."

(368)

1914: Salt Lake City

Songster of Angry Peoples

They condemn him for singing red ballads that make fun of God, that wake up the worker, that curse money. The sentence doesn't say that Joe Hill is a proletarian troubadour, or worse, a foreigner seeking to subvert the good order of business. The sentence speaks of assault and crime. There is no proof, the witnesses change their stories each time they testify, and the defense lawyers act as if they were the prosecutors. But these details lack importance for the judges and for all who make decisions in Salt Lake City. Joe Hill will be bound to a chair with a cardboard circle pinned over his heart as a target for the firing squad.

Joe Hill came from Sweden. In the United States he wandered the roads. In the cities he cleaned spittoons and built walls; in the countryside he stacked wheat and picked fruit, dug copper in the mines, toted sacks on the piers, slept under bridges and in barns, sang anywhere at any hour, and never stopped singing. He bids his comrades farewell singing, now that he's off to Mars to disturb its social peace.

(167)

1914: Torreón
By Rail They March to Battle

In the red car, which displays his name in big gilt letters, General Pancho Villa receives John Reed. He receives him in his underpants, pours him coffee, and studies him for a long moment. Deciding that this gringo deserves the truth, he begins to talk.

"The chocolate politicians want to win without dirtying their hands. Those perfumed . . ."

Then he takes him to visit the field hospital, a train with a surgery and doctors to heal their own men and others: and he shows him the cars that take corn, sugar, coffee, and tobacco to the front. He also shows him the platform on which traitors are shot.

The railroads were the work of Porfirio Díaz, the key to peace and order, masterkey to the progress of a country without rivers or roads. They had been created not to transport an armed people but cheap raw materials, docile workers, and the executioners of rebellions. But General Villa makes war by train. From Camargo he turns loose a locomotive at full speed and smashes a trainful of soldiers. Villa's men enter Ciudad Juárez crouching in innocent coal cars, and after firing a few shots occupy it, more out of fun than necessity. By train the Villista troops roll to the front lines of the war. The locomotive gasps, painfully climbing the bare northern slopes. From behind a plume of black smoke come creaking shaking cars filled with soldiers and horses. On their roofs sprout rifles, sombreros, and stoves. Up there, among soldiers singing *mañanitas* and shooting into the air, children bawl and women cook—the women, the *soldaderas*, dressed in bridal gowns and silk shoes from the last looting.

(246 and 368)

1914: The Fields of Morelos
It's Time to Get Moving and Fight,

and the roars and rifle shots echo like mountain landslides. The army of Zapata—*down with the haciendas, up with the villages*—opens the way to Mexico City.

Around chief Zapata, General Genovevo de la O meditates and cleans his rifle, his face like a mustachioed sun, while Otilio Montaño, anarchist, discusses a manifesto with Antonio Díaz Soto y Gama, socialist.

Among Zapata's officers and advisers there is but one woman. Colonel Rosa Bobadilla, who won her rank in battle, commands a troop of cavalrymen and maintains a ban on drinking so much as a drop of tequila. They obey her, mysteriously, although they remain convinced that women are only good for adorning the world, making children, and cooking corn, chili, beans, or whatever God provides and permits.

(296 and 468)

1914: Mexico City
Huerta Flees

on the same ship that took Porfirio Díaz from Mexico.

Rags are winning the war against lace. A campesino tide beats against the capital. Zapata, *the Attila of Morelos*, and Pancho Villa, *the orangutan who eats raw meat and gnaws bones*, attack from north and south, avenging wrongs. Just before Christmas, the front pages of Mexico City's newspapers appear with black borders, mourning the arrival of the outlaws, barbarian violators of young ladies and locks.

Turbulent years. Now nobody knows who is who. The city trembles in panic and sighs with nostalgia. Only yesterday at the hub of the world were the masters in their big houses with their lackeys and pianos, candelabra and Carrara marble baths; and all around, serfs, the poor of the barrios, dizzy with *pulque*, drowning in garbage, condemned to the wages or tips which barely bought some occasional watered milk or *frijol* coffee or burro meat.

(194 and 246)

1915: Mexico City
Power Ungrasped

A timid knock, somewhere between wanting and not wanting. A door that half opens. An uncovered head, enormous sombrero clutched in hands pleading, for the love of God, for water or tortillas. Zapata's men, Indians in white pants, cartridge belts crossed on chests, wander the streets of the city that scorns and fears them. Nowhere are they invited in. In no time they run into Villa's men, also foreigners lost, blind.

Soft click of sandals, chas-ches, chas-ches, on the marble stairways, feet that are frightened by the pleasure of carpets, faces staring bewildered at themselves in the mirrors of waxed floors: Zapata's and Villa's men enter the National Palace as if begging pardon. Pancho Villa sits on the gilt armchair that was Porfirio Díaz's throne *to see how it feels*, while at his side Zapata, in a very embroidered suit, with an expression of being there without being there, murmurs answers to the reporters' questions.

The campesino generals have triumphed, but they don't know what to do with their victory: *"This shack is pretty big for us."*

Power is something for doctors, a threatening mystery that can only be deciphered by the cultured, those who understand the high art of politics, *those who sleep on downy pillows.*

When night falls, Zapata goes to a seedy hotel just a step away from the railway that leads to his country, and Villa to a military train. After a few days, they bid farewell to Mexico City.

The hacienda peons, the Indians of the communities, the pariahs of the countryside, have discovered the center of power and occupied it for a moment, as if on a visit, on tiptoe, anxious to end as soon as possible this trip to the moon. Strangers to the glory of victory, they end up going home to the lands where they know how to move around without getting lost.

No better news could be imagined by Huerta's successor, Gen-

eral Venustiano Carranza, whose battered troops are recovering with
the aid of the United States.

(47, 194, 246, and 260)

1915: Tlaltizapán
Agrarian Reform

In an old mill in the village of Tlaltizapán, Zapata installs his headquarters. Here, in his native district, far from the sideburned lords
and their feathered ladies, far from the flashy, deceitful city, the
Morelos rebel chief liquidates the great estates, nationalizes sugar-
mills and distilleries without paying a centavo, and restores to the
communities lands stolen through the centuries. Free villages are
reborn, the conscience and memory of Indian traditions, and with
them local democracy. Here neither bureaucrats nor generals make
the decisions, but the assembled community in open forum. Selling
or renting land is forbidden. Covetousness is forbidden.

In the shade of the laurels, in the village plaza, the talk is of
more than fighting cocks, horses, and rain. Zapata's army, a league
of armed communities, watches over the recovered land; they oil
their guns and reload them with old Mauser and .30-.30 cartridges.

Young technicians are arriving in Morelos with tripods and other
strange instruments to help the agrarian reform. The campesinos
receive these budding engineers from Cuernavaca with a rain of flowers; but the dogs bark at the mounted messengers who gallop in from
the north with the grim news that Pancho Villa's army is being wiped
out.

(468)

1915: El Paso
Azuela

Exiled in Texas, a medic from Pancho Villa's army treats the Mexican
revolution as a pointless outburst. According to Mariano Azuela's
novel *The Underdogs*, this is a tale of drunken blind men who shoot
without knowing why or against whom, who lash out like animals

seeking things to steal or women to tumble on the ground in a land that stinks of gunpowder and frying grease.

(33)

1916: Tlaltizapán
Carranza

The clink of Villa's horsemen's spurs can still be heard in the mountains, but it is no longer an army. From trenches defended by barbed wire, machineguns have made a clean sweep in four long battles of Villa's fiery cavalry, ground to dust in stubbornly repeated suicide charges.

Venustiano Carranza, president in spite of Villa and Zapata, launches the war in the south: *"This business of dividing up the land is crazy,"* he says. One decree announces that lands distributed by Zapata will be returned to their old owners; another promises to shoot anyone who is, or looks like, a Zapatista.

Shooting and burning with rifles and torches, government forces swoop down on the flourishing fields of Morelos. They kill five hundred people in Tlaltizapán, and many more elsewhere. The prisoners are sold in Yucatán as slave labor for the henequén plantations, as in the days of Porfirio Díaz; and crops, herds, all war booty is taken to the markets of the capital.

In the mountains, Zapata resists. When the rainy season approaches, the revolution is suspended for planting; but later, stubbornly, incredibly, it goes on.

(246, 260, and 468)

1916: Buenos Aires
Isadora

Barefoot, naked, scantily draped in the Argentine flag, Isadora Duncan dances to the national anthem in a students' café in Buenos Aires, and the next morning the whole world knows of it. The impresario breaks his contract, good families cancel their reservations at the Colón Theater, and the press demands the immediate expulsion of this disgraceful North American who has come to Argentina to sully patriotic symbols.

Isadora cannot understand it. No Frenchman protested when she danced the Marseillaise in nothing but a red shawl. If one can dance an emotion, if one can dance an idea, why not an anthem?

Liberty offends. This woman with shining eyes is the declared enemy of schools, matrimony, classical dance, and everything that cages the wind. She dances for the joy of dancing; dances what she wants, when she wants, how she wants; and orchestras hush before the music that is born of her body.

(145)

1916: New Orleans

Jazz

From the slaves comes the freest of all music, jazz, which flies without asking permission. Its grandparents are the blacks who sang at their work on their owners' plantations in the southern United States, and its parents are the musicians of black New Orleans brothels. The whorehouse bands play all night without stopping, on balconies that keep them safe above the brawling in the street. From their improvisations is born the new music.

With his savings from delivering newspapers, milk, and coal, a short, timid lad has just bought his own trumpet for ten dollars. He blows and the music stretches out, out, greeting the day. Louis Armstrong, like jazz, is the grandson of slaves, and has been raised, like jazz, in the whorehouse.

(105)

1916: Columbus

Latin America Invades the United States

Rain falls upward. Hen bites fox and hare shoots hunter. For the first and only time in history, Mexican soldiers invade the United States.

With the tattered force remaining, five hundred men out of the many thousands he once had, Pancho Villa crosses the border and, crying *Viva Mexico!* showers bullets on the city of Columbus, Texas.

(206 and 260)

1916: León
Darío

In Nicaragua, occupied land, humiliated land, Rubén Darío dies.

The doctor kills him, fatally puncturing his liver. The embalmer, the hairdresser, the makeup man, and the tailor torment his remains.

A sumptuous funeral is inflicted upon him. The warm February air in the city of León smells of incense and myrrh. The most distinguished señoritas, festooned in lilies and heron feathers, serve as Canephoras and Virgins of Minerva strewing flowers along the route of the funeral procession.

Surrounded by candles and admirers, the corpse of Darío wears a Greek tunic and laurel crown by day, by night a formal black frock coat and gloves to match. For a whole week, day and night, night and day, he is scourged with never-ending recitals of shoddy verses, and regaled with speeches proclaiming him Immortal Swan, Messiah of the Spanish Lyre, and Samson of the Metaphor.

Guns roar. The government contributes to the martyrdom by piling War Ministry honors on the poet who preached peace. Bishops brandish crosses; steeple bells ring out. In the culminating moment of this flagellation, the poet who believed in divorce and lay education is dropped into the hole converted, a prince of the Church.

(129, 229, and 454)

1917: The Fields of Chihuahua and Durango
Eagles into Hens

A punitive expedition, ten thousand soldiers with plentiful artillery enter Mexico to make Pancho Villa pay for his impudent attack on the North American city of Columbus.

"We'll bring back that assassin in an iron cage," proclaims General John Pershing, and the thunder of his guns echoes the words.

Across the drought-stricken immensities of northern Mexico, General Pershing finds various graves—*Here lies Pancho Villa*—

without a Villa in any of them. He finds snakes and lizards and silent stones, and campesinos who murmur false leads when beaten, threatened, or offered all the gold in the world.

After some months, almost a year, Pershing returns to the United States. He brings back a long caravan of soldiers fed up with breathing dust, with the people throwing stones, with the lies in each little village in that gravelly desert. Two young lieutenants march at the head of the humbled procession. Both have had in Mexico their baptism of fire. For Dwight Eisenhower, newly graduated from West Point, it is an unlucky start on the road to military glory. George Patton spits as he leaves *this ignorant and half-savage country.*

From the crest of a hill, Pancho Villa looks down and comments: *"They came like eagles and they leave like wet hens."*

(206 and 260)

1918: Córdoba
Moldy Scholars

At the Argentine university of Córdoba degrees are no longer denied to those unable to prove their white lineage as was the case a few years ago, but *Duties toward Servants* is still a subject studied in the Philosophy of Law course, and students of medicine still graduate without having set eyes on a sick person.

The professors, venerable specters, copy a Europe several centuries gone, a lost world of gentlemen and pious ladies, the sinister beauty of a colonial past. The merits of the parrot and the virtues of the monkey are rewarded with trimmings and tassels.

The Córdoba students, fed up, explode with disgust. They go on strike against these jailers of the spirit, calling on students and workers throughout Latin America to fight for a culture of their own. From Mexico to Chile come mighty echoes.

(164)

1918: Córdoba

"The Pains That Linger Are the Liberties We Lack," Proclaims the Student Manifesto

. . . We have resolved to call all things by their right names. Córdoba is redeeming itself. From today we count for our country one shame less and one freedom more. The pains that linger are the liberties we lack. We believe we are not wrong, the resonances of the heart tell us so: we are treading on the skirts of the revolution, we are living an American hour . . .

The unversities have till now been a secular refuge for the mediocre, income of the ignorant, secure hospital for the invalid, and —which is even worse—the place where all forms of tyranny and insensitivity have found a professor to teach them. The universities thus faithfully reflect those decadent societies which offer the sad spectacle of senile immobility. For that reason, science, confronting these mute and shut-in establishments, passes by in silence or enters into bureaucratic service, mutilated and grotesque . . .

(164)

1918: Ilopango

Miguel at Thirteen

He arrives at the Ilopango barracks driven by a hunger that has sunk his eyes into the depths of his head.

In the barracks, in exchange for food, Miguel begins running errands and shining lieutenants' boots. He learns fast to split coconuts with one blow of the machete as if they were necks, and to fire a carbine without wasting cartridges. Thus he becomes a soldier.

At the end of a year of barracks life, the wretched boy gives out. After putting up for so long with drunken officers who beat him for no reason, Miguel escapes. And that night, the night of his flight, is the night of the Ilopango earthquake. Miguel hears it from far away.

For a whole day and the next day too, the earth shakes El Salvador, this little country of warm people, until between tremor and tremor the real quake comes, the super-earthquake that bursts and shatters everything. It brings down the barracks to the last stone, crushing officers and soldiers alike—but not Miguel.

And so occurs the third birth of Miguel Mármol, at thirteen years of age.

(126)

1918: *The Mountains of Morelos*
Ravaged Land, Living Land

The hogs, the cows, the chickens, are they Zapatistas? And the jugs, the pans, the stewpots, what of them? Government troops have exterminated half the population of Morelos in these years of stubborn peasant war, and taken away everything. Only stones and charred stalks remain in the fields; the wreckage of a house, a woman heaving a plow. Of the men, any not dead or exiled have become outlaws.

But the war continues. The war will continue as long as corn sprouts in secret mountain crannies, as long as Zapata's eyes flash.

(468)

1918: *Mexico City*
The New Bourgeoisie Is Born Lying

"We fight for the land," says Zapata, *"and not for illusions that give us nothing to eat . . . With or without elections, the people are chewing the cud of bitterness."*

While taking the land from the campesinos of Morelos and wrecking their villages, President Carranza talks about agrarian reform. While applying state terror against the poor, he grants them the right to vote for the rich and offers illiterates freedom of the press.

The new Mexican bourgeoisie, voracious child of war and plunder, sings hymns of praise to the Revolution while gobbling it down with knife and fork from an embroidered tablecloth.

(468)

1919: Cuautla

This Man Taught Them That Life Is Not Only Fear of Suffering and Hope for Death

It had to be done by treachery. Shamming friendship, a government officer leads him into the trap. A thousand soldiers are waiting, a thousand rifles tumble him from his horse.

Afterward they haul him to Cuautla and exhibit him face up.

Campesinos from everywhere flock there for the silent march-past, which lasts several days. Approaching the body, they remove their sombreros, look attentively, and shake their heads. No one believes it. There's a wart missing, a scar too many; that suit isn't his; this face swollen by so many bullets could be anybody's.

The campesinos talk in slow whispers, peeling off words like grains of corn:

"They say he went with a compadre to Arabia."

"Hell, Zapata doesn't chicken out."

"He's been seen on the Quilamula heights."

"I know he's sleeping in a cave in Cerro Prieto."

"Last night his horse was drinking in the river."

The Morelos campesinos don't now believe, nor will they ever believe, that Emiliano Zapata could have committed the infamy of dying and leaving them all alone.

(468)

Ballad of the Death of Zapata

Little star in the night
that rides the sky like a witch,
where is our chief Zapata
who was the scourge of the rich?

Little flower of the fields
and valleys of Morelos,
if they ask for Zapata,
say he's gone to try on halos.

Little bubbling brook,
what did that carnation say to you?
It says our chief didn't die.
that Zapata's on his way to you.

(293)

1919: Hollywood
Chaplin

In the beginning were rags.

From the rag bag of the Keystone studios, Charles Chaplin chose the most useless garments, the too big, too small, too ugly, and put them together, as if picking through a garbage can. Some outsized pants, a dwarf's jacket, a bowler hat, and some huge dilapidated shoes. To that he added a prop mustache and cane. Then this little heap of rejected rags stood up, saluted its author with a ridiculous bow, and set off walking like a duck. After a few steps he collided with a tree and asked its pardon, doffing his hat.

And so came to life Charlie the Tramp, outcast and poet.

(121 and 383)

1919: Hollywood
Keaton

The man who never laughs creates laughter.

Like Chaplin, Buster Keaton is a Hollywood magician. His outcast hero—straw hat, stone face, cat's body—in no way resembles Charlie the Tramp, but is caught in the same absurd war with cops, bullies, and machines. Always impassive, icy outside, burning inside, he walks with great dignity on walls, on air, on the bottom of the sea.

Keaton is not as popular as Chaplin. His films entertain, but with too much mystery, too much melancholy.

(128 and 382)

1919: Memphis

Thousands of People Flock to the Show,

and many are women with babies in their arms. The family performance reaches its high point when Ell Persons, tied to a stake, is
baptized with gasoline and the flames draw his first howls.

Not long afterward, the audience departs in an orderly fashion,
complaining of the brevity of these things. Some stir the cinders
seeking a bone as a souvenir.

Ell Persons is one of the seventy-seven blacks who have been
roasted alive or hanged by white crowds this year in the southern
United States for committing a murder or a rape—that is to say, for
looking at a white woman, possibly with a lascivious gleam; or for
saying "Yes" instead of "Yes, ma'am"; or for not removing his hat
before speaking.

Among these lynched "niggers," some have worn the military
uniform of the United States of America and hunted Pancho Villa
through Mexico's northern deserts, or are newly returned from the
world war.

(51, 113, and 242)

1921: Rio de Janeiro

Rice Powder

President Epitácio Pessoa makes a recommendation to the managers
of Brazilian football. For reasons of patriotic prestige, he suggests
that no player with black skin be sent to the coming South American
soccer championships.

It happens, however, that Brazil won last year thanks to the
mulatto Artur Friedenreich, who scored the winning goal and whose
boots, grimed with mud, are still on display in a jeweler's window.
Friedenreich, born of a German and a black, is Brazil's best player.
He always arrives on the field last. It takes him at least half an hour
in the dressingroom to iron out his frizz, so that during the game not
a hair will move, even when he heads the ball.

Football, that elegant after-Mass diversion, is something for whites.
"Rice powder! Rice powder!" yell the fans at Carlos Alberto,

another mulatto player on the Fluminense club who whitens his face with it.

(279)

1921: Rio de Janeiro
Pixinguinha

It is announced that the Batons will soon be appearing on the Paris stage, and indignation mounts in the Brazilian press. What will Europeans think? Will they imagine Brazil is an African colony? The Batons' repertory contains no operatic arias or waltzes, only *maxixes*, *lundús*, *cortajacas*, *batuques*, *cateretês*, *modinhas*, and the newborn *samba*. It is an orchestra of blacks who play black music. Articles exhort the government to head off the disgrace. The foreign ministry promptly explains that the Batons are not on an official mission.

Pixinguinha, one of the blacks in the ensemble, is the best musician in Brazil. He doesn't know it, nor does it interest him. He is too busy seeking on his flute, with devilish joy, sounds stolen from the birds.

(75)

1921: Rio de Janeiro
Brazil's Fashionable Author

inaugurates a swimming pool in a sports club. Coelho Neto's speech exalting the virtues of the pool draws tears and applause. Coelho Neto invokes the powers of sea, sky, and earth *on this solemn occasion of such magnitude that we cannot evaluate it without tracing, through the Shadows of Time, its projection into the Future.*

Sweets for the rich, denounces Lima Barreto, an author not in vogue and accursed both as a mulatto and a rebel, who, cursing back, dies in some godforsaken hospital.

Lima Barreto mocks the pomposities of writers who parrot the literature of ornamental culture. They sing the glories of a happy Brazil, without blacks, workers, or the poor; a Brazil populated with sage economists whose most original idea is to impose more taxes on the people, a Brazil with two hundred and sixty-two generals whose job is to design new uniforms for next year's parade.

(36)

1922: Toronto
This Reprieve

saves thousands condemned to early death. Neither royal nor presidential, it has been extended by a Canadian doctor who a week ago, with seven cents in his pocket, was looking for a job.

On a hunch that deprived him of sleep, and after much error and discouragement, Fred Banting discovers that insulin, secreted by the pancreas, reduces sugar in the blood; and thus he commutes the many death sentences imposed by diabetes.

(54)

1922: Leavenworth
For Continuing to Believe That
All Belongs to All

Ricardo, most talented and dangerous of the Flores Magón brothers, has been absent from the revolution he did so much to start. While Mexico's fate was played out on its battlefields, he was breaking stones, shackled in a North American prison.

A United States court had sentenced him to twenty years' hard labor for signing an anarchist manifesto against private property. He was many times offered a pardon, if only he would ask for it. He never asked.

"When I die, perhaps my friends will write on my grave: 'Here Lies a Dreamer,' and my enemies: 'Here Lies a Madman.' But no one will dare write: 'Here Lies a Coward and Traitor to his Ideas.' "

In his cell, far from his land, they strangle him. *Heart failure,* says the medical report.

(44 and 391)

1922: The Fields of Patagonia

The Worker-Shoot

Three years ago young aristocrats of the Argentine Patriotic League went hunting in the barrios of Buenos Aires. The safari was a success. The rich kids killed workers and Jews for a whole week without a license, and no one went to jail.

Now it's the army that is using workers for target practice in the frozen lands of the south. The boys of the Tenth Cavalry under Lieutenant Colonel Héctor Benigno Varela roam the great estates of Patagonia shooting peons on strike. Fervent Patriotic League volunteers accompany them. No one is executed without a trial. Each trial lasts less time than it takes to smoke a cigarette.

Estancia owners and officers act as judges. The condemned are buried by the heap in common graves they dig themselves.

President Hipólito Yrigoyen in general doesn't approve of this method of finishing off anarchists and reds, but lifts not a finger against the murderers.

(38 and 365)

1923: Guayas River

Crosses Float in the River,

hundreds of crosses crowned with mountain blossoms, flowery squadrons of tiny ships cruising on the swell of waves and memory. Each cross recalls a murdered worker. People have thrown these floating crosses into the water so that the workers lying in the riverbed may rest in peace.

It happened a year ago, in the port of Guayaquil, which for several hours was in the hands of the workers. Fed up with eating hunger, they had called the first general strike in Ecuador's history—not even government officials were able to circulate without a pass from the unions. The women—washerwomen, tobacco workers, cooks, peddlers—had formed the Rosa Luxemburg Committee; they were the most defiant.

"Today the rabble got up laughing. Tomorrow they'll go to bed crying," announced Carlos Arroyo, president of the Chamber of Deputies. And the president of the republic, José Luis Tamayo, ordered

General Enrique Barriga to take care of the matter: "At any cost."

At the first shots, many workers tried to escape, scattering like ants from an anthill squashed by a foot. These were the first to fall.

No one knows how many were thrown into the Guayas river to sink, their bellies slashed with bayonets.

(192, 332, and 472)

1923: Acapulco
The Function of the Forces of Order in the Democratic Process

As soon as the Tom Mix film ends, Juan Escudero surprises the audience by stepping in front of the screen of Acapulco's only cinema and delivering a harangue against bloodsucking merchants. By the time the boys in uniform pile on him, the Workers' Party of Acapulco has already been born, baptized by acclamation.

In no time at all, the Workers' Party has grown and won the elections and stuck its black-and-red flag over city hall. Juan Escudero—tall, thick sideburns, pointed mustache—is the new mayor, the socialist mayor. In the blink of an eye he turns the palace into a headquarters for cooperatives and unions, launches a literacy campaign, and defies the power of the three companies that own the water, air, ground, and grime of this filthy Mexican port abandoned by God and the federal government. Then the owners of everything organize new elections, so that the people may correct their error, but the Workers' Party of Acapulco wins again. So there's no way out but to call in the army, which promptly normalizes the situation. The victorious Juan Escudero receives two bullets, one in the arm and the other in the forehead, a mercy-shot from close range, while the soldiers set fire to city hall.

But Escudero survives, and continues winning elections. In a wheelchair, mutilated, hardly able to talk, Escudero conducts a victorious new campaign for deputy by dictating speeches to a youngster who deciphers his mumblings and repeats them aloud on campaign platforms.

The owners of Acapulco decide to pay thirty thousand pesos so that this time the military patrol will shoot properly. In the company ledgers these outlays are duly entered, but not their purpose. And

finally Juan Escudero falls, very much shot, dead of total death you
might say, thank you, gentlemen.

(441)

1923: Azángaro
Urviola

His family wanted him to be a doctor. Instead he became an Indian,
as if his double-humped back and dwarf stature were not curse enough.
Ezequiel Urviola quit his law career in Puno vowing to follow in the
footsteps of Túpac Amaru. Since then he speaks Quechua, wears
sandals, chews coca, and plays the *quena* flute. Day and night he
comes and goes, inciting revolt in the Peruvian sierra, where the
Indians have proprietors like the mules and the trees.

The police dream of catching the hunchback Urviola; the landlords pledge it; but the little shrimp turns into an eagle flying over
the mountains.

(370)

1923: Callao
Mariátegui

A ship brings José Carlos Mariátegui back to Peru after some years
in Europe. When he left he was a bohemian nighthawk from Lima
who wrote about horses, a mystical poet who felt deeply and understood little. Over in Europe he discovered America. Mariátegui found
Marxism and found Mariátegui, and this was how he learned to see
from afar the Peru he couldn't see close up.

Mariátegui believes that Marxism means human progress as in-
disputably as smallpox vaccine or the theory of relativity, but to Pe-
ruvianize Peru one has to start by Peruvianizing Marxism, which is
not a catechism or the tracing of some master plan, but a key to enter
deep into this country. And the clues to the depths of his country
are in the Indian communities, dispossessed by the sterile landowner
system but unconquered in their socialist traditions of work and life.

(321, 277, and 355)

1923: Buenos Aires

Snapshot of a Worker-Hunter

He peruses the firearms catalogs lasciviously, as if they were pornography. For him the uniform of the Argentine army is as beautiful as the smoothest of human skin. He likes skinning alive the foxes that fall into his traps, but prefers making target practice of fleeing workers, the more so if they are reds, and more yet if they are foreign reds.

Jorge Ernesto Pérez Millán Temperley enlisted as a volunteer in the troop of Lieutenant Colonel Varela, and last year marched to Patagonia for the sport of liquidating any strikers who came within range. Later, when the German anarchist Kurt Wilckens threw the bomb that blew up Lieutenant Colonel Varela, this hunter of workers swore loudly to avenge his superior.

And avenge him he does. In the name of the Argentine Patriotic League, Jorge Ernesto Pérez Millán Temperley fires a Mauser bullet into the chest of Wilckens as he sleeps in his cell, then has himself immediately photographed for posterity, gun in hand, striking a martial pose of duty done.

(38)

1923: Tampico

Traven

A phantom ship, an old hulk destined to be wrecked, arrives off the coast of Mexico. Among its crew, vagabonds without name or nation, is a survivor of the suppressed revolution in Germany.

This comrade of Rosa Luxemburg, fugitive from hunger and the police, writes his first novel in Tampico and signs it B. Traven. With that name he will become famous without anyone ever knowing which face or voice or footstep is his. Traven decides to be a mystery, so that no bureaucracy can label him. All the better to mock a world where the marriage contract and inheritance matter more than love and death.

(398)

1923: The Fields of Durango

Pancho Villa Reads the
Thousand and One Nights,

deciphering the words out loud by candlelight, because this is the book that gives him the best dreams; and afterward, he awakens early to pasture the cows with his old battle comrades.

Villa is still the most popular man in the fields of northern Mexico, and officialdom doesn't like it a bit. Today it is three years since his men turned the Canutillo hacienda into a cooperative, which now has a hospital and a school, and a world of people have come to celebrate.

Villa is listening to his favorite *corridos* when Don Fernando, a pilgrim from Granada, mentions that John Reed has just died in Moscow.

Pancho Villa orders the party stopped. Even the flies pause in flight.

"So old Juan died? My old pal, Juan?"

"Himself."

Villa half believes and half not.

"I saw it in the papers," Don Fernando says, excusing himself. "He's buried over there with the heroes of the revolution."

Nobody breathes. Nobody disturbs the silence. Don Fernando murmurs: "It was typhus, not a bullet."

And Villa nods his head: "So old Juan died."

Then repeats: "So old Juan's dead."

He falls silent. Looking into the distance, he finally says: "I never even heard the word 'socialism' until he explained it to me."

All at once he rises, and extending his arms, rebukes the silent guitar-players: "And the music? What happened to the music? Play!"

(206)

1923: Mexico City/Parral

The People Donated a Million Dead to the
Mexican Revolution

in ten years of war so that military chieftains could finally take possession of the best lands and the most profitable businesses. These officers of the revolution share power and glory with Indian-fleecing doctors and the politicos-for-hire, brilliant banquet orators who call Obregón *the Mexican Lenin.*

On this road to national reconciliation there is no problem that can't be overcome by a public-works contract, a land concession, or the sort of favor that flows out of an open purse. Álvaro Obregón, the president, defines his style of government with a phrase soon to become a classic in Mexico: *"There's no general who can resist a salvo of fifty thousand pesos."*

But Obregón gets it wrong with General Villa.

Nothing can be done with him except to shoot him down.

Villa arrives in Parral by car in the early morning. At the sight of him someone signals with a red scarf. Twelve men respond by squeezing triggers.

Parral was his favorite city. *"I like Parral so much, so much . . ."* And the day when the women and children of Parral chased out the gringo invaders with stones, the horses inside Pancho broke free, and he let out a tremendous yell of joy: *"I just love Parral to death!"*

(206, 246, and 260)

1924: Mérida, Yucatán

More on the Function of the Forces of Order in the Democratic Process

Felipe Carrillo Puerto, also invulnerable to the gun from which Obregón fires pesos, faces a firing squad one damp January morning.

"Do you want a confessor?"

"I'm not a Catholic."

"How about a notary?"

"I've nothing to leave."

He had been a colonel in Zapata's army in Morelos before founding the Socialist Workers' Party in Yucatán. There Carrillo Puerto delivered his speeches in Mayan, explaining that Marx was a brother of Jacinto Canek and Cecilio Chi and that socialism, the inheritor of the communitarian tradition, gave a future dimension to the glorious Indian past.

Until yesterday he headed the socialist government of Yucatán. Innumerable frauds and private interests had not been able to keep the socialists from an easy electoral victory, nor afterward keep them from fulfilling their promises. Their sacrileges against the hallowed big estates, the slave labor system and various imperial monopolies aroused the rage of those who ran the henequén plantations, not to speak of the International Harvester Company. The archbishop went into convulsions over lay education, free love, and red baptisms—so called because children received their names on a mattress of red flowers, and along with those names, wishes for a long life of socialist militancy. So what could be done, but call in the army to bring the scandal to an end?

The shooting of Felipe Carrillo Puerto repeats the history of Juan Escudero in Acapulco. The government of the humiliated has lasted a couple of years in Yucatán. The humiliated govern with the weapons of reason. The humiliators don't have the government, but they do have the reason of weapons. And as in all of Mexico, death rides the dice of destiny.

(330)

1924: Mexico City
Nationalizing the Walls

Easel art invites confinement. The mural, on the other hand, offers itself to the passing multitude. The people may be illiterate but they are not blind; so Rivera, Orozco, and Siqueiros assault the walls of México. They paint something new and different. On moist lime is born a truly national art, child of the Mexican revolution and of these days of births and funerals.

Mexican muralism crashes head on into the dwarfed, castrated art of a country trained to deny itself. All of a sudden, still lifes and defunct landscapes spring dizzily to life, and the wretched of the earth become subjects of art and history rather than objects of use, scorn, or pity.

Complaints pelt down on the muralists, but praise, not a drop. Still, mounted on their scaffoldings, they stick to their jobs. Sixteen hours without a break is the working day for Rivera, eyes and belly of a toad, teeth like a fish. He keeps a pistol at his waist.

"To set a line for the critics," he says.

(80 and 387)

1924: Mexico City
Diego Rivera

resurrects Felipe Carrillo Puerto, redeemer of Yucatán, with a bullet
wound in his chest but uninformed of his own death, and paints
Emiliano Zapata arousing his people, and paints the people, all the
peoples of Mexico, united in an epic of work and war and fiesta, on
sixteen hundred square meters of wall in the Ministry of Education.
While he washes the world with colors, Diego amuses himself by
lying. To anyone who wants to listen he tells lies as colossal as his
belly, as his passion for creating, and as his woman-devouring insa-
tiability.

Barely three years ago he returned from Europe. Over there in
Paris, Diego was a vanguard painter who got tired of the "isms"; and
just as his star was fading, and he was painting just from boredom,
he returned to Mexico and the lights of his country hit him in the
face, setting his eyes aflame.

(82)

1924: Mexico City
Orozco

Diego Rivera rounds out, José Clemente Orozco sharpens. Rivera
paints sensualities: bodies of corn flesh, voluptuous fruits. Orozco
paints desperations: skin-and-bone bodies, a maguey mutilated and
bleeding. What is happiness in Rivera is tragedy in Orozco. In Rivera
there is tenderness and radiant serenity; in Orozco, severity and
contortion. Orozco's Mexican revolution has grandeur, like Rivera's;
but where Rivera speaks to us of hope, Orozco seems to say that
whoever steals the sacred fire from the gods will deny it to his fellow
men.

(83 and 323)

1924: Mexico City
Siqueiros

Surly, withdrawn, turbulent inside—that's Orozco. Spectacular, bombastic, turbulent on the outside—that's David Alfaro Siqueiros. Orozco practices painting as a ceremony of solitude. For Siqueiros it is an act of militant solidarity. *"There is no other way except ours,"* says Siqueiros. To European culture, which he considers sick, he opposes his own muscular energy. Orozco doubts, lacks faith in what he does. Siqueiros bulls ahead, sure that his patriotic brashness is no bad medicine for a country with a severe inferiority complex.

(27)

The People Are the Hero of Mexican Mural Painting, Says Diego Rivera

The true novelty of Mexican painting, in the sense that we initiated it with Orozco and Siqueiros, was to make the people the hero of mural painting. Until then the heroes of mural painting had been gods, angels, archangels, saints, war heroes, kings and emperors, prelates, and great military and political chiefs, the people appearing as the chorus around the star personalities of the tragedy . . .

(79)

1924: Regla
Lenin

The mayor of the Cuban community of Regla calls everybody together. From the neighboring city of Havana has come news of the death of Lenin in the Soviet Union. The mayor issues a proclamation of mourning. The proclamation says that *the aforementioned Lenin won well-deserved sympathy among the proletarian and intellectual elements of this municipal district. Accordingly, at 5:00 P.M. Sunday next its residents will observe two minutes of silence and meditation, during which persons and vehicles will maintain absolute stillness.*

At precisely five o'clock on Sunday afternoon, the mayor of Regla climbs up Fortín hill. Despite a heavy downpour, over a thousand people accompany him to observe the two minutes of silence and meditation. Afterward, the mayor plants an olive tree on top of the hill in homage to the man who was always planting the red flag over there, in the middle of the snow.

(215)

1926: San Albino

Sandino

is short and thin as a rake. A stray wind would blow him away were he not so firmly planted in the soil of Nicaragua.

In this land, his land, Augusto César Sandino stands tall and speaks of what the land has said to him, for when Sandino stretches out to sleep, his land whispers sorrow and sweetness to him.

Sandino speaks of the secrets of his invaded and humiliated land, and asks, *How many of you love it as much as I do?*

Twenty-nine San Albino miners step forward.

These are the first soldiers in Nicaragua's army of liberation. Illiterate, they toil fifteen hours a day hacking gold out of the ground for a North American firm and sleep piled up in a shed. They blow up the mine with dynamite and follow Sandino into the mountains.

Sandino goes on a small white burro.

(118 and 361)

1926: Puerto Cabezas

The Most Admirable Women on Earth

are the whores of Puerto Cabezas. From pillow talk they know the exact spot under water where U.S. Marines have buried forty rifles and seven thousand cartridges. Thanks to these women, who risk their lives in defiance of the foreign occupation troops, Sandino and his men rescue from the waters, by torchlight, their first weapons and first ammunition.

(361)

1926: Juazeiro do Norte
Father Cicero

Once Juazeiro was a nothing of a hamlet—four shacks God seemed to have spat into the void when, one fine day, He pointed a finger at this garbage heap and decided it was to be a Holy City. Since then, the afflicted flock here by the thousands. Every road of martyrdom and miracle leads here. Squalid pilgrims from all Brazil, long lines of rags and stumps of limbs, have turned Juazeiro into the richest city of the northeastern hinterland. In this faith-restoring new Jerusalem, memorials to the forgotten, polestar of the lost, the modest Salgadinho stream is now known as the River Jordan. Surrounded by pious women brandishing their bleeding bronze crucifixes, Father Cicero announces that Jesus Christ is on his way.

Father Cicero Romão Baptista is the master of the lands and souls. This savior of the shipwrecked in the desert, tamer of madmen and criminals, gives children to sterile women, rain to dry ground, light to the blind, and, to the poor, some crumbs from the bread he eats.

(133)

1926: Juazeiro do Norte
By Divine Miracle a Bandit
Becomes a Captain

Lampião's warriors fire off bullets and sing songs. Tolling bells and fireworks welcome them to the city of Juazeiro. The *cangaceiros* display a complete arsenal and a luxuriance of medals on their leather armor.

At the foot of the statue of Father Cicero, Father Cicero blesses the chief of the gang. It is well known that the bandit Lampião never touches a house containing an image of Father Cicero, or kills any devotee of the miracle-working saint.

In the name of the government of Brazil, Father Cicero confers on Lampião the rank of captain, three blue stripes on either shoulder, and hands out to his men impeccable Mausers in exchange for their old Winchester rifles. In return, Captain Lampião promises to defeat the rebels under Lieutenant Luis Carlos Prestes, who roam Brazil preaching democracy and other devilish ideas; but he has hardly left this city before he forgets about the Prestes Column and returns to his old routine.

(120, 133, and 263)

1926: New York
Valentino

Last night, in an Italian bar, Rudolph Valentino collapsed, struck down by a pasta banquet.

Millions of women on five continents have been widowed. They adored the elegant, feline Latin on the screen-altar of the movie theater, itself a temple for all peoples in all cities. With him they galloped to the oasis, spurred by the wind of the desert, and with him participated in tragic bullfights, entered mysterious palaces, danced on mirrored floors, and undressed in the bedrooms of Indian Prince and Son of the Sheik. Pierced by the languid gimlet of his eyes and crushed by his arms, they swooned into deep silken beds.

He didn't even realize. Valentino, the Hollywood god who casually smoked while kissing and annihilated with a glance, he who daily received a thousand love letters, in reality slept alone and dreamed of Mother.

(443)

1927: Chicago
Louie

She lived on New Orleans' Perdido Street—the street of the lost—where the dead were laid out with a saucer on the chest for the neighbors' coins to pay for the funeral. When she dies, her son Louis takes pleasure in giving her a fine funeral—the deluxe funeral she would have dreamed of at the end of the dream in which God made her white and a millionaire.

Louis Armstrong, who grew up with no more to eat than leftovers and music, fled New Orleans for Chicago with only a trumpet for baggage and a fish sandwich for company. A few years have passed and he is getting fat. He eats to avenge himself. And if he returned to the South now, maybe he'd be welcomed in some of the places barred to blacks and out of bounds for the poor. He could probably walk down most any street in town. He's the king of jazz and no one argues it. His trumpet whispers, moans, wails, howls like a wounded beast, and laughs uproariously, celebrating with euphoria and immense power the absurdity of life.

(105)

1927: New York
Bessie

This woman sings her sufferings with the voice of glory and no one can listen and pretend he doesn't hear or he's not moved. Lungs of deep night: Bessie Smith, immensely fat, immensely black, curses the thieves of Creation. Her blues are the hymns of poor drunk black women of the slums. They announce that the whites and the supermen and the rich who humiliate the world will be dethroned.

(165)

1927: Rapallo
Pound

It is twenty years since Ezra Pound pulled out of America. Son of poets, father of poets, Pound seeks beneath the Italian sun new images, worthy accompaniments to the bison of Altamira, unknown words for talking to gods more ancient than the fish.

Along the road, he makes the wrong friends.

(261, 349, and 437)

1927: Charlestown
"Lovely day,"

says the governor of the state of Massachusetts.

At midnight on this August Monday, two Italian workers will occupy the electric chair of Charlestown prison's death house. Nicola Sacco, shoemaker, and Bartolomeo Vanzetti, fish peddler, will be executed for crimes they did not commit.

The lives of Sacco and Vanzetti are in the hands of a businessman who has made forty million dollars selling Packard cars. Alvan Tufts Fuller, governor of Massachusetts, a small man behind a big desk of carved wood, declines to yield to the protests rumbling from every direction. He honestly believes in the correctness of the trial and the validity of the evidence. He also believes that all the damned anarchists and filthy foreigners who come to ruin this country deserve to die.

(162 and 445)

1927: Araraquara
Mário de Andrade

challenges everything servile, saccharine, grandiloquent in official culture. He is a creator of words, words dying of envy for music, which nonetheless are capable of seeing and speaking everything to Brazil, and also of savoring it, Brazil the tasty hot peanut.

On holidays, for the fun of it, Mário de Andrade transcribes the sayings and deeds of one Macunaíma, a hero with no character, just as he hears them from the golden beak of a parrot. According to the parrot, Macunaíma was an ugly black man, born in the heart of the jungle, who didn't bother saying a word until he was six—for sheer laziness, and preoccupied as he was with decapitating ants, spitting in his brothers' faces, and fondling his female relatives. Macunaíma's wild adventures cover all times and all spaces in Brazil, while stripping saints of their robes, and puppets of their heads.

Macunaíma is more real than his author. Like every flesh-and-blood Brazilian, Mário de Andrade is a figment of the imagination.

(23)

1927: Paris
Villa-Lobos

From behind the enormous cigar floats a cloud of smoke. Enveloped within it, happy and in love, Heitor Villa-Lobos whistles a vagabond tune.

In Brazil, hostile critics claim he composes music to be played by epileptics for an audience of paranoiacs, but in France he is received with ovations. The Paris press enthusiastically applauds his audacious harmonies and his vigorous sense of nationality. They publish articles on the maestro's life. One newspaper recounts how Villa-Lobos was once bound to a grill and almost roasted alive by cannibal Indians while out strolling in the Amazon jungle with a Victrola in his arms playing Bach.

At one of the many parties they throw for him between concerts in Paris, a lady asks him if he has eaten people raw, and how he liked it.

(280)

1927: The Plains of Jalisco
Behind a Huge Cross of Sticks

charge the *Cristeros*, rebelling in Jalisco and other states of Mexico in search of martyrdom and glory. They shout *Vivas!* for a Christ the King crowned with jewels instead of thorns, and *Vivas!* for the Pope, who has not resigned himself to the loss of the few clerical privileges still remaining in Mexico.

These poor campesinos have just been dying for a revolution that promised them land. Now, condemned to a living death, they start dying for a Church that promises them heaven.

(297)

1927: San Gabriel de Jalisco
A Child Looks On

The mother covers his eyes so he cannot see his grandfather hanging by the feet. And then the mother's hands prevent his seeing his father's body riddled by the bandits' bullets, or his uncle's twisting in the wind over there on the telegraph posts.

Now the mother too has died, or perhaps has just tired of defending her child's eyes. Sitting on the stone fence that snakes over the slopes, Juan Rulfo contemplates his harsh land with a naked eye. He sees horsemen—federal police or *Cristeros*, it makes no difference—emerging from smoke, and behind them, in the distance, a fire. He sees bodies hanging in a row, nothing now but ragged clothing emptied by the vultures. He sees a procession of women dressed in black.

Juan Rulfo, a child of nine, is surrounded by ghosts who look like him.

Here there is nothing alive—the only voices those of howling coyotes, the only air the black wind that rises in gusts from the plains of Jalisco, where the survivors are only dead people pretending.

(48 and 400)

1927: El Chipote

The War of Jaguars and Birds

Fifteen years ago the Marines landed in Nicaragua for a while, *to protect the lives and properties of United States citizens,* and forgot to leave. Against them now loom these northern mountains. Villages are scarce here; but anyone who hasn't actually become one of Sandino's soldiers is his spy or messenger. Since the dynamiting of the San Albino mine and the first battle, at Muy Muy, the liberating force keeps growing.

The whole Honduran army is mobilized on the border to prevent arms from reaching Sandino from across the river, but the guerrillas, unconcerned, acquire rifles from fallen enemies and carve bullets out of the trees in which they imbed themselves; nor is there any shortage of machetes for chopping off heads, or sardine-can grenades filled with glass, nails, screws, and dynamite for scattering the enemy.

U.S. airplanes bomb haphazardly, destroying villages. And Marines roam the forests, between abysses and high peaks, roasted by the sun, drowned by the rain, asphyxiated by dust, burning and killing all they find. Even the little monkeys throw things at them.

They offer Sandino a pardon and ten dollars for every day he has been in rebellion. Captain Hatfield hints at a surrender.

From his stronghold in El Chipote, a mysterious peak wreathed in mist, comes the reply: *I don't sell out or surrender.* It closes: *Your obedient servant, who desires to put you in a handsome coffin with beautiful bouquets of flowers.* And then Sandino's signature.

His soldiers bite like jaguars and flit like birds. When least expected, they lash out in a single jaguar leap, and before the enemy can even react are already striking from the rear or the flanks, only to disappear with a flap of wings.

(118 and 361)

1928: San Rafael del Norte
Crazy Little Army

Four Corsairs bombard El Chipote, already encircled and harassed by salvos from Marine artillery. For days and nights now the whole region thunders and trembles, until the invaders fix bayonets and charge the stone trenches bristling with rifles. This heroic action ends with neither dead nor wounded, because the attackers find only soldiers of straw and guns of sticks.

U.S. papers promptly report the victory without mentioning that the Marines have demolished a legion of dolls with wide-brimmed hats and black-and-red kerchiefs. They do verify, however, that Sandino himself is among the victims.

In the remote village of San Rafael del Norte, Sandino listens to his men singing by the light of campfires. There he receives word of his death.

"*God and our mountains are with us. And after all is said and done, death is no more than a little moment of pain.*"

Over the past months thirty-six warships and six thousand more Marines have arrived as reinforcements in Nicaragua. Yet, of seventy-five big and small battles, almost all have been lost, and the quarry has slipped through their fingers, no one knows how.

Crazy little army, the Chilean poet Gabriela Mistral calls Sandino's battered warriors, these masters of daring and devilment.

(118, 361, and 419)

"It Was All Very Brotherly"

JUAN PABLO RAMÍREZ: *We made dolls of straw and stuck them there. As decoys we fixed up sticks topped by sombreros. And it was fun . . . They spent a week firing at them, bombing them, and I pissed in my pants laughing!*

ALFONSO ALEXANDER: *The invaders were like the elephant and we the snake. They were immobility, we were mobility.*

PEDRO ANTONIO ARAÚZ: *The Yanquis died sad deaths, the ingrates. They just didn't know how things work in our country's mountains.*

SINFOROSO GONZÁLEZ ZELEDÓN: *The campesinos helped us, they worked with us, they felt for us.*
COSME CASTRO ANDINO: *We weren't drawing any pay. When we got to a village and the campesinos gave us food, we shared it. It was all very brotherly.*

(236)

1928: Washington

Newsreel

In an emotional ceremony in Washington, ten Marine officers receive the Cross of Merit *for distinguished service and extraordinary heroism* in the war against Sandino.

The *Washington Herald* and other papers devote pages to the crimes of the *outlaw band* who slit Marines' throats. They also publish documents newly arrived from Mexico, with impressive numbers of spelling mistakes, proving that Mexican president Calles is sending bolshevik weapons and propaganda to Sandino through Soviet diplomats. Official State Department sources explain that Calles began revealing his communist sympathies when he raised taxes on U.S. oil companies operating in Mexico, and fully confirmed them when his government established diplomatic relations with the Soviet Union.

The U.S. government warns that it *will not permit Russian and Mexican soldiers to implant the Soviet in Nicaragua.* According to official State Department spokesmen, Mexico is *exporting bolshevism.* After Nicaragua the next target of Soviet expansion in Central America will be the Panama Canal.

Senator Shortridge declares that the citizens of the United States *deserve as much protection as those of ancient Rome,* and Senator Bingham says: *We are obliged to accept our function as international policemen.* Senator Bingham, the famous archaeologist who sixteen years ago discovered the ruins of Machu Picchu in Peru, has never concealed his admiration for the works of dead Indians.

For the opposition, Senator Borah denies his country's right to act as the censor of Central America, and Senator Wheeler suggests that the government send Marines to Chicago, not Nicaragua, if it really wants to take on bandits. The *Nation* magazine, for its part, takes the view that for the U.S. president to call Sandino a bandit is like George III of England labeling George Washington a thief.

(39 and 419)

1928: Managua

Profile of Colonial Power

North American children study geography from maps showing Nicaragua as a colored blob labeled *Protectorate of the United States of America.*

When the United States decided that Nicaragua could not govern itself, there were forty public schools in its Atlantic coast region. Now there are six. The tutelary power has not put in a railroad, opened a single highway, or founded a university. At the same time, the occupied country falls farther into debt, paying the costs of its own occupation, while the occupiers continue to occupy—to guarantee the payment of the expenses of the occupation.

The Nicaraguan customs offices are in the hands of North American creditor banks, which appoint Clifford D. Ham comptroller of customs and general tax collector. Ham is also the Nicaraguan correspondent for the United Press news agency, The vice-comptroller of customs and vice-collector of taxes, Irving Lindbergh, is the correspondent for the Associated Press. So Ham and Lindbergh not only usurp the tariffs of Nicaragua, they also usurp the information. It is they who inform international public opinion about the misdeeds of Sandino, *criminal bandit and bolshevik agent.* A North American colonel leads the Nicaraguan army—the National Guard—and a North American captain leads the Nicaraguan police.

North American General Frank McCoy administers the National Electoral Junta. Four hundred and thirty-two U.S. Marines and twelve U.S. airplanes preside over the voting tables. The Nicaraguans vote, the North Americans elect. The new president is barely chosen before he announces that the Marines will stay.

This unforgettable civic fiesta has been organized by General Logan Feland, commander of the occupation forces. General Feland, all muscle and eyebrows, crosses his feet under the desk. In the matter of Sandino, he yawns and says, *"This bird has to fall one day."*

(39 and 419)

1928: Mexico City

Obregón

At the Náinari hacienda in Mexico's Yaqui Valley, the dogs howled.

"*Shut them up!*" ordered General Álvaro Obregón.

But the dogs barked more than ever.

"*Have them fed!*" ordered the general.

But the dogs ignored the food and continued their uproar.

"*Throw them fresh meat!*"

But the fresh meat had no effect. Even when they were beaten, the din went on.

"*I know what they want,*" said Obregón with resignation.

This happened on May 17. On July 9, in Culiacán, Obregón was sipping a tamarind drink in the shade of a porch, when the cathedral bells tolled and the poet Chuy Andrade, slightly drunk, said, "*They're tolling for you, friend.*"

And the next day, in Escuinapa, after a banquet of shrimp tamales, Obregón was boarding a train when Elisa Beaven, a good friend, pressed his arm and pleaded with him in her hoarse voice, "*Don't go. They're going to kill you.*"

But Obregón entered the train anyway and rode to the capital. After all, he had known how to muscle and hustle his way ahead in the days when bullets buzzed like hornets. He was the killer of killers, the conqueror of conquerors, and had won power, and glory, and money, without losing anything but the hand that Pancho Villa blew off; so he wasn't about to back off now that he knew his days were numbered. He simply went ahead, blithely but sadly. He had, after all, lost his one innocence: the happiness of unconcern about his own death.

Today, July 17, 1928, two months after the dogs barked in Náinari, a Christ-the-King fanatic kills reelected President Álvaro Obregón in a Mexico City restaurant.

(4)

1928: Villahermosa

The Priest Eater

Obregón is hardly dead, felled by the bullets of an ultra-Catholic, when Governor Manuel Garrido of the Mexican state of Tabasco decrees vengeance. He orders the cathedral demolished to the last stone, and from the bronze of the bells erects a statue of the late lamented.

Garrido believes that Catholicism shuts workers into a cage of fear, terrorizing them with the threat of eternal fire. For freedom to come to Tabasco, says Garrido, religion must go; and he kicks it out, decapitating saints, wrecking churches, yanking crosses out of cemeteries, forcing priests to marry, and renaming all places named after saints. The state capital, San Juan Bautista, becomes Villahermosa. And in a solemn ceremony he has a stud bull called "Bishop" and an ass, "Pope."

(283)

1928: Southern Santa Marta

Bananization

They were no more than lost villages on the Colombian coast, a strip of dust between river and cemetery, a yawn between two siestas, when the yellow train of the United Fruit Company pulled in. Coughing smoke, the train had crossed the swamps and penetrated the jungle and emerged here in brilliant clarity, announcing with a whistle that the age of the banana had come.

The region awoke to find itself an immense plantation. Ciénaga, Aracataca, and Fundación got telegraph and post offices and new streets with poolrooms and brothels. Campesinos, who arrived by the thousands, left their mules at the hitching posts and went to work.

For years these workers proved obedient and cheap as they hacked at the undergrowth and roots with their machetes for less than a dollar a day, and consented to live in filthy sheds and die of malaria or tuberculosis.

Then they form a union.

(186 and 464)

1928: Aracataca

The Curse

Swelter and languor and rancor. Bananas rot on the trees. Oxen sleep before empty carts. Trains stand dead on their tracks, not a single bunch of fruit reaching them. Seven ships wait anchored at the Santa Marta piers: in their fruit-less holds, the ventilators have stopped whirring.

Four hundred strikers are behind bars, but the strike goes relentlessly on.

In Aracataca, United Fruit throws a supper in honor of the regional Civil and Military Chief. Over dessert, General Carlos Cortés Vargas curses the workers, *armed evildoers*, and their *bolshevik agitators*, and announces that tomorrow he'll march to Ciénaga at the head of the forces of order, to get on with the job.

(93 and 464)

1928: Ciénaga

Carnage

On the shores of Ciénaga, a high tide of banners. Men with machetes at their waists, women toting pots and children wait here amid the campfires. The company has promised that tonight it will sign an agreement ending the strike.

Instead of the manager of United Fruit comes General Cortés Vargas. Instead of an agreement he reads them an ultimatum.

No one moves. Three times the warning bugle blares. And then, in an instant, the world explodes, sudden thunder of thunders, as machineguns and rifles empty. The plaza is carpeted with dead.

The soldiers sweep and wash all night long, while corpses are thrown into the sea. In the morning there is nothing.

"In Macondo nothing has happened, nor is happening, nor ever will happen."

(93 and 464)

1928: Aracataca
García Márquez

The roundup is on for the wounded and hiding strikers. They are hunted like rabbits, with broadsides from a moving train, and in the stations netted like fish. One hundred and twenty are captured in Aracataca in a single night. The soldiers awaken the priest and grab the key to the cemetery. Trembling in his underwear, the priest listens as the shootings begin.

Not far away, a little boy bawls in his crib.

The years will pass and this child will reveal to the world the secrets of a region so attacked by a plague of forgetfulness that it lost the names of things. He will discover the documents that tell how the workers were shot in the plaza, and how Big Mamma is the owner of lives and haciendas and of the rain that has fallen and will fall, and how between rain and rain Remedios the Beautiful goes to heaven, and in the air passes a little old plucked angel who is falling into a henhouse.

(187 and 464)

1928: Bogotá
Newsreel

The press reports on recent events in the banana zone. According to official sources, the excesses of the strikers have left a total of forty plantations burned, thirty-five thousand meters of telegraph wires destroyed, and eight workers killed when they tried to attack the army.

The president of the republic charges the strikers with treason and felony. *With their poisoned dagger they have pierced the loving heart of the Fatherland,* he declares. By decree, the president appoints General Cortés Vargas head of the National Police, and announces promotions and rewards for the other officers who participated in the events.

In a spectacular speech, the young liberal legislator Jorge Eliécer Gaitán contradicts the official story. He accuses the Colombian army of committing butchery under the orders of a foreign company. The United Fruit Company, which directed the massacre, according to

Gaitán, has subsequently reduced the daily wage that it pays in coupons, not money. The legislator stresses that the company exploits lands donated by the Colombian state, which are not subject to taxes.

(174 and 464)

1929: Mexico City

Mella

The dictator of Cuba, Gerardo Machado, orders him killed. Julio Antonio Mella is just another expatriate student in Mexico, intensely busy chasing around and publishing articles—for very few readers—against racism and the hidden face of colonialism; but the dictator is not mistaken in thinking him his most dangerous enemy. He has been a marked man ever since his fiery speeches rocked Havana's students. Mella blazed as he denounced the dictatorship and mocked the decrepitude of the Cuban university, a factory of professionals with the mentality of a colonial convent.

One night Mella is strolling arm in arm with his friend Tina Modotti, when the murderers shoot him down.

Tina screams, but doesn't cry. Not until she returns home at dawn and sees Mella's empty shoes waiting for her under the bed.

Until a few hours ago, this woman was so happy she was jealous of herself.

(290)

1929: Mexico City

Tina Modotti

The Cuban government has nothing to do with it, insist the right-wing Mexican papers. Mella was the victim of a crime of passion, *whatever the Muscovite bolshevik yids may say.* The press reveals that Tina Modotti, *a woman of dubious decency,* reacted coldly to the tragic episode and subsequently, in her statements to the police, fell into suspicious contradictions.

Modotti, an Italian photographer, has dug her feet deeply into Mexico in the few years she has been here. Her photographs mirror a grandeur in everyday things, and in people who work with their hands.

But she is guilty of freedom. She was living alone when she found Mella mixed up in a crowd demonstrating for Sacco and Vanzetti and for Sandino, and she hitched up with him unceremoniously. Previously she had been a Hollywood actress, a model, and a lover of artists; and she makes every man who sees her nervous. In short, she is a harlot—and to top it off, a foreigner and a communist. The police circulate photos showing her unforgivable beauty in the nude, while proceedings begin to expel her from Mexico.

(112)

1929: Mexico City
Frida

Tina Modotti is not alone before her inquisitors. Accompanying her, one on each arm, are Diego Rivera and Frida Kahlo: the immense painter-Buddha and his little Frida, also a painter, Tina's best friend, who looks like a mysterious oriental princess but swears and drinks tequila like a Jalisco mariachi.

Kahlo has a wild laugh, and has painted splendid canvases in oils ever since the day she was condemned to pain without end. She had known other pain from infancy, when her parents dressed her up with straw wings. But constant and crippling agony has come only since her accident, when a shard from a shattered street car pierced her body, like a lance, tearing at her bones.

Now she is a pain that survives as a person. They have operated in vain several times; and it was in her hospital bed that she started painting self-portraits, desperate homage to the life that remains for her.

(224 and 444)

1929: Capela
Lampião

The most famous gang in northeast Brazil attacks the town of Capela. Its chief, Lampião, who never smiles, fixes a reasonable sum as ransom, then offers a reduction, because we are in the drought season. While the town notables drum up the money, he strolls the streets.

The whole town follows him. His horrifying crimes have won him general admiration.

Lampião, the one-eyed king, master of the open spaces, sparkles in the sun. His glittering gold-wire glasses give him the look of an absent-minded professor; his gleaming dagger is as long as a sword. On each finger shimmers a diamond ring, and to the hairband around his forehead are sewn English pound notes.

Lampião wanders into the cinema, where they are showing a Janet Gaynor film. That night he dines at the hotel. The town telegraph operator, seated beside him, tastes the first mouthful of each dish. Then Lampião has a few drinks while reading Ellen G. White's *Life of Jesus*. He ends the day in the whorehouse. He picks the plumpest one, a certain Enedina. With her he spends the whole night. By dawn, Enedina is famous. For years men will line up outside her door.

(120 and 348)

1929: Atlantic City

The Crime Trust

Organized crime in the United States holds its first national convention, in the salons of the President Hotel. Attending are the qualified representatives of mobs operating in each of the major cities.

Olive branch, white flag: The convention resolves that rival gangs will stop killing one another and decrees a general amnesty. To guarantee peace, the executives of the crime industry follow the example of the oil industry. As Standard Oil and Shell have just done, the powerful gangsters divide markets, fix prices, and agree to eliminate the competition of small and middle fry.

In recent years, crime's impresarios have diversified their activities and modernized their methods. Now they not only engage in extortion, murder, pimping, and smuggling, but also own distilleries, hotels, casinos, banks, and supermarkets. They use the latest-model machineguns and accounting machines. Engineers, economists, and publicity experts direct the teams of technicians that avoid waste of resources and ensure a constant rise in profits.

Al Capone chairs the board of the most lucrative company in the game. He earns a hundred million dollars a year.

(335)

1929: Chicago
Al Capone

Ten thousand students chant the name of Al Capone on the sports field of Northwestern University. The popular Capone greets the multitude with a two-handed wave. Twelve bodyguards escort him. At the gate an armored Cadillac awaits him. Capone sports a rose in his lapel and a diamond stickpin in his tie, but underneath he wears a steel vest, and his heart beats against a .45.

He is an idol. No one provides as much business for funeral parlors, flower shops, and tailors who do invisible mending on small holes; and he pays generous salaries to policemen, judges, legislators, and mayors. Exemplary family man, Capone abominates short skirts and cosmetics. He believes woman's place is in the kitchen. Fervent patriot, he exhibits portraits of George Washington and Abraham Lincoln on his desk. Influential professional, he offers the best available service for breaking strikes, beating up workers, and sending rebels to the other world. He is ever alert to the red menace.

(335)

Al Capone Calls for Defense Against
the Communist Danger

Bolshevism is knocking at our door. We must not let it in. We have to remain united and defend ourselves against it with full decisiveness. America must remain safe and uncorrupted. We must protect the workers from the red press and from red perfidy, and ensure that their minds stay healthy . . .

(153)

1929: New York
Euphoria

Millions are reading *The Man Nobody Knows*, the book by Bruce Barton that places heaven on Wall Street. According to the author, Jesus of Nazareth founded the modern world of business. Jesus, it turns out, was a market-conquering entrepreneur gifted with a genius for publicity, professionally assisted by twelve salesmen in his image and likeness.

With a faith bordering on the religious, capitalism believes in its own eternity. What North American citizen does not feel himself one of the elect? The Stock Exchange is a casino where everybody plays and no one loses. God has made them prosperous. The entrepreneur Henry Ford wishes he never had to sleep, so he could make more money.

(2 and 304)

From the Capitalist Manifesto of Henry Ford, Automobile Manufacturer

Bolshevism failed because it was both unnatural and immoral. Our system stands . . .

There can be no greater absurdity and no greater disservice to humanity in general, than to insist that all men are equal . . .

Money comes naturally as the result of service. And it is absolutely necessary to have money. But we do not want to forget that the end of money is not ease but the opportunity to perform more service. In my mind nothing is more abhorrent than a life of ease. None of us has any right to ease. There is no place in civilization for the idler . . .

In our first advertisement we showed that a motor car was a utility. We said: "We often hear quoted the old proverb, 'Time is money'—and yet how few business and professional men act as if they really believed its truth . . ."

(168)

1929: New York
The Crisis

Speculation grows faster than production and production faster than consumption, and everything grows at a giddy rhythm until, all of a sudden, in a single day, the collapse of the New York Stock Exchange reduces to ashes the profits of years. The most prized stocks become mere scraps of paper, useless even for wrapping fish.

Prices and salaries plummet along with stock quotations, and more than one businessman from his tower. Factories and banks close; farmers are ruined. Workers without jobs chafe their hands at burning garbage heaps and chew gum to pacify their stomachs. The largest enterprises collapse; and even Al Capone takes a fall.

(2 and 304)

1930: La Paz

A Touching Adventure of the Prince of Wales Among the Savages

The New York Stock Exchange pulls many governments down into the abyss. International prices crumble, and with them, one after another, the civilian presidents of Latin America—feathers plucked from the wings of the eagle—and new dictatorships are born, to make hunger hungrier.

In Bolivia, the collapse of the price of tin brings down President Hernando Siles and puts in his place a general on the payroll of Patiño, the tin king. A mob accompanying the military rises, attacks the government palace, is granted permission to loot it. Out of control, they make off with furniture, carpets, paintings, everything. Everything. They take whole bathrooms, including toilets, tubs, and drainpipes.

Just then the Prince of Wales visits Bolivia. The people expect a prince to arrive in the style God intended, riding on a white steed, a sword at his waist and golden locks streaming in the wind. They are disappointed by a gentleman with top hat and cane who gets off the train looking exhausted.

That evening the new president offers the prince a banquet in the stripped-down palace. At dessert, just when speeches are due to begin, His Highness whispers dramatic words into the ear of his interpreter, who transmits them to the aide-de-camp, who transmits them to the president. The president turns pale. The prince's foot nervously taps the floor. His wishes are commands; but in the palace there's no place, no way. Without hesitation the president appoints a committee, headed by the Foreign Minister and the Chief of the Armed Forces.

Impressively top-hatted and plumed, the retinue accompanies the prince at a dignified but brisk pace, almost a hop, across the Plaza de Armas. Arriving at the corner, they all enter the Paris Hotel. The

Foreign Minister opens the door marked GENTLEMEN and points the way for the heir to the imperial British crown.

(34)

1930: Buenos Aires

Yrigoyen

The world crisis also leaves Argentine president Hipólito Yrigoyen teetering at the edge of a precipice, doomed by the collapse of meat and wheat prices.

Silent and alone, a stubborn old hangover from another time, another world, Yrigoyen still refuses to use the telephone, has never entered a movie theater, distrusts automobiles, and doesn't believe in airplanes. He has conquered the people just by chatting, convincing them one by one, little by little, without speeches. Now the same people who yesterday unyoked the horses from his carriage and pulled him with their hands, revile him. The crowd actually throws his furniture into the street.

The military coup that overthrows him has been cooked up at the Jockey Club and the Círculo de Armas on the flames of this sudden crisis. The ailing patriarch, creaking with rheumatism, sealed his own fate when he refused to hand over Argentine petroleum to Standard Oil and Shell. Worse, he wanted to alleviate the price catastrophe by doing business with the Soviet Union.

Once more, for the good of the world, the hour of the sword has struck, writes the poet Leopoldo Lugones, ushering in the military era in Argentina.

At the height of the coup, a young captain, Juan Domingo Perón, observes some enthusiast dashing at top speed from the government palace, yelling, *"Long live the Fatherland! Long live the Revolution!"*

The enthusiast carries an Argentine flag rolled up under his arm. Inside the flag is a stolen typewriter.

(178, 341, and 365)

1930: Paris

Ortiz Echagüe, Journalist, Comments on the Fallen Price of Meat

Every time I return from Buenos Aires, the Argentines in Paris ask me: "How are the cows?"

One must come to Paris to appreciate the importance of the Argentine cow. Last night at El Garrón—a Montmartre cabaret where young Argentines experience the tough apprenticeship of life—some guys at a neighboring table asked me, with that small-hours familiarity, "Say, chum, how are the cows back home making out?"

"Pretty down and out," I said.

"And they can't get up?"

"Doesn't look good."

"You don't have any cows?"

I felt my pockets and said no.

"You don't know, old pal, how lucky you are." At that point three concertinas broke into sobs of nostalgia and cut the dialogue short.

"How are the cows?" I have been asked by maître d's and musicians, flower girls and waiters, pallid ballerinas, gold-braided porters, diligent grooms, and above all, by painted women, those poor baggy-eyed anemic women . . .

(325)

1930: Avellaneda

The Cow, the Sword, and the Cross

form the holy trinity of power in Argentina. Conservative Party toughs guard the altar.

In the heart of Buenos Aires, white-gloved gunmen use laws and decrees like machineguns in their holdups. Experts in double accounting and double morality, they needn't trouble themselves picking locks. They don't have doctorates for nothing. They know precisely what secret combinations will open the country's cashboxes.

Across the river, in Avellaneda, the Conservative Party sticks to honest shooting for its politics and business. Don Alberto Barceló, senator, makes and breaks lives from his throne there. Outcasts line up to receive from Don Alberto some small gratuity, fatherly advice, a chummy embrace. His brother, One-Arm Enrique, takes care of the brothel department. Don Alberto's responsibilities are lotteries and social peace. He smokes with a holder, spies on the world from beneath swollen lids. His henchmen break strikes, burn libraries, wreck printshops, and make short work of trade unionists, Jews, and all who forget to pay up and obey in this hour of crisis so conducive to disorder. Afterward, the good Don Alberto will give a hundred pesos to the orphans.

(166 and 176)

1930: Castex
The Last Rebel Gaucho

on the Argentine pampa is called Bairoletto, the son of peasants from Italy. He became an outlaw quite young, after shooting in the forehead a policeman who had humiliated him, and now he has no choice but to sleep outdoors. In the desert, beaten by the wind, he appears and disappears, lightning or mirage, riding an inky-black stallion that jumps seven-strand wire fences without effort. The poor protect him, and he avenges them against the powerful who abuse them and then swallow up their land. At the end of each raid, he engraves a B with bullets into the wings of the estancia's windmill, and seeds the wind with anarchist pamphlets foretelling revolution.

(123)

1930: Santo Domingo
The Hurricane

beats down with a roar, smashing ships against piers, shredding bridges, uprooting trees and whirling them through the air. Tin roofs, flying like crazy hatchets, decapitate people. This island is being leveled by winds, raked by lightning, drowned by rain and sea. The hurricane strikes as if revenging itself, or executing some fantastic curse. One might think that the Dominican Republic had been condemned, alone, to pay a debt due from the entire planet.

Later, when the hurricane moves on, the burning begins. Corpses and ruins have to be incinerated or plagues will finish off whatever remains alive and standing. For a week a vast cloud of black smoke hangs over the city of Santo Domingo.

So go the first days of the government of General Rafael Leónidas Trujillo, who has come to power on the eve of the cyclone, borne by a no less catastrophic fall in the international price of sugar.

(60 and 101)

1930: Ilopango
Miguel at Twenty-Five

The crisis also knocks the price of coffee for a loop. Beans spoil on the trees; a sickly odor of rotten coffee hangs in the air. Throughout Central America, growers put their workers out on the road. The few who still have work get the same rations as hogs.

In the worst of the crisis the Communist Party is born in El Salvador. Miguel, now a master shoemaker who works wherever he finds himself, is one of the founders. He stirs people up, wins recruits, hides and flees, the police always on his heels.

One morning Miguel, in disguise, approaches his house. It seems not to be watched. He hears his little boy crying and he enters. The child is alone, screaming his lungs out. Miguel has begun changing his diapers when he looks up and through the window sees police surrounding the place.

"Pardon me," he says to his shitty little half-changed boy, and springs up like a cat, slipping through a hole between some broken roof tiles just as the first shots ring out.

And so occurs the fourth birth of Miguel Mármol, at twenty-five years of age.

(126 and 404)

1930: New York
Daily Life in the Crisis

Unpleasantly, like a series of rude slaps in the face, the crisis wakes up North Americans. The disaster at the New York Stock Exchange has pricked the Great Dream, which promised to fill every pocket with money, every sky with planes, every inch of land with automobiles and skyscrapers.

Nobody is selling optimism in the market. Fashions sadden. Long faces, long dresses, long hair. The roaring twenties come to an end, and with them, the exposed leg and bobbed hair.

All consumption drops vertically. Sales are up only for cigarettes, horoscopes, and twenty-five-watt bulbs, which don't give much light, but don't draw much current. Hollywood prepares films about giant monsters on the loose: King Kong, Frankenstein, as inexplicable as the economy, as unstoppable as the crisis that sows terror in the streets of the city.

(15 and 331)

1930: Achuapa
Shrinking the Rainbow

Nicaragua, a country condemned to produce cheap desserts—bananas, coffee, and sugar—keeps on ruining the digestion of its customers.

The Sandinista chief Miguel Ángel Ortez celebrates the new year by wiping out a Marine patrol in the muddy ravines of Achuapa, and on the same day another patrol falls over a precipice in the vicinity of Ocotal.

In vain, the invaders seek victory through hunger, by burning huts and crops. Many families are forced to take to the mountains, wandering and unprotected. Behind them they leave pillars of smoke and bayonetted animals.

The campesinos believe that Sandino knows how to lure the rainbow to him; and as it comes it shrinks until he can pick it up with just two fingers.

(118 and 361)

1931: Bocay
The Trumpets Will Sound

By the light of aromatic pitch-pine chips, Sandino writes letters, orders, and reports to be read aloud in the camp on the military and political situation in Nicaragua (*Like a firecracker, the enemy will soon burn himself out* . . .), manifestos condemning traitors (*They will find no place to live, unless under seven spans of earth* . . .), and prophesies announcing that soon war trumpets will sound against oppressors everywhere, and sooner than later the Last Judgment will destroy injustice so that the world may at last be what it wanted to be when there was was still nothing.

(237)

Sandino Writes to One of His Officers: "We won't be able to walk for all the flowers . . ."

If sleep, hunger, or petty fears overtake you, ask God to comfort you . . . God will give us this other triumph, which will be the definitive one, because I am sure that after this battle they won't come back to get their change, and you will be covered with glory! When we enter Managua, we won't be able to walk for all the flowers . . .

(361)

1931: Bocay
Santos López

Whoever joins the liberating army gets no pay, no pay ever, only the right to be called *brother*. He has to find a rifle on his own, in battle, and maybe a uniform stripped from some dead Marine, to wear once the pants have been properly shortened.

Santos López has been with Sandino from day one. He had worked for the farmers who owned him since he was eight. He was twelve at the time of the San Albino mine rebellion, and became a water boy and messenger in Sandino's army, a spy among drunken or distracted enemies, and along with his other buddies, specialized in setting ambushes and creating diversions with cans and whatever noisy odds and ends he could lay his hands on to make a few people seem like a crowd.

Santos López turns seventeen on the day Sandino promotes him to colonel.

(236, 267, and 361)

1931: Bocay

Tranquilino

In Sandino's rickety arsenal the finest weapon is a Browning machine-gun of the latest model, rescued from a North American plane downed by rifle fire.

In the hands of Tranquilino Jarquín, this Browning shoots and sings.

Tranquilino is the cook. He shows one tooth when he smiles, sticks an orchid in his hat, and as he stirs the big steaming pot, meat-poor but rich in aroma, he tosses down a good swig of rum.

In Sandino's army drinking is forbidden, Tranquilino excepted. It took a lot to win that privilege. But without his little swigs this artist of wooden spoon and trigger doesn't function. When they put him on a water diet, his dishes are flat, his shots twisted and off-key.

(236 and 393)

1931: Bocay

Little Cabrera

Tranquilino makes music with the machinegun, Pedro Cabrera with the trumpet. For Tranquilino's Browning it's bursts of tangos, marches, and ballads, while Little Cabrera's trumpet moans protests of love and proclaims brave deeds.

To kiss his celestial trumpet each morning, Little Cabrera must freeze his body and shut his eyes. Before dawn he wakens the soldiers, and at night lulls them to sleep, blowing low, low, lingering notes.

Musician and poet, warm heart and itchy feet, Little Cabrera has been Sandino's assistant since the war began. Nature has given him a yard and a half of stature and seven women.

(393)

1931: Hanwell

The Winner

Charlie the Tramp visits Hanwell School. He walks on one leg, as if skating. He twists his ear and out spurts a stream of water. Hundreds of children, orphaned, poor, or abandoned, scream with laughter. Thirty-five years ago, Charlie Chaplin was one of these children. Now he recognizes the chair he used to sit on and the corner of the dismal gym where he was birched.

Later he had escaped to London. In those days, shop windows displayed sizzling pork chops and golden potatoes steeped in gravy; Chaplin's nose still remembers the smell that filtered through the glass to mock him. And still engraved in his memory are the prices of other unattainable treats: a cup of tea, one halfpenny; a bit of herring, one penny; a tart, twopence.

Twenty years ago he left England in a cattle boat. Now he returns, the most famous man in the world. A cloud of journalists follows him like his shadow, and wherever he goes crowds jostle to see him, touch him. He can do whatever he wants. At the height of the talkie euphoria, his silent films have a devastating success. And he can spend whatever he wants—although he never wants. On the screen, Charlie the Tramp, poor leaf in the wind, knows nothing of money; in reality, Charles Chaplin, who perspires millions, watches the pennies and is incapable of looking at a painting without calculating its price. He will never share the fate of Buster Keaton, a man with open pockets, from whom everything flies away as soon as he earns it.

(121 and 383)

1932: Hollywood

The Loser

Buster Keaton arrives at the Metro studios hours late, dragging the hangover of last night's drinking spree: feverish eyes, coppery tongue, dishrag muscles. Who knows how he manages to execute the clownish pirouettes and recite the idiotic jokes ordered by the script.

Now his films are talkies and Keaton is not allowed to improvise; nor may he do retakes in search of that elusive instant when poetry discovers imprisoned laughter and unchains it. Keaton, genius of liberty and silence, must follow to the letter the charlatan scenarios written by others. In this way costs are halved and talent eliminated, according to the production norms of the movie factories of the sound-film era. Left behind forever are the days when Hollywood was a mad adventure.

Every day Keaton feels more at home with dogs and cows. Every night he opens a bottle of bourbon and implores his own memory to drink and be still.

(128 and 382)

1932: Mexico City

Eisenstein

While in Mexico they accuse him of being a *bolshevik, homosexual, and libertine*; in Hollywood they call him a *red dog and friend of murderers*.

Sergei Eisenstein has come to Mexico to film an indigenous epic. Before it is half-produced, the guts are ripped out. The Mexican censor bans some scenes because the truth is all very well, but not so much of it, thank you. The North American producer leaves the filmed footage in the hands of whoever may want to cut it to pieces.

Eisenstein's film *Que Viva México* ends up as nothing but a pile of grandiose scraps, images lacking articulation put together incoherently or with deceit, dazzling letters torn loose from a word that was never before spoken about this country, this delirium sprung from the place where the bottom of the sea meets the center of the earth: pyramids that are volcanoes about to erupt, creepers interwoven like hungry bodies, stones that breathe . . .

(151 and 305)

1932: The Roads of Santa Fe

The Puppeteer

didn't know he was one until the evening when, high on a balcony in Buenos Aires with a friend, he noticed a haycart passing down the street. On the hay lay a young boy smoking, face to the sky, hands behind his neck, legs crossed. Both he and his friend felt an irrepressible urge to get away. The friend took off with a woman toward the mysterious frozen lands to the South of the South; and the puppeteer discovered puppeteering, craft of the free, and hit the road on a cart pulled by two horses.

From town to town along the banks of the River Paraná, the cart's wooden wheels leave long scars. The name of the puppeteer, conjurer of happiness, is Javier Villafañe. Javier travels with his children whose flesh is paper and paste. The best beloved of them is Master Globetrotter: long sad nose, black cape, flying necktie. During the show he is an extension of Javier's hand, and afterward, he sleeps and dreams at his feet, in a shoebox.

1932: Izalco

The Right to Vote and Its Painful Consequences

General Maximiliano Hernández Martínez, president by coup d'état, convokes the people of El Salvador to elect deputies and mayors. Despite a thousand traps, the tiny Communist Party wins the elections. The general takes umbrage. Scrutiny of ballots is suspended *sine die*.

Swindled, the Communists rebel. Salvadorans erupt on the same day that the Izalco volcano erupts. As boiling lava runs down the slopes and clouds of ashes blot out the sky, red campesinos attack the barracks with machetes in Izalco, Nahuizalco, Tacuba, Juayúa, and other towns. For three days America's first soviets come to power.

Three days. Three months of slaughter follow. Farabundo Martí and other Communist leaders face firing squads. Soldiers beat to death the Indian chief José Feliciano Ama, leader of the revolution in Izalco. They hang Ama's corpse in the main plaza and force schoolchildren to watch the show. Thirty thousand campesinos, denounced by their employers, or condemned on mere suspicion or old wives' tales, dig their own graves with their hands. Children die too, for Communists, like snakes, need to be killed young. Wherever a dog or pig scratches up the earth, remains of people appear. One of the firing-squad victims is the shoemaker Miguel Mármol.

(9, 21, and 404)

1932: Soyapango

Miguel at Twenty-Six

As they take them away bound in a truck, Miguel recognizes his childhood haunts.

"What luck," he thinks, *"I'm going to die where my umbilical cord was buried."*

They beat them to the ground with rifle butts, then shoot them in pairs. The truck's headlights and the moon give more than enough light.

After a few volleys, it's the turn of Miguel and a man who sells engravings, condemned for being Russian. The Russian and Miguel, standing before the firing squad, grip each other's hands, which are bound behind their backs. Miguel itches all over and desperately needs to scratch; this fills his mind as he hears: *"Ready! Aim! Fire!"*

Miguel regains consciousness under a pile of bodies dripping blood. He feels his head throbbing and bleeding, and the pain of the bullets in his body, soul, and clothes. He hears the click of a rifle reloading. A coup de grâce.

Another. Another. His eyes misted with blood, Miguel awaits the final shot, but feels a machete chopping at him instead.

The soldiers kick the bodies into a ditch and throw dirt over them. Hearing the trucks drive off, Miguel, wounded and cut, tries to move. It takes him centuries to crawl out from under so much death and earth. Finally, managing to walk at a ferociously slow pace, more falling than standing, he very gradually gets out, wearing the sombrero of a comrade whose name was Serafín.

And so occurs the fifth birth of Miguel Mármol, at twenty-six years of age.

(126)

1932: Managua

Sandino Is Advancing

in a great sweep that reaches the banks of Lake Managua. The occupation troops fall back in disarray. Meanwhile, two photographs appear in the world's newspapers. One shows Lieutenant Pensington of the United States Navy holding up a trophy, a head chopped from a Nicaraguan campesino. From the other smiles the entire general staff of the Nicaraguan National Guard, officers wearing high boots and safari headgear. At their center is seated the director of the Guard, Colonel Calvin B. Matthews. Behind them is the jungle. At the feet of the group, sprawled on the ground, is a dog. The jungle and the dog are the only Nicaraguans.

(118 and 361)

1932: San Salvador
Miguel at Twenty-Seven

Of those who saved Miguel, no one is left. Soldiers have riddled with bullets the comrades who found him in a ditch, those who carried him across the river on a chair of hands, those who hid him in a cave, and those who managed to bring him to his sister's home in San Salvador. When his sister saw the specter of Miguel stitched with bullets and crisscrossed with machete cuts, she had to be revived with a fan. Praying, she began a novena for his eternal rest.

The funeral service proceeds. Miguel begins to recover as best he can, hidden behind the altar set up in his memory, with nothing but the chichipince-juice ointment his sister applies with saintly patience to his purulent wounds. Lying behind the curtain, burning with fever, Miguel spends his birthday listening to disconsolate relatives and neighbors awash in oceans of tears, extolling his memory with nonstop prayers.

On one of these nights a military patrol stops at the door.

"Who are you praying for?"

"For the soul of my brother, the departed."

The soldiers enter, approach the altar, wrinkle their noses.

Miguel's sister clutches her rosary. The candles flicker before the image of our Lord Jesus Christ. Miguel has the sudden urge to cough. The soldiers cross themselves. "May he rest in peace," they say, and continue on their way.

And so occurs the sixth birth of Miguel Mármol, at twenty-seven years of age.

(126)

1933: Managua

The First U.S. Military Defeat
in Latin America

On the first day of the year the Marines leave Nicaragua with all their ships and planes. The scraggy general, the little man who looks like a capital T with his wide-brimmed sombrero, has humbled an empire.

The U.S. press deplores the many dead in so many years of occupation, but stresses the value of the training of their aviators. Thanks to the war against Sandino, the United States has for the first time been able to experiment with aerial bombing from Fokker and Curtiss planes specially designed to fight in Nicaragua.

The departing Colonel Matthews is replaced by a sympathetic and faithful native officer, Anastasio Tacho Somoza, as head of the National Guard, now called the Guardia Nacional.

As soon as he reaches Managua, the triumphant Sandino says: *"Now we're free. I won't fire another shot."*

The president of Nicaragua, Juan Bautista Sacasa, greets him with an embrace. General Somoza embraces him too.

(118 and 361)

1933: Camp Jordán

The Chaco War

Bolivia and Paraguay are at war. The two poorest countries in South America, the two with no ocean, the two most thoroughly conquered and looted, annihilate each other for a bit of map. Concealed in the folds of both flags, Standard Oil and Royal Dutch Shell are disputing the oil of the Chaco.

In this war, Paraguayans and Bolivians are compelled to hate each other in the name of a land they do not love, that nobody loves. The Chaco is a gray desert inhabited by thorns and snakes; not a songbird or a person in sight. Everything is thirsty in this world of horror. Butterflies form desperate clots on the few drops of water. For Bolivians, it is going from freezer to oven: They are hauled down from the heights of the Andes and dumped into these roasting scrublands. Here some die of bullets, but more die of thirst.

Clouds of flies and mosquitos pursue the soldiers, who charge through thickets, heads lowered, on forced marches against enemy lines. On both sides barefoot people are the down payment on the errors of their officers. The slaves of feudal landlord and rural priest die in different uniforms, at the service of imperial avarice.

One of the Bolivian soldiers marching to death speaks. He says nothing about glory, nothing about the Fatherland. He says, breathing heavily, *"A curse on the hour that I was born a man."*

(354 and 402)

Céspedes

On the Bolivian side, this pitiful epic will be related by Augusto Céspedes:

A squadron of soldiers in search of water start digging a well with picks and shovels. The little rain that has fallen has already evaporated, and there is no water anywhere. At twelve meters the water hunters come upon liquid mud. But at thirty meters, at forty-five, the pulley brings up bucketfuls of sand, each one drier than the last. The soldiers keep on digging, day after day, into that well of sand, ever deeper, ever more silent. And when the Paraguayans, likewise hounded by thirst, launch an attack, the Bolivians die defending the well as if it contained water.

(96)

Roa Bastos

From the Paraguayan side, Augusto Roa Bastos will tell the story. He too will speak of wells that become graves, and of the multitude of dead, and of the living who are only distinguishable from them by the fact that they move, though like drunkards who have forgotten the way home. He will accompany the lost soldiers, who haven't a drop of water, not even to shed as tears.

(380)

1934: Managua

Horror Film: Scenario for Two Actors
and a Few Extras

Somoza leaves the house of Arthur Bliss Lane, ambassador of the United States.

Sandino arrives at the house of Sacasa, president of Nicaragua.

While Somoza sits down to work with his officers, Sandino sits down to supper with the president.

Somoza tells his officers that the ambassador has just given his unconditional support to the killing of Sandino.

Sandino tells the president about the problems of the Wiwilí cooperative, where he and his soldiers have been working the land for over a year.

Somoza explains to his officers that Sandino is a communistic enemy of order, who has many more weapons concealed than those he has turned in.

Sandino explains to the president that Somoza won't let him work in peace.

Somoza discusses with his officers whether Sandino should die by poison, shooting, airplane accident, or ambush in the mountains.

Sandino discusses with the president the growing power of the Guardia Nacional, led by Somoza, and warns that Somoza will soon blow him away to sit in the presidential chair himself.

Somoza finishes settling some practical details and leaves his officers.

Sandino finishes his coffee and takes leave of the president.

Somoza goes off to a poetry reading and Sandino goes off to his death.

While Somoza listens to the sonnets of Zoila Rosa Cárdenas, young luminary of Peruvian letters who honors this country by her visit, Sandino is shot in a place called The Skull, on Lonesome Road.

(339 and 405)

1934: Managua

The Government Decides That Crime
Does Not Exist

That night, Colonel Santos López escapes the trap in Managua. On a bleeding leg, his seventh bullet wound in these years of war, he climbs over roofs, drops to the ground, jumps walls, and finally begins a nightmare crawl northward along the railroad tracks.

The next day, while Santos López is still dragging his wounded leg along the lake shore, a wholesale massacre takes place in the mountains. Somoza orders the Wiwilí cooperative destroyed, and the new Guardia Nacional strikes with total surprise, wiping out Sandino's former soldiers, who were sowing tobacco and bananas and had a hospital half built. The mules are saved, but not the children.

Soon after, banquets in homage to Somoza are given by the United States embassy in Managua and by the most exclusive clubs of León and Granada.

The government issues orders to forget. An amnesty wipes out all crimes committed since the eve of Sandino's death.

(267 and 405)

1934: San Salvador

Miguel at Twenty-Nine

Hunted as ever by the Salvadoran police, Miguel finds refuge in the house of the Spanish consul's lover.

One night a storm sweeps in. From the window, Miguel sees that, far over there where the river bends, the rising waters are threatening the mud-and-cane hut of his wife and children. Leaving his hideout in defiance of both gale and night patrol, Miguel hurries to his family.

They spend the night huddled together inside the fragile walls, listening to the roar of wind and river. At dawn, when winds and waters subside, the little hut is slightly askew and very damp, but still standing. And so Miguel says goodbye to his family and returns to his refuge.

But it is nowhere to be found. Of that solidly built house not a brick remains. The fury of the river has undermined the ravine, torn away the foundations, and carried off to the devil the house, the consul's lover, and the servant girl.

And so occurs the seventh birth of Miguel Mármol, at twenty-nine years of age.

(126)

1935: The Villamontes-Boyuibe Road
After Ninety Thousand Deaths

the Chaco War ends. It is three years since the first Paraguayan and Bolivian bullets were exchanged in a hamlet called Masamaclay, which in the Indian language means *place where two brothers fought.*

At noon the news reaches the front. The guns fall silent. The soldiers stand up, very slowly, and even more slowly emerge from the trenches. Ragged ghosts, blinded by the sun, they lurch across the no-man's-land between Bolivia's Santa Cruz regiment and Paraguay's Toledo regiment—the scraps, the shreds. Newly received orders prohibit fraternization with those who just now were enemies. Only the military salute is allowed; and so they salute each other. But someone lets loose a great howl, and then there is no stopping it. The soldiers break ranks, throw caps, weapons, anything, everything into the air and run in mad confusion, Paraguayans to Bolivians, Bolivians to Paraguayans, shouting, singing, weeping, embracing one another as they roll in the hot sand.

(354 and 402)

1935: Maracay
Gómez

The dictator of Venezuela, Juan Vicente Gómez, dies and keeps on ruling. For twenty-seven years no one has been able to budge him, and now no one dares crack a joke about his corpse. When the coffin of the terrible old man is unquestionably buried beneath a heap of earth, the prisoners finally break down the jail doors, and only then does the cheering and looting begin.

Gómez died a bachelor. He has sired mountains of children, loving as if relieving himself, but has never spent a whole night in a woman's arms. The dawn light always found him alone in his iron bed beneath the image of the Virgin Mary and alongside his chests filled with money.

He never spent a penny, paying for everything with oil. He distributed oil in gushers, to Gulf, Standard, Texaco, Shell, and with oil wells paid for the doctor who probed his bladder, for the poets whose sonnets hymned his glory, and for the executioners whose secret tasks kept his order.

(114, 333, and 366)

1935: Buenos Aires
Borges

Everything that brings people together, like football or politics, and everything that multiples them, like a mirror or the act of love, gives him the horrors. He recognizes no other reality than what exists in the past, in the past of his forefathers, and in books written by those who knew how to expound that reality. The rest is smoke.

With great delicacy and sharp wit, Jorge Luis Borges tells the *Universal History of Infamy*. About the national infamy that surrounds him, he doesn't even inquire.

(25 and 59)

1935: Buenos Aires
These Infamous Years

In London, the Argentine government signs a commercial treaty selling the country for halfpence. In the opulent estates north of Buenos Aires, the cattlocracy dance the waltz in shady arbors; but if the entire country is worth only halfpence, how much are its poorest children worth? Working hands go at bargain prices and you can find any number of girls who will strip for a cup of coffee. New factories sprout, and around them tin-can barrios, harried by police and tuberculosis, where yesterday's maté, dried in the sun, stifles hunger. The Argentine police invent the electric prod to convince those in doubt and straighten out those who buckle.

In the Buenos Aires night, the pimp seeks a girl wanting a good time, and the girl seeks a man who'll give her one; the racetrack gambler seeks a hot tip; the con man, a sucker; the jobless, a job in the early editions. Coming and going in the streets are the bohemian, the roué, and the cardsharp, all solitary in their solitude, while Discepolín's last tango sings that the world was and will continue to be a dirty joke.

(176, 365, and 412)

1935: Buenos Aires
Discepolín

He is one long bone with a nose, so thin that injections are put through his overcoat, the somber poet of Buenos Aires in the infamous years.

Enrique Santos Discépolo creates his first tangos, *sad thoughts that can be danced,* as a touring-company comedian lost in the provinces. In ramshackle dressing rooms he makes the acquaintance of huge, almost human-size fleas, and for them he hums tangos that speak of those with neither money nor faith.

(379)

1935: Buenos Aires
Evita

To look at, she's just a run-of-the-mill stick of a girl, pale, washed-out, not ugly, not pretty, who wears secondhand clothes and solemnly repeats the daily routines of poverty. Like the others, she lives hanging on to each episode of the radio soaps, dreams every Sunday of being Norma Shearer, and every evening goes to the railway station to see the Buenos Aires train pass by. But Eva Duarte has turned fifteen and she's fed up; she climbs aboard the train and takes off.

This little creature has nothing at all. No father, no money, no memories to hold on to. Since she was born in the town of Los Toldos, of an unmarried mother, she has been condemned to humiliation, and now she is a nobody among the thousands of nobodies the trains pour into Buenos Aires every day, a multitude of tousle-haired dark-skinned provincials, workers and servant girls who are sucked into the city's mouth and are promptly devoured. During the week Buenos Aires chews them up; on Sundays it spits out the pieces.

At the feet of the arrogant Moloch, great peaks of cement, Evita is paralyzed by a panic that only lets her clasp her hands, red and cold, and weep. Then she dries her tears, clenches her teeth, takes a firm grip of her cardboard valise, and buries herself in the city.

(311 and 417)

1935: Buenos Aires

Alfonsina

The ovaries of a woman who thinks dry up. Woman is born to produce milk and tears, not ideas; not to live life but to spy on it through slatted venetian blinds. A thousand times they have explained it to her but Alfonsina Storni never believed them, and her best-known verses protest against the macho jailer.

When she came to Buenos Aires from the provinces, all Alfonsina had were some down-at-heel shoes and, in her belly, a child with no legal father. In this city she worked at whatever she could get and stole blank telegram forms to write her sorrows. As she polished her words, verse by verse, night by night, she crossed her fingers and kissed the cards that announced journeys, inheritances, and loves.

Time has passed, almost a quarter of a century, and fate has given her no presents. But somehow Alfonsina has made her way in the male world. Her face, like a mischievous mouse, is never missing from group photos of Argentina's most illustrious writers.

This year, this summer, she finds she has cancer. So now she writes of the embrace of the sea and of the home that awaits her in the depths, on the avenue of Corals.

(310)

1935: Medellín

Gardel

Each time he sings, in that voice of many colors, he sings as never before. He makes dark notes, his opaque lyrics shine. He's the Magician, the Greatest, Carlos Gardel.

The shadow of a sombrero over his eyes, a perpetual and perfect smile forever young, he looks like a winner who has never been defeated. His origin is a mystery; his life, an enigma. Tragedy had no choice but to save him from explanation and decay. His worshippers would not have forgiven him for old age. The plane in which he is traveling takes off from Medellín airport and blows up in flight.

1936: Buenos Aires
Patoruzú

For ten years the Patoruzú comic strip, the work of Dante Quintero, has been published in the Buenos Aires dailies. Now, a monthly magazine appears wholly devoted to the character. Patoruzú is a big landlord, the owner of half of Patagonia, who lives in five-star hotels in Buenos Aires, squanders millions with both hands, and passionately believes in private property and the consumer civilization. Dante Quintero explains that Patoruzú is a typical Argentine Indian.

(446 and 456)

1936: Rio de Janeiro
Olga and He

With his rebel army Luis Carlos Prestes has crossed the immensity of Brazil on foot, end to end, there and back, southern prairies to northeastern deserts, the whole breadth of the Amazon jungle. In three years the Prestes Column has battled the coffee and sugar barons to a standstill, without a single defeat. So that Olga Benário imagined him as some devastating giant of a man, and is amazed when he turns out to be a fragile little fellow who blushes when she looks him in the eye.

She, toughened in the revolutionary struggles of Germany, a militant without frontiers, loves and sustains this rebel who has never known a woman. In time, both are taken prisoner. They are taken to different prisons.

From Germany, Hitler demands Olga, that Jew and Communist—vile blood, vile ideas—and Brazilian president Getulio Vargas turns her over. When soldiers come for her the prisoners riot. Olga stops them, seeing no point in useless slaughter, and lets herself be taken. Through the bars of his cell the novelist Graciliano Ramos sees her pass, handcuffed, with her pregnant belly.

At the docks a ship flying the swastika sits waiting for her; the captain has orders to head straight for Hamburg. There, Olga will be deposited in a concentration camp, asphyxiated in a gas chamber, carbonized in an oven.

(263, 302, and 364)

1936: Madrid
The Spanish War

The rising against the Spanish republic has been incubated in barracks, sacristies, and palaces. Generals, monks, lackeys of the king, and feudal lords of the gallows and the knife are its murky protagonists. The Chilean poet Pablo Neruda curses them, invoking the bullets that will one day find a home in their hearts. In Granada the fascists have just shot his beloved brother Federico García Lorca, the poet of Andalusía, *the ever-free flash of lightning,* for being or seeming to be homosexual and red.

Neruda roams the Spanish earth so soaked in blood and is transformed. The poet, distracted by politics, asks of poetry that it make itself useful like metal or flour, that it get ready to stain its face with coal dust and fight body to body.

(313 and 314)

1936: San Salvador
Martínez

At the head of the rebellion, Francisco Franco proclaims himself Generalisimo and Spanish Chief of State. The first diplomatic recognition comes to the city of Burgos from the remote Caribbean. General Maximiliano Hernández Martínez, dictator of El Salvador, congratulates the newly born dictatorship of his colleague.

Martínez, the kindly grandfather who murdered thirty thousand Salvadorans, believes killing ants more criminal than killing people; because ants, he says, cannot be reincarnated. Every Sunday Maestro Martínez speaks to the country on the radio about the international political situation, intestinal parasites, the reincarnation of souls, and the Communist peril. He routinely cures the ills of his ministers and officials with colored waters kept in big bottles on the patio of the presidential palace, and when the smallpox epidemic strikes he scares it off by wrapping the street lights in red cellophane.

To uncover conspiracies, he hangs a clock pendulum over steaming soup. For the gravest problems he resorts to President Roosevelt, communicating directly with the White House by telepathy.

(250)

1936: San Salvador
Miguel at Thirty-One

Miguel, just released from jail—almost two years handcuffed in solitary—wanders the roads, a ragged pariah with nothing. He has no party, because his Communist Party comrades suspect he made a deal with dictator Martínez. He has no work, because dictator Martínez sees to it that he can't get any. He has no wife, because she has left him and taken the children with her; no house either, or food, or shoes, or even a name. It has been officially established that Miguel Mármol does not exist, because he was executed in 1932.

He decides to put an end to it, once and for all. Enough of these thoughts. A single machete blow will open his veins. He is just raising the machete when a boy on a burro appears in the road. The boy greets him with a sweep of his enormous straw sombrero, asks to borrow the machete to split a coconut, then offers half the split nut, water to drink, coconut meat to eat. Miguel drinks and eats as if this unknown lad had invited him to a feast, and gets up and walks away from death.

And thus occurs the eighth birth of Miguel Mármol, at thirty-one years of age.

(126)

1936: Guatemala City
Ubico

Martínez has beaten him to it by a few hours, but Ubico is the second to recognize Franco. Ten days before Hitler and Mussolini, Ubico puts a stamp of legitimacy on the rising against Spanish democracy.

General Jorge Ubico, Chief of State of Guatemala, governs surrounded by effigies of Napoleon Bonaparte, whom he resembles, he says, like a twin. But Ubico rides motorcycles and the war he is waging has nothing to do with the conquest of Europe. His is a war against bad thoughts.

Against bad thoughts, military discipline. Ubico militarizes the post office employees, the symphony orchestra musicians, and the schoolchildren. Since a full belly is the mother of bad thoughts, he has United Fruit's plantation wages cut by half. He scourges idleness, father of bad thoughts, by forcing those guilty of it to work his lands for nothing. To expel the bad thoughts from the minds of revolutionaries, he invents a steel crown that squeezes their heads in police dungeons.

Ubico has imposed on the Indians a compulsory contribution of five centavos a month to raise a great monument to Ubico. Hand in jacket, he poses for the sculptor.

(250)

1936: Trujillo City
In the Year Six of the Trujillo Era

the name of the Dominican Republic's capital is corrected. Santo Domingo, so baptized by its founders, becomes Trujillo City. The port is now called Trujillo, as are many towns, plazas, markets, and avenues. From Trujillo City, Generalísimo Rafael Leónidas Trujillo sends Generalísimo Francisco Franco his most ardent support.

Trujillo, tireless bane of reds and heretics, was, like Anastasio Somoza, born of a U.S. military occupation. His natural modesty does not prevent him from allowing his name to appear on all automobile license plates and his likeness on all postage stamps, nor does he oppose the conferring of the rank of colonel on his three-year-old son Ramfis, as an act of simple justice. His sense of responsibility obliges him to appoint personally all ministers, porters, bishops, and beauty queens. To stimulate the spirit of enterprise, Trujillo grants the salt, tobacco, oil, cement, flour, and match monopolies to Trujillo. In defense of public health, Trujillo closes down businesses that do not sell meat from the Trujillo slaughterhouses or milk from his dairy farms; and for the sake of public security he makes obligatory the purchase of insurance policies sold by Trujillo. Firmly grasping the helm of progress, Trujillo releases the Trujillo enterprises from taxes, while providing his estates with irrigation and roads and his factories

with customers. By order of Trujillo, shoe manufacturer, anyone caught
barefoot on the streets of town or city goes to jail.

The all-powerful has a voice like a whistle, with which there is
no discussion. At supper, he clinks glasses with a governor or deputy
who will be off to the cemetery after coffee. When a piece of land
interests him, he doesn't buy it: he occupies it. When a woman appeals
to him, he doesn't seduce her; he points at her.

(89, 101, and 177)

Procedure Against Rain

What the Dominican Republic needs when torrential rains drown
crops is a proper supplicant who can walk in the rain without getting
wet to send up urgent pleas to God and the Blessed Saint Barbara.
Twins are especially good at leashing rain and scaring off thunder.

In the Dominican region of Salcedo they use another method.
They look for two big oval stones, the kind that get polished by the
river; they tie them firmly to a rope, one at each end, and hang them
from the bough of a tree. Giving the stone eggs a hard squeeze and
a sharp tug, they pray to God, who lets out a yell and moves on
somewhere else with his black clouds.

(251)

Procedure Against Disobedience

A woman of daily Masses and continual prayer and penitence, the
mother of María la O skinned her knees imploring God for the miracle
of making her daughter obedient and good, and begging pardon for
the brazen girl's insolences.

One Good Friday evening, María la O went down to the river.
Her mother tried in vain to stop her: *"Just think, they're killing Our
Lord Jesus Christ . . ."*

God's wrath leaves forever stuck together those who make love
on Good Friday, and though María la O was not going to meet a
lover, she did commit a sin. She swam naked in the river, and when
the water tickled the prohibited recesses of her body, she trembled
with pleasure.

Afterward she tried to get out of the river and couldn't because she was covered with scales and had a flipper where her feet had been.

And in the waters of Dominican rivers María la O swims to this day: she was never forgiven.

(251)

1937: Dajabón
Procedure Against the Black Menace

The condemned are Haitian blacks who work in the Dominican Republic. This military exorcism, planned to the last detail by General Trujillo, lasts a day and a half. In the sugar region, the soldiers shut up Haitian day-laborers in corrals—herds of men, women, and children—and finish them off then and there with machetes; or bind their hands and feet and drive them at bayonet point into the sea.

Trujillo, who powders his face several times a day, wants the Dominician Republic white.

(101, 177, and 286)

1937: Washington
Newsreel

Two weeks later, the government of Haiti conveys to the government of the Dominican Republic its *concern about the recent events at the border*. The government of the Dominican Republic promises *an exhaustive investigation*.

In the name of continental security, the government of the United States proposes to President Trujillo that he pay an indemnity to avoid possible friction in the zone. After prolonged negotiation Trujillo recognizes the death of eighteen thousand Haitians on Dominican territory. According to him, the figure of twenty-five thousand victims, put forward by some sources, reflects the intention to manipulate the events dishonestly. Trujillo agrees to pay the government of Haiti, by way of indemnity, $522,000, or twenty-nine dollars for every officially recognized death.

The White House congratulates itself on an agreement reached within the framework of established inter-American treaties and procedures. Secretary of State Cordell Hull declares in Washington that

President Trujillo is one of the greatest men in Central America and in most of South America.

The indemnity duly paid in cash, the presidents of the Dominican Republic and Haiti embrace each other at the border.

(101)

1937: Rio de Janeiro
Procedure Against the Red Menace

The president of Brazil, Getulio Vargas, has no alternative but to set up a dictatorship. A drumroll of press and radio reports discloses the sinister Cohen Plan, obliging Vargas to suppress Parliament and the electoral process. The Fatherland is not about to sit back and succumb to the advance of Moscow's hordes. The Cohen Plan, which the government has discovered in some cellar, gives the full details—tactics *and* strategy—of the Communist plot against Brazil.

The plan is called "Cohen" due to a stenographic error. The originator of the plan, Captain Olympio Mourão Filho, actually baptized it the Kun Plan, having based it on documents from the brief Hungarian revolution headed by Béla Kun.

But the name is secondary. Captain Mourão Filho gets a well-earned promotion to major.

(43)

1937: Cariri Valley
The Crime of Community

From planes, they bomb and machinegun them. On the ground, they cut their throats, burn them alive, crucify them. Forty years after it wiped out the community of Canudos, the Brazilian army does the same to Caldeirão, verdant island in the northeast, and for the same crime—denying the principle of private property.

In Caldeirão nothing belonged to anyone: neither textile looms, nor brick ovens, nor the sea of cornfields around the village, nor the snowy immensity of cotton fields beyond. The owners were everyone and no one, and there were no naked or hungry. The needy had formed this community at the call of the Holy Cross of the Desert, which saintly José Lourenço, desert pilgrim, had carried there on his shoulder. The Virgin Mary had chosen both the spot for the cross and the holy man to bring it. Where he stuck in the cross, water flowed continuously.

According to the newspapers of distant cities, this squalid holy man is the prosperous sultan of a harem of·eleven thousand virgins; and if that were not enough, also an agent of Moscow with a concealed arsenal in his granaries.

Of the community of·Caldeirão nothing and no one is left. The colt Trancelim, which only the holy man mounted, flees into the stony mountains. In vain it seeks some shrub offering shade under this infernal sun.

(3)

1937: Rio de Janeiro
Monteiro Lobato

The censors ban *The Oil Scandal* by Monteiro Lobato. The book offends the oil trust and its technicians, hired or purchased, who claim that Brazil has no oil.

The author has ruined himself trying to create a Brazilian oil company. Before that, he failed in the publishing business, when he had the crazy idea of selling books not only in bookstores, but also in pharmacies, bazaars, and newsstands.

Monteiro Lobato was born not to publish books but to write them. His forte is telling tales to children. On the Benteveo Amarillo farm a pig of small intelligence is the Marquis of Rabicó and an ear of corn becomes a distinguished viscount who can read the Bible in Latin and talk in English to Leghorn chickens. The Marquis casts a warm eye on Emilia, the rag doll, who chatters on nonstop, because she started so late in life and has so much chatter stored up.

(252)

1937: Madrid
Hemingway

The reports of Ernest Hemingway describe the war that is raging a step from his hotel in this capital besieged by Franco's soldiers and Hitler's airplanes.

Why has Hemingway gone to lonely Spain? He is not exactly a militant like the ones who have come from all parts of the world to join the International Brigades. What Hemingway reveals in his writings is something else—the desperate search for dignity among men. And dignity is the only thing that is not rationed in these trenches of the Spanish republic.

(220 and 312)

1937: Mexico City
The Bolero

Mexico's Ministry of Public Education prohibits the boleros of Agustín Lara in schools, because *their obscene, immoral, and degenerate lyrics* might corrupt children.

Lara exalts the Lost Woman, in whose eyes are seen sun-drunk palm trees; he beseeches love from the Decadent One, in whose pupils boredom spreads like a peacock's tail; he dreams of the sumptuous bed of the silky-skinned Courtesan; with sublime ecstasy he deposits roses at the feet of the Sinful One, and covers the Shameful Whore with incense and jewels in exchange for the honey of her mouth.

(299)

1937: Mexico City
Cantinflas

For laughter, the people flock into the suburban tents, poor little makeshift theaters, where all the footlights shine on Cantinflas.

"There are moments in life that are truly momentary," says Cantinflas, with his pencil mustache and baggy pants, reeling off his spiel at top speed. His fusillade of nonsense apes the rhetoric of half-baked intellectuals and politicians, doctors of verbal diarrhea who say nothing, who pursue a point with endless phrases, never catching up to it. In these lands, the economy suffers from monetary inflation; politics and culture from verbal inflation.

(205)

1937: Mexico City
Cárdenas

Mexico does not wash its hands of the war in Spain. Lázaro Cárdenas— rare president, friend of silence and enemy of verbosity—not only proclaims his solidarity, but practices it, sending arms to the republican front across the sea, and receiving orphaned children by the shipload.

Cárdenas listens as he governs. He gets around and listens. From town to town he goes, hearing complaints with infinite patience, and never promising more than is possible. A man of his word, he talks little. Until Cárdenas, the art of governing in Mexico consisted of moving the tongue; but when he says yes or no, people believe it. Last summer he announced an agrarian reform program and since then has not stopped allocating lands to native communities.

He is cordially hated by those for whom the revolution is a business. They say that Cárdenas keeps quiet because, spending so much time among the Indians, he has forgotten Spanish, and that one of these days he will appear in a loincloth and feathers.

(45, 78, and 201)

1938: Anenecuilco
Nicolás, Son of Zapata

Earlier than anyone else, harder than anyone else, the campesinos of Anenecuilco have fought for the land; but after so much time and bloodshed, little has changed in the community where Emiliano Zapata was born and rose in rebellion.

A bunch of papers, eaten by moths and centuries, lie at the heart of the struggle. These documents, with the seal of the viceroy on them, prove that this community is the owner of its own land. Emiliano Zapata left them in the hands of one of his soldiers, Pancho Franco: *"If you lose them, compadre, you'll dry up hanging from a branch."*

And, indeed, on several occasions, Pancho Franco has saved the papers and his life by a hair.

Anenecuilco's best friend is President Lázaro Cárdenas, who has visited, listened to the campesinos, and recognized and amplified their rights. Its worst enemy is deputy Nicolás Zapata, Emiliano's eldest son, who has taken possession of the richest lands and aims to get the rest too.

(468)

1938: Mexico City
The Nationalization of Oil

North of Tampico, Mexico's petroleum belongs to Standard Oil; to the south, Shell. Mexico pays dearly for its own oil, which Europe and the United States buy cheap. These companies have been looting the subsoil and robbing Mexico of taxes and salaries for thirty years— until one fine day Cárdenas decides that Mexico is the owner of Mexican oil.

Since that day, nobody can sleep a wink. The challenge wakes up the country. In never-ending demonstrations, enormous crowds stream into the streets carrying coffins for Standard and Shell on their backs. To a marimba beat and the tolling of bells, workers occupy wells and refineries. But the companies reply in kind: all the foreign technicians, those masters of mystery, are withdrawn. No one is left to tend the indecipherable instrument panels of management. The national flag flutters over silent towers. The drills are halted, the pipelines emptied, the fires extinguished. It is war: war against the Latin American tradition of impotence, the colonial custom of *don't know, no can do*.

(45, 201, 234, and 321)

1938: Mexico City
Showdown

Standard Oil demands an immediate invasion of Mexico.

If a single soldier shows up at the border, Cárdenas warns, he will order the wells set on fire. President Roosevelt whistles and looks the other way, but the British Crown, adopting the fury of Shell, announces it will not buy one more drop of Mexican oil. France concurs. Other countries join the blockade. Mexico can't find anyone to sell it a spare part, and the ships disappear from its ports.

Still, Cárdenas won't get off the mule. He looks for customers in the prohibited areas—Red Russia, Nazi Germany, Fascist Italy—while the abandoned installations revive bit by bit. The Mexican workers mend, improvise, invent, getting by on pure enthusiasm, and so the magic of creation begins to make dignity possible.

(45, 201, 234, and 321)

1938: Coyoacán
Trotsky

Every morning he is surprised to find himself alive. Although his house has guardtowers and electrified wire fences, Leon Trotsky knows it to be a futile fortress. The creator of the Red Army is grateful to Mexico for giving him refuge, but even more grateful to fate. "*See, Natasha?*" he says to his wife each morning. "*Last night they didn't kill us, and yet you're complaining.*"

Since Lenin's death, Stalin has liquidated, one after another, the men who had made the Russian revolution—to save it, says Stalin; to take it over, says Trotsky, a man marked for death.

Stubbornly, Trotsky continues to believe in socialism, fouled as it is by human mud; for when all is said, who can deny that Christianity is much more than the Inquisition?

(132)

1938: The Hinterland
The Cangaceiros

operate on a modest scale and never without motive. They don't rob towns with more than two churches, and kill only by specific order or for a vengeance sworn by kissing a dagger. They work in the burned lands of the desert, far from the sea and the salty breath of its dragons. They cross the lonely stretches of northeast Brazil, on horse or on foot, their half-moon sombreros dripping with decorations. They rarely linger anywhere. They neither raise their children nor bury their parents. They have made a pact with Heaven and Hell not to shelter their bodies from bullets or knives simply for the sake of dying a natural death; and sooner or later these hazardous, hazarded lives, a thousand times lauded in the couplets of blind singers, come to very bad ends: *God will say, God will give, high road, long road*—the epic of wandering bandits who go from fight to fight, without time for their sweat to go cold.

(136, 348, and 353)

1938: Angico
The *Cangaceiro* Hunters

To throw their enemies off the scent, the *cangaceiros* imitate the noises and tracks of animals or use trick soles with heel and toe reversed. But those who know, know. A good tracker recognizes the passage of humans through this dying landscape from what he sees, a broken branch or a stone out of place, and what he smells. The *cangaceiros* are crazy about perfume. They douse themselves by the liter, and this weakness betrays them.

Following tracks and scents, the hunters reach the hideout of Chief Lampião; and behind them the troops, so close they hear Lampião arguing with his wife. Seated on a stone at the entrance to a cave, María Bonita curses him, while smoking one cigarette after another; from within, he makes sad replies. The soldiers mount their machineguns and await the command to fire.

A light drizzle falls.

(52, 348, 352, and 353)

1939: São Salvador de Bahia
The Women of the Gods

Ruth Landes, North American anthropologist, comes to Brazil to learn about the lives of blacks in a country without racism. In Rio de Janeiro, Minister Osvaldo Aranha receives her. He explains that the government proposes to clean up the Brazilian race, soiled as it is by black blood, because black blood is to blame for national backwardness.

From Rio, Ruth goes to Bahia. In this city, where the sugar- and slave-rich viceroy once had his throne, blacks are an ample majority, and whether it's religion, music, or food, black is what is worthwhile here. Nevertheless, all Bahians, including blacks, think white skin is proof of good quality. No, not everyone. Ruth discovers pride of blackness in the women of the African temples.

There it is nearly always women, black priestesses, who receive in their bodies the gods from Africa. Resplendent and round as cannonballs, they offer their capacious bodies as homes where it is pleasant to visit, to linger. While the gods enter them, dance in them, from the hands of these possessed priestesses the people get encouragement and solace, and from their mouths hear the voices of fate.

The black priestesses of Bahia accept lovers, not husbands. What matrimony gives in prestige, it takes away in freedom and happiness. None of them is interested in formal marriage before priest or judge. None wants to be a handcuffed wife, a Mrs. Someone-or-other. Heads erect, with languid swings, the priestesses move like queens of Creation, condemning their men to the incomparable torment of jealousy of the gods.

(253)

Exú

An earthquake of drums disturbs Rio de Janeiro's sleep. From the backwoods, by firelight, Exú mocks the rich, sending against them his deadly curses. Perfidious avenger of the have-nots, he lights up the night and darkens the day. If he throws a stone into a thicket, the thicket bleeds.

The god of the poor is also a devil. He has two heads: one, Jesus of Nazareth; the other, Satan of Hell. In Bahia he is a pesky messenger from the other world, a little second-class god; but in the slums of Rio he is the powerful master of midnight. Capable of caress or crime, Exú can save or kill, sometimes both at once.

He comes from the bowels of the earth, entering violently, destructively, through the soles of unshod feet. He is lent body and voice by men and women who dance with rats in shacks perilously suspended over the void, people whom Exú redeems with such craziness that they roll on the ground laughing themselves to death.

(255)

María Padilha

She is both Exú and one of his women, mirror and lover: María Padilha, the most whorish of the female devils with whom Exú likes to roll in the bonfires.

She is not hard to recognize when she enters the body. María Padilha shrieks, howls insults, laughs crudely, and at the end of a trance demands expensive drinks and imported cigarettes. She has to be treated like a great lady and passionately implored before she will deign to use her well-known influence with the most important gods and devils.

María Padilha doesn't enter just any body. To manifest herself in this world, she chooses the women of the Rio slums who make a livelihood selling themselves for small change. Thus do the despised become worthy of devotion. Hired flesh mounts to the center of the altar. The garbage of the night shines brighter than the sun.

1939: Rio de Janeiro
The Samba

Brazil is Brazilian and so is God, proclaims Ari Barroso in the very patriotic and danceable music that is becoming the heart of Rio's carnival.

But the tastier samba lyrics offered at the carnival, far from exalting the virtues of this tropical paradise, perversely eulogize the bohemian life and the misdeeds of free souls, damn poverty and the police, and scorn work. Work is for idiots, because anyone can see that the bricklayer can never enter what his hands erect.

The samba, black rhythm, offspring of the chants that convoke the black gods of the slums, now dominates the carnivals, even if in respectable homes it is still scorned. It invites distrust because it is black and poor and born in the refuges of people hunted by the police. But the samba quickens the feet and caresses the soul and there is no disregarding it once it strikes up. The universe breathes to the rhythms of the samba until Ash Wednesday in a fiesta that turns every proletarian into a king, every paralytic into an athlete, and every bore into a beautiful madman.

(74 and 285)

1939: Rio de Janeiro
The Scoundrel

most feared in Rio is called Madame Satan.

When the child was seven, the mother swapped it for a horse. Since then, it has passed from hand to hand, master to master, until it ended up in a brothel where it learned the craft of cooking and the pleasures of the bed. There it became a professional tough, protector of whores, male and female, and of all defenseless bohemians. Beaten often enough and hard enough by the police to send several men to the cemetery, this fierce black never gets past hospital or jail.

Madame Satan is a he from Monday to Friday, a panama-hatted devil who with fist and razor dominates the night in the Lapa barrio, where he strolls about whistling a samba and marking time with a box of matches; but on the weekends he is a she, the very harpy who has just won the carnival fancy-dress contest with the campiest golden-bat cape, who wears a ring on every finger and moves her hips like her friend Carmen Miranda.

(146)

1939: Rio de Janeiro
Cartola

On the Mangueira knoll, Cartola is the soul of samba, and of practically everything else.

Often he passes by in a flash, waving his pants like a flag, pursued by some intolerant husband. Between his sprees and flights, melodies and protestations of love float up inside him, to be hummed and quickly forgotten.

Cartola sells his sambas to anyone who comes along and for whatever pittance he can get. He is always amazed that there are people who will pay anything at all for them.

(428)

1939: Montserrat

Vallejo

Mortally wounded, the Spanish republic staggers its final few steps. Little breath remains to it as Franco's exterminating army pushes on.

In the abbey of Montserrat, by way of farewell, the militias publish verses that two Latin Americans have written in homage to Spain and its tragedy. The poems of the Chilean Pablo Neruda and the Peruvian Vallejo are printed on paper made from rags of uniforms, enemy flags, and bandages.

César Vallejo has just died, hurt and alone, like Spain. He died in Paris, a day he had foreseen and recorded, and his last poems, written between four menacing walls, were for Spain. Vallejo sang of the heroism of the Spanish people in arms, of Spain's independent spirit, its beloved sun, beloved shade; and Spain was the last word he spoke in his death agony, this American poet, this most American of poets.

(457)

1939: Washington

Roosevelt

When Franklin Delano Roosevelt became president, the United States had fifteen million workless workers looking around with the eyes of lost children, raising a thumb on the highways as they wandered from city to city, barefoot or with cardboard tops on leaky soles, using public urinals and railroad stations for hotels.

To save his nation, Roosevelt's first act was to put money in a cage: He closed all the banks until the way ahead was clear. Since then he has governed the economy without letting it govern him, and has consolidated a democracy threatened by the crisis.

With Latin American dictators, however, he gets along fine. Roosevelt protects them, as he protects Ford automobiles, Kelvinator refrigerators, and other products of the United States.

(276 and 304)

1939: Washington

In the Year Nine of the Trujillo Era

a twenty-one-gun salute welcomes him to West Point, where Trujillo cools himself with a perfumed ivory fan and salutes the cadets with flutters of his ostrich-plume hat. A plump delegation of bishops, generals, and courtiers accompanies him, as well as a doctor and a sorcerer, both specializing in eye problems, not to speak of Brigadier General Ramfis Trujillo, age nine, dragging a sword longer than himself.

General George Marshall offers Trujillo a banquet on board the *Mayflower* and President Roosevelt receives him in the White House. Legislators, governors, and journalists shower this exemplary statesman with praise. Trujillo, who pays cash for murders, acquires his eulogies likewise, and lists the disbursements under the heading "Birdseed" in the executive budget of the Dominican Republic.

(60 and 177)

1939: Washington

Somoza

Before the Marines made him a general and the supreme boss of Nicaragua, Anastasio Tacho Somoza had pursued a successful career forging gold coins and cheating at poker and love.

Now that all power is his, Sandino's murderer has turned the national budget into his private bank account and has personally taken over the country's richest lands. He has liquidated his lukewarm enemies by firing National Bank loans at them, while his warmer enemies have providentially ended up in accidents or ambushes.

Somoza's visit to the United States is no less triumphant than Trujillo's. President Roosevelt and several cabinet members appear at Union Station to welcome him. A military band plays the anthems of both countries, and a rumble of guns and speeches follows. Somoza announces that the main avenue of Managua, which crosses the city from lake to lake, will be renamed Roosevelt Avenue.

(102)

1939: New York

Superman

Action Comics celebrates the first anniversary of the successful launch of Superman.

This Hercules of our time guards private property in the universe. From a place called Metropolis, flying faster than the speed of light and breaking time barriers, he travels to other epochs and galaxies. Wherever he goes, in this world or others, Superman restores order more efficiently and quickly than the whole Marine Corps put together. With a glance he melts steel, with a kick he fells a forest of trees, with a punch he perforates mountain chains.

In his other personality, Superman is timid Clark Kent, as meek as any of his readers.

(147)

1941: New York

Portrait of an Opinion Maker

At first, few theaters dare to show *Citizen Kane*, the movie in which Orson Welles tells the story of a man sick with power fever, a man who too closely resembles William Randolph Hearst.

Hearst owns eighteen newspapers, nine magazines, seven castles, and quite a few people. He is expert at stirring up public opinion. In his long life he has provoked wars and bankruptcies, made and destroyed fortunes, created idols and demolished reputations. Among his best inventions are the scandal campaign and the gossip column, so good for what he likes to do best—land a solid punch well below the belt.

The most powerful fabricator of opinion in the United States thinks that the white race is the only really human race; believes in the necessary victory of the strongest; is convinced that Communists are to blame for alcohol consumption among the young; and that Japanese are born traitors.

When Japan bombs the naval base at Pearl Harbor, Hearst's newspapers have already been beating a steady warning rhythm for half a century about the Yellow Peril. The United States enters the World War.

(130 and 441)

1942: New York
The Red Cross Doesn't Accept Black Blood

U.S. soldiers embark for the war fronts. Many are black under the command of white officers.

Those who survive will return home. The blacks will enter by the back door, and, in the Southern states, continue to live, work, and die apart, and even then will lie in separate graves. Hooded Ku Klux Klansmen will still insure that blacks do not intrude into the white world, and above all into the bedrooms of white women.

The war accepts blacks, thousands and thousands of them, but not the Red Cross. The Red Cross bans black blood in the plasma banks, so as to avoid the possibility that races might mix by tranfusion.

The research of Charles Drew, inventor of life, has finally made it possible to save blood. Thanks to him, plasma banks are reviving thousands of dying men on the battlefields of Europe.

When the Red Cross decides to reject the blood of blacks, Drew, director of the Red Cross plasma service, resigns. Drew is black.

(51, 218, and 262)

1942: Oxford, Mississippi
Faulkner

Seated on a rocker, on the columned porch of a decaying mansion, William Faulkner smokes his pipe and listens to the whispered confidences of ghosts.

The plantation masters tell Faulkner of their glories and their dreads. Nothing horrifies them like miscegenation. A drop of black blood, even one tiny drop, curses a whole life and ensures, after death, the fires of hell. The old Southern dynasties, born of crime and condemned to crime, watch anxiously over the pale splendor of their own twilight, affronted by the shadow of blackness, the slightest hint of blackness. These gentlemen would love to believe that purity of lineage will not die out, though its memory may fade and the trumpets of the horsemen defeated by Lincoln echo no more.

(163 and 247)

1942: Hollywood
Brecht

Hollywood manufactures films to turn the frightful vigil of humanity, on the point of annihilation, into sweet dreams. Bertolt Brecht, exiled from Hitler's Germany, is employed in this sleeping-pill industry. Founder of a theater that sought to open eyes wide, he earns his living at the United Artists studios, just one more writer who works office hours for Hollywood, competing to produce the biggest daily ration of idiocies.

On one of these days, Brecht buys a little God of Luck for forty cents in a Chinese store and puts it on his desk. Brecht has been told that the God of Luck licks his lips each time they make him take poison..

(66)

1942: Hollywood
The Good Neighbors to the South

accompany the United States into the World War. It is the time of *democratic prices*: Latin American countries supply cheap raw materials, cheap food, and a soldier or two.

The movies glorify the common cause. Rarely missing from a film is the South American number, sung and danced in Spanish or Portuguese. Donald Duck acquires a Brazilian sidekick, the little parrot José Carioca. On Pacific islands or in the fields of Europe, Hollywood Adonises wipe out Japanese and Germans by the heap. And how many Adonises have at their sides a simpatico, indolent, somewhat stupid Latin, who admires his blond northern brother and serves as his echo and shadow, faithful henchman, merry minstrel, messenger, and cook?

(467)

1942: María Barzola Pampa

A Latin American Method for Reducing Production Costs

Bolivia—subsisting, as ever, on hunger rations—is one of the countries that pays for the World War by selling its tin at a tenth of the normal price.

The mine workers finance this bargain price. Their wages go from almost nothing to nothing at all. And when a government decree calls for forced labor at gunpoint, the strikes begin. Another decree bans the strikes, but fails to stop them. So the president, Enrique Peñaranda, orders the army to take *severe and energetic* action. Patiño, king of the mines, issues his own orders: *Proceed without vacillation.* His viceroys, Aramayo and Hochschild, approve. The machineguns spit fire for hours and leave the ground strewn with people.

Patiño Mines pays for some coffins, but saves on indemnities. Death by machinegun is not an occupational hazard.

(97 and 474)

1943: Sans-Souci

Carpentier

Alejo Carpentier discovers the kingdom of Henri Christophe. The Cuban writer roams these majestic ruins, this memorial to the delirium of a slave cook who became monarch of Haiti and killed himself with the gold bullet that always hung around his neck. Ceremonial hymns and magic drums of invocation rise up to meet Carpentier as he visits the palace that King Christophe copied from Versailles, and walks around his invulnerable fortress, an immense bulk whose stones, cemented by the blood of bulls sacrificed to the gods, have resisted lightning and earthquakes.

In Haiti, Carpentier learns that there is no magic more prodigious and delightful than the voyage that leads through experience, through the body, to the depths of America. In Europe, magicians have become bureaucrats, and wonder, exhausted, has dwindled to a conjuring trick. But in America, surrealism is as natural as rain or madness.

(85)

1943: Port-au-Prince
Hands That Don't Lie

Dewitt Peters founds an open workshop and from it suddenly explodes Haitian art. Everybody paints everything: cloth, cardboard, cans, wooden boards, walls, whatever presents itself. They paint in a great outburst of splendor, with the seven souls of the rainbow. Everyone: the shoe repairman and fisherman, river washerwoman and market-stall holder. In America's poorest country, wrung out by Europe, invaded by the United States, torn apart by wars and dictatorships, the people shout colors and no one can shut them up.

(122, 142, and 385)

1943: Mount Rouis
A Little Grain of Salt

In a bar, surrounded by kids with bloated bellies and skeletal dogs, Hector Hyppolite paints gods with a brush of hens' feathers. Saint John the Baptist turns up in the evenings and helps him.

Hyppolite portrays the gods who paint through his hand. These Haitian gods, painted and painters, live simultaneously on earth and in heaven and hell: Capable of good and evil, they offer their children vengeance and solace.

Not all have come from Africa. Some were born here, like Baron Samedi, god of solemn stride, master of poisons and graves, his blackness enhanced by top hat and cane. That poison should kill and the dead rest in peace depends upon Baron Samedi. He turns many dead into zombies and condemns them to slave labor.

Zombies—dead people who walk or live ones who have lost their souls—have a look of hopeless stupidity. But in no time they can escape and recover their lost lives, their stolen souls. One little grain of salt is enough to awaken them. And how could salt be lacking in

the home of the slaves who defeated Napoleon and founded freedom
in America?

(146, 233, and 295)

1944: New York
Learning to See

It is noon and James Baldwin is walking with a friend through the
streets of downtown Manhattan. A red light stops them.

"*Look*," says the friend, pointing at the ground.

Baldwin looks. He sees nothing.

"*Look, look.*"

Nothing. There is nothing to look at but a filthy little puddle
of water against the curb.

His friend insists: "*See? Are you seeing?*"

And then Baldwin takes a good look and this time he sees, sees
a spot of oil spreading in the puddle. Then, in the spot of oil, a rainbow,
and even deeper down in the puddle, the street moving, and people
moving in the street: the shipwrecked, the madmen, the magicians,
the whole world moving, an astounding world full of worlds that glow
in the world. Baldwin sees. For the first time in his life, he sees.

(152)

1945: The Guatemala–El Salvador Border
Miguel at Forty

He sleeps in caves and cemeteries. Condemned by hunger to constant
hiccups, he competes with the magpies for scraps. His sister, who
meets him from time to time, says: "*God has given you many talents,
but he has punished you by making you a Communist.*"

Since Miguel recovered his party's confidence, the running and
suffering have only increased. Now the party has decided that its
most sacrificed member must go into exile in Guatemala.

Miguel manages to cross the border after a thousand hassles and
dangers. It is deepest night. He stretches out, exhausted, under a
tree. At daybreak, an enormous yellow cow wakens him by licking
his feet.

"*Good morning,*" Miguel says, and the cow, frightened, runs off at full tilt, into the forest, lowing. From the forest promptly emerge five vengeful bulls. There is no escape. Behind Miguel is an abyss and the tree at his back has a smooth trunk. The bulls charge, then stop dead and stand staring, panting, breathing fire and smoke, tossing their horns and pawing the ground, tearing up undergrowth and raising the dust.

Miguel trembles in a cold sweat. Tongue-tied with panic, he stammers an explanation. The bulls stare at him, a little man half hunger and half fear, and look at each other. He commends himself to Marx and Saint Francis of Assisi as the bulls slowly turn their backs on him and wander off, heads shaking.

And so occurs the ninth birth of Miguel Mármol, at forty years of age.

(126)

1945: Hiroshima and Nagasaki

A Sun of Fire,

a violent light never before seen in the world, rises slowly, cracks the sky open, and collapses. Three days later, a second sun of suns bursts over Japan. Beneath remain the cinders of two cities, a desert of rubble, tens of thousands dead and more thousands condemned to die little by little for years to come.

The war was nearly over, Hitler and Mussolini gone, when President Harry Truman gave the order to drop atomic bombs on the populations of Hiroshima and Nagasaki. In the United States, it is the culmination of a national clamor for the prompt annihilation of the Yellow Peril. It is high time to finish off once and for all the imperial conceits of this arrogant Asian country, never colonized by anyone. The only good one is a dead one, says the press of these treacherous little monkeys.

Now all doubt is dispelled. There is one great conqueror among the conquerors. The United States emerges from the war intact and more powerful than ever. It acts as if the whole world were its trophy.

(140 and 276)

1945: Princeton
Einstein

Albert Einstein feels as if his own hand had pressed the button. Although he didn't make it, the atomic bomb would not have been possible without his discoveries about the liberation of energy. Now Einstein would like to have been someone else, to have devoted himself to some inoffensive task like fixing drains or building walls instead of investigating the secrets of life that others now use to destroy it.

When he was a boy, a professor said to him: *"You'll never amount to anything."*

Daydreaming, with the expression of someone on the moon, he wondered how light would look to a person able to ride on a beam. When he became a man, he found the answer in the theory of relativity, won a Nobel Prize, and deserved many more for his answers to other questions born in his mind of the mysterious link between Mozart's sonatas and the theorem of Pythagoras, or of the defiant arabesques that the smoke from his extra-long pipe drew in the air.

Einstein believed that science was a way of revealing the beauty of the universe. The most famous of sages has the saddest eyes in human history.

(150 and 228)

1945: Buenos Aires
Perón

General MacArthur takes charge of the Japanese, and Spruille Braden of the Argentines. To lead Argentina down the good road to Democracy, U.S. ambassador Braden brings together all the parties, Conservative to Communist, in a united front against Juan Domingo Perón. According to the State Department, Colonel Perón, the government's minister of labor, is the chief of a gang of Nazis. *Look* magazine calls him a pervert who keeps photos of nude Patagonian Indian women in his desk drawer along with pictures of Hitler and Mussolini.

Nonetheless, Perón flies swiftly along the road to the presidency with Evita, the radio actress with the feverish eyes and enticing voice;

and when he gets tired, or doubtful, or scared, it is she who takes the bit in her teeth. Perón now attracts more people than all the parties put together. When they call him "agitator," he accepts the epithet as an honor. VIPs and the fashionably chic chant the name of Ambassador Braden on the street corners of Buenos Aires, waving hats and handkerchiefs; but in worker barrios, the shirtless shout the name Perón. These laboring people, exiles in their own land, dumb from so much shutting up, find both a fatherland and a voice in this unusual minister who always takes their side.

Perón's popularity climbs and climbs as he shakes the dust off forgotten social laws or creates new ones. His is the law that compels respect for the rights of those who break their backs on estancias and plantations. The law does not merely remain on paper; thus the country peon, almost a thing, becomes a rural worker complete with a trade union.

(311 and 327)

1945: The Fields of Tucumán
The Familiar

flies into a rage over these novelties that disturb his dominions. Workers' unions infuriate and scare him more than the hilt of a knife.

On the sugarcane plantations of northern Argentina, the Familiar is responsible for the obedience of the peons. If one answers back or acts impertinently, the Familiar devours him in a single gulp. He moves with a clank of chains and stinks of sulphur, but no one knows if he is the devil in person or just an official. Only his victims have seen him, and no one seems able to add up the accounts. It is rumored that at night the Familiar turns into an enormous snake and patrols the sheds where the peons sleep, or that he crouches in wait on the roads in the form of a dog with flaming eyes, all black, with huge teeth and claws.

(103 and 328)

A Wake for a Little Angel

In the northern provinces of Argentina, they don't weep for the death of small children. One less mouth on earth, one more angel in heaven. Death is drunk and dances from the first cock-crow, sucking in long draughts of carob-bean liquor and *chicha* to the rhythm of bass drum and guitar. While the dancers whirl and stomp their feet, the child is passed from arm to arm. Once the child has been well rocked and fully celebrated, everyone breaks into song to start it on its flight to Paradise. There goes the little traveler, clothed in its Sunday best, as the song swells; and they bid it farewell, setting off fireworks, taking great care not to burn its wings.

(104)

1945: *The Fields of Tucumán*
Yupanqui

He has the stony face of an Indian who stares impassively at the mountain that stares back at him, but he comes from the plains of the south, from the echoless pampa that hides nothing, this gaucho singer of the mysteries of the Argentine north. He comes on a horse, stopping anyplace, with anyone, at the whim of the road. To continue his journey he sings, singing what he has traveled, Atahualpa Yupanqui. And he sings to keep history going, because the history of the poor is either sung or lost as well he knows, he who is left-handed on the guitar and in his thinking about the world.

(202, 270, and 472)

1946: *La Paz*
The *Rosca*

At the summit there are three; at the foot of the mountain three million. The mountain is tin and is called Bolivia.

The three at the summit form the *rosca*: Simón Patiño in the center; on one side, Carlos Aramayo; on the other, Mauricio Hochschild. Half a century ago, Patiño was a down-and-out miner, but a fairy touched him with her magic wand and turned him into one of the world's richest men. Now he wears a vest with a gold chain, and kings and presidents sit at his table. Aramayo comes from the local aristocracy, Hochschild, from the airplane that brought him to Bolivia. Each of them has more money than the state.

All that the tin earns remains outside Bolivia. To avoid taxes, Patiño's headquarters are in the United States, Aramayo's in Switzerland, and Hochschild's in Chile. Patiño pays Bolivia fifty dollars a year in income tax, Aramayo twenty-two, Hochschild nothing. Of every two children born at the *rosca*'s mines, one doesn't survive.

Each member of the *rosca* has at his disposal a newspaper and various ministers and legislators. It is traditional for the foreign minister to receive a monthly salary from Patiño Mines. But now that President Gualberto Villarroel suggests the *rosca* pay taxes and salaries that are not merely symbolic, what is there to do but hatch a plot?

(97)

1946: La Paz

Villarroel

President Villarroel does not defend himself. He abandons himself to fate—as if it were a matter of fate.

He is attacked by paid gunmen followed by a great motley crowd of godly women and students. Brandishing torches, black flags, and bloody sheets, the insurgents invade the government palace, throw Villarroel off a balcony, then hang what's left of him, naked, from a lamppost.

Besides defying the *rosca*, Villarroel had wanted to give equal rights to whites and Indians, wives and lovers, legitimate and illegitimate children.

The world cheers the crime. The leaders of democracy commend the liquidation of a tyrant in the pay of Hitler, who with unpardonable insolence sought to raise the rock-bottom price of tin. And in Bolivia, a country that never stops toiling for its own misfortune, the fall of what is and the restoration of what was is wildly celebrated: happy days for the League of Morality, the Association of Mothers of Priests, the War Widows, the U.S. embassy, every complexion of rightist, nearly all of the left—left of the left of the moon!—and the *rosca*.

(97)

1946: Hollywood
Carmen Miranda

Sequined and dripping with necklaces, crowned by a tower of bananas, Carmen Miranda undulates against a cardboard tropical backdrop.

Born in Portugal, daughter of a penurious barber who crossed the ocean, Carmen is the chief export of Brazil. Next comes coffee.

This diminutive hussy has little voice, and what she has is out of tune, but she sings with her hands and with her gleaming eyes, and that is more than enough. She is one of the best-paid performers in Hollywood. She has ten houses and eight oil wells.

But Fox refuses to renew her contract. Senator Joseph McCarthy has called her obscene, because at the peak of one of her production numbers, a photographer revealed intolerable glimpses of bare flesh and who knows what else under her flying skirt. And the press has disclosed that in her tenderest infancy Carmen recited lines before King Albert of Belgium, accompanying them with wiggles and winks that scandalized the nuns and gave the king prolonged insomnia.

(401)

1948: Bogotá
On the Eve

In placid Bogotá, home of monks and jurists, General Marshall sits down with the foreign ministers of Latin America.

What gifts does he bring in his saddlebags, this Wise King of the Occident who irrigates with dollars the European lands devastated by the war? General Marshall, impassive, microphones stuck to his chest, resists the downpour of speeches. Without moving so much as an eyelid, he endures the protracted professions of democratic faith offered by many Latin American delegates anxious to sell themselves for the price of a dead rooster; while John McCloy, head of the World Bank, warns: *"I'm sorry, gentlemen, but I didn't bring my checkbook in my suitcase."*

Beyond the salons of the Ninth Pan-American Conference, even more florid speeches shower down throughout the length and breadth of the host country. Learned liberals announce that they will bring peace to Colombia *as the goddess Pallas Athena made the olive branch blossom on the hills of Athens,* and erudite conservatives promise *to draw unknown forces into the sunshine, and light up with the dark fire that is the entrails of the globe the timid votive light of the candelabra that is lit on the eve of treachery in the night of darkness.*

While foreign ministers clamor, proclaim, and declaim, reality persists. In the Colombian countryside the war between conservatives and liberals is fought with guns. Politicians provide the words, campesinos provide the corpses. And already the violence is filtering into Bogotá, knocking at the capital's doors and threatening its time-honored routines—always the same sins, always the same metaphors. At the bullfights last Sunday, the desperate crowd poured into the arena and tore to pieces a wretched bull that refused to fight.

(7)

1948: Bogotá

Gaitán

The political country, says Jorge Eliécer Gaitán, *has nothing to do with the national country.* Gaitán, head of the Liberal Party, is also its black sheep. Poor people of all persuasions adore him. *What is the difference between liberal hunger and conservative hunger? Malaria is neither conservative nor liberal!*

Gaitán's voice unbinds the poor who cry out through his mouth. He turns fear on its back. They come from everywhere to hear him—to hear themselves—the ragged ones, trekking through the jungle, spurring their horses down the roads. They say that when Gaitán speaks the fog splits in Bogotá; and that even in heaven Saint Peter listens and forbids the rain to fall on the gigantic crowds gathered by torchlight.

This dignified leader, with the austere face of a statue, does not hesitate to denounce the oligarchy and the imperial ventriloquist on whose knee the oligarchs sit without life of their own or words of their own. He calls for agrarian reform and articulates other truths to put an end to the long lie.

If they don't kill him, Gaitán will be Colombia's next president. He cannot be bought. To what temptation would he succumb, this man who scorns pleasure, sleeps alone, eats little, drinks nothing, and even refuses anesthesia when he has a tooth pulled?

(7)

1948: Bogotá
The *Bogotazo*

At 2:00 P.M. of this ninth of April, Gaitán has a date with one of the Latin American students who are gathering in Bogotá on the fringes of General Marshall's Pan-American ceremony.

At half past one, the student leaves his hotel, intending to stroll to Gaitán's office. But after a few steps a noise like an earthquake stops him, a human avalanche engulfs him. The people, pouring out of the barrios, streaming down from the hills, are rushing madly past him, a hurricane of pain and anger flooding the city, smashing store windows, overturning streetcars, setting buildings afire.

They've killed him! They've killed him!

It was done in the streets, with three bullets. Gaitán's watch stopped at 1:05 P.M.

The student, a corpulent Cuban named Fidel Castro, shoves his cap on his head and lets himself be blown along by the wind of people.

(7)

1948: Bogotá
Flames

Indian ponchos and workers' sandals invade the center of Bogotá, hands toughened by earth or stone, hands stained with machine oil or shoe polish, a tornado of porters, students, and waiters, washerwomen and market women, Jills of all beds and Jacks of all trades, ambulance chasers and fortune hunters. From the tornado a woman detaches herself, wearing four fur coats, clumsy and happy as a bear in love; running like a rabbit is a man with several pearl necklaces around his throat; walking like a tortoise, another with a refrigerator on his back.

At street corners, ragged kids direct traffic. Prisoners burst the bars of their cells. Someone cuts the fire hoses with a machete. Bogotá is an immense bonfire, the sky a vault of red; from the balconies of burning ministries typewriters plummet; from burning belltowers bullets rain. The police hide themselves or cross their arms before the fury.

At the presidential palace, a river of people is seen approaching. Machineguns have already repelled two of these attacks, although the crowd did succeed in hurling against the palace doors the disemboweled body of the puppet who killed Gaitán.

Doña Bertha, the first lady, sticks a revolver in her waistband and calls her confessor on the telephone: *"Father, be so good as to take my son to the American embassy."*

On another phone the president, Mariano Ospina Pérez, sees to the protection of General Marshall's house and dictates orders against the rebellious rabble. Then he sits and waits. The tumult grows in the streets.

Three tanks head the attack on the presidential palace. The tanks are swarming with people waving flags and yelling Gaitán's name, and behind them surges a multitude bristling with machetes, axes, and clubs. When they reach the palace the tanks halt. Their turrets turn slowly, aim to the rear, and commence mowing people down.

(7)

1948: Bogotá
Ashes

Someone wanders in search of a shoe. A woman howls, a dead child in her arms. The city smolders. Walk carefully or you'll step on bodies. A dismembered mannequin hangs on the streetcar cables. From the stairway of a burned monastery a naked, blackened Christ gazes skyward, arms outstretched. At the foot of that stairway, a beggar sits and drinks. The archbishop's mitre covers his head and a purple velvet curtain envelops his body. He further defends himself from the cold by sipping French cognac from a gold chalice, and offers drinks to passersby in a silver goblet. An army bullet ends the party.

The last shots ring out. The city, devastated by fire, regains order. After three days of vengeance and madness, a disarmed people returns to the old purgatory of work and woe.

General Marshall has no doubts. The *bogotazo* was the work of

Moscow. The government of Colombia breaks relations with the Soviet Union.

(7)

1948: Upar Valley
The *Vallenato*

"I want to let out a yell and they won't let me . . ."

The government of Colombia prohibits the "Vagabond Yell." Whoever sings it risks jail or a bullet. Along the Magdalena River, though, they keep singing.

The people of the Colombian coast defend themselves by making music. The "Vagabond Yell" is a *vallenato* rhythm, one of the cowboy songs that tell the story of the region and, incidentally, fill the air with joy.

Accordion to breast, the troubadours prance and navigate. Accordion on thigh, they receive the first drinks at all parties and challenge each other to a duel of couplets.

The *vallenato* verses born of accordions thrust back and forth like knives, like fusillades in daring musical battles that last for days and nights in markets and cockfight rings. The singers' most fearsome rival is Lucifer, that great musician, who gets bored in hell and comes to America at the drop of a hat, disguised, looking for fun.

(359)

1948: Wroclaw
Picasso

This painter embodies the best painters of all times. They cohabit in him, if rather uncomfortably. It is no easy task to assimilate such intractable folk, ancient and modern, who spend so much time in conflict with one another that the painter hasn't a free moment to listen to speeches, much less make them.

But for the first and only time in his life, Pablo Picasso makes a speech. This unheard-of event occurs in the Polish city of Wroclaw, at a world congress of intellectuals for peace: *"I have a friend who ought to be here . . ."*

Picasso pays homage to *the greatest poet of the Spanish language and one of the greatest poets on earth, who has always taken the side of the unfortunate: Pablo Neruda, persecuted by the police in Chile, cornered like a dog . . .*

(442)

1948: Somewhere in Chile
Neruda

The main headline in the daily *El Imparcial* reads: *Neruda Sought Throughout the Country;* and below: *Investigators locating his whereabouts will be rewarded.*

The poet goes from hideout to hideout, traveling by night. Neruda is one of many suffering persecution for being red or for being decent or for just being, and he doesn't complain of this fate, which he has chosen. Nor does he regret the solitude: He enjoys and celebrates this fighting passion, whatever trouble it brings him, as he enjoys and celebrates church bells, wine, eel broth, and flying comets with wings spreads wide.

(313 and 442)

1948: San José de Costa Rica
Figueres

After six weeks of civil war, and two thousand dead, the rural middle class comes to power in Costa Rica.

The head of the new government, José Figueres, outlaws the Communist Party and promises *unconditional support to the struggle of the free world against Russian imperialism.* But in an undertone he also promises to continue to expand the social reforms the Communists have promoted in recent years.

Under the protection of President Rafael Calderón, friend of the Communists, unions and cooperatives have multiplied in Costa Rica; small landowners have won land from the great estates; health has been improved and education extended.

The anticommunist Figueres does not touch the lands of the United Fruit Company, that most powerful mistress, but nationalizes the banks and dissolves the army, so that money will not speculate, nor arms conspire. Costa Rica wants out of the ferocious turbulence of Central America.

(42, 243, 414, and 438)

1949: Washington
The Chinese Revolution

Between yesterday and tomorrow, an abyss. The Chinese revolution springs into the air and leaps the gap.

The news from Peking provokes anger and fear in Washington. After their long march of armed poverty, Mao's reds have triumphed. General Chiang Kai-shek flees. The United States enthrones him on the island of Formosa.

The parks in China had been forbidden to dogs and the poor, and beggars still froze to death in the early mornings, as in the old days of the mandarins; but it was not from Peking that the orders came. It was not the Chinese who named their ministers and generals, wrote their laws and decrees, and fixed their tariffs and salaries. By a geographical error, China was not in the Caribbean.

(156 and 291)

1949: Havana
Radio Theater

"Don't kill me," pleads the actor to the author.

Onelio Jorge Cardoso had had it in mind to polish off Captain Hook in the next episode; but if the character dies of a sword-thrust on the pirate ship, the actor dies of hunger in the street. The author, a good friend of the actor, promises him eternal life.

Onelio devises breathtaking adventures, but his radio plays enjoy little success.

He doesn't pour it on thick enough, he doesn't know how to wring hearts out like laundry—to the last drop. José Sánchez Arcilla, by contrast, touches the most intimate fibers. In his serial "The Necklace of Tears," the characters struggle against perverse destiny in nine hundred and sixty-five episodes that bathe the audience in tears.

But the greatest success of all time is "The Right to Be Born," by Felix B. Caignet. Nothing like it has ever been heard in Cuba or anywhere else. At the scheduled nighttime hour, it alone gets a hearing, a unanimous Mass. Movies are interrupted, streets empty, lovers suspend their dalliances, cocks quit fighting, and even flies alight for the duration.

For seventy-four episodes, all Cuba has been waiting for Don Rafael del Junco to speak. This character possesses The Secret. But not only is he totally paralyzed, he lost his voice in episode 197. We've now made it to episode 271 and Don Rafael still can only clear his throat. When will he manage to reveal The Truth to the good woman who sinned but once, succumbing to Mad Passion's call? When will he have the voice to tell her that Albertico Limonta, her doctor, is really the fruit of that same illicit love, the baby she abandoned soon after birth into the hands of a black woman with a white soul? When, oh, when?

The public, dying of suspense, does not know that Don Rafael is on a silence strike. This cruel silence will continue until the actor who plays Don Rafael del Junco gets the raise he has been demanding for two and a half months.

(266)

1950: Rio de Janeiro
Obdulio

Although the dice are loaded against him, Obdulio steps firmly and kicks. The captain of the Uruguayans, this commanding, muscular black man does not lose heart. The more the hostile multitude roars from the stands, the more Obdulio grows.

Surprise and sorrow in Maracaná Stadium: Brazil, the great, pulverizing, goal-scoring machine, the favorite all along, loses this last match at the last minute. Uruguay, playing for its life, wins the world football championship.

That night Obdulio Varela flees from his hotel, besieged by journalists, fans, and the curious. Preferring to celebrate alone, he goes looking for a drink in some remote dive or other, but everywhere meets weeping Brazilians.

"*Obedulio is giving us the game,*" they were chanting in the stadium just hours ago, midway through the match. Now, bathed in tears, the same people cry, "*It was all Obedulio's fault.*"

And Obdulio, having so recently disliked them, is stunned to see them individually. The victory begins to weigh on him. He has ruined the party of these good folk and begins to wonder if he shouldn't beg their pardon for the tremendous sin of winning. So he keeps on wandering the Rio streets, from bar to bar. Dawn finds him still drinking, embracing the vanquished.

(131 and 191)

1950: Hollywood
Rita

Changing her name, weight, age, voice, lips, and eyebrows, she conquered Hollywood. Her hair was transformed from dull black into flaming red. To broaden her brow, they removed hair after hair by painful electrolysis. Over her eyes they put lashes like petals.

Rita Hayworth disguised herself as a goddess, and perhaps was one—for the forties, anyway. Now, the fifties demand something new.

(249)

1950: Hollywood
Marilyn

Like Rita, this girl has been improved. She had thick eyelashes and a double chin, a nose round at the tip, and large teeth. Hollywood reduced the fat, suppressed the cartilage, filed the teeth, and turned the mousy chestnut hair into a cascade of gleaming gold. Then the technicians baptized her Marilyn Monroe and invented a pathetic childhood story for her to tell the journalists.

This new Venus manufactured in Hollywood no longer needs to climb into strange beds seeking contracts for second-rate roles in third-rate films. She no longer lives on hot dogs and coffee, or suffers the cold of winter. Now she is a star; or rather a small personage in a mask who would like to remember, but cannot, that moment when she simply wanted to be saved from loneliness.

(214 and 274)

1951: Mexico City
Buñuel

Stones rain upon Luis Buñuel. Most of the newspapers and press syndicates insist that Mexico expel this Spanish ingrate who repays favors with infamy. The film that arouses national indignation, *Los Olvidados*, depicts the slums of Mexico City. Adolescents who live hand to mouth in this horrendous underworld eat whatever they find, including each other, with garbage heaps for their playground. They peck each other to pieces, bit by bit, these baby vultures, and so fulfill the dark destiny their city has chosen for them.

A mysterious resonance, a strange force, echoes in Buñuel's films. Some long, deep roll of drums, perhaps the drums of his infancy in Calanda, make the earth tremble, even if the sound track registers no noise, and the world simulates silence and forgiveness.

(70 and 71)

1952: San Fernando Hill
Sick unto Death

is Colombia since Gaitán was murdered on that Bogotá street. In mountains and plains, frozen prairies and steamy valleys—everywhere—campesinos kill each other, poor against poor, all against all. A tornado of vendettas and vengeance allows Blackblood, the Claw, Tarzan, Tough Luck, the Roach, and other artists of butchery to excel at their chosen trade, but more ferocious crimes are committed by the forces of order. The Tolima Battalion kills fifteen hundred, not counting rapes or mutilations, in its sweep of the area from Pantamillo to San Fernando Hill. To leave no seed from which the future might grow, soldiers toss children aloft and run them through with bayonet or machete.

"Don't bring me stories," say those who give the orders, *"bring me ears."*

Campesinos who manage to escape seek protection deep in the mountains, leaving their smoking shacks in cinders behind them. Before leaving, in a sad ceremony they kill the dog, because he makes noise.

(217, 227, and 408)

1952: La Paz

El Illimani

Though you can't see him, he watches you. Hide where you like, he watches over you. No cranny escapes him. The capital of Bolivia belongs to him, although they don't know it, the gentlemen who till last night thought themselves masters of these houses, these people.

El Illimani, proud king, washes himself with mist. At his feet, the city begins its day. Campfires die out, the last machinegun volleys are heard. The yellow hats of miners overwhelm the military caps. An army that has never won against those outside nor lost against those within, collapses. People dance on any street corner. Handkerchiefs flutter, braids and multilayered skirts undulate to the beat of the *cueca*.

In the absolute blueness of the sky gleams El Illimani's crown of three peaks: From the snowy summits the gods contemplate the happiness of their children in arms, at the end of this endless foot-by-foot struggle through the back streets.

(17, 172, and 473)

1952: La Paz

Drum of the People

that beats and rolls and rolls again, vengeance of the Indian who sleeps in the yard like a dog and greets the master with bended knee: The army of the underdogs fought with homemade bombs and sticks of dynamite until, finally, the arsenal of the military fell into their hands.

Víctor Paz Estenssoro promises that from this day Bolivia will be for all Bolivians. By the mines the workers fly the national flag at half-mast, where it will stay until the new president fulfills his promise to nationalize tin. In London they see it coming: As if by magic, the price of tin falls by two-thirds.

On the Pairumani estate, Indians roast on a grill the prize bulls Patiño imported from Holland.

Aramayo's tennis courts, surfaced with brick dust from England, are turned into mule corrals.

(17, 172, and 473)

A Woman of the Bolivian Mines Gives the Recipe for a Homemade Bomb

Look for a little milk can. Put the dynamite right in the middle, a capsule. Then, bits of iron, slag, a little dirt. Add glass and small nails. Then cover it up good. Like this, see? You light it right there and—shsss!—throw it. If you have a sling you can throw it farther. My husband can throw from here to six blocks away. For that you put in a longer wick.

(268)

1952: Cochabamba
Cries of Mockery and Grievance

All over the Bolivian countryside times are changing: a vast insurgency against the large estates and against fear. In the Cochabamba valley, the women too hurl their defiance, singing and dancing.

At ceremonies of homage to the Christ of the Holy Cross, Quechua campesinos from the whole valley light candles, drink *chicha*, sing ballads, and cavort to the sound of accordions and charangos, around the Crucified One.

The young girls implore Christ for a husband who won't make them cry, for a mule loaded with corn, a white sheep and a black sheep, a sewing machine, or as many rings as their hands have fingers. Afterward they sing stridently, always in the Indian language, their protest. To Christ, to father, to boyfriend and to husband they promise love and service, at table as well as in bed, but they don't want to be battered beasts of burden anymore.

Singing, they shoot bullets of mockery at the bull's eye of the naked macho, well ravaged by years and insects, who sleeps or pretends to sleep on the cross.

(5)

Shameless Verses Sung by Indian Women of Cochabamba to Jesus Christ

Little Father, to your flock,
"Daughter, daughter," you keep saying.
But how could you have fathered me
When you haven't got a cock?

"Lazy, lazy," you're reproving,
Little Father, Holy Cross,
But limp and lazy—look at you:
Standing up there, never moving.

Little fox with tail all curls,
Beady eyes on women spying,
Little old man with mousey face
And your nose so full of holes.

You won't put up with me unwed,
You condemn me to bear kids,
Dress and feed them while alive,
Bury them proper when they're dead.

Will you send to me a mate
Who would give me blows and kicks?
Why must every budding rose
Suffer the same wilted fate?

(5)

1952: Buenos Aires

The Argentine People Feel Naked Without Her

Long live cancer! wrote some hand on a wall in Buenos Aires. They hated her, they hate her, the well-fed—for being poor, a woman, and presumptuous. She challenged them in talk and offended them in life. Born to be a servant, or at best an actress in cheap melodramas, Evita refused to memorize her part.

They loved her, they love her, the unloved—through her mouth they spoke their minds and their curses. Evita was the blonde fairy who embraced the leprous and ragged and gave peace to the despairing, a bottomless spring that gushed jobs and mattresses, shoes and sewing machines, false teeth and bridal trousseaux. The poor received these charities at a side door, while Evita wore stunning jewelry and mink coats in midsummer. Not that they begrudged her the luxury: They celebrated it. They felt not humiliated but avenged by her queenly attire.

Before the body of Evita, surrounded by white carnations, people file by, weeping. Day after day, night after night, the line of torches: a procession two weeks long.

Bankers, businessmen, and landowners sigh with relief. With Evita dead, President Perón is a knife without a cutting edge.

(311 and 417)

1952: On the High Seas
Wanted: Charlie the Tramp

Charles Chaplin sails for London. On the second day at sea, news reaches the ship that he won't be able to return to the United States. The attorney general applies to his case a law aimed at foreigners suspected of communism, depravity, or insanity.

Some years earlier Chaplin had been interrogated by officials of the FBI and the Immigration and Naturalization Service:

Are you of Jewish origin?

Are you a Communist?

Have you ever committed adultery?

Senator Richard Nixon and the gossip columnist Hedda Hopper agree: *Chaplin is a menace to our institutions.* Outside theaters showing his films, the Legion of Decency and the American Legion picket with signs demanding: *Chaplin, go to Russia.*

The FBI has for nearly thirty years been seeking proof that Chaplin is really a Jew named Israel Thonstein and that he works as a spy for Moscow. Their suspicions were aroused in 1923 when *Pravda* printed the comment: *Chaplin is an actor of undoubted talent.*

(121 and 383)

1952: London

An Admirable Ghost

named Buster Keaton has returned to the screen after long years of oblivion, thanks to Chaplin. *Limelight* opens in London, and in it for a few precious minutes Keaton teams up with Chaplin in an absurd double act that steals the show.

This is the first time Keaton and Chaplin have worked together. They appear gray-haired and wrinkled, though with the same charm as in those moments long ago, when they made silence wittier than words.

Chaplin and Keaton are still the best. They know that there is nothing more serious than laughter, an art demanding infinite work, and that as long as the world revolves, making others laugh is the most splendid of activities.

(382 and 383)

1953: Washington

Newsreel

The United States explodes the first H-bomb at Eniwetok.

President Eisenhower names Charles Wilson secretary of defense. Wilson, an executive of General Motors, has recently declared: *What's good for General Motors is good for America.*

After a long trial, Ethel and Julius Rosenberg are executed in the electric chair. The Rosenbergs, accused of spying for the Russians, deny guilt to the end.

The American city of Moscow exhorts its Russian namesake to change its name. The authorities of this small city in Idaho claim the exclusive right to call themselves Muscovites, and ask that the Soviet capital be rebaptized *to avoid any embarrassing associations.*

Half the citizens of the United States decisively support Senator McCarthy's campaign against the Communist infiltration of democracy, according to opinion polls.

One of the suspects McCarthy plans to interrogate, engineer Raymond Kaplan, commits suicide by throwing himself under a truck.

The scientist Albert Einstein appeals to intellectuals to refuse to testify before the House Un-American Activities Committee and to be prepared for jail or economic ruin. Failing this, believes Einstein, *the intellectuals deserve nothing better than the slavery which is intended for them.*

(45)

1953: Washington
The Witch Hunt

Incorrigible Albert Einstein, according to Senator McCarthy's list, is America's foremost *fellow traveler*. To get on the list, all you need to do is have black friends or oppose sending U.S. troops to Korea; but the case of Einstein is a much weightier one. McCarthy has proof to spare that this ungrateful Jew has a heart that tilts left and pumps red blood.

The hearing room, where the fires of this Inquisition burn, becomes a celebrity circus. Einstein's is not the only famous name that echoes here. For some time the Un-American Activities Committee has had its eye on Hollywood. The Committee demands names, and Hollywood names cause scandal. Those who won't talk lose their jobs and find their careers ruined; or go to jail, like Dashiell Hammett; or lose their passports, like Lillian Hellman and Paul Robeson; or are expelled from the country, like Cedric Belfrage. Ronald Reagan, a minor leading man, brands the reds and pinks who don't deserve to be saved from the furies of Armageddon. Another leading man, Robert Taylor, publicly repents having acted in a film in which Russians smile. Playwright Clifford Odets begs pardon for his ideas and betrays his old comrades. Actor José Ferrer and director Elia Kazan point their fingers at colleagues. To dissociate himself clearly from Communists, Kazan makes a film about the Mexican leader Emiliano Zapata in which Zapata is not the silent campesino who championed agrarian reform, but a charlatan who shoots off bullets and speeches in an unceasing diarrhea.

(41, 219, and 467)

1953: Washington
Portrait of a Witch Hunter

His raw material is collective fear. He rolls up his sleeves and goes to work. Skillful molder of this clay, Joseph McCarthy turns fear into panic and panic into hysteria.

Feverishly he exhorts them to betray. He swears not to shut his mouth as long as his country is infected by the Marxist plague. For him all ambiguity has the ring of cowardice. First he accuses, then he investigates. He sells certainties to the vacillating and lashes out, knee to groin or knife to belly, at anyone who questions the right of private property or opposes war and business as usual.

(395)

1953: Seattle
Robeson

They bar him from traveling to Canada, or anywhere else. When some Canadians invite him to perform, Paul Robeson sings to them by telephone from Seattle, and by telephone he swears that he will stand firm as long as there is breath in his body.

Robeson, grandson of slaves, believes that Africa is a source of pride and not a zoo run by Tarzan. A black with red ideas, friend of the yellows who are resisting the white invasion in Korea, he sings in the name of his insulted people and of all insulted peoples who by singing lift their heads; and he sings with a voice full of thundering heaven and quaking earth.

(381)

1953: Santiago de Cuba
Fidel

At dawn on July 26, a handful of youths attack the Moncada barracks. Armed with dignity and Cuban bravura and a few bird guns, they assault the dictatorship of Fulgencio Batista and half a century of colonization masquerading as a republic.

A few die in battle, but more than seventy are finished off by the army after a week of torture. The torturers tear out the eyes of Abel Santamaría, among others.

The rebel leader, taken prisoner, offers his defense plea. Fidel Castro has the look of a man who gives all of himself without asking anything in return. The judges listen to him in astonishment, missing not a word. His words are not, however, for the ones kissed by the gods; he speaks for the ones pissed on by the devils, and for them, and in their name, he explains what he has done.

Fidel Castro claims the ancient right of rebellion against despotism: *"This island will sink in the ocean before we will consent to be anybody's slaves . . ."*

He tosses his head like a tree, accuses Batista and his officers of exchanging their uniforms for butchers' aprons, and sets forth a program of revolution. In Cuba there could be food and work for all, and more to spare.

"No, that is not inconceivable."

(90, 392, and 422)

1953: Santiago de Cuba
The Accused Turns Prosecutor and Announces: "History Will Absolve Me"

What is inconceivable is that there should be men going to bed hungry while an inch of land remains unsown; what is inconceivable is that there should be children who die without medical care; that thirty percent of our campesinos cannot sign their names and ninety-nine percent don't know the history of Cuba; that most families in our countryside should be living in worse conditions than the Indians Columbus found when he discovered the most beautiful land human eyes had ever seen . . .

From such wretchedness it is only possible to free oneself by death; and in that the state does help them: to die. Ninety percent of rural children are devoured by parasites that enter from the soil through the toenails of their unshod feet.

More than half of the best cultivated production lands are in foreign hands. In Oriente, the largest province, the lands of the United Fruit Company and the West Indian Company extend from the north coast to the south coast . . .

Cuba continues to be a factory producing raw materials. Sugar

*is exported to import candies; leather exported to import shoes; iron
exported to import plows . . .*

(90)

1953: Boston
United Fruit

Throne of bananas, crown of bananas, a banana held like a scepter:
Sam Zemurray, master of the lands and seas of the banana kingdom,
did not believe it possible that his Guatemalan vassals could give him
a headache. *"The Indians are too ignorant for Marxism,"* he used to
say, and was applauded by his court at his royal palace in Boston,
Massachusetts.

Thanks to the successive decrees of Manuel Estrada Cabrera,
who governed surrounded by sycophants and spies, seas of slobber,
forests of familiars; and of Jorge Ubico, who thought he was Napoleon
but wasn't, Guatemala has remained part of United Fruit's vast do-
minion for half a century. In Guatemala United Fruit can seize whatever land it wants—enormous unused tracts—and owns the railroad,
the telephone, the telegraph, the ports, and the ships, not to speak
of soldiers, politicians, and journalists.

Sam Zemurray's troubles began when president Juan Jośe Arévalo forced the company to respect the union and its right to strike.
From bad to worse: A new president, Jacobo Arbenz, introduces
agrarian reform, seizes United Fruit's uncultivated lands, begins
dividing them among a hundred thousand families, and acts as if
Guatemala were ruled by the landless, the letterless, the breadless,
the *less*.

(50 and 288)

1953: Guatemala City
Arbenz

President Truman howled when workers on Guatemala's banana plantations started to behave like people. Now President Eisenhower spits
lightning over the expropriation of United Fruit.

The government of the United States considers it an outrage that
the government of Guatemala should take United Fruit's account

books seriously. Arbenz proposes to pay as indemnity only the value that the company itself had placed on its lands to defraud the tax laws. John Foster Dulles, the secretary of state, demands twenty-five times that.

Jacobo Arbenz, accused of conspiring with Communists, draws his inspiration not from Lenin but from Abraham Lincoln. His agrarian reform, an attempt to modernize Guatemalan capitalism, is less radical than the North American rural laws of almost a century ago.

(81 and 416)

1953: San Salvador
Dictator Wanted

Guatemalan General Miguel Ydígoras Fuentes, distinguished killer of Indians, has lived in exile since the fall of dictator Ubico. Now, Walter Turnbull comes to San Salvador to offer him a deal. Turnbull, representative of both United Fruit and the CIA, proposes that Ydígoras take charge of Guatemala. There is money available for such a project, if he promises to destroy the unions, restore United Fruit's lands and privileges, and repay this loan to the last cent within a reasonable period. Ydígoras asks time to think it over, while making it clear he considers the conditions abusive.

In no time word gets around that a position is vacant. Guatemalan exiles, military and civilian, fly to Washington to offer their services; others knock at the doors of U.S. embassies. José Luis Arenas, "friend" of Vice-President Nixon, offers to overthrow President Arbenz for two hundred thousand dollars. General Federico Ponce says he has a ten-thousand-man army ready to attack the National Palace. His price would be quite modest, although he prefers not to talk figures yet. Just a small advance . . .

Throat cancer rules out United Fruit's preference, Juan Córdova Cerna. On his deathbed, however, Doctor Córdova rasps out the name of his own candidate: Colonel Carlos Castillo Armas, trained at Fort Leavenworth, Kansas, a cheap, obedient burro.

(416 and 471)

1954: Washington

The Deciding Machine, Piece by Piece

Dwight Eisenhower President of the United States. Overthrew the government of Mohammed Mossadegh in Iran because it nationalized oil. Has now given orders to overthrow the government of Jacobo Arbénz in Guatemala.

Sam Zemurray Principal stockholder in United Fruit. All his concerns automatically turn into U.S. government declarations, and ultimately into rifles, mortars, machineguns, and CIA airplanes.

John Foster Dulles U.S. Secretary of State. Former lawyer for United Fruit.

Allen Dulles Director of the CIA. Brother of John Foster Dulles. Like him, has done legal work for United Fruit. Together they organize "Operation Guatemala."

John Moors Cabot Secretary of State for Inter-American Affairs. Brother of Thomas Cabot, the president of United Fruit.

Walter Bedell Smith Under Secretary of State. Serves as liaison in Operation Guatemala. Future member of the board of United Fruit.

Henry Cabot Lodge Senator, U.S. representative to the United Nations. United Fruit shareholder. Has on various occasions received money from this company for speeches in the Senate.

Anne Whitman Personal secretary to President Eisenhower. Married to United Fruit public relations chief.

Spruille Braden Former U.S. ambassador to several Latin American countries. Has received a salary from United Fruit since 1948. Is widely reported in the press to have exhorted Eisenhower *to suppress communism by force in Guatemala*.

Robert Hill U.S. ambassador to Costa Rica. Collaborates on "Operation Guatemala." Future board member of United Fruit.

John Peurifoy U.S. ambassador to Guatemala. Known as *the butcher of Greece* for his past diplomatic service in Athens. Speaks no Spanish. Political background: the U.S. Senate, Washington, D.C., where he once worked as an elevator operator.

(416, 420, and 465)

1954: Boston

The Lie Machine, Piece by Piece

The Motor   The executioner becomes the victim; the victim, the executioner. Those who prepare the invasion of Guatemala from Honduras attribute to Guatemala the intention to invade Honduras and all Central America. *The tentacles of the Kremlin are plain to see*, says John Moors Cabot from the White House. Ambassador Peurifoy warns in Guatemala: *We cannot permit a Soviet republic to be established from Texas to the Panama Canal.* Behind this scandal lies a cargo of arms shipped from Czechoslovakia. The United States has forbidden the sale of arms to Guatemala.

Gear I   News and articles, declarations, pamphlets, photographs, films, and comic strips about Communist atrocities in Guatemala bombard the public. This educational material, whose origin is undisclosed, comes from the offices of United Fruit in Boston and from government offices in Washington.

Gear II   The Archbishop of Guatemala, Mariano Rossell Arellano, exhorts the populace to rise *against communism, enemy of God and the Fatherland.* Thirty CIA planes rain down his pastoral message over the whole country. The archbishop has the image of the popular Christ of Esquipulas, which will be named Captain General of the Liberating Brigade, brought to the capital.

Gear III   At the Pan-American Conference, John Foster Dulles pounds the table with his fist and gets the blessing of the Organization of American States for the projected invasion. At the United Nations, Henry Cabot Lodge blocks Jacobo Arbenz's demands for help. U.S. diplomacy is mobilized throughout the world. The complicity of England and France is obtained in exchange for a U.S. commitment to silence over the delicate matters of the Suez Canal, Cyprus, and Indochina.

Gear IV   The dictators of Nicaragua, Honduras, Venezuela, and the Dominican Republic not only lend training camps, radio transmitters, and airports to "Operation Guatemala," they also make a contribution to the propaganda campaign. Somoza I calls together the international press in Managua and displays some pistols with hammers and sickles stamped on them. They are, he says, from a Russian submarine intercepted en route to Guatemala.

(416, 420, and 447)

The Reconquest of Guatemala

Guatemala has neither planes nor antiaircraft installations, so U.S. pilots in U.S. planes bomb the country with the greatest of ease.

A powerful CIA transmitter, installed on the roof of the U.S. embassy, spreads confusion and panic: the Lie Machine informs the world that this is the rebel radio, the Voice of Liberation, transmitting the triumphal march of Colonel Castillo Armas from the jungles of Guatemala. Meanwhile, Castillo Armas, encamped on a United Fruit plantation in Honduras, awaits orders from the Deciding Machine.

Arbenz's government, paralyzed, attends the ceremony of its own collapse. The aerial bombings reach the capital and blow up the fuel deposits. The government confines itself to burying the dead. The mercenary army, *God, Fatherland, Liberty*, crosses the border. It meets no resistance. Is it money or fear that explains how Guatemala's military chiefs could surrender their troops without firing a shot? An Argentine doctor in his early twenties, Ernesto Guevara, tries in vain to organize popular defense of the capital: he doesn't know how or with what. Improvised militias wander the streets unarmed. When Arbenz finally orders the arsenals opened, army officers refuse to obey. On one of these dark ignoble days, Guevara has an attack of asthma and indignation; on another, one midnight after two weeks of bombings, President Arbenz slowly descends the steps of the National Palace, crosses the street, and seeks asylum in the Mexican embassy.

(81, 416, 420, and 447)

1954: Mazatenango
Miguel at Forty-Nine

As soon as the birds started singing, before first light, they sharpened their machetes, and now they reach Mazatenango at a gallop, in search of Miguel. The executioners are making crosses on a long list of those marked to die, while the army of Castillo Armas takes over Guatemala. Miguel is number five on the most-wanted list, condemned for being a red and a foreign troublemaker. Since his arrival on the run from El Salvador, he has not stopped for an instant his work of labor agitation.

They sic dogs on him. They aim to parade his body hanging from a horse along the roads, his throat slit by a machete. But Miguel, one very experienced and knowing animal, loses himself in the scrub.

And so occurs the tenth birth of Miguel Mármol, at forty-nine years of age.

(222)

1954: Guatemala City
Newsreel

The archbishop of Guatemala declares: *"I admire the sincere and ardent patriotism of President Castillo Armas."* Amid a formidable display of gibberish, Castillo Armas receives the blessing of the papal nuncio, Monsignor Genaro Verrolino.

President Eisenhower congratulates the CIA chiefs at the White House: *"Thanks to all of you. You've averted a Soviet beachhead in our hemisphere."*

The head of the CIA, Allen Dulles, assigns to a *Time* journalist the job of framing Guatemala's new constitution.

Time publishes a poem by the wife of the U.S. ambassador to Guatemala. The poem says that Mr. and Mrs. Peurifoy are *optimistic* because Guatemala is no longer *communistic*.

At his first meeting with the ambassador after the victory, President Castillo Armas expresses his concern at the insufficiency of local jails and the lack of necessary cells for all the Communists. According to lists sent from Washington by the State Department, Guatemala's Communists total seventy-two thousand.

The embassy throws a party. Four hundred Guatemalan guests sing in unison "The Star-Spangled Banner."

(416 and 420)

1954: Rio de Janeiro
Getulio

He wants to erase the memory of his own dictatorship, those bad old police-state days, and so in his final years governs Brazil as no one ever has before.

He takes the side of the wage earner. Immediately the profit-makers declare war.

To stop Brazil from being a colander, he corks up the hemorrhage of wealth. Immediately foreign capital takes to economic sabotage.

He recovers for Brazil its own oil and energy, which are as national a patrimony as anthem and flag. The offended monopolies immediately respond with a fierce counteroffensive.

He defends the price of coffee instead of burning half the crop, as was customary. The United States immediately cuts its purchases in half.

In Brazil, journalists and politicians of all colors and areas join the scandalized chorus.

Getulio Vargas has governed with dignity. When he is forced to bow down, he chooses the dignity of death. He raises the revolver, aims at his own heart, and fires.

(427, 429, and 432)

1955: Medellín
Nostalgia

It is almost twenty years since Carlos Gardel burned to death, and the Colombian city of Medellín, where the tragedy occurred, has become a place of pilgrimage and the focus of a cult.

The devotees of Gardel are known by their tilted hats, striped pants, and swaying walk. They slick down their hair, look out of the corners of their eyes, and have twisted smiles. They bow and sweep, as if in a constant dance, when shaking hands, lighting a cigarette, or chalking a billiard cue. They spend the night leaning against some suburban lamp-post, whistling or humming tangos which explain that all women are whores except mother, that sainted old lady whom God has taken to his glory.

Some local devotees, and certain visiting cultists from Buenos

Aires, sell relics of the idol. One offers genuine Gardel teeth, acquired
on the spot when the plane blew up. He has sold more than thirteen
hundred at an average of twelve dollars apiece. It was some years
ago that he found his first buyer, a tourist from New York, a member
of the Gardel Fan Club. On seeing the souvenir, how could the
customer help but burst into tears?

(184)

1955: Asunción
Withdrawal Symptoms

When he commits the unforgivable sin of promulgating a divorce law,
the Church makes the missing sign of the cross over him, and the
military begin to conspire, in full daylight, to overthrow him.

The news is celebrated in drawing rooms and mourned in kitch-
ens; Perón has fallen. Offering no resistance, he leaves Argentina,
for Paraguay and exile.

In Asunción, his days are sad. He feels beaten, old, alone. He
claims that by his act of renunciation a million deaths have been
avoided. But he also says that the people didn't know how to defend
what he gave them, that the ingrates deserve whatever misfortunes
befall them, that they think with their bellies, not with their heads
or hearts.

One morning Perón is confiding his bitterness to his host, Ricardo
Gayol, when suddenly he half-closes his eyes and whispers: *"My smile
used to drive them crazy. My smile . . ."*

He raises his arms and smiles as if he were on the palace balcony,
greeting a plaza filled with cheering people. *"Would you like my
smile?"*

His host looks at him, stupefied.

"Take it, it's yours," says Perón. He takes it out of his mouth
and puts it in his host's hand—his false teeth.

(327)

1955: Guatemala City

One Year after the Reconquest of Guatemala,

Richard Nixon visits this occupied land. The union of United Fruit workers and five hundred and thirty-two other unions have been banned by the new government. The new penal code punishes with death anyone who calls a strike. Political parties are outlawed. The books of Dostoyevsky and other Soviet writers have been thrown onto the bonfire.

The banana kingdom has been saved from agrarian reform. The vice-president of the United States congratulates President Castillo Armas. For the first time in history, says Nixon, a Communist government has been replaced by a free one.

(416 and 420)

1956: Buenos Aires

The Government Decides That Peronism Doesn't Exist

While shooting workers on garbage dumps, the Argentine military decrees the nonexistence of Perón, Evita, and Peronism. It is forbidden to mention their names or their deeds. Possessing images of them is a crime. The presidential residence is demolished to the last stone, as though the disease were contagious.

But what about the embalmed body of Evita? She is the most dangerous symbol of the arrogance of the rabble who have sauntered the corridors of power as if in their own homes. The generals dump the body in a box labeled "Radio Equipment" and send it into exile. Just where is a secret. To Europe, rumor has it, or maybe to an island in mid-ocean. Evita becomes a wandering body traveling secretly through remote cemeteries, expelled from the country by generals who don't know—or don't want to know—that she lies within the people.

(311 and 327)

1956: León

Son of Somoza

Santa Marta, Santa Marta has a train, sing the musicmakers, dance the dancers, *Santa Marta has a train but has no tram*; and in the middle of the song and the fiesta, Rigoberto López Pérez, poet, owner of nothing, fells the owner of everything with four bullets.

A North American plane carries off the dying Anastasio Somoza to a North American hospital in the North American Panama Canal Zone, and he dies in a North American bed. They bury him in Nicaragua, with the honors of a prince of the Church.

Somoza I held power for twenty years. Every six years he lifted his state of siege for one day and held the elections that kept him on the throne. Luis, eldest son and heir, is now the richest and most powerful man in Central America. From Washington, President Eisenhower congratulates him.

Luis Somoza bows before the statue of his father, the bronze hero who gallops motionlessly in the very center of Managua. In the shadow of the horse's hoofs he seeks advice from the founder of the dynasty, guide to good government, proliferator of jails and businesses, then covers the monumental tomb with flowers.

Evading the vigilance of an honor guard, the hand of somebody, anybody, everybody, has hurriedly scrawled this epitaph on the marble tomb: *Here lies Somoza, a bit rottener than in life.*

(10, 102, and 460)

1956: Santo Domingo

In the Year Twenty-Six of the Trujillo Era

his likeness is sold in the markets, among the little engravings of the Virgin Mary, Saint George, and other miracle workers.

"Saints, cheap saints!"

Nothing Dominican is beyond his grasp. All belongs to him: the first night of the virgins, the last wish of the dying, the people and the cows, the air fleet and the chain of brothels, the sugar and wheat mills, the beer factory and the virility-potion bottling plant.

For twenty-six years Trujillo has occupied God's vice-presidency.

Every four years, this formula has been blessed by democratic elections: *God and Trujillo,* proclaim all walls.

In her work *Moral Meditations,* which earns her the title of First Lady of Caribbean Letters, Doña María de Trujillo compares her husband to El Cid and Napoleon Bonaparte. Plump Doña María, who practices usury during the week and mysticism on Sundays, has in turn been compared with Saint Teresa de Jesus by local critics.

With El Cid's sword or Napoleon's hat, Trujillo poses for statues. Statues multiply him in bronze and marble, with a chin he doesn't have and without the double chin he does. Thousands of statues: From high on their pedestals, Trujillo straddles the most remote corner of every city or village, watching. In this country not a fly shits without his permission.

(63 and 101)

1956: Havana

Newsreel

The Cuban army has thwarted an armed expedition from Mexico, surrounding the invaders, machinegunning and bombing them at a place called Alegría de Pío in Oriente province. Among the many dead are Fidel Castro, leader of the gang, and an Argentine Communist agitator, Ernesto Guevara.

After enjoying a long stay in the city of New York, Dr. Ernesto Sarrá and his very attractive and elegant wife, Loló, figures of the highest rank in this capital's social circles, have returned to Havana.

Also arriving from New York is Bing Crosby, the popular singer who, without removing his topcoat or beaver hat, declared at the airport: *"I have come to Cuba to play golf."*

A young Havanan, on the point of winning the grand prize in the "TV School Contest," fails to answer the next to last question. The final question, which remained unasked, was: *What is the name of the river that crosses Paris?*

An exceptional lineup will run tomorrow at the Marianao Racecourse.

(98)

1956: At the Foot of the Sierra Maestra

Twelve Lunatics

They go a week without sleep, huddled together like sardines in a can, vomiting, while the north wind toys playfully with the little boat *Granma*. After much seesawing in the Gulf of Mexico, they disembark in the wrong place, and a few steps ashore are swept by machinegun fire or burned alive by incendiary bombs, a slaughter in which almost all of them fall. The survivors consult the sky for directions but get the stars mixed up. The swamps swallow their backpacks and their arms. They have no food except sugarcane, and they leave its betraying refuse strewn along the trail. They lose their condensed milk by carrying the cans holes down. In a careless moment they mix their little remaining fresh water with sea water. They get lost and search aimlessly for one another. Finally, one small group discovers another small group on these slopes, by chance, and so the twelve saved from annihilation join together.

These men, or shadows of men, have a total of seven rifles, a little damp ammunition, and uncounted sores and wounds. Since the invasion began there is hardly a mistake they haven't made. But on this starless night they breathe fresher, cleaner air, and Fidel says, standing before the foothills of the Sierra Maestra: *"We've already won the war. Batista is fucked!"*

(98 and 209)

1957: Benidorm

Marked Cards

Between liberals and conservatives, a conjugal agreement. On a beach in the Mediterranean, Colombia's politicians sign the compromise that puts an end to ten years of mutual extermination. The two main parties offer each other an amnesty. From now on, they will alternate the presidency and divvy up the other jobs. Colombians will be able to vote, but not elect. Liberals and conservatives are to take turns in power, to guarantee the property and inheritance rights over the country that their families have brought or received as gifts.

In this pact among the wealthy there is no good news for the poor.

(8, 217, and 408)

1957: Majagual
Colombia's Sainted Egg

Burning towns and killing Indians, leveling forests and erecting wire fences, the masters of the land have pushed the campesinos right up against the river banks in this coastal region of Colombia. Many campesinos have nonetheless refused to serve as slaves on the haciendas and have instead become fishermen—artists at gritting their teeth and living on what they can find. Eating so much turtle, they learn from him: The turtle never lets go what he catches in his mouth and knows how to bury himself on the beaches in the dry season when the seagulls threaten. With that and God's help they get by.

Few monks remain in these hot regions. Here on the coast no one takes the Mass seriously. Whoever isn't paralyzed runs from marriage and work, and, the better to enjoy the seven deadly sins, indulges in endless siestas in endless hammocks. Here God is a good fellow, not a grouchy, carping police chief.

The boring Christ of Jegua is dead—a broken doll that neither sweats nor bleeds nor performs miracles. No one has even wiped the bat shit off him since the priest fled with all the silver. But very much alive, sweating and bleeding and miracle-working, is Our Little Black Lord, the dark Christ of San Benito Abad, giving counsel to anyone who will stroke him affectionately. Alive, too, and wagging their tails, are the frisky saints who appear on the Colombian coast at the drop of a hat and stick around.

One stormy night, some fishermen discover God's face, agleam in lightning flashes, on a stone the shape of an egg. Since then they celebrate the miracles of Saint Egg, dancing the *cumbia* and drinking to his health.

The parish priest of Majagual announces that he will go up river at the head of a battalion of crusaders, throw the sacrilegious stone to the bottom of the waters, and set fire to their little palm-frond chapel.

In the tiny chapel, where Masses are celebrated with lively music, the fishermen stand guard around Saint Egg. Ax in hand, day and night.

(159)

1957: Sucre
Saint Lucío

While the Majagual priest declares war on Saint Egg, the priest of Sucre expels Saint Lucía from his church, because a female saint with a penis is unheard of.

At first it looked like a cyst, or a bump on the neck; but it kept moving lower and lower, and growing, bulging beneath the sacred tunic that shortened every day. Everyone pretended not to notice, until one day a child suddenly blurted out: *"Saint Lucía has a dick!"*

Exiled, Saint Lucío finds refuge in a hut not far from the little temple of Saint Egg. In time, the fishermen put up an altar to him, because Saint Lucío is a fun-loving, trustworthy guy who joins the binges of his devotees, listens to their secrets, and is happy when summer comes and the fish begin to rise.

This he, who used to be she, doesn't figure among the saints listed in the Bristol Almanac, nor has Saint Egg been canonized by the Pope of Rome. Neither has Saint Board, unhinged from the box of soap in which a laundrywoman found the Virgin Mary; or Saint Kidney, the humble kidney of a cow in which a slaughterer saw Christ's crown of thorns. Nor Saint Domingo Vidal . . .

(159)

1957: The Sinú River Banks
Saint Domingo Vidal

He had been a dwarf and a paralytic. The people had named him a saint, Saint Domingo Vidal, because with his prophetic hunches he had known just where on this Colombian coast a lost horse had strayed, and which cock would win the next fight, and because he had asked nothing for teaching the poor how to read and defend themselves from locusts and omnivorous landlords.

Son of Lucifer, the Church called him. A priest hauled him out of his grave inside the chapel of Chimá and broke his bones with an ax and hammer. His shattered remains ended up in a corner of the plaza, and another priest wanted to throw them in the garbage. The first priest died a writhing death, his hands turning into claws; the other suffocated, wallowing in his own excrement.

Like Saint Egg, Saint Lucío, and many of their local colleagues, Saint Domingo Vidal remains happily alive in the fervor of all those hereabouts who love—either in or out of wedlock—and in the noisy throng of people who share the grim battle for land and the joys of its fruits.

Saint Domingo Vidal protects the ancient custom of the Sinú River villagers, who visit each other bearing gifts of food. The people of one village bear litters to another loaded with flowers and delicacies from the river and its banks: dorado or shad stews, slices of catfish, iguana eggs, riced coconut, cheese, sweet *mongomongo*; and while the recipients eat, the donors sing and dance around them.

(160)

1957: Pino del Agua
Crucito

Batista offers three hundred pesos and a cow with calf to anyone who brings him Fidel Castro, alive or dead.

On the other side of the crests of the Sierra Maestra, the guerrillas sweat and multiply. They quickly learn the rules of war in the brush: to mistrust, to move by night, never to sleep twice in the same place, and above all, to make friends with the local people.

When the twelve bedraggled survivors arrived in this sierra, they knew not a single campesino, and the River Yara only through the song that mentions it. A few months later there are a few campesinos in the rebel ranks, the kind of men who cut cane for a while at harvest time and then are left to starve in unknown territory; and now the guerrillas know these areas as if they had been born in them. They know the names of the places, and when they don't, they baptize them after their own fashion. They have given the Arroyo of Death its name because there a guerrilla deserted who had sworn to fight to the death.

Others die fighting, without having sworn anything.

While smoking his pipe during the rest periods, José de la Cruz— "Crucito"—sierra troubadour, composes in ten-verse *guajira* stanzas the entire history of the Cuban revolution. For lack of paper he commits it to memory, but has it taken from him by a bullet, on the heights of Pino del Agua during an ambush of army trucks.

(209)

1957: El Uvero
Almeida

Juan Almeida claims he has a joy inside him that keeps tickling, making him laugh and jump. A very stubborn joy if one considers that Almeida was born poor and black on this island of private beaches which are closed to the poor because they are poor and to blacks because they stain the water; and that, to make matters worse, he decided to be a bricklayer's helper and a poet; and that, as if those were not complications enough, he rolled his life into this crap game of the Cuban revolution, and as one of the Moncada assailants was sentenced to jail and exile, and was navigator of the *Granma* before becoming the guerrilla that he is now; and that he has just stopped two bullets—not mortal, but motherfuckers—one in the left leg and one in the shoulder, during the three-hour attack on the Uvero barracks, down by the shore.

(209)

1957: Santiago de Cuba
Portrait of an Imperial Ambassador

Earl Smith, ambassador of the United States, receives the keys to the city of Santiago de Cuba. As the ceremony proceeds and the speeches pour forth, a commotion is heard through the curtains. Discreetly, the ambassador peers out the window and observes a number of women approaching, clad in black, chanting the national anthem and shouting *"Liberty!"* The police club them down.

The next day, the ambassador visits the U.S. military base at Guantánamo. Then he tours the iron and nickel mines of the Freeport Sulphur Company, which, thanks to his efforts, have just been exempted from taxes.

The ambassador publicly expresses his disgust with the police beatings, although he recognizes that the government has a right to defend itself from Communist aggression. Advisers have explained to the ambassador that Fidel has been abnormal since childhood, from having fallen off a moving motorcycle.

The ambassador, who was a champion boxer in his student days, believes General Batista must be defended at any cost. With Batista in power, tourists can pick from photos handed them on the airplane their pretty mulatta for the weekend. Havana is a North American city, full of one-armed bandits from Nevada and mafia bosses from Chicago, and with plenty of telephones to order a nice hot supper to be brought on the next flight out of Miami.

(431)

1957: El Hombrito
Che

In the Hombrito Valley, the rebels have installed an oven for baking bread, a printshop consisting of an old mimeograph machine, and a clinic that functions in a one-room hut. The doctor is Ernesto Guevara, known as Che, who apart from his nickname has retained certain Argentine customs, like maté and irony. American pilgrim, he joined Fidel's forces in Mexico, where he settled after the fall of Guatemala to earn a living as a photographer at one peso per photo, and as a peddler of little engravings of the Virgin of Guadalupe.

In the Hombrito clinic, Che attends a series of children with bloated bellies, almost dwarfs, and aged girls worn out from too many births and too little food, and men as dry and empty as gourds, because poverty turns everyone into a living mummy.

Last year, when machineguns mowed down the newly landed guerrillas, Che had to choose between a case of bullets and a case of medicines. He couldn't carry both and decided on the bullets. Now he strokes his old Thompson rifle, the only surgical instrument he really believes in.

(209)

Old Chana, Campesina of the
Sierra Maestra, Remembers:

Poor dear Che! I always saw him with that curse of his asthma and said, "Ay, Holy Virgin!" With the asthma he would get all quiet, breathing low. Some folks with asthma get hysterical, cough and open their eyes and open their mouth. But Che tried to soften up the asthma. He would throw himself in a corner to rest the asthma.

He didn't like sympathy. If you said, "Poor guy," he gave you a quick look that didn't mean anything, and meant a lot.

I used to warm him up a bit of water to rub on his chest for relief. He, the big flatterer, would say, "Oh, my girlfriend." But he was such a rascal.

(338)

1958: Stockholm
Pelé

Brazilian football glows. It dances and makes one dance. At the World Cup in Sweden, Pelé and Garrincha are the heroes, proving wrong those who say blacks can't play in a cold climate.

Pelé, thin as a rake, almost a boy, puffs out his chest and raises his chin to make an impression. He plays football as God would play it, if God decided to devote himself seriously to the game. Pelé makes a date with the ball anywhere, any time, and she never stands him up. He sends her high in the air. She makes a full curve and returns to his foot, obedient, grateful, or perhaps tied by an invisible elastic band. Pelé lifts her up, puffs out his chest, and she rolls smoothly down his body. Without letting her touch the ground he flips her to the other foot as he flings himself, running like a hare, toward the goal. No one can catch him, with lasso or bullet, until he leaves the ball, shining, white, tight against the back of the net.

On and off the field, he takes care of himself. He never wastes a minute of his time, nor lets a penny fall from his pocket. Until recently he was shining shoes down at the docks. Pelé was born to rise; and he knows it.

(279)

1958: Stockholm

Garrincha

Garrincha plays havoc with the other teams, always threatening to break through. Half turn, full turn, he looks like he's coming, but he's going! He acts like he's going, but he's coming. Flabbergasted opponents fall on their asses as if Garrincha were scattering banana peels along the field. At the goal line, when he has eluded them all, including the goalie, he sits on the ball. Then he backs up and starts again. The fans are amused, but the managers go crazy. Garrincha, carefree bird with bandy legs, plays for laughs, not to win, and forgets the results. He still thinks soccer's a party, not a job or a business. He likes to play for nothing, or a few beers, on beaches or ragged little fields.

He has many children, his own and other people's. He drinks and eats as if for the last time. Openhanded, he gives everything away, loses the works. Garrincha was born to fall; and he doesn't know it.

(22)

1958: Sierra Maestra

The Revolution Is an Unstoppable Centipede

As the war reaches its height, beneath the bullets Fidel introduces agrarian reform in the Sierra Maestra. Campesinos get their first land, not to speak of their first doctor, their first teacher, even their first judge—which is said to be a less dangerous way to settle a dispute than the machete.

Batista's more than ten thousand soldiers can't seem to do anything but lose. The rebel army is infinitely smaller and still poorly armed, but under it, above it, within it, ahead of and behind it, are the people.

The future is now. Fidel launches a final offensive: Cuba from end to end. In two columns, one under the command of Che Guevara, the other under Camilo Cienfuegos, a hundred and sixty guerrillas descend from the mountains to conquer the plain.

(98 and 209)

1958: Yaguajay

Camilo

Magically eluding bombardment and ambush, the invading columns strike for the island's gut, slicing Cuba in two as Camilo Cienfuegos takes the Yaguajay barracks after eleven days of fighting and Che enters the city of Santa Clara. Suddenly, half of Batista's island has disappeared.

Camilo Cienfuegos, brave and greedy, fights at such close quarters that, killing an enemy soldier, he catches his rifle in mid-air without its touching the ground. Several times the fatal bullet that should have been his just barely wasn't, and once he nearly died from gobbling down a whole kid after two days of eating nothing at all.

Camilo has the beard and mane of a biblical prophet, but where a worry-creased face should be, there's only an ear-to-ear grin. The feat he is most proud of is that time up in the mountains when he fooled a light military plane by painting himself red with iodine and lying still with his arms crossed.

(179 and 210)

1959: Havana

Cuba Wakes Up Without Batista

on the first day of the year. The dictator lands in Santo Domingo and seeks refuge with his colleague Trujillo; back in Havana, for the former hangmen, it's *sauve qui peut*, a stampede.

U.S. Ambassador Earl Smith is appalled. The streets have been taken over by rabble and by a few dirty, hairy, barefoot guerrillas, just a Latin Dillinger gang who dance the *guaguancó*, marking time with rifle shots.

(98 and 431)

The Rumba

The *guaguancó* is a kind of rumba, and every self-respecting Cuban has the rumba under his belt, in peace, war, and anything between. Even when picking a fight, the Cuban rumbas, so now he joins the dance of the bullets without a second thought, and the crowds surge behind the drums that summon them.

"I'm enjoying it. And if they get me, too bad. At least I'm enjoying it."

On any street or field the music lets loose. There's no stopping it—that rumba rhythm on drums and crates, or, if there are no drums or crates, on bodies, or just in the air. Even ears dance.

(86, 198, and 324)

1959: Havana

Portrait of a Caribbean Casanova

Porfirio Rubirosa, the Dominican ambassador, looks with dread on this horrifying spectacle. He has nothing for breakfast but a cup of coffee. The news has taken away his appetite. While servants by the dozen nail down boxes and close trunks and suitcases, Rubirosa nervously lights a cigarette and puts his favorite song, "Taste of Me," on the phonograph.

The sun, they say, never sets on his bed. Trujillo's man in Cuba is a famous enchanter of princesses, heiresses, and movie stars. Rubirosa beguiles them with flattery and plays the ukulele to them before loving or beating them.

Some say his tremendous energy derives from the milk of his infancy, which came from sirens' tits. Dominican patriots insist that his secret is a virility elixir Trujillo concocts from the *pega-palo* plant and exports to the United States.

Rubirosa's career began when Trujillo made him his son-in-law; continued when, as Dominican ambassador to Paris, he sold visas to Jews persecuted by Hitler; and was perfected in his marriages to multi-millionairesses Doris Duke and Barbara Hutton. It is the smell of money that excites the tropical Casanova, as the smell of blood excites sharks.

(100)

1959: Havana

"We have only won the right to begin,"

says Fidel, who rides into town on top of a tank, direct from the Sierra Maestra. To a surging crowd he explains that all this, while it might look like a conclusion, is no more than a beginning.

Half of Cuba's land is uncultivated. According to the statistics, last year was the most prosperous in the island's history; but the campesinos, who can't read statistics or anything else, haven't noticed. From now on, a different cock will crow, with agrarian reform and a literacy campaign, as in the sierra, the most urgent tasks. But before that, the dismantling of an army of butchers. The worst torturers go up against a wall. The aptly named "Bonebreaker" faints each time the firing squad takes aim. They have to bind him to a post.

(91)

1960: Brasília

A City, or Delirium in the Midst of Nothing

Brazil lifts the curtain on its new capital. Suddenly, Brasília is born at the center of a cross traced on the red dust of the desert, very far from the coast, very far from everything, out at the end of the world— or perhaps its beginning.

The city has been built at a dizzying speed. For three years this was an anthill where workers and technicians labored shoulder to shoulder, night and day, sharing jobs, food, and shelter. But when Brasília is finished, the fleeting illusion of brotherhood is finished, too. Doors slam: This city is not for servants. Brasília locks out those who raised it with their own hands. Their place is piled together in shacks that blossom by God's grace on the outskirts of town.

This is the government's city, house of power. No people in its plazas, no paths to walk on. Brasília is on the moon: white, luminous, floating way up, high above Brazil, shielded from its dirt and its follies.

Oscar Niemeyer, architect of its palaces, did not dream of it that way. When the great inaugural fiesta occurs, Niemeyer does not appear on the podium.

(69 and 315)

1960: Rio de Janeiro
Niemeyer

He hates right angles and capitalism. Against capitalism there's not much he can do; but against the right angle, that oppressor, constrictor of space, his architecture triumphs. It's free and sensual and light as clouds.

Niemeyer imagines human habitations in the form of a woman's body, a sinuous shoreline, or a tropical fruit. Also in the form of a mountain, if the mountain breaks up into beautiful curves against the sky, as do the mountains of Rio de Janeiro, designed by God on that day when God thought he was Niemeyer.

(315)

1960: Rio de Janeiro
Guimaraes Rosa

Daring and undulating, too, is the language of Guimaraes Rosa, who builds houses with words.

Works warm with passion are created by this formal gentleman, metronomically punctual, incapable of crossing a street against the light. Tragedy blows ferociously through the stories and novels of the smiling career diplomat. When he writes he violates all literary rules, this bourgeois conservative who dreams of entering the Academy.

1960: Artemisa
Thousands and Thousands of Machetes

wave in the air, brushing, rubbing, colliding, clashing, providing a background of battle-music for Fidel's speech—or, rather, for the song he is singing from the platform. Here, on the eastern end of the island, he explains to sugar workers why his government has expropriated Texaco Oil.

Cuba reacts to each successive blow with neither trepidation nor deference. The State Department refuses to accept the agrarian reform: Cuba divides the U.S.-owned estates among campesinos. Eisenhower sends planes to set fire to canefields and threatens not to

buy Cuban sugar: Cuba breaks the commercial monopoly and ex-
changes sugar for oil with the Soviet Union. U.S. oil companies refuse
to refine Soviet oil: Cuba nationalizes them.

Every discourse is a course. For hours and hours Fidel reasons
and asks, teaches and learns, defends and accuses, while Cuba gropes
forward, each step a search for the way.

(91)

1961: Santo Domingo

In the Year Thirty-One of the Trujillo Era

The paperweight on his desk, lying amid gilt cupids and dancing girls,
is a porcelain baseball glove. Surrounded by busts of Trujillo and
photos of Trujillo, Trujillo scans the latest lists of conspirators sub-
mitted by his spies. With a disdainful flick of the wrist he crosses out
names, men and women who will not wake up tomorrow, while his
torturers wrench new names from prisoners who scream in the Ozama
fortress.

The lists give Trujillo cause for sad reflection. Leading the
conspirators arrayed against him are the U.S. ambassador and the
archbishop primate of the Indies, who only yesterday shared his government. Now Empire and Church are repudiating their faithful son,
who has become unpresentable in the eyes of the world, and whose
prodigal hand they now reject. Such ingratitude from the authors of
capitalist development in the Dominican Republic hurts him deeply.
Nevertheless, among all the decorations that hang from his breast,
his belly, and the walls, Trujillo still loves best the Grand Cross
of the Order of Saint Gregory, which he received from the Vatican,
and the little medal which, many years ago, recognized his services
to the U.S. Marines.

Until death he will be the Sentinel of the West, despite all the
grief, this man who has dubbed himself Benefactor of the Fatherland,
Savior of the Fatherland, Father of the Fatherland, Restorer of Financial Independence, Champion of World Peace, Protector of Culture, First Anticommunist of the Americas, Outstanding and Most
Illustrious Generalísimo.

(60, 63, and 101)

1961: Santo Domingo

The Defunctísimo

leaves as his bequest an entire country—in addition to nine thousand six hundred neckties, two thousand suits, three hundred and fifty uniforms, and six hundred pairs of shoes in his closets in Santo Domingo, and five hundred and thirty million dollars in his private Swiss bank accounts.

Rafael Leónidas Trujillo has fallen in an ambush, bullets tattooing his car. His son, Ramfis, flies in from Paris to take charge of the legacy, the burial, and vengeance.

Colleague and buddy of Porfirio Rubirosa, Ramfis Trujillo has acquired a certain notoriety since a recent cultural mission to Hollywood. There, he presented Mercedes Benzes and chinchilla coats to Kim Novak and Zsa Zsa Gabor in the name of the hungry but generous Dominican people.

(60, 63, and 101)

1961: Bay of Pigs

Against the Wind,

against death, moving ahead, never back, the Cuban revolution remains scandalously alive no more than eight minutes' flying time from Miami.

To put an end to this effrontery, the CIA organizes an invasion to be launched from the United States, Guatemala, and Nicaragua. Somoza II sees the expeditionary force off at the pier. In the Cuban Liberation Army, machine-tooled, oiled, and greased by the CIA, soldiers and policemen from the Batista dictatorship cohabit with displaced inheritors of sugar plantations, banks, newspapers, gambling casinos, brothels, and political parties.

"Bring me back some hairs from Castro's beard!" Somoza instructs them.

U.S. planes, camouflaged and decorated with the star of the Cuban Air Force, enter Cuban skies. These planes, flying low, strafe the people who greet them, then bomb the cities. After this softening-up operation, the invaders land haplessly in the swamps of the Bay of Pigs.

Meanwhile, President Kennedy golfs in Virginia. He has issued the invasion order, but it was Eisenhower who had set the plan in motion, Eisenhower who gave it the green light at the same desk where he approved the invasion of Guatemala. Allen Dulles, head of the CIA, assured him it would be as simple to do away with Fidel as it was with Arbenz. A matter of a couple of weeks, give or take a day or two; even the same CIA team to take charge of it. Same men, same bases. The landing of the liberators would unleash popular insurrection on this island under the boot of red tyranny. U.S. intelligence operatives report exactly that. The people of Cuba, fed up with forming queues, await the signal to rise.

(415 and 469)

1961: Playa Girón

The Second U.S. Military Defeat
in Latin America

It takes Cuba only three days to finish off the invaders. Among the dead are four U.S. pilots. The seven ships of the invasion fleet, escorted by the United States Navy, flee or sink in the Bay of Pigs.

President Kennedy assumes full responsibility for this CIA fiasco.

The Agency believed, as always, in the reports of its local spies, whom it paid to say what it was desperate to hear; and, as always, it confused geography with a military map unrelated to people or to history. The marshes the CIA chose for the landing had been the most miserable spot in all Cuba, a kingdom of crocodiles and mosquitos—that is, until the revolution. Then human enthusiasm had transformed these quagmires, peppering them with schools, hospitals, and roads.

The people here are the first to face the bullets of the invaders who have come to save them.

(88, 435, and 469)

1961: Havana

Portrait of the Past

The invaders—hangers-on and hangmen, young millionaires, veterans of a thousand crimes—answer the journalists' questions. No one assumes responsibility for Playa Girón; no one assumes responsibility for anything. They were all cooks.

Ramón Calvino, famous torturer of the Batista regime, suffers total amnesia when confronted by the women he had beaten, kicked and raped, who identify and revile him. Father Ismael de Lugo, chaplain of the assault brigade, seeks shelter beneath the Virgin's cloak. He had fought on Franco's side in the Spanish war—on the Virgin's advice, he says—and joined the invasion force to keep the Virgin from having to suffer any more the spectacle of communism. Father Lugo invokes the tycoon Virgin, owner of some bank or nationalized plantation, who thinks and feels like the other twelve hundred prisoners: that right is the right of property and inheritance; freedom, the freedom of enterprise; the model society, a business corporation; exemplary democracy, a shareholders' meeting.

All the invaders have been educated in the ethics of impunity. None admit to having killed anybody; but then, like them, poverty doesn't exactly sign its name to its crimes either. Some journalists question them about social injustice, but they wash their hands of it, the system washes its hands. After all, children in Cuba—in all of Latin America—who die soon after birth, die of gastroenteritis, not capitalism.

(397)

1961: Washington

Who Invaded Cuba? A Dialogue in the U.S. Senate

SENATOR CAPEHART: *How many [planes] did we have?*
ALLEN DULLES (director of the CIA): *How many did the Cubans have?*
SENATOR SPARKMAN: *No, the Americans had how many?*
DULLES: *Well, these are Cubans.*
SPARKMAN: *The rebels.*

DULLES: *We do not call them rebels.*
CAPEHART: *I mean, the revolutionary forces.*
SPARKMAN: *When he said how many did we have, that is what we are referring to, anti-Castro forces.*
RICHARD M. BISSELL (deputy director of the CIA): *We started out, sir, with sixteen B-26s . . .*

(108)

1961: Havana
María de la Cruz

Soon after the invasion, a vast crowd assembles in the plaza to hear Fidel announce that the prisoners will be exchanged for children's medicines. Then he gives out diplomas to forty thousand campesinos who have learned to read and write.

An old woman insists on mounting the platform, insists so energetically that finally they bring her up. She flaps vainly at the too-high microphone, until Fidel hands it down to her.

"I wanted to meet you, Fidel. I wanted to tell you . . ."

"Look, you'll make me blush."

But the old woman, all wrinkles and little bones, isn't about to be put off. She says she's finally learned to read and write at the age of a hundred and six. She introduces herself. Her Christian name is María de la Cruz, because she was born on the day that the Holy Cross was invented; her surname is Semanat, after the sugar plantation on which she was born a slave, the daughter of slaves, granddaughter of slaves. In those days the masters sent blacks who tried to get an education to the pillory, María de la Cruz explains, because blacks were supposed to be machines that went into action at the sound of a bell, to the rhythm of whips, and that was why she took so long to learn.

María de la Cruz takes over the platform. After speaking, she sings. After singing, she dances. It's been more than a century since María de la Cruz began dancing. Dancing she emerged from her mother's belly and dancing she journeyed through pain and horror until she arrived here, where she should have been long ago. Now no one can stop her.

(298)

1961: Punta del Este

Latrine Diplomacy

After the fiasco of the military landing in Cuba, the United States changes its tune, announcing a massive landing of dollars in Latin America.

To isolate Cuba's bearded ones, President Kennedy floods Latin America with a torrent of donations, loans, investments.

"Cuba is the hen that laid your golden eggs," Che Guevara tells the Pan-American Conference at Punta del Este, calling this proposed program of bribery an enormous joke on Latin America.

So that nothing should change, the rhetoric of change is unleashed. The conference's official reports run to half a million pages, not one of which neglects to mention "revolution," "agrarian reform," or "development." While the United States knocks down the prices of Latin American products, it promises latrines for the poor, for Indians, for blacks—no machinery, no equipment, just latrines.

"For the technical gentlemen," says Che, *"planning amounts to the planning of latrines. If we took them seriously, Cuba could be . . . a paradise of the latrine!"*

(213)

1961: Escuinapa

The Tale Spinner

Once he saddled and mounted a tiger, thinking it was a burro. Another time he belted his pants with a live snake—only noticing because it had no buckle. Everyone believes him when he explains that no plane can land unless grains of corn are thrown on the runway, or when he describes the terrible bloodbath the day the train went mad and started running sideways. *"I never lie,"* lies Wily Humbug.

Wily, a shrimp fisherman in the Escuinapa estuaries, is a typical loose tongue in this region. He is of that splendid Latin American breed of tale spinners, magicians of crackerbarrel talk that's always spoken, never written down.

At seventy, his eyes still dance. He even laughed at Death, who came one night to seek him out.

"Toc toc toc," Death knocked.

"Come in," Wily coaxed from his bed. *"I was expecting you."*
But when he tried to take her pants down, Death fled in panic.

(309)

1961: São Salvador de Bahia
Amado

While Wily Humbug scares off death in Mexico, in Brazil novelist
Jorge Amado invents a captain who scares off solitude. According to
Amado, this captain defies hurricanes and will-o'-the-wisps, bestrides
seaquakes and black whirlpools, while treating his barrio neighbors
to drinks prepared from the recipes of an old Hong Kong sea-wolf.

When the captain is shipwrecked off the coast of Peru, his neighbors are shipwrecked too. It wrings their hearts, timid retired officials
that they are, sick with boredom and rheumatism, to see a mountain
of ice advancing toward the ship, off the port bow, on the foggy North
Sea; or the monsoon blowing furiously on the Sea of Bengal. All shiver
with pleasure as the captain evokes once again the Arab beauty who
bit juicy grapes as she danced on the sands of Alexandria, wearing
nothing but a white flower in her navel.

The captain has never left Brazil, nor set foot on any kind of
boat, because the sea makes him sick. He sits in the living room
of his house and the house sails off, drifting farther than Marco Polo
or Columbus or the astronauts ever dreamed.

(19)

1962: Cosalá
One Plus One Is One

Hitched to the same post, overloaded with dry wood, they look at
each other. He, amorously; she, dizzily. As the male and the female
burro consider and reconsider each other, devout women cross the
plaza, heading toward church, wrapped up in prayer. Because it's
Good Friday they chant mournful Masses for Our Lord Jesus Christ
as they go by, all in black: black mantillas, black stockings, black
gloves. They become frantic when the two burros, breaking their
bonds, romp over to enjoy themselves right there, in the plaza, facing
the church, rumps to city hall.

Screams resound across Mexico. The mayor of Cosalá, José Antonio Ochoa, emerges onto the balcony, lets out a shriek, and covers his eyes. He promptly orders the rebellious burros shot. They fall dead, hooked together in love.

(308 and 329)

1962: Villa de Jesús María
One Plus One Is All

In another mountain village not far away, the Cora Indians don masks and paint their naked bodies. As on every Good Friday, they give things new names while the fiesta lasts—passion of Christ, magic deer-hunt, murder of the god Sun, that crime from which human life on earth began.

"Let him die, let him kill, let him beget."

At the foot of the cross, dancing lovers offer themselves, embrace, enter one another, while the clown dancers skip about imitating them. Everyone joins in love-play, caressing, tickling, teasing. Everyone eats as they play: Fruits become projectiles, eggs bombs, and this great banquet ends in a war of hurled tortillas and showering honey. The Cora Indians enjoy themselves like lunatics, dancing, loving, eating in homage to the first agonies of the dying Christ. From the cross he smiles his thanks.

(46)

1963: Bayamo
Hurricane Flora

pounds Cuba for more than a week. The longest hurricane in the nation's history attacks, retreats, then returns as if realizing it had forgotten to smash a few last things. Everything spins around this giant, furious snake which twists and strikes suddenly, where least expected.

Useless to nail up doors and windows. The hurricane rips everything off, playing with houses and trees, flipping them into the air. The sky empties of panicky birds, while the sea floods the whole east of the island. From a base at Bayamo, brigades venture forth in launches and helicopters; volunteers come and go rescuing people and animals, vaccinating whatever they find alive and burying or burning the rest.

(18)

1963: Havana

Everyone a Jack-of-All-Trades

On this hurricane-devastated island, blockaded and harassed by the United States, getting through the day is a feat. Store windows display Vietnam solidarity posters but not shoes or shirts, and to buy the smallest thing, you wait hours in line. The occasional automobile runs on piston rings made of ox horns, and in art schools pencil graphite is ground up to approximate paint. In the factories, cobwebs cover some new machines, because a particular spare part has not yet completed its six-thousand-mile journey to get here. From remote Baltic ports come the oil and everything else Cuba needs, and a letter to Venezuela has to circle the globe before reaching its nearby destination.

And it's not only things that are lacking. Many know-it-alls have gone to Miami on the heels of the have-it-alls.

And now?

"Now we have to invent."

At eighteen, Ricardo Gutiérrez paraded into Havana, rifle held high, amid a tide of rifles, machetes, and palm-frond sombreros celebrating the end of Batista's dictatorship. On the following day he had to take charge of various enterprises abandoned by their owners. A women's underwear factory, among others, fell to his lot. Immediately the raw-material problems began. There was no latex foam for the brassieres. The workers discussed the matter at a meeting and decided to rip up pillows. It was a disaster. The pillow stuffing couldn't be washed because it never dried.

Ricardo was twenty when they put two pesos in his pocket and sent him to administer a sugar mill. He had never seen a sugar mill in his life, even from a distance. There he discovered that cane juice has a dark color. The previous administrator, a faithful servant with a half-century of experience, had disappeared over the horizon carrying under his arm the oil portrait of Julio Lobo, lord of these canefields which the revolution has expropriated.

Now the foreign minister sends for him. Raúl Roa sits on the floor before a big map of Spain spread over the carpet, and starts to draw little crosses. This is how Ricardo finds out, at twenty-two, that they have made him a consul.

"*But I type with only two fingers,*" he stammers.

"*I type with one and I'm a minister,*" says Roa, putting an end to the matter.

1963: Havana
Portrait of the Bureaucrat

A black time engenders a red time that will make possible a green time: Solidarity slowly replaces greed and fear. Because it is capable of invention, of creation and madness, the Cuban revolution is making out. But it has enemies to spare. Among those most to be feared is the bureaucrat, devastating as the hurricane, asphyxiating as imperialism. There is no revolution without this germ in its belly.

The bureaucrat is the wooden man, that bloodless error of the gods, neither decisive nor indecisive, an echo with no voice, a transmitter of orders, not ideas. He considers any doubt heresy, any contradiction treason; confuses unity with unanimity, and sees the people as an eternal child to be led by the ear.

It is highly improbable that the bureaucrat will put his life on the line. It is absolutely impossible that he'll put his job on the line.

1963: Havana
Bola de Nieve

"*This is Yoruba-Marxism-Leninism,*" says Bola de Nieve, singer of Guanabacoa, son of Domingo the cook and Mama Inés. He says it in a sort of murmur, in his enormous little hoarse, fleshy voice. *Yoruba-Marxism-Leninism* is the name Bola de Nieve gives to the ardor and jubilation of these people who dance the Internationale with swaying hips, in this revolution born of the fierce embrace of Europe and Africa on the sands of America. In this place, gods made by men are crossed with men made by gods, the former descending to earth, the latter launched to conquer heaven; and Bola de Nieve celebrates it all with his salty songs.

1963: Río Coco

On His Shoulders He Carries
the Embrace of Sandino,

which time has not obliterated. Thirty years later, Colonel Santos López returns to war in the northern forests, so that Nicaragua may *be*.

A few years ago, the Sandinista Front was born. Carlos Fonseca Amador and Tomás Borge gave it birth along with Santos López and others who'd never known Sandino but wanted to perpetuate him.

The job will cost them blood, and they know it: *"So much filth can't be washed with water, no matter how holy,"* says Carlos Fonseca.

Lost, weaponless, drenched by the eternal rain, with nothing to eat—but eaten up, fucked over, and frustrated—the guerrillas wander the forest. There is no worse moment than sunset. Day is day and night is night, but dusk is the hour of agony, of frightful loneliness, and the Sandinistas are nothing yet, or nearly nothing.

(58 and 267)

1963: San Salvador

Miguel at Fifty-Eight

Miguel is living, as usual, from hand to mouth, unionizing campesinos and making mischief, when the police catch him in some little town and haul him, hands and feet bound, into the city of San Salvador.

Here he gets a protracted beating. For eight days they beat him hung up, and for eight nights they beat him on the floor. His bones creak, his flesh cries out, but he utters no sound as they torture him for his secrets. Yet when the captain insults the people he loves, the defiant old man heaves up his bleeding remains; the plucked rooster lifts his crest and crows.

Miguel orders the captain to shut his swinish trap. The captain buries a revolver barrel in his neck. Miguel defies him to shoot. The two remain face to face, ferocious, both gasping as if blowing on embers: the soldier, finger on trigger, eyes fixed on Miguel's; Miguel unblinking, counting the seconds, the centuries, as they pass, listening to the pounding of his heart as it rises into his head. Miguel gives himself up for dead now, really dead, when suddenly a shadow dims the furious glitter of the torturer's eyes, a weariness, or who knows what, and Miguel takes those eyes by storm. The torturer blinks, as if surprised to be where he is. Slowly, he lowers the gun, and with it, his eyes.

And so occurs the eleventh birth of Miguel Mármol, at fifty-eight years of age.

(222)

1963: Dallas

The Government Decides That Truth Doesn't Exist

At noon, on a street in Dallas, the president of the United States is assassinated. He is hardly dead when the official version is broadcast. In that version, which will be the definitive one, Lee Harvey Oswald alone has killed John Kennedy.

The weapon does not coincide with the bullet, nor the bullet with the holes. The accused does not coincide with the accusation: Oswald is an exceptionally bad shot of mediocre physique, but according to the official version, his acts were those of a champion marksman and Olympic sprinter. He has fired an old rifle with impossible speed and his magic bullet, turning and twisting acrobatically to penetrate Kennedy and John Connally, the governor of Texas, remains miraculously intact.

Oswald strenuously denies it. But no one knows, no one will ever know what he has to say. Two days later he collapses before the television cameras, the whole world witness to the spectacle, his mouth shut by Jack Ruby, a two-bit gangster and minor trafficker in women and drugs. Ruby says he has avenged Kennedy out of patriotism and pity for the poor widow.

(232)

1963: Santo Domingo

A Chronicle of Latin American Customs

From the sands of Sosúa, he used to swim out to sea, with a band playing to scare off the sharks.

Now, General Toni Imbert, potbellied and slack, rarely goes into the water; but he still returns to the beach of his childhood. He likes to sit on the waterfront, take aim, and shoot sharks. In Sosúa, the sharks compete with the poor for the leftovers from the slaughter-house. General Imbert is sorry for the poor. From the beach, he throws ten-dollar bills at them.

General Imbert greatly resembles his bosom friend, General Wessin y Wessin. Even with a cold, both can smell a Communist a mile off; and both have won many medals for getting up early and killing shackled people. When they say *"el presidente,"* both refer to the president of the United States.

Dominican graduates of the U.S. School of the Americas in Panama, Generals Imbert and Wessin y Wessin both fattened up under Trujillo's protection. Then both betrayed him. When, after Trujillo's death, elections were held and the people voted *en masse* for Juan Bosch, they could not stand still. Bosch refused to buy planes for the Air Force, announced agrarian reform, supported a divorce law, and raised wages.

The red lasted seven months. Imbert, Wessin y Wessin, and other generals of the nation have recovered power, that rich honey-comb, in an easy barracks revolt at dawn.

The United States loses no time recognizing the new government.

(61 and 281)

1964: Panama

Twenty-Three Boys Are Pumped Full of Lead

when they try to hoist the flag of Panama on Panamanian soil.

"We only used bird-shot," the commander of the North American occupation forces says defensively.

Another flag flies over the strip that slits Panama from sea to sea. Another law prevails, another police keep watch, another language is spoken. Panamanians may not enter the Canal Zone without permission, even to pick up fallen fruit from a mango tree, and they work here at second-class pay, like blacks and women.

The Canal Zone, North American colony, is both a business and a military base. The School of the Americas' courses are financed with the tolls ships pay. In the Canal Zone barracks, Pentagon officers teach anticommunist surgery to Latin American military men who will soon, in their own countries, occupy presidencies, ministries, commands, and embassies.

"They are the leaders of the future," explains Robert McNamara, secretary of defense of the United States.

Wary of the cancer that lies in wait for them, these military men will cut off the hands of anyone who dares to commit agrarian reform or nationalization, and tear out the tongues of the impudent or the inquisitive.

(248)

1964: Rio de Janeiro
"There are dark clouds,"

says Lincoln Gordon:

"Dark clouds are closing in on our economic interests in Brazil . . ."

President João Goulart has just introduced agrarian reform, the nationalization of oil refineries, and an end to the flight of capital. The indignant ambassador of the United States loudly attacks him. From the embassy, rivers of money flow to pollute public opinion, and the military prepare to seize power. A shrill call for a coup d'état is publicized by the media. Even the Lions Club signs it.

Ten years after Vargas's suicide the same furor erupts again, several times stronger. Politicians and journalists call for a uniformed Messiah who can put some order into the chaos. The TV broadcasts a film showing Berlin walls cutting Brazilian cities in two. Newspapers and radios exalt the virtues of private capital, which turns deserts into oases, and the merits of the armed forces, who keep Communists from stealing the water. Down the avenues of the chief cities the March of the Family with God for Liberty pleads to heaven for mercy.

Ambassador Lincoln Gordon excoriates the Communist plot: Goulart, estancia owner, is betraying his class at the moment of choice between devourers and devoured, between the makers and the objects of opinions, between the freedom of money and the freedom of people.

(115 and 141)

1964: Juiz de Fora

The Reconquest of Brazil

Almost thirty years after Captain Olympio Mourão Filho fabricated a Communist plot at the orders of President Vargas, General Mourão Filho buys a Communist plot fabricated by Ambassador Lincoln Gordon. The modest general confesses that in political matters he is just a uniformed ox, but he does understand about Communist conspiracies.

In the Juiz de Fora barracks he raises his sword: *"I'll snatch Brazil from the abyss!"*

Mourão has been awake since before dawn. While shaving he recites the psalm of David, the one that declares that all verdure will perish. Then he eats breakfast, congratulates his wife on being married to a hero, and at the head of his troops sets out to march on Rio de Janeiro.

The rest of the generals fall into line, and from the United States, already heading for Brazil, come one aircraft carrier, numerous planes and warships, and four fuel-supply ships. It's "Operation Brother Sam," to assist the rising.

João Goulart, irresolute, watches it happen. His colleague Lyndon Johnson sends warmest approval to the authors of the coup, even though Goulart still occupies the presidency; the State Department immediately offers generous loans to the new government. From the south, Leonel Brizola's attempt at resistance produces no echo. At last, Goulart heads into exile.

Some anonymous hand writes on a wall in Rio de Janeiro: *"No more middlemen! Lincoln Gordon for president!"*

But the triumphant generals choose Marshall Castelo Branco, a solemn military man without a sense of humor or a neck.

(115, 141, and 307)

1964: La Paz
Without Shame or Glory,

like the president of Brazil, President Víctor Paz Estenssoro boards a plane that will take him into exile.

He leaves behind him René Barrientos, babbling aviator, as dictator of Bolivia. Now the U.S. ambassador participates in cabinet meetings, seated among the ministers, and the manager of Gulf Oil draws up economic decrees.

Paz Estenssoro had been left devastatingly alone, and along with him falls the national revolution after twelve years in power. Bit by bit the revolution had turned around until it had shown its back to the workers, the better to suckle the new rich and the bureaucrats who squeezed it dry. Now, a slight puff suffices to blow it over.

Meanwhile, the divided workers fight among themselves, as if they were Laime and Jucumani tribesmen.

(16, 17, 26, and 473)

1964: North of Potosí
With Savage Fury

the Laime Indians fight the Jucumanis. The poorest of poor Bolivia, pariahs among pariahs, they devote themselves to killing one another on the frozen steppe north of Potosí. Five hundred from both tribes have died in the past ten years; the burned huts are beyond counting. Battles continue for weeks, without letup or mercy. The Indians cut one another to pieces to avenge petty grievances or disputes over scraps of sterile land in these lofty solitudes to which they were banished long, long ago.

Laimes and Jucumanis live on potatoes and barley, all the steppe with great effort will yield them. They sleep on sheepskins, accompanied by lice that welcome the warmth of their bodies.

For the ceremonies of mutual extermination they cover their heads with rawhide caps in the exact shape of the conquistadors' helmets.

(180)

Hats

in today's Bolivia are descended from Europe, brought by conquistadors and merchants; but they have been adapted to belong to this land and this people. Originally they were like cattle brands, compulsory disguises that helped each Spanish master recognize the Indians he owned. As time passed, communities began to deck out their headgear with their own stamps of pride, symbols of joy: stars and little moons of silver, colored feathers, glass beads, paper flowers, crowns of corn . . . Later, the English flooded Bolivia with bowlers and top hats: the black stovepipe hat of the Potosí Indian women, the white one of those of Cochabamba. By some mistake, the borsalino hat arrived from Italy and settled down on the heads of La Paz's Indian women.

The Bolivian Indian, man or woman, boy or girl, may go barefoot, but never hatless. The hat prolongs the head it protects; and when the soul falls, the hat picks it up off the ground.

(161)

1965: San Juan, Puerto Rico
Bosch

People stream into the streets of Santo Domingo, armed with whatever they can find, and pitch themselves against the tanks. "Thieves, get out!" they yell. "Come back, Juan Bosch, our president!"

The United States holds Bosch prisoner in Puerto Rico, preventing his return to his country in flames. A man of strong fiber, all tendon and tension, Bosch, alone in his anger, bites his fists, and his blue eyes pierce walls.

A journalist asks him over the phone if he is an enemy of the United States. No, he is only an enemy of U.S. imperialism.

"No one who has read Mark Twain," says Bosch, *"can be an enemy of the United States."*

(62 and 269)

1965: Santo Domingo

Caamaño

Into the melee pour students, soldiers, women in hair curlers. With barricades of barrels and overturned trucks, the rumbling advance of the tanks is stopped. Stones and bottles fly, while from the wingtips of swooping planes machinegun fire sweeps the Ozama River bridge and the thronged streets. The tide of people rises, and rising, separates the soldiers who had formerly served Trujillo: on one side, those commanded by Imbert and Wessin y Wessin, who are shooting people; on the other, the followers of Francisco Caamaño, who break open the arsenals and begin distributing rifles.

This morning, Colonel Caamaño set off the uprising for Bosch's return, believing it would be a matter of minutes. By midday, he realized it was a long job, that he would have to confront his comrades-in-arms, that blood was flowing; and had a horrifying presentiment of national tragedy. At nightfall he sought asylum in the Salvadoran embassy.

Collapsed in an armchair, Caamaño tries to sleep. He takes sedatives, his usual dose and more, but nothing works. Insomnia, teeth-grinding, nail-biting: Trujillo's legacy to him from the time when he was an officer in the dictator's army and performed, or saw performed, dark, sometimes atrocious deeds. Tonight it's worse than ever. He no sooner closes his eyes than he starts to dream. Dreaming, he is honest with himself; awakening he trembles, weeps, rages with shame for his fear.

Morning comes and his exile ends: It has lasted just one night. Colonel Caamaño wets his face and leaves the embassy. He walks staring at the ground, through the smoke of the fires, thick smoke that casts a shadow, and emerges into the shimmering light of day to return to his post at the head of the rebellion.

(223)

1965: Santo Domingo

The Invasion

Not by air, not by land, not by sea. General Wessin y Wessin's planes and General Imbert's tanks cannot still the free-for-all in the burning city any more than the ships that fire on the Government Palace, occupied by Caamaño, but kill housewives.

The United States embassy, which calls the rebels *Communist scum* and *a gang of thugs*, reports that there is no way to stop the disturbance and requests urgent aid from Washington. The Marines land.

Next day, the first invader dies: a boy from the mountains of northern New York State, shot from a roof, in a narrow street of this city whose name he had never heard in all his life. The first Dominican victim is a child of five. He dies on a balcony from a grenade explosion. The invaders had mistaken him for a sniper.

President Lyndon Johnson warns that he will not tolerate another Cuba in the Caribbean. More troops land. And more. Twenty thousand, thirty-five thousand, forty-two thousand. As U.S. soldiers tear up Dominicans, North American volunteers stitch them together in hospitals. Johnson exhorts his allies to join this Western Crusade. The military dictatorship of Brazil, the military dictatorship of Paraguay, the military dictatorship of Honduras, and the military dictatorship of Nicaragua all send troops to the Dominican Republic to save the democracy threatened by its people.

Trapped between river and sea, in the old barrio of Santo Domingo, its people resist.

José Mora Otero, secretary general of the Organization of American States, meets privately with Colonel Caamaño. He offers him six million dollars to leave the country, and is told to go to hell.

(62, 269, and 421)

1965: Santo Domingo

One Hundred Thirty-Two Nights

and this war of sticks and knives and carbines against mortars and machineguns still goes on. The city smells of gunpowder, garbage, and death.

Unable to force a surrender, the invaders, all-powerful as they are, have no alternative but agreement. The nobodies, the nothings have not let themselves be beaten. They have fought fierce battles by night, every night, house to house, body to body, yard by yard, until the moment the sun raised his flaming flag from the bottom of the sea, when they lowered themselves into darkness until the next night. And after so many nights of horror and glory, the invading troops do not succeed in installing General Imbert in power, nor General Wessin y Wessin, nor any other general.

(269 and 421)

1965: Havana

This Multiplier of Revolutions,

Spartan *guerrillero*, sets out for other lands. Fidel makes public Che Guevara's letter of farewell. *"Now nothing legal ties me to Cuba,"* says Che, *"only the bonds that cannot be broken."*

Che also writes to his parents and to his children. He asks his children to be able to feel in their deepest hearts any injustice committed against anyone in any part of the world.

Here in Cuba, asthma and all, Che has been the first to arrive and the last to go, in war and in peace, without the slightest weakening.

Everyone has fallen in love with him—the women, the men, the children, the dogs, and the plants.

(213)

Che Guevara Bids Farewell to His Parents

Once again I feel under my heels the ribs of Rocinante: I return to the road with shield on arm . . .

Many will call me an adventurer, and that I am; only of a different type—of those who risk their hides to demonstrate their truths. This may be the decisive one. I do not seek it but it is within the logical estimate of probabilities. If that's how it is, this is my last embrace.

I have loved you a lot, only haven't known how to express my affection; I am extremely rigid in my actions and I think you sometimes didn't understand me. It wasn't easy to understand me, but just believe me today.

Now the will that I have polished with the delight of an artist will sustain this flabby pair of legs and these weary lungs. I will do it. Think once in a while about this little twentieth-century condottiere.

(213)

1966: Patiocemento
"We know that hunger is mortal,"

said the priest Camilo Torres. "And if we know that, does it make sense to waste time arguing whether the soul is immortal?"

Camilo believed in Christianity as the practice of loving one's neighbor, and wanted that love to be effective. He had an obsession about effective love. That obsession made him take up arms, and because of it, he has died, in an unknown corner of Colombia, fighting with the guerrillas.

(448)

1967: Llallagua
The Feast of San Juan

Bolivian miners are sons of the Virgin and nephews of the Devil, but neither can save them from early death. They are buried in the bowels of the earth, an implacable rain of mine dust annihilating them: In just a moment, a few short years, their lungs turn to stone and their tracheas close. Even before the lungs forget to breathe, the nose forgets smells and the tongue forgets tastes, the legs become like lead and the mouth discharges nothing but insult and vengefulness.

When they emerge from the pit, the miners look for a party. While their short life lasts and their legs still move, they need to eat spicy stews and swallow strong drink and sing and dance by the light of the bonfires that warm the barren plain.

On this night of San Juan, as the greatest of all fiestas is in progress, the army crouches in the mountains. Almost nothing is known here about the guerrillas of the distant Ñancahuazú River, although the story goes that they are fighting for a revolution so beautiful that, like the ocean, it has never been seen. But General Barrientos believes that a sly terrorist is lurking within every miner.

Before dawn, just as the Feast of San Juan is ending, a hurricane of bullets slashes through the town of Llallagua.

(16, 17, and 458)

1967: Catavi

The Day After

The light of the new day is like a glitter of bones. Then the sun hides behind clouds as the outcasts of the earth count their dead and carry them off in little carts. The miners march down a narrow muddy road in Llallagua. The procession crosses the river, dirty saliva flowing among stones of ash, and threads onto the vast pampa heading toward Catavi cemetery.

The sky, immense roof of tin, has no sun, and the earth no bonfires to warm it. Never was this steppe so frozen.

Many graves have to be dug. Bodies of every size are lined up, stretched out, waiting.

From the top of the cemetery wall, a woman screams.

(458)

1967: Catavi

Domitila

cries out against the murderers from the top of the wall.

She lives in two rooms without latrine or running water with her miner husband and seven children. The eighth child is eager to be born. Every day Domitila cooks, washes, sweeps, weaves, sews, teaches what she knows, cures what she can, prepares a hundred meat pies, and roams the streets looking for buyers.

For insulting the Bolivian army, they arrest her. A soldier spits in her face.

(458)

The Interrogation of Domitila

He spat in my face. Then he kicked me. I wouldn't take it and I slapped him. He punched me again. I scratched his face. And he was hitting me, hitting me . . . He put his knee here on my belly. He squeezed my neck and I almost choked. It seemed like he wanted to make my belly burst. He tightened his hold more and more . . . Then, with my two hands, with all my two hands, with all my strength I pulled his hands down. And I don't remember how, but I had grabbed him with my fist and was biting him, biting . . . I was horribly disgusted tasting his blood in my mouth . . . Then, with all my fury— tchá—I spat his blood all over his face. A tremendous howling started. He grabbed me, kicked me, hollered at me . . . He called the soldiers and had me seized by four or more of them . . .

When I woke up as if from a dream, I'd been swallowing a piece of my tooth. I felt it here in my throat. Then I noticed that this monster had broken six of my teeth. The blood was pouring over me and I couldn't open my eyes or my nose . . .

Then, as if fate ordained it, I began to give birth. I started to feel pains, pains and pains, and sometimes the baby that was coming seemed too much for me . . . I couldn't stand it any more. And I went to kneel down in a corner. I supported myself and covered my face, because I couldn't muster even a bit of strength. My face felt as if it was going to burst. And in one of those moments it came. I saw that the baby's head was already out . . . And right there I fainted.

How long afterward I don't know: "Where am I? Where am I?"

I was completely wet. The blood and the liquid that comes when you give birth had soaked me all over. Then I made an effort and somehow I got hold of the baby's cord. And pulling up the cord, at the end of the cord I found my little baby, cold, frozen, there on the floor.

(458)

1967: Catavi

The God in the Stone

After the gale of bullets, a gale of wind sweeps through the mining town of Llallagua removing all the roofs. In the neighboring parish of Catavi, the same wind topples and breaks the statue of the Virgin.

Its stone pedestal, however, remains intact. The priest comes to pick off the floor the pieces of the Immaculate One.

Look, father, say the workers, and they show him how the pedestal has shrugged off the burdensome Virgin.

Inside this pedestal the conquered ancient gods still sleep, dream, breathe, care for petitioners, and remind the mine workers that the great day will come: *Our day, the one we're waiting for.*

From the day it was originally found and worshipped by the workers the priest had condemned the miracle-working stone. He had shut it up in a cement cage so that the workers couldn't parade it in processions; then he put the Virgin on top of it. The mason who caged the stone at the priest's order has been shaking with fever and squinting ever since that fateful day.

(268)

1967: On the Ñancahuazú River Banks
Seventeen Men March to Annihilation

Cardinal Maurer arrives in Bolivia. From Rome he brings the Pope's blessings and word that God unequivocally backs General Barrientos against the guerrillas.

Meanwhile, hungry and disoriented, the guerrillas twist and turn through the Ñancahuazú River scrub. There are few campesinos in these immense solitudes; and not one, not a single one, has joined the little troop of Che Guevara. His forces dwindle from ambush to ambush. Che does not weaken, won't let himself weaken, although he feels that his body is a stone among stones, a heavy stone he drags along at the head of the others; nor does he let himself be tempted by the idea of saving the group by abandoning the wounded. By Che's order they all move at the pace of those least able to move: Together they will all be saved or lost.

Lost. Eighteen hundred soldiers, led by U.S. Rangers, are treading on their shadow. A ring is drawing tighter and tighter. Finally, a couple of campesino informers and the radar of the U.S. National Security Agency reveal their exact location.

(212 and 455)

1967: Yuro Ravine

The Fall of Che

Machinegun bullets break his legs. Sitting, he fights until the rifle is blown from his hands.

The conquering soldiers fall to blows over his watch, his canteen, his belt, his pipe. Several officers interrogate him, one after another. Che keeps quiet as his blood flows. Vice Admiral Ugarteche, daring land-wolf, head of the navy in a country without an ocean, insults and threatens him. Che spits in his face.

From La Paz comes the order to finish off the prisoner. A burst of gunfire. Che dies from a treacherous bullet shortly before his fortieth birthday, the age at which Zapata and Sandino died, also from treacherous bullets.

In the little town of Higueras, General Barrientos exhibits his trophy to journalists. Che lies on a laundry sink. They shoot him a final time, with flashbulbs. This last face has accusing eyes and a melancholy smile.

(212 and 455)

1967: Higueras

Bells Toll for Him

Did he die in 1967 in Bolivia because he guessed wrong about the when and the where and the how? Or did he not die at all, not anywhere, because he wasn't wrong about what really matters despite all the whens and wheres and hows?

He believed that one must defend oneself from the traps of greed without ever letting down one's guard. When he was president of the National Bank of Cuba, he signed the banknotes "Che," in mockery of money. For love of people, he scorned things. Sick is the world, he thought, in which to have and to be mean the same thing. He never kept anything for himself, nor ever asked for anything.

Living is giving oneself, he thought; and he gave himself.

1967: La Paz

Portrait of a Supermacho

On the shoulders of Nene, his giant bodyguard, General Barrientos crosses the city of La Paz. From Nene's shoulders he greets those who applaud him. He enters the government palace. Seated at his desk, with Nene behind him, he signs decrees that sell at bargain prices the sky, the soil, and the subsoil of Bolivia.

Ten years ago, Barrientos was putting in time in a Washington, D.C., psychiatric clinic when the idea of being president of Bolivia entered his head. He'd already made a career for himself as an athlete. Disguising himself as a North American aviator, he laid siege to power; and now he exercises it, machinegunning workers and pulling down libraries and wages.

The killer of Che is a cock with a loud crow, a man with three balls, a hundred women, and a thousand children. No Bolivian has flown so high, made so many speeches, or stolen so much.

In Miami, the Cuban exiles elect him Man of the Year.

(16, 17, 337, and 474)

1967: Estoril

Society Notes

Pinned to the hostess's gleaming coiffure are some of the world's largest diamonds. The cross on her granddaughter's necklace displays one of the world's largest emeralds. The Patiños, inheritors of one of the world's largest fortunes, throw one of the world's largest parties.

To make a thousand people happy night and day for a week, the Patiños collect *all* the elegant flowers and fine drinks buyable in Portugal. The invitations have gone out well ahead, so that the fashion-designers and society reporters could do their jobs properly. Several times a day the ladies change their dresses, all exclusive designs, and when two similar gowns appear in one salon, someone observes that she will fry Yves Saint-Laurent in oil. The orchestras come by charter from New York. The guests come in yachts or private planes.

Europe's nobility is out in force. The late lamented Simón Patiño, the anthropophagous Bolivian, devourer of miners, bought top-quality alliances. He married his daughters to a count and a marquis, and his son to a king's first cousin.

(34)

1967: Houston
Ali

They called him Cassius Clay: He chooses to call himself Muhammad Ali.

They made him a Christian: He chooses to make himself a Muslim.

They made him defend himself: No one punches like Ali, so fierce and fast, light tank, bulldozing feather, indestructible possessor of the world crown.

They told him that a good boxer confines his fighting to the ring: He says the real ring is something else, where a triumphant black fights for defeated blacks, for those who eat leftovers in the kitchen.

They advised discretion: From then on he yells.

They tapped his phone: From then on he yells on the phone, too.

They put a uniform on him to send him to Vietnam: He pulls it off and yells that he isn't going, because he has nothing against the Vietnamese, who have done no harm to him or to any other black American.

They took away his world title, they stopped him from boxing, they sentenced him to jail and a fine: He yells his thanks for these compliments to his human dignity.

(14 and 149)

1968: Memphis
Portrait of a Dangerous Man

The Reverend Martin Luther King preaches against the Vietnam War. He protests that twice as many blacks as whites are dying there, cannon fodder for an imperial adventure comparable to the Nazi crimes. The poisoning of water and land, the destruction of people and harvests are part of a plan of extermination. Of the million Vietnamese dead, says the preacher, the majority are children. The United States, he claims, is suffering from an infection of the soul; and any autopsy would show that the name of that infection is Vietnam.

Six years ago the FBI put this man in Section A of the Reserved List, among those dangerous individuals who must be watched and jailed in case of emergency. Since then the police hound him, spying on him day and night, threatening and provoking him.

Martin Luther King collapses on the balcony of a Memphis hotel. A bullet full in the face puts an end to this nuisance.

(254)

1968: San Jose, California
The Chicanos

Judge Gerald Chargin passes sentence on a lad accused of incest, and while he's at it, advises the young man to commit suicide and tells him, *"You Chicanos are worse than animals, miserable, lousy, rotten people . . ."*

The Chicanos are the descendants of those who came across the border river from Mexico to harvest cotton, oranges, tomatoes, and potatoes at dirt-cheap wages, and who stayed on in these southwestern and western states, which until little more than a century ago were the north of Mexico. In these lands, no longer theirs, they are used and despised.

Of every ten North Americans killed in Vietnam, six are blacks or Hispanics. And to them they say:

If you're so tough and strong, you go to the front lines first.

(182, 282, 369, and 403)

1968: San Juan, Puerto Rico
Albizu

Puerto Ricans are also good at dying in Vietnam in the name of those who took away their country.

The island of Puerto Rico, North American colony, consumes what it doesn't produce and produces what it doesn't consume. On its abandoned lands not even the rice and beans of the national dish are grown. Washington teaches the Puerto Ricans to breathe refrigerated air, eat canned food, drive long, well-chromed cars, sink up to the neck in debt, and lose their souls watching television.

Pedro Albizu Campos died a while back after almost twenty years spent in U.S. jails for his unceasing activities as an agitator. To win back the fatherland, one should love it with one's soul and one's life, he thought, as if it were a woman; to make it breathe again, one should rescue it with bullets.

He always wore a black tie for the lost fatherland. He was more and more alone.

(87, 116, 199, and 275)

1968: Mexico City
The Students

invade the streets. Such demonstrations have never been seen before in Mexico, so huge, so joyous, everyone linked arm in arm, singing and laughing. The students cry out against President Díaz Ordaz and his ministerial mummies, and all the others who have taken over Zapata's and Pancho Villa's revolution.

In Tlatelolco, a plaza where Indians and conquistadors once fought to the death, a trap is sprung. The army blocks every exit with strategically placed tanks and machineguns. Inside the corral, readied for the sacrifice, the students are hopelessly jammed together. A continuous wall of rifles with fixed bayonets advances to seal the trap.

Flares, one green, one red, give the signal. Hours later, a woman searches for her child, her shoes leaving bloody tracks on the ground.

(299 and 347)

"There was much, much blood," says the mother of a student,

"so much that I felt it thick on my hands. There was also blood on the walls. I think the walls of Tlatelolco have their pores full of blood; all Tlatelolco breathes blood . . . The bodies lay on the concrete waiting to be removed. I counted many from the window, about sixty-eight. They were piling them up in the rain. I remembered that my

son Carlitos was wearing a green corduroy jacket and I thought I saw it on each body . . ."

(347)

1968: Mexico City
Revueltas

He has been around for half a century, but repeats daily the crime of being young. Always at the center of any uproar, José Revueltas now denounces the owners of power in Mexico, who, out of incurable hatred for all that pulses, grows, and changes, have murdered three hundred students in Tlatelolco.

"The gentlemen of the government are dead. For that they kill us."

In Mexico, power assimilates or annihilates, shoots deadly lightning with a hug or a slug, consigns to grave or prison the impudent ones who will not be bought off with a sinecure. The incorrigible Revueltas rarely sleeps outside a cell; and when he does, he spends the night stretched out on some bench in a park, or on a desk at the university. Hated by the police for being a revolutionary and by dogmatists of all types for being free, he is condemned by pious leftists for his predilection for cheap bars. Not long ago, his comrades provided him with a guardian angel to save him from temptation, but the angel had to pawn his wings to pay for the sprees they enjoyed together.

(373)

1968: Banks of the River Yaqui
The Mexican Revolution Isn't There Anymore

The Yaqui Indians, warriors for centuries, call upon Lázaro Cárdenas. They meet him on a bright sunny prairie in northern Mexico, near their ancestral river.

Standing in the shade of a leafy breadfruit tree, the chiefs of the eight Yaqui tribes welcome him. On their heads gleam the plumes reserved for great occasions.

"Remember, Tata?" Thirty years have passed and this is a great

occasion. The top chief speaks: *"Tata Lázaro, do you remember? You gave us back the lands. You gave us hospitals and schools."*

At the end of each sentence the chiefs beat the ground with their staves, and the dry echo reverberates across the prairie.

"You remember? We want you to know, the rich have taken back the lands. The hospitals have been turned into barracks. The schools are cantinas."

Cárdenas listens and says nothing.

(45)

1968: Mexico City
Rulfo

In the silence, the heartbeat of another Mexico. Juan Rulfo, teller of tales about the misadventures of the dead and the living, keeps silent. Fifteen years ago he said what he had to say, in a small novel and a few short stories, and since then he says nothing. Or rather, he made the deepest kind of love, and then went to sleep.

1969: Lima
Arguedas

splits his skull with a bullet. His story is the story of Peru: Sick with Peru, he kills himself.

The son of whites, José María Arguedas was raised by Indians and spoke Quechua throughout his childhood. At seventeen, he was torn away from the sierra and thrust into the coastal area—from the small communal towns to the proprietorial cities.

He learned the language of the victors and spoke and wrote it. He never wrote *about* the vanquished, rather *from* them. He knew how to express them; but his feat was his curse. He felt that everything about him was treachery or failure; he felt torn apart. He couldn't be Indian; he didn't want to be white. He couldn't endure both the scorning and the being scorned.

This lonely wayfarer walked at the edge of an abyss, between two enemy worlds that divided his soul. Many an avalanche of anguish swept down on him, worse than any landslide of mud and rocks, until finally he was overwhelmed.

(30 and 256)

1969: Sea of Tranquillity
The Discovery of the Earth

The space ship from Houston, Texas, puts down its long spider legs on the Moon. Astronauts Armstrong and Aldrin see the Earth as no one has seen it before, an Earth that is not the generous breast that gives us milk and poison to suck, but a handsome frozen stone rotating in the solitude of the universe. The Earth seems to be childless, uninhabited, perhaps even indifferent, as if it didn't feel a single tickle from the human passions that swarm on its soil.

Via television and radio, the astronauts send us preprogrammed words about the great step that humanity is taking, while they stick the flag of the United States of America into the stony Sea of Tranquillity.

1969: Bogotá
The Urchins

They have the street for a home. They are cats made for jumping and slapping, sparrows for flying, little cocks for fighting. They go about in packs, in gangs. They sleep in clusters, bunched together against the freezing dawns. They eat what they steal or the leftovers they beg or the garbage they find; they have grey teeth and faces burned by the cold.

Arturo Dueñas, of the Twenty-second Street gang, leaves his pack, fed up with offering his bottom to be spanked just because he's the smallest, the bedbug, the tick. He decides he'll fare better on his own.

One night, a night like any other, Arturo slips under a restaurant table, grabs a chicken leg, and brandishing it like a flag, scoots off down an alley. When he finds some obscure nook, he sits down to have supper. A little dog watches him and licks its chops. Several times Arturo pushes it away, but the dog returns. They examine each other: The two are equals, sons of nobody, beaten, pure bone and grime. Arturo resigns himself and shares.

Since then they've gone together on winged feet, sharing the danger, the booty, and the lice. Arturo, who has never talked to anybody, opens up, and the little dog sleeps curled up at his feet.

One accursed day the police catch Arturo robbing buns and haul him to the Fifth Precinct for a tremendous beating. When, in time, Arturo returns to the street, all battered, the little dog is nowhere to be seen. Arturo runs back and forth, searching wildly everywhere, but it doesn't appear. A lot of questions, and nothing. A lot of calling, and nothing. No one in the world is so alone as this child of seven who is alone on the streets of the city of Bogotá, hoarse from so much screaming.

(68 and 342)

1969: Any City
Someone

On a corner, by a red light, someone swallows fire, someone washes windshields, someone sells Kleenex, chewing gum, little flags, and dolls that make pee-pee. Someone listens to the horoscope on the radio, pleased that the stars are concerned about him. Walking between the tall buildings, someone would like to buy silence or air, but doesn't have the cash. In a filthy barrio, amid swarms of flies above and armies of rats below, someone hires a woman for three minutes. In a whorehouse cell the raped becomes the rapist, better than making it with a donkey in the river. Someone talks to no one on the phone, after hanging up the receiver. Someone talks to no one in front of the TV set. Someone talks to no one in front of a one-armed bandit. Someone waters a pot of plastic flowers. Someone climbs on an empty bus, at dawn, and the bus stays empty.

1969: Rio de Janeiro
Expulsion from the Slums

They refuse to go. They have been the poorest of the poor in the countryside and now they're the poorest in the city, always the last in line, people with cheap hands and dancing feet. Here, at least, they live near the places where they earn their bread. The inhabitants of Praia do Pinto and the other slums covering Rio de Janeiro's mountains have turned stubborn. But the military has long eyed these tracts, highly salable and resalable and well-suited for speculation, and so the problem will be solved by means of an opportune fire. The firemen never turn up. Dawn is the hour of tears and cinders. After fire destroys the houses made of garbage, they sweep up the people like garbage and take them far away for dumping.

(340)

1969: Baixo Grande
A Castle of Garbage

Old man Gabriel dos Santos does what his dreams tell him to do. He dreams the same crazy dreams in Brazil that Antonio Gaudí dreamed decades ago in Catalonia, in far-off Barcelona, although old Gabriel has never heard of Gaudí or seen his works.

As soon as he awakes, old Gabriel starts modeling with his hands the marvels he sees in his dreams, before they get away from him. Thus he has built the House of the Flower. In it he lives, on the slope of a hill beaten by the ocean wind. From dream to dream, through the years, old Gabriel's home keeps growing, this strange castle or beast of bright colors and sinuous forms, all made of garbage.

Old Gabriel, worker in the salt mines, never went to school, never watched television, never had money. He knows no rules, has no models. He plays around, in his own free style, with whatever leftovers the nearby city of Cabo Frío throws his way: fenders, headlights, splintered windows and smashed bottles, broken dishes, bits of old iron, chair legs, wheels . . .

(171)

1969: Arque Pass
The Last Stunt of Aviator Barrientos

Cardinal Maurer says that President Barrientos is like Saint Paul, because he roams the Bolivian countryside handing out truths. Barrientos also hands out money and soccer balls. He comes and goes, raining banknotes by helicopter. Gulf Oil gave the helicopter to Barrientos in exchange for the two billion dollars' worth of gas and one billion of petroleum that Barrientos gave Gulf Oil.

On this same helicopter, Barrientos paraded with Che Guevara's body tied to its skids through the skies of Bolivia. On this helicopter Barrientos arrives at Arque Pass on one of his incessant junkets, and as usual tosses money down on the campesinos; but on taking off, he collides with a wire fence and crashes against some rocks, burning himself alive. After burning so many pictures and books, fiery Barrientos dies cooked to a crisp in his helicopter, filled to the brim with banknotes that burn with him.

(16, 17, and 474)

1969: San Salvador and Tegucigalpa
Two Turbulent Soccer Matches

are played between Honduras and El Salvador. Ambulances remove the dead and wounded from the stands, while fans continue the stadium uproar in the streets.

Immediately, the two countries break relations. In Tegucigalpa, automobile windshields carry stickers that say: *Honduran—grab a stick, be a man, kill a Sal-va-dor-e-an.* In San Salvador, the newspapers urge the army to invade Honduras *to teach those barbarians a lesson.* Honduras expels Salvadoran campesinos, who are mostly unaware they are foreigners, having never seen an identity document. The Honduran government forces the Salvadorans to leave with nothing but what they have on, and then burns their shacks, describing the expulsion as "agrarian reform." The government of San Salvador considers all Hondurans who live there to be spies.

War soon breaks out. The army of El Salvador crosses into Honduras and advances, machinegunning border villages.

(84, 125, and 396)

1969: San Salvador and Tegucigalpa
The Soccer War

pits as enemies two fragments of Central America, shreds of what was a single republic a century and a half ago.

Honduras, a small agrarian country, is dominated by big landlords.

El Salvador, a small agrarian country, is dominated by big land-lords.

The campesinos of Honduras have neither land nor work.

The campesinos of El Salvador have neither land nor work.

In Honduras there is a military dictatorship born of a coup d'état.

In El Salvador there is a military dictatorship born of a coup d'état.

The general who governs Honduras was trained at the School of the Americas in Panama.

The general who governs El Salvador was trained at the School of the Americas in Panama.

From the United States come the weapons and advisers of the dictator of Honduras.

From the United States come the weapons and advisers of the dictator of El Salvador.

The dictator of Honduras accuses the dictator of El Salvador of being a Communist in the pay of Fidel Castro.

The dictator of El Salvador accuses the dictator of Honduras of being a Communist in the pay of Fidel Castro.

The war lasts one week. While war continues, the people of Honduras think their enemy is the people of El Salvador and the people of El Salvador think their enemy is the people of Honduras. They leave four thousand dead on the battlefields.

(84 and 125)

1969: Port-au-Prince

A Law Condemns to Death Anyone Who Says or Writes Red Words in Haiti

Article One: Communist activities are declared to be crimes against the security of the state, in whatsoever form: any profession of Communist faith, verbal or written, public or private, any propagation of Communist or anarchist doctrines through lectures, speeches, conversations, readings, public or private meetings, by way of pamphlets, posters, newspapers, magazines, books, and pictures; any oral or written correspondence with local or foreign associations, or with persons dedicated to the diffusion of Communist or anarchist ideas; and furthermore, the act of receiving, collecting, or giving funds directly or indirectly destined for the propagation of said ideas.

Article Two: The authors and accomplices of these crimes shall be sentenced to death. Their movable and immovable property shall be confiscated and sold for the benefit of the state.

> Dr. François Duvalier
> President-for-Life
> of the Republic of Haiti
> (351)

1970: Montevideo
Portrait of a Torture Trainer

The Tupamaro guerrillas execute Dan Anthony Mitrione, one of the North American instructors of the Uruguayan police.

The dead man gave his courses to officers in a soundproof basement. For his practical lessons he used beggars and prostitutes pulled off the street. He showed his pupils the effects of various electric voltages on the most sensitive parts of the human body, and how to apply emetics and other chemical substances efficaciously. In recent months three men and a woman died during these classes in the Technique of Interrogation.

Mitrione despised disorder and dirt. A torture chamber should be as aseptic as an operating room. And he detested incorrect language: *"Not balls, commissioner. Testicles."*

He also abominated useless expense, unnecessary movement, avoidable damage.

"It's an art, more than a technique," he said. *"The precise pain in the precise place, in the precise amount."*

(225)

1970: Managua
Rugama

A distinguished poet, a little man in a surplice who received Holy Communion standing up, shoots his last bullet and dies resisting a whole battalion of Somoza's troops.

Leonel Rugama was twenty.

Of friends, he preferred chess players.

Of chess players, those who lose because of the girl passing by.
Of those who pass by, the one who stays.
Of those who stay, the one who has yet to come.
Of heroes, he preferred those who don't say they are dying for
their country.
Of countries, the one born of his death.

(399)

1970: Santiago de Chile
Landscape after Elections

In a display of unpardonably bad conduct, the Chilean people elect
Salvador Allende president. Another president, of the International
Telephone and Telegraph Corporation, offers a million dollars to
whoever can put an end to this disgrace, while the president of the
United States earmarks ten million for the affair. Richard Nixon instructs the CIA to prevent Allende from sitting in the presidential
chair; or, should he sit, to see that the chair doesn't stay under him
long.

General René Schneider, head of the army, rejects the call for
a coup d'état and is struck down in an ambush: *"Those bullets were
for me,"* says Allende.

Loans from the World Bank and all other official and private
banks are suspended, except those for the military. The price of
copper plummets.

From Washington, Secretary of State Henry Kissinger explains:
*"I don't see why we should have to stand by and let a country go
Communist due to the irresponsibility of its own people."*

(138, 181, and 278)

1971: Santiago de Chile
Donald Duck

and his nephews spread the virtues of consumer civilization among
the savages of an underdeveloped country with picture-postcard landscapes. Donald's nephews offer soap bubbles to the stupid natives in
exchange for nuggets of pure gold, while Uncle Donald fights outlaw
revolutionaries who disturb order.

From Chile, Walt Disney's comic strips are distributed throughout South America and enter the souls of millions of children. Donald Duck does not come out against Allende and his red friends; he doesn't need to. The world of Disney is already the lovable zoo of capitalism: Ducks, mice, dogs, wolves, and piglets do business, buy, sell, respond to advertising, get credit, pay dues, collect dividends, dream of bequests, and compete among themselves to have more and get more.

(139 and 287)

1971: Santiago de Chile
"Shoot at Fidel,"

the CIA has ordered two of its agents. Certain TV cameras that appear to be busy filming Fidel Castro's visit to Chile conceal automatic pistols. The agents zoom in on Fidel, they have him in their sights—but neither shoots.

For many years now, specialists of the CIA's technical services division have been dreaming up attacks on Fidel. They've spent fortunes trying out cyanide capsules in chocolate malteds, and pills that dissolve in beer and rum and are untraceable in an autopsy. They've tried bazookas and telescopic rifles, a thirty-kilo plastic bomb that an agent was to put in a drain beneath a speaker's platform. Even poisoned cigars: They fixed up a special Havana for Fidel—supposed to kill the moment it touched his lips. But it didn't work, so they tried another guaranteed to produce nausea and, worse yet, a high-pitched voice—if they couldn't kill *him*, they hoped at least to kill his prestige. To this end also they tried spraying the microphone with a powder guaranteed to provoke in mid-speech an irresistible tendency to talk nonsense, and then, as the coup de grâce, concocted a depilatory potion to make his beard fall out, leaving him naked before the crowd.

(109, 137, and 350)

1972: Managua
Nicaragua, Inc.

The tourist arrives in Somoza's plane or ship and lodges in one of Somoza's hotels in the capital. Tired, he falls asleep on a bed and mattress manufactured by Somoza. On awaking, he drinks Presto coffee, property of Somoza, with milk from Somoza's cows and sugar harvested on a Somoza plantation and refined in a Somoza mill. He lights a match produced by Somoza's firm, Momotombo, and tries a cigarette from the Nicaraguan Tobacco Company, which Somoza owns in association with the British-American Tobacco Company.

The tourist goes out to change money at a Somoza bank and buys the Somoza daily *Novedades* on the corner. Reading *Novedades* is an impossible feat, so he throws the paper into the garbage which, tomorrow morning, will be collected by a Mercedes truck imported by Somoza.

The tourist climbs on one of Somoza's Condor buses, which will take him to the mouth of the Masaya volcano. Rolling toward the fiery crest, he sees through the window the barrios of tin cans and mud where live the dirt-cheap hands used by Somoza.

The tourist returns at nightfall. He drinks a rum distilled by Somoza, with ice from the Somoza Polar company, eats meat from one of his calves, butchered in one of his slaughterhouses, with rice from one of his farms and salad dressed with Corona oil, which belongs jointly to Somoza and United Brands.

Half past midnight, the earthquake explodes. Perhaps the tourist is one of the twelve thousand dead. If he doesn't end in some common grave, he will rest in peace in a coffin from Somoza's mortuary concern, wrapped in a shroud from El Porvenir textile mill, property of . . . .

(10 and 102)

1972: Managua
Somoza's Other Son

The cathedral clock stops forever at the hour the earthquake lifts the city into the air. The quake shakes Managua and destroys it.

In the face of this catastrophe Tachito Somoza proves his virtues both as statesman and as businessman. He decrees that bricklayers shall work sixty hours a week without a centavo more in pay and declares: *"This is the revolution of opportunities."*

Tachito, son of Tacho Somoza, has displaced his brother Luis from the throne of Nicaragua. A graduate of West Point, he has sharper claws. At the head of a voracious band of second cousins and third uncles, he swoops down on the ruins. He didn't invent the earthquake, but he gets his out of it.

The tragedy of half a million homeless people is a splendid gift for this Somoza, who traffics outrageously in debris and lands; and, as if that weren't enough, he sells in the United States the blood donated to victims of the quake by the International Red Cross. Later, he extends this profitable scam: Showing more initiative and enterprising spirit than Count Dracula, Tachito Somoza founds a limited company to buy blood cheap in Nicaragua and sell it dear on the North American market.

(10 and 102)

Tachito Somoza's Pearl of Wisdom

I don't show off my money as a symbol of power, but as a symbol of job opportunities for Nicaraguans.

(434)

1972: Santiago de Chile
Chile Trying to Be Born

A million people parade through the streets of Santiago in support of Salvador Allende and against the embalmed bourgeoisie who pretend to be alive and Chilean.

A people on fire, a people breaking the custom of suffering: In search of itself, Chile recovers its copper, iron, nitrates, banks, foreign trade, and industrial monopolies. It also nationalizes the ITT telephone system, paying for it the small amount that ITT said it was worth in its tax returns.

(278 and 449)

1972: Santiago de Chile
Portrait of a Multinational Company

ITT has invented a night scope to detect guerrillas in the dark, but doesn't need it to find them in the government of Chile—just money, of which the company is spending plenty against President Allende.

Recent experience shows how worthwhile it is: The generals who now rule Brazil have repaid ITT several times over the dollars invested to overthrow President Goulart.

ITT, with its four hundred thousand workers and officials in seventy countries, earns much more than Chile. On its board of directors sit men who were previously directors of the CIA and the World Bank. ITT conducts multiple businesses on all the continents: It produces electronic equipment and sophisticated weapons, organizes national and international communication systems, participates in space flights, lends money, works out insurance deals, exploits forests, provides tourists with automobiles and hotels, and manufactures telephones and dictators.

(138 and 407)

1973: Santiago de Chile
The Trap

By diplomatic pouch come the dollars that finance strikes, sabotage, and lies. Businessmen paralyze Chile and deny it food. There is no other market than the black market. People have to form long lines for a pack of cigarettes or a kilo of sugar. Getting meat or oil requires a miracle of the Most Sainted Virgin Mary. The Christian Democrats and the newspaper *El Mercurio* abuse the government and openly demand a redemptory coup d'état, since the time has come to finish with this red tyranny. Newspapers, magazines, and radio and TV stations echo the cry. For the government it is tough to make any move whatsoever: judges and parliamentarians dig in their heels, while in the barracks key military men whom Allende believes loyal conspire against him.

In these difficult times, workers are discovering the secrets of the economy. They're learning it isn't impossible to produce without bosses or supply themselves without merchants. But they march without weapons, empty-handed, down this freedom road.

Across the horizon sail U.S. warships preparing to exhibit themselves off the Chilean coast. The military coup, so much heralded, occurs.

(181, 278, and 449)

1973: Santiago de Chile

Allende

He likes the good life. He has said many times that he doesn't have what it takes to be an apostle or a martyr. But he has also said that it's worthwhile to die for that without which it's not worthwhile to live.

The rebel generals demand his resignation. They offer him a plane to take him out of Chile. They warn him that the presidential palace will be bombarded.

Together with a handful of men, Salvador Allende listens to the news. The generals have taken over the country. Allende dons a helmet and readies his rifle. The first bombs fall with a shuddering crash. The president speaks on the radio for the last time:

"*I am not going to resign . . .*"

(449 and 466)

1973: Santiago de Chile

Great Avenues Will Open Up, Announces Salvador Allende in His Final Message

I am not going to resign. Placed in a critical moment of history, I will pay with my life for the loyalty of the people. And let me tell you that I am sure the seed we sowed in the dignified conscience of Chileans will definitely not be destroyed. They have the force. They might be able to overcome us, but social processes cannot be stopped with crime or force. History is ours and the people make it . . .

Workers of my country: I have faith in Chile and its destiny. Other men will surmount this gray and bitter moment when treason seeks to impose itself. Rest assured that, much sooner than later, great avenues will once again open up through which free mankind shall pass to build a better society. Long live Chile, long live the people, long live the workers! These are my last words. I am certain that my sacrifice will not be in vain.

1973: Santiago de Chile
The Reconquest of Chile

A great black cloud rises from the flaming palace. President Allende dies at his post as the generals kill Chileans by the thousands. The Civil Registry does not record the deaths, because the books don't have room enough for them, but General Tomás Opazo Santander offers assurances that the victims do not exceed .01 percent of the population, which is not, after all, a high social cost, and CIA director William Colby explains in Washington that, thanks to the executions, Chile is avoiding a civil war. Señora Pinochet declares that the tears of mothers will redeem the country.

Power, all power, is assumed by a military junta of four members, formed in the School of the Americas in Panama. Heading it is General Augusto Pinochet, professor of geopolitics. Martial music resounds against a background of explosions and machinegun fire. Radios broadcast decrees and proclamations which promise more bloodshed, while the price of copper suddenly rises on the world market.

The poet Pablo Neruda, dying, asks for news of the terror. At moments he manages to sleep, and raves in his sleep. The vigil and the dream are one great nightmare. Since he heard Salvador Allende's proud farewell on the radio, the poet has begun his death-throes.

(278, 442, and 449)

1973: Santiago de Chile
The Home of Allende

Before attacking the presidential palace, they bombarded Allende's house.

Afterward, the soldiers wiped out whatever remained. With bayonets they ripped up paintings by Matta, Guayasamín, and Porto-carrero; with axes they smashed furniture.

A week has passed. The house is a garbage heap. Arms and legs from the suits of armor that adorned the staircase are littered everywhere. In the bedroom a soldier snores, sleeping off a hangover, his legs flung apart, surrounded by empty bottles.

From the living room comes a moaning and panting. There, in a big yellow armchair, torn apart but still standing, the Allendes' bitch is giving birth. The puppies, still blind, grope for her warmth and milk. She licks them.

(345)

1973: Santiago de Chile

The Home of Neruda

Amid the devastation, in a home likewise chopped to bits, lies Neruda, dead from cancer, dead from sorrow. His death isn't enough, though, Neruda being a man so stubbornly alive, so the military must kill his things. They splinter his happy bed and happy table, they disembowel his mattress and burn his books, smash his lamps and his colored bottles, his pots, his paintings, his seashells. They tear the pendulum and the hands off his wall clock; and with a bayonet gouge out the eye of the portrait of his wife.

From his devastated home, flooded with water and mud, the poet leaves for the cemetery. A cortege of intimate friends escorts him, led by Matilde Urrutia. (He once said to her: *It was so beautiful to live when you were living.*)

Block by block, the cortege grows. On every street corner it is joined by people who fall into step despite the military trucks bristling with machineguns and the carabineros and soldiers who come and go on motorcycles and in armored cars, exuding noise and fear. Behind some window, a hand salutes. High on some balcony a handkerchief waves. This is the twelfth day since the coup, twelve days of shutting up and dying, and for the first time the Internationale is heard in Chile—the Internationale hummed, groaned, wept, but not sung until the cortege becomes a procession and the procession a demonstration, and the people, marching against fear, break into song in the streets of Santiago, at the top of their lungs, with all their voices, to accompany in a fitting way Neruda, the poet, their poet, on his last journey.

(314 and 442)

1973: Miami

Sacred Consumerism Against
the Dragon of Communism

The bloodbath in Chile inspires fear and disgust everywhere, but not in Miami: A jubilant demonstration of exiled Cubans celebrates the murder of Allende and all the others.

Miami now has the greatest concentration of Cubans in the world, Havana excepted. Eighth Street is the Cuba that was. The dreams of bringing down Fidel have faded, but walking down Eighth Street one returns to the good old lost days.

Bankers and mafiosi run the show here; anyone who thinks is crazy or a dangerous Communist, and blacks still know their place. Even the silence is strident. Plastic souls and flesh-and-blood automobiles are manufactured. In the supermarkets, things buy people.

(207)

1973: Recife

Eulogy of Humiliation

In the capital of northeast Brazil, Gilberto Freyre attends the opening of a restaurant named for his famous book, *Great House and Slave Quarters*. Here, the writer celebrates the fortieth anniversary of the book's first edition.

The waiters serving the tables are dressed as slaves. Atmosphere is created by whips, shackles, pillories, chains, and iron collars hanging from the walls. The guests feel they have returned to a superior age when black served white without any joking, as the son served the father, the woman her husband, the civilian the soldier, and the colony the motherland.

The dictatorship of Brazil is doing everything possible to further this end. Gilberto Freyre applauds it.

(170 and 306)

1974: Brasília

Ten Years after the Reconquest of Brazil

the economy is doing very well. The people, very badly. According to official statistics, the military dictatorship has made Brazil an economic power, with a high growth index for its gross national product. They also show that the number of undernourished Brazilians has risen from twenty-seven million to seventy-two million, of whom thirteen million are so weakened by hunger that they can no longer run.

(371, 377, and 378)

1974: Rio de Janeiro

Chico

This dictatorship hurts people and decomposes music. Chico Buarque, made of music and people, sings against it.

Of every three songs he writes, the censor bans or mutilates two. Almost daily, the political police make him undergo long interrogations. As he enters their offices, they search his clothing. As he leaves, Chico searches his innards to see if the police have put a censor in his soul or, in an unguarded moment, confiscated his joy.

1974: Guatemala City

Twenty Years after the Reconquest of Guatemala

In towns and cities chalk crosses appear on doors, and by the roadsides heads are stuck on stakes. As a lesson and a warning, crime is turned into a public spectacle. The victims are stripped of name and history, then thrown into the mouth of a volcano or to the bottom of the sea, or buried in a common grave under the inscription *NN*, which means *non nato*, which means not born. For the most part this state terrorism functions without uniform. It is called the Hand, the Shadow, the Lightning Flash, the Secret Anticommunist Army, the Order of Death, the Squadron of Death.

General Kjell Laugerud, newly come to the presidency after

faked elections, commits himself to a continued application in Guatemala of the techniques pioneered by the Pentagon in Vietnam. Guatemala is the first Latin American laboratory for dirty war.

(450)

1974: Forests of Guatemala
The Quetzal

was always the joy of the air in Guatemala. The most resplendent of birds continues to be the symbol of this country, although now rarely if ever seen in the high forests where it once flourished. The quetzal is dying out while vultures are multiplying. The vulture, who has a good nose for death from afar, completes the work of the army, following the executioners from village to village, circling anxiously.

Will the vulture, shame of the sky, replace the quetzal on banknotes, in the national anthem, on the flag?

1974: Ixcán
A Political Education Class in Guatemala

Full of worms and uncertainties, the guerrillas cross the forest. These famished shadows have been walking in the dark for many days beneath a roof of trees, shut off from the sun. For a clock, they use the voices of the thicket: The nightjar sings from the river announcing dawn; at dusk the parrots and macaws begin their scandalous chatter; when night falls the badgers scream and the coatis cough. On this occasion, for the first time in months, the guerrillas hear a cock crow. A village is close by.

In this village on this sierra, a landlord known as the Tiger of Ixcán is boss. Like the other masters of this land, he is exempted from the law and criminal responsibility. On his farms are gallows, whips, and pillories. When the local labor force is insufficient, the army sends him Indians by helicopter, to cut down trees or pick coffee for nothing.

Few have seen the Tiger of Ixcán. All fear him. He has killed many, has had many killed.

The guerrillas bring the Indians together and show them. The Tiger, dead, looks like an empty costume.

(336)

1974: Yoro
Rain

In Chile he has seen a lot of dying, his dearest friends shot, beaten, or kicked to death. Juan Bustos, one of President Allende's advisers, has saved himself by a hair.

Exiled in Honduras, Juan drags out his days. Of those who died in Chile, how many died instead of him? From whom is he stealing the air he breathes? He has been this way for months, dragging himself from sorrow to sorrow, ashamed of surviving, when one evening his feet take him to a town called Yoro, in the central depths of Honduras.

He arrives in Yoro for no particular reason, and in Yoro spends the night under any old roof. He gets up very early and starts walking half-heartedly through the dirt streets, fearing melancholy, staring without seeing.

Suddenly, the rain hits him, so violent that Juan covers his head, though noticing right away that this prodigious rain isn't water or hail. Crazy silver lights bounce off the ground and jump through the air.

"*It's raining fish!*" cries Juan, slapping at the live fish that dive down from the clouds and leap and sparkle around him. Never again will it occur to him to curse the miracle of being alive, never again will he forget that he had the luck to be born in America.

"*That's right,*" says a neighbor, quietly, as if it were nothing. "*Here in Yoro it rains fish.*"

1975: San Salvador
Miguel at Seventy

Each day of life is an unrepeatable chord of a music that laughs at death. With the dangerous Miguel still alive, El Salvador's masters decide to hire an assassin to send his life and his music somewhere else.

The assassin has a dagger hidden beneath his shirt. Miguel sits talking to students at the university. He is telling them that young people must take the place of their jaded elders, that they must act, risk their necks, and do what must be done without cackling like hens each time they lay an egg. The assassin slowly slips through the audience until he's right behind Miguel. But as he raises the blade, a woman screams and Miguel automatically flings himself to the ground, just avoiding the blow.

And thus occurs the twelfth birth of Miguel Mármol, at seventy years of age.

(222)

1975: San Salvador
Roque

Roque Dalton, Miguel Mármol's pupil in the art of resurrection, has twice escaped death up against the wall. Once he was saved because the government fell; the second time because the wall itself fell, thanks to an opportune earthquake. He also escaped from the torturers, who left him in bad shape but alive, and from the police, who chased him with blazing guns. He even escaped from stone-throwing soccer fans, from the fury of a woman scorned, and from numerous husbands thirsting for revenge.

Profound yet playful, the poet Roque preferred to laugh at himself than take life too seriously, and so saved himself from grandiloquence, solemnity, and other ailments so gravely afflicting Latin American political poetry.

Only from his comrades can he not save himself. It is they who condemn him, for the crime of Difference of Opinion. This bullet, the only one that could find Roque, had to come from right beside him.

(127)

1975: Amazon River
Tropical Landscape

The ship chugs slowly up the Amazon on this endless voyage from Belém to Manaos. Now and then, some shack masked by tangled lianas comes into view, and a naked child waves his hand at the crew.

On the jammed deck someone reads the Bible aloud, sonorous praises to God, but most people prefer to laugh and sing as bottles and cigarettes pass from mouth to mouth. A tame cobra entwines itself on iron crossbeams, brushing against the skins of dead brothers drying in the air. The owner of the cobra, seated on the deck, challenges the other passengers to a game of cards.

A Swiss journalist traveling on this ship has for hours been watching a poor, bony old man embracing a large carton he never unclutches, even in his sleep. Stung by curiosity, the Swiss offers cigarettes, cookies, and conversation, but the old fellow is one without vices who isn't hungry and has nothing to say.

In the middle of the voyage, in mid-jungle, the old man disembarks. The Swiss, helping him take the big carton ashore, peeks through the half-open lid and sees inside, wrapped in cellophane, a plastic palm tree.

(264)

1975: Amazon River

This Is the Father of All Rivers,

the mightiest river in the world, and the jungle sprouting from its breath is the last lung of this planet. The adventurous and the avaricious have flocked to Amazonia since the first Europeans who came this way discovered Indians with reversed feet, who walked backward instead of forward over these lands promising prodigious fortunes.

Since then, all business in Amazonia starts with a massacre. At an air-conditioned desk in São Paulo or New York, a corporate executive signs a check which amounts to an extermination order, for the initial job of clearing the jungle begins with Indians and other wild beasts.

They give the Indians sugar or salt mixed with rat poison, or bomb them from the air, or hang them by the feet to bleed to death without bothering to skin them, because who would buy the hides?

The job is finished off by Dow Chemical's defoliants, which devastated Vietnam's forests and now Brazil's. Blind tortoises stumble about where trees used to be.

(55, 65, 67, and 375)

1975: Ribeirão Bonito
A Day of Justice

Large as countries are the lands of the cattle companies, conquerors of Amazonia. The Brazilian generals exempt them from taxes, open up roads for them, give them credits and permission to kill.

The companies use tattered campesinos from the northeast transplanted here by rivers and poverty. The campesinos kill Indians, and are killed in turn; they steal the Indians' lands, and are stolen from in turn. They drive off the Indians' cattle, whose flesh they will never taste.

When the highway reaches the village of Ribeirão Bonito, the police begin the expulsion. Campesinos who resist are persuaded in jail. Pulverizing them with clubs or sticking needles under their fingernails prove useful techniques. The priest João Bosco Burnier arrives in the village, enters the jail, asks for the torturers. A cop replies by blowing his head off with a bullet.

The next day, furious women—Carmesinha, Naide, Margarida—erect an enormous cross. Behind them, six hundred campesinos brandish axes, picks, sticks. The whole village joins the attack, singing in chorus, a magnificent voice of voices; and now, where the jail stood, a small pile of rubble remains.

(65 and 375)

1975: Huayanay
Another Day of Justice

For some years the community of Huayanay in the Peruvian Andes has had a terrible affliction: Matías Escobar. This scoundrel, thief of goats and women, arsonist and murderer, does much harm before the community catches, judges, sentences, and executes him. Matías dies of two hundred and thirty blows in the village Plaza de Armas: Each member of the community contributes one blow, and afterward two hundred and thirty thumbprints sign the confession.

No one has paid the slightest attention to General Velasco Alvarado's decree that made Quechua an official language. Quechua is not taught in the schools or accepted in the courts. In the incomprehensible Castilian tongue a judge interrogates various Huayanay Indians, jailed in Lima. He asks them, as if it wasn't known, who killed Matías Escobar.

(203)

1975: Cuzco
Condori Measures Time by Bread

He works as a mule. At cockcrow the first cargo is already loaded on his back at the market or the station, and until nightfall he is on the streets of Cuzco transporting whatever he can get in exchange for whatever he can get. Crushed beneath the weight of bundles and years, his clothing in shreds, a man in shreds, Gregorio Condori works and remembers as long as his back and his memory hold out.

Since his bones hardened as a boy, he has been shepherd and pilgrim, laborer and soldier. In Urcos he was jailed for nine months for accepting a little broth made from a stolen cow. In Sicuani he saw his first train, a black snake snorting fire out of its head, and years later he fell on his knees as a plane crossed the sky like a condor announcing with hoarse screams the end of the world.

Condori remembers the history of Peru in terms of loaves: *"When five big loaves of pure wheat bread cost one real, and three cost half a real, Odría took the presidency from Bustamante."*

And then someone else came along who seized power from Odría, and then someone else, and another, and another, until finally Velasco threw out Belaúnde. And now who'll throw out Velasco? Condori has heard that Velasco sides with the poor.

(111)

1975: Lima
Velasco

A rooster crows out of tune. Hungry birds peck at dry grains. Blackbirds flap their wings over others' nests. Not exactly thrown out, he leaves anyway. Sick, pecked to pieces, discouraged, General Juan Velasco Alvarado quits the presidency of Peru.

The Peru he leaves is less unjust than the one he found; he took on the imperial monopolies and the feudal lords, and tried to enable Indians to be something more than exiles in their own land.

The Indians, tough as esparto grass, keep hoping their day will come. By Velasco's decree the Quechua language now has the same rights as Spanish, and is equally official, though no official cares. The Academy of the Quechua Language gets a subsidy from the state— the equivalent of six dollars and seventy-five cents a year.

1975: Lima
The Altarpieces of Huamanga

In Lima painters and scholars are indignant; even the avant-garde registers shock. The National Art Prize has been given to Joaquín López Antay, altarpiece-maker of Huamanga. A scandal. Artisanship is okay, say the Peruvian artists, as long as it knows its place.

The altarpieces of Huamanga, first created as portable altars, have been changing their casts of characters with the passage of time. Saints and apostles have given way to sheep suckling their lambs with the condor watching over the world, laborers and shepherds, punitive bosses, hatmakers in their workshops, and singers mournfully caressing their charangos.

López Antay, intruder into Art Heaven, learned from his Indian grandmother how to make altarpieces. More than half a century ago she taught him to do saints, and now she watches him at work, from the peace of her grave.

(31 and 258)

The Molas of San Blas

The Cuna Indians, on Panama's San Blas islands, make molas to be shown off from back or breast. With needle and thread, talent and patience, they combine scraps of colored cloth in unrepeatable patterns. Sometimes they imitate reality; sometimes they invent it. And sometimes, wanting to copy, just copy, some bird they have seen, they cut and sew, stitch by stitch, and end up discovering a new creature more colorful and melodious and fleet than any bird that's ever soared in the sky.

The Bark Paintings of the Balsas River

Before the rains, in the season of the new moon, they strip off the bark of the amate tree. The stripped tree dies. On its skin the Mexican Indians of the Balsas River region paint flowers and fantasies, radiant mountain birds and monsters lying in wait, or they paint the daily round of events in communities which greet the Virgin in devout procession and summon the rain in secret ceremonies.

Before the European conquest, other Indians had painted on amate bark the codices that told of people's lives and of the stars. When the conquistadors imposed their paper and their images, amates disappeared. For more than four centuries no one in the land of Mexico painted on this forbidden paper. Not long ago, in the middle of our century, amates returned: *"All the people are painters. All. Everyone."*

Ancient life breathes through these amates, which come from afar, from so very far away, but never arrive tired.

(57)

The Arpilleras of Santiago

The children, sleeping three to a bed, stretch out their arms toward a flying cow. Santa Claus has a bag of bread, not toys, slung over his shoulder. At the foot of a tree a woman begs. Under the red sun a skeleton drives a garbage cart. On endless roads go men without faces. An enormous eye watches. At the center of the silence and the fear steams the communal stewpot.

Chile is this world of colored rags against a background of flour sacks. With scraps of wool and old cloth, women from Santiago's wretched slums embroider arpilleras. The arpilleras are sold in churches. That anyone buys them is incredible. The women are amazed: *"We embroider our problems, and our problems are ugly."*

This was first done by the wives of prisoners. Then others took it up—for money, which is a help, but not just for money. Embroidering arpilleras brings the women together, eases their loneliness and sadness, and for a few short hours breaks the routine of obedience to husband, father, macho son, and General Pinochet.

The Little Devils of Ocumicho

Like the Chilean arpilleras, the little clay devils of the Mexican village of Ocumicho are the creations of women. These devils make love, in pairs or in groups, go to school, drive motorcycles or airplanes, sneak into Noah's Ark, hide among the rays of the moon-loving sun, and intrude into Christmas nativity scenes. They lie in wait under the table at the Last Supper, while Jesus Christ, nailed to the cross, shares a meal of Patzcuaro lakefish with his Indian disciples. Eating, Christ laughs from ear to ear as if he had suddenly discovered that this world is more easily redeemed by pleasure than by pain.

In dark, windowless houses the Ocumicho potters model these luminous figures. Women tied to an endless chain of children, prisoners of drunken husbands who beat them, practice a new free-style art. Condemned to submission, destined for sadness, they create each day a new rebellion.

On Private Property and the Right of Creation

Buyers want the Ocumicho potters to sign their works, so they use stamps to engrave their names at the foot of their little devils. But often they forget, or use a neighbor's stamp if their own isn't handy, so that María comes out as the artist of a work by Nicolasa, or vice versa.

They don't understand this business of solitary glory. In their Tarascan Indian community, all are one when it comes to this sort of thing. Outside the community, like the tooth that falls from a mouth, one is nobody.

(183)

1975: Cabimas

Vargas

Oil, passing along the banks of Lake Maracaibo, has taken away the colors. In this Venezuelan garbage dump of sordid streets, dirty air, and oily waters, Rafael Vargas lives and paints.

Grass does not grow in Cabimas, dead city, emptied land, nor do fish remain in its waters, nor birds in its air, nor roosters in its dawns; but in Vargas's paintings the world is in fiesta, the earth breathes at the top of its lungs, the greenest of trees burst with fruit and flowers, and prodigious fish, birds, and roosters jostle one another like people.

Vargas hardly knows how to read or write. He does know how to earn a living as a carpenter, and how as a painter to earn the clean light of his days: His is the revenge, the prophecy of one who paints not the reality he knows but the reality he needs.

1975: Salta

Happy Colors of Change

As in a painting by the Venezuelan Vargas, in the Argentine province of Salta police patrol cars were painted yellow and orange. Instead of sirens, they had music, and instead of prisoners, children: Patrol cars rolled along filled with children who came and went from remote shacks to the city's schools. Punishment cells and torture chambers were demolished. The police withdrew from soccer games and demonstrations. The tortured went free and the torturers, officers who specialized in breaking bones with hammers, disappeared behind bars. Police dogs, which once had terrorized the poor, began giving acrobatic performances in the slums.

This happened a couple of years ago, when Rubén Fortuny was Salta's chief of police. Fortuny didn't last long. While he did what he did, though, other men like him were committing similar insanities throughout Argentina, as if the whole country were clasped in some euphoric embrace.

Sad epilogue to this newest Peronist episode: Perón, having returned to power, has died, and the hangmen are once again free and busy.

They kill Fortuny with a bullet in the heart. Then they kidnap the governor who appointed him, Miguel Ragone. All they leave of Ragone is a bloodstain and a shoe.

1975: Buenos Aires

Against the Children of Evita and Marx

But for Argentines the dangerous wind of change refuses to die down. The military see the threat of social revolution peeking out of every door and prepare to save the nation. They have been saving the nation for nearly half a century; and more recently, in courses in Panama, have found support in the Doctrine of National Security, which confirms for them that the enemy is within. Certain finishing touches are added to the next coup d'état. The program of national purification will be applied *by every means*: This is a war, a war against the children of Evita and Marx, and in war the only sin is inefficiency.

(106, 107, and 134)

1976: Madrid

Onetti

He doesn't expect to find any messages in any bottles in any sea. But the despairing Juan Carlos Onetti refuses to be alone. He would be alone, of course, if it weren't for the inhabitants of the town of Santa María, sad like himself, invented by him to keep him company.

Onetti has lived in Madrid since he came out of prison. The military rulers of Uruguay had jailed him because a story to which he had given a prize in a competition he was judging was not to their liking.

Hands clasped behind his neck, the exile contemplates the damp stains on the ceiling of his room in Santa María or Madrid or Montevideo or who knows where. From time to time he picks himself up and writes shouts that only seem like whispers.

1976: San José

A Country Stripped of Words

President Aparicio Méndez declares that *the Democratic Party of the United States and the Kennedy family are sedition's best partners in Uruguay*. A journalist tapes this sensational revelation, in the presence of the bishop of the city of San José and other witnesses.

Aparicio Méndez was chosen president in an election in which twenty-two citizens voted: fourteen generals, five brigadiers, and three admirals. The military have forbidden their president to talk to journalists, to anyone, in fact, except his wife. For this particular indiscretion they punish the newspaper that publishes his declaration with two days' suspension; and the journalist is fired.

Before silencing their president, the military took the reasonable precaution of silencing the rest of Uruguay. Every word that is not a lie is subversive. No one may mention any of the thousands of politicians, trade unionists, artists, and scientists who have been placed outside the law. The word *guerrilla* is officially banned; instead, one must say *lowlife*, *criminal*, *delinquent*, or *evildoer*. Carnival musicians, typically cheeky and disrespectful, may not sing the words *agrarian reform*, *sovereignty*, *hunger*, *clandestine*, *dove*, *green*, *summer*, or *contracanto*. Nor may they sing the word *pueblo*, even when it means a small city.

In the kingdom of silence the chief jail for political prisoners is called Liberty. The prisoners, held in isolation, invent codes to speak without voices, knocking on the walls from cell to cell to form letters and words so they can continue liking and teasing each other.

(124 and 235)

A Uruguayan Political Prisoner, Mauricio Rosencof, Says His Piece

It is like the struggle of a man who resists being turned into a cow. Because they put us in a cow-making machine and told us that instead of talking we should moo. And that is the question: How a prisoner can resist being animalized in such a situation. It is a battle for dignity . . . There was one compañero who got hold of a bit of sugarcane, bored a hole in it with his fingernail, and made a flute. And this clumsy, rudimentary thing stammers a sort of music . . .

(394)

1976: Liberty
Forbidden Birds

The Uruguayan political prisoners may not talk without permission, or whistle, smile, sing, walk fast, or greet other prisoners; nor may they make or receive drawings of pregnant women, couples, butterflies, stars, or birds.

One Sunday, Didaskó Pérez, school teacher, tortured and jailed *for having ideological ideas*, is visited by his daughter Milay, age five. She brings him a drawing of birds. The guards destroy it at the entrance to the jail.

On the following Sunday, Milay brings him a drawing of trees. Trees are not forbidden, and the drawing gets through. Didaskó praises her work and asks about the colored circles scattered in the treetops, many small circles half-hidden among the branches: *"Are they oranges? What fruit is it?"*

The child puts a finger on his mouth. *"Sssssshhh."*

And she whispers in his ear: *"Silly. Don't you see they're eyes? They're the eyes of the birds that I've smuggled in for you."*

(204 and 459)

1976: Montevideo
Seventy-Five Methods of Torture,

some copied, others invented thanks to the creativity of the Uruguayan military, punish solidarity. Anyone doubting property rights or the law of obedience ends up in jail, grave, or exile. The danger-meter classifies citizens in three categories, A, B, or C, according to whether they are "dangerous," "potentially dangerous," or "not dangerous." Trade unions become police stations, and wages are cut in half. Whoever thinks or has ever thought loses his or her job. In primary schools, high schools, even the university, speaking of José Artigas's agrarian reform program is prohibited. Who cares if it was the first in America? Nothing is allowed to contradict this order of the deaf and dumb. Obligatory new texts impose military pedagogy on the students.

(235)

1976: Montevideo

"One Must Obey," the New Official Texts
Teach Uruguayan Students

The existence of political parties is not essential for a democracy. We have the clear example of the Vatican, where political parties do not exist and nevertheless there is a real democracy . . .

The equality of women, badly interpreted, means stimulating her sex and her intellectuality, while postponing her mission as mother and wife. If from the juridical standpoint man and woman are evidently equal, such is not the case from the biological standpoint. The woman as such is subject to her husband and hence owes him obedience. It is necessary that in any society there be a head who serves as guide, and the family is a society . . .

It is necessary for some to obey in order that others may exercise command. If no one obeyed, it would be impossible to rule . . .

(76)

1976: Montevideo

The Head Shrinkers

Dedicated to the prohibition of reality and the arson of memory, the Uruguayan military have beaten the world record for newspaper closures.

The weekly *Marcha*, after a long life, has ceased to be. One of its editors, Julio Castro, has been tortured to death, then disappeared—a dead man without a corpse. The other editors have been sentenced to prison, exile, or silence.

One night Hugo Alfaro, a movie critic condemned to wordlessness, sees a film that excites him. As soon as it ends he runs home and types a few pages, in a big hurry because it's late and *Marcha* closes its entertainment pages in the early hours. As he pecks out the last period, Alfaro suddenly realizes that *Marcha* hasn't existed for two years. Ashamed, he drops his review in a desk drawer.

This review, written for no one, deals with a Joseph Losey film set during the Nazi occupation of France, a film which shows how the machinery of repression grinds up not just the persecuted but also those who think they are safe, those who know what is happening, and even those who prefer not to know.

Meanwhile, on the River Plata's other bank, the Argentine military make their own coup d'état. One of the heads of the new dictatorship, General Ibérico Saint-Jean, clarifies things: *"First we'll kill all the subversives. Then we'll kill the collaborators. Then the sympathizers. Then the undecided. And finally, we'll kill the indifferent."*

(13 and 106)

1976: La Perla
The Third World War

From the top of a hill, on a chestnut mount, an Argentine gaucho looks on. José Julián Solanille sees a long military caravan approaching. He recognizes General Menéndez dismounting from a Ford Falcon. Out of trucks, shoved by clubs, tumble men and women, hoods over their heads, hands tied behind their backs. The gaucho sees one of the hooded ones make a break for it. He hears the shots. The fugitive falls, gets up, and falls, several times before falling for the last time. When the fusillade begins, men and women collapse like rag dolls. The gaucho spurs his horse and takes off. Behind him black smoke rises.

This valley, in the first undulations of the Córdoba sierra, is one of the many dumps for corpses. When it rains, smoke drifts up from the pits because of the quicklime they throw on the bodies.

In this holy war, the victims *disappear*. Those not swallowed by the earth are devoured by fish at the bottoms of rivers or the sea. Many have committed no greater crimes than appearing on a list of phone numbers. They march into nothingness, into the fog, into death, after torture in the barracks. *No one is innocent*, says Monseñor Plaza, bishop of La Plata, and General Camps says it is right to liquidate a hundred suspects if only five of them turn out to be guilty. Guilty of terrorism.

Terrorists, explains General Videla, *are not only those who plant bombs, but also those who act with ideas contrary to our Western and Christian civilization*. This is vengeance for the defeat of the West in Vietnam:

"*We are winning the Third World War,*" crows General Menéndez.

(100, 107, and 134)

1976: Buenos Aires
The Choice

One prisoner, pregnant, is offered the choice between rape or the electric prod. She chooses the prod, but after an hour can no longer endure the pain. They all rape her. As they rape her, they sing the Wedding March.

"*Well, this is war,*" says Monseñor Gracelli.

The men who burn breasts with blowtorches in the barracks wear scapulars and take communion every Sunday.

"*Above us all is God,*" says General Videla.

Monseñor Tortolo, president of the Episcopate, compares General Videla with Jesus Christ, and the military dictatorship with the Easter Resurrection. In the name of the Holy Father, nuncio Pío Laghi visits the extermination camps, exalts the military's love of God, Fatherland, and Family, and justifies state terrorism on the grounds that civilization has the right to defend itself.

(106, 107, and 134)

1976: La Plata
Bent over the Ruins, a Woman Looks

for something in her home that has not been destroyed. The forces of order have shattered María Isabel de Mariani's home, and she pokes through the remains in vain. What they have not stolen, they have pulverized. Only one record, Verdi's *Requiem*, is intact.

María Isabel would like to find in the litter some memento of her children and of her granddaughter, a photo or toy, book, ashtray, anything. Her children, suspected of running a clandestine press, have been gunned down. Her three-month-old granddaughter has been given away or sold as war booty by the officers.

It is summer, and the smell of gunpowder mixes with the aroma of flowering lindens. That aroma will forever be unbearable. María Isabel has no one to be with. She is the mother of subversives. Seeing her coming, her friends cross the street or avert their eyes. Her telephone is silent. No one tells her anything, even lies. Without help she proceeds to put the shreds of her destroyed home in boxes. Well after nightfall she pulls the boxes onto the sidewalk. Very early in the morning the garbage men collect the boxes, one by one, gently, without knocking them over. The garbage men treat the boxes with great care, as if aware they are full of the bits of a broken life. Silently peering through the remains of a venetian blind, María Isabel thanks them for this caress, the only one she has had since the sorrow began.

(317)

1976: Forest of Zinica
Carlos

He criticized you to your face, praised you behind your back.

He had the myopic, fanatical gaze of an angry rooster, sharp brown eyes from which he saw farther than others, a man of all or nothing; but moments of joy made him jump like a small child, and when he gave orders he seemed to be asking favors.

Carlos Fonseca Amador, leader of the Nicaraguan revolution, has died fighting in the jungle.

A colonel brings the news to the cell where Tomás Borge lies shattered.

Together they had traveled a long road, Carlos and Tomás, since the days when Carlos sold newspapers and candy in Matagalpa. Together they founded, in Tegucigalpa, the Sandinista Front.

"He's dead," says the colonel.

"You're wrong, colonel," says Tomás.

(58)

1977: Managua
Tomás

Bound to an iron ring, teeth chattering, drenched in shit, blood, and vomit, Tomás Borge is a pile of broken bones and stripped nerves, a scrap lying on the floor waiting for the next round of torture.

But this remnant of himself can still sail down secret rivers that take him beyond pain and madness. Letting himself go, he drifts into another Nicaragua. He sees it.

Through the hood that squeezes his face swollen by blows, he sees it: He counts the beds in each hospital, the windows in each school, the trees in each park, and sees the sleepers fluttering their eyelids, bewildered, those long dead from hunger and everything else that kills now being awakened by newly born suns.

(58)

1977: Solentiname Archipelago
Cardenal

The herons, looking at themselves in the shimmering mirror, lift their beaks. The fishermen's boats are already returning, and behind them swim the turtles that come here to give birth on the beach.

In a wooden cabin, Jesus is seated at the fishermen's table. He eats turtle eggs, fresh-caught *guapote,* and cassava. The forest, searching for him, slips its arms through the windows.

To the glory of this Jesus, Ernesto Cardenal, the poet-monk of Solentiname, writes. To his glory sings the trumpeter *zanate,* the homeless bird, always flying among the poor, that freshens its wings in the lake waters. And to his glory the fishermen paint. They paint brilliant pictures that announce Paradise—all brothers, no bosses, no peons—until one night the fishermen who paint Paradise decide to start making it, and cross the lake to attack the San Carlos barracks.

From the darkness, the owl promises trouble: *"Screwed . . . screwed . . ."*

The dictatorship kills many as these seekers of Paradise pass through the mountains and valleys and islands of Nicaragua. *The dough rises, the big loaf swells . . .*

(6 and 77)

Omar Cabezas Tells of the Mountain's Mourning for the Death of a Guerrilla in Nicaragua

I never forgave Tello for being killed with one bullet, just one bullet . . . I felt a great fear, and it was as if the mountain, too, felt fear. The wind dropped and the trees stopped swaying, not a leaf stirred, the birds stopped singing. Everything froze, awaiting that moment when they'd come and kill the lot of us.

And we set out. When we broke into a marching pace up the ravine, it was as if we were shaking the mountain, as if we were grabbing her and telling her: Who the hell does this bitch think she is?

Tello lived with the mountain. I'm convinced he had relations with her, she bore him sons; and when Tello died she felt that all was over, her commitment was gone, that all the rest was foolishness . . . But when she saw the will to fight of the men marching there over her, in her heart she realized that Tello was not the beginning and end of the world. Though Tello may have been her son, though he may have been her life, her secret lover, her brother, her creature, her stone, though Tello may have been her river . . . he was not the end of the world, and that after him came all of us who could still light a fire in her heart.

(73)

1977: Brasília
Scissors

Over a thousand Brazilian intellectuals sign a manifesto against censorship.

In July of last year, the military dictatorship stopped the weekly *Movimiento* from publishing the United States Declaration of Independence, because in it is said that the people have the right and the duty to abolish despotic governments. Since then the censorship has banned: the Bolshoi Ballet, because it is Russian; the erotic prints of Pablo Picasso, because they are erotic; and the *History of Surrealism,* because one of its chapters has the word *revolution* in its title ("Revolution in Poetry").

(371)

1977: Buenos Aires

Walsh

He mails a letter and several copies. The original letter, to the military junta that rules Argentina. The copies, to foreign press agencies. On the first anniversary of the coup d'état, he is sending a sort of statement of grievances, a record of the infamies committed by a regime that can only stagger in its dance of death. At the bottom he puts his signature and number (Rodolfo Walsh, I.D. 2845022). He is only steps from the post office when their bullets cut him down; and he is carried off wounded, not to be seen again.

His naked words were scandalous where such fear reigns, dangerous while the great masked ball continues.

(461)

1977: Río Cuarto

The Burned Books of Walsh and Other Authors Are Declared Nonexistent

IN VIEW OF the measure taken by the ex–Military Intervention of this National University in fulfillment of express superior orders, with respect to withdrawing from the Library Area all reading material of an antisocial nature and whose contents exuded ideologies alien to the Argentine National Being, constituting a source of extreme Marxist and subversive indoctrination, and
WHEREAS: Said literature having been opportunely incinerated, it is fitting to strike it from the patrimony of this House of Advanced Studies, the Rector of the National University of Río Cuarto
RESOLVES: To strike from the patrimony of the National University of Río Cuarto (Library Area) all the bibliography listed below: [Long list follows of books by Rodolfo Walsh, Bertrand Russell, Wilhelm Dilthey, Maurice Dobb, Karl Marx, Paulo Freire, and others].

(452)

1977: Buenos Aires

The Mothers of the Plaza de Mayo,

women born of their children, are the Greek chorus of this tragedy. Brandishing photos of their disappeared ones, they circle round and round the obelisk, before the Pink House of the government, as obstinately as they make pilgrimages to barracks, police stations, and sacristies, dried up from so much weeping, desperate from so much waiting for those who were and are no longer, or perhaps still are . . . who knows?

"I wake up believing he's alive," says one, say all. "I begin to disbelieve as the morning goes on. He dies on me again at noon. He revives in the evening, I begin to believe he'll come soon, and I set a place for him at the table, but he dies again and at night I fall asleep without hope. When I wake up, I feel he's alive . . ."

They call them *madwomen*. Normally no one speaks of them. With the situation normalized, the dollar is cheap and certain people, too. Mad poets go to their deaths, and normal poets kiss the sword while praising silence. With total normality the Minister of Finance hunts lions and giraffes in Africa and the generals hunt workers in the suburbs of Buenos Aires. New language rules make it compulsory to call the military dictatorship *Proceso de Reorganización Nacional*.

(106 and 107)

1977: Buenos Aires

Alicia Moreau

Sometimes she goes overboard in her faith, anticipating social revolution in a none too realistic way, or explodes publicly in tirades against military power and the Pope of Rome. But what would become of the Plaza de Mayo mothers without the enthusiasm of this sprite woman? She never lets them grow discouraged or feel defeated by so much indifference and jeering: *"One can always do something,"* she tells them. *"Together. Each one on her own, no. Let's—we have to—"*

She grasps her cane and is the first to move.

Alicia Moreau is nearly a hundred years old. She has been in the struggle since the days when socialists drank only water and sang only the Internationale. She has witnessed many marvels and betrayals, births and deaths,, and whatever her momentary troubles, she keeps believing that it's worthwhile to believe. Alicia Moreau is as lively now as she was when the century began and she made speeches from soapboxes between red flags in the worker barrios of Buenos Aires, or crossed the Andes on muleback, hurrying the animal so as not to arrive late at a feminist congress.

(221)

1977: Buenos Aires
Portrait of a Croupier

The Minister of Finance of the Argentine dictatorship is a pious devotee of private enterprise. He thinks about it on Sundays, when he kneels at the Mass, and also on weekdays, when he gives courses at the Military School. Nevertheless, the minister correctly withdraws from the company he directs, generously ceding it to the state for ten times its worth.

The generals turn the country into a barracks. The minister turns it into a casino. Argentina is deluged with dollars and consumer goods. It is the time of the hangman, but also of the conman and the conjurer. The generals order the country to shut up and obey, while the minister orders it to speculate and consume. Anyone who works is a sucker, anyone who protests, a corpse. To cut wages in half and reduce rebellious workers to nothing, the minister slips sweet silver bribes to the middle class, who fly to Miami and return loaded with mountains of gadgets and gimmickry. In the face of the daily massacre, people shrug their shoulders: *"They must have done something. It's for a good reason."*

Or they whistle and look the other way: *"Don't get involved."*

(143)

1977: Caracas

The Exodus of the Intruders

The prophet spoke in a café on Caracas's Calle Real de Sabana Grande. An extraterrestrial with flaming eyes appeared for a moment and announced that on a certain August Sunday a furious ocean would split the mountains and wipe out the city.

Bishops, witches, astronomers, and astrologers repeatedly issued reassurances that there was nothing to worry about, but they couldn't stop the panic from growing, from rolling like a ball through the barrios of Caracas.

Yesterday was the Sunday in question. The president of the republic ordered the police to take charge of the city. More than a million Caracans stampeded, fled with their belongings on their backs. More automobiles than people remained in the city.

Today, Monday, the fugitives begin to return. The ocean is where it always was, the mountains too. In the valley, Caracas continues to exist. And so the oil capital recovers its terrified citizens. They reenter as if begging pardon, because they know now that they are superfluous, that this is a world of wheels, not legs. Caracas belongs to its prepotent automobiles, not to whoever dares cross its streets to the annoyance of the machines. What would become of these people, condemned to live in a city that doesn't belong to them, if María Lionza didn't protect them and José Gregorio didn't cure them?

(135)

María Lionza

Her breasts rise above the center of Caracas and reign, nakedly, over the frenzy. In Caracas, in all Venezuela, María Lionza is a goddess.

Her invisible palace is far from the capital on a mountain in the Sorte chain. The rocks scattered over this mountain were once María Lionza's lovers, men who paid for a night of embraces by being converted into breathing stones.

Simón Bolívar and Jesus of Nazareth work for her in the sanctuary. Also helping her are three secretaries: one black, one Indian, one white. They attend to the faithful, who come loaded with offerings of fruit, perfumes, and undergarments.

María Lionza, untamed woman, feared and desired by God and Satan, has the powers of heaven and hell. She can inspire happiness or unhappiness; she saves if she feels like saving, and thunders if she feels like thundering.

(190 and 346)

José Gregorio

He is chastest of the chaste, María Lionza's white secretary. Doctor José Gregorio Hernández has never yielded to the temptations of the flesh. All the insinuating women who approached him ended up in convents, repenting, bathed in tears. This virtuous Physician of the Poor, this Apostle of Medicine, ended his days in 1919, undefeated. His immaculate body was pitilessly crushed by one of the two or three automobiles that circulated in Caracas at a snail's pace in those happy days. After death, the miraculous hands of José Gregorio have continued prescribing remedies and operating on the sick.

In the sanctuary of María Lionza, José Gregorio busies himself with public health problems. He has never failed to turn up from the Great Beyond at the call of sufferers, the only saint ever in a necktie and hat.

(363)

1977: Graceland

Elvis

Once, his way of shaking his left leg evoked screams. His lips, his eyes, his sideburns were sexual organs.

Now a soft ball of flab, Elvis Presley, dethroned king of rock 'n' roll, lies in bed, his glance floating between six television screens. The TVs, suspended from the ceiling, are each tuned to a different channel. Between sleep and dreams, always more asleep than awake, Elvis fires unloaded pistols, click, click, at the images he doesn't like. The suet ball of his body covers a soul made of Codeine, Morphine, Valium, Seconal, Placidyl, Quaalude, Nembutal, Valmid, Demerol, Elavil, Aventyl, Carbrital, Sinutab, and Amytal.

(197 and 409)

1978: San Salvador

Romero

The archbishop offers her a chair. Marianela prefers to talk standing up. She always comes for others; but this time Marianela comes for herself. Marianela García Vilas, attorney for the tortured and disappeared of El Salvador, does not come this time to ask the archbishop's solidarity with one of the victims of D'Aubuisson, Captain Torch, who burns your body with a blowtorch, or of some other military horror specialist. Marianela doesn't come to ask help for anyone else's investigation or denunciation. This time she has something personal to say to him. As mildly as she can she tells him that the police have kidnapped her, bound, beaten, humiliated, stripped her—and that they raped her. She tells it without tears or agitation, with her usual calm, but Archbishop Arnulfo Romero has never before heard in Marianela's voice these vibrations of hatred, echoes of disgust, calls for vengeance. When Marianela finishes, the archbishop, astounded, falls silent too.

After a long silence, he begins to tell her that the Church does not hate or have enemies, that every infamy and every action against God forms part of a divine order, that criminals are also our brothers and must be prayed for, that one must forgive one's persecutors, one must accept pain, one must . . . Suddenly, Archbishop Romero stops.

He lowers his glance, buries his head in his hands. He shakes his head, denying it all, and says: *"No, I don't want to know."*

"I don't want to know," he says, and his voice cracks.

Archbishop Romero, who always gives advice and comfort, is weeping like a child without mother or home. Archbishop Romero, who always gives assurance, the tranquillizing assurance of a neutral God who knows all and embraces all—Archbishop Romero doubts.

Romero weeps and doubts and Marianela strokes his head.

(259 and 301)

1978: La Paz

Five Women

"What is the main enemy? The military dictatorship? The Bolivian bourgeoisie? Imperialism? No, compañeros. I want to tell you just this: Our main enemy is fear. We have it inside us."

This is what Domitila said at the Catavi tin mine, and then she came to the capital with four other women and more than twenty kids. On Christmas Day they started their hunger strike. No one believed in them. Some thought it a ridiculous joke: *"So five women are going to overthrow the dictatorship?"*

The priest Luis Espinal is the first to join them. In no time there are fifteen hundred people starving themselves all over Bolivia. The five women, accustomed to hunger since they were born, call water *chicken* or *turkey* and salt *pork chop*, and feed on laughter. Meanwhile the hunger strikers multiply—three thousand, ten thousand—until the Bolivians who have stopped eating and working can no longer be counted, and twenty-three days after the start of the hunger strike the people invade the streets, and now nothing can be done to stop them.

The five women have overthrown the military dictatorship.

(1)

1978: Managua

"The Pigsty"

is what Nicaraguans call the National Palace. On the first floor of this pretentious Parthenon senators spout off. On the second, deputies.

One midday in August, a handful of guerrillas led by Edén Pastora and Dora María Téllez attack the Pigsty and in three minutes capture all of Somoza's legislators. To get them released, Somoza has but to free Sandinista prisoners. People line the airport road to cheer them.

This is turning out to be a year of continuous war. Somoza started it with the murder of the journalist Pedro Joaquín Chamorro. Infuriated people promptly incinerate several of the dictator's businesses. Flames consume the prosperous Plasmaféresis, Inc., which exports Nicaraguan blood to the United States. The people swear that they won't rest until the vampire himself is buried in some place darker than the night, with a stake impaling his heart.

(10 and 460)

Tachito Somoza's Pearl of Wisdom

I am a businessman, but humble.

(434)

1978: Panama City
Torrijos

General Omar Torrijos says he does not want to enter history. He only wants to enter the Canal Zone, stolen by the United States at the turn of the century. Thus he wanders the world from country to country, government to government, platform to platform. When accused of serving Moscow or Havana, Torrijos laughs. Every people, he says, swallows its own aspirins for its own headache. If it comes to that, he says, he gets along better with the Castristas than with the castrati.

Finally the canal's fences fall. The United States, pressured by the world, signs a treaty that restores to Panama, by degrees, the canal and the prohibited zone that encloses it.

"It's better this way," says Torrijos, relieved. They've saved him the disagreeable task of blowing up the canal and all its installations.

(154)

1979: Madrid
Intruders Disturb the Quiet Ingestion of the Body of God

In a big church in Madrid, a special Mass celebrates the anniversary of Argentine independence. Diplomats, business executives, and military men have been invited by General Leandro Anaya, ambassador of the dictatorship which is so busy across the sea protecting the Argentine heritage of fatherland, faith, and other proprieties.

Through the stained-glass windows rich lights illumine the faces and fashions of the ladies and gentlemen. On Sundays like this, God is worthy of confidence. Very occasionally a timid cough decorates the silence, as the priest performs the rite: imperturbable silence of eternity, eternity of the Lord's elect.

The moment of communion comes. Ringed by bodyguards, the Argentine ambassador approaches the altar. He kneels, closes his eyes, opens his mouth. Instantly the flutter of white handkerchiefs unfurling, covering the heads of the women who walk up the aisles, all the aisles. The mothers of the Plaza de Mayo advance softly, cottony rustle, until they surround the bodyguards who surround the ambassador. Then they stare at him. Simply stare. The ambassador opens his eyes, looks at all these women looking at him without blinking, and swallows his saliva, while the priest's hand remains paralyzed in midair, the Host between his fingers.

The whole church is filled with these women. Suddenly there are no longer saints or merchants in this temple, nothing more than a multitude of uninvited women: black dresses, white handkerchiefs, all silent, all on their feet.

(173)

1979: New York
Banker Rockefeller Congratulates Dictator Videla

His Excellency Jorge Rafael Videla
President of Argentina
Buenos Aires, Argentina

Dear Mr. President,
I am very grateful to you for taking time to receive me during my recent visit to Argentina. Not having been there for seven years, it was encouraging to see what progress your government has made during the past three years, both in controlling terrorism and strengthening the economy. I congratulate you on what you have achieved and wish you every success for the future . . .
With warm good wishes,

Sincerely,

David Rockefeller

(384)

1979: Siuna

Portrait of a Nicaraguan Worker

José Villarreina, married, three children. Works for the North American company Rosario Mines, which seventy years ago overthrew President Zelaya. Since 1952, Villarreina has been scraping gold from the excavations at Siuna; even so, his lungs are not yet entirely rotted out.

At 1:30 P.M. on July 3, 1979, Villarreina looks out from one of the mineshafts and a mineral-loaded cart tears off his head. Thirty-five minutes later, the company notifies the dead man that in accordance with articles 18, 115, and 119 of the Labor Code, he is discharged for nonfulfillment of his contract.

(362)

1979: In All Nicaragua

The Earth Buckles

and shakes worse than in all the earthquakes put together. Airplanes fly over immense stretches of jungle dropping napalm, and bomb cities crisscrossed with barricades and trenches. The Sandinistas take over León, Masaya, Jinotega, Chinandega, Estelí, Carazo, Jinotepe . . .

While Somoza awaits a sixty-five-million-dollar loan, approved by the International Monetary Fund, in Nicaragua they fight tree by tree, house by house. With masks or handkerchiefs covering their faces, the youths attack with rifles or machetes, sticks or stones; even a toy gun serves to make an impression.

In Masaya, which in the language of the Indians means *city that burns*, the fighters, adept in pyrotechnics, turn drainpipes into mortars and invent a fuseless contact bomb which explodes on striking. Old women weave between the bullets carrying large bags full of bombs, which they hand around like loaves of bread.

(10, 238, 239, and 320)

1979: In All Nicaragua
Get It Together, Everyone,

don't lose it, the big one is here, the shit has hit the fan, hell has broken loose, we're at fever heat, fighting with nothing but a home-made arsenal against tanks, armored cars, and planes, so everyone get into it, from here on no one ducks out, it's our war, the real thing, if you don't die killing you'll die dying, shoulder to shoulder makes us bolder, all together now, the people is us.

(10, 238, and 239)

From the Datebook of Tachito Somoza

1979
Thursday, July 12,
Love

1979: Managua
"Tourism must be stimulated,"

orders the dictator while Managua's eastern barrios burn, set ablaze by the air force.

From his bunker, great steel and cement uterus, Somoza rules. Here nothing penetrates, not the thunder of bombs, not the screams of people, nothing to ruffle the perfect silence. Here one sees nothing, smells nothing. In this bunker Somoza has lived for some time, right in the center of Managua but about as far from Nicaragua as you can get; and in this bunker, he now sits down with Fausto Amador.

Fausto Amador is the father of Carlos Fonseca Amador. The son, founder of the Sandinista Front, understood patriotism; the father, administrator general for the richest man in Central America, understands patrimony.

Surrounded by mirrors and plastic flowers, seated before a computer, Somoza, with Fausto Amador's help, organizes the liquidation of his businesses, which means the total pillage of Nicaragua.

Afterward, Somoza says on the telephone: *"I'm not going and they're not throwing me out."*

(10, 320, and 460)

1979: *Managua*
Somoza's Grandson

They're throwing him out and he's going. At dawn, Somoza boards a plane for Miami. In these final days the United States abandons him, but he does not abandon the United States: *"In my heart, I will always be part of this great nation."*

Somoza takes with him the gold ingots of the Central Bank, eight brightly colored parrots, and the coffins of his father and brother. He also takes the living body of the crown prince.

Anastasio Somoza Portocarrero, grandson of the founder of the dynasty, is a corpulent military man who has learned the arts of command and good government in the United States. In Nicaragua, he founded, and until today directed, the Basic Infantry Training School, a juvenile army group specializing in interrogations of prisoners—and famous for its skill. Armed with pincers and spoons, these lads can tear out fingernails without breaking the roots and eyes without injuring the lids.

The Somoza clan goes into exile as Augusto César Sandino strolls through Nicaragua beneath a rain of flowers, a half century after they shot him. This country has gone mad; lead floats, cork sinks, the dead escape from the cemetery, and women from the kitchen.

(10, 322, and 460)

1979: *Granada*
The Comandantes

Behind them, an abyss. Ahead and to either side, an armed people on the attack. La Pólvora barracks in the city of Granada, last stronghold of the dictatorship, is falling.

When the colonel in command hears of Somoza's flight, he orders the machineguns silenced. The Sandinistas also stop firing.

Soon the iron gate of the barracks opens and the colonel appears, waving a white rag. *"Don't fire."*

The colonel crosses the street. *"I want to talk to the comandante."*
A kerchief covering one of the faces drops. *"I'm the comandante,"* says Mónica Baltodano, one of the Sandinista women who lead troops.
"What?"
Through the mouth of the colonel, this haughty macho, speaks the military institution, defeated but dignified. Virility of the pants, honor of the uniform. *"I don't surrender to a woman!"* roars the colonel.
And he surrenders.

1979: In All Nicaragua
Birth

The Nicaragua newly born in the rubble is only a few hours old, fresh new greenery among the looted ruins of war; and the singing light of the first day of Creation fills the air that smells of fire.

1979: Paris
Darcy

The Sorbonne confers the title of Doctor Honoris Causa on Darcy Ribeiro. He accepts, he says, on the merit of his failures.

Darcy has failed as an anthropologist, because the Indians of Brazil are still being annihilated. He has failed as rector of the university because the reality he wanted it to transform proved obdurate. He has failed as Minister of Education in a country where illiteracy never stops multiplying. He has failed as a member of a government that tried and failed either to make agrarian reform or to control the cannibalistic habits of foreign capital. He has failed as a writer who dreamed of forbidding history to repeat itself.

These are his failures. These are his dignities.

(376)

1979: Santiago de Chile

Stubborn Faith

General Pinochet stamps his signature on a decree that imposes private property on the Mapuche Indians. The government offers funds, fencing, and seeds to those who agree to parcel out their communities with good grace. If not, the government warns, they'll accept without any grace.

Pinochet is not the first to believe that greed is part of human nature and that God wants it that way. Long ago, the conquistador Pedro de Valdivia had tried to break up the indigenous communities of Chile. Since then, by fire and sword everything has been seized from the Indians, everything: land, language, religion, customs. But the Indians, hemmed in, trapped in poverty, exhausted by so much war and so much swindling, persist in believing that the world is a shared home.

1979: Chajul

Another Kind of Political Education in Guatemala

Patrocinio Menchú, Maya-Quiché Indian, born in the village of Chimel, had, along with his parents, defended the lands of his harassed community. From his parents he learned to walk the heights without slipping, to greet the sun according to ancient custom, to clear and fertilize the ground, and to stake his life on it.

Now, he is one of the prisoners that the army trucks have brought to the village of Chajul for the people to see. Rigoberta, his sister, recognizes him, although his face is swollen from beatings and he bleeds from his eyes, his tongueless mouth, and his nail-less fingers.

Five hundred soldiers—Indians too, Indians of other regions—stand guard over the ceremony. Herded into a circle, the whole population of Chajul is forced to watch. Rigoberta has to watch, while within her, as in everyone, a silent, moist curse blooms. The captain displays the nude bodies, flayed, mutilated, still alive, and says that these are Cubans who have come to stir up trouble in Guatemala. Showing off the details of the punishments that each one earned, the captain yells:

"Have a good look at what's in store for guerrillas!"
Then he soaks the prisoners with gasoline and sets fire to them.
Patrocinio Menchú was still tender corn. It was only sixteen years
ago that he was planted.

(72)

The Mayas Plant Each Child That Is Born

High up in the mountains, the Indians of Guatemala bury the umbilical cord while presenting the child to Grandpa Vólcano, Mother
Earth, Father Sun, Grandma Moon, all the powerful grandparents,
and asking them to protect the newly born from danger and error.

*Before the rain that irrigates us and before the wind that bears
us witness, we, who are part of you, plant this new child, this new
compañero, in this place . . .*

1980: La Paz
The Cococracy

General Luis García Meza, author of the 189th coup d'état in a century
and a half of Bolivia's history, announces that he will establish a free
economy, as in Chile, and make sure all extremists disappear, as in
Argentina.

With García Meza, the cocaine traffickers take over the state.
His brand-new Interior Minister, Colonel Luis Arce Gómez, divides
his time and energy between drug smuggling and heading up the
Bolivian Section of the World Anticommunist League. He will not
rest, he says, never rest, *until the cancer of Marxism is extirpated.*

The military government raises the curtain by assassinating Marcelo Quiroga Santa Cruz, enemy of Gulf Oil and its forty thieves,
implacable foe of hidden filth.

(157 and 257)

1980: Santa Ana de Yacuma
Portrait of a Modern Businessman

He fires from the hip, both bullets and bribes. At his waist he carries a golden pistol, in his mouth a golden smile. His bodyguards use machineguns with telescopic sights. He has twelve missile-armed combat planes and thirty cargo planes that take off early each morning from the Bolivian jungle loaded with cocaine paste. Roberto Suárez, cousin and colleague of the new Interior Minister, exports a ton a month.

"My philosophy," he says, *"is to do good."*

He claims that the money he has given to the Bolivian military would suffice to pay the country's external debt.

Like a good Latin American businessman, Suárez sends his winnings to Switzerland, where they find refuge in banking secrecy. But in Santa Ana de Yacuma, the town where he was born, he has paved the main street, restored the church, and given sewing machines to widows and orphans; and when he turns up there he bets thousands of dollars on a roll of the dice or a cockfight.

Suárez is the most important Bolivian capitalist in a huge multinational enterprise. In his hands, the price of a coca leaf is multiplied by ten as it changes into paste and leaves the country. Later, as it becomes powder and reaches the nose that inhales it, its price soars two hundred times. Like any raw material from a poor country, coca lines the pockets of intermediaries, and above all intermediaries in the rich country that consumes it transformed into cocaine, the white goddess.

(157, 257, and 439)

The White Goddess

is the most expensive of the divinities. She costs five times as much as gold. In the United States, ten million devotees yearn and burn, ready to kill, and kill themselves for her. Every year they throw thirty billion dollars at the foot of her shining altar of pure snow. In the long run she will annihilate them; from the start she steals their souls; but in exchange she offers to make them, by her good grace, supermen for a moment.

(257 and 372)

1980: Santa Marta

Marijuana

Out of each dollar of dreams that a U.S. marijuana smoker buys, barely one cent reaches the hands of the Colombian campesinos who grow it. The other ninety-nine cents go to the traffickers, who in Colombia have fifteen hundred airports, five hundred airplanes, and a hundred ships.

On the outskirts of Medellín or Santa Marta, the drug mafiosi live in ostentatious mansions. In front they like to display on granite pedestals the small planes they used in their first operation. They rock their children in gold cradles, give golden fingernails to their lovers, and on ring finger or necktie wear diamonds as discreet as headlights.

The mafiosi habitually fumigate their forces. Four years ago they machinegunned Lucho Barranquilla, most popular of the traffickers, on a street corner in the city of Santa Marta. The murderers sent to the funeral a floral wreath in the form of a heart and took up a collection to erect a statue of the departed in the main plaza.

(95 and 406)

1980: Santa Marta

Saint Agatón

Lucho Barranquilla was widely mourned. The children who played in his amusement park wept for him, as did the widows and orphans he protected, and the cops who ate from his hand. In fact, the whole city of Santa Marta, which lived thanks to his loans and donations, wept. And Saint Agatón wept for him, too.

Saint Agatón is the patron saint of drunkards. On Carnival Sunday, drunks from the whole Colombian coast descend on the village of Mamatoco, on Santa Marta's outskirts. There they take Saint Agatón out of his church and parade him, singing dirty songs and spraying him with firewater, just the way he likes.

But what the drunks are parading is only a white-bearded impostor brought from Spain. The true Saint Agatón, who had an Indian face and a straw hat, was kidnapped half a century ago by a temperance priest who fled with the saint under his surplice. God punished that priest with leprosy and crossed the eyes of the sacristan who accompanied him, but left the real Saint Agatón hidden in the remote village of Sucre.

A committee has gone to Sucre in recent days to plead with him to return: *"Since you left,"* they tell him, *"there's no more miracles or fun."*

Saint Agatón refuses. He says he won't go back to Santa Marta, because there they killed his friend Lucho Barranquilla.

1980: Guatemala City

Newsreel

It was General Romeo Lucas García, president of Guatemala, who gave the order to set fire to the Spanish embassy with its occupants inside. This statement comes from Elías Barahona, official spokesman for the Ministry of the Interior, who calls a press conference after seeking asylum in Panama.

According to Barahona, General Lucas García is personally responsible for the deaths of the thirty-nine persons roasted alive by the police bombs. Among the victims were twenty-seven Indian leaders who had peacefully occupied the embassy to denounce the massacres in the Quiché region.

Barahona also states that General Lucas García commands the paramilitary and parapolice bands known as the Squadrons of Death, and helps draw up the lists of opponents condemned to disappear.

The former press secretary of the Interior Ministry claims that in Guatemala a "Program of Pacification and Eradication of Communism" is being carried out, based on a four-hundred-and-twenty-page document drawn up by specialists in the United States on the basis of their experience in the Vietnam war.

In the first half of 1980 in Guatemala, twenty-seven university professors, thirteen journalists, and seventy campesino leaders, mainly Indians, have been murdered. The repression has had a special intensity for Indian communities in the Quiché region, where large oil deposits have recently been discovered.

(450)

1980: Uspantán

Rigoberta

She is a Maya-Quiché Indian, born in the village of Chimel, who has been picking coffee and cotton on the coastal plantations since she learned to walk. In the cotton fields she saw two of her brothers die—Nicolás and Felipe, the youngest—and also her best friend, still only half grown. All fell victim to pesticide spraying.

Last year in the village of Chajul, Rigoberta Menchú saw how the army burned alive her brother Patrocinio. Soon afterward, her father suffered the same fate in the Spanish embassy. Now, in Uspantán, the soldiers have killed her mother, very gradually, cutting her to pieces bit by bit after dressing her up in guerrilla's clothing.

Of the community of Chimel, where Rigoberta was born, no one remains alive.

Rigoberta, who is a Christian, has been taught that true Christians forgive their persecutors and pray for the souls of their executioners. When they strike you on one cheek, she was taught, the true Christian offers the other.

"I no longer have a cheek to offer," says Rigoberta.

(72)

1980: San Salvador

The Offering

Until a couple of years ago, he only got along well with God. Now he speaks with and for everyone. Each child of the people tormented by the powerful is a child of God crucified; and in the people God is renewed after each crime the powerful commit. Now Monseñor Romero, archbishop of El Salvador, world-breaker, world-revealer, bears no resemblance to the babbling shepherd of souls whom the powerful used to applaud. Now ordinary people interrupt with ovations his sermons denouncing state terrorism.

Yesterday, Sunday, the archbishop exhorted the police and soldiers to disobey the order to kill their campesino brothers. In the name of Christ, Romero told the Salvadoran people: *Arise and go.*

Today, Monday, the murderer arrives at the church escorted by two police patrols. He enters and waits, hidden behind a pillar. Romero is celebrating Mass. When he opens his arms and offers the bread and the wine, body and blood of the people, the murderer pulls the trigger.

(259 and 301)

1980: Montevideo
A People Who Say No

The dictatorship of Uruguay calls a plebiscite and loses.

This people forced into silence seemed dumb; but when it opens its mouth, it says no. The silence of these years has been so deafening that the military mistook it for resignation. They never expected such a response. They asked only for the sake of asking, like a chef who orders his chickens to say with what sauce they prefer to be eaten.

1980: In All Nicaragua
On Its Way

The Sandinista revolution doesn't shoot anybody; but of Somoza's army not a brass band remains. The rifles pass into everybody's hands, while the banner of agrarian reform is unfurled over desolate fields.

An army of volunteers, whose weapons are pencils and vaccines, invades its own country. Revolution, revelation, of those who believe and create; not infallible gods of majestic stride, but ordinary people, for centuries forced into obedience and trained for impotence. Now, even when they trip, they keep on walking. They go in search of bread and the word: This land, which opened its mouth, is eager to eat and speak.

1980: Asunción
Stroessner

Tachito Somoza, dethroned, exiled, is blown to pieces on a street corner in Asunción.

"Who did it?" ask the journalists in Managua.

*"Fuenteovejuna,"** replies comandante Tomás Borge.

Tachito had found refuge in the capital of Paraguay, the only city in the world where there was still a bronze bust of his father, Tacho Somoza, and where a street was still named "Generalisimo Franco."

Paraguay, or the little that is left of Paraguay after so much war and plunder, belongs to General Alfredo Stroessner. Every five years this veteran colleague of Somoza and Franco holds elections to confirm his power. So that people can vote, he suspends for twenty-four hours Paraguay's eternal state of siege.

Stroessner believes himself invulnerable because he loves no one. The State is him. Every day, at precisely 6:00 P.M., he phones the president of the Central Bank and asks him:

"How much did we make today?"

1980: In All Nicaragua
Discovering

Riding horseback, rowing, walking, the brigadistas of the literacy campaigns penetrate the most hidden corners of Nicaragua. By lamplight they teach the handling of a pencil to those who don't know, so that they'll never again be fooled by people who think they're so smart.

While they teach, the brigadistas share what little food they have, stoop down to weed and harvest crops, skin their hands chopping wood, and spend the night on the floor slapping at mosquitos. They discover wild honey in the trees, and in the people legends, verses, lost wisdom; bit by bit they get to know the secret languages of the herbs that enliven flavors, cure pains, and heal snake bites. Teaching, the brigadistas learn the marvel and malevolence of this country, their country, inhabited by survivors; in Nicaragua, anyone who doesn't die of hunger, disease, or a bullet, dies of laughter.

(11)

* The allusion is to the play *Fuenteovejuna* by the Spanish playwright Lope de Vega (1562–1635), in which all the people of the town of that name claim collective responsibility for the death of a tyrant. The most famous passage in the play reads: "Who killed the Comendador? Fuenteovejuna, señor."

1980: New York

The Statue of Liberty Seems
Pitted with Smallpox

because of the poisonous gases so many factories throw into the sky, and which rain and snow bring back to earth. One hundred and seventy lakes have been murdered by this acid rain in New York State alone, but the director of the Federal Office of Management and Budget says it's not worth bothering about. After all, those lakes are only four percent of the state total.

The world is a racetrack. Nature, an obstacle. The deadly breath of the smokestacks has left four thousand lakes without fish or plants in Ontario, Canada.

"We'd better ask God to start over," says a fisherman.

1980: New York

Lennon

A shirt hung out on a roof flaps its arms. The wind complains. The roaring and screaming of city life is joined by the shriek of a siren rushing through the streets. On this dirty day in Manhattan, John Lennon, musical innovator, has been murdered.

He didn't want to win or kill. He didn't agree that the world should be a stock market or a barracks. Lennon was on the sidelines of the track. Singing or whistling with a distracted look, he watched the wheels of others turn in the perpetual vertigo that comes and goes between madhouse and slaughterhouse.

1981: Surahammar

Exile

What is the distance that separates a Bolivian mining camp from a city in Sweden? How many miles, how many centuries, how many worlds?

Domitila, one of the five women who overthrew a military dictatorship, has been sentenced to exile by another military dictatorship and has ended up, with her miner husband and her many children, in the snows of northern Europe.

From where there's too little anything to where there's too much everything, from lowest poverty to highest opulence. Eyes full of wonder in these faces of clay: Here in Sweden they throw in the garbage nearly new TVs, hardly used clothing and furniture, and refrigerators and dishwashers that work perfectly. To the junkyard goes last year's automobile.

Domitila is grateful for the support of the Swedes and admires them for their liberty, but the waste offends her and the loneliness troubles her. These poor rich folk live all alone before the television, drinking alone, eating alone, talking to themselves:

"Over there in Bolivia," says—recommends—Domitila, *"even if it's for a fight, we get together."*

(1)

1981: Celica Canton
"Bad Luck, Human Error, Bad Weather"

A plane crashes at the end of May, and so ends the life of Jaime Roldós, president of Ecuador. Some campesinos hear the explosion and see the plane in flames before it crashes.

Doctors are not permitted to examine the body. No autopsy is attempted. The black box never turns up; they say the plane had none. Tractors smooth over the scene of the disaster. Tapes from the Quito, Guayaquil, and Loja control towers are erased. Various witnesses die in accidents. The Air Force's report discounts in advance any crime.

Bad luck, human error, bad weather. But President Roldós was defending Ecuador's coveted oil, had restored relations with prohibited Cuba, and backed accursed revolutions in Nicaragua, El Salvador, Palestine.

Two months later another plane crashes, in Panama. *Bad luck, human error, bad weather.* Two campesinos who heard the plane explode in the air disappear. Omar Torrijos, guilty of rescuing the Panama Canal, knew he wasn't going to die in bed of old age.

Almost simultaneously, a helicopter crashes in Peru. *Bad luck, human error, bad weather.* This time the victim is the head of the

Peruvian army, General Rafael Hoyos Rubio, an old enemy of Standard Oil and other benevolent multinational corporations.

(154 and 175)

1982: South Georgia Islands
Portrait of a Brave Fellow

The mothers of the Plaza de Mayo called him *the Angel*, because of his pink baby face. He had spent some months working with them, always smiling, always ready to lend a hand, when, one evening, the soldiers pick up several of the movement's most active militants as they leave a meeting. These mothers disappear, like their sons and daughters, and nothing more is heard of them.

The kidnapped mothers have been fingered by *the Angel*; that is, Frigate Lieutenant Alfredo Astiz, member of Task Force 3-3-2 of the Navy's Mechanics School, who has a long and brilliant record in the torture chambers.

This spy and torturer, now a lieutenant on a warship, is the first to surrender to the English in the Malvinas war. He surrenders without firing a shot.

(107, 134, 143, and 388)

1982: Malvinas Islands
The Malvinas War,

patriotic war that for a moment united trampled and tramplers, ends with the victory of Great Britain's colonial army.

The Argentine generals and colonels who promised to shed their last drops of blood have not so much as cut a finger. Those who declared war haven't even put in a guest appearance. So that the Argentine flag might fly over these ice cubes, a just cause in unjust hands, the high command sent to the slaughterhouse youngsters roped into compulsory service, who died more of cold than of bullets.

Their pulses do not flicker. With firm hands, these rapers of bound women, hangmen of disarmed workers, sign the surrender.

(185)

1982: The Roads of La Mancha

Master Globetrotter

completes his first half century of life far from where he was born. In a Castilian village, in front of one of the windmills that challenged Don Quixote, Javier Villafañe, patriarch of America's puppeteers, celebrates the birthday of his favorite son. To be worthy of this great date, Javier decides to marry a pretty gypsy he has just met; and Master Globetrotter presides over the ceremony and banquet with his characteristic melancholy dignity.

They've gone through life together, these two, puppeteering along the roads of the world, sweetness and mischief, Master Globetrotter and the pilgrim Javier. Whenever Master Globetrotter gets sick, a victim of worms or moths, Javier heals his wounds with infinite patience and afterward watches over his sleep.

At the start of each performance, before an expectant crowd of children, the two tremble as if at their first show.

1982: Stockholm

Novelist García Márquez Receives the Nobel Prize and Speaks of our Lands Condemned to One Hundred Years of Solitude

I dare to think that it is this outsized reality, and not just its literary expression, that has deserved the attention of the Swedish Academy of Letters. A reality not of paper, but one that lives within us and determines each instant of our countless daily deaths, and that nourishes a source of insatiable creativity full of sorrow and beauty, of which this roving and nostalgic Colombian is but one cipher more, singled out by fortune. Poets and beggars, musicians and prophets, warriors and scoundrels, all creatures of that unbridled reality, we have had to ask but little of our imagination, for our crucial problem has been a lack of conventional means to render our lives believable. This, my friends, is the crux of our solitude . . .

The interpretation of our reality through patterns not our own serves only to make us ever more unknown, ever less free, ever more solitary . . .

No: the immeasurable violence and pain of our history are the result of age-old inequities and untold bitterness, and not a conspiracy plotted three thousand leagues from our homes. But many European leaders and thinkers have thought so, this with the childishness of old-timers who have forgotten the fruitful excesses of their youth, as if it were impossible to find another destiny than to live at the mercy of the two great masters of the world. This, friends, is the very scale of our solitude . . .

(189)

1983: Saint George's

The Reconquest of the Island of Grenada

Tiny Grenada, hardly visible speck of green in the immensity of the Caribbean, suffers a spectacular invasion of Marines. President Ronald Reagan sends them to murder socialism, but the Marines kill a corpse. Some days earlier, certain native military men, greedy for power, had already assassinated socialism, in the name of socialism.

Behind the Marines lands North American secretary of state George Shultz. At a press conference he says: *"At first sight I realized that this island could be a splendid real estate prospect."*

1983: La Bermuda

Marianela

Every morning at dawn, they lined up, these relatives, friends, and lovers of the disappeared of El Salvador. They came looking for or offering news; they had no other place to ask about the lost or bear witness. The door of the Human Rights Commission was always open; or one could simply step through the hole the last bomb had opened in its wall.

Since the guerrilla movement started growing in the countryside, the army has no longer bothered to use prisons. The Commission denounced them before the world: *July: fifteen children under fourteen who had been detained charged with terrorism are found decapitated. August: thirteen thousand five hundred civilians murdered or disappeared so far this year* . . .

Of the Commission's workers, Magdalena Enríquez, the one who laughed most, was the first to fall. Soldiers dumped her flayed body on the beach. Then came the turn of Ramón Valladares, found riddled with bullets in the roadside mud. Only Marianela García Vilas remained: *"The bad weed never dies,"* she said.

They kill her near the village of La Bermuda in the burned lands of Cuscatlán. She was walking with her camera and tape recorder collecting proof that the army fires white phosphorus at rebellious campesinos.

(259)

1983: Santiago de Chile

Ten Years after the Reconquest of Chile

"You have the right to import a camel," says the Minister of Finance. From the TV screen the minister exhorts Chileans to make use of free trade. In Chile anyone can decorate his home with an authentic African crocodile, and democracy consists of choosing between Chivas Regal and Johnnie Walker Black Label.

Everything is imported: brooms, birdcage swings, corn, water for the whiskey. Baguette loaves come by air from Paris. The economic system, imported from the United States, obliges Chileans to scratch at the entrails of their mountains for copper, and nothing more. Not a pin can they manufacture, because South Korean pins come cheaper. Any creative act is a crime against the laws of the market—that is, the laws of fate.

From the United States come television programs, cars, machineguns, and plastic flowers. In the upper-class neighborhoods of Santiago, one cannot move without bumping into Japanese computers, German videocassettes, Dutch TVs, Swiss chocolates, English marmalade, Danish hams, clothing from Taiwan, French perfumes, Spanish tuna, Italian oil . . .

He who does not consume does not exist. Everyone else is simply used and discarded, although they pay the bills for this credit-card fiesta.

The unemployed scavenge through refuse. Everywhere one sees signs that say: *No openings. Do not insist.*

The foreign debt and the suicide rate have increased six-fold.

(169 and 231)

1983: A Ravine Between Cabildo and Petorca
Television

The Escárates had nothing—until Armando brought that box on his mule.

Armando Escárate had been away a whole year, working at sea as a cook for fishermen, and also in the town of La Ligua, doing odd jobs and eating leftovers, toiling night and day until he could put together enough money to pay for it.

When Armando got off his mule and opened the box, the family was struck dumb with fright. No one had ever seen the like of it in these regions of the Chilean cordillera. From afar people came, as if on pilgrimage, to examine the full-color Sony that ran off a truck battery.

The Escárates had nothing. They still have nothing, and continue to sleep huddled together, barely getting by on the cheese they make, the wool they spin, and the flocks of goats they graze for the boss of the hacienda. But the television rises like a totem in the middle of their mud shanty roofed with reeds. From the screen Coca-Cola offers them the sparkle of life, and Sprite, bubbles of youth; Marlboro cigarettes give them virility; Cadbury candies, human communication; Visa credit cards, wealth; Dior perfumes and Cardin shirts, distinction; Cinzano vermouth, social status; the Martini, passionate love. Nestlé powdered milk provides them with eternal vigor, and the Renault automobile with a new way to live.

(230)

1983: Buenos Aires
The Granny Detectives

While the military dictatorship disintegrates in Argentina, the Plaza de Mayo grandmothers go looking for their lost grandchildren. These children, imprisoned with their parents or born in concentration camps, have been distributed as war booty, and more than one has for parents his own parents' murderers. The grannies investigate on the basis of whatever they can dig up—photos, stray data, a birthmark, someone who saw something—and so, beating out a path with native shrewdness and umbrella blows, they have recovered a few children.

Tamara Arze, who disappeared at one-and-a-half, did not end up in military hands. She is in a suburban barrio, in the home of the good folk who picked her up where she was dumped. At the mother's appeal, the grannies undertook the search for her. They had only a few leads, but after a long, complicated sweep, they have located her. Every morning Tamara sells kerosene from a horse-drawn cart, but she doesn't complain of her fate. At first she doesn't even want to hear about her real mother. Very gradually the grannies explain to her that she is the daughter of Rosa, a Bolivian worker who never abandoned her. That one night her mother was seized at the factory gate, in Buenos Aires . . .

(317)

1983: Lima

Tamara Flies Twice

Rosa was tortured—under the supervision of a doctor who indicated when to stop—and raped, and shot at with blank cartridges. She spent eight years in prison, without trial or explanation, and only last year was expelled from Argentina. Now, in Lima airport, she waits while her daughter Tamara flies over the Andes toward her.

Accompanying Tamara on the flight are two of the grannies who found her.

She devours every bit of food she is served on the plane, not leaving a crumb of bread or a grain of sugar.

In Lima, Rosa and Tamara discover each other. They look in the mirror together. They are identical: same eyes, same mouth, same marks in the same places.

When night comes, Rosa bathes her daughter. Putting her to bed, she smells a milky, sweetish smell on her; and so she bathes her again. And again. But however much soap she uses, there is no way to wash off the smell. It's an odd smell . . . And suddenly Rosa remembers. This is the smell of little babies when they finish nursing: Tamara is ten, and tonight she smells like a newly born infant.

(317)

1983: Buenos Aires

What If the Desert Were Ocean and the Earth Were Sky?

The mothers and grandmothers of the Plaza de Mayo are frightening. For what would happen if they tired of circling in front of the Pink House and began signing government decrees? And if the beggars on the cathedral steps grabbed the archbishop's tunic and biretta and began preaching sermons from the pulpit? And if honest circus clowns began giving orders in the barracks and courses in the universities? And if they did? And if?

(317)

1983: Plateau of Petitions

The Mexican Theater of Dreams

As they do every year, the Zapotec Indians come to the Plateau of Petitions.

On one side is the sea, on the other, peaks and precipices.

Here dreams are turned loose. A kneeling man gets up and goes into the wood, an invisible bride on his arm. Someone moves like a languid jellyfish, navigating in an aerial ship. One makes drawings in the wind and another rides by with slow majesty, astride a tree branch. Pebbles become grains of corn, and acorns, hen's eggs. Old people become children, and children, giants; the leaf of a tree becomes a mirror that imparts a handsome face to anyone looking at it.

The spell is broken should anyone dare not be serious about this dress rehearsal of life.

(418)

1983: Tuma River

Realization

In Nicaragua, bullets whiz back and forth between dignity and scorn; and the war extinguishes many lives.

This is one of the battalions fighting the invaders. These volunteers have come from the poorest barrios of Managua to the far plains of the Tuma River.

Whenever there is a quiet moment, Beto, *the prof*, spreads the contagion of letters. The contagion occurs when some militiaman asks him to write a letter for him. Beto does it, and then: *"This is the last one I'll write for you. I'm offering you something better."*

Sebastián Fuertes, iron soldier from El Maldito barrio, a middle-aged man of many wars and women, is one of those who came up and was sentenced to alphabetization. For some days he has been breaking pencils and tearing up sheets of paper in the respites from shooting, and standing up to a lot of heavy teasing. And when May First arrives, his comrades elect him to make the speech.

The meeting is held in a paddock full of dung and ticks. Sebastián gets up on a box, takes from his pocket a folded paper, and reads the first words ever born from his hands. He reads from a distance, stretching out his arm, because his sight is little help and he has no glasses.

"Brothers of Battalion 8221! . . ."

1983: Managua

Defiance

Plumes of smoke rise from the mouths of volcanos and the barrels of guns. The campesino goes to war on a burro, with a parrot on his shoulder. God must have been a primitive painter the day he dreamed up this land of gentle speech, condemned to die and to kill by the United States, which trains and pays the contras. From Honduras, the Somocistas attack it; from Costa Rica, Edén Pastora betrays it.

And now, here comes the Pope of Rome. The Pope scolds those priests who love Nicaragua more than heaven, and abruptly silences those who ask him to pray for the souls of murdered patriots. After quarreling with the Catholic multitude gathered in the plaza, he takes off in a fury from this bedeviled land.

1983: Mérida

The People Set God on His Feet,

and the people know that to stand up in the world, God needs their help.

Every year, the child Jesus is born in Mérida and elsewhere in Venezuela. Choristers sing to the strains of violins, mandolins, and guitars, while the godparents gather up in a big cloth the child lying in the manger—delicate task, serious business—and take him for a walk.

The godparents walk the child through the streets. The kings and shepherds follow, and the crowd throws flowers and kisses. After such a warm welcome into the world, the godparents put Jesus back in the manger where Mary and Joseph are waiting for him.

Then, in the name of the community, the godparents stand him up for the first time, and make sure he remains upright between his parents. Finally the rosary is sung and all present get a little cake of the old-fashioned kind with twelve egg yolks, and some sweet mistela wine.

(463)

1983: Managua

Newsreel

In a Managua barrio, a woman has given birth to a hen, according to the Nicaraguan daily *La Prensa*. Sources close to the ecclesiastical hierarchy do not deny that this extraordinary event may be a sign of God's anger. The behavior of the crowd before the Pope may have exhausted the Divine Patience, these sources believe.

Back in 1981, two miracles with equally broad repercussions occurred in Nicaragua. The Virgin of Cuapa made a spectacular appearance that year in the fields of Chontales. Barefoot, crowned with stars, and enveloped in a glowing aura that blinded witnesses, the Virgin made declarations to a sacristan named Bernardo. The Mother of God expressed her support for President Reagan's policies against atheistic, Communist-inspired Sandinismo.

Shortly afterward, the Virgin of the Conception sweated and wept copiously for several days in a Managua house. The archbishop, Monseñor Obando, appeared before his altar and exhorted the faithful to pray for the forgiveness of the Most Pure. The Virgin of the Conception's emanations stopped only when the police discovered that the owners of the plaster image were submerging it in water and shutting it in a refrigerator at night so that it would perspire when exposed to the intense local heat, before the crowd of pilgrims.

1984: The Vatican
The Holy Office of the Inquisition

now bears the more discreet name of the Congregation for the Doctrine of the Faith. It no longer burns heretics alive, although it might like to. Its chief headache these days comes from America. In the name of the Holy Father, the inquisitors summon Latin American theologians Leonardo Boff and Gustavo Gutiérrez, and the Vatican sharply reprimands them for lacking respect for the Church of Fear.

The Church of Fear, opulent multinational enterprise, devotee of pain and death, is anxious to nail on a cross any son of a carpenter of the breed that now circulates within America's coasts inciting fishermen and defying empires.

1984: London
Gold and Frankincense

Top officials of the United States, Japan, West Germany, England, France, Italy, and Canada, forgather at Lancaster House to congratulate the organization that guarantees the freedom of money. The seven powers of the capitalist world unanimously applaud *the work of the International Monetary Fund in the developing countries*.

The congratulations do not mention the executioners, torturers, inquisitors, jailers, and informers who are the functionaries of the Fund in these *developing countries*.

A Circular Symphony for Poor Countries, in Six Successive Movements

So that labor may be increasingly obedient and cheap, the poor countries need legions of executioners, torturers, inquisitors, jailers, and informers.

To feed and arm these legions, the poor countries need loans from the rich countries.

To pay the interest on these loans, the poor countries need more loans.

To pay the interest on the loans on top of loans, the poor countries need to increase their exports.

To increase their exports, products condemned to perpetually collapsing prices, the poor countries need to lower production costs.

To lower production costs, the poor countries need increasingly obedient and cheap labor.

To make labor increasingly obedient and cheap, the poor countries need legions of executioners, torturers, inquisitors . . .

1984: Washington

1984

The U.S. State Department decides to suppress the word *murder* in its reports on violations of human rights in Latin America and other regions. Instead of *murder*, one must say: *illegal or arbitrary deprivation of life.*

For some time now, the CIA has avoided the word *murder* in its manuals on practical terrorism. When the CIA murders an enemy or has him murdered, it *neutralizes* him.

The State Department calls any war forces it lands south of its borders *peace-keeping forces*; and the killers who fight to restore its business interests in Nicaragua *freedom fighters.*

(94)

1984: Washington

We Are All Hostages

Nicaragua and other insolent countries still act as if unaware that history has been ordered not to budge, under pain of total destruction of the world.

"*We will not tolerate . . .*" warns President Reagan.

Above the clouds hover the nuclear bombers. Farther up, the military satellites. Beneath the earth and beneath the sea, the missiles. The Earth still rotates because the great powers permit it to do so. A plutonium bomb the size of an orange would suffice to explode the entire planet, and a good-size discharge of radiation could turn it into a desert populated by cockroaches.

President Reagan says Saint Luke (14:31) advises increasing military funding to confront the Communist hordes. The economy is militarized; weapons shoot money to buy weapons to shoot money. They manufacture arms, hamburgers, and fear. There is no better business than the sale of fear. The president announces, jubilantly, the militarization of the stars.

(430)

1984: São Paulo

Twenty Years after the Reconquest of Brazil

The last president of the military dictatorship, General Figueiredo, leaves the government to civilians.

When they ask him what he would do if he were a worker earning the minimum wage, General Figueiredo replies: "*I would put a bullet through my head.*"

Brazil suffers a famished prosperity. Among countries selling food to the world, it stands in fourth place; among countries suffering hunger in the world, sixth place. Now Brazil exports arms and automobiles as well as coffee, and produces more steel than France; but Brazilians are shorter and weigh less than they did twenty years ago.

Millions of homeless children wander the streets of cities like São Paulo, hunting for food. Buildings are turning into fortresses, doormen into armed guards. Every citizen is either an assailant or assailed.

(371)

1984: Guatemala City
Thirty Years after the Reconquest of Guatemala,

the Bank of the Army is the country's most important, after the Bank of America. Generals take turns in power, overthrowing each other, transforming dictatorship into dictatorship; but all apply the same policy of land seizure against the Indians guilty of inhabiting areas rich in oil, nickel, or whatever else turns out to be of value.

These are no longer the days of United Fruit, but rather of Getty Oil, Texaco, and the International Nickel Company. The generals wipe out many Indian communities wholesale and expel even more from their lands. Multitudes of hungry Indians, stripped of everything, wander the mountains. They come from horror, but they are not going to horror. They walk slowly, guided by the ancient certainty that someday greed and arrogance will be punished. That's what the old people of corn assure the children of corn in the stories they tell them when night falls.

(367 and 450)

1984: Rio de Janeiro
Mishaps of Collective Memory in Latin America

Public accountant João David dos Santos jumped for joy when he managed to collect his many overdue accounts. Only payment in kind, but something. For lack of funds, a social science research center paid him its whole library of nine thousand books and over five thousand magazines and pamphlets devoted to contemporary Brazilian history. It contained very valuable material on the peasant leagues of the Northeast and the Getulio Vargas administration, among other subjects.

Then accountant dos Santos put the library up for sale. He offered it to cultural organizations, historical institutes, and various ministries. No one had the money. He tried universities, state and private, one after another. No takers. He left the library on loan at one university for a few months, until they started demanding rent. Then he tried private citizens. No one showed the slightest interest. The nation's history is an enigma, a lie, or a yawn.

The unhappy accountant dos Santos feels great relief when he finally succeeds in selling his library to the Tijuca Paper Factory, which turns all these books, magazines, and pamphlets into tinted toilet paper.

(371)

1984: Mexico City

Against Forgetting,

the only death that really kills, Carlos Quijano wrote what he wrote. This grouch and troublemaker was born in Montevideo as the century was born, and dies in exile, as Uruguay's military dictatorship is falling. He dies at work, preparing a new Mexican edition of his magazine *Marcha*.

Quijano celebrated contradictions. Heresy for others to him was a sign of life. He condemned imperialism, humiliator of nations and multitudes, and proclaimed that Latin America is destined to create a socialism worthy of the hopes of its prophets.

(356)

1984: Mexico City

The Resurrection of the Living

The Mexicans make a custom of eating death, a sugar or chocolate skeleton dripping with colored caramel. In addition to eating it, they sing it, dance it, drink it, and sleep it. Sometimes, to mock power and money, the people dress death in a monocle and frock coat, epaulettes and medals, but they prefer it stripped naked, racy, a bit drunk, their companion on festive outings.

Day of the Living, this Day of the Dead should be called, although on reflection it's all the same, because whatever comes goes and whatever goes comes, and in the last analysis the beginning of what begins is always the end of what ends.

"My grandfather is so tiny because he was born after me," says a child who knows what he's talking about.

1984: Estelí
Believing

They preside over childbirth. Giving life and light is their profession. With practiced hands they straighten the child if it's coming out wrong, and communicate strength and peace to the mother.

Today, the midwives of the Estelí villages and mountains close to Nicaragua's border are having a party to celebrate something that truly deserves joy: For a year now not one new baby in this region has died of tetanus. The midwives no longer cut umbilical cords with a machete, or burn them with tallow, or tie them off without disinfectant; and pregnant women get vaccines that protect the child living inside. Now no one here believes that vaccines are Russian witches' brews meant to turn Christians into Communists; and no one, or almost no one, believes that a newborn can die from the fixed stare of a drunken man or a menstruating woman.

This region, this war zone, suffers continuous harassment by the invaders.

"Here, we are in the alligator's mouth."

Many mothers go off to fight. The ones who stay share their breasts.

1984: Havana
Miguel at Seventy-Nine

Since the dawn of the century, this man has gone through hell and died several times over. Now, from exile, he still energetically accompanies his people in their war.

The dawn light always finds him up, shaved and conspiring. He could just as easily keep turning in the revolving door of memory;

but he doesn't know how to be deaf when the voices of these new times and the roads he still hasn't traveled call out to him.

And so at seventy-nine every day is a new birth for Miguel Mármol, old master of the art of constant rebirth.

1984: Paris

The Echoes Go Searching for the Voice

While writing words that loved people, Julio Cortázar was making his own journey, a journey backward through the tunnel of time. He was traveling from the end to the beginning, from discouragement to enthusiasm, from indifference to passion, from solitariness to solidarity. At almost seventy, he was a child of all ages at once.

A bird that flew toward the egg, Cortázar went forward by going back, year after year, day after day, toward the embrace of lovers who make the love that makes them. And now he dies, now he enters the earth, like a man who, entering a woman, returns to the place he comes from.

1984: Punta Santa Elena

The Eternal Embrace

They were found only recently in the wasteland that once was Zumpa beach in Ecuador. And here they are, in full sunlight, for anyone who wants to see: a man and a woman lying in embrace, sleeping lovers, out of eternity.

Excavating an Indian cemetery, an archaeologist came upon this pair of skeletons bound together by love. It was eight thousand years ago that the lovers of Zumpa committed the irreverence of dying without separating themselves, and anyone who approaches can see that death does not cause them the slightest concern.

Their splendid beauty is surprising, considering that they are such ugly bones in such an ugly desert, pure dryness and grayness; and more surprising is their modesty. These lovers, sleeping in the wind, seem not to have grasped that they have more mystery and grandeur than the pyramids of Teotihuacán or the sanctuary of Machu Picchu or the waterfalls of Iguazú.

1984: Violeta Parra Community

The Stolen Name

The dictatorship of General Pinochet changes the names of twenty bone-poor communities, tin and cardboard houses, on the outskirts of Santiago de Chile. In the rebaptism, the Violeta Parra community gets the name of some military hero. But its inhabitants refuse to bear this unchosen name. They are Violeta Parra or nothing.

A while back they had decided in unanimous assembly to name themselves after the campesina singer with the raspy voice who in her songs of struggle knew how to celebrate Chile's mysteries.

Violeta was sinful and saucy, given to guitar-strumming and long talks and falling in love, and with all her dancing and clowning around she kept burning the empanadas. *Thanks to life, which has given me so much,* she sang in her last song; and a turbulent love affair sent her off to her death.

(334 and 440)

1984: Tepic

The Found Name

In the mountains of Nayarit in Mexico, there was a community that had no name. For centuries this community of Huichol Indians had been looking for a name. Carlos González found one by sheer accident.

This Huichol had come to the city of Tepic to buy seeds and visit relatives. Crossing a garbage dump, he picked up a book thrown into the rubbish. It was years ago that Carlos had learned to read the Castilian language, and he could still just about manage it. Sitting in the shade of a projecting roof, he began to decipher the pages. The book spoke of a country with a strange name, which Carlos couldn't place but which had to be far from Mexico, and told a story of recent occurrence.

On the way home, walking up the mountain, Carlos continued reading. He couldn't tear himself away from this story of horror and bravery. The central character of the book was a man who had kept his word. Arriving at the village, Carlos announced euphorically: *"At last we have a name!"*

And he read the book aloud to everyone. This halting recital took him almost a week. Afterward, the hundred and fifty families voted. All in favor. Dancing and singing they performed the baptism.

So finally they have a name for themselves. This community bears the name of a worthy man who did not doubt at the moment of choice between treachery and death.

"I'm going to Salvador Allende," the wayfarers say now.

(466)

1984: Bluefields

Flying

Deep root, lofty trunk, dense foliage: from the center of the world rises a thornless tree, one of those trees that know how to give themselves to the birds. Around the tree whirl dancing couples, navel to navel, undulating to a music that wakens stones and sets fire to ice. As they dance, they dress and undress the tree with streaming ribbons of every color. On this tormented, continuously invaded, continuously bombarded coast of Nicaragua, the Maypole fiesta is celebrated as usual.

The tree of life knows that, whatever happens, the warm music spinning around it will never stop. However much death may come, however much blood may flow, the music will dance men and women as long as the air breathes them and the land plows and loves them.

1986: Montevideo

A Letter

Cedric Belfrage
Apartado Postal 630
Cuernavaca, Morelos
Mexico

My Dear Cedric:
    Here goes the last volume of Memory of Fire. *As you'll see, it ends in 1984. Why not before, or after, I don't know. Perhaps because that was the last year of my exile, the end of a cycle, the end of a century;*

or perhaps because the book and I know that the last page is also the first.

Forgive me if it came out too long. Writing it was a joy for my hand; and now I feel more than ever proud of having been born in America, in this shit, in this marvel, during the century of the wind.

No more now, because I don't want to bury the sacred in palaver. Abrazos,

Eduardo

(End of the third volume of
Memory of Fire.)

The Sources

1. Acebey, David. *Aquí también Domitila*. La Paz: n.p., 1984.
2. Adams, Willi Paul. *Los Estados Unidos de América*. Madrid: Siglo XXI, 1979.
3. Aguiar, Cláudio. *Caldeirão*. Rio de Janeiro: José Olympio, 1982.
4. Aguilar Camín, Héctor. *Saldos de la revolución. Cultura y política de México, 1910–1980*. Mexico City: Nueva Imagen, 1982.
5. Aguiló, Federico. *Significado socio-antropológico de las coplas al Cristo de Santa Vera Cruz*. Paper presented at the second Conference of Bolivian Studies, Cochabamba, 1984.
6. Agudelo, William. *El asalto a San Carlos. Testimonios de Solentiname*. Managua: Asoc. para el Desarrollo de Solentiname, 1982.
7. Alape, Arturo. *El bogotazo. Memorias del olvido*. Bogotá: Pluma, 1983.
8. ———. *La Paz, la violencia: testigos de excepción*. Bogotá: Planeta, 1985.
9. Alegría, Claribel, and D. J. Flakoll. *Cenizas de Izalco*. Barcelona; Seix Barral, 1966.
10. ———. *Nicaragua: la revolución sandinista. Una crónica política, 1855–1979*. Mexico: Era, 1982.
11. Alemán Ocampo, Carlos. *Y también enséñenles a leer*. Managua: Nueva Nicaragua, 1984.
12. Alfaro, Eloy, *Narraciones históricas*. (Preface by Malcolm D. Deas.) Quito: Editora Nacional, 1983.
13. Alfaro, Hugo. *Navegar es necesario*. Montevideo: Banda Oriental, 1985.
14. Ali, Muhammad. *The Greatest: My Own Story*. New York: Random House, 1975.
15. Allen, Frederick Lewis. *Apenas ayer. Historia informal de la decada del 20*. Buenos Aires: EUDEBA, 1964.
16. Almaraz Paz, Sergio. *Requiem para una república*. La Paz: Universidad, 1969.
17. ———. *El poder y la caída*. La Paz and Cochabamba: Amigos del Libro, 1969.
18. Almeida Bosque, Juan. *Contra el agua y el viento*. Havana: Casa de las Américas, 1985.
19. Amado, Jorge. *Los viejos marineros*. Barcelona: Seix Barral, 1983.
20. Amorim, Enrique. *El Quiroga que yo conocí*. Montevideo: Arca, 1983.
21. Anderson, Thomas. *El Salvador. Los sucesos políticos de 1932*. San José de Costa Rica: EDUCA, 1982.
22. Andrade, Joaquim Pedro de. *Garrincha, alegria do povo*. (Film produced by Barreto, Nogueira, and Richers.) Rio de Janeiro, 1963.

23. Andrade, Mário de. *Macunaíma, o herói sem nenhum caráter*. Belo Horizonte and Brasília: Itatiaia, 1984.

24. Andrade, Roberto. *Vida y muerte de Eloy Alfaro*. Quito: El Conejo, 1985.

25. Andreu, Jean. "Borges, escritor comprometido," in *Texto crítico*, No. 13, Veracruz, April–June 1979.

26. Antezana, Luis E. *Proceso y sentencia de la reforma agraria en Bolivia*. La Paz: Puerta del Sol, 1979.

27. Arenales, Angélica. *Siqueiros*. Mexico City: Bellas Artes, 1947.

28. Arévalo Martínez, Rafael. *Ecce Pericles. La tiranía de Manuel Estrada Cabrera en Guatemala*. San José de Costa Rica: EDUCA, 1983.

29. Arguedas, Alcides. *Pueblo enfermo*. La Paz: Juventud, 1985.

30. Arguedas, José María. *El zorro de arriba y el zorro de abajo*. Buenos Aires: Losada, 1971.

31. ———. *Formación de una cultura nacional indoamericana*. Mexico City: Siglo XXI, 1975.

32. Aricó, José (ed.). *Mariátegui y los orígenes del marxismo latinoamericano*. Mexico City: Pasado y Presente, 1980.

33. Azuela, Mariano. *Los de abajo*. Mexico City: FCE, 1960.

34. Baptista Gumucio, Mariano. *Historia contemporánea de Bolivia, 1930–1978*. La Paz: Gisbert, 1978.

35. Barrán, José P., and Benjamín Nahum. *Batlle, los estancieros y el Imperio Británico. Las primeras reformas, 1911–1913*. Montevideo: Banda Oriental, 1983.

36. Barreto, Lima. *Os bruzundangas*. São Paulo: Ática, 1985.

37. Barrett, Rafael. *El dolor paraguayo*. (Preface by Augusto Roa Bastos.) Caracas: Ayacucho, 1978.

38. Bayer, Osvaldo. *Los vengadores de la Patagonia trágica*. Buenos Aires: Galerna, 1972, 1974; and Wuppertal: Hammer, 1977.

39. Beals, Carleton. *Banana Gold*. Managua: Nueva Nicaragua, 1983.

40. ———. *Porfirio Díaz*. Mexico City: Domés, 1982.

41. Belfrage, Cedric. *The American Inquisition, 1945–1960*. Indianapolis: Bobbs-Merrill, 1973.

42. Bell, John Patrick. *Guerra civil en Costa Rica. Los sucesos políticos de 1948*. San José de Costa Rica: EDUCA, 1981.

43. Beloch, Israel, and Alzira Alves de Abreu. *Dicionário histórico-biográfico brasileiro, 1930–1983*. Rio de Janeiro: Fundação Getúlio Vargas, 1984.

44. Benítez, Fernando. *Lázaro Cárdenas y la revolución mexicana. El porfirismo*. Mexico City: FCE, 1977.

45. ———. *Lázaro Cárdenas y la revolución mexicana. El cardenismo*. Mexico City: FCE, 1980.

46. ———. *Los indios de México* (Vol. 3). Mexico City: Era, 1979.

47. ———. *La ciudad de México, 1325–1982*. Barcelona and Mexico City: Salvat, 1981, 1982.
48. Benítez, Fernando, *et al. Juan Rulfo, homenaje nacional*. Mexico City: Bellas Artes/SEP, 1980.
49. Benvenuto, Ofelia Machado de. *Delmira Agustini*. Montevideo: Ministerio de Instrucción Pública, 1944.
50. Bernays, Edward. *Biography of an Idea*. New York: Simon and Schuster, 1965.
51. Berry, Mary Frances, and John W. Blassingame. *Long Memory: The Black Experience in America*. New York and Oxford: Oxford University Press, 1982.
52. Bezerra, João. *Como dei cabo de Lampião*. Recife: Massangana, 1983.
53. Bingham, Hiram. *Machu Picchu, la ciudad perdida de los incas*. Madrid: Rodas, 1972.
54. Bliss, Michael. *The Discovery of Insulin*. Toronto: McClelland and Stewart, 1982.
55. Bodard, Lucien. *Masacre de indios en el Amazonas*. Caracas: Tiempo Nuevo, 1970.
56. Bolaños, Pío. *Génesis de la intervención norteamericana en Nicaragua*. Managua: Nueva Nicaragua, 1984.
57. Bonfil Batalla, Guillermo. *El universo del amate*. Mexico City: Museo de Culturas Populares, 1982.
58. Borge, Tomás. *Carlos, el amanecer ya no es una tentación*. Havana: Casa de las Américas, 1980.
59. Borges, Jorge Luis. *Obras completas, 1923–1972*. Buenos Aires: Emecé, 1974.
60. Bosch, Juan. *Trujillo: causas de una tiranía sin ejemplo*. Caracas: Las Novedades, 1959.
61. ———. "Crisis de la democracia de América en la República Dominicana," in *Panoramas*, No. 14, supplement, Mexico City, 1964.
62. ———. *La revolución de abril*. Santo Domingo: Alfa y Omega, 1981.
63. ———. *Clases sociales en la República Dominicana*. Santo Domingo: PLD, 1982.
64. Bravo-Elizondo, Pedro. "La gran huelga del salitre en 1907," in *Araucaria*, No. 33, Madrid, 1986.
65. Branford, Sue, and Oriel Glock. *The Last Frontier, Fighting Over Land in the Amazon*. London: Zed, 1985.
66. Brecht, Bertolt. *Diario de trabajo*. Buenos Aires: Nueva Visión, 1977.
67. Buarque de Holanda, Sérgio. *Visão do paraíso*. São Paulo: Universidad, 1969.
68. Buitrago, Alejandra. *Conversando con los gamines*. (Unpublished.)
69. Bullrich, Francisco, *et al. América Latina en su arquitectura*. Mexico City: Siglo XXI, 1983.

70. Buñuel, Luis. *Mi último suspiro (memorias)*. Barcelona: Plaza y Janés, 1982.

71. ———. *Los olvidados*. Mexico City: Era, 1980.

72. Burgos, Elisabeth. *Me llamo Rigoberta Menchú y así me nació la conciencia*. Barcelona: Argos-Vergara, 1983.

73. Cabezas, Omar. *La montaña es algo más que una inmensa estepa verde*. Managua: Nueva Nicaragua, 1982.

74. Cabral, Sergio. *As escolas de samba: o quê, quem, como, quando e porquê*. Rio de Janeiro: Fontana, 1974.

75. ———. *Pixinguinha. Vida e obra*. Rio de Janeiro: Lidador, 1980.

76. Caputo, Alfredo. *Educación moral y cívica*. Montevideo: Casa del Estudiante, 1978. See also textbooks by Dora Noblía and Graciela Márquez, and by Sofía Corchs and Alex Pereyra Formoso.

77. Cardenal, Ernesto. *Antología*. Managua: Nueva Nicaragua, 1984.

78. Cárdenas, Lázaro. *Ideario político*. Mexico City: Era, 1976.

79. Cardona Pena, Alfredo. *El monstruo en el laberinto. Conversaciones con Diego Rivera*. Mexico City: Diana, 1980.

80. Cardoza y Aragón, Luis. *La nube y el reloj. Pintura mexicana contemporánea*. Mexico City, UNAM, 1940.

81. ———. *La revolución guatemalteca*. Mexico City: Cuadernos Americanos, 1955.

82. ———. *Diego Rivera. Los frescos en la Secretaría de Educación Pública*. Mexico City: SEP, 1980.

83. ———. *Orozco*. Mexico City: FCE, 1983.

84. Carías, Marco Virgilio, and Daniel Slutzky. *La guerra inútil. Análisis socio-económico del conflicto entre Honduras y El Salvador*. San José de Costa Rica: EDUCA, 1971.

85. Carpentier, Alejo. *Tientos y diferencias*. Montevideo: Arca, 1967.

86. ———. *La música en Cuba*. Havana: Letras Cubanas, 1979.

87. Carr, Raymond. *Puerto Rico: A Colonial Experiment*. New York: Vintage, 1984.

88. Casaus, Víctor. *Girón en la memoria*. Havana: Casa de las Américas. 1970.

89. Cassá, Roberto. *Capitalismo y dictadura*. Santo Domingo: Universidad, 1982.

90. Castro, Fidel. *La revolución cubana, 1953–1962*. Mexico City: Era, 1972.

91. ———. *Hoy somos un pueblo entero*. Mexico City: Siglo XXI, 1973.

92. Castro, Josué de. *Geografia da fome*. Rio de Janeiro: O Cruzeiro, 1946.

93. Cepeda Samudio, Álvaro. *La casa grande*. Buenos Aires: Jorge Álvarez, 1967.

94. Central Intelligence Agency. *Manuales de sabotaje y guerra psicológica*

para derrocar al gobierno sandinista. (Preface by Philip Agee.) Madrid: Fundamentos, 1985.

95. Cervantes Angulo, José. *La noche de las luciérnagas.* Bogotá: Plaza y Janés, 1980.

96. Céspedes, Augusto. *Sangre de mestizos. Relatos de la guerra del Chaco.* La Paz: Juventud, 1983.

97. ———. *El presidente colgado.* La Paz: Juventud, 1985.

98. "Cien años de lucha." Various authors, special edition of *Cuba*, Havana, October 1968.

99. Clark, Ronald William. *Edison: The Man Who Made the Future.* New York: Putnam, 1977.

100. Clase, Pablo. *Rubi. La vida de Porfirio Rubirosa.* Santo Domingo: Cosmos, 1979.

101. Crassweller, Robert D. *Trujillo. La tragica aventura del poder personal.* Barcelona: Bruguera, 1968.

102. Crawley, Eduardo. *Dictators Never Die: A Portrait of Nicaragua and the Somozas.* London: Hurst, 1979.

103. Colombres, Adolfo. *Seres sobrenaturales de la cultura popular argentina.* Buenos Aires: Del Sol, 1984.

104. Coluccio, Félix. *Diccionario folklórico argentino.* Buenos Aires: n.p., 1948.

105. Collier, James Lincoln. *Louis Armstrong: An American Genius.* New York: Oxford University Press, 1983.

106. Comisión Argentina por los Derechos Humanos. *Argentina: proceso al genocidio.* Madrid: Querejeta, 1977.

107. Comisión Nacional sobre la Desaparición de Personas. *Nunca más.* Buenos Aires: EUDEBA, 1984.

108. Committee on Foreign Relations, U.S. Senate. *Briefing on the Cuban Situation.* Washington, D.C., May 2, 1961.

109. Committee to Study Governmental Operations with Respect to Intelligence Activities, U.S. Senate. *Alleged Assassination Plots Involving Foreign Leaders: An Interim Report.* Washington, D.C., November 20, 1975.

110. Condarco Morales, Ramiro. *Zárate, el temible Willka. Historia de la rebelión indígena de 1899.* La Paz: n.p., 1982.

111. Condori Mamani, Gregorio. *De nosotros, los runas.* (Testimonies collected by Ricardo Valderrama and Carmen Escalante.) Madrid: Alfaguara, 1983.

112. Constantine, Mildred. *Tina Modotti. Una vida frágil.* Mexico City: FCE, 1979.

113. Cooke, Alistair. *America.* New York: Knopf, 1977.

114. Cordero Velásquez, Luis. *Gómez y las fuerzas vivas.* Caracas: Lumego, 1985.

115. Corrêa, Marcos Sá. *1964 visto e comentado pela Casa Branca*. Porto Alegre: L y PM, 1977.
116. Corretger, Juan Antonio. *Albizu Campos*. Montevideo: El Siglo Ilustrado, 1969.
117. Cueva, Gabriela de la. *Memorias de una caraqueña de antes del diluvio*. San Sebastián: n.p., 1982.
118. Cummins, Lejeune. *Don Quijote en burro*. Managua: Nueva Nicaragua, 1983.
119. Cunha, Euclides da. "A margem da história," in *Obra completa*. Rio de Janeiro: Aguilar, 1966.
120. Chandler, Billy Jaynes. *Lampião, o rei dos cangaceiros*. Rio de Janeiro: Paz e Terra, 1980.
121. Chaplin, Charles. *My Autobiography*. New York: Simon and Schuster, 1964.
122. Christensen, Eleanor Ingalls. *The Art of Haiti*. Philadelphia: Art Alliance, 1975.
123. Chumbita, Hugo. *Bairoletto. Prontuario y leyenda*. Buenos Aires: Marlona, 1974.
124. Daher, José Miguel. "Méndez: el Partido Demócrata de EE. UU. es socio de la sedición," in *La Mañana*, Montevideo, October 9, 1976.
125. Dalton, Roque. *Las historias prohibidas del Pulgarcito*. Mexico City: Siglo XXI, 1974.
126. ———. *Miguel Mármol. Los sucesos de 1932 en El Salvador*. Havana: Casa de las Américas, 1983.
127. ———. *Poesía*. (Mario Benedetti, ed.) Havana: Casa de las Américas, 1980.
128. Dardis, Tom. *Keaton: The Man Who Wouldn't Lie Down*. New York: Scribners, 1979.
129. Darío, Rubén. *Poesía*. (Preface by Angel Rama.) Caracas: Ayacucho, 1977.
130. Davies, Marion. *The Times We Had: Life With William Randolph Hearst*. Indianapolis and New York: Bobbs–Merrill, 1975.
131. Delgado Aparaín, Mario. "Mire que sos loco, Obdulio," in *Jaque*, Montevideo, January 25, 1985.
132. Deutscher, Isaac. *The Prophet Outcast: Trotsky, 1929–1940*. London: Oxford University Press, 1963.
133. Della Cava, Ralph. *Milagre em Joaseiro*. Rio de Janeiro: Paz e Terra, 1977.
134. *Diario de Juicio, El*. (Court record of trial of heads of Argentine dictatorship.) Buenos Aires: Perfil, 1985.
135. *El Nacional* and *Ultimas Noticias*, Caracas, August 28–29, 1977.
136. Dias, José Humberto. "Benjamin Abrahão, o mascate que filmou Lam-

pião," in *Cadernos de Pesquisa*, No. 1, Rio de Janeiro, Embrafilme, September 1984.

137. *Documentos de la CIA. Cuba acusa.* Havana: Ministerio de Cultura, 1981.
138. *Documentos secretos de la I.T.T.* Santiago de Chile: Quimantú, 1972.
139. Dorfman, Ariel, and Armand Mattelart. *Para leer al Pato Donald.* Mexico City: Siglo XXI, 1978.
140. Dower, John. *War Without Mercy: Race and Power in the Pacific War.* New York: Pantheon, 1986.
141. Dreifuss, René Armand. *1964: A conquista do Estado. Ação política, poder e golpe de classe.* Petrópolis: Vozes, 1981.
142. Drot, Jean-Marie. *Journal de voyage chez les peintres de la Fête et du vaudou en Haiti.* Geneva: Skira, 1974.
143. Duhalde, Eduardo Luis. *El estado terrorista argentino.* Buenos Aires: El Caballito, 1983.
144. Dumont, Alberto Santos. *O que eu vi, o que nós veremos.* Rio de Janeiro: Tribunal de Contas, 1983.
145. Duncan, Isadora. *My Life.* New York: Liveright, 1955.
146. Durst, Rogério. *Madame Satã: com o diabo no corpo.* São Paulo: Brasiliense, 1985.
147. Eco, Umberto. *Apocalíptis e integrados ante la cultura de masas.* Barcelona: Lumen, 1968.
148. Edison, Thomas Alva. *Diary.* Old Greenwich: Chatham, 1971.
149. Edwards, Audrey, and Gary Wohl. *Muhammad Ali. The People's Champ.* Boston and Toronto: Little Brown, 1977.
150. Einstein, Albert. *Notas autobiográficas.* Madrid: Alianza, 1984.
151. Eisenstein, S. M. *¡Que viva México!.* (Preface by José de la Colina.) Mexico City: Era, 1971.
152. Elgrably, Jordan. "A través del fuego. Entrevista con James Baldwin," in *Quimera*, No. 41, Barcelona, 1984.
153. Enzensberger, Hans Magnus. *Política y delito.* Barcelona: Seix Barral, 1968.
154. Escobar Bethancourt, Rómulo. *Torrijos: ¡colonia americana, no!* Bogotá: Valencia, 1981.
155. Faingold, Raquel Zimerman de. *Memorias de una familia inmigrante.* (Unpublished.)
156. Fairbank, John K. *The United States and China.* Cambridge: Harvard University Press, 1958.
157. Fajardo Sainz, Humberto. *La herencia de la coca. Pasado y presente de la cocaína.* La Paz: Universo, 1984.
158. Falcão, Edgard de Cerqueira. *A incompreensão de uma época.* São Paulo: Tribunais, 1971.

159. Fals Borda, Orlando. *Historia doble de la Costa. Resistencia en el San Jorge.* Bogotá: Valencia, 1984.

160. ———. *Historia doble de la Costa. Retorno a la tierra.* Bogotá: Valencia, 1986.

161. Faría Castro, Haroldo and Flavia de. "Los mil y un sombreros de la cultura boliviana," in *Geomundo*, Vol. 8, No. 6, Santiago de Chile, June 1984.

162. Fast, Howard. *The Passion of Sacco and Vanzetti: A New England Legend.* Westport, Conn.: Greenwood, 1972.

163. Faulkner, William. *Absalom, Absalom.* New York: Modern Library, 1951.

164. Federación Universitaria de Córdoba. *La reforma universitaria.* Buenos Aires: FUBA, 1959.

165. Feinstein, Elaine. *Bessie Smith, Empress of the Blues.* New York: Viking, 1985.

166. Folino, Norberto. *Barceló, Ruggierito y el populismo oligárquico.* Buenos Aires: Falbo, 1966.

167. Foner, Philip S. *The Case of Joe Hill.* New York: International Publications, 1965.

168. Ford, Henry (with Samuel Crowther). *My Life and Work.* New York: Doubleday, 1926.

169. Foxley, A. *Experimentos neoliberales en América Latina.* Santiago de Chile: CIEPLAN, 1982.

170. Freyre, Gilberto. *Casa grande e senzala.* Rio de Janeiro: José Olympio, 1966.

171. Fróes, Leonardo. *A casa de flor.* Rio de Janeiro: Funarte, 1978.

172. Frontaura Argandoña, Manuel. *La revolución boliviana.* La Paz and Cochabama: Amigos del Libro, 1974.

173. Gabetta, Carlos. *Todos somos subversivos.* Buenos Aires: Bruguera, 1983.

174. Gaitán, Jorge Eliécer. *1928. La masacre de las bananeras.* Bogotá: Los Comuneros, n.d.

175. Galarza Zavala, Jaime. *Quiénes mataron a Roldós.* Quito: Solitierra, 1982.

176. Galasso, Norberto, *et al. La década infame.* Buenos Aires: Carlos Pérez, 1969.

177. Galíndez, Jesús. *La era de Trujillo.* Buenos Aires: Sudamericana, 1962.

178. Gálvez, Manuel. *Vida de Hipólito Yrigoyen.* Buenos Aires: Tor, 1951.

179. Gálvez, William. *Camilo, señor de la vanguardia.* Havana: Ciencias Sociales, 1979.

180. Gandarillas, Arturo G. "Detrás de linderos del odio: laimes y jucumanis," in *Hoy*, La Paz, October 16, 1973.

181. Garcés, Joan. *El estado y los problemas tácticos en el gobierno de Allende.* Mexico City: Siglo XXI, 1974.
182. García, F. Chris. *Chicano Politics: Readings.* New York: n.p., 1973.
183. García Canclini, Néstor. *Las culturas populares en el capitalismo.* Havana: Casa de las Américas, 1982.
184. García Lupo, Rogelio. "Mil trescientos dientes de Gardel," in *Marcha,* No. 1004, Montevideo, April 8, 1960.
185. ———. *Diplomacia secreta y rendición incondicional.* Buenos Aires: Legasa, 1983.
186. García Márquez, Gabriel. *La hojarasca.* Buenos Aires: Sudamericana, 1969.
187. ———. *Cien años de soledad.* Buenos Aires: Sudamericana, 1967.
188. ———. "Algo más sobre literatura y realidad," in *El País,* Madrid, July 1, 1981.
189. ———. "La soledad de la América Latina" (Nobel Prize acceptance speech), in *Casa,* No. 137, Havana, March–April 1983.
190. Garmendia, Hermann. *María Lionza, ángel y demonio.* Caracas: Seleven, 1980.
191. Garrido, Atilio. "Obdulio Varela. Su vida, su gloria y su leyenda," in *El Diario,* "Estrellas deportivas" supplement, Montevideo, September 20, 1977.
192. Gallegos Lara, Joaquín. *Las cruces sobre el agua.* Quito: El Conejo, 1985.
193. Gil, Pío. *El Cabito.* Caracas: Biblioteca de autores y temas tachirenses, 1971.
194. Gilly, Adolfo. *La revolución interrumpida.* Mexico City: El Caballito, 1971.
195. Gilman, Charlotte Perkins. *Herland.* (Preface by Ann J. Lane.) New York: Pantheon, 1979.
196. ———. *The Yellow Wallpaper.* New York: Feminist Press, 1973.
197. Goldman, Albert. *Elvis.* New York: McGraw-Hill, 1981.
198. Gómez Yera, Sara. "La rumba," in *Cuba,* Havana, December 1964.
199. González, José Luis. *El país de cuatro pisos y otros ensayos.* San Juan de Puerto Rico: Huracán, 1980.
200. González, Luis. *Pueblos en vilo.* Mexico City: FCE, 1984.
201. ———. *Historia de la Revolución Mexicana, 1934–1940: Los días del presidente Cárdenas.* Mexico City: Colegio de México, 1981.
202. González Bermejo, Ernesto. "Interview with Atahualpa Yupanqui," in *Crisis,* No. 29, Buenos Aires, September 1975.
203. ———. "¿Qué pasa hoy en el Perú?," in *Crisis,* No. 36, Buenos Aires, April 1976.
204. ———. *Las manos en el fuego.* Montevideo: Banda Oriental, 1985.

205. Granados, Pedro. *Carpas de México. Leyendas, anécdotas e historia del teatro popular*. Mexico City: Universo, 1984.
206. Grigulevich, José. *Pancho Villa*. Havana: Casa de las Américas, n.d.
207. Grupo, Areíto. *Contra viento y marea*. Havana: Casa de las Américas, 1978.
208. Guerra, Ramiro. *La expansión territorial de los Estados Unidos*. Havana: Ciencias Sociales, 1975.
209. Guevara, Ernesto Che. *Pasajes de la guerra revolucionaria*. Havana: Arte y Literatura, 1975.
210. ———. "Camilo, imagen del pueblo," in *Granma*, Havana, October 25, 1967.
211. ———. *El socialismo y el hombre nuevo*. Mexico City: Siglo XXI, 1977.
212. ———. *El diario del Che en Bolivia*. Bilbao: Zalla, 1968.
213. ———. *Escritos y discursos*. Havana: Ciencias Sociales, 1977.
214. Guiles, Fred Lawrence. *Norma Jean*. New York: McGaw-Hill, 1969.
215. Guillén, Nicolás. "Un olivo en la colina," in *Hoy*, Havana, April 24, 1960.
216. Guzmán, Martín Luis. *El águila y la serpiente*. Mexico City: Cía. General de Ediciones, 1977.
217. Guzmán Campos, Germán (with Orlando Fals Borda and Eduardo Umaña Luna). *La violencia en Colombia*. Bogotá: Valencia, 1980.
218. Hardwick, Richard. *Charles Richard Drew: Pioneer in Blood Research*. New York: Scribners, 1967.
219. Hellman, Lillian. *Scoundrel Time*. Boston: Little Brown, 1976.
220. Hemingway, Ernest. *Enviado especial*. Barcelona, Planeta, 1968.
221. Henault, Mirta. *Alicia Moreau de Justo*. Buenos Aires: Centro Editor, 1983.
222. Heras León, Eduardo. Interview with Miguel Mármol. (Unpublished.)
223. Hermann, Hamlet. *Francis Caamaño*. Santo Domingo: Alfa y Omega, 1983.
224. Herrera, Hayden. *Frida. A Biography of Frida Kahlo*. New York: Harper and Row, 1983.
225. Hervia Cosculluela, Manuel. *Pasaporte 11.333. Ocho años con la CIA*. Havana: Ciencias Sociales, 1978.
226. Hidrovo Velasquez, Horacio. *Un hombre y un río*. Portoviejo: Gregorio: 1982.
227. Hobsbawm, Eric J. *Primitive Rebels*. New York: Norton, 1965.
228. Hoffman, Banesh. *Einstein*. Barcelona: Salvat, 1984.
229. Huezo, Francisco. *Últimos días de Rubén Darío*. Managua: Renacimiento, 1925.
230. Huneeus, Pablo. *La cultura huachaca o el aporte de la televisión*. Santiago de Chile: Nueva Generación, 1981.

231. ———. *Lo comido y lo bailado.* . . . Santiago de Chile: Nueva Generación, 1984.
232. Hurt, Henry. *Reasonable Doubt: An Investigation into the Assassination of John F. Kennedy.* New York: Holt, Rinehart, and Winston, 1986.
233. Huxley, Francis. *The Invisibiles.* London: Hart-Davis, 1966.
234. Ianni, Octavio. *El Estado capitalista en la época de Cárdenas.* Mexico City: Era, 1985.
235. Informes sobre la violación de derechos humanos en el Uruguay, realizados por Amnesty International, la Comisión de Derechos Humanos y el Comité de Derechos Humanos de las Naciones Unidas y La Comisión Interamericana de Derechos Humanos de la OEA. [Accounts of the violation of human rights in Uruguay. Collected by Amnesty International; the Committee on Human Rights of the United Nations; and the Inter-American Commission on Human Rights of the OAS.]
236. Instituto de Edustios del Sandinismo. *Ni vamos a poder caminar de tantas flores.* (Testimonies of Sandino's soldiers; unpublished).
237. ———. *El sandinismo. Documentos básicos.* Managua: Nueva Nicaragua, 1983.
238. ———. *La insurrección popular sandinista en Masaya.* Managua: Nueva Nicaragua, 1982.
239. ———. *¡Y se armó la runga!* Managua: Nueva Nicaragua, 1982.
240. Jaramillo-Levi, Enrique, *et al. Una explosión en América: el canal de Panamá.* Mexico City: Siglo XXI, 1976.
241. Jenks, Leland H. *Nuestra colonia de Cuba.* Buenos Aires: Palestra, 1961.
242. Johnson, James Weldon. *Along This Way.* New York: Viking, 1933.
243. Jonas Bodenheimer, Susanne. *La ideología socialdemócrata en Costa Rica.* San José de Costa Rica: EDUCA, 1984.
244. Julião, Francisco, and Angélica Rodríguez. Testimony of Gregoria Zúñiga in "Los últimos soldados de Zapata," in *Crisis,* No. 21, Buenos Aires, January 1975.
245. Katz, Friedrich. *La servidumbre agraria en México en la época porfiriana.* Mexico City: Era, 1982.
246. ———. *La guerra secreta en México.* Mexico City: Era, 1983.
247. Kerr, Elizabeth M. *William Faulkner's Gothic Domain.* Port Washington, New York: Kennikat, 1979.
248. Klare, Michael T., and Nancy Stein. *Armas y poder en América Latina.* Mexico City: Era, 1978.
249. Kobal, John. *Rita Hayworth: The Time, the Place, and the Woman.* Norton, 1978.
250. Krehm, William. *Democracia y tiranías en el Caribe.* Buenos Aires: Palestra, 1959.

251. Labourt, José. *Sana, sana, culito de rana.* . . . Santo Domingo: Taller, 1979.
252. Landaburu, Jon, and Roberto Pineda. "Cuentos del diluvio de fuego," in *Maguaré*, No. 1, Bogotá, Universidad Nacional, June 1981.
253. Landes, Ruth. *A cidade das mulheres.* Rio de Janeiro: Civilização Brasileira, 1967.
254. Lane, Mark, and Dick Gregory. *Code Name Zorro: The Murder of Martin Luther King.* Englewood Cliffs, N.J.: Prentice-Hall, 1977.
255. Lapassade, Georges, and Marco Aurélio Luz. *O segredo da macumba.* Rio de Janeiro: Paz e Terra, 1972.
256. Larco, Juan. *et al. Recopilación de textos sobre José María Arguedas.* Havana: Casa de las Américas, 1976.
257. Latin America Bureau. *Narcotráfico y política.* Madrid: IEPALA, 1982.
258. Lauer, Mirko. *Crítica de la artesanía. Plástica y sociedad en los Andes peruanos.* Lima: DESCO, 1982.
259. La Valle, Raniero, and Linda Bimbi. *Marianella e i suoi fratelli. Una storia latinoamericana.* Milan: Feltrinelli, 1983.
260. Lavretski, I., and Adolfo Gilly. *Francisco Villa.* Mexico City: Macehual, 1978.
261. Levy, Alan. *Ezra Pound: The Voice of Silence.* Sag Harbor, N.Y.: Permanent, 1983.
262. Lichello, Robert. *Pioneer in Blood Plasma: Dr. Charles R. Drew.* New York: Messner, 1968.
263. Lima, Lourenço Moreira. *A coluna Prestes (marchas e combates).* São Paulo: Alfa-Omega, 1979.
264. Loetscher, Hugo. *El descubrimiento de Suiza por los indios.* Cochabamba: Amigos del Libro, 1983.
265. Loor, Wilfrido. *Eloy Alfaro.* Quito: n.p., 1982.
266. López, Oscar Luis. *La radio en Cuba.* Havana: Letras Cubanas, 1981.
267. López, Santos. *Memorias de un soldado.* Managua: FER, 1974.
268. López Virgil, José Ignacio. *Radio Pío XII: una mina de coraje.* Quito: Aler/Pío XII, 1984.
269. Lowenthal, Abraham F. *The Dominican Intervention.* Cambridge: Harvard University Press, 1972.
270. Luna, Félix. *Atahualpa Yupanqui.* Madrid: Júcar, 1974.
271. Machado, Carlos. *Historia de los orientales.* Montevideo: Banda Oriental, 1985.
272. Magalhães Júnior, R. *Rui. O homem e o mito.* Rio de Janeiro: Civilização Brasileira, 1964.
273. Maggiolo, Oscar J. "Política de desarrollo científico y tecnológico de América Latina," in *Gaceta de la Universidad*, Montevideo, March–April 1968.
274. Mailer, Norman. *Marilyn.* New York: Grossett and Dunlap, 1973.

275. Maldonado-Denis, Manuel. *Puerto Rico: mito y realidad*. San Juan de Puerto Rico: Antillana, 1969.

276. Manchester, William. *The Glory and the Dream: A Narrative History of America*. Boston: Little Brown, 1972.

277. Mariátegui, José Carlos. *Obras*. Havana: Casa de las Américas, 1982.

278. Marín, Germán. *Una historia fantástica y calculada: la CIA en el país de los chilenos*. Mexico City: Siglo XXI, 1976.

279. Mário Filho. *O negro no futebol brasileiro*. Rio de Janeiro: Civilização Brasileira, 1964.

280. Mariz, Vasco. *Heitor Villa-Lobos, compositor brasileiro*. Rio de Janeiro: Zahar, 1983.

281. Martin, John Bartlow. *El destino dominicano. La crisis dominicana desde la caída de Trujillo hasta la guerra civil*. Santo Domingo: Editora Santo Domingo, 1975.

282. Martínez, Thomas M. "Advertising and Racism: The Case of the Mexican-American," in *El Grito*, Summer 1969.

283. Martínez Assad, Carlos. *El laboratorio de la revolución: el Tabasco garridista*. Mexico City: Siglo XXI, 1979.

284. Martínez Moreno, Carlos. "Color del 900," in *Capítulo oriental*. Montevideo: CEDAL, 1968.

285. Matos, Cláudia. *Acertei no milhar. Samba e malandragem no tempo de Getúlio*. Rio de Janeiro: Paz e Terra, 1982.

286. Matos Díaz, Eduardo. *Anecdotario de una tiranía*. Santo Domingo: Taller, 1976.

287. Mattelart, Armand. *La cultura como empresa multinacional*. Mexico City: Era, 1974.

288. May, Stacy, and Galo Plaza. *United States Business Performance Abroad: The Case Study of United Fruit Company in Latin America*. Washington, D.C.: National Planning, 1958.

289. Medina Castro, Manuel. *Estados Unidos y América Latina, siglo XIX*. Havana: Casa de las Américas, 1968.

290. Mella, Julio Antonio. *Escritos revolucionarios*. Mexico City: Siglo XXI, 1978.

291. Mende, Tibor. *La Chine et son ombre*. Paris: Seuil, 1960.

292. Méndez Capote, Renée. *Memorias de una cubanita que nació con el siglo*. Santa Clara (de Cuba): Universidad, 1963.

293. Mendoza, Vincente T. *El corrido mexicano*. Mexico City: FCE, 1976.

294. Mera, Juan León. *Cantares del pueblo ecuatoriano*. Quito: Banco Central, n.d.

295. Métraux, Alfred. *Haiti. La terre, les hommes et les dieux*. Neuchâtel: La Baconnière, 1957.

296. Meyer, Eugenia. Interview with Juan Olivera López. (Unpublished.)

297. Meyer, Jean. *La cristiada. La guerra de los cristeros.* Mexico City: Siglo XXI, 1973.
298. Molina, Gabriel. *Diario de Girón.* Havana: Política, 1983.
299. Monsiváis, Carlos. *Días de guardar.* Mexico City: Era, 1970.
300. ———. *Amor perdido.* Mexico City: Era, 1977.
301. Mora, Arnoldo. *Monseñor Romero.* San José de Costa Rica: EDUCA, 1981.
302. Morais, Fernando. *Olga.* São Paulo: Alfa-Omega, 1985.
303. Morel, Edmar. *A revolta da chibata.* Rio de Janeiro: Graal, 1979.
304. Morison, Samuel E., and Henry S. Commager. *A Concise History of the American Republic.* New York: Oxford University Press, 1977.
305. Moussinac, Léon. *Sergei Michailovitch Eisenstein.* Paris: Seghers, 1964.
306. Mota, Carlos Guilherme. *Ideologia da cultura brasileira, 1933–1974.* São Paulo: Ática, 1980.
307. Maurão Filho, Olympio. *Memórias: a verdade de um revolucionário.* Porto Alegre: L y PM, 1978.
308. Murúa, Dámaso. *En Brasil crece un almendro.* Mexico City: El Caballito, 1984.
309. ———. *40 cuentos del Güilo Mentiras.* Mexico City: Crea, 1984.
310. Nalé Roxlo, Conrado, and Mabel Mármol. *Genio y figura de Alfonsina Storni.* Buenos Aires: EUDEBA, 1966.
311. Navarro, Marysa. *Evita.* Buenos Aires: Corregidor, 1981.
312. Nepomuceno, Eric. *Hemingway: Madrid no era una fiesta.* Madrid: Altalena, 1978.
313. Neruda, Pablo. *Confieso que he vivido.* Barcelona: Seix Barral, 1974.
314. ———. *Obras completas.* Buenos Aires: Losada, 1973.
315. Niemeyer, Oscar. Texts, drawings, and photos in a special edition of *Módulo,* Rio de Janeiro, June 1983.
316. Nimuendajú, Curt. *Mapa etno-histórico.* Rio de Janeiro: Fundaçao Nacional Pró-Memória, 1981.
317. Nosiglia, Julio E. *Botín de guerra.* Buenos Aires: Tierra Fértil, 1985.
318. Novo, Salvador. *Cocina mexicana. Historia gastronómica de la ciudad de México.* Mexico City: Porrúa, 1979.
319. Núñez Jiménez, Antonio. *Wifredo Lam.* Havana: Letras Cubanas, 1982.
320. Núñez Téllez, Carlos. *Un pueblo en armas.* Managua: FSLN, 1980.
321. O'Connor, Harvey. *La crisis mundial del petróleo.* Buenos Aires: Platina, 1963.
322. Olmo, Rosa del. *Los chigüines de Somoza.* Caracas: Ateneo, 1980.
323. Orozco, José Clemente. *Autobiografía.* Mexico: Era, 1979.
324. Ortiz, Fernando. *Los bailes y el teatro de los negros en el folklore de Cuba.* Havana: Letras Cubanas, 1981.
325. Ortiz Echagüe, Fernando. "Sobre la importancia de la vaca argentina

en París." Originally published in 1930; republished by Rogelio García Lupo in *Crisis*," No. 29, Buenos Aires, September 1975.
326. Ortiz Letelier, Fernando. *El movimiento obrero en Chile. Antecedentes 1891–1919.* Madrid: Michay, 1985.
327. Page, Joseph A. *Perón.* Buenos Aires: Vergara, 1984.
328. Paleari, Antonio. *Diccionario mágico jujeño.* San Salvador de Jujuy: Pachamama, 1982.
329. Paliza, Héctor. "Los burros fusilados," in *Presagio*, Culiacán, Sinaloa, No. 10, April 1978.
330. Paoli, Francisco J., and Enrique Montalvo. *El socialismo olvidado de Yucatán.* Mexico City: Siglo XXI, 1980.
331. Paramio, Ludolfo. *Mito e ideología.* Madrid: Corazón, 1971.
332. Pareja Diezcanseco, Alfredo. *Ecuador. La república de 1830 a nuestros días.* Quito: Universidad, 1979.
333. Pareja y Paz Soldán, José. *Juan Vicente Gómez. Un fenómeno telúrico.* Caracas: Ávila Gráfica, 1951.
334. Parra, Violeta. *Violeta del pueblo.* (Javier Martínez Reverte, ed.) Madrid: Visor, 1983.
335. Pasley, F. D. *Al Capone.* (Preface by Andrew Sinclair.) Madrid: Alianza, 1970.
336. Payeras, Mario. *Los días de la selva.* Havana: Casa de las Américas, 1981.
337. Peña Bravo, Raúl. *Hecos y dichos del general Barrientos.* La Paz: n.p., 1982.
338. Pérez, Ponciana (known as Chana la Vieja). Public testimony in *Cuba*, Havana, May–June 1970.
339. Pérez Valle, Eduardo. *El martirio del héroe. La muerte de Sandino.* Managua: Banco Central, 1980.
340. Perlman, Janice, E. *O mito da marginalidade. Favelas e política no Rio de Janeiro.* Rio de Janeiro: Paz e Terra, 1981.
341. Perón, Juan Domingo. *Tres revoluciones militares.* Buenos Aires: Síntesis, 1974.
342. Pineda, Virginia Gutiérriz de, et al. *El gamín.* Bogotá: UNICEF/Instituto Colombiano de Bienestar Familiar, 1978.
343. Pinto, L. A. Costa. *Lutas de famílias no Brasil.* São Paulo: Editora Nacional, 1949.
344. Pocaterra, José Rafael. *Memorias de un venezolano de la decadencia.* Caracas: Monte Ávila, 1979.
345. Politzer, Patricia. *Miedo en Chile.* (Testimonies of Moy de Tohá and others.) Santiago de Chile: CESOC, 1985.
346. Pollak-Eltz, Angelina. "María Lionza, mito y culto venezolano," in *Montalbán*, No. 2, Caracas, UCAB, 1973.
347. Poniatowska, Elena. *La noche de Tlatelolco.* Mexico City: Era, 1984.

348. Portela, Fernando, and Cláudio Bojunga. *Lampião. O cangaceiro e o outro.* São Paulo: Traço, 1982.
349. Pound, Ezra, *Selected Cantos.* New York: New Directions, 1970.
350. Powers, Thomas. *The Man Who Kept the Secrets: Richard Helms and the CIA.* New York: Knopf, 1979.
351. Presidency of the Republic of Haiti. Law of April 29, 1969. Palais National, Port-au-Prince.
352. Queiroz, María Isaura Pereira de. *Os cangaceiros.* São Paulo: Duas Cidades, 1977.
353. ———. *História do cangaço.* São Paulo: Global, 1982.
354. Querejazu Calvo, Roberto, *Masamaclay. Historia política, diplomática y militar de la guerra del Chaco.* Cochabamba and La Paz: Amigos del Libro, 1981.
355. Quijano, Aníbal. *Introducción a Mariátegui.* Mexico City: Era, 1982.
356. Quijano, Carlos. Various articles from *Cuadernos de Marcha,* Mexico City and Montevideo: CEUAL, 1984–85.
357. Quiroga, Horacio. *Selección de cuentos.* (Preface by Emir Rodríguez Monegal.) Montevideo: Ministerio de Instrucción Pública, 1966.
358. ———. *Sobre literatura.* (Preface by Roberto Ibáñez.) Montevideo: Arca, 1970.
359. Quiroz Otero, Ciro. *Vallenato. Hombre y canto.* Bogotá: Icaro, 1983.
360. Rama, Ángel. *Las máscaras democráticas del modernismo.* Montevideo: Fundación Ángel Rama, 1985.
361. Ramírez, Sergio, ed. *Augusto C. Sandino. El pensamiento vivo.* Managua: Nueva Nicaragua, 1984.
362. ———. *Estás en Nicaragua.* Barcelona: Muchnik, 1985.
363. Ramírez, Pedro Felipe. *La vida maravillosa del Siervo de Dios.* Caracas: n.p., 1985.
364. Ramos, Graciliano. *Memórias do cárcere.* Rio de Janeiro: José Olympio, 1954.
365. Ramos, Jorge Abelardo. *Revolución y contrarevolución en la Argentina.* Buenos Aires: Plus Ultra, 1976.
366. Rangel, Domingo Alberto. *Gómez, el amo del poder.* Caracas: Vadell, 1980.
367. Recinos, Adrián, trans. *Popol Vuh. Las antiguas historias del Quiché.* Mexico City: FCE, 1976.
368. Reed, John. *Insurgent Mexico.* New York: Simon and Schuster, 1969.
369. Rendón, Armando B. *Chicano manifesto.* New York: Macmillan, 1971.
370. Rengifo, Antonio. "Esbozo biográfico de Ezequiel Urviola y Rivero," in *Los movimientos campesinos en el Perú, 1879–1965.* Lima: Delva, 1977.
371. *Retrato do Brasil.* (Various authors.) São Paulo: Tres, 1984.
372. See 445a.

373. Revueltas, José. *México 68: Juventud y revolución*. Mexico City, Era, 1978.
374. Ribeiro, Berta G. "O mapa etno-histórico de Curt Nimuendajú," in *Revista de Antropologia*, Vol. XXV, São Paulo: Universidad, 1982..
375. Ribeiro, Darcy. *Os índios e a civilização*. Petrópolis: Vozes, 1982.
376. ———. Reception Speech on the Occasion of Receiving Doctorate honoris causa at the University of Paris VII, May 3, 1979; in *Módulo*, Rio de Janeiro, 1979..
377. ———. *Ensaios insólitos*. Porto Alegre: L y PM, 1979.
378. ———. *Aos trancos e barrancos. Como o Brasil deu no que deu*. Rio de Janeiro: Guanabara, 1986.
379. Rivera, Jorge B. "Discépolo," in *Cuadernos de Crisis*, No. 3, Buenos Aires, December 1973.
380. Roa Bastos, Augusto. *Hijo de hombre*. Buenos Aires: Losada, 1960.
381. Robeson, Paul. *Paul Robeson Speaks*. (Edited and with preface by Philip S. Foner.) Secaucus: Citadel, 1978.
382. Robinson, David. *Buster Keaton*. Bloomington: University of Indiana Press, 1970.
383. ———. *Chaplin: His Life and Art*. London: Collins, 1985.
384. Rockefeller, David. Letter to Gen. Jorge Rafael Videla, in *El Periodista*, No. 71, Buenos Aires, January 17–23, 1986.
385. Rodman, Selden. *Renaissance in Haiti: Popular Painters in the Black Republic*. New York: Pellegrini and Cudahy, 1948.
386. Rodó, José Enrique. *Ariel*. Madrid: Espasa-Calpe, 1971.
387. Rodríguez, Antonio. *A History of Mexican Mural Painting*. London: Thames and Hudson, 1969.
388. Rodríguez, Carlos. "Astiz el ángel exterminador," in *Madres de Plaza de Mayo*, No. 2, Buenos Aires, January 1985.
389. Rodríguez Monegal, Emir. *Sexo y poesía en el 900*. Montevideo: Alfa, 1969.
390. ———. *El desterrado. Vida y obra de Horacio Quiroga*. Buenos Aires: Losada, 1968.
391. Roeder, Ralph. *Hacia el México moderno: Porfirio Díaz*. Mexico City: FCE, 1973.
392. Rojas, Marta. *El que debe vivir*. Havana: Casa de las Américas, 1978.
393. Román, José. *Maldito país*. Managua: El pez y la serpiente, 1983.
394. Rosencof, Mauricio. Statement to Mercedes Ramírez and Laura Oreggioni, in *Asamblea*, No. 38, Montevideo, April 1985.
395. Rovere, Richard H. *Senator Joe McCarthy*. New York: Harcourt Brace Jovanovich, 1959.
396. Rowles, James. *El conflicto Honduras–El Salvador y el orden jurídico internacional*. San José de Costa Rica: EDUCA, 1980.

397. Rozitchner, León. *Moral burguesa y revolución*. Buenos Aires: Procyón, 1963.
398. Ruffinelli, Jorge. *El otro México. México en la obra de Traven, Lawrence y Lowry*. Mexico City: Nueva Imagen, 1978.
399. Rugama, Leonel. *La tierra es un satélite de la luna*. Managua: Nueva Nicaragua, 1983.
400. Rulfo, Juan. *Pedro Páramo* and *El llano en llamas*. Barcelona: Planeta, 1982.
401. Saia, Luiz Henrique. *Carmen Miranda*. São Paulo: Brasiliense, 1984.
402. Salamanca, Daniel. *Documentos para una historia de la guerra del Chaco*. La Paz: Don Bosco, 1951.
403. Salazar, Ruben. Articles in *Los Angeles Times*, February–August 1970.
404. Salazar Valiente, Mario. "El Salvador: crisis, dictadura, lucha, 1920–1980," in *América Latina: historia de medio siglo*. Mexico City: Siglo XXI, 1981.
405. Salvatierra, Sofonías. *Sandino o la tragedia de un pueblo*. Madrid: Talleres Europa, 1934.
406. Samper Pizano, Ernesto, *et al*. *Legalización de la marihuana*. Bogotá: Tercer Mundo, 1980.
407. Sampson, Anthony. *The Sovereign State of ITT*. Greenwich, Conn., Fawcett, 1974.
408. Sánchez, Gonzalo, and Donny Meertens. *Bandoleros, gamonales y campesinos. El caso de la violencia en Colombia*. Bogotá: El Áncora, 1983.
409. Sante, Luc. "Relic," in *The New York Review of Books*, Vol. 28, No. 20, New York, December 17, 1981.
410. Saume Barrios, Jesús. *Silleta de cuero*. Caracas: n.p., 1985.
411. Schaden, Egon. "Curt Nimuendajú. Quarenta anos a servico do índio brasileiro e ao estudo de suas culturas," in *Problemas brasileiros*, São Paulo, December 1973.
412. Scalabrini Ortiz, Raúl. *El hombre que está solo y espera*. Buenos Aires: Plus Ultra, 1964.
413. Schinca, Milton. *Boulevard Sarandí. Anécdotas, gentes, sucesos, del pasado montevideano*. Montevideo: Banda Oriental, 1979.
414. Schifter, Jacobo. *La fase oculta de la guerra civil en Costa Rica*. San José de Costa Rica: EDUCA, 1981.
415. Schlesinger, Arthur M. *The Thousand Days: John F. Kennedy in the White House*. Boston: Houghton Mifflin, 1965.
416. Schlesinger, Stephen, and Stephen Kinzer. *Bitter Fruit: The Untold Story of the American Coup in Guatemala*. New York: Anchor, 1983.
417. Sebreli, Juan José. *Eva Perón: ¿aventurera o militante?*. Buenos Aires: Siglo Veinte, 1966.

418. Séjourné, Laurette. *Supervivencias de un mundo mágico*. Mexico: FCE, 1953.
419. Selser, Gregorio. *El pequeño ejército loco*. Managua: Nueva Nicaragua, 1983.
420. ———. *El guatemalazo*. Buenos Aires: Iguazú, 1961.
421. ———. *¡Aquí, Santo Domingo! La tercera guerra sucia*. Buenos Aires: Palestra, 1966.
422. ———. "A veinte años del Moncada," in *Cuadernos de Marcha*, No. 72, Montevideo, July 1973.
423. ———. *El rapto de Panamá*. San José de Costa Rica: EDUCA, 1982.
424. Senna, Orlando. *Alberto Santos Dumont*. São Paulo: Brasiliense, 1984.
425. Serpa, Phoción. *Oswaldo Cruz. El Pasteur del Brasil, vencedor de la fiebre amarilla*. Buenos Aires: Claridad, 1945.
426. Silva, Clara. *Genio y figura de Delmira Agustini*. Buenos Aires: EUDEBA, 1968.
427. Silva, José Dias da. *Brasil, país ocupado*. Rio de Janeiro: Record, 1963.
428. Silva, Marília T. Barboza da, and Arthur L. de Oliveira Filho. *Cartola. Os tempos idos*. Rio de Janeiro: Funarte, 1983.
429. Silveira, Cid. *Café: um drama na economia nacional*. Rio de Janeiro: Civilização Brasileira, 1962.
430. Slosser, Bob. *Reagan Inside Out*. New York: World Books, 1984.
431. Smith, Earl E. T. *El cuarto piso. Relato sobre la revolución comunista de Castro*. Mexico City: Diana, 1963.
432. Sodré, Nelson Werneck. *Oscar Niemeyer*. Rio de Janeiro: Graal, 1978.
433. ———. *História militar do Brasil*. Rio de Janeiro: Civilização Brasileira, 1965.
434. Somoza Debayle, Anastasio. *Filosofía social*. (Armando Luna Sulva, ed.) Managua: Presidencia de la República, 1976.
435. Sorensen, Theodore C. *Kennedy*. New York: Harper and Row, 1965.
436. Souza, Tárik de. *O som nosso de cada dia*. Porto Alegre: L y PM, 1983.
437. Stock, Noel. *Poet in Exile: Ezra Pound*. New York: Barnes and Noble, 1964.
438. Stone, Samuel. *La dinastía de los conquistadores. La crisis del poder en la Costa Rica contemporánea*. San José de Costa Rica: EDUCA, 1982.
439. Suárez, Roberto. *Statements to El Diario and Hoy*, La Paz, July 3, 1983.
440. Subercaseau, Bernardo (with Patricia Stambuk and Jaime Londoño). *Violeta Parra: Gracias a la vida. Testimonios*. Buenos Aires: Galerna, 1985.
441. Taibo, Paco Ignacio II, and Roberto Vizcaíno. *El socialismo en un solo puerto, Acapulco, 1919–1923*. Mexico City: Extemporáneos, 1983.
442. Teitelboim, Volodia. *Neruda*. Madrid: Michay, 1984.

443. Tello, Antonio, and Gonzalo Otero Pizarro. *Valentino, La seducción manipulada*. Barcelona: Bruguera, 1978.
444. Tibol, Raquel. *Frida Kahlo. Crónica, testimonio y aproximaciones*. Mexico City: Cultura Popular, 1977.
445. *Time Capsule, 1927: A History of the Year Condensed from the Pages of Time*. New York: Time-Life, 1928.
445a. *Time*. "High on Cocaine: A $30 Billion U.S. Habit," July 6, 1981.
446. Toqo. *Indiomanual*. Humahuaca: Instituto de Cultura Indígena, 1985.
447. Toriello, Guillermo. *La batalla de Guatemala*. Mexico City: Cuadernos Americanos, 1955.
448. Torres, Camilo. *Cristianismo y revolución*. Mexico City: Era, 1970.
449. Touraine, Alain. *Vida y muerte del Chile popular*. Mexico City: Siglo XXI, 1974.
450. Tribunal Permanente de los Pueblos. *El caso Guatemala*. Madrid: IEP-ALA, 1984.
451. Turner, John Kenneth. *Barbarous Mexico*. Austin: Univesity of Texas Press, 1969.
452. Universidad Nacional de Río Cuarto, Córdoba, Argentina. Resolution No. 0092 of February 22, 1977, signed by rector Eduardo José Pesoa; in *Soco Soco*, No. 2, Río Cuarto, April 1986.
453. Valcárcel, Luis E. *Machu Picchu*. Buenos Aires: EUDEBA, 1964.
454. Valle-Castillo, Julio. Introduction to Rubén Darío, *Prosas políticas*. Managua: Ministerio de Cultura, 1983.
455. Vásquez Díaz, Rubén. *Bolivia a la hora del Che*. Mexico City: Siglo XXI, 1968.
456. Vásquez Lucio, Oscar E. (Siulnas). *Historia del humor gráfico y escrito en la Argentina, 1801–1939*. Buenos Aires: EUDEBA, 1985.
457. Vélez, Julio, and A. Merino. *España en César Vallejo*. Madrid: Fundamentos, 1984.
458. Viezzer, Moema. *Si me permiten hablar: testimonio de Domitila, una mujer de las minas de Bolivia*. Mexico City: Siglo XXI, 1978.
459. Vignar, Maren. "Los ojos de los pájaros." In Maren and Marcelo Vignar, *Exilio y tortura*. (Unpublished.)
460. Waksman Schinca, Daniel, *et al. La batalla de Nicaragua*. Mexico City: Bruguera, 1980.
461. Walsh, Rodolfo. Letter to the Military Junta, in *Operación masacre*. Buenos Aires: De la Flor, 1984.
462. Weinstein, Barbara. *The Amazon Rubber Boom, 1850–1920*. Stanford: Stanford University Press, 1983.
463. Wettstein, Germán. "La tradición de la Paradura del Niño," in *Geomundo* (special edition on Venezuela), Panama City: 1983.
464. White, Judith. *Historia de una ignominia: La United Fruit Company en Colombia*. Bogotá: Presencia, 1978.

465. Wise, David, and Thomas B. Ross. *The Invisible Government*. New York: Random House, 1964.
466. Witker, Alejandro. *Salvador Allende, 1908–1973. Prócer de la liberación nacional*. Mexico City: UNAM, 1980.
467. Woll, Allen L. *The Latin Image in American Film*. Los Angeles: UCLA Press, 1977.
468. Womack, John, Jr. *Zapata and the Mexican Revolution*. New York: Knopf, 1968.
469. Wyden, Peter. *Bay of Pigs: The Untold Story*. New York: Simon and Schuster, 1980.
470. Ycaza, Patricio. *Historia del movimiento obrero ecuatoriano*. Quito: Cedime, 1984.
471. Ydígoras Fuentes, Miguel (with Mario Rosenthal). *My War with Communism*. Englewood Cliffs, N.J.: Prentice-Hall, 1963.
472. Yupanqui, Atahualpa. *Aires indios*. Buenos Aires: Siglo Veinte, 1985.
473. Zavaleta Mercado, René. *El desarrollo de la conciencia nacional*. Montevideo: Diálogo, 1967.
474. ———. "Consideraciones generales sobre la historia de Bolivia, 1932–1971." In *América Latina: historia de medio siglo*, (various authors). Mexico City: Siglo XXI, 1982.
475. ———. "El estupor de los siglos," in *Quimera* No. 1, Cochabamba, September 1985.

Index

About the Author

The author was born in Montevideo, Uruguay, in 1940. His full name is Eduardo Hughes Galeano. He entered journalism as a political caricaturist for the socialist weekly *El Sol*, signing himself "Gius," the nearest approximation to the Spanish pronunciation of his paternal surname. Later he was an editor of the weekly *Marcha*, and he edited the daily *Epoca* and various Montevideo weeklies. In 1973 he went into exile in Argentina, where he founded and edited the magazine *Crisis*. He lived in Spain from 1976 to 1984, but has now returned to Uruguay.

Among his books, *Open Veins of Latin America* (1971), *Days and Nights of Love and War* (1978), and the first two volumes of this trilogy: *Genesis* (1982) and *Faces and Masks* (1984), have been published in English, and both *Days and Nights* and *The Song of Ourselves* (a novel, 1975) have won the Cuban Casa de las Américas prizes.

About the Translator

Born in London in 1904, Cedric Belfrage came to the U.S. in 1925 and began writing about movies in Hollywood. He was a co-founder of the *National Guardian* in 1948 and its editor until 1955, when a brush with McCarthy led to his deportation. He has written ten books and novels, published in this country, including *Away from It All*, *Abide with Me*, *My Master Columbus*, and *The American Inquisition*, *1945–1960*. He lives with his wife, Mary, in Cuernavaca, Mexico.